Anthony Boucher

The Case of the Seven of Calvary

Nine Times Nine

Rocket to the Morgue

The Case of the Crumpled Knave

A Black Box Thriller from Zomba Books

FIRST PUBLISHED IN GREAT BRITAIN IN 1984
BY ZOMBA BOOKS, ZOMBA HOUSE, 165–167 WILLESDEN
HIGH ROAD, LONDON NW10 2SG

The Case of the Seven of Calvary © 1937 renewed 1961

Nine Times Nine © 1940 by H. H. Holmes

Rocket to the Morgue © 1942 by H. H. Holmes

The Case of the Crumpled Knave © 1939

Anthology © Estate of Anthony Boucher, 1984

ISBN 0 946391 29 7 (pb)
0 946391 30 0 (hc)

All Rights Reserved. No Part Of This Book May Be
Reproduced In Any Form Or By Any Means, Except For
The Inclusion Of Brief Quotations In A Review, Without
Prior Permission In Writing From The Publisher

Phototypeset by Input Typesetting Ltd, London
Printed by Richard Clay (The Chaucer Press)
Cover Designed by John Gordon
Cover Painting by Robin Harris

Production Services by Book Production Consultants,
Cambridge
General Editor Black Box Thrillers: Maxim Jakubowski

FIRST EDITION

INTRODUCTION
(David Langford)   v

THE CASE OF THE SEVEN OF CALVARY   1

NINE TIMES NINE   147

ROCKET TO THE MORGUE   323

THE CASE OF THE CRUMPLED KNAVE   469

Introduction
By David Langford

Do you remember the days of detection's Golden Age—when again and again the impossible crime would be committed in the locked room, when the merest dust-grain of a clue would successively point to four different murderers, when the Detection Club's code of fair play solemnly proscribed such plot devices as Secret Passages, Identical Twins, Mysterious Chinamen and Poisons Hitherto Unknown To Science? For sufficient reasons I don't remember that time too well myself, but these four novels of Anthony Boucher's gave me again that feeling of nostalgia for a day when I happened not to have been born.

Golden Ages are awkward things to pin down. Writing in the mid-forties, Edmund Wilson (*Who Cares Who Killed Roger Ackroyd?*) enthusiastically put the boot into practically all crime fiction since Sherlock Holmes. Some other critics assume a sort of linear progression of literary wonderfulness, whereby the top writers of today are by definition better than those of yesterday because we've come a long way since then. (You know, the way Mozart was cast into eternal oblivion by the coming of the Beatles.) In another genre it's been perceptively said, "The golden age of science fiction is about fifteen." Tastes may change in later life, but what you read when you're first hooked is likely to stay with you as a pattern of the *real thing* in SF or in crime.

The age whose reprints hooked me was that of the classical "fair-play" detective story which flourished from, say, the early thirties to the Second World War. (Drawing these lines across the century always irritates by what it leaves out—notably most of G. K. Chesterton, the best detective writer of all, who as in other things was ahead of his time.) Ellery Queen was publishing his murderously exhaustive logic-problem novels. Agatha Christie, like a con man inviting you to find the lady, kept shuffling and reshuffling her tatty pack of characters, and even as you admired the legerdemain there was the weary knowledge that the old dear would cheat you at denouement time. John Dickson Carr and his alias Carter Dickson, boasting between them more than eighty distinct solutions to the traditional locked-room puzzle, ran the most dazzling magic-show of this age but later went mysteriously into eclipse. Tastes had changed.

The trademark of the period, visible in Boucher's four novels here, was a conscious artificiality, an awareness that this kind of detective story was an elaborate game with the reader. Half the fun was leading you up the garden path by playing with unspoken conventions. Does the great detective usually confide in a harmless Watson who tells the story and thus plainly can't be the murderer? Very well, let's boggle the reader with a story where Watson *is* the murderer. Is medical evidence about the body normally accepted as infallible? Very well, let's make the doctor's time-of-death estimate, based on blood clotting, completely and excusably wrong because the deceased was a haemophiliac. Does John Dickson Carr's essay on locked room mysteries (in *The Hollow Man*, known in America and thus to Boucher herein as *The Three Coffins*) seem completely exhaustive? Surely we can dream up *another* means whereby the corpse is found murdered in a sealed room which no murderer could have entered, from which no murderer could have escaped . . .?

You might imagine that this Golden Age passed because writers ran out of permutations and perversions of the old plot devices like locked rooms, mirrors, fiddled clocks, mistaken identities, cryptic dying messages, forged fingerprints, infernal machines and hints of the supernatural (which, said the conventions, may be introduced only to be rationally explained away). But far more formalized puzzles are still popular: chess problems, crosswords, and those incredibly boring and repetitive "logic problems". The puzzle-plot could almost be said to have survived without the traditional detective novel of which it was a part.

What happened was that conscious flamboyance of plot seemed to slip out of fashion. Somebody has probably written a frighteningly intelligent thesis about the effects of post-war austerity on realism in detective stories, leading to the argument, maybe not overtly expressed but lurking there somewhere all the same—

(1) Everyday life is practically devoid of plot.
(2) Good books ought to reflect everday life.
(3) So books with intricate plotting, elaborately prepared fireworks in the final chapters, and other flashy evidences of the author's manipulating hand, are pretty damned unrespectable.

The Joy of Plot was OK in science fiction, or upmarket, avant-garde novels, or crime stories by authors who'd crashed the fame barrier to orbit like Agatha Christie (especially with her *Mousetrap* which was beyond the reach of changes in fashion's climate). But when SF author John Sladek wrote a couple of enjoyable and traditionally intricate detective puzzles in the seventies, he found that "I was turning out a product the supermarkets didn't need any more—stove polish or yellow cakes of laundry soap. One could starve very quickly writing locked-room mysteries now. SF has much more glamour and glitter attached to it, in these high-tech days."

Fashions continue to alter, though. Crime authors from the thirties and forties come and go, bursting back into paperback for a few years and lying low again for a few years more. Here, back in print after a gap which in Britain has lasted since the Golden Age, are four of the best novels by the man who most often wrote as Anthony Boucher.

*

The references above to science fiction aren't just happenstance. William Anthony Parker White, to give him his full name, was well-known in both SF and detection circles. He was born in Oakland, California, in 1911, and until his death in 1968 spent most of his working days as an author, editor and critic of these two genres and—another major interest—opera and music. Thus he regularly reviewed detective stories for *Ellery Queen's Mystery Magazine* and the *New York Times Book Review*; fantasy and SF for the *New York Times* and (under his other byline H. H. Holmes) the Chicago *Sun-Times* and *New York Herald Tribune*; and it shouldn't take a lifelong diet of crime fiction to deduce what he reviewed for *Opera News*.

From 1949 to 1958 he edited the newly-founded *Magazine of Fantasy and Science Fiction* (*F&SF*), then and now the most literate of SF magazines, which together with his intelligent and sympathetic reviewing was a major force in boosting the respectability of American magazine SF. The last years of his editorship brought *F&SF* the first of many Hugo awards as Best Professional SF Magazine.

One of his editorial quirks was a fascination with Catholicism (as well as detection, opera and cats): his own most noted SF story *The Quest for St Aquin* features a superhumanly intelligent robot which embraces the Catholic faith through sheer logical reasoning. Two *F&SF* authors, Robert Silverberg and Randall Garrett, tried to profit from the editorial obsessions, with a story about a nun's cat which solves a detective puzzle—"I think we worked opera into it somewhere, too," confesses Silverberg—but Boucher restrained himself from buying the spoof story. This Catholic interest appears in three of the four novels here.

Anthony Boucher also edited *True Crime Detective* magazine (1952–53), half a dozen detection anthologies and, in succession, three major American lines of crime fiction: the Mercury Mysteries (1952–55), the Dell Great Mystery Library (1957–60) and the Collier Mystery Classics (1962–68). Between 1945 and 1948 he wrote radio plays for the *Sherlock Holmes* and *Case Book of Gregory Hood* series in the USA. The Mystery Writers of America elected him their President for 1951, and three times voted him the Edgar Allan Poe award for excellence in criticism (1946, 1950, 1953). In 1970, after his death, American detective fans began annual conventions in his memory—"Bouchercons"—and the 1973 event was marked by the publication of Boucher's selected criticism under the title *Multiplying Villainies*. Another nonfiction book, published during his lifetime, was *Ellery Queen: A Double Profile* (1951); this of course dealt with the two authors who between them were the late Ellery Queen.

Boucher's fictional output wasn't huge. Apart from the multiple collaboration *The Marble Forest* (1951, as by "Theo Durrant", also known as *The Big Fear*), it consists of seven detective novels and barely fifty short stories, some mysteries, some SF/fantasy and some a mixture of both.

The novels are: *The Case of the Seven of Calvary* (1937), *The Case of the Crumpled Knave* (1939), *Nine Times Nine* (1940), *The Case of the Baker Street Irregulars* (1940, reprinted as *Blood on Baker Street*), *The Case of the Solid Key* (1941), *Rocket to the Morgue* (1942) and *The Case of the Seven Sneezes* (1942). Three collections of the short stories exist—*Far and Away; Eleven Fantasy and SF Stories* (1955), *The Compleat Werewolf and Other Stories of Fantasy and SF* (1969) and *Exeunt Murderers (The Best Mystery Stories of Anthony Boucher)* edited by Francis M. Nevins Jr and Martin H. Greenberg (1983).

Boucher himself didn't draw a hard and fast line between his crime and his SF. The popular character Fergus O'Breen, an Irish private detective with an erratic line in brashness and blarney, is introduced in the *Crumpled Knave* and reappears not only in three more detective novels (*Baker Street Irregulars*, *Solid Key*, *Seven Sneezes*) but also in lighthearted fantasies like "Elsewhen", when the fiendish killer sneaks in and out of the locked room by time machine, and "Gandolphus", featuring a disembodied extraterrestrial to do the dirty work in a similar case. It's hard to read these without imagining the outraged faces of Detection Club members, like something in H. M. Bateman's riper cartoons: The Man Who Introduced The Supernatural into A Detective Story And Failed To Explain It Away! In *The Compleat Werewolf*, O'Breen duly meets a Professor of Philology who develops this tendency to turn into a wolf, and . . . but perhaps I should stop and assure readers that the novels in this collection contain only the purest and most legitimate jiggery-pokery. They'll lead you up the garden path and pull whole skeins of wool over your eyes, but they'll do it fairly.

A closer look, then, at the four novels here: two locked-room mysteries in the Carr tradition and two Queenlike stories with multifaced clues and suspicion skipping round the circle of suspects in a deadly game of pass-the-parcel. Despite the awful temptation to reveal Too Much (like cabbies who take you to the *Mousetrap* theatre and shout the murderer's name after you if your tip's too mingy), I think this bit can be safely read without spoiling your first encounter with the books themselves.

The Case of the Seven of Calvary was Boucher's first novel, and excellent fun it is. Armchair detective Dr John Ashwin is full of tantalizing erudition in such matters as Sanskrit—one up on the don-detectives with their Latin and Greek quotations!—Thomas Hood, *The Mystery of Edwin Drood*, detective stories in general . . . As Dr Fell remarks in *The Hollow Man*: "We're in a detective story, and we don't fool the reader by pretending we're not. Let's not invent elaborate excuses to drag in a discussion of detective stories. Let's candidly glory in the noblest pursuits possible to characters in a book." Bravo. And Dr Ashwin plainly feels the same.

"Holmes, of course, would begin by deducing from the ice pick that the murderer was a cuckold; but I think that a bit far-fetched."

"A cuckold? Just how—"

"Because his household still employs an icebox in these days of electric refrigeration, a fact most probably occasioned by his wife's intrigue with the proverbial iceman. Elementary, my dear Lamb . . ."

Meanwhile that Catholic fascination comes out in the account of the Seven of Calvary, symbol of a weird heretical cult which deserves its place besides other such sinisterly practical groups as the Red-headed League or the Ten Teacups. I particularly like the footnote towards the end of chapter three, in which a grinning Anthony Boucher pours cold water over the one safe guess the reader has made so far . . . prior to jolting complacency even further by ruthless application of the principle quoted tongue-in-cheek by James Thurber: "The person you suspect of the first murder should always be the second victim."

A footnote in the penultimate chapter issues the Queenian Challenge to the Reader, inviting you to unravel the whole tangle of misdirection before Dr Ashwin. What could be more traditional? It's a pity that despite the hints on the final page, there were no more stories of Ashwin.

Nine Times Nine and *Rocket to the Morgue* appeared under Boucher's pseudonym H. H. Holmes: both feature the somewhat unlikely detective Sister Ursula, a nun (yes!) of the spurious Order of St Martha of Bethany. Both are locked-room mysteries with original solutions. *Nine Times Nine*, the better of the two, again indulges in the "noblest pursuits possible to characters in a book." Chapter fourteen features a discussion of the locked-room problem in terms of fiction—specifically, in terms of Carr's famous analysis "The Locked-Room Lecture" in *The Hollow Man*. Which is putting the cards on the table with a vengeance, since in retrospect you can see (you won't see it at the time) that the whole locked-room trick of *Nine Times Nine* is a clever fusion of (a) a stage property from *The Hollow Man* itself and (b) a throwaway line in that book, concerning Ellery Queen's *Chinese Orange Mystery* . . .

Other assets like Boucher's usual witty dialogue, and the enjoyable loony "Children of Light" cult—headed, if you please, by the Wandering Jew—help make this the author's best work.

Sister Ursula, the harassed cop Lt. Marshall, and other characters from *Nine Times Nine* return in *Rocket to the Morgue*. Here the locked-room puzzle is weaker, and indeed proves to be a spoof of one favourite Golden Age cliché-cum-plot-device. This story is the one most popular with the SF fans, since it's set in the world of awful "pulp" SF writing which Boucher knew so well and (via *F& SF*) helped raise from the gutter.

Several SF authors and editors appear thinly disguised under their own pen-names: even Anthony Boucher is there, this book being by "H. H. Holmes". Anson Macdonald and Lyle Monroe were pseudonyms of Robert Heinlein; Don Stuart, editor of *Surprising Stories* and *Worlds Beyond* magazines, was John W. Campbell of *Astounding SF* and *Unknown*; René Lafayette was one named used by L. (for Lafayette) Ron Hubbard while still a humble hack, before he made his dubious pile by inventing Scientology. The injokes are strictly for the fans, but Boucher's SF shop-talk paints a lurid picture of those days' combined ghastliness and delusive grandeur, with unpolished authors mapping the Future of the Human Race at 1¢ per word!

Chapter three has a jolly discussion of SF and the detective story, pushing Campbell's belief that the genres couldn't be mixed . . . since there's no such thing as a locked room when you can have time-machines, psychic powers and fourth-dimensional snickersnees to reach through the walls. Boucher's character doesn't realize (I suspect Boucher did) that an ad-hoc gadget like this is precisely the same cheat as the last-chapter introduction of a hitherto unmentioned secret passage which allows whole platoons of murderers to stalk in and out of the "locked" room with their poison vials and blunt instruments. Asimov and others later wrote fair-play detection in the SF genre, with some success.

Besides two mysterious stabbings, *Rocket to the Morgue* boasts a properly science-fictional though strictly prosaic murder by rocket. Now there's a novelty.

Finally, *The Case of the Crumpled Knave* pits private eye Fergus O'Breen against one of those Ellery Queen riddles where an enigmatic dying message and a puzzling scatter of clues are suddenly marshalled into a murderous pattern, precise as a mathematical equation. Only, of course, the clues are two-faced at the very least, and the equation is one of those with several solutions. This one is difficult to discuss further without giving too much away—but keep your eye on apoplectic old Colonel Rand, who is not what he seems!

Again the book is conscious of its own artificiality, with even the detective musing in literary terms: "She's read too many of those novels where the person who Knows Too Much is the second victim . . ." The classical detective story is an artificial literary form, all right, but not to be despised as such. So, after all, is the sonnet.

*

There is one supposedly crushing criticism you hear about Golden Age detection. It's approximately the same as the criticism of landscape gardening in this exchange from Thomas Love Peacock:
 "I distinguish the picturesque and the beautiful, and I add to them, in the laying out of grounds, a third and distinct quality, which I call *unexpectedness*."
 "Pray, sir," said Mr Milestone, "by what name do you distinguish this character, when a person walks round the grounds for a second time?"
Or: where is the charm of an intricate detective story when you read it again with full knowledge of whodunnit? Isn't there something inferior about a novel which can only be read once?
 There are two replies. Firstly comes the snide one: with most of,

say, Agatha Christie's novels you'll have forgotten the details next day, just as you wouldn't remember where the queen actually *was* after being fooled again by the three-card trick. The second and better answer applies equally to landscape gardening. If properly done, that quality of "unexpectedness" brings new satisfaction the second time round, since now you can appreciate the subtleties of design and misdirection which lead up to what *was* a pure surprise but now reveals itself as the culmination of good craftsmanship. To take an outrageously lofty example, does *Hamlet* lose its force when you watch it and happen to know that all the main characters are going to get it in the neck?

This makes detective stories sound far more pretentious than they are. Let's just conclude that, if not one of the Greats, Boucher stands high above the rabble of thirties/forties crime writers. He writes amusingly and well, his plots are nicely constructed along the classical lines of the Golden Age, and these four books will stand being read a second time.

Now go and read them.

The Case Of The Seven Of Calvary

DEDICATED TO

Dr. Ashwin

[Arthur William Ryder, 1877–1938]

The characters, institutions, and action of this novel are completely fictional, and have no reference to actual people or events—with one exception. That one is Dr. Ashwin, who is accurately reproduced from reality, and whose name in this book is a sanskrit translation of his own.

Anthony Boucher

Characters

I. Students at the University of California
    A. Residents of International House
        *Martin Lamb, *research fellow in German*
        *Alex Bruce, *research fellow in chemistry*
        *Kurt Ross, *a Swiss*
        Paul Boritsin, *a White Russian*
        Richard Worthing, *a Canadian*
        Remigio Morales, *a Bolivian*
        *Mona, *his sister*
        *Guadalupe Sanchez (Lupe), *a Mexican*
    B. Other Students
        *Cynthia Wood, *Bruce's fiancée*
        Mary Roberts
        Chuck Withers

II. Faculty members of the University of California
    *John Ashwin, Ph.D., *professor of Sanskrit*
    *Paul Lennox, M.A., *instructor in history*
    *Ivan Leshin, Ph.D., *exchange professor of Slavic history*
    *Tatyana (Tanya), *his wife*
    *Joseph Griswold, Ph.D., *professor of Spanish*
    Lawrence Drexel, *director of the Little Theatre*

III. Others
    *Sergeant Cutting, *of the Berkeley police*
    Davis, *a policeman*
    Warren Blakely, *head of International House*
    Morris, *a hospitable philologist*
    Dr. Evans, *of the Memorial Hospital*
    A young internee
    An elderly clerk at Zolotoy's ("Theatrical Accessories")
    *Hugo Schaedel, Ph.D., *Kurt Ross's uncle and unofficial ambassador of the Swiss Republic*

* The reader who approaches a mystery novel as a puzzle and a challenge is cautioned that he need keep his eye only on those characters marked by an asterisk; the rest are merely necessary extras.—*A. B.*

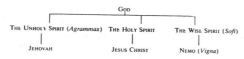

THE SEVEN OF CALVARY

(*diagram prepared by Martin Lamb after the researches of Paul Lennox*)

Prelude

An admirable crab cocktail and two bottles of beer had, I confess, made me more than usually argumentative. I had reached the point of maintaining, for the sheer pleasure of argument, an untenable position quite contrary to my own belief.

"The Watson," I expounded, "is an outworn device. In the early days of detective fiction he was essential. The unaccustomed reader would never have seen what the detective was driving at without him; hence the need of Dupin's unnamed friend and of Watson himself. But now the reader of mystery stories is so inoculated, like Betteredge, with detective fever that he needs—as you might say, Martin—no 'stooge' to act as interpreter to the master mind."

Martin Lamb summoned his attention from the fishing boats outside the window and from the Japanese children who seemed in imminent danger of plunging from the pier. "Logical," he commented. "But writers still use them."

"Do they?" I asked. "Roger Sheringham, Reggie Fortune, Lord Peter Wimsey—these almost too bright young men don't seem to find a Watson necessary. Philo Vance's Van Dine is a figurehead who never utters a word, a phantom first person, as every producer has realized in omitting him on the screen. Can you conceive of any Holmes novel filmed with Watson omitted? Dr. Thorndyke has so many Watsons that he may be said to have none. Dr. Fell, that magnificently bawdy toper—"

"You see, Tony," Martin interrupted, "I'm a trifle prejudiced on this question of Watsons. I was one myself once, and I flatter myself that I was damned indispensable."

"And when was this?" I asked the question reluctantly, fully expecting a more or less elaborate bit of leg pulling.

Martin had taken out his pencil and was drawing something on the back of the menu. "When? Were you in Berkeley when Dr. Schaedel was killed?"

Schaedel . . . The name was familiar. I seemed to remember fragments of some complicated and unsolved mystery. "Something about Switzerland, wasn't it?" I finally answered. "And an ice pick?"

"Switzerland and an ice pick . . ." Martin smiled. "That combination makes about as much sense as the whole problem seemed to at first. And as it still seems to the Berkeley police . . . Have you ever heard of the Seven of Calvary?" he asked abruptly, handing me the menu.

I looked at the curious figure for several moments. A sort of Italic F over three rectangles. I shook my head. "Now I see," I said. "In order to disprove my own argument I am now to play Watson to you. Well, tell the story."

"First," said Martin, "we will have some more beer and some more crab. We'd be idiots to eat only a single crab cocktail apiece in one of the few places in the world which serve whole crab instead of shredded. Then I'll begin the story and continue it over dinner at—shall we say La Favorite?"

I agreed gladly. The mixed smell of fish, fishing boats, and salt water had roused an appetite not easily satisfied. But an equally strong appetite had been stirred by Martin's casual reference to his playing Watson. More details of the Schaedel case returned to my mind. There had been another murder—or was it two?—in Berkeley around the same time. As best I could remember, the cases had seemed linked, but no solution had ever been found.

The crab and the beer arrived. Martin took a large swig, lifted one perfect crab leg out of its sauce, and sat regarding the end of his fork. "I scarcely know what is the logical beginning of the story," he said. "We should start, I suppose, with the fons et origo mali, as Ashwin might say. You know Ashwin, of course?"

"I met him once." And who does not know the translations from the Sanskrit of John Ashwin? The Panchatantra, the dramas of Kalidasa, the racy Ten Princes, the sublime Bhagavad Gita—a library would be poor indeed which contained no Ashwin.

"Good," Martin went on. "But where should I begin? With the day that Ashwin first read a mystery novel? That would be logical enough. Or the day that Dr. Schaedel discovered the delights of an evening walk? Or the day that I began my translation of José María Fonseca? Or—most logical of all perhaps—the day that the noted Eastbay businessman, Robert R. Wood, decided to change his religion?"

"Please, Martin," I begged, "stop being mystifying and tell the story. Remember you're the Watson, not the Master Mind."

Martin finished his cocktail deliberately. "All right," he said. "I'll begin with myself on the day of the murder. That should allow me to bring in everything. And this I promise you—nothing irrelevant and everything relevant. This shall be a model of fair play." He took another draught of beer and offered me his cigarette case. And as we began to add tobacco smoke to the fish-laden air, he commenced the story of the murder of Dr. Hugo Schaedel, which is also the story of Dr. John Ashwin, scholar, poet, translator, and detective.

ONE

PRELIMINARIES TO A MURDER

"*atha nalopākhyānam. brhadaçva uvāca.*"
" 'Here begins the episode of Nala. Brihadashva speaks,' " Martin translated almost automatically. The warm spring air entering through the open windows of the classroom was quite enough to distract his attention from the *Mahabharata*.
Dr. Ashwin rose somewhat heavily from behind the desk and began to pace the room as he recited the opening shloka. His voice took on a booming richness which fitted equally well his imposing figure and the magnificent Sanskrit verse.

Martin was sincerely eager to keep his attention fixed upon his translation. As the sole student of first year Sanskrit in the entire university, he had a reputation to maintain. But his thoughts insisted on wandering. Rehearsal that afternoon. Could he possibly persuade Drexel to make Paul change his reading of the death speech? Just what were the rights of a translator against those of a director? And that evening the reception for Dr. Schaedel. Why the devil had he let himself be roped in on a reception committee? As if he didn't have enough . . . " 'Thus speaking, the king released the swan,' " he translated.

" 'Thus having spoken,' " Ashwin amended.

When half an hour of this had passed, Ashwin laid the text on the table and sat down. "You did very well, Mr. Lamb," he commented. "How do you like your first contact with Sanskrit narrative verse?"

"Very much indeed," Martin admitted honestly. "It has a splendid roll."

"In all literature," said Ashwin, "I have found only three verse meters which I can read indefinitely without tiring: English blank verse, the Latin and Greek hexameter, and the Sanskrit shloka." Like all of Ashwin's frequent *ex cathedra* statements, this came forth with an impression of superpontifical infallibility. And in the same manner, without a pause, he asked, "Have you found any interesting mystery novels of late?"

Dr. Ashwin's perturbingly catholic tastes rarely failed to startle Martin slightly. He was quite likely to turn from a stringent critique of Virgil to extravagant praise of Ogden Nash, who, in his estimation, held first place among American poets. The unpredictable jump from metrical technique to mystery novels took Martin a little aback. "Interesting, possibly," he answered, "but not good. An atrocious modern solution to *Edwin Drood,* in which the Princess Puffer turns out to be Jasper's mother."

"The Princess Puffer," Ashwin began, "is to me the only mystery in the unfinished novel. The main points of the plot are entirely too obvious, which is, of course, exactly why there is so much discussion about them:

"Edwin Drood was murdered by John Jasper, who, as a member of the cult of Phansigars, employed his black kerchief for strangling. Datchery, who, needless to say, is Bazzard, discovers the facts of the crime from Deputy and Durdles. Grewgious evolves an elaborate plot to force a confession from Jasper. Helena Landless, disguised as her twin Neville, leads Jasper to the Sapsea monument under pretext of threats—Jasper naturally planning to kill this supposed Neville. At the tomb he is confronted with Neville himself posing as the dead Drood. In terror he admits his guilt and attacks the ghost. Before Grewgious and Bazzard-Datchery, hidden nearby, can seize him, he has given Neville a mortal wound. Drood's bones are identified by the ring, Jasper hangs for both deaths, and Helena and Rosa marry Crisparkle and Tartar. It is all too obvious, although I admit that the Princess Puffer still puzzles me."

"But if it is so obvious why has it been a literary crux for years?"

"As I said, *because* it is obvious. It is the blatantly obvious that defies this muddle-headed world, which chooses what is quite possibly so in preference to what is obviously truth. This 'quite possibly so' is rarely entirely wrong; it is simply confused. And truth can issue far more readily from error than from confusion. Moha rules the world." A bell rang at this pronouncement, and Ashwin rose. "Should you care to lunch with me, Mr. Lamb?" he asked.

Gratefully free now from academic responsibilities, they lit cigarettes as they walked out onto the vernal campus. Martin nodded to several friends as they passed, noting on the face of each the expression of slight surprise always caused by his companionship with Dr. Ashwin. They did make a curious pair. A difference of thirty years in age, an utter contrariety in upbringing and attitude, and certain striking divergences in taste were more than balanced by an essential similarity in the way their minds worked and a common devotion to beer and whisky.

It was beer that was on Martin's mind now as they passed through Sather Gate onto Telegraph Avenue. Ashwin paused a moment and looked at the entrance to the campus. "When I first came to this university," he observed, "there was a frieze of naked athletes on that gate. Since they were not only naked but somewhat ithyphallic, the pure people of Berkeley demanded the removal of the frieze. But what most rejoiced me was this: Underneath this group of males, apparently rearing for action, was the inscription: ERECTED BY JANE K. SATHER."

Happily sated with a good lunch and good talk, Martin entered the history classroom. Fortunately there was a vacant seat next to Cynthia Wood, and he took it. Seats near Cynthia were usually at something of a premium.

"Hello, Martin," she smiled.

"Hello," he answered. "How's Alex?"

"How should I know?" Her tone was sharp.

"Sorry. I just thought you might have seen him at lunch."

"Well, I didn't."

Despite Cynthia's abruptness, Martin relaxed in the stiff wooden chair and looked at her with pleasure. She was enough to relieve the tedium of any class. In earliest adolescence Cynthia had decided to become exotic, and she had succeeded almost without trying. The natural development of her body had produced a more exotic result than any effort could have managed. She used no make-up, and as a consequence her black lashes, her white cheeks, and her full red lips were far more striking than the best Max Factor effects. Her breasts were the only living ones which had ever reminded Martin of the half-pomegranates which grace the chests of every maiden (in the widest sense) in the Arabian Nights; he fully expected that her navel, by analogy, would hold an ounce of ointment. He had, in fact, once expressed that idea in an imitation of Arabic verse, which had fortunately been lost long since in his infinite mess of papers.

"Tell me, Cyn," he asked abstractedly, "how on earth did you come to be taking this course? Slavic History's an odd bit of knowledge for a rich girl who is going to justify her existence by teaching English."

Cynthia shrugged her round shoulders. "I don't know. I had a free elective, and I thought Dr. Leshin ought to be interesting."

"Well, isn't he?"

"Yes," she admitted reluctantly, "but I'm funny. I'd sooner get my grades on a sheet of paper than on a sheet of linen."

Martin nodded sympathetically. Dr. Ivan Leshin, half Russian and half Czech, was an attractive man, and resolutely determined to use that attractiveness for all it was worth. His private coaching lessons, despite his charming young Russian wife, had already become a byword during his brief sojourn in Berkeley as Exchange Professor of Slavic History.

"But why the devil do you always ask me where Alex is?" Cynthia broke out abruptly.

"You're generally with him for lunch. I don't see what there is to make a scene about, Cyn."

"And don't call me Cyn."

"It was Paul's gag. I think he started it so that he could say a picture was pretty as Cyn."

"I don't like Paul's gags. In fact," Cynthia added in unconscious paraphrase of Groucho Marx, "I don't like Paul."

Of course, Martin thought, as the entrance of Dr. Leshin cut off the conversation, it was easy enough not to like Paul Lennox. His superficial cynicism and methodical carelessness could put one off all too easily. And Martin had special reason for dislike at present; there was Paul's atrocious reading of his last line, to say nothing of the absurdly unnatural way in which he crumpled into death in the big strangulation scene. But Martin knew Paul rather better than most of his acquaintances, and found in him something strangely fascinating. He really seemed more apt to appeal to Cynthia than the pleasant and undistinguished chemist Alex Bruce to whom she was engaged. Or was it an actual engagement? It is so difficult to make absolutely accurate statements concerning campus romances.

And Martin's mind continued to wander on subjects from romance to *The Mystery of Edwin Drood* while the professor from the University of Prague, Dr. Leshin, lectured on the defenestration of 1618. Tantalizing word, defenestration. It should mean something far more glamorous than throwing royal secretaries out of windows—and onto dunghills at that. Dr. Leshin's mind was also evidently wandering. His sharp black eyes betrayed far more interest in the evening's coaching lesson (and what does Mrs. Leshin do with her evenings, Martin wondered) than in the afternoon's lecture.

Martin was relieved when the lecture was over. There was now an hour's breathing space in the midst of a painfully busy day. He selected a sunny spot of lawn and lay in idle luxury, thinking vaguely about people.

"I should have been a Brantôme," he murmured, "or at least a Winchell. I always manage to know more things about people's complications, and I never have any of my own. Cyn and Alex . . . the Leshins . . . Kurt and Lupe . . . Paul in lonely splendor . . ."

It was his prophetic soul that soliloquized as he thus grouped all the principal figures of the coming tragedy—all, that is, save one, and that one already marked for death.

He was half asleep when the Campanile struck three. With a minor mental curse, he rose and walked into the auditorium. The rehearsal was late in starting. The cast wandered about with the futile look peculiar to amateur actors wondering if they know their lines. Martin was sure that they did not.

Paul Lennox sat alone in the middle of the hall, trying to light a particularly recalcitrant pipe. It was almost unprecedented that an instructor in history should take part in campus dramatics; but Martin, as translator of the play, had persuaded the director to hear Paul read. In the stirring blank verse into which Martin had rendered Fonseca's tirades, there appeared a new Paul Lennox—a sixteenth century cloak-and-sword figure. His dramatic training was slight (hence the lapses that so annoyed Martin), but his feeling for the character of Don Juan was amazing.

Martin strolled up to him as a glow at last appeared in the large pipe bowl. "Hello," said Paul, looking up. "Drexel's late again."

"I'm just as glad. I wish the rehearsal were called off. I've got to dress for dinner tonight."

"What do you mean, 'dress'? Tails and things?"

"Not quite." Martin was thankful. "Just tuxedo. It's the private dinner for that Swiss deputy or whatever—you know, Kurt Ross's uncle."

"I'd heard there was some sort of a grand panjandrum coming to International House, but I didn't know it had anything to do with Kurt. Maybe that's why he's so worried."

"Kurt?"

"Yes. Goes around looking as though he were ready to take the last great step or something. What's uncle's name? Ross?"

"No, Schaedel, I think. Dr. Hugo Schaedel."

And that was the first time that Paul Lennox ever heard the name of the man whose face he was never to see but whose fate was so tightly linked with his own.

Martin's hopes had been dashed. The rehearsal was not called off. It started late and lasted far beyond its usual limits. As a result, he was delayed in getting back to International House and was forced to dress at a most uncomfortable rate of speed. He had just succeeded, after Houdinesque efforts, in getting the third tricky stud into his dress shirt when he was interrupted by a knock on his door.

"Who is it?" he called.

"Kurt," came the answer. "Are you not dressed?"

"Will be in a minute. Come in."

Paul was right, Martin reflected as Kurt Ross entered. Something was wrong. The tall blond young Swiss looked somewhat like the Spartan boy just as the fox reached the juiciest tidbits. Martin almost expected to see a vulpine head rear itself from behind the black waistcoat, just about where the Phi Beta Kappa key dangled.

"Sit down. I'll be ready in a second. Cigarettes are there by the typewriter."

"Thanks." Kurt sat in the one comfortable chair and lit a cigarette. Its smoke seemed slightly to allay the fox pains.

"How's Lupe?" Martin asked casually as he adjusted his suspenders.

"All right. Why?" Kurt snapped out the answer with sudden viciousness as though the fox had just discovered a new and more sensitive line of attack.

Oh, damn, thought Martin, why *can't* I ask a harmless question without being barked at? First Cyn, now Kurt. . . . "I just thought I'd ask. After all—"

"I said that she is all right, did I not?" In his annoyance Kurt's accent, usually barely perceptible, became thicker.

"That's good." Martin continued dressing in silence. He scarcely knew what to say after being rebuffed on such an obvious conversational opening. He hoped nothing was really the matter with Lupe Sanchez. International House was a curious place with its incredible assortment of nationalities, leavened by a few ordinary Americans such as Paul Lennox, Alex Bruce, or Martin himself. And if the founder's high ideals of promoting international good feeling were not always fully realized, at least the house produced some strange interracial romances. Kurt and Lupe, Swiss and Mexican, formed one of the oddest of these mixed couples and, to Martin's mind, one of the most charming. It would be a pity if anything had happened.

After a careful brushing, Martin slipped on his coat and looked in the mirror. He would do, he decided. Possibly not exactly a model of the well dressed reception committee, but good enough. As he turned from the mirror, Kurt spoke. "Aren't you going to wear your Phi Beta Kappa key?"

"Hell, no. Mind handing me those cigarettes? Thanks. No; I'd rather not decorate my stomach with a blatant atrocity like that. If they were some decent size, maybe yes, but as it is . . . " He finished filling his cigarette case.

"It would be a mark of courtesy to our distinguished visitor."

"Put on swank for Uncle Hugo? Show him what a brilliant reception committee it is?"

"It is not because he is my uncle. It is simply as a token of—"

"All right." It was less trouble to wear the damned thing than to argue with Kurt. Martin slipped the key on his watch chain and prepared to go. As Kurt rose, there was a slight clink on the floor. Martin laughed. "Serves you right, Kurt. You would lecture me on wearing one."

Kurt's internal agony allowed him a shamefaced smile. "It often falls off," he admitted. "I must have the ring fixed."

Martin experienced a sense of growing discomfort as they went down to the small dining room to welcome Dr. Schaedel. The other members of the reception committee were there already—a quiet and bespectacled young Chinese; a White Russian aristocrat who had never quite got over his visit to the National Students' League because he had heard that he would find other Russians there; a swarthy Bolivian who had seriously threatened the peace of International House when appointed to a committee containing two Paraguayans; a Canadian who had at first been so often thought an American that he had developed an astounding B.B.C. manner of speech; and a young French Jew who kept glancing nervously at Kurt, who managed, quite unconsciously, to look far too Aryan for M. Bernstein's peace of mind.

Martin exchanged cigarettes with Boritsin, who had equipped himself with long thin ones fitted with mouthpieces. On such occasions International House expects its members to be as distinctively national as possible.

"You look uncomfortably formal, Mr. Lamb," the Russian aristocrat remarked.

Martin admitted that he was.

"For my part," said Boritsin, "I am glad that the dinner is formal. For were it not so, I should doubtless be expected to wear a Russian blouse, which I never did before coming to this International House. I assure you that it was with great difficulty that my mother the Princess succeeded in securing one for me."

"Yes," observed the Bolivian, who had joined them, "I remember when Lupe Sanchez and my sister sang for a Sunday-night supper. They had to search through every costumer in San Francisco to find dresses characteristic enough to please the committee."

"By the way," Martin asked, "how is Miss Sanchez?"

"Unwell, my sister tells me. She has retired early to her room. My sister is worried."

"Damn it, stop worrying." Kurt stood behind the Bolivian and looked down on him in anger. "She's all right, I tell you, Morales. That is, she will be. After tonight."

At that moment Mr. Blakely, head of International House, entered, followed by Dr. Schaedel. Martin observed the unofficial Swiss representative with curiosity. If his tour was, as Kurt had said, in the interests of world peace, no more fitting person could have been chosen, so far as appearance went. Utterly unlike his young-Siegfried nephew, he resembled a quiet monk with no interests beyond his garden, his breviary, and the poor. He was of average height, but the mild beneficence which radiated from him gave you the curious impression that he was small. His features were sharp, but his kind expression softened them. He acknowledged Mr. Blakely's Rotarian introductions with a smile, but no words beyond a polite repetition of the name. There followed an awkward pause, as though both honored guest and reception committee expected the first words to come from the other, and then a general movement, as a gesture from Blakely, toward the table.

The dinner was competent but dull, and of course unrelieved by wine. Martin sat between Boritsin and Worthing, listening alternately to the Russian's plaints against the Soviet and the Canadian's violent bursts of Anglophilia. At that, he felt, he was better off than Dr. Schaedel, who maintained a polite smile through a lengthy discourse on international brotherhood as exemplified by the House. It was fairly obvious that Dr. Schaedel's understanding of English was none too good, which was, Martin thought, just as well.

At last the dessert was cleared away, and Martin settled down to wholehearted enjoyment of coffee and a cigarette. Mr. Blakely rose and launched forth into a speech, for which his monologue to Dr. Schaedel had evidently been in the nature of a rehearsal, ending with a peroration which served to introduce "that worthy scholar and gentleman who has devoted his life to furthering that cause which is, we may safely say, the cause of prime importance to all the world and above all, perhaps, in these troublous times, to we of America" (Martin winced), "the cause of World Peace." (Here came a five-minute digression and recapitulation.) "Friends of International House, my words cannot do justice to this man. In fact, the less said about him, the better." (Martin repressed a snort at this typical Blakely infelicity.) "Gentlemen, Dr. Hugo Schaedel."

Dr. Schaedel spoke in a soft voice and with a strongly marked accent. "Gentlemen," he said, "it is with great difficulty that I in this language speak. My nephew tells me that already among you one is who can for me interpret. *Herr Lamb, möchten Sie vielleicht übersetzen was ich auf Deutsch sage?*"

"*Sehr gerne, Herr Doktor,*" Martin answered.

"*Besten Dank, mein Freund. Also...*" Dr. Schaedel paused a moment, and then began his impromptu speech, pausing frequently for Martin's translations.

It was a simple, direct talk, an appeal to mankind, as exemplified by these representatives of divers races, to forget its evil nature and allow itself to be won by the good. Warming to his topic, he grew slightly mystical and referred to the Black and White powers which rule the world. The Black, he said, reward evil, but their rewards are evil; the White reward good with good rewards. Therefore we should abstain from Evil, if only that we may win the rewards of Good. "I know that this is bad Christianity," he added, "but it is meant for bad Christians."

There was silence when he had finished. Some inherent goodness in his thought and character had communicated itself to the group. Then Mr. Blakely thanked Dr. Schaedel, and the spell was broken.

As the reception committee filed out of the dining room, Kurt approached Martin. "It was very good of you to interpret for my uncle," he said. "He has many difficulties with the language, and I myself felt unable this evening . . . "

"I was glad to," Martin answered. "It's the devil's own language anyway, and doubtless spoken exclusively in the seventh circle of Hell. Please tell your uncle that I'd be very glad to be of help to him whenever I could."

"Thanks, Martin. I will." Kurt moved away. Martin saw him pluck Dr. Schaedel by the sleeve and detach him for a moment from Mr. Blakely. "*Darf ich einen Augenblick mit dir sprechen?*"[1] he heard Kurt ask.

"*Später, Kurt. Sagen wir um halb sehn bei mir,*"[2] was the Herr Doktor's reply.

Whether Kurt repeated his offer of assistance to Dr. Schaedel in their appointed interview at nine thirty, Martin never learned. Surely neither the Swiss emissary nor Martin himself could then have imagined what form that assistance would take.

Relieved of his committee costume and comfortable again in a dressing robe, Martin spent a quiet evening brooding over a tremendously complicated alibi. By ten thirty he had reached the point where the detective remarks to his stooge, "All the facts are now in your hands. Let us see if you reach the same conclusions as I." Such challenges always stimulated Martin. He laid the book aside, lit a cigarette, and leaned back in his chair to destroy the alibi.

Martin broke off his cogitations in annoyance. Why the devil did authors always suppose that a man who has been on the stage, even in amateur dramatics at Oxford, must *ipso facto* be able to wander about the streets in a completely convincing false character? From what he knew of actors, especially amateurs, and even more from what he knew of make-up, the whole proposition seemed preposterous.

"Come in," Martin called in answer to a knock on the door.

The visitor was Paul Lennox, whose room was next to Martin's. Pipe, slippers, and all, he seemed a model of scholarly placidity. No eye could have discerned in this quiet man the flamboyant Spanish gallant of the afternoon's rehearsal. "I got some new discs yesterday from the record library in San Francisco," he began. "I thought you might like to hear them."

"Good," said Martin, rising. "I've been trying to break down an excellent alibi, and I'm tired."

"You've been what?"

---

[1] "May I speak with you a moment?"
[2] "Later, Kurt. Shall we say at nine thirty in my room."

"Breaking down a murderer's alibi. You've no idea how complex they can be. What are your records?"

"An album by the Hugo Wolf Society. Kipnis and Rethberg singing."

"Fine."

So Martin spent a pleasant half-hour in Paul's room listening to Wolf *Lieder* with interpolated conversation. The phonograph was an electric model which bulked up large in the small room; but the excellence of its tone apparently compensated Paul for the inconvenience. After the last record Paul remarked, "You know, Martin, that play of yours has set me off on an interesting track of research. I've decided to do a paper on *Possible Historical Originals of the Don Juan Legend*. It should do for publication, and that always helps one's academic standing here."

"Have you found any new material?" Martin asked.

"A suggestion or two that may build into something. I say—would you like to see my tentative outline? I think you'd find it interesting. It's rather rough, but if you'll give me fifteen minutes I'll type it out for you."

"You needn't bother."

"No bother at all. Unless of course you're sleepy. I always find music stimulating; I could spend the rest of the night talking."

"All right," Martin agreed. "I'll dig out some bourbon that I carefully hid away from the chambermaid, and we'll have an all-night discussion on Don Juan."

"It's fairly early yet anyway." Paul glanced at his clock. "Eleven fifteen."

"You're slow," said Martin. "I have eleven twenty."

"Damn. Are you sure? That clock is one of my special prides. Well, anyhow, I'll get this thing finished in about twenty minutes and bring it over."

"And bring your glass, unless you don't mind the bottle."

Paul was truly industrious when once he became interested in the matter in hand. No sooner had Martin returned to his own room than he could hear the click of the typewriter and the ping of its bell.

He dug the bourbon out from under a pile of shorts. Most of the chambermaids were very decent, but there was no use risking a report for violation of the rule against liquor. He poured himself a sizable drink and decided to finish *The Boat Train Murders*. A quarter of an hour later he set the book aside in disgust.

In rhythm to the still clicking typewriter, Martin poured himself another drink and sat down at the desk. He had just had a lovely idea for a parody on "Gunga Din," but before he could get beyond the first line ("*Wee timorous cowering bheestie...*") Paul rapped on the door.

"There!" he said as he entered. "I think I did that in nearly record time." And he waved a sizable outline.

"Twenty minutes," Martin checked on his watch. "Not bad at all. Did you bring a glass?"

"Just hand me the bottle." Martin did so. "I need a drink after a job like that."

Martin also dispensed with a glass this time. After a healthy swig, he sat on the bed and lit a cigarette. "Now," he said, "let's have your theory."

"First a match, please. I forgot mine. Thanks. . . . Now," Paul expounded in puffs as he lit his pipe, "you realize that the first appearance in literature of Don Juan is in Tirso's *El Burlador de Sevilla*—that is, in the early seventeenth century." Martin nodded. "Now I have here —" He broke off as another knock came on the door.

"Come in," Martin called.

"I heard voices so I thought I'd drop in. Hello, Paul—" and Alex Bruce interrupted his speech of greeting to make a grab for the whisky bottle which Paul, in rising, had knocked from the desk.

"Sorry, Martin," Paul apologized. "I'm getting clumsy. How are you, Alex?"

"Fine. What are you fellows discussing?"

"A pint of bourbon," Martin answered. "Join us?"

"Of course."

"How's Cynthia?" Paul asked.

From his previous experiences of that day, Martin was a little afraid of what the answer might be. But Alex smiled, wiped a drop of whisky from his lip, and replied, "Fine, I guess. I haven't seen her today."

"She said you were going over this evening." Something in Paul's tone puzzled Martin. There was a slight touch of inconsistent emotion. Jealousy? he thought vaguely. Is that perhaps why Cyn dislikes Paul—because he is too interested in her?

"Come to think of it, I did say I might drop in," Alex was saying, "but I was tired after working at the lab—How about another drink, Martin?"

The bottle went the rounds, and there was a moment's silence. Martin took a cigarette and passed one to Alex, who accepted. Paul leisurely relit his pipe. The silence was not the oppressive emptiness of uncongeniality; it was simply the quiet that can be enjoyed by three men blessed with whisky and tobacco.

Martin indulged in his frequent habit of unspoken soliloquy as he looked about the room, rapidly filling with smoke. They made a curious trio—Paul, instructor in history, amateur cynic, and scorner of emotional entanglements; Alex, research worker in chemistry, essentially earnest, and quite openly in love with the exotic Cynthia; and Martin himself, graduate fellow in German with writing ambitions and dabbler in all things including emotions.

Alex broke the silence. "It's funny your asking me about Cynthia, Paul. I had an idea that there was something I should do tonight and—"

"Damn!" Martin exclaimed. "Somebody else at the door. I seem to be keeping open house tonight."

The new arrival was Kurt Ross, and a very different Kurt from the self-contained, if internally anguished, member of the reception committee. His tie was askew and his movements were jerky. Martin noticed inconsequentially that the Phi Beta key had evidently fallen off again and this time gone unnoticed. Kurt's eye wandered from Martin to the whisky bottle. "I thought so," he muttered. "Do you mind, Martin?"

"Of course not."

"There," Kurt gasped after a long drag at the bottle. "I thought you'd have something like that. I needed it."

"What the devil's the matter with you?" Paul asked.

"Oh, hello, Paul. Nothing. Nothing. I was just a little nervous, that is all."

"It's the most melodramatic entrance I've seen in years. You look as though—"

"Oh, let him be, Paul," Alex put in soothingly. "Who cares why he was nervous? He was, and he's had a shot of bourbon, and he'll soon have another, and that's that."

Martin held up the bottle for a sorrowful examination. "I'm not sure he will have another."

"Wait a minute," Alex suggested. "I've got about half a pint. Be back in a minute."

As Alex left, Martin handed the bottle to Kurt. "Here," he said. "Kill it, Kurt."

Kurt obeyed gratefully. "Thank you, Martin. You don't know what you've done for me."

"Don't worry, Kurt," Paul interposed. "He will know. You see, Martin reads mystery novels. He breaks down alibis. In short, he's a dangerous person to have around where there are secrets."

The hour that passed after Alex returned with his whisky, the quantity of which he had underestimated grossly, was a little vague when Martin tried to recall it the next morning. The chief memory was that of a glorious glow, in which Paul lost his dignity, Alex his earnestness, and Kurt his nerves. On such occasions there was very little for Martin to lose; instead he found somewhere what seemed at the time to be a singing voice, and joined in lustily on "Blow the Man Down" and "The Bastard King of England."

Kurt, whose English vocabulary was limited to printable words, got a little lost, but sought revenge with a song in Swiss dialect which was, he assured them seriously, the bawdiest song ever invented. None of them understood a word of it, but they believed Kurt implicitly and found it colossally panicking. Then Paul, who had, as a sign of general laxity, abandoned his pipe for Martin's cigarettes, gave them the story of Anthony Claire, who was a notable conjurer of surprising articles. All three others joined in on the lusty chorus until a banging on the wall and on the ceiling led Martin to suggest adjournment of the session.

He stumbled into bed, leaving his clothes on odd portions of furniture, and reviewed the day's events in his mind. He finally came to the conclusion, which seemed at the time to be of some subtle importance, that it had been a Full Day.

It was not until the next morning that he learned that the day (Friday, April 6th, to be precise) had included among its many events the murder of Dr. Hugo Schaedel, at approximately 11:30 P.M.

TWO

THE OBSERVATIONS OF DR. ASHWIN

SAVANT SLAIN WITH STILETTO
Berkeley Murder By Unknown Fiend
Mystery Killer Leaves Cryptic Warning

An unknown hand dealt death last night to a man who has given his life to fighting death. Dr. Hugo Schaedel, unofficial ambassador of the Swiss Republic, who was scheduled to give several public addresses in the Bay Region on the subject of World Peace, was found dead last night in front of a private residence at 27 Panoramic Way, Berkeley. He had been stabbed from behind by some instrument with a long thin blade which had pierced the heart. Death must have been almost instantaneous, police surgeons report.

The body was discovered by Miss Cynthia Wood of 27 Panoramic Way, graduate student at the University of California and daughter of Robert R. Wood, prominent Eastbay financier. Miss Wood states that a man unknown to her called at her house at 11:28 last night. She is able to give the exact time because the stranger asked the time and also how to find his way to International House. Immediately after he had left, Miss Wood heard a cry and rushed outside, accompanied by Miss Mary Roberts. On the sidewalk in front of her house she found the body of the man she had just spoken with.

Miss Roberts called Dr. H. D. Calvert and the police, but the man was already dead. Because of his question to Miss Wood, Sergeant Cutting requested Warren Blakely, head of International House, to inspect the body. Blakely identified it as that of Dr. Schaedel.

Although Miss Wood rushed from the house immediately upon hearing the cry, she did not see the mysterious assailant. There is no clue to his identity beyond a piece of paper left beside the corpse on which a symbol is written, the meaning of which has not yet been discovered. Sergeant Cutting reports that the police have several indications which will not as yet be made public. An arrest is expected shortly.

Martin read this surprising account over a very late breakfast in the House cafeteria. The shock served to dissipate completely his random fears lest some stern disciplinarian might have reported last night's binge to the House authorities. When a large glass of tomato juice and several cups of black coffee had cleared away the haze of his hangover, he lit a cigarette and reread the article carefully.

It was impossible nonsense. No one could want to kill that inoffensive and charming little man. "An arrest is expected shortly." That was obviously padding, partly to maintain official reputation, partly, perhaps, to frighten the murderer into a false move. There seemed to be no doubt that it was murder. Stabbing from behind could scarcely be accident or suicide, nor yet self-defense—as though anyone should need to defend himself against Dr. Schaedel. It seemed necessarily to be cold-blooded murder. But why?

Martin turned to the second page of the newspaper. Here there were many photographs; one of the exterior of 27 Panoramic Way, a little house familiar to Martin, with the conventional X marking a spot on the sidewalk just to the left of the path leading to the porch; one of the "cryptic warning" (Martin could scarcely see the element of warning involved in leaving a note beside a corpse—unless—and he suddenly paused—it were as a warning to the next victim); and one of Cynthia registering horror at the discovery of the body. It was a good picture of Cyn. Martin played momentarily with the thought of a Hollywood executive picking up this San Francisco paper and instantly wiring Cynthia to come at once.

The warning, or whatever one chose to call it, attracted Martin's attention again. It was drawn, apparently in pencil, on what looked like half of an ordinary sheet of typing paper. Despite the scientific leanings of the Berkeley police, that would not be easy to trace, unless there were fingerprints. And fingerprints would be useless save as corroboration, unless the murderer were a professional criminal, which seemed unlikely.

The figure itself was a strange one. It consisted of what looked

like a curious sort of italic *F,* mounted upon three rectangles shaped like steps. The arrangement, for some reason, brought a cross to Martin's mind, although he could not see the connection. The symbol fascinated him. It brought the final touch of melodrama to the nonsensical story-book murder of this good man. He stared at it intently:

"Ah, I see that you interest yourself in our local murder, Mr. Lamb," Boritsin remarked as he seated himself at Martin's table.

"Yes. I'm trying vainly to make any sort of sense out of it."

The Russian removed his coffee from the tray and shoved the latter onto an empty table. "You think it makes no sense?" he asked, lighting a cigarette.

"None at all. You met Dr. Schaedel last night. You know his reputation. Why should he be killed?"

"In the first place, Mr. Lamb," Boritsin replied, "you assume too much. You assume that he was as blameless as you—and I, too, I admit—thought him." Having thus, for variety, uttered two sensible sentences, the aristocrat reverted to a more characteristic type of reasoning. "But in the second place, may one not see in his very blamelessness a sufficient motive for killing him?"

"What on earth do you mean?"

"He was preaching Peace, was he not? And most sincerely and effectively. Well?"

"Yes?"

"He came here from New York and he was going on to China and to Russia. Well?"

"Well what?"

Boritsin was enjoying himself. He settled back in his chair and blew an admirable smoke ring before he answered. "Who is behind the movement for World Peace?" he asked.

"I wish that I could answer, 'Everyone.' But certainly a great many forces, from Francis Lederer to the Society against War and Fascism."

"Aha!" Boritsin gleamed. "There you have it. The Society against War and Fascism. That is a Communist organization. Now you see it all!"

"Do I?"

"It is a Soviet plot. These Communists, they spread peace, peace, everywhere, and why? So that there may be no more munitions, no more armies; and then these Communists will conquer all. They are happy to see Dr. Schaedel convert Europe, convert America to peace. But then he proposes to visit China, visit Russia itself. Suppose he converts the red soldiers of China to peace? Suppose he makes converts to the glory of peace in very St. Petersburg—I will not speak its accursed new name—what then? So, they say, we must kill him. And *voilà*—it is done!"

Martin was polite. He made some vague comment, looked impressed, gulped his coffee, and hurried out into the lounge where he could laugh to his heart's content. It was such a wonderful theory, and so superbly Boritsin. He expected that the Russian would soon discover that the F stood for Fascism, and that the three steps represented Lenin, Stalin, and Trotsky—for the aristocrat's mind would doubtless lump them all together. And then the police would receive an anonymous letter advising them to search the National Students' League headquarters for the murderer of Dr. Schaedel.

"What are you laughing about, Lamb?"

There was no mistaking that pseudo-Oxonian accent. Martin controlled himself a little as he looked up at Worthing. "The . . . the murder," he spluttered.

"Really?" The Canadian raised his voice and his eyebrows "I can't say that I find it so excruciatingly funny, old man."

"It's not that. It's Boritsin. He was just telling me how Dr. Schaedel was murdered by Moscow Gold."

"Oh, I say. That is a bit thick. Especially when the whole ruddy thing is so blasted simple." Worthing, having never visited the Mother Country which he so worshipped, had picked up his British colloquialisms chiefly from popular novels, and never bothered to notice the level of society at which they were used.

"So simple?"

"Oh, I've heard rumors. There's a lot more of that sort of thing goes on than one knows about, you know."

"What sort of thing?"

"You understand, old man, I'm not saying anything. But you know what one means." He lowered his voice, if not his eyebrows. "*Cherchez la femme!* What?" And he discarded his Oxford elegance to the extent of a broad wink.

As Worthing made his exit on this effective line, Martin began thinking. The Canadian's theory, if it could be called that, was as preposterous as Boritsin's. Lechery did, of course, crop up in unexpected places; a life in academic circles had accustomed Martin to that phenomenon. But he could not associate it with Dr. Schaedel. It was wrong. There was in fact something damnably wrong about the whole thing. Martin picked up the paper again and read over the brief biography of Dr. Schaedel.

There was nothing there to help him. It simply gave the dates marking the doctor's slow rise to fame and a moderate fortune. Beginning as a humble private tutor, he had finally become Professor of Economics at the University of Berne. During the World War, he entered politics and was elected to the National Council on a platform of maintaining Switzerland's neutrality. Later he became a member of the Federal Council itself, finally retiring in order to devote his time as an unofficial envoy to the cause of world peace. His political life had been quiet. He had given active support to the expulsion of Hoffmann from the Federal Council; but surely no quarrel so old could have anything to do with the present. He was unmarried, and left no living relatives save his sister's son, Kurt Ross.

There was nothing in all this, Martin decided. If he were to carry out his sudden whim of evolving a theory of the murder, he must seek elsewhere. He put a cigarette in his mouth and struck a match, then paused suddenly and reread the last statement in the biography. He stared curiously at the paper until the forgotten match burned his finger.

"Have you seen Cyn today?" Martin asked Alex Bruce over lunch.

"I went over as soon as I'd seen the papers, but I couldn't see her. She's had a nervous collapse. Mary was with her and wouldn't let anyone in. There are policemen, uniformed and plain-clothes both, scattered all over Panoramic Way. They're trying to find the direction in which the murderer vanished."

"Cynthia didn't see him?"

"That's right. Neither did Mary."

"Neither did I what?" Mary Roberts stood beside the luncheon table, looking surprisingly fresh and sensible.

"Sit down, Mary," Martin said. "Three guesses what we're talking about."

"Is anybody on campus talking about anything else? If it keeps on much longer, I'll be having a breakdown like Cynthia." Mary paused to give her order, and went on. "I've been up there all morning—I stayed the night, of course—more to keep away from people than to help Cynthia. Sorry she couldn't see you this morning, Alex. I told her you were there, and it just seemed to make her worse than ever."

"I think she's annoyed with me," Alex confessed. "I said I'd go over last night, and I worked so hard in the lab that I forgot all about it. While you were finding corpses, I was starting off on a fairish binge with Martin. My conscience hurts me a little."

"Maybe that's why she was so worried. She called me up, you

know, about ten last night and said she was alone and would I please come over right away. She wanted to talk to me about something."

"What was it? Or ought you to tell me?"

"I don't know." Mary paused in her attack upon a lamb chop. "All evening it seemed as though she were just going to say something important. And then it all happened, and of course she hasn't said anything since."

Martin finished his pie and lit a cigarette. "Mind if I ask you a question, Mary?"

"I suppose I'll have to get used to it. Go ahead."

"This murderer seems to be a very elusive person. You rush right out—only a couple of yards—and there's not a soul in sight. Either he's the Invisible Man or he must have popped into one of the houses around."

"But we didn't rush right out. Rather, we did, but we didn't get there. Cynthia tripped on the porch and came a cropper. So what with me helping her to her feet and her testing her ankle, which wasn't sprained after all, the man had plenty of time to get away."

"Why is it people always say 'the man'?" Alex wondered. "It seems like a definite double standard."

"When in doubt, use the masculine," Martin replied. "Besides, this looks like a male crime."

"What do you mean by that?" Mary asked through a mouthful of jello.

"I'm not quite sure. But I think one may safely generalize—"

Martin's generalization, whatever it may have been, was interrupted by two new arrivals at the table—Remingio Morales, the Bolivian, and his sister Mona.

"Do you know where we seek the answer to this riddle?" Morales was asking almost immediately after the mutual greetings.

"In the Gran Chaco?" Martin ventured, tongue in cheek, mindful of Boritsin's ingenuity.

"But exactly," Morales replied seriously. "How did you guess it?" And he launched into an elaborate explanation of the dastardly Paraguayan plot which had destroyed the inoffensive Dr. Schaedel.

Martin did not dare listen too closely, for fear of a return of the laughing attack which had so shocked Worthing. At last he interposed a cautious question. "Have you seen Kurt Ross this morning? What does he think of it all?"

"I have not seen him," and Morales continued his exposition.

"But I have," Mona interrupted. "I have forgotten to tell you, Remigio. I was sitting in the lounge after breakfast when Kurt came through with a tall man in an overcoat."

"With a cigar?" Martin asked.

"No. Why?"

"The traditions are being shamefully neglected. Go on, Mona."
"I had not yet heard of the death, and I said, 'Where do you go so early?' He said, 'They want to ask me some questions,' and went on. I think that it was the police."
There was sudden silence at the luncheon table. Martin wondered if anyone else had been already struck by that sentence in the newspaper biography.
"Poor Lupe," Mary sighed. "She must be dreadfully worried."
"Had you not heard about Lupe Sanchez?" Mona, usually quiet, was enjoying to the full her possession of exclusive news. Her brother was becoming impatient; he had not yet fully explained about the Argentinian millionaires who were backing Paraguay in the Chaco.
"What about Lupe?"
"She is ill. She left this morning for a hospital in San Francisco."
"What's the matter with her?"
"Anything serious?"
"Why not the hospital here on campus?"
"That is a question which answers itself, I think." Mona smiled cryptically and hoped that she would not be pressed for an explanation. In her black eyes Martin noticed the glint of a modest girl flirting pleasantly with an immodest topic.
He leaned back in his chair while Morales resumed his revelations. It all fitted together too nicely. Motive, opportunity, and, he supposed, means. It was disappointingly simple. There were only two things against it: one, that idiotic symbol; and two, the fact that he liked Kurt Ross.

Martin spent the afternoon in the library poring over old volumes of the *Jahrbuch der Shakespeare-Gesellschaft,* trying to find if anyone had anticipated his theory that Caspar Wilhelm von Borcke, first German translator of Shakespeare, had used the Theobald edition. It was a doubly useful afternoon. First, it established beyond a doubt that his theory, well backed by internal evidence, was new and probably worth publishing; second, it kept his mind off Dr. Schaedel and Kurt Ross.

But his worries returned to him during dinner. He brushed them away with the thought that the police would doubtless find whatever there was to discover; but this was small consolation. At last he decided that he must give way to the obvious.

As he left the dining room, he heard the sound of music from the Home Room upstairs. He thought he recognized the voice, and he was sure that he recognized the song, a plaintive Bolivian folktune.

Mona Morales looked up from the piano with a smile as Martin entered. *"Buenas tardes,"* she said.

"Don't let me bother you," Martin answered in Spanish. "Just go on singing. I like to listen."

"*Gracias, señor. Es muy amable.*" Mona wandered from one folksong to another, in a clear and sweet, if untrained voice, while Martin smoked even more persistently than usual. Mona was as pleasant to look at as she was to hear. The light of the floor lamp gleamed on her black hair as softly as on the deep polish of the piano. Her simple white dress was a charming contrast to her dark skin. But try though he might to enjoy her voice and her appearance, Martin's mind kept returning to her remarks at lunch.

"You will forgive me if I pause?" she said at last. "I am tired and I think that I would sooner talk for a while. May I have a cigarette?"

"You know," Martin began, offering her a light, "I was wondering . . . that is . . . something you said at lunch today . . ."

"Yes?"

"I want to ask you a frank question, Mona."

"But of course."

"Why—"

And the omnipresent Boritsin wandered into the room. To find a piano not in use was joy enough, but to find a ready-made audience beside it was bliss overflowing. For ten minutes Martin listened to a disquisition on the musical superiority of the *ancien régime* in Russia. Lush Tchaikovsky was contrasted with badly played Shostakovich to make a point—Martin was not quite sure what.

Finally, he leaned over and whispered to Mona, "I have to go now. I hate to leave you at Boritsin's mercy, but Dr. Ashwin's expecting me. When can I see you again?"

"Am I not always here?"

"I know, but . . . There's a Mexican film playing at a little house down on Broadway. It might be rather fun. Could you go?"

"When?"

"Tomorrow?"

"Remigio and I are going to San Francisco. There is a ball at the Bolivian Consulate. I must go over early because—" She paused abruptly. "Monday?"

"Fine."

"I am through at two. Shall we meet at Sather Gate?"

"Good." And Martin slipped out unnoticed by Boritsin, who was at the moment explaining the musical degeneration of the Russian ballet.

Martin walked down Channing Way in a state of suspense—a suspense that must last for two more days at least. Mona was Lupe Sanchez's best friend; she, if anyone, would definitely. And suppose it did turn out to be a genuine illness? There went motive. And Martin knew that he would feel much better.

He climbed the twisting steps of the rooming house and knocked on Dr. Ashwin's door. In a few moments he was comfortably settled in a chair by the desk while Ashwin produced a fifth of Teacher's Highland Cream and excused himself to rinse a pair of glasses. Martin looked about the single room in which John Ashwin lived. In one corner stood a small bed, obviously made by male hands. Aside from a few chairs and a heater, the only other article of furniture was the huge roll-top desk with its swivel-chair, the throne from which Ashwin launched his best dicta. And the books—bookcases ran around two sides of the room, crammed with volumes, mostly old and well worn. The very richness of Ashwin's tastes resembled poverty in its quality of making strange bedfellows. The best available edition of Valmiki's great epic, the *Ramayana,* leaned top-heavily upon a cheap copy of Conan Doyle. The historical romances of the elder Dumas were scattered among bulky dictionaries of the classical languages. And Ashwin's own translations from the Sanskrit rubbed figurative elbows with Rider Haggard's epics of the Zulu dynasty. As the little round button on top of this heap of miscellany, Martin noticed an authoritative work on military tactics set beside *Alice in Wonderland.*

When the scotch had been poured, tasted, and found good, Martin opened the conversation with his conventional gambit. "How is Elizabeth?" he asked.

Ashwin's general aversion to women did not extend to those below the age of six. For many years he had been in the habit of selecting some female child of around three or four to whom he would act as unofficial godfather, abandoning her with the ruthlessness of a Schnitzler lieutenant when she reached the critical age of six. Elizabeth, however, seemed to possess some secret charm lacking in her predecessors; she was by now almost eight years old, and Ashwin was still devoted to her.

"She is well, thank you," Dr. Ashwin replied. "I spent last night and this morning with her family in San Rafael. She thanks you very much for the toy which you sent her."

"I'm glad she liked it. I do want to meet her some time."

"She seemed impressed by your gift in the manner usual to womankind."

"What do you mean?"

"She was asking after all the Berkeley people of whom she has heard me speak. 'How is Dr. McIntyre?' she asked. 'Fine,' I said. 'How are the Revkins?' and so forth. At last she asked, 'How is Mr. Lamb?' And when I said 'Fine,' she added, 'Give *him* my love.' "

Martin smiled. "I must remember. A wooden penguin is a simple means of conquest."

"And Elizabeth is learning Sanskrit."

"At the age of eight?"

"Yes. She asked me to say something Sanskrit for her. It is a confusing request, as I take it you know from similar experiences."

Martin nodded. "There's something tongue-tying about it. I imagine we'd be equally speechless if a man from Mars calmly asked us to 'say something English.' What did you do?"

"After some puzzling, I decided to recite that ingenious tongue-twister which consists entirely of *n*s and vowels. You remember?—

"*na nonanunno nunnono
na nā nānānanā nanu
nunno 'nunno nununneno
nānenā nunnanunnanut.*[1]

"She was so delighted with it that nothing would do but I must spend hours reciting it. At last she knew it almost as well as I, and will probably amaze her playmates with her classical knowledge."

Thus the conversation passed from Elizabeth to the extraordinary ingenuities of the Sanskrit language, its amazing tongue-twisters, and especially the incredible feat of Dandin in the twelfth chapter of *The Ten Princes,* wherein Mantragupta relates a sizable narrative without employing any labial sounds because his lips "twitched with the soreness left by a charming mistress' kisses." "I lacked character for this achievement in my translation," Ashwin confessed ruefully, "and was forced to adopt the shabby substitute of a somewhat more highfalutin style."

After that came a discussion of the perfections and imperfections of Haggard's *Finished,* and a gradual divergence to the topic of Conan Doyle, which brought Martin, around the end of the third glass of scotch, to the subject which had been on his mind all evening. He finished his glass and poured another—Ashwin being the ideal host who allows his guest to serve himself. Then, settling down comfortably with a fresh cigarette, he began: "We're both very much interested in murder—that is, from an historical or fictional viewpoint. How do you feel about our sudden contact with it here on campus?"

"I know almost nothing of it," Ashwin admitted. "As you know, I was in San Rafael, and I barely glanced at the morning paper save to read the comics to Elizabeth."

Martin smiled at the picture of the translator of Kalidasa reading

[1] Literally:
    He is not a man who is struck by an inferior:
    He by whom an inferior is struck is no man, by the gods!
    He who is struck is not struck if his master is not struck.
    He is not sinless who strikes one struck again and again.

out the exploits of Buck Rogers. "You should have read the newspaper accounts," he said. "But I thought you mightn't have, so I brought them along." He fished from his pocket the articles in the morning paper and handed them over.

Ashwin winced slightly at SAVANT SLAIN WITH STILETTO, and glanced at Martin as though to say, "Must I?" Instead he asked, "Have you any especial reason to be interested in this murder?"

"Yes. I met Dr. Schaedel shortly before his death and liked him very much. Besides, I think I know the murderer."

Martin was pleased with the effect of this melodramatic sentence. Ashwin said nothing, but began to read the clipping carefully. He reread it, then turned to the photographs and the biography. "Did not this young lady join us at lunch a week or two ago?" he asked.

Martin nodded.

"Yes." Ashwin thought back. "I remember it was a Friday, and she took a peculiar relish in eating meat—a silly gesture of defiance against her home life. And she swore stupidly." He frowned. Enough of Dr. Ashwin's New England upbringing persisted to make him disapprove strongly of girls who swore even when they were as attractive as Cynthia Wood. "The picture almost does her justice," he resumed. "I begin to see the reason for your unusual interest."

He went over the group of clippings again and laid them on the table. "Now," he said, "is there anything more? That is this morning's paper. Was there anything in this evening's news?"

"Only one thing of importance. They've found the weapon."

"Was it a stiletto?"

"No. An ice pick."

"How unfortunate for the alliterative caption writer. Where was it found?"

"A few yards up Panoramic Way away from Cynthia's toward the hills. Which doesn't mean that the murderer went that way. It could have been thrown from where the body was found. It was caked with blood and regrettably free from fingerprints."

"That is all, then, from the newspapers. And have you any news of your own? How many of these people do you know, aside from Miss Wood?"

"I know Mary Roberts fairly well, and Kurt Ross."

"That is the nephew?"

"Yes."

Ashwin leaned back in the swivel chair. "Now, just what is it you want me to do? Play detective with you?"

"I simply thought that if we discussed all the points of the case we might make it clear in our own minds and possibly discover something so obvious that it had been overlooked."

This reference to his own pet contention pleased Dr. Ashwin.

"It should at least be an interesting mental exercise," he said. "So tell me all that you have heard from your friends."

Martin began with his minor binge of the preceding evening, so that he might be able to include the surprising entrance of Kurt Ross. He then told of the luncheon-table remarks of Mary and of Mona, and closed, by way of comedy relief, with the theories of Boritsin, Worthing, and Morales, at which Ashwin smiled.

"That is all your information?" he asked.

Martin assented.

"And you have already satisfied yourself as to the murderer? In that case you should hardly have any need of my observations. But let us begin, in the conventional manner of detective fiction, with that immortal trinity: Motive, Means, and Opportunity." Dr. Ashwin filled his glass and opened a fresh pack of cigarettes, which he offered to Martin. After the business of lighting, he resumed. "I think we may begin by discarding Means as unlikely to be of any aid to us. An ice pick is a decidedly uncharacteristic and unidentifiable weapon, if none the less deadly. Even the organized forces of Scotland Yard could hardly hope to capture a murderer by inquiring into all suspicious purchases of ice picks during the last fortnight. Holmes, of course, would begin by deducing from the ice pick that the murderer was a cuckold; but I think that a bit far-fetched."

"A cuckold? Just how—?"

"Because his household still employs an icebox in these days of electric refrigeration, a fact most probably occasioned by his wife's intrigue with the proverbial iceman. Elementary, my dear Lamb; but we file this hint away, thinking it more likely that the ice pick was bought with its deadly nature in mind. One might, with somewhat more justice, observe that the murderer probably possesses an elementary knowledge of surgery, since a slight error in locating the heart would make the wound merely dangerous and not fatal. This is not, however, too helpful a point; the requisite knowledge could have been acquired for the occasion by a layman. Now since, as you say, the handle reveals no fingerprints—the refinement of the science of fingerprinting must have been a great boon to the glove industry—we have, I believe, exhausted the possibilities of Means. Next we come to—"

"Motive?"

"Let us save that for the last. Next, I say, we come to Opportunity to ill-annexéd Opportunity, that foul abettor, that notorious bawd. There is much justice, if little poetry, in Lucree's famous rant against Opportunity, but in this case, I fear, it does not apply. This crime is not one in which a sudden opportunity presented itself for a murder which might not otherwise have occurred. People do not wander innocently about Panoramic Way carrying a handy ice pick. By the way, Mr. Lamb, how did Dr. Schaedel himself happen to be wandering about there?"

"Kurt mentioned to me," Martin replied, "that his uncle was fond of walking at night. He probably had been strolling about the hills, and lost his way coming home."

"Then how did the murderer know where he would be—unless of course, the murderer were following him? There is a point under Opportunity. But it is not a limiting point. The scene of the crime is one to which anyone in Berkeley could have ready access. A perfect—or, perhaps preferably, not quite perfect—alibi for eleven thirty would be the only possible elimination under Opportunity. What can you tell me about that?"

"Well, I am a suspect myself then. I have no alibi for that hour. I was simply drinking and reading *The Boat Train Murders*. Of the people I know, Mary Roberts and Cynthia provide each other with alibis. Kurt Ross, so far as I know, has none. It was around a quarter or ten minutes of twelve when he came to my room."

"Mr. Lamb," said Dr. Ashwin reproachfully, "please do not indulge in the smartalecky ingenuity of proving yourself a likely suspect. For your other information, I thank you. I believe that we have extracted most of the juice from Opportunity."

"And now we come to Motive?"

"Yes." Ashwin rose ponderously and moved about the room. "It is, I believe, Miss Tennyson Jesse who conveniently classified the motives for murder under six heads. I cannot remember her order, but the heads are these: Jealousy, Revenge, Elimination, Gain, Conviction, and Lust for Killing. Of these the last is of no use to the reasoning of a self-appointed detective. The most unlikely murderer may kill the most unlikely victim from sheer homicidal madness. The murderer may be, as it was insinuated that Jack the Ripper was, a respected individual completely normal in all other respects. If Dr. Schaedel was killed by a maniac, all our further reasoning is absurd and futile. Let us remember that possibility and continue."

"Jealousy," Martin suggested, "is what I suppose Worthing meant to imply. But to judge, not only from my impression of Dr. Schaedel, but from all Kurt's references to his uncle in the past, it is a ridiculous suggestion."

"Quite aside from that," Ashwin added, "if it be sexual jealousy—Dr. Schaedel arrived in California yesterday for the first time in his life. Either the jealousy must date back to some remote Swiss affair, or the old gentleman must, with all due reverence, have been a very fast worker. Somewhat the same objection applies to revenge. A revenge which chases its victim across two continents and an ocean is a trifle too early Doyle for my taste. I admit that it is possible, but I prefer not to consider it as yet. What have we left now?"

"Murder from conviction?"

"In other words, assassination. Yes. But Dr. Schaedel's political career seems to have been placid enough, and, as a matter of fact, he holds no official position at present. His assassination would seem to be a very empty gesture. There is obviously no need of considering seriously Mr. Boritsin's theory, although one might, if one leaned leftward, evolve a very pretty counter-theory to the effect that Dr. Schaedel was murdered by a conspiracy between the House of Morgan and the sage of San Simeon."

Martin laughed.

"Let us fill our glasses on that," Dr. Ashwin suggested. The suggestion obeyed, he continued. "That leaves us, I believe, two motives, Elimination and Gain. The motive of elimination is generally the result of fear, as in the case of the murder of a blackmailer, the device to which all novelists resort when they wish their murderer to be sympathetic. From what you tell me, I can hardly imagine anyone fearing Dr. Schaedel. We now have left the motive which you have your heart on—Gain."

Martin acquiesced.

"You believe that Kurt Ross needed a sum of money for an urgent purpose whose existence, it seems to me, you have deduced from flimsy and largely hearsay evidence."

"I expect to find confirmation on Monday," Martin added.

"Very well. You think further that Kurt Ross approached his uncle for the money after the dinner—"

"At nine thirty," Martin put in. "I heard the arrangement."

"—at nine thirty, and that his uncle refused, possibly upon learning the cause of the need for money. Here is your first snag. Granting Dr. Schaedel the character which you give him, such a refusal seems to me most unlikely, unless occasioned by religious scruples. But let that go. Allow a half-hour for this stormy scene. At ten Uncle Hugo sets off for a walk in the hills. Does Kurt then accompany him or shadow him? If the former, what has become of Kurt when Dr. Schaedel is lost and asks his way of Miss Wood? And in either case where does Kurt acquire the ice pick? And, if Kurt has just committed a cold-blooded murder—I say cold-blooded advisedly because of the careful wound in the back, something that could scarcely occur in an ordinary fight—why does he come dashing into your room to beg for whisky? Why is he perfectly willing to let three men know that he has just been through some harrowing experience? The theory does not hold water, Mr. Lamb."

"I could add one more point against my own theory," Martin admitted. "I can conceive of Kurt killing someone, even his own uncle, in the heat of a moment. But I cannot conceive of him lurking around dark corners with an ice pick. Still you cannot deny that his motive is obvious—the one obvious thing in this whole case."

Ashwin abruptly ceased his pacing and seated himself. There was a worried look in his eyes. "The more we discuss this affair, Mr. Lamb," he said, "the more I realize that one thing, and only one, is obvious. And that one thing frightens me."

He was silent for so long a time that Martin began to wonder if, for the first time, he was seeing Dr. Ashwin affected by whisky. At last Ashwin moved to reach for his cigarettes. He lit the match with a gesture as though he hoped by its light to dispel the gloom that had descended. When he finally spoke, it was in a fresher tone of voice.

"Let us now consider that symbol," he said.

Martin looked again at the curious device. "I can't make any sense out of it," he offered at last. "I've thought of all the words, printable and unprintable, for which the *F* could stand, and they're not in the least helpful."

Ashwin contemplated the photograph for a moment. "And small wonder that they are not. Although I cannot offhand give a meaning to the symbol, I can at least offer one suggestion. I do not believe that it is an *F*."

"Then what is it?"

"A seven."

Martin looked blank.[1] "A seven? I can't quite see . . . "

"Surely, Mr. Lamb, you are acquainted with the continental habit of crossing a seven to distinguish it from a one? The head of the one in European calligraphy, to dignify it by a flattering name, is so far extended as to make it resemble our seven. The seven, therefore, is adorned with this crossbar as a distinguishing mark."

He drew several examples on a scrap of paper and passed it to Martin, who nodded after a moment's study.

"Yes," he admitted, "I think you may be right. And I admit that a seven, with all its strange associations, is more apt to figure in such a symbol than an *F*. But we still don't know what the symbol means."

"Let us disregard for the moment the meaning of the symbol, and see what conclusions we can draw merely from the fact that a symbol was left by the murderer. There are several possible reasons for such an act."

"We seem to be returning to early Doyle," Martin commented.

---

[1] This is the reader's opportunity to feel triumphant, since he will already have guessed as much from the title of the novel.—*A. B.*

"One's first thoughts are of dastardly secret societies and tremendously elaborate vengeances."

"There is of course that possibility, distasteful though it may be. The nature of the seven and the circumstances of Dr. Schaedel's life both lead one to conclude that the society is a European one. And why then should they wait until he is in Berkeley to murder him? What else does the use of a symbol suggest to you, Mr. Lamb?"

"The act, perhaps, of an inherently melodramatic person, who wishes to embellish his crime with a colorful touch of bright bravado."

"Plausible," Ashwin smiled. "I can imagine you, for instance, feeling the need of some such theatrical device. And in that case the symbol might have no meaning whatsoever, but be a creation of the murderer's. What else?"

"Suppose . . ." Martin found this idea a little difficult to express. "Suppose that you wanted to kill several people for identical or similar reasons. You kill the first and leave a symbol beside the body which will mean nothing to the investigators, but will be too intelligible to the rest of your proposed victims. To them it will mean either, 'Prepare to die!' or, 'Mend your ways, lest you too die!'"

"Ingenious, although I fail to see how a seven mounted on a flight of steps could convey either of those meanings. But then, you specified that the symbol should be unintelligible to an investigator. According to that idea, Mr. Lamb, you expect more murders in Berkeley?"

"Not necessarily. I was just suggesting—"

"Perhaps you were right. Perhaps we should expect more murders—one more at least. But have you any further suggestions as to the use of the symbol?"

"Not at the moment."

"Then allow me to offer one. The symbol might have been used as a blind, so that the police or any other investigating agency might attribute its use to one of the reasons which we have just discussed. That is, a murderer killing from strictly private reasons might use a symbol to suggest the work of a society. A quiet, unmelodramatic, efficient murderer might leave a symbol simply because he reasons that its use is, to use one of your theatrical terms, out of character for him, and therefore likely to create a false scent."

"Ingenious," Martin smiled in mimicry of Ashwin. "But I somehow distrust these intricacies. Next I could reason that the murderer really was flamboyantly melodramatic, and left the symbol so that a detective might be deluded into thinking that a quiet person had left it in order to delude him (the detective) into thinking that he (the murderer)—"

Dr. Ashwin held up his hand. "Mercy, Mr. Lamb, mercy! Forgive me my ingenuities and fill your glass in token of peace."

"This will be the last," Martin said as he complied. "I got to bed terribly late last night, what with Kurt and the others."

"I understand now your intense desire to prove poor Herr Ross guilty. It is simply so that you may one day boast of how you caroused with a murderer whose hands still reeked of figurative blood."

It was now Martin's turn to cry mercy. "I admit that I still think Kurt is a possible suspect, but I certainly can't fit him in with any of our ideas of the symbol. He is neither flamboyant nor subtle, and he surely is not the emissary of that fatal secret society, the Stepping Seven—which sounds like a vaudeville team. But I can't get away from the fact that he seems to have such a good motive—need of immediate money—sole heir to a moderately good sum—"

Dr. Ashwin interrupted. "I think you will find before long, Mr. Lamb," he said, "that no one had a possible motive for killing Dr. Schaedel."

THREE

THE SEVEN OF CALVARY

On his way to a reasonably early breakfast the following morning, Martin bought a Sunday newspaper. Despite his keen interest in the matter in hand, his loyalty to his lower tastes made him read first of all the comics. These lasted him well through the cereal and poached eggs; it was not until he had lighted the day's first cigarette to accompany his second cup of coffee that he turned to the news section.

But although a feature writer had spread the Ice Pick Murder over a long front-page double column, there were no new facts of interest. Martin read carefully how Sergeant Cutting had deduced from the cash and jewelry present on the corpse that robbery had not been the motive for the crime, how the Swiss Consul in San Francisco was berating the laxity of American justice and insinuating that international complications might result, how the radio program of World Peaceways had resolved to make its next half-hour a memorial to Dr. Schaedel, and how an appeal to come forward with their information was being broadcast to all who might know the meaning of the cryptic symbol. There was no reference to the questioning of Kurt Ross by the police—in fact no mention of Kurt whatsoever.

Through Martin's mind kept coursing, like a striking musical theme, Dr. Ashwin's words: *"No one had a possible motive for killing Dr. Schaedel."* And again: *"Perhaps we should expect more murders—one at least."* Could this mean that Ashwin believed in the existence of a homicidal maniac running loose in Berkeley? But why should such a maniac rest content with one more murder? And why the symbol?

Martin finished his coffee, extinguished his cigarette, and left the paper for a later breakfaster to find. Then he set out on a leisurely stroll across the campus to Newman Hall. Many of Martin's friends and among them Dr. Ashwin, had never quite made up their minds as to the sincerity of Martin's religious devotion; but none had been able to suggest any alternative motive for his constant attendance a Mass. Surely it was not for the sake of Father O'Moore's oleaginous sermons, nor yet for the too hearty goodfellowship of the Newman Club.

Quite aside from any question of religion, it was fortunate that Martin went to Mass on that particular Sunday morning, for there he saw Cynthia Wood. It was after Mass, as he descended the stairs from the chapel, that he felt a light hand on his shoulder and looked up into Cynthia's face.

"Hello, Cyn," he smiled. "I didn't think you were up and around yet."

"Had to be," she answered. "Going back to the House now?"

"Yes."

"I'll walk over with you."

As they left the church, Martin caught a glimpse of the Morales entering Remigio's car. Mona turned, saw him, and waved gaily. *"Mañana a las dos,"* she called, and smiled. Such a smile, Martin foresaw, would make the matter of questioning her extremely difficult.

He turned as the car drove off to see Cynthia regarding him with amusement. "So you're going in for Latins, Martin?" she queried with raised eyebrows. "Naughty-naughty!"

"What did you mean by 'had to be up and around'?" Martin asked, chiefly to change the subject. He had suddenly realized that such ribbing, which he would ordinarily have answered lightly in kind, was decidedly not to his taste when Mona Morales was concerned.

"Dad again," Cynthia replied shortly. "He and Father O'Moore are just like *that*—It was the darling Father, damn him, who converted Dad to the Church. And if Father doesn't see me after Mass, he passes the word on to Dad—oh, ever so casually—and damned if he doesn't cut my allowance. I even have to make little weekly reports on the sermon to prove I got in early."

"I must confess," said Martin, "you're in a devil of a fix if you have to tell every week what Father O'Moore's sermons are about. I'm sure I never know even while they're going on."

"So I had to come to church today. A mere thing like nerves wouldn't be an excuse for Dad." She was lighting a cigarette with jerky fingers.

"It must have been an awful shock," Martin faltered.

"Shock? For once, darling, your fine vocabulary is pitifully weak. Shock? To have a nice sweet little old man drop in to ask his way, and then two minutes later to see him lying dead on the sidewalk . . . Shock?" Cynthia laughed jarringly. "And it all seems so damned impossible this morning. The campus is green and bright and lovely. The sun is warm, and there's a nice breeze from the bay. It's spring and everything's wonderful. And somewhere that sweet old man is lying on a slab . . . maybe they're putting things in him now to keep him from rotting . . . rotting away like a—"

"Don't be a damned fool, Cyn." Martin was surprisingly abrupt. "You're just talking yourself into a state of nerves. It's not your fault you got mixed up in his death. And thinking about it won't do you or him any good."

"All right." Cynthia sighed. "It's such a surprise to hear you talking like a sensible person, Martin, that I'll have to try acting like one." They walked on in silence a bit, and then she spoke again. "Be a sweet child, Martin, and drop in for tea this afternoon. There's a lamb—sorry, didn't mean the pun, but with a name like yours . . . Pop around and cheer me up. Bring anybody I know. I'll ask Alex and Mary, and we'll just sit around and talk. It'll do me good."

"A swell idea, Cyn. About what time?"

"Oh, around three. Shall I ask your Latin?"

"She's going to San Francisco this afternoon," Martin began quickly, and stopped to see Cynthia smiling at him in a most annoying manner.

"Well, bring anyone. And be prepared to talk and talk and talk and talk. I've got to listen to people or I'll go mad—very literally."

Martin left her at International House and watched her light a fresh cigarette from the old one as she started up toward Panoramic Way. He was sorry for Cynthia, but not surprised to see how quickly her superficial brightness had faded at an unpleasant contact with reality. He looked after her for a moment, and then suddenly realized that he wanted lunch.

A little before three Martin left his room, where he had been working industriously on his Borcke-Shakespeare-Theobald paper, and descended to the main hall, remembering Cynthia's injunction to bring someone along with him. He dodged behind a pillar for a moment to escape Boritsin. and then stepped forward to survey the possibilities.

He nodded to the serious young Chinese who had attended the reception dinner and who was now frowning over an economics text; he exchanged a few words with the tall girl at the reception desk; and was rather abrupt to one of the leading æsthetes of the House.

He had practically given up finding a possible tea guest when he saw Paul Lennox reclining in a comfortable chair puffing unconcernedly at a curved pipe which had gone out some time before.

"Hello," said Martin, sitting down beside him. "The Hall's almost deserted today."

"Everybody's out in the hills reveling in the spring. I suppose I should be too, but I found this new book on the Albigensians too interesting." He paused to relight his pipe. "And where are you off to?"

"Cynthia's for tea. Like to come along?"

Paul shrugged his shoulders. "I doubt if Cynthia would be exactly wild about seeing me."

"She told me to ask you," Martin said, with courageous disregard for accuracy. After all, if there were some slight animosity between Cynthia and Paul, that very friction might serve to take her mind off the murder and the state of her nerves.

"All right," Paul agreed indifferently. "A cup of tea would be rather pleasant." His pipe was satisfactorily alight now. Slipping the Albigensian volume under his arm, he started off with Martin.

Martin paused on the steps to light a cigarette. "By the bye, Paul," he said, annoyedly tossing away a match which had gone out too soon, "there's one little thing—don't say anything about Dr. Schaedel or ice picks or anything. Cyn's nerves are in a hell of a state. Just keep up a running fire of stuff—you know, your present research—that Don Juan business—anything."

"Right." Paul nodded sympathetically.

At that moment, just as Martin finally lit his cigarette, Worthing bounded up the stairs. "Ah there old man," he chirped, "and where might you be headed?"

"Going out to tea," Martin admitted.

"It's so good to see anyone in the States who really appreciates that custom, what? I was just going to have a spot myself in here."

Martin was rash. He said, "Why don't you come along with us?" Worthing's inanities, he thought. might be a possible diversion. And poor Richard Worthing leaped at the invitation. little suspecting what strange mental anguish and physical fear he was later to reap in consequence of that eager acceptance.

Throughout the short stroll to Cynthia's house Worthing talked, while Paul cast reproachful glances at Martin. It was very blithe talk, liberally larded with I say's and What?'s, with an occasional "blasted" just to show that Worthing was a Man among Men.

As they reached the house, Worthing paused and looked at the sidewalk in fascinated horror. "The poor old chap," he moaned. "Think of him lying there! And that spot . . . I say, old man, do you think that's blood?"

Martin remarked that he thought it was more likely canine excrement, but he couched his remark in solid Anglo-Saxon words which caused Worthing to wince slightly.

"I say, really now, old man! I feel gooseflesh all over. Could you let me have a fag, what?"

Martin took out his cigarette case. At the moment that he was offering it to Worthing, Cynthia appeared on the porch and called, "Aren't you ever coming in?" Turning to look at her, he dropped the case and saw it fall under a bush by the sidewalk. "Go on in," he said to the others. "I'll get this damned thing."

It was several minutes later that Martin entered the living room. Mary Roberts was trying vainly to stem Worthing's reminiscences of Rugby games in Canada, and his entrance was more than welcome. It was a good entrance. There was dirt on the knees of his otherwise spotless flannels, and bits of twigs and leaves stuck out of his hair. But his cigarette case was safe in his pocket, and even safer in another pocket was something which he had seen dangling from an inner branch of the bush, something easily enough overlooked in a police search concentrated on stilettos. Martin had discovered where Kurt Ross had lost his Phi Beta Kappa key.

"Twenty minutes of," Mary Roberts observed in the midst of a sudden silence. There followed the usual ritual comparison of watches and several comments on how strange it was that silences always came at twenty of or twenty after the hour. And then the silence descended again.

"You know, Martin," Alex began, in a brave effort to keep things going, "I've been wondering just what sort of a play of yours Little Theatre's doing."

"I wouldn't exactly say of mine. I just translated it. It's a Spanish play by José María Fonseca. Last of the early nineteenth century romanticists. Very colorful, fairly bawdy. He called it *Don Juan Redivivo*. That's a swell title, but I couldn't translate it; so I called it *Don Juan Returns,* and let it go at that."

"And Paul's your star?" Cynthia's tone was skeptical.

"Yes, but he's still the scholarly historian. He's started doing a paper on the Don Juan legend."

"Oh, do tell us about it, Paul." Mary was not particularly interested in the Don Juan legend, but her pet superstition demanded that there should not be another dead pause until twenty after.

Paul told them about it, briefly and interestingly. As he finished and poured himself a fresh cup of tea, the thing happened that everyone had been waiting for.

"I say, Paul old man, you've so much information and rot on strange things—perhaps you could tell us something about that symbol." It was Worthing, of course. Martin remembered now, too late, that he had not warned him.

"What symbol?" Paul's carelessness was a little too studied.

"What symbol! Why, dash it all, you know—the blasted symbol that was beside Dr. Schaedel's body."

That's done it! thought Martin. Cynthia's lips seemed to grow thin while she clenched her teacup as though she would crush it. Alex and Paul glared at Worthing with concentrated dislike. Silence took possession of the group with fine disregard of the fact that it was only five minutes after.

At last Mary spoke. "For heaven's sake," she said forcibly, "let's not all be such ninnies. We all know that the poor dear old man is dead, and we all know how Cynthia and I feel about finding him. So why not be open?"

A feeling of relief passed over them all. Cynthia set down her cup and reached for a cigarette. She even managed a smile. "Well," she asked evenly, tapping the cigarette, "well, Paul, do you?"

"Do I what?"

"Know anything about that symbol?"

"It's very strange that you should ask me that. I think that I am quite possibly the only man in Berkeley who does know."

The calm statement produced all the sensation which Paul could conceivably have desired. After a moment Martin amended, "The only other man, you mean. There is, of course, the person who left it."

"I don't know, Martin. I think it quite possible that he himself did not know the full meaning of the Seven of Calvary."

At the word *Calvary*, Martin suddenly knew why the symbol had at first made him think of a cross. He saw in his mind the heraldic device of a cross mounted upon three steps. "The Cross Calvary," he murmured.

"Exactly," Paul agreed. "I was keeping quiet because, as Mary correctly put it, I was a ninny. But since we've broached the subject now, should you like to hear the story of that symbol?"

There was a general assent, and a momentary pause for the

lighting of cigarettes and pipes, during which Martin fingered reflectively the gold key in his pocket. Then Paul began his narrative.

"I warn you," he said, "it's a long story—good for the rest of the afternoon. Anyone not feeling up to that can walk, or preferably run, to the nearest exit. No one? Then here goes:

"I found out all this business when I was at the University of Chicago last summer doing some research work. Some of you know how much I've always been interested in the heresies of the early Church, to give them their usual name—although I must say that some of my studies almost lead me to call the Church itself the Pauline heresy."

"Bless you, Paul Lennox," Cynthia interrupted, grimacing at Martin as the sole available representative of the Church. "For that I'm going to ask you home to dinner some time. If Dad heard that, he'd have piebald kittens right at the table."

"Thanks, Cyn. Well, one evening in Chicago I was sitting up late over various bottles of beer with a young fellow named Jean Stauffacher. He was a Swiss from somewhere around Lausanne, an exchange student. And heresies were something of a hobby of his, too. We had been wandering along in our discussion from Neminians to Mandaeans, from Manichaeans to Catharists. I think it was in connection with the Neminians that he suddenly asked, 'and have you ever heard of the Vignards?'

"It is a confusing name spoken aloud. Most of you probably think I said *Vineyards,* and that is exactly what I thought when Stauffacher spoke. 'Whose vineyards?' I asked. 'Naboth's?' "

" 'No, no, no,' he reproached me. 'Not vineyards—Vignards. It is a curious Swiss sect, named after Anton Vigna.' And he proceeded to tell me a little about them, most of which he had learned from his grandfather, who had been a member of the sect and had later died as a result of his apostasy. He also referred me to a couple of rare books in the university library, where I found more corroborative details."

"Grandfather died, you say?" Martin asked.

"Yes. It was in 1920, at the time of the plebiscite on the League of Nations. The Vignards—for they are active politically as well as in religion, as you shall shortly hear —the Vignards were conducting a secret campaign against the League. Grandfather Stauffacher, who had renounced his membership many years before, threatened to make certain revelations concerning the *sub rosa* activities of the Vignards. So Grandfather Stauffacher died."

"How?" asked Alex.

Paul hesitated a moment and looked at Cynthia.

"Go on," said Mary. "I suppose he was stabbed in the back with an ice pick."

"Not with an ice pick, Mary, but he was stabbed, and in the

back. Beside him was found the Seven of Calvary. His murderer was never apprehended."

"Worthing had been silent long enough. "I say, Lennox old man," he burst in, "just where is all this getting us? You go on talking about Vignards and Seven of Calvary's and grandfathers and you don't tell us anything."

"Be patient, Worthing," Martin remarked. "Paul's simply building it dramatically—my Machiavellian influence. Let him go on. You say, Paul, you found two rare books on the subject in the university library?"

"Yes. Werner Kurbrand's *Volksmythologie der Schweiz* and Ludwig Urmayer's *Nachgeschichte des gnostischen Glaubens*. Both published in Germany in the late eighties and long since out of print."

"Pardon me, Paul," Alex interrupted. "These rolling German titles are all very well for you and Martin, but let the rest of us in on it."

Paul smiled. "All right. Kurband's *Folk Mythology of Switzerland*, and Urmayer's *Later History of Gnostic Belief*. It was by piecing together bits from these books—just minor references—with what Jean Stauffacher had told me, that I arrived at some knowledge of the Vignards. I made a great many notes—force of academic habit—and naturally, when I recognized the Seven of Calvary in yesterday's papers, I refreshed my memory. Damn this pipe; it always goes out."

Such was the curiosity of the group that no one spoke—not even Richard Worthing—while Paul carefully relit his pipe, lingering over the process a little longer than was strictly necessary.

"Swiss history, you know," he said at last, "is not nearly such a calm matter as you might perhaps imagine from its present uneventfulness. Both religiously and politically, things have been pretty complicated. This particular complication dates back to the early fourth century, when Christianity was first established in Switzerland.

"Those early bishops had a pretty hard time of things. Not only did they have to combat the pagan worship, but they also had the devil's own time with the Gnostic heretics inside their flocks. Then the barbarians came, and Christianity in Switzerland was fairly well wiped out—on the surface, that is—until St. Columbanus came on missionary work in the late sixth century.

"But during all this period of apparently successful barbarian hegemony, the faith was retained by a few priests and the families of faithful early converts. And since Christianity itself kept alive, it was only natural that in certain places Gnosticism too was cherished."

"Just a moment, Paul." It was Alex again, whose scientific mind wanted to keep things straight and clear. "I'm a little vague on heresies and things. Just what is Gnosticism?"

"My dear Alex, it is going to take me the best, or at least the largest, part of an afternoon to explain Vignardism. If I start to explain Gnosticism too, you'd best ask Cyn to put us up for the night. But I can say briefly that Gnosticism—with a G—was once a noble philosophy, based largely on the works of the mystic Valentinus, which rapidly degenerated into an elaborate mythology, half Christian, half pagan, and finally became mere magical hocus-pocus."

Alex nodded satisfied. "Thanks. Go on."

"Now the doctrine of the Seven of Calvary originated apparently in a small community near Altdorf, in the Canton of Uri. Here there was strong mental and physical inbreeding of a small and isolated group which had come under the influence of some early Gnostic. They had not fully understood his teachings—possibly he himself was none too clear—and as the centuries passed they built up what might almost be called their own religion.

"It was technically Christian, though heretical—but then the Mandaeans are technically heretical Christians, even though they call Christ *Nbu* and think him an evil spirit. This Urian sect (they were not called Vignards yet) did not go quite so far as that, but they did relegate Christ to a comparatively unimportant post in their septenity."

"Septenity?" This time it was Martin who was puzzled.

Paul shrugged deprecatingly. "I admit I coined the word myself, in order to translate the *Siebenfältigkeit* of my sources. A septenity is to a trinity as seven to three—in other words, there are seven persons in their godhead."

"And the symbol denotes that?"

"Yes. Most of you must have realized by now that the mark is a continental seven and not the italic *F* which the papers have called it. The three steps have two possible meanings—Urmayer and Kurbrand disagree there. Urmayer claims that it denotes seven triumphing over three—that is, their septenity over the Christian trinity. Kurbrand claims that it is a reminiscence of the Cross Calvary mounted on three steps. The former seems more likely, in view of the sect's history, but its name, the Seven of Calvary, inclines one toward the latter."

"Is that its official name in the sect?" Martin asked.

"So Jean Stauffacher called it."

"And who are the seven persons?" Mary was becoming more interested.

"This is their mythical cosmogony. You have a smattering of such knowledge, Martin; you will notice the very definite Gnostic touches. In the beginning there was Something—the Allfather, what Valentinus calls the Deep. This sect, being too naïve to elaborate such terms as Cosmos or *Urmacht,* called this primordial Something simply God. This God, apparently, did nothing but think. He had no desire to create. But one day, if we can speak of days in such a connection, he had a thought which displeased him—what we should call an evil thought. He cast it from him, and it assumed independent existence and powers.

"This was the *Unholy Spirit,* corresponding roughly to the Satan of the Christians. The Unholy Spirit felt the creative impulse lacking in its contemplative parent, and created the World. Moreover, through some strange parthenogenesis, it had a child. That child was *Jehovah,* the god of the Hebrews, who seemed to these simple folk, as he must indeed to many of us, a very evil and unholy sort of god."

"Two dinner invitations . . . " Cynthia murmured.

"Now God—the Ur-God, that is—looked on the World and saw that it displeased him. So he cast out another thought, this time a good one, to save the World. This second thought was the *Holy Spirit.* After a period of warring with the Unholy One, it also had a child, *Jesus Christ.* Now the Holy Spirit, for all its goodness, was cunning. It made a bargain with the Unholy One—'I will let my child die if you will do the same for yours.' The bargain was made, and ratified before the Ur-God, who foresaw the duplicity of his Holy Offspring and approved. Then the Holy Spirit made its child flesh, so that he could die as a man but still live as a god. Jehovah, who was not made flesh, had to die as a god, although, in some manner which I do not follow, he remained a member of the septenity."

"But that's only five," Mary objected as Paul paused.

"We now come to the most important pair. Seeing that the conflict of good and evil was wrecking the world, the Ur-God had another thought. This third thought was neither good nor evil, but wise, and her name was *Sofi.* She is, of course, the Sophia of Valentinus and the heroine of the *Pistis Sophia,* which accounts for her being definitely feminine while the other thought emanations, especially the Holy Spirit, are vaguely neuter.

"Sofi, naturally. carrying on the traditions of the Ur-God's family, also had a child, named *Nemo.* In this name, the sect anticipated Rodulphus and his Neminians by many centuries, basing its ideas on the same passages of scripture (*No man hath ascended into heaven—No man hath seen God—*and so forth), in which, they claim, *Nemo* does not mean *no man,* but is a proper name. Sofi's child Nemo, then, was to reconcile good and evil and to prepare the world for its end.

"Centuries passed after the idea and possibly, in some earlier shape, the symbol were once formulated. Villagers moved from

Uri to other parts of Switzerland and took their strange faith with them. People waited for the coming of Sofi's child, and meanwhile sought to placate equally the children of the Holy and the Unholy Spirits. The Unholy Spirit was at first supposed to have some name which could never be spoken or written (even as his son Jehovah had the unpronounceable tetragrammaton), and was thence called *Agrammatos,* the Unwritten One. With the years this became *Agrammax,* and was looked upon as a proper name. The final *x,* of course, reminds one of Gnostic magic formulae.

"Now since the Holy and Unholy Spirits were apparently of equal power, this dualistic concept gave rise to a sort of devil worship, for which authority was found in a misunderstanding of the parable in Luke—you know, the one about *Make to yourselves friends of the Mammon of unrighteousness.*"

"I have yet to hear a sermon by a priest who understands that parable," Martin observed.

"But you've probably never heard it twisted so beautifully as they did. They took it as a direct injunction to devil-worship, with all its concomitants of necromancy, anthropomancy, and whatever other mancies you can think of. So the sect went on, worshiping Agrammax and awaiting Nemo, until the end of the thirteenth century. Some time around then, some thirty years before the episode of William Tell, Anton Vigna was born.

"That period is perhaps the darkest in all of Swiss history—that is, darkest in the sense of most obscure. We shall probably never know definitely whether or not there was a William Tell or a meeting on the Rütli, and Anton Vigna belongs in the same quasi-legendary category. He was born near Altdorf and lived a quiet life until he was twenty-seven. He then calmly proclaimed that he was Nemo.

"Then everything proceeded to happen that should happen when one-seventh of God comes to earth. There were miracles and conversions and sermons and parables and disciples. He had studied his New Testament well, and patterned his life carefully on that of Christ, even to the forty days' retirement—using an Alp for lack of an available desert. But martyrdom in his thirtieth year was a resemblance which he had probably not foreseen. The Austrian bailiff, aided by a group of monks, stirred up the people against him, and he was stoned to death. As he lay dying, the mob continued to pelt him with stones, only to realize suddenly that some unseen force was pelting them. Some providential hailstorm had occurred just at the right time to be a Vignard miracle. A particularly large stone struck the bailiff on the forehead with such force as to kill him outright. And on all the stones which fell could be seen, as though carefully graven, a small seven.

"Vigna was dead, but, largely because of this miracle, the

Vignards lived on. In revenge for the death of their God, they swore toward the Christians the same hatred which the early Christians felt for the Jews. Some even pledged themselves to Agrammax if he would help them against the Holy Spirit and his son Christ. They bound themselves to destruction, and from this vow results their political importance.

"They have survived through the years, a small group, gaining few converts outside of their hereditary ranks, but they have fomented, or at least fostered, most of the dissensions which have torn Switzerland. Vigna's brother Leopold is reported to have been present at the Rütli. Those strange burgomasters of Zürich—Brun, Stüssi, Waldmann—are said to have been Vignards. That heroic and quixotic madman, Major Davel, was an apostate who had refused allegiance to Agrammax, and therefore failed.

"Especially have the Vignards rejoiced in causing religious disturbances. They hated Catholic and Protestant equally, and have supported movements as various as the expulsion of the Jesuits and the formation of the Sonderbund simply for the sake of setting two kinds of Christians at each other's throats.

"No . . . " he summed up, "definitely the Vignards are not nice people. So you see, I don't like the Seven of Calvary in Berkeley."

In the pause that followed, Paul Lennox calmly refilled his pipe. The others sat in silence. It was not a pretty picture, this story of the Vignards. Sofi and Nemo and Agrammax were ludicrous enough, as was the hailstone marked with a seven which had killed the Austrian bailiff. But Dr. Schaedel was dead, and Grandfather Stauffacher, and God knows how many others had lain dead, with the Seven of Calvary beside them. And how many more were yet to die?

Martin shuddered slightly and reached for a cigarette. In his pocket his fingers touched once more the gold key. He was reassured. There could be no mad sectarian loose in Berkeley. As Dr. Ashwin would say, it was too early Doyle. Someone who knew of the existence of the Seven of Calvary had planted it to create a false track. And who would know? Someone from Switzerland. . . .

"You know, Paul," Alex was saying, "you really should go to the police with all that information. They're begging for someone who can explain the symbol."

"No, no, Alex. I'm in no mood for suicide. If the Vignards thought that I knew too much—no, really, Alex. Besides, the police may find out anyway. The Swiss Consul might possibly know, or some other research worker—although I could never have pieced together those bits out of Urmayer and Kurbrand if it hadn't been for my talk with Jean Stauffacher. I think that they were a little afraid too."

"Dash it all, old man," Worthing exploded, "you've a public duty as a citizen."

"Have I?" Paul smiled.

"Don't you want this blasted murderer-chappie hanged?"

"Not if it should cost me my own life."

"Why, it's . . . it's . . . " The Canadian spluttered with indignation and ended lamely, "Well, hang it all, old man, it *is!*" And he reluctantly subsided again, but Martin could see that he was thinking very concentratedly.

Martin and Paul took a long walk through the hills together after supper that evening. It was a pleasantly silent walk, but through it all one thought kept recurring to Martin's mind. When, around ten o'clock, they were seated in the White Tavern with coffee and hamburgers, Martin at last spoke it out.

"Paul . . . " he began.

"I ordered black coffee," Paul remarked on a tangent, looking in annoyance at the milk-defiled contents of his mug. "Oh, well . . . What is it, Martin?"

"That business you were telling us this afternoon—I can understand your reluctance to broadcast the fact that you know so much about it, but there is one person who would like very much to hear it."

"Who?" Paul asked between bites of hamburger.

"Dr. Ashwin."

"And why not? Yes, I suppose a brand-new heresy like that might appeal to him—bit of variety from the Vedas. All right—I'll give him the full story."

"Should you like to drop over there now? He's probably still up."

"Very well—just a few minutes."

The few minutes, it is almost needless to say, became an hour and a half. Dr. Ashwin welcomed them cordially—he had met Paul two or three times before—and produced a bottle of his never-failing scotch. He listened to the story with great interest, and made a few notes from time to time. He smoked a multitude of cigarettes, but made no comment until Paul had quite finished.

"Thank you very much, Mr. Lennox," he said then. "That was a fascinating story. It should explain a great deal. I had thought myself reasonably well versed on the subject of heretical folklore, but this strange narrative shakes my belief in my near omniscience. I can scarcely understand how so curious a legend could have escaped me. Still, I repeat, fascinating."

Paul smiled wryly. "I'm afraid it's a little more than a fascinating story, Dr. Ashwin. You forget that Death is a leading character."

"I have not forgotten that." Dr. Ashwin lit a fresh cigarette, and started to refill all three glasses.

"No, thanks." Paul placed his hand over his glass. "I have to stop in at Finch's before it's too late."

"Finch's?" Dr. Ashwin queried.

"Finch Ralton," Martin answered, "has a good phonograph and reputedly the most beautiful male stomach in Berkeley. But that doesn't explain, Paul, why on earth you should go out of your way to listen to him."

Paul shrugged his shoulders. "I promised to return his record-repeater and forgot it."

"Oh." Martin was satisfied. "As long as it isn't for the sheer masochistic pleasure of hearing him misquote MacLeish . . . I think I'll stay a bit, if you don't mind, Dr. Ashwin. See you tomorrow evening at rehearsal, Paul."

Paul nodded, thanked Ashwin for his attention and his whisky, and left for the apartment of Finch Ralton, who will probably be quite surprised, if he ever reads this, to learn that he figured, even so indirectly, in the investigation of the Schaedel murder.

Ashwin revolved slightly in his chair. "Mr Lennox has a great many phonograph records?"

"A fine collection of his own," Martin explained, "and then he rents a good many from the disc library in San Francisco. His phonograph's really quite a consolation to me."

Ashwin nodded. "And what sort of records interest him?"

"Mostly symphonies and chamber music—a few *Lieder* —on the whole practically nothing but album sets."

"No dance records?"

"No. I'm afraid Paul is a trifle austere in his tastes."

Dr. Ashwin leaned back in his swivel chair and drained his whisky glass. "That austerity, Mr. Lamb," he said, "is in my opinion the most curious portion of the narrative of Mr. Lennox."

FOUR

MARTIN ACCUSES

Mona smiled.

Martin's premonitions were fully justified. That smile did make the impartial attitude of an investigator damnably difficult. He began to wonder why he had ever decided to play detective in this murder, which was, after all, no concern of his.

To be sure, if he had not had his investigations as a basis for rationalizing, he might never have taken Mona to see the Mexican film when he really should have been conventionally studious in the stacks of the library, and should have missed thereby two pleasures. One was the picture itself, a concoction of subtle horror such as only the Mexicans seem able to create; the other, of course, was Mona.

Ordinarily so quiet and reserved, she had changed amazingly in the theatre. She shuddered quite unrepressedly at the more shuddersome moments, and clutched Martin's arm when the black letters of an evil book changed to crawling death worms. With the strange closing line of the film still sounding in his mind, still possessed of the curious sense of unreality which the mad plot had instilled in him, Martin had suddenly awakened to the fact that Mona's hand lay in his. Her hand was warm and very real.

Mona smiled and consented to another glass of sherry. For his part, Martin ordered more beer.

They were seated in a booth at a cheap beer joint near the little theatre, refreshing themselves after the horrors of the picture and fortifying themselves for the long streetcar ride back to the campus.

"One does not know what to believe," Mona murmured. "It leaves a strange mood, that picture. It is as the husband said, 'Perhaps those dead monks came to life, or perhaps we three died for one night. Who knows?'"

"Death in itself is strange," Martin observed. "Perhaps a strange death is less so—the two strangenesses canceling each other. . . ."

The drinks arrived—which was perhaps just as well, since Martin's conceit of death threatened to become painfully muddled. Mona sipped her sherry silently, then said, "I saw Kurt Ross at noon. He is sad because of his uncle."

The death of Dr. Schaedel was something which Martin did not wish to discuss directly at the moment. Instead he asked, "And Lupe Sanchez? How is she?"

"I saw her on Sunday afternoon. That is why I went to San Francisco early. She is much better, thank you, Martin."

"Was her illness serious?"

"N-no." Mona appeared to be about to say more, but changed her mind. Martin waited a moment, and then, deciding that that approach was closed, offered Mona a cigarette, took one himself, and returned to the subject of the picture.

But even as he elaborated his theories of the horror film Martin was watching Mona closely. She obviously wished to say something. Finally, thinking the moment right, he paused in his dissertation and drained his glass of beer.

"Martin . . . " Mona began hesitantly.

"Yes?" He did not wish to seem eager.

"You are a friend of Kurt's?"

"Of course," Martin replied evenly, despite a slight twinge of conscience.

"Then please be nice to him."

"I always am." Martin was a little puzzled by this approach.

"Should you care for another drop of sherry?"

"Please." Martin pantomimed the order as Mona falteringly continued. "But I mean . . . very nice . . . comforting. He is unhappy, and he has so few friends. You and Remigio and one or two others. And Remigio is not of much help," she added with true sisterly skepticism.

"I can understand," Martin nodded sympathetically. "His uncle dead . . . Lupe in the hospital . . . " Inwardly he cursed himself for a trebly damned hypocrite.

Mona was not smiling now, but the serious expression of her mobile face seemed almost sweeter. "He needs someone, Martin. And he does not dare to go to visit Lupe for fear that someone might suspect—"

The arrival of the sherry and beer cut off the sentence, to Martin's irritation. "Suspect what?" he asked with apparent indifference, when the waiter was gone.

Mona took a large drink of her sherry as though to strengthen herself. "Another cigarette, please, Martin," she asked. The sherry had combined with the fact that they were speaking Spanish to make her unusually confidential. She blew a cloud of smoke and began. "It is perhaps better that I tell you all. Only Kurt and Lupe and I know, but if you too know it may help you with Kurt. It is no illness that Lupe has."

Martin nodded. "I had thought as much."

"I am sorry for her. I know that it is wrong, but she and Kurt—they love each other so. They were so happy. . . And then she discovered this. There was only this way out. One of Lupe's friends had told her of this doctor in San Francisco—I will not tell you the friend's name, but she had been to him twice. He was sure and safe. And then—they had no money."

Mona fell silent and returned to her sherry. Martin continued looking as much like a father confessor as possible.

"You said that death is strange, Martin," she resumed suddenly. "To me love is quite as strange, and far more terrifying. I think of Lupe, and I do not want to love. Not ever. If such a thing were to happen to me—Remigio would—I do not know what he would do. And if the General were to learn of this . . . "

"The General?"

"Lupe's father."

Then Martin remembered. General Pompilio Sánchez y Lárreda once a famous and daring Mexican rebel, now led a life of painful enforced quiet in Los Angeles. A proud man, claiming that in his veins flowed the blood of Conquistador and Aztec alike, the vigor of the conqueror and the nobility of the conquered.

"Why did they not marry?" Martin asked.

"Lupe is engaged to the son of an old aide of the General's. Him she must some day marry, and return with him to Mexico. It would kill her father else."

"But if they had no money, how does it happen that she's in San Francisco now?"

"That I do not know. Saturday morning Lupe tells me that all is well, she can go to the doctor. That is all I know."

It was almost too perfect, Martin thought. Everything dovetailed together. Everything but the fact that Kurt Ross was such a decent, likeable fellow.

"And you will be nice to Kurt, and try to help him?" Mona was asking. Martin suddenly noticed with surprise that somewhere in their confidential talk she abandoned the formality of *usted* and was addressing him familiarly as *tú*.

"If only for your sake," he answered gallantly in the same form. She shook her head. "Not for my sake, Martin. For his."

"I shall go to see him as soon as we get back to International House." That at least, Martin thought ruefully, was the truth.

"That is good. I like you, Martin." And he was rewarded with another smile and a light pressure of his hand as they rose from the table.

The serious mood dispelled, they chatted so gaily on the streetcar in an irresponsible mixture of Spanish and English, that Martin quite forgot his twinges of conscience. But the key still lay in his pocket.

"I'll go right up to Kurt," Martin had promised Mona as they parted in the hall of International House. But the stimulating effects of her smile wore off quickly, and instead he went to his own room.

Sitting disconsolate on the bed, he held a lengthy silent soliloquy. What was he to do? He had no desire to give his evidence, such as it was—the key, Kurt's wild entrance Friday evening, Lupe's abortion—to the police without allowing Kurt a chance to explain things. But he could hardly walk in upon the young Swiss and say, "Look here. I'm pretty certain that you murdered your uncle, and I'd just like to hear what you have to say about it."

If only he were dead certain that Kurt was the murderer. He could write out his evidence in an impressive document, leave it for Kurt with a note saying, "Tomorrow I deliver this to the police," and wait for Kurt to complete the conventional gambit by committing suicide. But he was not certain.

Damn it, one didn't know murderers. He had once played with a pet theory that every person, in the course of a lifetime, knows at least one murderer. He remembered once shocking a girl's parents at the dinner table with this pronouncement. They were incredulous until the girl's mother suddenly recalled some curious facts concerning a onetime neighbor and revealed to Martin the most ingenious case of unprovable faked suicide that he had ever heard.

But this was different. A congenial, relatively intimate friend . . . It was as though Paul or Alex or he himself should be a murderer. And it was—this was what bothered him the most—it was out of character. It was a subtle murder from an open person.

He began to wish that some of the bourbon were left from Friday's binge. Three beers are very little to fortify you for an accusation of murder.

And then another thought struck him. Was he himself safe? His mind, filled with mystery novels, recalled that the man who, in the conventional phrase, Knew Too Much was always the victim of the second murder. If he hinted his knowledge to Kurt, might not he himself be killed before he could inform the police? He saw a pretty picture of himself lying on a sidewalk—probably with the Seven of Calvary beside him—and wondered just how an ice pick felt.

Suddenly he rose, extinguished his cigarette, and hurried down the corridor. He did not even bother to knock on Kurt's door. He opened it, and walked to the dresser before which Kurt was combing his hair. He laid the gold Phi Beta Kappa key on the table and said, "I found this. I thought you might want it." Then he turned to leave the room.

Martin himself did not know why he had done this. It merely seemed the simplest way of washing one's hands of the whole business. Relief was already on his face when Kurt's hand stopped him at the door. The thought of the second victim flashed absurdly across his mind; but the expression on Kurt's face was puzzlement rather than anger.

"Don't rush off like that, Martin," the tall Swiss was saying. "Stay and talk while I finish dressing. Then we might dine together."

Martin smiled. "*Dine* is a queer word for the usual food here," he said. "But we might eat together."

Kurt nodded. "Sit down, then." Martin obeyed, wondering what the next move was. "Where," Kurt asked, with an unsuccessful attempt at nonchalance, "where did you find that key?"

"Under a bush."

"What bush? Where?"
"The bush beside which they found the Seven of Calvary."
The puzzlement on Kurt's face grew deeper. The name seemed entirely strange to him. "The Seven of Calvary?" he repeated slowly. "What has that to do with my key?"
If this were mere acting, Martin decided, the Little Theatre had lost a brilliant star. "You don't know the Seven of Calvary?" he asked, penciling idly on a scrap of paper.
"No." Kurt's voice sounded completely sincere. Then he started back as he saw what Martin was sketching. "That!" he gasped. "That is what you mean?" Martin nodded. "I see . . . I see . . . " Kurt sank into a chair. "So that is it. You too, Martin . . . You think . . . "
"Yes?"
"You think that I murdered my uncle."
This was all wrong, Martin thought. Nothing in his previous calculations had come out quite like this. The accusation was proceeding from the suspect himself, not from the brilliant young amateur investigator. He swallowed with a good deal of effort and finally blurted forth, "Yes." He was surprised by his own voice.
Kurt spoke softly, but his tone was sorrowful. "I was not surprised by the police," he said. "To them I was just a possibility, not a person—just something that had to be investigated. But you, Martin—I had thought that you were a friend."
Martin tried to summon up the logical attitude of the righteous accuser. It was no go. He could only feel sorry for Kurt. The tall blond youth no longer resembled Young Siegfried. Rather he looked like an older Siegfried, at the moment wherein he realizes that Hagen has struck him through. And Martin did not like to be Hagen. He sought for words that would be comforting, and thought of Mona's request, and of her smile.
"Why?" Kurt was asking. "Why could you think that of me?"
Martin forgot the phrases that he was hunting for and spoke straight out. "I didn't want to," he said. "But I simply couldn't help it. Everything pointed that way. Your terrified entrance to my room Friday evening—I noticed then that you'd lost your key—then finding the key in the bush in front of Cynthia's . . . And the symbol was Swiss—that pointed to you. Besides, I knew about Lupe—"
"You knew?" Kurt interrupted.
"That is," Martin hurried to make clear, "I guessed. From various little references that people made." He had quickly realized that Kurt would not appreciate Mona's confidences.
Kurt rose slowly. "I suppose I cannot blame you," he said. "If you knew all that. That is more than the police knew. But you, Martin, you knew *me*."

"That was what worried me so much. The whole thing wasn't like you. I couldn't feel sure. That is why I told nothing to the police."

"Thank you, Martin." Kurt was looking more nearly happy. "I spoke too soon. I should have known that you were kind when you returned to me the key. And to be grateful now I shall tell it all to you."

"Tell it all?" Martin wondered what fresh revelation was forthcoming.

"But first of all—Why do you speak of this symbol as the Seven of—was it Calvary? Yes. The Seven of Calvary. I have not seen that name in any newspaper."

"Haven't you ever heard of the Vignards?"

"No."

So Martin gave a highly condensed version of Paul Lennox's narrative. When he had finished, Kurt shook his head reflectively.

"It might be," he said doubtfully. "History I know little of, and of heresies nothing. It might be. But never in Switzerland have I heard of these—what do you call them?—Vignards, nor of their Seven. And I do not think that Uncle Hugo had ever a political enemy.

"But now I shall tell you my story. You say you know about Lupe. You are clever, Martin, to have put little things together so. She is well, Mona tells me. I wish that I could myself see her. I need her—ah, terribly. But if someone were to suspect, and the General ever to learn—You will be secret, Martin?"

"You can trust me."

"Good. You know perhaps that I have loved Lupe for many months—almost since I met her in the last autumn. We have been . . . " He paused and groped for a word. Finding none and reassured by Martin's sympathetic glance, he resumed. ". . . since the Christmas holidays. It happened just before she went to Los Angeles for Christmas. We have loved each other in that way ever since." He paused again. Kurt was not a man who talked freely of his love life—which was one reason why Martin liked him—and he found his confession extremely painful.

"It was a month ago that she knew what had happened. We were both frightened. We thought that we had been so careful. And now—if it were learned, the General would go mad. And there would be a *Skandal*, and all would be terrible. We did not know what to do.

"We needed a doctor, and we did not know one who would do—what we needed. Lupe feared to ask anyone, because it might be suspected what had happened. Then one night she heard one girl—I do not think that she was sober—telling another of the luck that she had had two times, and Lupe learned the name of the doctor. We knew he would be good but expensive, because the girl was wealthy.

"In the meantime, I had written to my uncle, who was just arrived in New York, telling him that I needed some money badly and asking him for a loan. I will show you his answer." Kurt rose and opened the drawer of his desk. Martin waited expectantly. On this letter depended, apparently, the entire question of motive.

"Here it is," Kurt said, handing it to him.

"*Lieber Kurt,*" Martin read silently, deciphering with some difficulty the outmoded German script, "*Du kannst ja garnicht wissen, wies es mich freut, zum erstenmale in Amerika anzukommen. Die frische Luft dieses freien, friedlichen Landes...*" Martin smiled ironically and skipped hurriedly through three paragraphs of rejoicing in the peaceful freedom of America. Dr. Schaedel seemed to have been a curious combination of wisdom and innocence. "*In Bezug auf Deinen letzten Brief...*" he read at last, and concentrated his attention. His eyes opened wide as he read on.

"In regard to your last letter" (thus Dr. Schaedel said, freely translated), "I realize that I have long been remiss toward my only living relation. While I have enjoyed to the full your letters and your company, I have never thought how I might aid you in any way. I am not a wealthy man, but I am of comfortable means. As I believe I have told you, my fortune (if I may dignify it by such a word) goes at my death to several Swiss universities and charitable organizations, in addition to a fund to provide a Schaedel Chair of World Peace at my own university (a selfish whim to immortalize my name perhaps, but certainly a worthy immortality). Even in view of my previous remissness, I cannot see my way clear to altering my will and depriving any of these institutions of their allotments; but I am resolved to do what I can for you during my life. I shall be in Berkeley within two weeks, and you can then explain to me your need if you desire, or keep it secret if that seem necessary. In either case, please consider my aid as a gift, not as a loan. If your need be too urgent to wait the two weeks, wire me here."

At this point the letter went off into a discussion of Dr. Schaedel's plans for his lecture tour, and Martin laid it aside. "You have shown this to the police?" he asked.

"Yes. They secured other documents of my uncle and gave them to an expert of handwriting, who did me the honor of deciding that this letter was genuine. It was then that they told me to return home."

"Of course," Martin muttered. This letter removed any possible motive that Kurt might have had. With Dr. Schaedel alive, he could expect financial aid whenever he needed it. With Dr.

Schaedel dead, he would have no claim whatsoever upon any of his uncle's money.

Kurt roused himself from silence and said, "I had best tell you the rest, too, even as I told it to Sergeant Cutting."

"Is there more?"

"You still do not know why you found my key, Martin," Kurt reminded him.

Martin nodded. His sympathy for Kurt had for the moment dispelled his detective fever.

"Very well," Kurt resumed. "It is now Friday evening. After the dinner I speak to my uncle, and he tells me that he will see me at half after nine."

"I know. I heard you."

"So? You knew that too? Martin, I am surprised that you have not by now hanged me." Kurt's laughter was forced. "I went to his room at that hour. We talked a little and then he said,

" 'Kurt, take this.'

"He seemed awkward and unhappy, as though he were embarrassed by his gift. I took it. It was twenty-five twenty-dollar bills.

" 'I do not want to know your trouble,' he said. 'I have decided that it is better that I only give you this. If it is enough,' he added.

"I said, 'More than enough,' and then I was telling to him all the story. Martin, he was a kind man. Things let themselves be told to him. . . .

"When I had finished, he said, 'I do not like death, even of one not yet truly alive. But it is perhaps wise if it saves the happiness of those living.' And he smiled and got up and said, 'Now I am going for my evening walk. Send your Lupe to the hospital tomorrow, and bring me to see her when she is better. She must be a charming girl, Kurt.'

"I could not say anything. I took his hand and . . . and kissed it, like a peasant kissing the hand of his emperor. I felt like that. He was so good, and I was . . .

"That was the last time I spoke to him alive."

Kurt, deeply moved, ceased to speak, while Martin, moved almost as deeply, could find nothing to say that would not sound intolerably stupid. He was surprised to hear Kurt, after a short pause, continue his story.

"That was some time after ten o'clock. I hurried from his room to mine and there . . . there I wept. Then I hid the money deep back in a drawer and went for a walk myself. I walked about an hour in the hills, and then was coming back along Panoramic Way. I had just looked at my watch about five minutes earlier; it must have been around eleven thirty.

"I saw a man who might have been my uncle go into Cynthia Wood's house. I was not sure. You know he was of ordinary height, but looked so small because he stooped. On his evening walks, he kept very straight. And he was in an ordinary gray suit. It might have been anyone, and since he went into Cynthia's I thought for a minute it might be Alex. He has a suit like that. But I waited for a moment, and saw him come out again. I was about ten meters away, and I started forward, and then . . . " Kurt broke off. His emotion was too great.

"You mean—you saw him killed?" Martin exclaimed.

"Yes!" Kurt burst out. "Yes! I saw that good man killed. It was someone who was behind that bush where you found my key. He rushed out and seized my uncle. Then my uncle fell. It was all over before I could even move. I hurried and seized the man. I was not afraid, only for my uncle. He did not try to stab me. He only slipped away and vanished. I bent over my uncle. He was dead. Then I heard people coming out of the house, and then . . . now this I do not like to tell, no, not even to you, Martin, I am not proud of it. But . . . I was afraid. There was my uncle, dead—there was nothing that I could do for him. But those who were coming—what might they not think on finding me? It was foolish, that I know—but it was . . . hysteria almost. I ran. I left that dear dead man and ran away from a fear that did not exist. For ten, fifteen minutes I do not know what I did. I wandered helpless, hopeless, mad. . . . And then I forced myself to come back among people. I came to your room. And the rest you know. . . ." He paused with something almost a sob.

"And it was while you were struggling with the murderer that you lost your key?"

"I think so."

"You told this to the police too?"

"Just as to you, Martin."

"What was he like, this man?"

"That I cannot tell you. He wore a rough mask from a handkerchief. He was smaller than I—about my uncle's height, and wore a gray suit much like his. It was dark; you could not recognize people."

"And how did this keep out of the papers?"

"Sergeant Cutting said: 'If I say through the papers that you saw the murderer and could not identify him, he will feel too safe. If I say a lie that could identify him, perhaps you will not be safe yourself. It is best I say nothing. He may become worried and make a mistake.' "

Martin mentally noted that Sergeant Cutting was a much shrewder man than his statements to the newspapers might lead one to believe.

"Now that is all that I know," Kurt concluded. "I do not quite know why I have told you so much, Martin. Sergeant Cutting wished that I should say nothing of it. But you were very kind to me"—he glanced at the gold key—"and I wished to thank you."

"I should thank you, Kurt. It was most interesting," Martin said lamely. It was so much more than interesting, and still it led nowhere that he could see.

Kurt picked up the key and adjusted it on his watch chain. "I must have this repaired," he said. "God knows where I might lose it next."

"I only hope that I'll find it again, and not—" Martin broke off, realizing that the remark was tactless.

"Shall we now dine—pardon me, Martin—eat?" Kurt asked.

Martin glanced at his watch. "I'm sorry," he replied. "It's late and I've got to get to rehearsal. I'll just have time for a hamburger at the White Tavern." He paused embarrassedly, and finally held out his hand—an uncommon gesture for Martin. "Well," he said, "good luck, Kurt. And I hope Lupe gets on all right."

"I am sure that she will. I have much trust in a doctor recommended by Cynthia."

"Cynthia!"

"I am sorry. I had not meant to let the name slip. Goodbye, Martin, and thank you."

So that was that, thought Martin on his way to rehearsal. His beautifully built-up case had collapsed completely. With all trace of motive ripped out, the other details explained themselves readily enough.

And he was glad—terrifically glad that his feelings had been right and his reasoning wrong. But if Kurt was innocent, who was the murderer? Kurt's description might fit anyone—a masked man of medium height—it meant nothing. There seemed to remain only the two possibilities—the homicidal maniac and the emissary of the Vignards. Martin admitted that both ideas, however possible, or even plausible, were distasteful to him. He had certain aesthetic ideals of murder, in which neither madness nor secret societies played any part.

Irrelevant though it was to the murder, his thoughts recurred to Kurt's involuntary mention of Cynthia. He could hardly believe the staid Alex responsible for Cynthia's visits to the abortionist. And what then would Alex think if he knew of them? It was an amusingly bawdy topic for wonder, and a relief from the murder. Some day he should write a mystery novel in which the entire mystery should consist of such a question as paternity. Better yet, a mysterious rape. There could be a wonderful scene in which the crime was reconstructed, with the detective, as is conventional, performing the actions of the criminal.

Martin reached Wheeler Hall a little late, despite the speed with which he had gulped his hamburger. Rehearsal was already in progress, and Drexel greeted him with anything but the proper respect due to a translator-actor. Paul was on the stage, looking, as always, slightly annoyed that he was not allowed to go through the part with a pipe in his mouth.

"Come on, Lamb," Drexel called petulantly. "After all, it is *your* play, you know, and you've got to snap into it."

Martin snapped obediently, and so effectively that in his preoccupation over *Don Juan Returns* he quite forgot his preoccupation over the Seven of Calvary. He had little notion how soon those two preoccupations were to become one.

FIVE

WATSON AS LOTHARIO

"Arthur Machen, in his brief study of the Islington mystery," Dr. Ashwin pronounced, "has stated that the public taste in murders is undependable and vagarious. Surely we have here a case in point."

It was late on Friday evening, a week, almost to the hour, after the murder of Dr. Hugo Schaedel. Martin, wearied by a strenuous rehearsal, had encountered Alex, almost equally weary from long hours of experimenting in the laboratory; and together they had decided to pay a brief visit to Dr. Ashwin.

Inevitably the conversation, which had first lingered upon such topics as the recent amusing remarks of Elizabeth or Dr. Ashwin's eminently sound reasons for not translating the masterpieces of Bravabhuti, had come round to murder and the Seven of Calvary. Ashwin, who had begun to take an almost personal pride in the intricacies of the local murder, was now venting his grievance against the newspaper-reading public.

"The murder of Dr. Schaedel," he continued, "was a skillful and fascinating crime. The character of the victim, the lack of motive, the curious symbol left beside the corpse—all these combined to make it a puzzle of unusual interest. By the way, Mr. Lamb, how did it happen that the newspapers secured the story of the Seven of Calvary? Mr. Lennox seemed firmly resolved not to make it public."

"I suspect Worthing," Martin said. "There was a fierce light of resolution in his eyes when Paul announced that he respected his life more than his public duty. You remember, Alex?"

Alex nodded silently.

"Besides," Martin added, "he probably got space rates."

"That does seem likely," Ashwin admitted. "Was Mr. Lennox much perturbed by the publication of his dangerous knowledge?"

"I was with him when he read it," said Alex. "When he saw that his name was mentioned he was relieved. But he did seem puzzled when the Swiss Consul said he'd never heard of the Vignards."

Martin smiled. "I think he suspects the Swiss Consul of being a Vignard himself. The Seven of Calvary is approaching the proportions of a monomania with Paul."

"So." Ashwin settled farther into the swivel chair. "And yet even that wildly romantic revelation failed to keep the newspaper public interested. Over the last week end, the Ice Pick Murder was spread on the front pages of every Bay Region newspaper. It is still unsolved, and yet, within a week—"

"Yes," Martin agreed regretfully, "all that the papers are interested in now is the Twin Peaks Murder."

"And what is there in that for a connoisseur of murder? A common, brutal *crime passionel,* utterly deficient in mystery or subtleties of psychology." Ashwin sighed. "A naked female body is found in a parked car on Twin Peaks. The woman has been shot. Five yards down the road, the gun is found. The car and the gun are both traced to a married man who is known to have been the woman's lover. His fingerprints are on the gun—that such negligence should be possible in this age of mystery-novel readers!—and he confesses to the crime. There is your Twin Peaks Murder, and it absorbs every copywriter to the entire exclusion of the Seven of Calvary." Ashwin sighed again and shifted about in discomfort. "Gentlemen," he announced, "only another glass of scotch can keep me from tears at the thought of this shameful decadence of modern taste. Will you join me?"

Martin and Alex joined him, with suitably doleful countenances.

"I can see but one explanation," Dr. Ashwin reflected aloud. "In view of the naked female body involved in the Twin Peaks Murder, the public must suppose the *twin peaks* to have a physiological, rather than a geographical, reference. Lubricity is indeed the lubricant of social thought." He relapsed into mournful silence.

"Dr. Ashwin . . . " Alex began tentatively.

"Yes, Mr. Bruce?"

"Martin tells me that you were rather interested in poor Dr. Schaedel's death. I wonder if you have any new ideas on it by now?"

"I have no ideas on it, Mr. Bruce, beyond the perception of certain obvious facts. That these have not been perceived by the authorities is doubtless unfortunate; for that means that this first murder will in all likelihood remain unsolved."

"This first murder . . . ?" Alex sounded a little frightened.

"Consider the facts as they stand, Mr. Bruce. Mr Lamb will remember that he and I ran through a little list of possible motives. We eliminated Jealousy, Revenge, and Elimination because of the character of the victim. Gain was considered for a time—at least, Mr. Lamb did—thinking that Kurt Ross stood to gain by his uncle's death. But Mr. Lamb spent the greater part of a recent class period, which might better have been devoted to the *Mahabharata*" (Ashwin's look of stern reproof was not a complete success), "in explaining to me why Mr. Ross could have no motive. We can hardly suspect the emissaries of Swiss charities of having committed this murder; and they alone stood to gain by it.

"Thus we are left with Conviction and Lust for Killing as motives. Conviction could result only in the case of the Vignards, and I begin to feel that there Mr. Lennox's imagination and zeal for research have twisted a too elaborate explanation from probably simple sources. I deeply regret that those works of Urmayer's and Kurbrand's are not available here. There remains, of course, the last possibility—the crime of a homicidal maniac. But that a maniac who has never struck before in Berkeley should kill a Swiss emissary just arrived in the city and leave beside him a symbol connected with Swiss history—to believe this is to stretch the laws of chance too far." Ashwin paused to find a cigarette.

"Then what is there left?" Alex asked not illogically.

"What is there left, Mr. Bruce? The fact—the glaring, horrifying fact—the fact, indeed, in the Elizabethan sense—the deepest of deep damnations of this taking-off—the fact that the wrong man was murdered."

Alex's mouth fell open, and was not closed until he had finished off his glass of scotch. Martin, who had half expected the idea, felt none the less the need of whisky.

"The wrong man?" Alex mumbled.

"Dr. Schaedel was of ordinary height and ordinarily attired. It was a dark night, and a dozen men in Berkeley must have looked exactly as he did. The murderer simply made the trifling error of killing the wrong person. That accounts completely for the absence of motive, and that is why I spoke of Dr. Schaedel's death as the first murder."

"You mean . . . ?"

"I mean, Mr. Bruce, that the murderer will, in all probability, still carry out his original intention, and kill his planned victim. Whatever his motive may have been, Dr. Schaedel's death has certainly not satisfied it. The fact that his accidental murder has been a complete success, in so far as his personal safety is concerned, will merely be a stimulus to him in his second effort.

"I have never put much stock," Ashwin continued, "in the oft-stated theory that murder breeds murder—that is, that a once-successful murderer is more apt to kill than any other man. Most people pass through life without having a real reason for killing more than one or two people. The necessary killing once accomplished, they are, in my opinion, if anything, less apt than a nonmurderer to kill again. Your Landrus and Smith, men to whom killing became more or less a profession, or at least a hobby, are of course in a class apart.

"But in this case the necessary murder was not accomplished. Someone still lives who, in the mind of the gentleman who left the Seven of Calvary, needs killing. It will surprise me very much if another strange death in Berkeley does not in its turn supersede the Twin Peaks Murder."

"You know," said Alex to Martin as they walked home together, "I think he's right."

Saturday, Martin, with no rehearsal to worry him, spent the day with Mona. They lunched together—for the third time that week—and boated on Lake Merrit in the afternoon. Martin rowed over the sunny lake while Mona sang plaintive South American folksongs from time to time, and grew every moment more charming to him.

They dined—and on this occasion, Martin thought, the word was properly used—at the Capri, with a bottle of Chianti to aid digestion and other things. When they had reached the stage of coffee, liqueurs, and cigarettes—Martin had rather wanted a cigar, but realized in time that he looked somewhat ludicrous smoking one—Mona asked, "And what sort of party is it that you're taking me to tonight?"

"A Morris party," Martin replied.

"Is that an idiom?" Mona looked delightfully puzzled.

"It's a Berkeley idiom," he explained; "or perhaps an idiotism, as you call it in Spanish. Haven't I mentioned Mr. Morris before?"

"I do not think so. Who is he?"

"I'm none too sure myself. I don't even know his first name. He's moderately wealthy and thinks he's a philologist. He lives in a pleasant house in the hills and does pseudophilological research at the university. His hobby is parties."

"Does he give so many?"

"He practically never gives any. The rest of us do at his house. You call him up and say, 'Mr. Morris? Martin speaking. Will you be home Saturday evening?' He says, 'Yes. Why don't you get together some friends and have a party?' So you give a Morris party."

Mona laughed. "That should be fun."

And it was fun. About a dozen people were there when Martin

and Mona arrived, and a dozen or so more dropped in in the course of the evening—during which time some of the original dozen vanished. It was a kaleidoscopic gathering. There were Cynthia and Alex, Mary Roberts and a boy named Chuck Withers (who never liked any of Mary's friends, but insisted on coming to their parties to assert his own superiority), Paul in his usual celibate loneliness, and various assorted couples, among them Dr. Ivan Leshin and his attractive wife Tanya. Kurt had been invited, but had stayed at home with his worries. (Lupe, Mona had confided to Martin, was getting on as well as could be expected.) Boritsin had not been invited, but had come anyway.

No one noticed especially the entrance of Mona and Martin. The phonograph was playing and Boritsin was attempting a tango with Cynthia. The spectacle was quite enough to distract anyone from new arrivals.

Martin nodded random greetings here and there and struggled through to the host, who, oblivious to the dance, was explaining to an extremely uninterested Chuck Withers how the golf term *stymie* was derived from the Greek *stigma* in the sense of *fault* or *blame*. Martin interrupted long enough to introduce Mona, and Morris, with a glance of approval and the question "Wine or whisky?" slipped off to the kitchen.

He returned with whisky for Martin and Angelica for Mona, and relapsed almost instantly into his discussion. This derivation, he was apparently maintaining, clearly proved that golf was known to the Greeks.

Martin drew Mona after him through the crowd and found a large cushion on the floor by a welcome open window. There they sat, with more comfort than grace, as the ballet number ended and applause broke out. Someone changed the record and substituted Strauss's *Wienerblut*. Martin finished his whisky, stretched out almost his full length, and looked up at Mona. She smiled down on him, and he began mentally to quote "The Blessèd Damozel."

But his pre-Raphaelite musings were interrupted by a voice which gave him good evening with a harsh Slavic accent. He looked up to see Dr. Leshin, who was smiling condescendingly at Martin's pose of sprawling devotion.

"Hello," he responded, with something less than a proper attitude of respect for an Exchange Professor. "Having a good time?"

"Ah, yes." Dr. Leshin's white teeth glittered. "It is an amusing party, is it not?"

"These parties usually are. Nobody tries to make people enjoy themselves, and as a result they generally do. Oh, pardon me. Miss Morales—Dr. Leshin."

The Slav bowed gracefully, with no attempt at hiding the gleam in his eyes. Martin realized with some annoyance why the visitor from Prague had singled him out of the party. Mona smiled in slight confusion.

"How is Mrs. Leshin?" Martin asked unfairly.

"Very well." Dr. Leshin's gaze wandered across the room. "She seems to be enjoying herself."

Martin followed Leshin's glance and saw Tanya Leshin, slim and striking in a flaming gown, dancing the Strauss waltz with a seemingly reluctant Paul Lennox. The inflection of Dr. Leshin's last sentence amused him. It showed that a consummate rake was perfectly capable of jealousy where his wife was concerned —jealousy even of Paul, or more probably merely of Strauss.

"Have you seen the current Soviet film in San Francisco, Mr. Lamb?" Dr. Leshin asked, forcibly removing his gaze from the dancers. On Martin's negative reply, he proceeded into a long, but keen, analysis of its merits, interrupted by the arrival of Boritsin.

"Of what is it that you speak, Dr. Leshin?" the exiled aristocrat asked.

"The newest Soviet film—to my mind perhaps the most—"

"Dr. Leshin!" Boritsin seemed wounded. "Can it be that a man of your intellectual attainments can be intaken by the pseudo-art of propaganda which they of the Soviet seek to foist upon us? To me—"

"Martin . . ." Mona whispered.

"Yes?"

"If they are going on for long like this . . . I think I need more wine."

Quite unnoticed by the Russian disputants, who were fast reaching such a heat that English words no longer sufficed to express their feelings, Martin slipped away with Mona's glass and his own. Cynthia, he noted in passing, was the current unwilling victim of Mr. Morris's philological vagaries.

He entered the kitchen, looked about, and finally found the bottles. As he was filling the glasses, he felt a tap on his shoulder and looked around to find Cynthia.

"Got a cigarette, Martin? Like an idiot, I've run out." He obliged her gladly. "And while you're pouring, you might pour me one too."

"Angelica?"

"Hell, no. Is that what your little Latin's drinking?" She shuddered, and added, "Bourbon. Straight."

The glasses filled, Cynthia lifted hers, exclaimed, "Here's to philology!" and she gulped the whisky down. Martin joined her. "Ouf!" she gasped. "For ten minutes by anybody's clock and ten hours by my feeling I've been listening to how *bosom* is originally the same word as *besom* because the peasants of Swabia were flat-chested and filled out their bosoms with broom straw. Thank God

I'm not a peasant of Swabia!" She looked down with not unjustified satisfaction at her own full breasts.

"You are not alone in being thankful for that," Martin ventured awkwardly.

"Sweet of you, Martin. I didn't think you noticed such things. And to think that this man actually believes all this rot about words . . . ! Tell me, Martin," she switched abruptly, "do you like Mrs. Leshin?"

"I scarcely know her. I've been to their house once or twice. She's a pleasant hostess—seems intelligent—"

"You know that's not what I mean. I mean do you think she's—well, attractive?"

"That's a matter of taste. To my mind, she's a trifle slim—"

"Slim? Martin, you're always too damned betwixt-and-between to please everybody. Slim? She's thin—she's scrawny—she's—she's—a peasant of Swabia, that's what she is!" Cynthia had poured another drink, and downed it triumphantly at this *mot juste*.

Martin was puzzled by the violence of Cynthia's outburst. "I don't quite see . . . " he began.

"Martin darling, do you ever quite see anything? Run along and take your Latin her Angelica. Auntie Cynthia's staying right here for a while with the bourbon."

Precariously bearing the two filled glasses, Martin re-entered the main room. Some kind soul, in the midst of the general confusion, was keeping the phonograph in action, holding its repertory fairly steadily to Strauss, Lehar, and Kalman. Seeing that the cushion by the window was vacant, Martin looked over the dancers until he spied Mona waltzing with Dr. Leshin. He felt annoyed, and then annoyed with himself for being annoyed.

"What do you think, Martin?" he heard Alex's voice at his side.

It was on the tip of his tongue to say, "I think you'd better go out to the kitchen and keep Cyn from making a fool of herself," but he controlled his impulse—it was none of his business—and merely asked, "What do I think about what?"

"This absurd theory of your Dr. Ashwin's," Paul replied.

"I was telling Paul," Alex explained, "about the ideas that Dr. Ashwin was expounding last night."

"They seem reasonable enough," said Martin.

"Reasonable?" Paul puffed on his pipe with extra vigor. "My dear Martin, this isn't a detective novel. You can't reason things out in actual life with such absolute precision. If a thing is reasonable and yet fantastic, it's not worth considering."

"And still I think he may be right," Alex said quietly.

"Our opinion can make very little difference to the murderer," Paul observed conclusively. "It's a futile discussion."

That was the only mention of the murder in the course of the evening, and yet Martin felt that this brief snatch of dialogue contained some important meaning which he was unable to grasp. Perhaps, he consoled himself, it was only the bourbon.

The music stopped momentarily, and he saw Mona coming toward him. Dr. Leshin, after a polite adieu to his partner, had hurried off to rescue his wife from Boritsin, who seemed, to judge from his gestures, engaged in another of his periodic dissertations on the decadence of the Russian ballet.

"Thanks, Martin," Mona smiled as he handed her the glass. "Let's sit down."

Their window cushion was now occupied by Chuck and Mary, but they finally found sitting space on the floor behind the piano.

"Please, Martin," Mona begged earnestly as she sipped her wine, "don't leave me alone with him again, not even if I want another glass."

"Was he so dull?"

"No, no. Not dull." She paused. "I only do not like to dance with him. He . . . he is not a nice dancer. . . ."

Martin nodded. He had heard that commentary on Dr. Leshin before, and reproached himself for deserting Mona, even at her own request.

They sat in silence for a while, smoking and sipping and listening to the waltzes. Somehow Mona's hand had slipped into Martin's. Suddenly she spoke.

"Please, Martin, dance with me."

"I'm an atrocious dancer, I warn you—"

"That is no matter. I see your Russian doctor coming this way, and I think—"

Dr. Leshin looked a trifle disconcerted. He arrived from across the room just in time to see Martin waltz off with Mona. The music was Kalman's magnificent *Sari* waltz, and its surging rhythm brought to Martin a sense of surprising abandon. Paul, he noticed, was dancing again with Tanya Leshin, and her husband had been trapped by the host for a little give-and-take on Slavic philology. Dr. Leshin's dark glances wandered appealingly around the room, resting in turn on each attractive girl, while he vainly tried to correct Mr. Morris's fixed impression that Finnish was a Russian dialect. Martin laughed and swung joyously in the rhythmic compulsion of the music. He reveled in international joy—a joy compounded of American bourbon, Hungarian music, and a Bolivian smile.

"Martin," Mona whispered, brushing her cheek lightly against his, "you were right. You are atrocious."

The joy collapsed. Martin stopped dancing and stood still with a comically rueful countenance.

Mona laughed softly. "I am sorry. But you are, you know." And then, as though to make amends, "Where is it that we might find fresh air?"

Fresh air, indeed, was sorely needed. No amount of open windows can prevent partial suffocation in a room of a dozen constant smokers. Taking her hand, Martin led her up the stairs, through an unused room, and out onto a small balcony. The night was cool. There was no moon; but here, high in the hills, far from disturbing street lights, the light of the stars was bright. Over on the bay the ferryboats crawled, and beyond them glowed the lights of San Francisco. From the party below came a faint sound of waltzes.

Mona sighed deeply. "It is beautiful. It is of the beauty that is ever sadness. . . ."

Martin looked at her face. Her olive skin seemed ivory in the starlight and her hair jet. "And your beauty . . . is that sadness too, Mona?"

"Please do not talk."

As they sat silently on the balustrade, watching the glimmer of distant lights, Mona began softly to sing. Her song was *Las Cuatro Milpas,* the Mexican lament—the saddest, Martin had often thought, of all the world's folksongs. To the beat of a slow waltz of tragedy, its sadness seemed to envelop them both:

". . . *toditito se acobó. ¡Ay! . . .* "

Martin took her hand as she sang. It was cold and lifeless.

". . . *ni heidras, ni flores. Todito murió...*"

Her voice rose in the impassioned appeal of the second part:

". . . *Me prestaras tus ojos, morena,
en el alma los llevo que miren allá . . .* "

Her parted lips were black in the starlight. Her small breasts trembled.

". . . *los despojos de aquella casita
tan linda y bonita...*"

Martin felt her hand grow warm in his.

". . . *lo triste que está. . . .* "

Martin kissed her.

It was a surprising kiss. For one moment her lips were pressed warmly against his, as though the strong emotion of the song had continued into the kiss. The next moment she was sitting on the balustrade a foot away from him and gazing at him reproachfully.

"Martin . . . " was all she said. But when he tried to approach her she waved him away. "You do not love me, Martin," she said after an unhappy pause.

"No," Martin admitted frankly, "I don't." He had always been rather skeptical as to the possibility of his ever falling in love. "But is that all that matters? I like you. I think you are sweet, charming, lovely—"

"Nor do I love you," she continued as though he had not spoken. "Martin, one does not kiss without love."

To Martin this seemed an indefensibly exaggerated statement, but he said nothing.

"It was better that Lupe did . . . what she did with love, than that I do only this without love." She paused again, and finally added, "Martin, are we friends?"

"Of course, Mona."

"Let us go in."

She held out her hand.

By common consent, Mona and Martin separated when they returned to the party. While Mona danced with Chuck, Martin wandered into the kitchen.

Paul was sitting here, in pipe-equipped placidity, listening to a long tirade from Cynthia, who had given up by now any pretense to sobriety. The tirade broke off as Martin entered, but he gathered that it still concerned the boyish figure of Tanya Leshin, a subject that seemed to agitate Cynthia quite disproportionately.

Paul rose and sauntered back to the main room. "You're in for it, Martin," he observed. "She's got to tell her troubles to somebody."

Without a word, Martin crossed to the whisky bottle, filled with a childish resolve to get good and plastered just to prove that scenes on balconies didn't bother him one little bit.

"What's the matter, Martin?" Cynthia inquired in practically one syllable, as he resolutely swallowed a large dose of bourbon.

"Nothing."

"Something's the matter. Tell Cynthia."

"Nothing, damn it."

"Mm. He's angry. Nice quiet Martin's angry. Is it the little Latin? I thought she looked like a nice girl, Martin. And were you naughty? Should have fed her bourbon; you'll never get any place with Angelica."

Martin poured himself another drink.

"That's the idea, Martin. We'll have another drink. One for you and one for me and one for—No. Just you and me. Here's to—here's—well, anyway, here's!"

They drank in unison. Martin produced an amazing glurping noise as aftermath; it was really pretty bad bourbon.

"Don't make faces, Martin. Isn't nice. Are we downhearted? No! No! A thousand times no!" And Cynthia was singing in a loud voice to no apparent tune that she'd rather diiiiiiie than say yes.

Martin began to feel better. The immortal spirit of Mehitabel was permeating him. "Wotthell, Archie!" he exclaimed. "*Toujours gai,* kid; *toujours gai!*"

"Once a lady, always a lady," Cynthia responded duly. "How's about maybe another drink maybe?"

From that point on, with one strongly marked exception, the entire evening became rather vague in Martin's memory. How long he and Cynthia were in the kitchen God only knew. The time could be calculated only approximately from the size of the whisky bottle which they resolutely depleted.

It was when the bottle was about empty that Mona appeared in the doorway. Martin thought it was at the moment when Cynthia was teaching him to tango, a process which resulted in their both collapsing on the floor in hysterics.

"I'm going home now, Martin," Mona said. She was not smiling.

Martin rose with extreme dignity. "In an instant," he announced, "I shall have secured my cat and hoat. Then I shall escort you, Mona."

"Martin," Cynthia shrieked, "you said 'cat and hoat'!"

"What is so amusing about that?"

" 'Cat and hoat'!"

"Ah, I see. It was silly of me. I never wear a cat. Very diverting error, Mona. Now if you will await me here till I get my hoat and—"

"Do not mind," Mona said calmly. "Mr. Boritsin has a car and will drive me home. If you wish to come with us, you may; but I do not want to spoil your fun."

And she left the room.

The next thing that Martin remembered at all distinctly, as he attempted the next morning to review events, was a very loud chorus of *Tavern in the Town,* with Mary at the piano. Then there was a shadowy recollection of Alex looking pained and unhappy, and a picture of the terrific blush on the face of a girl Martin had never seen before as she came down from a session on the balcony with Dr. Leshin.

Then, too, there was the astounding moment when Martin and Cynthia, stumbling into a passage off the main room, saw Mrs. Leshin being kissed with unmistakable vigor. Dr. Leshin's roving black eyes had by now discovered an object which interested him more than his jealousy of his own wife; and she had apparently decided to have a little fun on her own. At first Cynthia sniffed, seemingly in disgust at anyone who could find amorous pleasure in a peasant of Swabia; and then she gasped, as did Martin, to recognize in Tanya's partner the ordinarily staid Paul Lennox. His pipe was nowhere to be seen, and he was quite evidently entering wholeheartedly into the spirit of the occasion.

It was some indefinite time after this vision that Martin found himself on the balcony with Cynthia. It was a very different matter from his first balcony scene of the evening. This time there was no abstract discussion of love; there was nothing but lusty kisses and warm caresses. Martin's head was swimming through an uncertain ocean of bourbon; but he realized that he was discovering a marked taste for decidedly un-Swabian pomegranates.

As Martin's caresses grew even more intimate, Cynthia sighed luxuriously. "Darling . . . " she moaned, running her fingers through his rumpled hair. "Paul darling . . . Paul. . . ."

For one instant Martin was, in his astonishment, completely sober. Paul. . . . Paul's name was Cynthia's unconscious and automatic response to the warmest love-making. Martin's hands ceased to wander and his lips grew unresponsive as he tried to piece this together with other things. Dozens of other things. Cynthia's tirades against Tanya Leshin . . . the brief conversation earlier in the evening between Paul and Alex . . . Cynthia's two visits to the doctor in San Francisco. Cynthia, finding herself suddenly quite uncaressed, began to express her chagrin in purest Billingsgate.

Alex was standing at the entrance to the balcony and saying something about time to go home now. Martin was glad. He was frightened and could no longer remember why.

It was Chuck Withers, he discovered later, who drove them all home, and Alex who helped him to bed. And no one realized, least of all Martin, that he had established a new precedent by showing how drunkenness and its consequent lechery may prove invaluable to the incipient Watson.

SIX

THE SUPERFLUOUS ALIBI

All this was on Saturday. Sunday was, as a natural result, as dismal a day as Martin had ever passed. He awoke in the early afternoon with a head of fabulous proportions. His alarm clock, he discovered, had run down completely without in the least disturbing his sleep. He had missed Mass, and his mouth—none of the conventional similes involving birdcages or motorman's gloves were in the least adequate to describe his mouth.

Things were very confused in his mind as he dressed. The one clear idea was that he owed Mona an apology. He rehearsed several possible openings while he steadied himself with vast quantities of black coffee and tomato juice (with Worcestershire sauce), only to find that Mona had left for San Francisco—probably to see Lupe, he thought—and would be gone all day.

On his way to the library he ran into Paul, who looked almost equally low, and Alex, who made unpleasant remarks about people who had to be put to bed. At last, in absolute desperation, he lost himself in the stacks and read a complete novel by Gutzkow at one sitting.

Since he had gone that far, he determined to cap the wretchedness of the day by attending the Sunday Supper at International House. He even sat through the speeches, then hurried to bed and a mercifully quick sleep.

He felt better on Monday. Even the dullness of Hagemann's course on Young Germany, for which he had gobbled the Gutzkow, did not particularly disturb him, and by the time he had reached Dr. Ashwin's class he was his own bright self.

When the translation from the *Mahabharata* had been concluded (and none too successfully, for he had not prepared it well), he entered into a spirited discussion concerning the relative merits of the imperishable Master of Baker Street in novels and in short stories, and decided to look upon Saturday night and Sunday as simply not having been.

As the hour drew to a close, Dr. Ashwin glanced at his watch and said, "I regret that I have an appointment, Mr. Lamb, or I should ask you to lunch with me. I wish, frankly, to pick your brains for certain specialized information. Could you come to see me this evening?"

"I'll be rehearsing. The show goes on Friday, you know, and I'll be busy as the devil all week."

"Come after rehearsal for a half-hour or an hour."

"It'll be late."

"That is all right. If it will not be too inconvenient for you?"

"Oh, no."

"Good. And please, Mr. Lamb—come alone."

Martin nodded, a trifle puzzled.

The rest of the day was a busy one. Dr. Leshin's class—wherein the doctor cast at Martin several knowing and reminiscent glances, of the one-man-of-the-world-to-another sort, which were rather embarrassing—then most of the afternoon in conference with Drexel and his costume designer; a hurried dinner hour, mostly spent in a vain search for Mona; and then the rehearsal. It was the first rehearsal with sets and props, and as confusing as such occasions usually are. Its one redeeming feature was the fact that Paul Lennox at last was good in his death scene.

Dog-tired but persistent, Martin climbed the stairs to Dr. Ashwin's room. He sank into a chair without a word and gratefully accepted the whisky glass which Ashwin had already filled for him.

"You look tired," Dr. Ashwin observed.

Martin emptied the glass at a gulp. "I know you love to enunciate the obvious," he said, "but that's even a little too much so." He lit a cigarette and half closed his eyes.

"I am sorry to bother you when you are so busy," Ashwin continued, "but my mind has kept itself too much occupied with this problem of murder. Your presenting me with that problem, Mr. Lamb, was as though I should offer a glass of this scotch to a teetotaler who had within him the potentialities of an extreme dipsomaniac. You have corrupted me."

"*Mea culpa* . . . " Martin murmured.

"I have no work to do at present, beyond my familiar teaching routine, which is light. I am working on no translation, as I have generally been in the past, for there is nothing left in Sanskrit at once worthy of translation and suited to my abilities and limitations. Thus this problem of murder has furnished me with something to work at, and I cannot stop."

Martin made a wearily inarticulate questioning noise as Ashwin paused.

"You wonder then why I have insisted on your visiting me tonight? It is because I need facts concerning people, and I think that you can give them to me."

" 'Who's Who in Berkeley, or, The Traveler's Compendium of Fascinating Facts.' Go on." Martin settled himself more comfortably.

"You must also forgive me," Ashwin resumed, "if I employ you as an accessory to my reasoning, in the Socratic method. I feel the need of—shall we say, a Watson?"

"A stooge," Martin emended.

"Your alternations, Mr. Lamb, between the diction of the eighteenth century and that of the theatrical periodical, *Variety,* which you once showed me, never cease to astound me. But to continue: We agreed, I believe, on the occasion of your last visit, that the murdered Dr. Schaedel was in all likelihood a mere innocent bystander. Do you still think that plausible?"

"Quite. So does Alex. He was very much impressed, and got into quite an argument with Paul about your theory."

Dr. Ashwin was markedly interested. "So? Mr. Lennox does not think my theory tenable?"

"Not in the least."

"Now that, Mr. Lamb, is an example of the sort of fact which I hope to elicit from you. But to resume the logical course of discussion—If Dr. Schaedel was indeed the wrong man, the next step would be to decide who was the right man. It should be far simpler to find who the murderer was once we know who was the intended victim.

"There are, in this murder, three separate possibilities in explaining the confusion of victims. Let us be methodical and letter them. A: The murderer, having long since resolved to kill his victim, accidentally encounters Dr. Schaedel coming from Miss Wood's door and does the deed then and there. B: The murderer is deliberately shadowing his victim with murder in mind; but the victim's evening wanderings cross those of Dr. Schaedel and the murderer follows the wrong man. C: The murderer is lying in wait for his victim in front of Miss Wood's home. Can you suggest any further possibilities?"

"No," Martin admitted. "But I can make objections to those, which is, I suppose, what you want me to do."

"Go on," Ashwin prompted.

"Well . . . As to A, it's too damned improbable. I grant Dr. Schaedel looked very ordinary at night and might be taken for anyone, but only if you had a definite reason for thinking he was someone else—such a reason as knowing that your intended victim would be in that place at that time. Just a chance encounter won't do."

Ashwin nodded. "And you see, of course, that sometimes the same objection applies to B. If the murderer had lost the trail unwittingly, he would not have killed at that precise moment unless Dr. Schaedel was doing something which the real victim would have done."

"In other words," Martin interposed, "what you're getting at is this: Whoever the intended victim was, he was someone whom the murderer might expect to see coming out of Cynthia's house at that hour."

"Exactly. And now you see, Mr. Lamb, why I wish to question you. Who would fulfill that condition and at the same time resemble Dr. Schaedel sufficiently?"

Martin pondered. "Let's see . . . Of course, the most frequent male visitor to Cynthia's is Alex Bruce. And he's about the right height. In fact, Kurt told me that he thought for a moment his uncle was Alex, seeing him go into Cynthia's." Dr. Ashwin noted down the name. "No one else goes there regularly, but lots of us drop in, even at late hours. Paul Lennox, if I remember aright, is even closer to Dr. Schaedel's height than Alex. He and Cynthia aren't exactly friendly, but—" He stopped abruptly. Cynthia's unconscious revelation on the balcony he had forgotten completely up to that moment. Now it leaped suddenly and dominatingly into his mind.

"Go on." Dr. Ashwin held his pencil ready. "Who else?"

"Several other men—but all the wrong build. Worthing's too small; anyway, he scarcely knows Cyn. Kurt and Chuck are both tall and heavy. Boritsin is tall and thin. Of course, there's me."

"Mr. Lamb," said Ashwin reprovingly, "I am not such a purist as to object to your grammar, but I do object, and strongly, to your habit of dragging yourself into every discussion. None the less, I suppose that I should write down your name." He did so reluctantly.

"One thing, though," Martin went on undaunted, "it couldn't very well have been me—I—whatever—because I never wear a hat. Dr. Schaedel did. Paul and Alex both wear one about half the time."

"A good point, Mr. Lamb, and one which spares me the necessity of asking why anyone should bother to kill you. Can you think of any other likely candidates?"

"Cyn's father comes to see her once in a while. He's about the right height, but much heavier. Anyway, I don't think he'd ever come at that hour of the night or on foot."

"The list, then, seems to consist solely of Alex Bruce and Paul Lennox. I am glad that they are both men whom I have met. Now, Mr. Lamb, please tell me everything you can about these two."

Martin paused and refilled his glass. "Well," he began, "first we have, in this corner, Alex Bruce. Age: twenty-six. Nationality: American of Scotch descent. Political affiliation, if that means anything in these days: Democrat. Religion: Presbyterian, but never does anything about it. Profession: research fellow in chemistry, University of California. Degrees: B.S., M.S. Character: quiet, but determined. Sports: swimming, tennis. Rumored engaged to Cynthia Wood. Satisfactory?"

"Not precisely helpful," Ashwin commented, "but continue."

"Next, Paul Lennox. Age: twenty-eight. Nationality: American, of vague antecedents. Political affiliation: none. Religion: none. Profession: instructor in history, University of California. Degrees. B.A., M.A. Character: sardonic, reserved, a little cryptic. Sports: hiking, chess."

"For statements of succinct fact, Mr. Lamb," Dr. Ashwin observed, "these brief biographies are no doubt admirable, but they scarcely aid in determining why either man should be killed. Have they money?"

"None so far as I know, beyond their respective salaries."

"No marked enmities, I take it, or you would have mentioned them. Once more we seem forced back upon Miss Wood as a starting point. Tell me something about their relations with her."

"As I said, Alex is with her a great deal and there seems to be some sort of an understanding. In public, she and Paul don't get on at all well."

"In public?"

Martin hesitated a moment, and then told the story of Saturday evening—as much, that, is as seemed pertinent and he could remember.

"From that, then," Dr. Ashwin mused, when he had finished, "we may conclude with some certainty that Miss Wood is deceiving Bruce with Lennox, and that Lennox in turn is carrying on some slight affair with this professor's wife—you were doubtless right, Mr. Lamb, to withhold the professor's name."

"That seems to sum it up," Martin agreed.

"And there we have a plentiful supply of motives. Sexual jealousy dictates so many crimes—even the Twin Peaks Murder," Ashwin admitted regretfully. "Either Bruce or your nameless professor might wish to kill Lennox out of jealousy, as might also Miss Wood herself."

"But Mary Roberts was with Cynthia at the time of the killing," Martin objected.

"True. If I remember correctly, Miss Wood herself summoned Miss Robert to her home that evening for reasons which were never fully explained. Is that not true?"

"Yes."

"There we have the first example of what might be termed the Incident of the Supererogatory Alibi. But I shall return to that later. The set of facts which you have just given me suggests also that Mr. Lennox may have motivation for killing Mr. Bruce."

"Paul kill Alex? Why? If Paul is enjoying Cynthia's favors and at the same time carrying on an affair with a married woman, why should he want to kill Cynthia's public lover? Alex is too good and useful a blind for him to dispense with."

"There, Mr. Lamb, I am tempted to toy with a theory unsupported by any known facts, and yet logically enough arrived at. I am, unfortunately, possessed of sufficient natural vanity to desire not to appear ridiculous, but not enough to make me feel omniscient and infallible as a detective. For that reason, I do not care as yet to state the theory, for fear that the facts may prove it absurd. But let me direct your attention to two facts concerning Miss Wood's father: He is extremely rich, and he is a fanatically strict converted Catholic."

Martin nodded with an appearance of intelligent comprehension, although the two facts conveyed no theory to his mind.

"I have evolved this theory," Dr. Ashwin continued, "because to me it seems almost inevitable that Mr. Lennox is the criminal and Mr. Bruce the intended victim. For one thing, you will remember telling me that Alex Bruce expected to be at Miss Wood's on that Friday evening, but forgot the appointment because of his laboratory work. Anyone knowing of that engagement, as you said that Paul Lennox knew, would naturally expect him to be leaving the house somewhere around the hour of the crime."

"But look," Martin broke in. "If you're casting Paul for the murderer, it simply won't do. I can give him a perfect alibi."

"That, Mr. Lamb, is why I suspect Mr. Lennox."

"What do you mean?"

Dr. Ashwin, despite his occasional sarcastic references to Martin's love of the theatre, fully appreciated the value of dramatic pause. Before he answered the question, he emptied his glass, refilled it, and lit a cigarette. Then he said, "An alibi, Mr. Lamb, is in ordinary existence an extremely rare event. We are generally quite unable to prove where we were at a particular hour. Let us take, for example, the exact moment of Dr. Schaedel's murder—11:30 P.M. Friday, April 6th.

"I shall not use your shoddy device of personal reference, for it chances that I do have a relatively satisfactory alibi. At ten o'clock I left Elizabeth's home to go to my hotel; to have reached Berkeley from San Rafael in an hour and a half, unable as I am to drive either an automobile or an aeroplane, would have been little short of a miracle. But observe that even that is not an alibi to the minute. Now let us take the other persons involved:

"You, Mr. Lamb, were sitting alone in your room, drinking bourbon (I have never been able to understand your strange preference for that liquor) and finishing *The Boat Train Murders*. You are utterly unalibied. Kurt Ross was wandering alone in the hills. Alex Bruce was walking across campus from the chemistry laboratories to International House. Any one of you might have been at Panoramic Way (Mr. Ross, indeed, was there) for all that you can prove to the contrary.

"But one person is accounted for, to the very minute, and that person is Paul Lennox. When you first told me of that evening, I jotted down the times and have them here. Are you sure of your watch on that occasion?"

"I set it by the radio after dinner. It never loses more than a minute or so a week. And Mary Roberts told me that she and Cynthia had set the clock—also by radio—at ten thirty that night."

"Good. Now here are the times:

10:45 (*approximately*) Lamb goes to Lennox's room.
11:20 (*exactly*) Lamb leaves Lennox's room. Lennox calls direct attention to clock, which Lamb corrects from his watch.
11:28 (*exactly*) Dr. Schaedel asks Miss Wood his way and the time.
11:30 (*approximately*) Dr. Schaedel leaves Miss Wood and is instantly killed. (This time is also checked by Kurt Ross's narrative.)

11:40 (*exactly*) Lennox reenters Lamb's room. He calls attention to the time by commenting on his speed in typing.
11:42 (*approximately*) Bruce enters Lamb's room. Lennox is surprised that he is not at Miss Wood's.
11:45 (*approximately*) Kurt Ross enters Lamb's room in a terrific state of nerves."

Dr. Ashwin handed the paper to Martin. "Is that roughly correct?"

Martin nodded. "I know that leaves Paul the time between eleven twenty and eleven forty. That's plenty of time to get to Cynthia's and back again. But that would mean he'd have to know exactly when Alex would leave Cynthia's. After all, lovers don't say good night by clockwork."

"True. But not an insuperable objection."

"You think not? But this is. All that time, from eleven twenty to eleven forty, I could hear Paul typing away like the devil. The walls are thin, you know; there's no doubt that the sound came from Paul's room. And if you're going to suggest that he had an accomplice come in and type for him—that's too damned much. Whoever it was would realize what it was about as soon as a murder occurred during that exact time."

"I am not suggesting an accomplice, Mr. Lamb. I am simply suggesting that the alibi is not a perfect one. Again I have a theory, which I shall ask you later to substantiate for me. Meanwhile, you have all the facts upon which I have based my two theories. Indeed, your specialized interest in the theatre should predispose you to this second one."

Martin sat silent for a moment. "In short," he said at last, "what you believe is this: That Paul Lennox sought to kill Alex Bruce for a motive which I cannot guess and by means of a faked alibi to which I am the deceived witness. And how about the Seven of Calvary? You think Paul made up the whole story?"

"Yes. As a red herring. The symbol was probably left originally, as I suggested in our first discussion, to hint at some strange motive and at a different type of murderer. When Lennox learned who his victim really was, he invented this fantastic tale, the truth of which could not readily be checked."

"Then why didn't he go to the police with it?"

"He was far more subtle. If he seemed anxious to have it known, its truth might be doubted. Instead, he told it to a group of five people, enjoining them to secrecy after the police had broadcast a request for information. The chances were certainly in favor of the secret's betrayal by at least one of those people."

"And you expect him still to carry out his original intention?"

"Of course. And what can I do about it? I have no certain evidence with which to satisfy the police. I cannot even warn Mr.

Bruce on such grounds of theoretical reasoning. All that I can do . . ."

"Yes?"

"All that I can do, Mr. Lamb, is to request you to keep an eye upon these two gentlemen and to see if you can discover anything further. Be with them even more than you ordinarily are."

"Keeping an eye on Paul will be easy enough for me this week. We'll be at rehearsal together every night, and probably eat together too. I'll be with him every evening from about six until we go to bed. And Alex is in the chem lab all afternoon."

Ashwin smiled. "I feel like Jehovah setting a guardian angel to watch over potential malefactors and victims. You make a curious angel, Mr. Lamb."

"I wonder if guardian angels drink scotch?" Martin asked.

Martin left Dr. Ashwin's room a half-hour later in a state of sore bewilderment. Ashwin's case against Paul as murderer was certainly plausible, even cogent; and Paul was surely far better cast as a subtle murderer than Kurt had been. Still, Martin felt the same instinctive reaction against believing that he numbered a murderer among his intimates. It was idiotic and yet . . . None the less he resolved to be most vigilant in his new role as guardian angel.

As he reached the entrance to International House, he was relieved to see a sound and healthy Alex Bruce approaching him.

"Hello. Been to Cynthia's?" he asked.

"Yes," Alex answered somewhat abruptly.

"A scene? You look it."

"A little. Partly your fault, Martin. We were fighting about Saturday night."

"I am sorry, Alex. It was stupid of me to—"

"That's all right. I don't blame you for that balcony scene. Why shouldn't you make love to Cynthia? You might as well join the crowd."

They entered the elevator and rode to their floor without another word. Martin felt too embarrassed to say anything; a guardian angel is not generally rebuked for his accidental amorousness.

As Martin went to his room after a curt good night, he thought back over Ashwin's new theory and found it good, if disquieting. Thus for the second time Martin found himself possessed of a relatively satisfactory explanation of Dr. Schaedel's death; and this time he was not nearly so afflicted with instinctive qualms against his own belief.

But this, of course, was before the second murder.

INTERLUDE

Martin timed the sentence with which I have concluded the last chapter so that it came just as we descended from the streetcar.

"I thought you were holding a second murder up your sleeve, Martin," I observed. "Are we then to wait until enough characters have been killed and the list of suspects narrowed down to one?"

"I don't quite know whether that method would work here, Tony," he answered me. "Wait and see. Besides, remember I'm not trying to tell a technically perfect story; all this really happened to me. Now let's not say anything for a while; I'm out of breath after all that narration."

To be sure, I too was a little weary, and not sorry for a momentary pause. We walked along in silence, gazing at the fascinatingly crowded windows of Italian importers' shops, and dodging occasionally to avoid the rapid career of a youthful fascist on skates.

When we were comfortably settled in a booth at La Favorite and had ordered cocktails while we examined the menu, I asked, "Have you got your breath back yet?"

"Tony, you're positively avid!"

"It's simply natural curiosity—my first meeting with a Watson." I did not bother to state that I was already considering the novelistic possibilities of Martin's narrative.

"And how do you like me as Watson?"

I reflected judiciously. "Hm-m . . . A little unconventional. It's disconcerting to have a rather ponderous Holmes and a decidedly erratic Watson."

The drinks arrived, and we returned to our study of the menu. Our orders given, Martin resumed:

"And Ashwin?"

"A little too good to be true, if I hadn't met him once when I was at Berkeley. Such a pity he wasn't born in the eighteenth century. You expect him to include a 'sir' in every sentence."

Martin looked up quizzically. "Are you laying any wagers on the murderer?"

"I don't trust you, Martin."

"Now, now, Tony, I'm being perfectly fair. I'm telling you everything—everything, that is, that Ashwin and I knew. I don't think I'm even using much false emphasis. Now, who's the murderer?"

I shook my head. "I have such a weakness for the formula of the least suspected person—short of detectives, doctors, and butlers, who are beyond the pale—and I don't see how you can use it here. There isn't any unsuspected person save you and Ashwin. Of course, Kurt and Paul are innocent; you've laid so much stress on them. Then there's Alex . . . Dr. Leshin. . . . Martin, if the murderer turns out to be anyone like Worthing or Boritsin, I'll make you pay for dinner even though you are my guest."

"I told you I was playing fair," said Martin.

The waiter brought the hors d'œuvres and a steaming tureen of soup, and stood in expectancy. Martin caught the meaning of his attitude and looked at me.

"Should we?" he asked.

"Should we what?"

"Order wine after all our beer?"

I shrugged my shoulders. I never can remember the technicalities of precedence.

"Bier auf Wein
Ist nicht fein . . . " Martin was murmuring.

"Wein auf Bier."

Rat' ich Dir . . . A bottle of Chablis, waiter. —It's the only way to remember," he added turning to me.

When the wine had been brought and poured, I lifted my glass. "To the Unknown Murderer!" I declaimed. After the toast was drunk, "Now go on, Martin," I should like to know whom I was toasting."

"Excellent soup," Martin remarked irrelevantly. "Well . . . that was on Monday. Nothing particular happened after that until dress rehearsal. . . ."

SEVEN

STRANGULATION SCENE

Dress rehearsal was scheduled for Thursday evening, which meant that Martin calmly cut all of his Thursday classes and spent the entire day in Wheeler Auditorium with Drexel. There were last-minute alterations in the sets, questions as to the proper shades of grease paint for different characters, minor problems of costuming and hand props; and in all these matters Drexel wished his decision to bear the authoritative *cachet* of the translator. Martin found this attitude flattering but wearisome, and breathed intense relief when Drexel finally called it a day at four o'clock.

This preoccupation with details had caused Martin quite to neglect his post as guardian angel; but he was far too weary to feel

any pangs of conscience. As he came out of the auditorium, however, he found himself confronted with another problem which he had been neglecting for *Don Juan Returns*. On the sunlit stone steps sat Mona Morales.
 She was alone, and studying intently. She was not aware of Martin's presence until he stood beside her and spoke her name. Then she stood up, a trifle awkwardly, and looked disconcerted for the first time in Martin's knowledge of her. There followed a pause which threatened to be of indefinite length. Martin sought for the perfect phrase which would put everything right again. It was not to be found, but fortunately it was not needed. Suddenly Mona smiled and extended her hand.
 "It's nice to see you again, Martin," she said.
 Martin took her hand gratefully. That smile had sufficed to set the times perfectly in joint again. "I've been working with Drexel all day," he said, "and I'm half dead. Won't you have tea with me? Sorry I can't offer anything more stimulating near campus."
 "I'd love to. Do you like the Black Sheep?"
 "Very much." They started off, and stopped in sudden embarrassment. Martin reluctantly freed her hand, which had remained so naturally in his.
 The tea was good, and so were the cinnamon rolls which Martin had ordered in preference to cinnamon toast. "No restaurant," he expounded in a manner which he noticed with surprise was almost Ashwinian, "no restaurant knows how to make cinnamon toast. The secret is to use a broiling rack, not a toaster, and to toast only one side of the bread before spreading the butter, sugar, and cinnamon. That gives you the perfect glaze. It's my own invention . . . " he added in a faltering echo of the White Knight. His pontifical manner was rapidly fading before the steady, cool gaze of Mona. He looked down at the cinnamon rolls with an intentness which even the admirable presence of pecans did not justify.
 Mona spoke. Her voice was as cool and steady as her gaze. "I know what you want to say, Martin, and that you seek some way that you may come to it. Do not say it, Martin. It is no need."
 Martin looked up in surprise. "I don't know . . . "
 "Yes, you do. You wish to say, 'Mona, I was a fool. Please forgive me,' or something as silly as that. Why should one forgive people? If one likes them not, why to bother? And if one does like them . . . it is no need."
 Martin was at a loss for words—a rare state indeed for him. He finished a cinnamon roll, took a gulp of tea, which was much hotter than he had expected, and produced his cigarettes, offering one to Mona. "You're very kind," he said.
 "Thank you. That is, for the cigarette—not for the compliment. I am not kind, Martin; I am sensible. I like you, and I tell you so

to keep you from worry. Thank you," she said again as he offered her a match flame. "I admit that I was a little . . . irritated. Perhaps if I had seen you Sunday morning, I should not have spoken as now I speak. That is why I avoided you. I knew that I too can be silly—oh, very silly. Now I am not."

Martin drank his tea in silence. He was intensely grateful for having been spared an apologetic scene, and he was unable to express his gratitude.

"Besides," Mona continued with a light smile, "I have not forgotten the balcony. No, no," she added quickly as Martin looked up. "I do not mean that as perhaps it sounds. I mean—you stopped when I told you. That does not always happen. I remember two months ago—it was a great unpleasantness, Martin, a young man who would not stop . . . " Her voice trailed off. "I speak too much, Martin," she resumed. "That is a long story and not a nice one. You shall not hear it until you know me much better."

"Then assuredly I shall hear it," Martin said with a determination which surprised himself.

Tea did not keep Martin from eating a hearty dinner. He knew that he had a strenuous evening before him, and he resolved to fortify himself as best he could. But his concentration on food make him a little late, and he was hurrying through the Great Hall as Alex called to him.

"Why the terrific rush, Martin?"

"It's almost quarter of, and I've got to be in costume and make-up by seven. Not that we'll start on time of course. Hello, Cyn," he added a little shortly.

"I do wish you luck with the play, Martin," Cynthia said. "I'm terribly sorry I shan't be able to see it. I'm dreadfully loaded with engagements this week end."

"So am I," Alex added. "That is, not engagements exactly, but a few social appointments with test tubes and retorts. What we were wondering was—do you think you could sneak us in to the dress rehearsal?"

"I don't see why not. Drexel may give you hell and throw you out, and he may be glad to have some sort of an audience to give reactions. Nothing guaranteed. As a matter of fact, I asked Mona to drop in tonight; she can't make the performance either."

"And you want your little Latin to see your great triumph?" Cynthia smiled maliciously.

"Yes," Martin answered simply. It was easier than an exchange of sarcasm. "You can just slip in at the back of the auditorium. We'll probably get things started some time between seven-thirty and eight." With a nod of farewell, he set off for the auditorium.

Martin fingered his beard doubtfully. The make-up mirror

assured him that it was convincing, but it felt so damned artificial. With the scissors he snipped a bit of hair from one side and regarded it again. As Paul Lennox came into the little classroom which had been forced into theatrical service, he looked up. "Do you think that's any better?" he asked.

"I couldn't tell." Paul sank into a one-armed class chair and produced a briar pipe from somewhere in his sixteenth century doublet. "You know, Martin," he went on during the process of filling and lighting, "I think I've got stage fright. I've lectured before huge classes, I've read a paper before a learned association, and never a quiver. I know this play's just fun, nothing that really matters—"

"Thanks," Martin interrupted.

"I mean nothing that really matters so far as I'm concerned—my career and what not—and yet somehow I feel as though tonight were the most important night in my life."

"Stage fright's a good sign," said Martin. "Only lousy actors are ever quite free from it." He lit a cigarette after a last regretful glance at the reflection of his beard. "But if you're jittery tonight, what will you be tomorrow with an audience out front?"

"There's enough of an audience tonight. People have kept dribbling in at the back of the auditorium. Drexel began to blow up, and then suddenly decided that their reactions might be valuable. I think he said it with capital letters."

They smoked in silence for a minute or so. "By the way," Martin said, "you were swell in the death scene last night. Keep it up."

"Thanks." Paul smiled quietly. "You've no idea how strange you look, Martin. The cigarette itself goes queerly enough with your costume and your beard, but when the tip of the cigarette is stained with lip rouge . . . "

Martin was glaring at the results of make-up when a head popped in at the door, called "Places!" and vanished. Paul rose leisurely and knocked the ashes out of his pipe. His hand was none too steady.

"Well, good luck, Paul. I've got to the end of the first scene to enjoy my own private jitters. You'll knock 'em dead with that first curtain."

Paul nodded a little dubiously and left. Martin had finished his cigarette and was again considering the beard question when a tap came on the door. "Come in," he said.

It was Mona. "I did not think I was supposed to come behind the stage," she began. "But I do want to wish you luck. It has begun. The setting looks lovely. Paul is a little frightened. . . ." She paused.

"Thank you, Mona," Martin said, and pressed her hand. "*¡Buena suerte, amigo!*" she exclaimed, kissed him impulsively, and hurried away. For once it was the girl and not the man who carried off telltale traces of make-up.

For the remainder of his off-stage wait, Martin forgot his beard, his role, his play, and his status as guardian angel; and thought only of Mona until the detached head appeared once more to call "Places for scene two!"

He was still in something of a daze as he began what was to prove the most momentous stage appearance of his life.

"Watch your next extrance cue, Elvira. You miss it nine times out of ten."

"Tell Harold to check your make-up, Paul. We can't see your eyes at all under that spot."

"Now by the Mass, Don Juan, this time you lie!"
"If it were but to lie with thee, my chick . . ."

"Even money we have to cut that line the second night. . . ."

"Check that green spot for the statue's entrance. It's not center stage; it's right center."

"Then let blood flow, Don Félix. What care I,
Be it from sword-pierced hearts or shattered maidenheads?"

"It's a classic. I guess you can get by with any kind of line in a classic. . . ."

"Maybe someday we'll have an honest-to-god theatre in this university. I'm so God-damned sick of horsing around on a lousy lecture platform—"

"Did you see the notice in the Daily *Cal.*?"

"Did I? They got my name wrong and they forgot to say I played in *Death Takes a Holiday*."

"Maybe they were just being charitable, darling. . . ."

"God's doom has hung ere this so close o'er me
That I could feel Jehovah's awful breath
Searing my cheecks. . . ."

"My God, he's cut five pages of the script!"

"How can I make my entrance?"

"Ad-lib. Do anything. But get on there!"

"You were wonderful in the love scene, Laurel."

"Thanks loads."

"I've never seen anyone look so completely seduced. Drexel's marvelous at casting. . . ."

"I thought I'd blow for sure when Nathan said, 'And is this puny wench the side of Preville?'"

"He's muffed that line at every rehearsal. There's always one hitch like that in every show."

"I don't give a good God damn if your mother and your grandmother and your grandmother's illegitimate great-aunt are going to be out front. You can *not* wear a brassiere with that low-necked second-act bodice!"

> "*Two blades I bear, Don Sancho; one is victor
> In death—in love, the other...*"

"Has anybody got a drink for God's sake?"

"What I want to know is, how did Don Juan ever get anywhere in clothes like these?"

"That's a quick black-out on the convent scene, Roy. If you dim, you kill the whole effect."

"I'm damned if I see why Drexel dragged in this Lennox person. Just because he's a friend of Lamb's—I've been in ten shows here on this stage, and if I haven't earned a good lead by now . . . "

"I don't know what happened. My mind just went blank. I'll have that speech cold tomorrow."

"Lights!"

"Snap up your cues there!"

"Places!"

"That last scene drags like hell in the middle. Speed it up tomorrow!"

"Check that!"

"Stand by to help Elvira on that quick change!"

"If you're prompting this show, Miss Davis, for God's sake prompt it!"

"Speed up that change!"

"Mark that cross!"

"Places!"

"Fix that spot!"

"Okay?"

"Check!"

In short, a dress rehearsal, as such undistinguishable from any other. Undistinguishable, that is, up to eleven thirty.

The second act was finished a little before eleven, which was not half bad. Martin had had nightmares of rehearsal till three or four—a not unheard-of occurrence. The cast was still fairly chipper, but Drexel none the less advised a fifteen-minute rest before taking up the third act, which was short but strenuous in the extreme.

The house lights went on, and Martin, standing beside a table of third-act props, looked out into the auditorium. Alex and Cynthia had apparently come over with Mona. At least, the three were sitting together and talking excitedly. All of the small audience, in fact, seemed to be deeply interested in the play, which, despite its great and lasting popularity in Spain and Latin America, had hitherto been completely unknown to English-speaking audiences.

Some of the audience began drifting backstage during this informal pause. Among them Martin noticed Dr. Griswold of the Spanish Department and with him, to Martin's surprise, the Leshins. It was the first time that he had ever seen them apparently satisfied with each other's company.

Dr. Griswold peered through the backstage mob, looking more than ever like Don Quixote in modern dress, until he caught sight of Martin.

"I like it," he said, as he slipped between a pair of Sevillian gallants, nearly tripping over their clumsily adjusted swords. "I don't think much of the play, as you may remember from the seminar, but I like your translation."

"Thanks," Martin answered. "That means something from you. And I still think it's a swell piece of theatre, even if it isn't Literature for seminars."

Dr. Griswold blinked an appreciative smile.

"It is very interesting, Mr. Lamb," Dr. Leshin added. "I know next to nothing of the Spanish theatre, but I find this piece fascinating."

"And you, Mrs. Leshin?"

"Chiefly I am surprised that Mr. Lennox can act so well."

Martin repressed several comments at once.

"So am I," Dr. Griswold agreed. "The only chance for acting that I had as an instructor was in controlling myself at faculty meetings."

Cynthia, Alex, and Mona now joined the group at the prop table. Cynthia was gushing with excitement, and even Alex was interested. "I think it's too damned thrilling for words, Martin!" Cynthia was exclaiming. "And Paul is simply swelegant. Don't you think so, Mrs. Leshin?" she added in a voice that was markedly not calm.

"Mr. Lennox has indeed greatly surprised me," the doctor's wife replied.

"Now *you* surprise *me,* Mrs. Leshin," said Cynthia a little too sweetly.

Martin was uncomfortable. As the little group around him shifted to allow for the flowings of the rest of the crowd, he felt that they all moved around one axis—the direct line of antagonism between these two women. He was glad that Paul had remained in the dressing room for the brief rest.

Dr. Griswold's dry voice broke the tension. "I've been telling

Martin," he was saying to Dr. Leshin, "that he ought to try his hand at something of Lope de Vega's. *Fuenteovejuna* has been sorely neglected in view of its sociological interest to—"

There was a tinkle of breaking glass. Martin turned and saw one of the two glasses that had stood on the prop table now lying in fragments on the floor. "God damn it!" he exclaimed. "Who the devil knocked that down?"

"Mr. Lamb . . . !" Mrs. Leshin was regarding him with raised eyebrows.

"Sorry. You can scarcely help barking at people in a hubbub like this. Oh, well, it doesn't much matter. Only one glass is really used in this scene, so the one that's left will be enough. The other's just for looks—not a real hand prop. But these little things are so damned annoying at a rehearsal."

"Places for act three!"

The helterskelter backstage wanderings began to assume obedient order to the disembodied voice.

Dr. Griswold, the Leshins, Cynthia, Alex,—all slipped back into the auditorium with murmured congratulations and good wishes. Mona, who had not spoken a word, remained behind for an instant.

"You do bring luck, Mona," said Martin, touching her hand lightly.

"I'm glad," and she was gone.

Martin's gaze returned to the fragments of glass lying on the floor, and the little pool of coloured water which the audience had been supposed to take for sherry. He had turned around the instant he heard the crash, but no one had been standing near the table. Or was there one? For some reason at the moment obscure to him, he was very badly puzzled by this trifling incident, possibly simply because it freed his mind for an instant of the major worries of the evening.

But there was no need for such worrying. Martin's statement had been perfectly true. The glass that was left was quite enough.

The brief first scene of the third act, in which Martin, as Don Félix, hears the confession of his sister Elvira and swears vengeance upon her betrayer, went off with admirable tension. The audience lost all pretense of informality and indifference; they were enjoying Theatre in its most exciting aspect, and thrilled to the chill of imminent death which pervaded the auditorium.

As the lights dimmed and Martin left the stage, there was even a brief patter of applause. Paul, waiting in the wings, seized his hand. "Grand work, Martin."

"I surprised myself," Martin admitted. "If we can only keep it up for the strangulation scene. . . ."

"I've never been so moved in my life as tonight. If this is the theatre, even amateur, I'm damned if I'll ever teach history again."

The lights slowly went up on the stage—act three, scene two, a room in the ancestral home of Don Juan. The low comedian who was playing Don Juan's manservant got a sizable laugh on his opening business.

"Well," said Paul, "here goes." He shook Martin's hand firmly and strode onto the stage. Martin looked after him with warm admiration. Ashwin's reasonings had vanished completely from his mind.

Dialogue between Don Juan and his manservant. Fairly bawdy, but it got the laughs. The stage manager rapped loudly on a wooden board, and the servant exited. Don Juan's soliloquy—an inspired moment, which evoked almost involuntary applause. The servant re-entered, ushering in Don Félix (Martin), and exited again. The big scene of the play began.

The brief stichomythy between Don Juan and Don Félix moved well; but then came an awkward moment.

"*Though, as you say, you come to murder me,*"

spoke Paul—Don Juan,

"*Let us rejoice our gullets ere we die.
Sherry's the life-blood of your true Sevillian.
Honor my celler, sir, if not my soul.*"

After which speech, he was supposed to take one glass from the center table, offering the other with a gesture to Don Félix. Paul carelessly took the one glass which stood there, then gestured hospitably at the empty table. A mild titter rippled over the audience.

"*Ay, if I knew it to be only sherry,*"

Martin replied regardless,

"*But death has hid in greater wines than yours.*"

The momentary amusement of the audience passed off, and the scene continued. Paul drained the pseudo-sherry at one vicious gulp, and launched into his big speech, a magnificent tirade in which, facing instant death at the hands of Don Félix, he still rails at virtue and glorifies impenitence. Despite the vigor with which he delivered the speech, Paul's stage fright, Martin noticed, was becoming curiously obvious. His pupils were dilated, and his arms were twitched by odd jerks and shudders.

At last the long speech, which ran fully four minutes, was ended, and Martin, with a raging snarl, tossed aside his sword.

*"With fœtid blood I will not stain my steel,
But rather wrest life from thy lying throat!"*

With a leap, he seized Paul by the throat.

Now a strangulation scene is a difficult piece of theatrical business. The strangler must give the effect of great effort while exerting none at all, and the victim must preserve the appearance of passivity in the midst of extravagant contortions. Martin was accustomed in this scene simply to set his face in an expression of great and virulent hatred, and to let Paul do all the work.

Tonight Paul was superb. His limbs jerked briefly, then suddenly stretched out stiff. His head fell back, and his very face seemed to change. It might, thought Martin, be just the lighting; but his cheeks grew dusky and congested, his eyes threatened to pop from their sockets.

Martin released the body to speak his curtain-line of vengeance accomplished, and Paul fell into a curious position which he had not used at any rehearsal. It was at once grotesque and terrifying. His body seemed rod-stiff and arched, resting on the head and the heels. It was an oddly convincing and yet slightly shocking death pose.

Martin stepped backstage from the body, pantomiming the awful reaction of the justified murderer after his accomplished crime. The lights dimmed, but the scene remained sharp in his mind. He saw the terrible stiffness of the corpse and the macabre fixed smile on its face—another new touch of Paul's which blended the satirically unreal with ghastly actuality. He felt for an instant the truth of the whole scene. The feeling of full indentification with a character came upon him as he had never known it before. He *was* Don Félix, the killer. And he noticed two discordant and irrelevant details. Paul's modern briar pipe had fallen from his costume in the struggle and lay beneath the arched back, and on the table, where the glass had stood, was a small scrap of paper unspecified in any prop list.

The lights had dimmed to complete darkness. There was an instant of perfect silence, and then a burst of the loudest applause that had ever come from such a miniature audience. So gradual had been the dimming that Martin could still see vaguely. He could see that Paul had relaxed from his amazing rigidity, but still lay on the stage. Martin was puzzled and stepped forward. Behind him he could hear the stagehands rapidly striking the set. He bent over Paul, scarcely knowing what he expected.

Paul Lennox lay very still. He was breathing heavily as though in utter physical exhaustion. Martin touched his face lightly. His skin was covered with sweat and his lips trembled.

"Lights!" Martin did not remember rising, nor could he recognize the voice as his own. "Lights for God's sake!" The anguished shriek poured into silence and dissipated it. The auditorium began to fill with murmurs. Suddenly the lights came on, a blinding flood of brightness. Gazing at him with terrified fixity, Martin saw Paul's limbs begin to twitch again, his head to jerk. A groan of agony came from him.

"Martin!" he cried. "Rub my arms! They're . . . Oh, Christ! Hold me! Hold me! I can't . . ." The twitching grew worse. Martin knew what would follow. That unhuman arch again. The fixed smile was returning to Paul's face.

People were crowding onto the little stage. Drexel was trying desperately to assert his authority, without the slightest idea of what to do with it when once asserted. Martin shuddered and turned away, bumping into a stagehand who, himself caught up in the general confusion, had decided simply to disregard it and go on about his business. He was carrying the table which had stood center stage. The bit of paper was still on it.

Martin seized the stagehand by the arm. "For God's sake, Mac," he cried, "leave that table here!"

"What the hell's biting you?"

For answer Martin pointed to the piece of paper. The stagehand set the table down suddenly and moved to a respectful distance. Even he had read of the Seven of Calvary.

Paul Lennox died in convulsions at the university hospital at six minutes after one on the morning of Friday, April 20th, thirteen days and an hour or so after the murder of Dr. Hugo Schaedel.

It was the retiring scholar, Dr. Joseph Griswold, who had taken charge of the confusion in the auditorium and, aided by Mac and another stagehand, had himself driven Paul to the hospital. Martin followed on foot, accompanied by Alex, Cynthia, and Mona. He was glad to leave the auditorium. Everyone there seemed to take it for granted that Paul was simply suffering some queer sudden seizure brought on by Martin's rough handling in the strangulation scene; and all looked on him with a mixture of reproach and wonder.

Martin all but wished that the general opinion were indeed correct. He himself, he thought, as they walked across the campus, might be wrong; but there were the symptoms, recognized by him too late, there was that strange business of the glasses, and above all there was that piece of paper with the dreadful mark of the Vignards.

None of the four spoke a word until they had reached the hospital. In the hall Dr. Griswold and a young interne were awaiting them. Dr. Griswold spoke first.

"It is no use," he said, "to hold out false hopes. Dr. Evans cannot give him more than an hour or two."

"Where is he?" in anguish from Cynthia, all pretense of indifference or animosity to Paul now vanished.

"Dr. Evans is with him now," the interne answered. "It would be better if you waited out here."

Then Cynthia broke down. It was the most complete and honest expression of emotion that Martin had ever seen from her. She sank on a bench in the hallway, abandoned to her grief. Alex sat beside her and let her head fall on his shoulder. Suppressing whatever jealousy he might naturally have felt, he tried to comfort her.

Dr. Griswold drew Martin aside. "I know the things that they had begun to say in the auditorium," he began. "There seemed to be a feeling that you had . . . carried realism a bit too far."

Martin nodded.

"You do not need to fear any responsibility, Martin. Mr. Lennox is dying from no such simple cause."

"I know," Martin broke in.

Dr. Griswold questioned him in silence.

"Strychnine," said Martin.

"True." Dr. Griswold touched his Quixotic beard in slight confusion. "On the advice of Dr. Evans, I have telephoned to the police. Sergeant Cutting will be here shortly."

By that time the auditorium was almost empty. Drexel and a couple of the crew had cleared the stage at last.

"This probably means no performance tomorrow," Drexel was complaining. "It's a damnable disappointment after all these weeks. I simply can't understand it from Lamb. I can't imagine him doing a thing like that. I suppose it just goes to show that there's a little of the beast in all of us."

He stood back and surveyed the stage. "There," he said. "I guess that'll do for a lecture platform for tomorrow's eight o'clock . . . Joe! What's that scrap of paper over there? Get rid of it."

And Joe, who never read a newspaper, picked up the scrap, glanced uncuriously at the peculiar F on it, and dropped it in the wastebasket.

EIGHT

TEMPEST IN A WINEGLASS

Sergeant Cutting looked like a policeman and talked like a gentleman. He arrived at the hospital about ten minutes before Paul's death and closeted himself almost at once with Dr. Evans and Dr. Griswold.

The two policemen who had accompanied him remained in the hall. "You'd better all stick around," one of them said. "The sergeant's got a lot of questions to ask." With which he relapsed into silence.

It was a grotesque group that waited in the mercilessly white hall. The young interne and the policemen in the uniforms of their respective professions . . . Martin looking strangely helpless and forlorn for all the bravado of his sixteenth century doublet, hose, and beard . . . Cynthia weak from crying, her eyes swollen and all her claims to exoticism vanished for the moment. . . . Only Alex and Mona looked quietly ordinary, and even they showed manifest signs of sorrow and discomfort.

Sergeant Cutting had been gone five minutes when the young interne had his inspiration. "Officer," he suggested, "would it be all right if I offered these people a drink of whisky? They've been through an awful shock, you know, and I think it would really help when it comes around to the sergeant's questioning."

The two policemen looked at each other dubiously, and finally the more loquacious of the pair (the one who had actually spoken once before) said, "I guess it'll be okay."

Martin was grateful for the whisky. The hospital's stock (for medicinal use only) was fine bonded bourbon, far better than he was accustomed to, and his twisted nerves began to straighten themselves out. Everyone, even the policemen, seemed to feel the same beneficial effect; and when the interne topped his hospitality by producing cigarettes, there was a general unbending. The group was still relatively silent, but when Sergeant Cutting returned, the heavy atmosphere of dread had been largely dispelled.

His first words sufficed to restore it. "Mr. Lennox is dead," he told them quietly. Martin could see that he was watching their faces closely. The announcement was received in silence, save for a shocked gasp from Cynthia. They had known that Paul must die; the exact news of his death meant little.

"Poor fellow . . . " said Alex softly.

Sergeant Cutting turned to one of his men. "You know where Wheeler Auditorium is, Davis?"

"Yes, sir."

"Well, get on over there right away. I've phoned the station; they're sending three more men out. See that nothing's disturbed, and hold anybody that's still there for questioning."

"Yes, sir." And Davis left.

"I'll have to ask the rest of you to stay here a while," Sergeant Cutting continued in the same calm and pleasing voice; "I'll want to ask you a few questions. Dr. Evans is letting me use his office; I'll see you in there one at a time. First of all, I'm going to tell you this: According to Dr. Griswold, the idea seemed to get around that Mr. Lennox's death was accidental. I warn you now, it was murder."

Again Sergeant Cutting was disappointed, if he had expected any spectacular and informative reactions. To Martin the fact was no news; and the other three, knowing Martin as well as they did, could never for a moment have entertained the accident theory.

"I'll talk to you first, Mr. Lamb," added the sergeant after a brief pause. "You must have been with him when he was poisoned." He led the way into a little office, and Martin began to wish that the interne had suggested a second round of whisky.

The sergeant seated himself at Dr. Evans' desk and waved Martin to a chair. Their respective position reminded Martin curiously of his sessions with Dr. Ashwin.

"You were a close friend of Mr. Lennox?" Sergeant Cutting began, after the formalities of name and address.

"As close as anyone was."

"Mm . . . Will you please tell me, Mr. Lamb, just what happened on the stage of Wheeler Auditorium?"

Martin described the scene, the drinking of the pseudo-sherry, and Paul's delivery of his big speech. "It is a long speech," he said. "It must have been about five minutes after he took the drink that I noticed the beginning of the strychnine convulsions." And he continued to describe, as best he could, the rest of that terrible scene, reserving for the moment any mention of the Seven of Calvary.

"Mr. Lamb . . . " Sergeant Cutting paused. "You said 'strychnine convulsions.' I told you only that Mr. Lennox had been poisoned."

"Sorry to disappoint you, but it's nothing suspicious. As I looked back, I recognized the symptoms, and Dr. Griswold confirmed my recognition."

"And how do you happen to be so familiar with the symptoms of strychnine poisoning?"

"Harmless again. I'm a devoted reader of mystery novels and dabble a bit in criminology and toxicology."

"You've read too many mystery novels, Mr. Lamb," Sergeant Cutting said, "if you think that I'm trying to trap you or jump to conclusions. Now, have you any idea when that poison could have been administered?"

"I think in that glass of stage sherry. I don't know how else. It couldn't have been more than an hour or so before the convulsions. The water we drink backstage is from drinking fountains, and Paul wasn't taking any liquor—he was afraid it might make him muff his performance."

"Mr. Lennox did not leave the auditorium?"

"Not since eight o'clock. He couldn't have. The time he wasn't on the stage—and it's a prominent starring part—he had costume changes that took every minute of it."

"Good. That's a helpful point." Sergeant Cutting lit a cigarette and passed one to Martin. "This glass—what was supposed to be in it?"

"Colored water—not very tasty. Drexel spent almost an hour doctoring a solution to the color he thought was right for sherry."

"Drexel?"

"Lawrence Drexel. Little Theatre Director. He tried iced tea first, but its color struck him as aesthetically wrong."

"Damn Mr. Drexel's aesthetic sensibilities, if you will forgive me, Mr. Lamb. You realize, of course, that tannic acid is an antidote for strychnine, and that Mr. Lennox might be alive now if Drexel had used iced tea. Where was this solution kept?"

"You'll have to ask the prop man. I don't know. The glasses were filled and set on a table backstage before the third act began."

"The glasses?"

"There was supposed to be another one. It was broken by accident."

Sergeant Cutting looked a trifle quizzical as he made his notes. "Who could have put the poison in that glass?"

"Anyone. Dozens of people were backstage before the third act. I was near that table myself most of the time, but I wouldn't necessarily have noticed it."

"Whom did you see particularly near that table?"

Martin blinked slightly at the *whom* (Only in the Berkeley police force . . . he thought), but answered, "A group of my friends. The four people outside—Dr. Griswold, Mr. Bruce, Miss Wood, and Miss Morales—and Dr. Leshin of the History department and his wife."

"What connection did any of these people have with Mr. Lennox?"

Martin paused imperceptibly. "We all knew him," he said,

"except possibly Dr. Griswold. He and Mr. Bruce and I have been boon companions at various times. Miss Wood is Mr. Bruce's fiancée and knew Paul only through him, so far as I know. Dr. Leshin is in the same department—History—that Paul teaches . . . taught in. Miss Morales and Mrs. Leshin have met him at parties and things."

Sergeant Cutting looked up from his notes. "You described yourself as a devoted reader of mystery novels, Mr. Lamb. Doubtless you've been waiting on tenterhooks for this question, so I'd better ask it. Do you know any reason for which anyone would kill Mr. Lennox?"

"Sergeant Cutting," Martin replied, "first I want to tell you one more thing about this evening. After Paul had fallen and people were rushing around, I saw a piece of paper on the table where the glass had been. It had the same mark on it as you and your men found beside Dr. Schaedel's body."

The sergeant looked up and with an expression of frank surprise and interest, which suddenly turned into a laugh. "Mr. Lamb," he said, "that's absurd. Utterly absurd. You've confessed yourself to a mystery-novel mind; it's simply run away with you. What possible connection could there be between Mr. Lennox and a Swiss secret society—if such a society ever existed in the first place?"

"Just this," Martin answered quietly. He was not surprised by the sergeant's reaction. "It was Paul Lennox who furnished indirectly all the information that was printed about the Seven of Calvary. And he told us that his life would not be safe if the Vignards knew he had revealed their secrets."

"Of course you can substantiate that?"

"Five or six of us heard him."

"We'll check it. . . . But do you know of any other—I shan't say more plausible, but any more personal motive that anyone could have for killing Paul Lennox?"

"No," said Martin.

Martin awoke about eleven the next morning. His first thought, after a glance at the unset alarm clock, was regret that he was missing Ashwin's class for the first time. Then all the memories of the past night came over him. He sat up in bed, shuddered slightly, and reached for a cigarette.

After his questioning by the sergeant, he had waited in the hall, under the watchful eye of the remaining policeman, to see Mona home. Her interrogation had been the last and the briefest. He remembered Alex walking in and out of Dr. Evans' office with an imperturbable calm almost worthy of Paul himself. He remembered half stifled sobs from the office during Cynthia's interview, and wondered just what Sergeant Cutting had learned from her. The young interne had obligingly produced cold cream and alcohol, and Martin had spent most of the time during the others' sessions in removing beard, spirit gum, and grease paint from his face. When at last he escorted Mona home, he looked an ordinary twentieth century young man again, despite doublet and hose. And to crown this evening of Spanish melodrama, sudden death, and suspicion, he remembered kissing Mona good night, quite as though it were the most natural thing on earth to do (as indeed it was), and remembered her cool voice whispering, "Much nicer without the beard."

But even at such a sweet memory as this, the prickings of his conscience returned to bother him. Should he have told Sergeant Cutting what he knew of the complex emotional relations of Paul Lennox with Cynthia, Alex, and the Leshins? It was obviously of the greatest importance, and yet . . . what evidence did he have for it? A few words of Cynthia's while drunk and amorous, an embrace in a dark hallway, an atmosphere of tenseness under the casual speeches of two women—the sergeant would probably have found the idea only a trifle less amusing than the appearance of the Seven of Calvary.

And as to the carefully evolved Ashwinian theory that Dr. Hugo Schaedel had been killed (as was now apparent) in error for Paul Lennox—what would that amount to in a police court? It was so completely obvious, and yet what proof was there? It was, Martin thought, like the rabbit which the Hindus see in the moon. It is next to impossible to make people see it: but once they have recognized it, they will never see a face or a man or a woman there again. It is obvious that there is a rabbit in the moon; but obviousness seems too often unsusceptible of proof.

As Martin was thus easing his conscience, he heard a sound which for a moment terrified him. Someone was moving around in the room next to his—the room which had once been that of Paul Lennox. It was not the maid; those were a man's footsteps—or was it two men? Martin's first instinctive fear passed almost instantly into curiosity. He threw on his bathrobe, slipped his feet into a pair of slippers, and tiptoed into the hall. He paused a moment before the door to which Paul's card was still affixed. The footsteps were in there definitely—two pairs of male feet. As Martin stood wavering, the door opened and he was face to face with Sergeant Cutting.

"Good morning, Mr. Lamb. I was just going to knock on your door again. You seem a heavy sleeper."

Martin was too surprised to reply at first, and then suddenly realized how natural it was that the police should search Paul's quarters.

"Come in," Sergeant Cutting continued. "I have several things to tell and to ask you."

Martin obeyed, seating himself reluctantly on the edge of the bed. The room was in a topsyturvy state of search. Davis, the more voluble policeman, was at the moment silently examining the record albums—with what hopes, Martin had no idea. Neither, it may be added, had Davis.

"You will be pleased to know, Mr. Lamb," Sergeant Cutting began, "that everyone seems to agree with you. No one can suggest any reason for killing Paul Lennox. I wouldn't say that he was well liked—people seem to have have disliked him for any cause from his sarcasm to his pipe—but men aren't murdered from simple dislike. But there is no support for your Vignard idea. Not that I disbelieve you, but only that I think you unconsciously exaggerated."

"Didn't you find anything at the auditorium?"

Sergeant Cutting shook his head. "Davis here got there too late. The stage crew had been all too efficient, and the whole place was clean as a whistle. They'd swept the stage, emptied the waste baskets—even, damn them, washed the glass that must have held the poison. Your Mr. Drexel was the only person still there, and Davis followed my instructions. He held him for three solid hours while I was at the hospital."

The picture of the mercurial Drexel sitting beside the stolid Davis for three hours was too much for Martin.

"I can't quite blame you for laughing, Mr. Lamb. Myself, I think it served Drexel damned well right for being so officiously active. He might have suspected something was wrong—but he didn't, and any hopes we might have had for facts from the auditorium have gone up in smoke. You will notice I say 'facts,' Mr. Lamb; you would say 'clues.' "

Martin rose somewhat excited. "But surely, Sergeant, this doesn't disprove my seeing that paper. Some idiot of a stagehand probably chucked it away. It was no imagination. Mac saw it too—Don MacKinley, he's on the crew—ask him. And God knows I of all people ought to recognize the Seven of Calvary—"

"Just what do you mean by that, Mr. Lamb?"

Martin told the partial truth. "I knew Dr. Schaedel and I liked him," he said. "Naturally I was particularly interested in the circumstances of his murder. And I was one of the group to which Paul Lennox told the story of the Vignards before it got into the papers. I've been quite fascinated by that strange symbol."

"I'm afraid you just have the unhappy faculty of making incriminating remarks." Sergeant Cutting smiled, while Davis snorted half audibly. He never had liked the way Sarge talked to them college mugs. The sergeant continued, disregarding the snort, "But now to the question: Mr. Lamb, why were you coming into this room just now?"

"I heard sounds in here. First I was a little scared; it seemed as though Paul . . . but that's nonsense. Then I thought it might be someone who . . . who had no business here . . . "

"You mean . . . ?"

"The murderer. Yes. I never thought of the police. I simply thought I ought to investigate."

"And had you heard any noises in here earlier this morning?"

"No. I was sound asleep. As you know, Sergeant, I got home late."

"I know. I've knocked on your door three times in the past hour. But the point I'm making is this, Mr. Lamb—Davis and I were not the first people to search this room."

Martin looked up in surprise.

"The maid came in here at nine thirty to make up the room. She's a stolid soul, and hadn't even heard that Paul Lennox was dead. She found the door unlocked, which surprised her, and the bed unslept in. The whole room was in perfect order, excepting the papers on the lowest shelf of the bookcase. Those were scattered all over the floor. She said Mr. Lennox never left them that way."

"That's true," Martin observed. "Paul went in for the strictest order. His room and mine were models for the study of contrast. To be sure, he was excited last night, but even at that—" Martin paused abruptly.

"Yes, Mr. Lamb?"

"I wonder if I might see those papers. I know something about his work; I might be able—"

"Certainly. As a matter of fact, that's why I tried to wake you up. I thought you might give us a line on why anyone should want to rummage through those things."

Davis finished the last phonograph album and relinquished the floor to Martin, who squatted in a corner by the bookcase and began to examine the papers on the first shelf, where they had been replaced.

They were a curious assortment of stuff—seminar papers, notes for seminar papers, papers read before societies, outlines of projected papers (among these the well remembered outline on *Possible Historical Originals for the Don Juan Legend**), notebooks, and all the mess of stuff that an academic man keeps because he never knows when he might need it. Anything could have been

---

* This paper, which was to cause so much discussion among scholars, was published posthumously (edited and revised by Joseph Griswold, Ph.D., and Martin Lamb) in *Modern Language Notes* for April, 1935 (50:4:230/42).

in this assorted pile—anything, that is, of scholastic interest, but nothing remotely connected with a murder.

Then Martin noticed that several of the notebooks bore the imprint of the students' store at the University of Chicago. The first two contained vague random jottings on books not available elsewhere, including some curious bits of information concerning the Mandaeans and the Neminians over which Martin would gladly have lingered, had not the constant glances of the two policemen kept his search purposeful.

The third University of Chicago notebook began with a titlepage. *The History of the City of Lausanne,* it read; *notes from conversation with Jean Stauffacher.* Martin gave an involuntary cry of triumph, and read on. The next four pages contained various facts and dates, with an occasional anecdote apparently from the Stauffacher family legends. The fifth page ended with the words: *Far more interesting, however, than this historical material is the information which I have obtained from Jean concern—*

The remaining pages of the notebook had been torn out.

It was with something of exultation that Martin showed this notebook to Sergeant Cutting. "You see, Sergeant," he explained, "this must be what they were after. Stauffacher is the man he told us about who put him on the track of the Vignards. This notebook must have been where he kept his material. I remember he spoke of refreshing his memory from his notes. And there are no notes on the Vignards anywhere in all this pile of stuff."

"Thanks, Mr. Lamb." The sergeant took the notebook. "You may be right. But if you are, it's damned funny your Swiss emissary tore out those sheets. Why didn't he just lift the notebook? And besides, how did he get in?"

"I can help you there. These doors have Yale locks, as you've noticed, but there's no catch to make them lock automatically. You have to remember to lock them with your key. Paul was in no state to remember such trifles last night, and the door was probably left unlocked."

"Thanks again. Well, Mr. Lamb, I expect I'll see you at the inquest Monday, and maybe before that. But if I were you, I wouldn't say anything about this Seven of Calvary business at the inquest. It'll just confuse the jury. Myself, I'll keep it in mind; but I won't be able to act on it as I would if there were surer evidence."

Davis suddenly spoke for the first time since Martin had come in. "I think this Swiss business is a lot of bull," he said.

Sergeant Cutting grinned at Martin. "For once I think Davis is right. At least I hope so. It'll be a lot easier for me if he is."

Martin took the sergeant's proffered hand, smiled in reply, and returned to his room. He dressed rapidly, for he was by now painfully hungry, and wondered just what he himself thought about this Vignard business. Thoughts and theories tumbled through his mind. . . .

"I must see Dr. Ashwin tonight," he finally decided.

"Good evening, Mr. Lamb," Dr. Ashwin welcomed him. "I was not surprised by your absence from class this morning; I thought that you would sleep well after life's particularly fitful fever last night."

"I hate to object," Martin replied, "but the quotation seems to me as inappropriate as it is ominous. I hope it will be a long time before I sleep the sleep of Duncan."

Dr. Ashwin smiled. "Well," he said, "let me make amends for my infelicity. Sit down, and I shall rinse the glasses."

When the ceremony of the first drink was concluded, Ashwin spoke. "Tonight, I think, we need indulge in none of our customary beating-around-the-bush. Doubtless you've come to talk about last night and for my part, I postponed a trip to visit Elizabeth simply because I felt sure that you would come. I have read the newspaper accounts of Mr. Lennox's death and have gathered little more than that he was poisoned by strychnine during the dress rehearsal of your play. Now tell me all the details."

Martin told his entire narrative, from the meeting with Alex and Cynthia in the Great Hall up to his interview that morning with Sergeant Cutting. Ashwin followed it all with intense interest, interrupting only when Martin described the appearance of the Seven of Calvary.

"I cannot understand it," Dr. Ashwin exclaimed with surprise. "How could so glaring a piece of sensation be omitted from the newspapers?"

"Because Sergeant Cutting thinks I was seeing things," Martin answered, and went on to a fuller explanation. When he had finished the whole story, Ashwin sat for a while in silence.

"I like your Sergeant Cutting," he said finally. "To be sure, his own too strict logic makes him muddle-headed, but I like him. He saw the point of the notebook."

"You mean the Stauffacher notebook?" Martin asked. "That's one of a lot of things that worry me. You said you thought that Paul invented that whole story, but of course that was when you believed him the agent and not the victim. We'll have to rearrange all our ideas now."

"I know." Dr. Ashwin shook his head sadly. "It is most inconsiderate of a mere murderer to upset so completely my applecart of obvious conclusions. But let us say this: before, we were reasoning only from a partial set of facts. Now that the real murder has at last taken place, we have a more nearly complete set, and our conclusions will therefore be so much nearer the truth. Now let us see what we make of the new points."

He settled back in the swivel chair and waved to Martin to fill the glasses. "First," he began didactically, "we know that Dr. Schaedel was killed in error for Paul Lennox, who was, you will remember, one of the only two people for whom the Herr Doktor could have been mistaken. We concluded before that four persons had possible motives for killing Mr. Lennox—the four being, of course, Mr. Bruce, Miss Wood, and (now that you have finally revealed their names to me) the Leshins, all these motives springing from varying forms of jealousy. And all four of these people, according to you, had equal opportunities of slipping strychnine into the false sherry. As to whether they had an opportunity to secure the strychnine, that is the sort of question which only formal police investigation can cover adequately."

"Alex undoubtedly had," Martin interposed. "As a research fellow in chemistry, he could probably lay his hands on whatever he wanted."

"Very well then. On motive and opportunity, our four possible suspects run neck and neck; Mr. Bruce has a slight, but by no means conclusive, edge in the matter of means. Another point: whoever committed this crime must have known your play, known that Don Juan drinks a glass of sherry in act three, scene two. To whom would that condition apply?"

"Both Alex and Cynthia read the play while I was working on it. I don't know about the Leshins. They could, of course, have borrowed a script from Drexel or from Paul. He had a complete script instead of just sides, since his part was so long. Or they could have read the original in the library; they're both rather talented linguists, like most Slavs, and I've made practically no changes in that particular scene."

"One more question concerning this glass of pseudo-sherry, Mr. Lamb. Does any one of these four people possess theatrical experience—professional or amateur?"

Martin pondered briefly. "I know Alex doesn't. I can't say about the Leshins, but I doubt it extremely. Cynthia doesn't act, but she has done props and back-stage work for Thalian—that's sort of a Women's Auxiliary to Little Theatre."

"And would it have been quite usual if Drexel had, as you say he once intended, used cold tea to represent the sherry?"

"Quite."

"Then we have a small point to aid in clearing Miss Wood of suspicion. She alone of our quartet would know that the sherry was likely to be really tea, and that therefore it would be an inadvisable vehicle in which to administer strychnine. The point is indicative rather than conclusive; her knowledge of toxicology might be so slight as to cause her to make an error which succeeded in spite of itself. And now this matter of the Seven of Calvary—the most damnably confusing point of all. First tell me, Mr. Lamb, just what do you think of it?"

"Chiefly that it just doesn't make sense."

"I agree with you in the main, but go on."

Martin found the confusion of his thoughts difficult to sort into words. "In the first place . . . " he began, and paused.

"A sound beginning," Dr. Ashwin observed.

"In the first place," Martin went on, with growing confidence, "it seems that there really must be such a society as the Vignards. Paul would scarcely have concocted a fable to aid a murderer whose intended victim he himself unwittingly was."

"A somewhat Teutonic sentence, but the idea is plausible."

"Then, if our idea of the murder-by-mistake is correct, it follows that the murderer also knew about the Vignards, unless you choose the improbable alternative of his lighting by chance on their symbol."

"Let me interpose a point," said Dr. Ashwin. "He might know the symbol without knowing anything about the Vignards *qua* Vignards. A European might have seen the Seven in connection with some Vignard assassination years ago and have remembered the symbol although he never learned the story behind the killing."

"Possible," Martin admitted. "But again we run up against a coincidence—that the accidental victim of the first murder should be a man whom the Vignards would have a possible reason for assassinating."

"Allow me to hypothesize again." Ashwin emptied his glass. "Suppose that the murderer recognized Dr. Schaedel when it was too late, suddenly remembered the symbol and its Swiss associations, and hurriedly drew it and left it there."

Martin moved as though to speak, and Ashwin continued. "No . . . I see your objection, Mr. Lamb. There was neither time nor light for such an action. And besides, why should he then leave the symbol beside the body of Mr. Lennox, who was quite unconnected with Switzerland?"

"Unless he knew that it was Paul from whom, indirectly, the newspaper stories came. Alex and Cynthia both knew that; I doubt as to the Leshins, but Paul himself might have told one or both of them of the incident."

"We are going around in circles, Mr. Lamb," murmured Dr. Ashwin regretfully. "Calvary seems to mix both history and geography, our Waterloo. . . ."

After a short silence, Martin began on a fresh tack. "You know," he suggested, "it almost seems to me that we're disregarding an entirely obvious solution. Why shouldn't the whole affair be a pair of genuine Vignard assassinations? Dr. Schaedel was killed because he was spreading the gospel of peace, displeasing to Agrammax, and possibly for older reasons of Swiss politics; and Paul was killed because he knew too much about the sect. I know your ethical objections to such melodrama, but that doesn't prevent the occurrence of melodramatic happenings."

Ashwin shook his head. "No, Mr. Lamb," he said, "my objection to an emissary of the Vignards is no simple matter of taste now, as it was when we first discussed Dr. Schaedel's death. The affair of the notebook has proved conclusively that the murderer was not a Vignard."

"But how? I should think that if anything—"

"Please. Sergeant Cutting was absolutely right in saying that the thief should have carried off the whole notebook. A Vignard could have only one motive for rifling Mr. Lennox's papers—the desire to make it appear that the whole story of the sect had no foundation in fact and that no such notes as Mr. Lennox had described were actually among his effects. To do that, he would simply have taken the book, leaving the remaining papers in perfect order."

Martin nodded agreement.

"But what does our thief do? First he leaves the papers in terrific disorder, so that no one can fail to observe that the room has been searched. Second, he tears from the notebook those leaves dealing with the Vignards, while there remains on the preceding page an incomplete sentence making perfectly clear the content of the missing leaves. In brief, the purpose of a true Vignard would have been to make the world believe the story of the society false; the actual thief did his best to make it appear true."

Martin admitted regretfully that he was convinced. "I'm afraid," he said, "that washes up the Vignards."

"I am afraid that it does, as you say, wash them up. But there is another point in that notebook. The fact that it dealt with the Vignards would be clear, from what remains of it, only to someone who knew that Paul Lennox received his information from one Jean Stauffacher, a fact which the thief could easily expect you, as Mr. Lennox's neighbor and closest friend, to explain to the police. That fact could not be gathered from the newspaper accounts."

"Then that comes back again to the group of us that heard Paul's story—Alex, Cynthia, and me. Mary Roberts and Worthing are irrelevant, of course. Excepting," and Martin began to smile reflectively, "that if it really were the Vignards, Worthing would be the next victim. It must have been he who gave Paul's story to the papers. And I wouldn't be surprised if he were suffering from a very nice bunch of jitters right now."

Dr. Ashwin rose—an unusual action on his part and one which marked considerable stress. "Mr. Lamb," he announced, "I am at times almost shocked by the flippancy with which you and I look on these murders. To us they seem only parts of an entertaining intellectual game. And yet two men have been cruelly killed, the second one in the very face of my reasoning from the obvious. If we could force certainty out of this tangle of facts, if we could make our intellectual puzzle a weapon of justice—"

"Paul was my friend," Martin said. He suddenly realized, not exactly a thirst for vengeance, but a simple desire for retribution.

"Let us for the time being," Ashwin proposed, "forget all this complex business of symbols and sects. The notebook has shown us that it is assuredly a blind, if we cannot understand its exact purpose. Let us concentrate on the people, and above all on the poisoning. Mr. Lamb, do you have a good visual memory?"

"Fair. Why?"

"I want you to make me a chart of the relative positions of the people around that—'prop table' I believe you called it—at the moment when the glass broke. Ask Miss Morales to do the same, and bring me the charts after lunch tomorrow. Then you and I shall call on Dr. Griswold, and ask him the same question. His will probably be the sharpest observation. After that, we can really begin to reason."

"Lupe will be back this afternoon," Mona remarked at lunch.

"She's all right now?" Martin asked.

"Perfectly. It will be nice to see her with Kurt again. But now that she is once more well, she hears from Los Angeles that her father the General is perhaps gravely ill. It is an unhappy compensation."

"I haven't seen Kurt in ages."

"No?" Mona refilled her teacup. "Then you did not see him backstage Thursday night?"

Martin almost dropped a forkful of good apple pie. "Kurt, too? Was everybody I know backstage that night?"

"Is it all not natural? We are your friends; we like to see your work."

"When did you see him?"

"He was in all that crowd behind the stage. I spoke to him when he passed the table where we stood. I thought that you too saw him."

"No . . . " Martin was rebuking himself for his sudden excitement. Whatever imaginary motive Kurt Ross might have had for desiring his uncle's death, surely he could have no earthly interest in that of Paul Lennox. It was just a coincidence. Martin collected his thoughts and turned again to his companion. "Which reminds me, Mona," he said. "You may have gathered that I've been taking a lot of interest in these deaths. Well, I'm that worst abortion of nature an amateur detective—and besides, I liked Paul. . . ."

Mona finished her tea and looked up curiously. "Yes?"

"The police think" (it gave Martin an odd sense of satisfaction to quote Sergeant Cutting so authoritatively) "that Paul must have taken the poison in that glass of stage sherry. Now someone—I know I can trust you to be quiet about this, Mona—someone probably put the poison there when that other glass was knocked over. You remember?"

"Yes . . . " There was hesitation in Mona's voice.

"I want you, Mona, to draw me a chart of how the people were standing around the prop table at that moment. Do you think you could do that?"

"You must know better than I do, Martin."

"Possibly I do. I just want to check my own memory."

"Ask Dr. Griswold then."

"I intend to."

"Then is not that enough?" Mona's sweet voice was trembling slightly.

"Yes, but . . . What is the matter, Mona?"

"Please give me a cigarette, Martin."

He obeyed, took another for himself, and lit them both. There was a pause while Mona seemed to grope blindly for words.

"I think that I know, Martin," she began at last, "why you ask me and Dr. Griswold instead of Alex or Cynthia or even the Leshins. It is because you think that we two could not have any possible connection with Paul in life or in death."

"Yes," Martin admitted.

"*Pues bien* . . . ask Dr. Griswold."

"Mona . . . What do you mean?"

"On Thursday—oh, such years ago—when we had tea, Martin, I told you a little about a man who . . . would not stop." Martin nodded encouragement as Mona faltered, then resumed. "It was at a very stupid party in the hills where everyone drank and was like the animals. They were friends of Remigio's; I never went again. I do not know if he was drunk or not; I think it was only that he was with people who did not know him too well. The house is very lonely. This was in the garden. I do not know what could have happened had not Remigio come. Remigio did not see him to know him, I thank God; he fled when he heard my brother's footsteps . . . It was just like the Marines in the pictures." She smiled a very pale un-Mona-like smile, but her voice dropped to almost inaudible silence as she added, "I think that I hated Paul Lennox."

And Martin realized that he was not nearly so anxious to bring Paul's murderer to justice.

They sat in silence, an understanding silence as comforting as the touch of hand to hand, until suddenly the loud accents of the British Broadcasting Company rang through the dining room.

"Lamb! I say, Lamb, old boy, I've been looking everywhere for you. Hang it all, you know more about this blasted thing than anyone else."

Martin looked up at Worthing with an aversion even greater than usual. "What is it?" he asked restrainedly.

"It was pinned to my door when I went upstairs after lunch. Found it ten minutes ago. Might have been put there any time all forenoon. Been looking for you everywhere. I say, old man, can't you help me? I mean, should I ask the bobbies for a spot of protection, what? Do you think I'm in danger of my ruddy neck?"

"I do not understand," Mona murmured, lost in the maze of Worthingesque Britishisms.

"Just what did you find?" Martin asked quietly, nobly suppressing an intense desire to wring that ruddy neck then and there.

"This." And Worthing laid on the luncheon table the third exemplar of the Seven of Calvary.

NINE

THE LAST SEVEN

Dr. Griswold was at the piano, playing excerpts of Gilbert and Sullivan for his own delectation, when Martin and Dr. Ashwin arrived that afternoon. While they waited on the porch for the housekeeper to answer their ring, Ashwin beamed with joy. Sullivan's tunes were the only ones that appealed to his anti-musical tastes, only because he remembered the accompanying lyrics.

As the housekeeper opened the door, the scholar-pianist modulated abruptly from an *Iolanthe* chorus into the Mikado's solo, and the two amateur detectives entered the living room to the notes of

> *My object all sublime*
> *I shall achieve in time:*
> *To let the punishment fit the crime,*
> *The punishment fit the crime* . . .

Dr. Griswold broke off and rose from the piano. "This is a pleasant surprise visit," he blinked. "Very glad to see you both." And he gestured them to chairs.

Ashwin plunged into the middle of things with unaccustomed abruptness. "You've no idea, Griswold, what appropriate music you provided for our entrance."

Dr. Griswold stroked his beard in quiet amusement. "I see Martin's corrupting you already, Ashwin; you speak in terms of the theatre just like him. By the way," he added, turning to Martin, "I came across a curious little squib in *La abeja* last night—a theatrical reviewer speaking of Fonseca's *Don Juan Redivivo* as '*un drama maldito,*' an accursed play—I suppose you would say 'a jinx show'?"

"So?" Martin asked curiously. "When was this notice?"

"In 1848, I think. I jotted down the reference; I thought you might want it." He handed Martin one of those small bits of paper (known among the scholastic, Heaven knows why, as P-slips) with which his pockets always bulged. "The reviewer told of various incidents of deaths, accidents, and other catastrophes in connection with revivals of the play—sometimes the same legend as is told of the opera *La Forza del destino.*"

Ashwin was becoming a little impatient. "It is precisely in connection with *Don Juan Returns* that we've come to see you, Griswold."

"You sound sternly official. What can I do for you?"

"I'm quite sure that the dean and the president and several other worthies would not approve of what I am doing; but I've worked with you on committees, and I know that you are no hidebound academician."

"Thank you." Dr. Griswold blinked mildly and placed his fingers together, wondering what on earth was coming of all this.

"The fact is, Griswold" (and for once Dr. Ashwin's aplomb very nearly deserted him), "the fact is, I've turned detective."

Dr. Griswold turned a rebuking smile on Martin. "You've corrupted him quite thoroughly, haven't you?"

"I'm afraid I have," Martin answered, "but it's really not a gag. It's serious, and it may be damned important."

"You see," Dr. Ashwin resumed, "Mr. Lamb has come across several things in connection with these deaths here which are not straightforward, acceptable, police-court evidence, but which have set me thinking along some peculiar lines. If we can learn just a little bit more, I think that we can know the whole thing."

"And then do your duties as citizens?" Dr. Griswold suggested. "Well, whatever information I can furnish you, you may have."

"Thank you." Ashwin was visibly relieved at having completed the confession of his new hobby. "All that we want of you is this: a diagram of how people were standing around that little table backstage when the glass was broken."

Dr. Griswold looked at them with a quizzical expression, and

Martin hastened to explain the business of the stage sherry. When he had finished, Dr. Griswold removed his glasses and polished them absently.

"Why yes . . . " he said at last. "I think I could do that." He found a pencil and paper and began his chart, making it slowly with many pauses for a careful check of his memory.

When the sketch was almost complete, Dr. Ashwin broke the silence with another question. "Do you know how the Leshins happened to attend the dress rehearsal?"

"Let me see . . . I ran into Leshin in the library. He said he was meeting his wife at the auditorium to see the play, and I decided to go along, even though I had tickets for tonight. Fortunate that I did."

"You helped us through a bad time," Martin said warmly.

"I didn't mean that." Dr. Griswold was thoroughly embarrassed. "Simply that I should not have seen your play otherwise."

"But why were the Leshins going to the dress rehearsal, rather than to one of the performances?" Ashwin asked.

"I don't know. It wasn't mentioned. We spoke very little. I scarcely know Mrs. Leshin, and there seemed to be some coolness between her and her husband. In fact, unless I am quite mistaken, she seemed surprised to see him there. Although he had told me that he was supposed to meet her."

Martin and Ashwin exchanged a glance of understanding. The obvious meaning was that Tanya Leshin had come alone, planning to meet Paul afterwards, if for no more sinister reason, and that Ivan Leshin had suspected and followed her, bringing Dr. Griswold possibly to avoid a scene.

Dr. Griswold laid down the pencil. "There," he said, "I think that is correct. I have as a rule an excellent visual memory." He handed his chart to Ashwin, who produced from his pocket the one which Martin had previously drawn for him.

The three men sat on the couch by the window, the bright April sunlight shining on the two charts of death. Dr. Griswold was the first to speak.

"We seem to agree well enough, Martin. I believe we can conclude that both diagrams are approximately accurate."

" 'Approximately,' " Ashwin repeated with noticeable irritation.

"If you want to discuss them with your Watson," said Dr. Griswold, "go right ahead. I promise discretion."

"How far across would you say that table was?" Dr. Ashwin asked.

"About three or four feet. Do you agree, Martin?"

"Right."

"Then anyone reaching across the table would have been conspicuous. To be sure, you might not have noticed it; but it would have meant running a needless risk. That means that only Miss Wood or Mr. Bruce could have knocked that glass off the table."

"I thought Mr. Bruce was rather far from the table for that," Dr. Griswold objected.

"To my mind he seemed close enough," Martin countered.

"Then that . . . Ah!" Ashwin looked up with something of satisfaction. "You, Mr. Lamb, were facing toward Mr. Bruce and would have seen him the instant the glass fell. But you, Dr. Griswold, were faced toward Leshin, and had to turn a bit toward the sound before you could see Bruce. He had moved back in that moment."

"But just a minute!" Dr. Griswold had another objection. "You say you think that the other glass received the poison at the same time that this one was knocked over. But the poisoned glass was on the other side of the table from Bruce, nearer to Leshin and me."

"Of course!" Ashwin's face bore a look of strong self-reproach. "The obvious has been staring me in the face and I have disregarded it. Breaking this glass was no accident. It had to be broken, deliberately."

"Why?" asked Martin. "Breaking it seems to me merely to draw unnecessary attention to the glasses."

"It had to be broken to make absolutely certain that Mr. Lennox would drink the strychnine-filled glass."

"Couldn't both glasses have been poisoned?"

"Then there would be the bare possibility of some harmless third person's drinking off the second glass of poison. Our murderer was discriminating."

Martin nodded. "Then you think the other glass was poisoned earlier?"

"Yes. Probably when people were milling about before you assumed these fairly fixed positions indicated on your diagrams. Possibly even after the glass was broken."

Dr. Griswold blinked several times. "You have no idea how I enjoy watching a deductive detective at work—or is this induction?—especially when I have seen him apply not dissimilar principles to scholarship applications in committee—among them yours, Martin. But would you mind telling me exactly what conclusions you reach from all this?"

"Just this," Ashwin replied deliberately, "and I'm afraid it is only a matter of probabilities. It is probable that Alex Bruce knocked over that glass. (It is almost certain that either he or Miss Wood did so.) Since destroying that glass must have been an essential part of the poisoner's plot, it is therefore probable that Alex Bruce was the poisoner. But this is no matter of obvious certainty. It is barely possible that Mr. Bruce or Miss Wood may have knocked over that glass by accident, simply forestalling the poisoner's intent. We need more facts, and I don't see where to find them."

"Since there is no immediate hurry in securing those facts," said Dr. Griswold, "or at least I hope that there is none, why don't you and Martin stay for tea and rest your minds of this problem? My daughter Marjorie should be home at any moment and—"

Dr. Ashwin rose ponderously. It was not merely the presence of a quiet young girl for tea that was sending him away; he wanted to be alone, free even of his loyal Watson, and struggle through this problem again. "I'm sorry," he said; "I think I must be going. You stay, Mr. Lamb. I shall see you on Monday." And after brief farewells, he left.

"Ashwin needed an interest like this," Dr. Griswold observed. "He seemed to be going a little stale after he stopped translating. He gave up chess, gave up billiards—he used to be quite a champion at the Faculty Club, you know—and lost interest in most things aside from the little girl—Elizabeth or whatever her name is. I'm glad you've corrupted him."

"I'm a little worried about him," Martin replied. "He seems suddenly to be much more serious about the whole thing. And that abrupt, 'I shall see you on Monday, Mr. Lamb. . . .' Things have come to a pretty pass when Holmes dismisses Watson as peremptorily as that."

At this point Marjorie Griswold came home. The tea was good; Dr. Griswold resumed his piano playing; and Marjorie had various anecdotes, not unmalicious, concerning her instructors, which amused both Martin and her father.

"And Dr. Leshin wasn't at class this morning," she mentioned. "Not that I blame him, because lots of times I'm not at a Saturday morning nine o'clock myself, but they say it's because his wife is having a nervous breakdown and needs him with her or something."

Aside from the sudden little shock he felt on hearing that piece of news, Martin spent a pleasant and quiet afternoon, unperturbed by thoughts of strychnine, symbols, or sudden death. The subject was not recalled to his mind until, returning home, he chanced to see Worthing sitting in the Great Hall. Beside him on the sofa sat Davis, the corporeal result of Worthing's request for police protection. It had taken a call to the British Consulate in San Francisco to persuade Sergeant Cutting to give him a guard; and the more he looked at the stolid policeman, the less Worthing thought it worth the effort.

His request and an inadvertent reference by the sergeant to what Martin had seen had caused the evening papers to blossom out in headlines.

SWISS SECT STRIKES AGAIN
SCHAEDEL SLAYER ELUDES POLICE

"Despite efforts of the police," Martin read, "to disregard or suppress this important fact, it has been ascertained that the symbol of the Seven of Calvary was found beside the body of Paul Lennox, poisoned on the stage of Wheeler Auditorium at the University of California Thursday night. Lennox, it is now learned, was the original source of the information published exclusively in this paper concerning the Seven of Calvary and the activities of the Swiss sect known as the Vignards."

Here followed a rewrite of the original story, ending, "Richard Worthing, a close friend of Lennox" (Martin was a little dazed by this statement), "who supplied the information to this paper, has received the symbol of death and only with great difficulty could secure police protection."

Guessing what he might find, Martin turned to the editorial page. Yes, there it was: a half-column of scathing denunciation of the police, together with certain remarks which would probably work the Swiss Consulate into a beautiful lather of indignation.

The whole idea of the Vignards seemed damnably plausible—far more plausible, certainly, than the idea that Alex had committed two cold-blooded murders out of jealousy. To be sure, you never know how sexual rage will affect anyone, but still it seemed an insufficient motive for a person of Alex's sympathetic quietness. And then there was the new symbol delivered to Worthing—a blind, or . . . ?

Martin wondered.

Sunday afternoon Martin went for a walk in the hills with Mona, Lupe Sanchez, and Kurt Ross. Lupe seemed in the best of health again, although worried by her father's illness and expecting at any moment an urgent call to Los Angeles. As the two girls chatted together in rapid Spanish, Kurt took Martin's arm and held him back a moment.

"Martin," he began hesitantly, "is it true what is in the papers?"

"Practically never."

"No, no. I mean, what is in the papers of what you saw—that symbol?"

"Yes. I saw it right enough, and Mac will back me up on it, no matter what Sergeant Cutting thinks about my imagination running away with me."

"It was exactly the same as the one beside my uncle?"

"As to exactly, I can't say. I got only a brief glimpse of it at a very confused moment. But it was certainly the same symbol."

Kurt was worried. "Martin," he said at last, "I cannot understand it. I am Swiss; surely I should know if such a sect there were. And what connection could Paul have with my uncle, unless all this be true?"

"Mona said you were backstage that night." Martin's inflection was halfway between statement and question.

"Yes, but I saw nothing. How could I in that mass of people?"

"You were near the table?"

"Where the glasses were? Yes. I did not speak to you because you seemed to be so surrounded; I could not catch your eye."

"Didn't you see anything unusual?"

"No."

"Come on!" Mona's clear voice sounded from twenty yards ahead of them. In puzzled silence they quickened their steps.

Suddenly Kurt paused again. "Unusual . . . ! Yes, Martin. One little thing. It returns suddenly. As I passed the table I heard the lady in red say, 'Where is there a drinking fountain?' I noticed because I too was seeking one. And the small dark man—that is Dr. Leshin, is it not?—said, 'Why do you not drink of this?' meaning the glass on the table."

"Which glass?" Martin interrupted eagerly.

"How should I know? I only thought it was strange to suggest drinking what stands about on stage tables. I was not noticing it much."

"And did she?"

"She said, 'I am not so thirsty as that,' or something like it—I do not know. I was only going by."

Martin was silent. Was this some significant new clue or the merest coincidence? Had Dr. Leshin had some mad idea of poisoning his wife as well as her lover? Was he aware of her plot and taunting her with it? Or was it simply a rather stupid conversation-making remark? And her refusal to drink—did it result from knowledge of what the glass contained or merely a quite natural disinclination to taste what passes for wine on the stage?

"Are not you ever coming, you two?" Lupe called.

"What do you believe of all this?" Kurt asked as they approached the girls.

"I don't know what I believe," Martin replied. And that at least was the truth.

After an hour of pleasant walking, Martin found himself stretched full length beneath a shady tree, with Mona sitting at his side. Kurt and Lupe had wandered off with the ostensible purpose of gathering wild flowers.

Mona broke a long contented silence by asking, "And how are you progressing as an amateur detective?"

"Lousily."

"How so, 'lousily'?" The word sounded strange indeed when spoken with a Bolivian accent.

"I can't make sense out of anything. . . ." He plucked irritably at a blade of grass. "Besides, I've violated the first rule of a good detective story."

"What do you mean, Martin?"

"Detectives don't fall in love." He kissed her hand tenderly.

Mona leaned over. "*Pero, ¡qué tonterías me dices!*" she murmured. "*¿Enamorado tú?*"

It was a subject best discussed in Spanish, Martin decided, and taking the cue from Mona he continued the discussion in that language until both simultaneously decided that no speech at all was even preferable. And Martin quite forgot that the inquest on Paul Lennox was to take place on the following day.

It would have mattered little if he had continued to forget the inquest, since it brought out no new facts of interest.

Martin himself, in the absence of any relatives, gave formal identification of the body. For some reason, he found this a peculiarly unpleasant task. Then followed questions concerning what had taken place on the stage of Wheeler Auditorium, covering practically the same ground as his first interview with Sergeant Cutting. At last he sat down, not entirely surprised that the Seven of Calvary had not once been mentioned in the questioning. The news break caused by Worthing's request for protection had, he imagined, so irritated Sergeant Cutting that he was more than ever determined to disregard the incongruous symbol.

The autopsy had revealed the size of the dose of poison administered—three grains, well over a toxic dose. No witnesses as to possible motives were called, and the jury brought in the inevitable verdict—that Paul Lennox had died of strychnine, given as willful murder by person or persons unknown.

Not that this affected the case in the least, Martin realized. The verdict of the coroner's jury was a formality, with no defined legal standing as a finding of facts. Sergeant Cutting would continue his investigation, and perhaps . . . Looking up, Martin noticed among the few people in court Richard Worthing (still accompanied by the long-suffering Davis) and seeming woefully as though he expected to be the next protagonist in a coroner's inquest.

"Murder plays hell with Sanskrit," Martin remarked as he settled himself in the chair beside Ashwin's desk.

"Yes. It seems almost as though I should have to pass you more on your Watsonian abilities than on your knowledge of the *Mahabharata*."

"There's one consolation at least . . ." Martin could see that Dr.

Ashwin was not in the mood for a plunge into discussion; a brief period of light conversation seemed indicated.* "Murder and Sanskrit make a unique combination."

"There, Mr. Lamb, you are guilty of a grievous error." Ashwin seemed glad of an opportunity to deliver a few *ex cathedra* dicta. "Do you not remember Eugene Aram? One of the world's most curiously solved murders, and surprisingly well celebrated by Thomas Hood."

"Curiously solved?" Martin repeated. "I remember that Aram was something of a philologist, but I thought his crime was revealed simply by someone's finding the skeleton of his victim."

"The case, Mr. Lamb, is a curious reversal of the situation which we have to deal with here in Berkeley. In the Aram affair, the right man was killed, but the wrong body was found. That is, the body of Aram's victim was discovered only after suspicion and a search had been provoked by the finding of a skeleton which was never identified and which had no connection with the crime."

Ashwin's eyes had been roving the book-lined walls. "Ah, here!" he exclaimed, and took down a small well-worn volume in blue cloth. With great relish, he began to read of

> *how the sprites of injur'd men*
>   *Shriek upward from the sod*
> *Aye, how the ghostly hand will point*
>   *To show the burial clod;*
> *And unknown facts of guilty acts*
>   *Are seen in dreams from God!*

It was a curious performance, its half-singsong clearly influenced by the metric quantities of Sanskrit verse, yet oddly effective.

"And that, Mr. Lamb," he observed in conclusion, "was written by possibly the greatest punster of the English language—by a man who could conceive and carry out the idea of writing blank verses in rhyme—by a man of sheerly Sanskrit verbal ingenuity. How can Thomas Hood go unappreciated today? But how did we come to Hood?

"Oh, of course: Eugene Aram. Ridiculously overestimated as a philologer simply because he happened to be also a murderer (even as your party-giving Mr. Morris, should he chance to commit a capital crime, would doubtless be ranked along with Aram and Edward Ruloff as a 'learned' man), still, Mr. Lamb, Aram invalidates your contention that murder and Sanskrit form a unique combination. And George Borrow, who knew at least a smattering of

---

* If too impatient of this unusual display of Ashwinian temperament, the reader may pick up the plot again on page 112 at the asterisk.

Sanskrit, whatever one may think of the uses to which he put it, describes in one of his books several meetings with John Thurtell."
"Thurtell?"
"I cannot remember in which book. You must ask Dr. Griswold—he is far more of a Borrovian than I, if indeed there be such a word as Borrovian."
"Borrowgove," Martin suggested.
"Thurtell, the gigman, was a common enough murderer who would, today, be known principally from Borrow's references had not he also inspired a poet by his crime. Less fortunate than Aram, Thurtell is not mentioned by name in the anonymous verse born of his action, but the stanza itself is to my mind of immortal succinctness." And he recited:

> *"They cut his throat from ear to ear,*
> *His brains they batter'd in;*
> *His name was Mr. William Weare,*
> *He dwelt in Lyon's Inn."*

Pleased by Martin's amused reception of the great quatrain, Ashwin relaxed in the swivel chair and finished his drink. Then, in deliberate silence, he opened a fresh pack of cigarettes, took one, offered another to Martin, lit both, and exhaled a large cloud of smoke.

*"I was worried," he said at last, "when I left you at Dr. Griswold's Saturday, and I am still no less worried. I have slept very little over the week end. I have smoked far more than I should, and I have drunk near-Gargantuan quantities. And, as I have said, I am still worried. Have you anything new to tell me?"

Martin briefly described the uneventful inquest and added Kurt's not particularly helpful account of the dialogue between the Leshins.

"Unless there is some peculiarly subtle point hidden in Mr. Ross's story, Mr. Lamb, I fear that we are no further advanced than we were. You have suggested several interpretations of that episode—the most probable, of course, being that it means nothing. Another interpretation would be that Mr. Ross was lying."

"But why?"

"I had expected that to be your first thought. After all, he was long your favored suspect."

"But we disproved that motive completely. Oh . . . !" Martin paused abruptly.

"Yes?"

---

* Here the impatient reader, if not too discouraged, may resume the course of the plot.

"You mean that Kurt might have another motive? That he is, of all the people involved, the one most likely to be a Vignard?"

"I mean nothing of the sort, Mr. Lamb. I was just curious to see whether or not you would suggest the idea. As I said to you before, the notebook conclusively disposes of the Vignards—or rather, washes them up, to use the phrase for which you seem to have a preference. No, I give you Mr. Ross; but I think you have bothered that harmless young man enough."

"But who do you think—"

"Mr. Lamb, I am in a state where to me nothing seems obvious but the fact that things are wrong. Whether the Leshins, Miss Wood, or, as seems most likely, Mr. Bruce poisoned Paul Lennox, the killing of Dr. Schaedel is still a mystery. Why did Mr. Lennox establish so careful an alibi for the evening when he was scheduled to be a victim—an alibi, moreover, which could so easily have been faked? And why did he later tell an elaborate piece of unsubstantiated rigmarole about an obscure Swiss sect? There is no sense in it at all.

"But one question above all others—why did the murderer change his weapons? To carry on and commit the desired elimination after a murderous failure argues a strong criminal mind. And yet your true criminal . . . Cream was fond of strychnine and faithful to it. Jack the Ripper used a knife well, and continued to use it, despite the absurd theories of those who insist that he later became Dr. Cream.

"You will say, perhaps, that these are only deranged criminals following an *idée fixe*. But look on Brides-in-the-Bath Smith (more entitled, possibly, than the great Sidney to the appellation 'the Smith of Smiths'), look on Dr. Pritchard, look on Lydia Sherman, Sarah Jane Robinson, 'dear Aunt Jane' Toppan, even Mr. Pearson's beloved Lizzie Borden, whose only variance in method, according to the quatrain which ranks with Mr. William Weare's epitaph, was the difference between forty and forty-one whacks. What would cause a murderer to switch from an ice pick in one instance to strychnine in another?"

"Most of those people you mention," Martin suggested, "were caught exactly because they used the same method over and over. That's certainly true of Cream and Smith and Pritchard, even though Jack the Ripper got away with it. Perhaps our murderer wanted to avoid that danger."

"That won't wash, Mr. Lamb. He varies his method to conceal his identity and so leaves exactly the same symbol beside both corpses?"

Martin reflected. "If there were some particular reason why the murder had to take place at the rehearsal of my play, strychnine might have presented itself as the only possibility. You can't use an ice pick on a stage in full view of an audience. Or the murderer might suddenly have got access to a poison which he couldn't get hold of when he made his first attempt."

"Both suggestions are plausible enough, and yet . . . Will you bring me a copy of your play, Mr. Lamb? There might be something suggestive that we've overlooked."

"God knows there's enough in it that's suggestive, but in a somewhat different sense than you mean. But I'll bring it anyway."

"Good. I wonder if it is true that murder goes to a murderer's head?"

"What do you mean?"

"Our X has committed one accidental murder and one (from his point of view) necessary one. So far he seems safe enough as regards both, unless Sergeant Cutting is concealing something exceptionally revealing (an oddly contradictory phrase). Now if this seeming security should tempt him into disposing neatly of anyone else who at all encumbers him . . . "

"It seems hardly likely."

Dr. Ashwin smiled an almost macabre smile. "Delusions of absolute safety could lead our X into a very curious crime. Even though I disbelieve entirely in the Vignards, or at least in their supposed activities in Berkeley, I none the less think Mr. Worthing justified in requesting police protection. To murder him would seem to everyone the surest proof of the existence of the sect, since no one else could possibly wish to kill such a harmless ass."

"Though God knows I've wanted to often enough," Martin murmured.

"Well, Mr. Lamb, I make hypotheses for my own amusement and to conceal my worry. I think we can feel certain that the Seven of Calvary has killed its last victim."

In which dictum Dr. Ashwin was approximately half right.

For four days after that Monday evening interview, nothing happened. Martin received one visit from Sergeant Cutting, liked him more than ever, and answered a great many questions, particularly concerning any possible connection between Paul Lennox and Dr. Hugo Schaedel; for evidently the sergeant was beginning to take the Seven of Calvary a little more seriously. Twice Martin attended Sanskrit class and concluded with fair success the reading of the *Nala* episode; but his discussions with Ashwin at these sessions turned merely upon such subjects as the relative contributions of Rider Haggard and Andrew Lang to *The World's Desire,* or anecdotes of the pleasantly precocious Elizabeth. "She has been telling her schoolmates about Sanskrit," her mother had written. "I heard her say to one little girl, 'It goes *"nana nana nut,"* and it's a language!'"

"I have been writing letters myself," Dr. Ashwin remarked as he folded the note from which he had read this excerpt. "You may be extremely interested in the reply which I expect from the University of Chicago library."

After class on Wednesday afternoon, Martin approached Dr. Leshin. "Miss Griswold tells me that Mrs. Leshin is ill. I hope it is nothing serious."

"Not at all, Mr. Lamb, I thank you. Nervous strain—the shock of seeing Mr. Lennox poisoned—it understands itself, I think. She is now at a rest home in Marin County."

"Please offer her my condolence," Martin said confusedly, and cursed himself the remainder of the afternoon for uttering such a stupid word.

On Friday morning Lupe Sanchez received a message that her father the General was much worse, and made her plans to leave for Los Angeles on Saturday.

On Friday evening Martin and Mona went to the United Artists Theatre to see a film already being mentioned for the Academy award. It had three stars, ran a hundred and ten minutes, and bored them both to petrifaction. (In brief, the award was in the bag.)

"No, thank you," Mona replied to Martin's offer of refreshment as they left the theatre. "I need much fresh air after that film. Let us walk in the hills."

They strolled quietly and pleasantly up Bancroft and past International House to Panoramic, while Martin praised Mexican films, so snootily scorned by American critics, in contrast to such arrant bosh as the super-production they had just seen. The lecture, which Mona received with admirable patience, was interrupted as they passed Cynthia's house by the appearance of Alex Bruce.

"Hello," he said. "Going for a walk in the hills even without moonlight?"

"It is not always necessary, the moonlight," Mona whispered softly.

"No, I suppose not. And sometimes it just wouldn't do any good. I've been talking with Cynthia," he added to Martin.

"So?"

"I guess that's over with. We sort of called each other by our real names tonight. Had a couple of drinks—just enough to loosen up our repressions—and started in saying all the things we've always meant to say. So if you ever had any idea, Martin, of my playing Maecenas to struggling young authors after I married into the Wood fortune—well, that's out."

"Too bad, Alex. But I guess it was just one of those things that don't work out."

Alex shrugged his shoulders. "And at that it's no reason for me to bother other people. '*And all third parties who on spoiling tête-à-têtes insist...,*' you know. I need a walk in the hills to clear my brain, but I won't inflict myself on you. Besides, I want to walk at a good stiff pace; I almost feel as though I were running away from something . . . "

" '*But at my back I always hear...*' 'Martin quoted.

"Something like that. So long." And Alex set off toward the hills at a nervous speed that brought to Martin's mind yet another quotation, telling of

> . . . *one that on a lonesome road*
> *Doth walk in fear and dread,*
> *And having once turn'd round, walks on,*
> *And turns no more his head;*
> *Because he knows a fearful fiend*
> *Doth close behind him tread.*

But just then Martin and Mona were passing along a stretch of road where the street lamp did not shine, and in the embrace which logically ensued they let pass them unnoticed whatever might have been treading close behind Alex Bruce.

In the absence of the moon, the hills were enfolded in dark quietude. It was in the same spot which had witnessed their discussion in Spanish on Sunday that Mona and Martin at last established themselves. They spoke now—when they spoke at all—in odd comminglings of English and Spanish, little fragments of whichever best suited the moment. And Martin, in disregarding what he had cited as the first rule of a fictional detective, was gloriously happy.

It all happened at once and broke with its suddenness into the very middle of a kiss. First there was the sound of footsteps coming down the path, then the appearance of the quickly walking figure, then the shot, the figure falling to the ground, and the tall shape moving abruptly on the other side of the path. It happened too quickly, too confusedly, for Martin to make any sense of it; but a sudden impulse sent him across the path to seize the tall shape, despite Mona's restraining hand.

His reasoning mind, at the moment notably absent, should have been astounded and relieved that the shape neither fired nor fled. Instead it rushed at him and seized him with strong arms. Martin was neither an experienced fighter nor a strong one; the shape was both. Still Martin, with a fragmentary memory of jiu-jitsu and a dash of ingenuity, managed, after a long and heavy-breathed struggle, to make at least some impression on the shape—enough, indeed, to set it swearing in fluent German with a marked Swiss accent.

"Kurt!" Martin exclaimed, and the amazed shape loosed its hold.

"Martin! *Du! Um Gottes willen...!*"

In the darkness they stared at each other. Suspicion ... Disbelief ... Fear ... Kurt felt his aching thumb regretfully.

"The shot came from farther down, on your side of the path," Kurt said at last.

"But who... what...?" With an unwarranted access of sense, Martin turned at last to the form lying on the path. Two girls knelt beside it.

"I heard footsteps running down the path," Mona said as Kurt and Martin approached. He now indistinctly recognized the other girl as Lupe Sanchez.

"It's no use trying to follow, then," Martin reflected. "Whoever it was could have vanished any place in these hills while Kurt and I were trying to catch each other."

"And the shot was not all," Mona added. "He threw this at the body before he ran." She handed Martin a stone around which was wrapped a piece of paper, secured by a rubber band.

Martin did not need to be told what symbol he would find when he unwrapped the paper, nor did he need to light a match to know that the motionless body on the path was that of Alex Bruce.

INTERLUDE

"*It is the Vance method!*" *I exclaimed. "One by one you kill them off, and lo—!"*

"*I'm afraid,*" *said Martin reflectively, "that I have just been guilty, for the first time in this narrative, of the undue sensationalism for which Holmes used to reproach Watson. You see, Alex Bruce was not dead.*"

"*No?*" *I confess that I felt a trifle let down.*

"*No.*" *Martin sipped his glass of liqueur Grand Marnier as the waiter cleared away the remains of dessert. "The bullet grazed his skull and laid him unconscious. But the fact that he was shot at is the important thing, not whether he lived or died. Important, of course, from the point of view of the mystery; I should have been very sorry to lose Alex as a friend.*"

"*And what happened next?*" *I prompted.*

"*Nothing.*"

"*What on earth do you mean, nothing?*"

"*Just that. Nothing more happened. Aside from two or three of what Ashwin might call corroborative minutiae, I have told you the* whole case. When I was telling about the absurd novel on the boat-train murders, I mentioned the point in the story where the detective says to his stooge, 'You are now in possession of all the facts. Let us see if you reach the same conclusions as I.' Well, this is that point."

"For my part, Martin," I mumbled through the process of lighting a cigarette, "I don't reach any conclusions at all."

"You needn't feel bad about it, Tony. Neither did I. And yet Ashwin knew no more than I have just told you when he evolved his complete solution of the case."

"You've been quite fair in telling it?"

"Scrupulously. The facts were fortunately such that I was able to be fair; there were no startling last-minute disclosures. We knew everything; it just happened that Ashwin was the only man in Berkeley who could piece it together."

I finished my liqueur and sat disconsolate. Try as I might, the thing didn't make sense; I was as mystified as I dare hope that my reader may be now. Even if one accepts Dr. Ashwin's explanation of the Schaedel killing as accidental, who could desire the lives of both Paul Lennox and Alex Bruce? Who, for that matter, his rival Lennox being dead, could conceivably want Bruce's life at all?

Martin roused me from my meditations. "Come on," he said. "We've talked enough about the Seven of Calvary for one night. Let's wander down to the Chinese Theatre—it's a pleasant short walk from here—and see an hour or so of their endless performance. I never like to visit San Francisco without seeing it; some day I may make sense of it."

"All right. But if you can puzzle out the plot of a Chinese play, you don't need Dr. Ashwin to solve murders."

"Then, Tony, you can spend the night in lonely cogitation, and I'll drop around for breakfast and tell you all the fascinating facts. Right?"

"Fine."

Martin was a punctual breakfast guest. At the appointed eight-thirty, he arrived, to find me with the grapefruit juice squeezed, the coffee made, the bacon frying, and the French toast ready to go in the pan. He sniffed the bacon aroma appreciatively, and nodded at the French toast. "Breakfast promises well," he said. "And are you as good a deductionist as you are a cook, Tony?"

"Three more minutes of silence, Martin, or you'll have burned French toast."

The threat silenced him, but he returned to the subject as soon as I had served the meal.

"I didn't do so well," I replied. "Like M. P. Shiel's nurse-detective, I dreamed a complete solution of the case, but unlike her, I haven't remembered even a punning symbol of what that solution might be. Besides, I rather think it was all mixed up with Chinese robes and long white beards. Now be a good lad, Martin, and Tell All."

"Very well," said Martin, as he poured maple syrup liberally over the toast. "First the corroborative minutiae—that phrase grows on me—and then the Ashwinian solution itself. Damned good French toast, by the way. Use flour? I thought not. Well, Alex, as I said last night, was not killed. . . ."

TEN

TRUTH DOES A STRIPTEASE

Martin had unwrapped the paper and was staring at it in bewilderment when he was roused by Lupe's voice.

"I think he is all right," she was saying. "I cannot find a wound."

Martin turned and knelt beside Alex. His heart was beating, and he was breathing reassuringly.

"Come on, Kurt. Give me a hand, and we'll get him down to the hospital."

The two men propped Alex up between them and, the girls following, started down the trail. After a few minutes of silent walking, they heard groans and unintelligible mutterings from the figure they were supporting.

"He's coming around," said Martin. "Let's stop a minute."

They lowered Alex into a relatively comfortable position at the foot of a tree, his head in Mona's lap. Martin, with vague memories of "What To Do in Emergencies," began chafing his wrists while Mona stroked his forehead. Kurt and Lupe stood apart, Kurt glancing now and then, with a slight shudder, at the Vignard-inscribed paper which Martin had handed to him.

Alex opened his eyes at last and rose unsteadily to a sitting posture. "What the hell . . . "he muttered.

"God bless you, Alex!" Martin exclaimed, "I was afraid you'd say, 'Where am I?'"

"Martin!"

"Yes."

Alex rubbed his aching head with the back of his hand. "I think I know where I am, all right. Some place in the hills, isn't it?"

"Right."

"But just what in hell's happened to me? My head feels like a walnut that's quarreled with a steam roller. And what are you doing here and who are these other people? I can't see very well, and to be honest, I don't much care." His head sank back in Mona's lap.

"I don't know myself just what happened. Mona and I were—well, that is, we were—and you came down the path. Suddenly there was a shot from some place a little farther down the path, and you fell. Kurt and Lupe were near there and heard and saw the same thing. Kurt and I each thought that the other was your assailant, and gaily tackled each other. During the melee, whoever it was got smoothly away."

Alex managed to rise a little, his hand still at his head. "Must have grazed me. There's a place here on my temple that hurts like a lot of words I won't use at the moment. Did you see who it was?"

"No."

"Man or a woman?"

"I don't know."

"I think," Lupe interrupted, "I think I saw it when it threw the stone. It was small, and I think—to this I will not swear—it was a woman."

"Threw the stone? What's this all about, Martin? It's bad enough to have people taking pot shots at you in the hills; but if they're going to throw stones at you to boot—"

"It was a stone with a paper wrapped around it," Martin explained.

"Paper?" Alex shook his dazed head worriedly. "Is this a gag?" Then a quick look of comprehension came, and with it something approaching terror. "Martin! That paper . . . It wasn't . . . "He choked, and left the sentence unfinished.

"I think it was. Kurt!"

Obediently Kurt advanced. He handed the Seven of Calvary to Alex and struck a match. In the light of the flickering flame, Martin saw on Alex's face an expression which might have denoted anything from utter fright to complete resignation. Then Alex's head fell back and he seemed for a moment to lose consciousness again.

Mona looked up at Martin with concern. "Had you not best take him to the hospital?"

"Right. Come on, Kurt."

But as they bent over Alex to raise him, he roused himself and struggled unaided to his feet. "No!" he cried. "Leave me alone. No hospital for me—thanks all the same. That means they'd recognize the bullet scratch, and that—God bless the laws—would mean the police. And that's out—out, do you hear?"

"But Alex—"

"I'm all right. Just a scratch. I can settle this." He wavered a little, and caught Martin's arm. "If you've just got to do something helpful, you can help me back to the House. My legs don't seem to be quite themselves yet. And if you've got any whisky lying around . . ."

It was a strange and silent procession that approached the south entrance of International House. The girls went on to the women's entrance, and Martin and Kurt helped Alex into the elevator and on to his room. There he sat, still a trifle dazed, on the edge of the bed while Martin hurried to his own room for whisky and Kurt fetched a cold damp towel from the washroom.

The whisky braced Alex no end, and the cold towel helped in the transformation. In a few moments he looked almost normal again.

"Have you got a cigarette, Martin?" he asked. "That's the worst of this whole damned episode—I lost a pack of cigarettes some place on the trail up there."

Martin handed over his pack. For himself, he took a large swig from the bottle—he felt he needed it almost as much as Alex—and passed it on to Kurt.

"Thanks. That smoke feels good." Alex leaned back on the bed. "And my head's better now."

"But Alex," Martin insisted, "this must come to the police eventually."

"And why?"

"Damn it all, Alex, how can you ask why? That paper —this isn't something that involves just you. It concerns Dr. Schaedel and Paul Lennox. If we can check on the person who shot at you—"

"—you won't find out one damned thing."

"Martin is right, Alex," Kurt put in.

"Martin is wrong, Kurt." Alex sat up vigorously and reached again for the whisky. "Martin is so damned wrong he'll never even know how wrong he is. And meanwhile both of you are going to promise me here and now that you'll never mention a word of this to anyone. Do you promise?"

But both hesitated.

"Come on! After all, it's my cause, isn't it? I'm the injured party. And if I know—as I do know—that I can settle it, just what the hell is it to you?"

"Alex," said Martin, "I'm going to be frank with you. I'll promise not to say a word to the police or to anyone else, but I make one exception."

"Yes?"

"Dr. Ashwin."

"The loyal Watson. My compliments, Martin, for your fidelity.

All right. If your great Sanskrit amateur detective wants to know about this, let him. After all, I owe him a good turn. And much good may it do him. Now how about you, Kurt?"

"I shall be as the grave."

"Not a very cheery comparison, but let it pass. All right, gentlemen. You give me your word not to whisper this to anyone at all—with Martin's exception?"

"I give you my word," said Martin, and Kurt echoed him.

It was the battlements of Elsinore Castle. "*This not to do, swear, so grace and mercy at your most need help you*". Martin as Horatio, Kurt as Marcellus, Alex as an oddly colloquial Hamlet . . . all that was lacking was the Ghost in the cellarage. And Martin was not so sure that he was indeed lacking.

"That's that." Alex passed the whisky back to his friends. "Now let's be cheerful. We can't go to sleep at once after that gay little scene. We'll kill that bottle and tell stories."

Reluctantly, Martin drank. Kurt hesitated. Martin knew what was in his mind. He was thinking of the night he had seen his uncle killed, and of how they had all sat in Martin's room drinking and rollicking while the police carried off what had been a man of love and peace.

It had been a night just like this. The Seven had struck in the hills, and the blow had been followed by stag carousing in a room of International House. Martin and Alex and Kurt—but the group was smaller by one now. Paul Lennox was not there, to abandon his pipe for cigarettes and deliver the great saga of Anthony Claire.

There *was* a ghost in the cellarage.

Martin rose early the next morning and hurried down Channing Way to the rooming house where Dr. Ashwin lived, only to learn that his master had left for the week end, presumably to stay in San Rafael with Elizabeth and her mother. He would be back some time Sunday.

It proved an intolerable week end for Martin. He wanted to bring this newest factor of the case to Dr. Ashwin's attention immediately, and he was helpless. He did not even know Elizabeth's last name nor where to reach Ashwin in Marin County. Moreover, Mona had left with Remigio, to spend the week end with friends in San Francisco —*attachés* of the Bolivian Consulate or some such thing. Lupe had departed for Los Angeles early Saturday morning, and Kurt, as a result, proved a moping and dull companion. And Martin felt an odd disinclination to see Alex.

There was only one thing left to do—work. And heaven knows it was necessary. Seminar papers had been piling up right and left while Martin had labored on *Don Juan Returns* or held conferences with Ashwin. So, for this last week end before the dénouement of the Schaedel case, Martin slaved alternately at Caspar Wilhelm von Borcke and at the influence of Saint-Simonianism on the *Jung Deutschland* movement, and heard or spoke scarcely a word upon the Seven of Calvary.

The one exception occurred after dinner on Saturday when he encountered Paul Boritsin in the Great Hall. It was too soon after food to settle down anew to the letters of Georg Büchner, and a chat with the Russian, Martin thought, might effectively drive him to industry.

After desultory remarks on the Tchernavins, Carveth Wells, and Mr. Hearst's latest starvation statistics, Martin could not resist a mild bit of ribbing. "You remember your extremely acute theory concerning the murder of Dr. Schaedel?" he asked. "Just how do you square that up with later developments?"

"Later developments, Mr. Lamb?"

"The poisoning of Paul Lennox. Why should the dirty Reds want to polish him off?"

"Mr. Lamb!" Boritsin smiled a smile of aristocratic superiority. "But it is of a simplicity which amazes me you do not comprehend."

Martin struggled his way through the sentence and finally prompted, "So?"

"But of course. It is notorious that Mr. Lennox was a Communist."

Martin gulped. "Paul a Communist?"

"Have I not seen him to emerge from a theatre at which was showing *Peasants?* Have I not heard him to whistle an air by Hanns Eisler while that he was shaving? Above all, have I not heard him to praise highly what is called the 'music' of Shotstakovich? Mr. Lamb, I ask you, could anyone not a Communist do these things?"

Martin gulped doubly and said nothing.

"I see you doubt. Mr. Lamb, I will now contribute the clinching nail to my argument. I happen to know—mind you, Mr. Lamb, this is no vagrom calumny—I happen to *know* that Mr. Lennox was subscriber to the *Nation!*" Boritsin leaned back, blew out a great puff of smoke (which had been intended as a ring), and beamed complacently. "The rest follows of itself. He knew something of the assassination. Perhaps he was not all bad, and threatened to make a revelation. So." the aristocrat concluded, adding a nice Nazi touch to his scheme, "he was purged."

Martin rose. "Today, Boritsin," he said sternly, "I bought a copy of the *Daily Worker*."

He walked off quietly. It may be added that Boritsin never spoke to him again.

Martin, nervously watching Dr. Ashwin's rooming house, saw him return about eight thirty Sunday evening. Allowing a decent pause, he hurried up the stairs and knocked on the doctor's door.

Ashwin welcomed him with a broad smile which ill accorded with Martin's eager impatience. "Why are you so amused?" Martin could not help asking.

Ashwin settled himself comfortably and laughed. "Over the week end," he explained, "I have learned a profound secret. I have learned the invaluable quality of an inflatable rubber duck."

Without waiting for Martin's prompting, he continued his narrative. "Elizabeth's mother, as I believe I have told you, is a still young, attractive, and quite remarriagable woman. In fact, a sturdy young man is at present courting her. But he was not present at dinner last night; there were only Elizabeth, her mother, and I. A silence fell briefly in the midst of the dinner-table conversation; and of a sudden Elizabeth remarked, 'Dr. Ashwin, Mother thinks you're an awfully nice man. Why don't you marry her?' "

The remembrance of the painful situation brought renewed laughter to Dr. Ashwin, laughter in which Martin could not help joining as he pictured Elizabeth looking alternately at her mother and at her patron and wondering why so logical a question should affect them both so strangely.

"What on earth did you do?" Martin asked at last.

"In my pocket," Dr. Ashwin replied, "there reposed a rubber duck which I had bought that afternoon for Elizabeth. I had found it in a drugstore on the counter next to the whisky. While Elizabeth's mother blushed into her napkin, I extracted the rubber duck and gravely inflated it. So delighted was Elizabeth with this exhibition that the awkward subject was quite forgotten. I must remember never to travel again in perilous mixed company without an inflatable rubber duck."

Ashwin finally broke off his laughter to fetch the whisky. As he poured it, he asked, "And what has happened in Berkeley during my absence? My landlady tells me that you called yesterday at an hour surprisingly early for you, and seemed very anxious to see me."

So Martin told the detailed story of Friday night. "And it leaves me," he concluded, "more confused than ever. Even with a Vignard theory, you can't account for anyone wanting to kill Alex. And don't get any wild ideas of its being a plan to ward off suspicion. If that were it, he certainly wouldn't have sworn Kurt and me to secrecy; and besides, that bullet was meant to kill. No one's a good-enough shot to graze the head like that on purpose; it's mere accident that Alex is alive."

"True. But continue, Mr. Lamb. I want to see what other ideas this attack suggests to you."

"Well . . . It eliminates the Leshins pretty thoroughly, I should say, even aside from Mrs. Leshin's being in Marin County. Alex has only the slightest acquaintance with either of them. Unless he saw something backstage that night—but Alex in the role of secret blackmailer just doesn't make sense."

"And what else?"

"He quarreled violently with Cynthia that night. She might . . . But then she is the one person with a completely sound alibi for the murder of Dr. Schaedel."

"True."

"That lets out . . . Well, among them, the three killings —I count the attack on Alex as one because it certainly was so in intent—the three killings let out everyone. The first one lets out Cynthia; the second eliminates Paul, all too literally; and this third disposes of Alex, the Leshins, and the Vignards—even if your beloved notebook hadn't done that already. What we need, Dr. Ashwin, is a whole new set of suspects."

"Yes?"

"For God's sake don't be so omnisciently monosyllabic. Tell me what you think."

"I do not think, Mr. Lamb. Now I know."

"What?" Martin reached swiftly for the bottle.

"Yes, Mr. Lamb, I know. This attack on Mr. Bruce was the one thing needed to make the pattern complete, the one touch to render the whole series of crimes obvious."

"Then you know who the murderer is?"

"I might logically answer your question with another, but I shall not."

"And what are you going to do?"

"I need one or two facts before I can do anything. To be exact, I need three facts. One I expect to receive tomorrow from the University of Chicago library. Since I wrote via airmail special delivery and enclosed an envelope for an answer of similar speed, I should hear from them tomorrow. The second fact you shall secure for me in San Francisco either tomorrow or Tuesday, if you will be so good as to perform an errand for me."

"Gladly. Tuesday would be better."

"Fine. And the third fact I shall learn from Mr. Bruce himself at the little conference which I propose to hold here on Wednesday evening."

"A conference?"

"Yes. I should like to expound my ideas to those interested before I make definite use of them. Not that I doubt myself; I think that, in my heart of hearts, it is simply a desire for an appreciative audience."

"Who is to be there?"

"Yourself, of course; you need not fear being cheated. Mr. Ross, as representing the interests of the first victim—his discretion can be trusted, can it not?"

"Of course."

"You may be considered as representing Mr. Lennox, and the third victim, Mr. Bruce, can of course represent himself. I shall also invite Dr. Griswold. His mind shows the most admirable combination of scholarship and intellect that I have ever encountered; he should be the ideal critical audience. You will doubtless remember the *Panchatantra:*

"*Scholarship is less than sense;
Therefore seek intelligence.*"

"But why don't you tell me what you know?"

Dr. Ashwin smiled. "Griswold observed very justly that you have corrupted me. I have now developed such a taste for the theatrical that my lips are sealed until Wednesday night."

Martin swore under his breath and consoled himself with another drink.

"You will of course see to inviting Mr. Ross and Mr. Bruce. I shall myself speak with Dr. Griswold. Now as to your errand on Tuesday . . ."

Martin jotted down his instructions and slipped them into his pocket. "I'm afraid I must go now," he said rising. "I've got to finish off Gutzkow tonight."

"You look quite ludicrous, Mr. Lamb, in your sheepish disappointment—your pardon, yours was a name born to create bad accidental puns. It is, I grant you, cruel, the manner in which we detectives treat our Watsons."

"Oh, well, I can wait," Martin muttered with an assumed indifference.

"But let me be at least more helpfully cryptic, Mr. Lamb, and direct your attention to these points." Ashwin ticked them off on his fingers as he enumerated them.

"A: THE POINT OF THE FATHER'S RELIGION.
B: THE POINT OF THE SUPERFLUOUS ALIBI
(*which is two points*).
C: THE POINT OF THE FORTUNATE STUMBLE.
D: THE POINT OF THE DISPUTED THEORY.
E: THE POINT OF THE VARYING WEAPONS.
F: THE POINT OF THE SEVILLIAN TIRADE.
G: THE POINT OF THE EYE AND THE TOOTH.

And above all—
H: THE POINT OF THE SEVEN OF CALVARY.

"You see," Dr. Ashwin concluded, "I am well conversant with

my Stuart Palmer and my Erle Stanley Gardner, to say nothing of my never-to-be-sufficiently-praised John Dickson Carr."

"You are a help," added Martin disgruntedly, and left.[1]

The ferry ride to San Francisco Tuesday morning was, as it always is, a pleasant interval of quiet surcease. Martin had bought a copy of *Variety* to enjoy on the trip, but it lay neglected beside him as he sat on the front of the upper deck and watched the San Francisco skyline materialize into clarity. The morning was at once cold and warm; the sun was bright, and a chill breeze blew across the bay.

Martin left the Ferry Building, besieged by the usual swarm of newsboys and taxi drivers, and walked leisurely up Mission Street. At last he paused before a store bearing the inscription "I. Goldfarb, Theatrical Accessories."

A little Jewish clerk beamed at Martin from behind a long glass counter containing everything from crepe hair to collapsible daggers. "Yes, sir? What can we do for you?"

"Do you carry sound-effect records—phonograph transcriptions for offstage noises?"

"Yes, sir. Just what would you be wanting?"

"Do you have a record of typing?"

"Yes, sir. A very good one. If you'll just step this way, sir—"

He led Martin into a small room containing an electric phonograph, vanished a moment, and reappeared with a record. "Here you are, sir," he announced. "Recorded in a genuine office, thirty typewriters going at once."

Martin's face fell. "You don't have a record of just one typewriter?"

"Sorry, sir, we don't. No call for it. For just one machine, it's easier and cheaper to use a real typewriter. You want it for amateur theatricals, I suppose?"

"Yes."

"Well, take my advice and have your prop man use a real typewriter offstage. If there was much professional demand out here, we might carry it—using a genuine typewriter would mean another union man—but you amateurs don't have to worry about that."

---

[1] I feel that this brief list provides the proper place to issue a challenge to the reader, in the manner of the admirable Ellery Queen. To be sure, all the essential facts had been told when Martin challenged me after dinner to equal Ashwin's solution; but it was not until I had, between mouthfuls of French toast, heard these eight points that I suddenly understood the tangled web of plot that lay behind the deaths of Dr. Hugo Schaedel and Paul Lennox. Here, then, I challenge my readers (in a confident plural), and urge them on to check their solutions against the obvious certainty of Dr. John Ashwin.—*A. B.*

And the clerk continued a discourse on the troubles of union regulations in the theatre as he bowed Martin out. "You might try Zolotoy's," he concluded. "About two blocks west; they carry anything."

Somewhat less hopefully, Martin approached the white-haired old man at Zolotoy's with the same opening gambit. He was surprised by the result of his question; the old man smiled a very broad smile and seemed secretly pleased about something.

"I told him," he chuckled. "Many's the time I've told him. He wouldn't believe me, but I'm right. He'll see." He continued muttering as he led Martin into another little room almost identical with that of Goldfarb's. "You're sure it's *one* typewriter you want?"

"Yes. One."

"Just a moment, young man, just a moment. I'll have it right here for you."

He returned promptly and started the record. It was an excellent transcription, sharp and clear, and the record was so unusually free from surface noises as to be completely convincing. Click-click-click-click-click-click-click-click-*ping!* Martin was again drinking his bourbon and reading *The Boat Train Murders*. The rate was the same—just a little better than Paul Lennox's normal speed. . . .

Martin shuddered.

The old man stopped the record. "Would that be satisfactory now, young man?"

"Too damned satisfactory."

"What?"

"Nothing. But I'd like to ask you a couple of questions."

"All right." The old man sat down and devoted himself to a venerable and oddly colored clay pipe. "What is it, young man?"

"You see," Martin began, "I'm from the U.C. Experimental Theatre in Berkeley. We used a record just like that in our last show. Now, somebody's been playing around with the books of the theatre, doctoring up expense accounts and what not, and I'm trying to check up on things. Could you tell me if our record was rented here?"

"When was your show?"

"Friday, April 6th."

"Just a minute, young man." The stooped figure disappeared into an inner office and returned with a ledger marked *Sound Transcriptions, N—Z*. After a few moments' search he announced, "Here we are; *No. T 321. Single typewriter. Rented April 5. Returned April 7.* I guess that's the one you want. Here, you can copy it down if you need it for your books."

Martin jotted down the entry and noticed the renter's name—Frank Hellmuth. Grudgingly, he applauded Paul for avoiding the usual obvious self-betrayals made by those who choose false names.

"Will that be all?" the old man was saying.

"One thing more. I'm not sure it was really Frank who rented this record; there've been some funny things happening in our theatre, and I just want to check." He took up his briefcase and extracted a group of photographs—mostly snaps, but good ones. Several of them were blanks—people, that is, quite unconnected with the case—but among them Ashwin had insisted, for some strange reason, on including Alex Bruce as well as Paul Lennox.

The old man looked over the photos slowly, sucking on the clay. The first two he discarded instantly (one of them was Boritsin). Over the third, that of Alex, he paused, and thoughtfully laid it aside. The next three he skipped over without interest. Then he seized on Paul's, and let fall two more that he had not even glanced at.

"This is the one," he said definitely. "Is that your Frank, young man?"

"No," said Martin truthfully. "There's something funny here. How can you be so sure? How can you remember one rental weeks ago so clearly?"

"Ah." A long puff on the clay. "Now you're asking something. Well, young man, I'll tell you." A still longer puff. "Two years ago we got that record. I wanted to get it; I thought it'd be useful maybe. But the boss, he was against it; he said people could use a typewriter if they wanted a typewriter. Well, I ordered the record without telling him, see; and when it came he kicked up hell. And for two years we didn't rent it. Every time I gave him any advice about anything he'd say, 'Oh yeah? You knew about the typing record too, didn't you?' So you can see why I remembered it when I finally rented the record. I told that young man in the picture all about the boss and he laughed and we was what you might call chummy about it; so I remember him." He settled back to relight his pipe after so long a speech.

Martin picked up Alex's picture. "Then why did you set this one aside? It doesn't look anything like the other."

"Because I've seen him too, only not then. I couldn't think where, but now I remember. He come in here about a week after the other one, and did pretty much like you did. First he wanted to know did we have a record like that, and then had anybody rented it lately, and then what kind of a looking person it was. He didn't talk about no theatre, though."

"And you told him?"

"Just what I told you, young man, only no pictures."

"Thanks." Martin repacked his briefcase. "I'm afraid I won't want the record after all, but you needn't tell your boss that. Here—have a couple of beers on me and forget the boss."

The old man glowed contentedly and puffed firmly at the clay. "Thanks, young man," he grinned. "Any time I can do anything for you—"

Martin walked slowly down to the Embarcadero and over to Bernstein's for lunch. Today's discoveries seemed at first almost to make things more complicated. And then, as he attacked an excellent lobster louie, reinforced by beer, he remembered the seventh of Ashwin's cryptic points.

Things began to grow clearer.

Turning his swivel chair away from the desk, Dr. Ashwin faced the little group assembled in his room on Wednesday evening. Martin was in his usual chair, and Alex Bruce sat in another and equally stiff one. Dr. Griswold had made himself fairly comfortable at the head of the couch, and Kurt Ross sat awkwardly at its foot. Ashtrays and glasses of scotch were disposed hospitably beside each of them, save for the abstemious professor of Spanish.

"You all know," Ashwin began in his most rounded voice, "why we are gathered together here. Three sensational crimes have been committed on or near the campus of this university, and no plausible explanation of them has been publicly advanced. I have, to my own satisfaction, evolved a complete solution of this series of crimes, and I have asked you gentlemen to hear and criticize my explanation.

"You, Dr. Griswold, I ask to serve as a check-and-balance to myself. You other three represent indirectly or, in one case, directly, the three victims, and as such representatives are entitled to know my construction of the facts. When you have heard that construction, we can, as a group, decide what use to make of it."

Martin looked around the group. It was an uneasy lot of people, realizing that they were assembled on a matter of life and death and worrying as to what decision it might fall to their lot to make.

Dr. Ashwin resumed his prefatory discourse. "The basic facts of these crimes are, I believe, known to all of you, at least since I spent the greater portion of the afternoon relating them to Dr. Griswold. Certain other less known facts will be brought out in my discussion, for many of which I am indebted to Mr. Lamb's sometimes purposeful but more often accidental researches. These will clarify themselves as the occasion arises.

"On Sunday last I told Mr. Lamb that my reconstruction of the case still needed the answers to three questions. The first answer I received Monday in an express package from the head librarian of the University of Chicago. In a way, it was anything but satisfactory. I had committed the grievous error of underestimating the astuteness of the murderer; I had hoped for a far simpler clue than he had left me. But that I shall explain further at the proper time."

"Never underestimate a murderer, Dr. Ashwin," Alex observed quietly.

"I assure you, Mr. Bruce, I shall avoid that fault in the future. The answer to my second question Mr. Lamb found in San Francisco on Tuesday; this too we shall take up in its proper place. This answer, I may add, serves strongly to corroborate my theory. There remains but one question before I can feel upon sure ground and continue my exposition; that question, Mr. Bruce, I must ask of you."

Alex lifted his glass and took a quick drink of the scotch. "Yes?" he said.

"I think you will find it best to answer me truthfully, Mr. Bruce, although the question may seem a random shot." Dr. Ashwin paused. "Mr. Bruce, were you secretly married to Cynthia Wood?"

Alex dropped his glass to the floor and let the whisky flow unheeded. For a moment he was silent, and then gasped, "How did you know?"

Kurt and Martin looked at each other in speechless amazement. Dr. Griswold stroked his beard unmoved and seemed to wonder quietly what could happen next.

Dr. Ashwin settled back in the swivel chair and again surveyed the group. "The third question is answered satisfactorily. Now, Mr. Bruce, with your permission, I shall proceed to explain why you poisoned Paul Lennox."

ELEVEN

THE NAKED TRUTH

There was a moment of tense silence. Even Dr. Griswold leaned forward in surprise. Kurt started from the couch with clenched fists, then sank back, swearing beneath his breath. Martin watched Alex closely.

Whatever reaction he might have expected from a man suddenly accused of murder, he did not perceive the slightest discomposure. Ashwin's abrupt question had moved Alex far more than the subsequent accusation.

The young chemist leaned over and picked up his glass. "I shall be curious to hear your reasoning, Dr. Ashwin," he said softly.

"When you have quite finished and the others of the group have made their comments, then I shall reply as I see fit. In the meanwhile, do you mind if I refill my glass?"

"Not at all." Dr. Ashwin handed him the bottle. "A mere accusation of murder, Mr. Bruce, should never stand in the way of hospitality."

Alex filled his glass, emptied it swiftly, refilled it, and returned the bottle. "Go on," he said.

"You gentlemen will understand," Ashwin began, "that whatever is said in this room tonight is to remain forever a secret among the five of us, unless we should jointly decide otherwise. Now, in order to explain how I reached this conclusion which has so startled three of you, I believe I shall find it best to rehearse the case from its very beginning, and explain what seemed obvious at every step. This matter of obviousness is, as Mr. Lamb well knows, my *idée fixe*. It was my belief in it that tempted me to theorize when your uncle, Mr. Ross, was found murdered; and it is my pursuit of this belief that has drawn me now so deeply into this strange series of crimes.

"Let us begin with the death of Dr. Schaedel. Here was a man, as Mr. Lamb has assured me and as you, Mr. Ross, are doubtless equally convinced—a man, I say, utterly free from guile, a noble, admirable, even lovable man, who had led a clear, uncomplicated life. And this man was found foully murdered. As his letter to Mr. Ross fortunately proved, only certain worthy Swiss institutions stood to profit financially by his death. When I first approached this problem, I did so, as Mr. Lamb will remember, by means of a famous list of the possible motives for murder: Gain, Jealousy, Revenge, Elimination, Lust for Killing, and Conviction. Of these, the first four were obviously inapplicable in the case of Dr. Schaedel. Lust for Killing I frankly chose not to consider, for no amount of mental ingenuity can discover the obvious when dealing with a psychopathic criminal; if the murderer was a lust-killer, my reasoning efforts would then be clearly futile.

"There remained, to be sure, murder from conviction—a theory substantiated by the symbol found beside the body and by Mr. Lennox's later revelations concerning that symbol. But even from the first I was skeptical of the Vignards. That a man should live in Switzerland almost all of his life, and be slain by a Swiss sect only when he arrives in Berkeley is a concept to strain one's credulity; and the utter ignorance of Vignardism on the part of Mr. Ross and of the Swiss Consulate confirmed me in my disbelief. Later events, of course, eliminated the Vignards completely—to my great relief.

"The crime itself, you will remember, left no hint of the murderer's identity. The weapon bore no fingerprints and was itself unidentifiable; and Mr. Ross, the only eyewitness, gave such a vague description of his uncle's assailant that almost anyone short of my corpulence might have been suspect. The police were, in the classic phrase, baffled. Here we were with the corpse of a man whom no one could want to kill and with no trace of the identity of his killer.

"It was then that the first obvious point in this case occurred to me; and I simply asserted to Mr. Lamb and Mr. Bruce, whom the most melodramatic of the fates must have sent to my room that night, that the wrong man had been killed. The question then to be answered was, '*Who was the right man?*' We could make no guesses as to the identity of the murderer until we knew that of his intended victim.

"Now the requirements for the right man were these: He must be of average height and build. He must, at least frequently, wear a gray suit and hat. And, most essential, he must be a fairly regular visitor of Cynthia Wood's. Only if these conditions were fulfilled could Dr. Schaedel, so built, so garbed, and leaving Miss Wood's door at eleven thirty, have been mistaken for him. Two men and only two answered all of these requirements. Those two were Alex Bruce and Paul Lennox."

Dr. Ashwin paused for a drink and a fresh cigarette. "I fear," he smiled, "that this is becoming the longest monologue I have ever delivered or any of you have ever heard. How are you holding up?"

"Go on," said Kurt. "It is of great importance to me that I know how my uncle was killed." And he cast a glance of hate at Alex.

"I too find it intensely interesting. Do go on," from Alex.

Dr. Griswold smiled and blinked. "It reminds me very much of the method which I used in disproving the authenticity of certain plays supposedly by Lope de Vego. I shall continue to listen with great interest if only I may have a glass of water. Your admirable hospitality of whisky and tobacco is of little use to me."

At a nod from Ashwin, Martin left the room and fetched a glass of water, which seemed almost sacrilege beneath the Ashwinian roof. When he returned, the exposition had already been resumed.

"Meanwhile," Ashwin was saying, "my attention had been strongly attracted by the very curious fact that two people entirely unconnected with Dr. Schaedel had perfect alibis for the time that he was killed, alibis, moreover, whose perfection had been quite needlessly emphasized. Miss Wood had urgently begged her friend Mary Roberts to visit her that evening. The extreme urgency of this request struck Miss Roberts as unusual, and was never explained. Also, at the exact moment of the murder Paul Lennox was typing within earshot of Mr. Lamb. His excuse for his sudden spurt of industry seemed trumped-up, and he was very careful to call Mr. Lamb's attention to the clock immediately before and after the typing period.

"These alibis needed consideration. Miss Wood's was undoubtedly genuine, but her unneeded rush call to Miss Roberts suggested that she knew that something was about to happen for which she would need an alibi. Mr. Lennox's alibi, however, did not have such a genuine ring, especially when I learned of his owning an electric phonograph and an automatic repeater for records—an attachment for which the serious music lover has very little use. The time that he was out of Mr. Lamb's sight would have been ample for him to reach Miss Wood's home, strike his blow, and return. He could place upon the phonograph a theatrical sound-effect record of a typewriter, adjust the repeater, and go calmly off—having, of course, previously typed the paper which he was later to show Mr. Lamb as the result of his twenty minutes' work.

"Two things more made me suspicious of Mr. Lennox. One was—a minor detail—his unwarranted surprise when Mr. Bruce entered Mr. Lamb's room on the night of the murder. The other was his elaborate narrative of the Seven of Calvary, which, as I have already explained, I tended to consider fictitious.

"Now, if I was inclined to believe Mr. Lennox the murderer, and he and Mr. Bruce had already been shown to be the only possible victims, it followed that Mr. Lennox had intended to murder Mr. Bruce. The one remaining question was: Why?"

Dr. Ashwin paused. The explanation so far was familiar ground to Martin; his chief interest lay in watching the expressions of the others. Kurt grew more intense with each moment; Martin had never realized how fond the young Swiss was of his dead uncle until he saw his reactions to this narrative of murder. Dr. Griswold nodded with scholarly appreciation at each fresh point which Ashwin made. Alex looked on impassive; he might have been the merest curious auditor rather than a central figure in the story.

"Liquor," Dr. Ashwin resumed didactically, "is, in my opinion, man's greatest friend. A dog I have never thought comparable to a bottle of good scotch. But dogs are at least faithful creatures, and liquor is notoriously treacherous, despite its many kindnesses. If it were not for the treachery of (if I remember aright) bad bourbon, I might never have been able to answer that question: *Why?* Even to those who knew them well, Paul Lennox and Cynthia Wood seemed only superficial, if mildly antagonistic, acquaintances. But Mr. Lamb, on the occasion of what he describes as a 'Morris party', discovered and fortunately, despite his own condition, remembered the following facts: That Cynthia Wood was in love with Lennox and in all likelihood his mistress, and that Lennox was instituting an affair of sorts with the wife of a faculty member. This latter point seemed at times, in my consideration of the case, to offer a promising lead; but since it proved a blind alley, there is no need to provoke further scandal than necessary by naming names.

"But even knowing that Mr. Lennox was Miss Wood's lover, I was not much forrader. If he had attained her favors without interference from Mr. Bruce, the holder of a prior claim, and if, moreover, he was already casually unfaithful to Miss Wood, why in God's name should he wish to kill Mr. Bruce? And then I committed my one act of rash hypothesizing. Miss Wood, I remembered, was an heiress to no inconsiderable fortune. Let us suppose, I thought, that Mr. Lennox's true object is not Miss Wood's doubtless delectable exotic body, but rather her father's even more delectable money. Then he should marry her. Well, why doesn't he? Query: A previous marriage? Second query: To Mr. Bruce, the most likely candidate? Objection: But even so, couldn't he persuade Miss Wood (or Mrs. Bruce, if you prefer), who is so obviously—from Mr. Lamb's narrative—passionately enamoured of him, to divorce this unnecessary husband? Why kill him?

"And then I remembered the religion of Robert R. Wood. Not only is Mr. Wood a Roman Catholic, he is a convert to the faith, with all the rabid fanaticism which characterizes the convert. He is insistent that his daughter follow rigidly every precept of the Church. To eat ham on Friday delights her because it is a wild defiance of parental authority. She is forced to report to him each week on the subject of the sermon for the preceding Sunday. Obviously, if his daughter were to be guilty of divorce and remarriage, both she and her second husband would be disinherited forever from the Wood fortune.

"You will object that all this is mere hypothesis. But I have shown already the practical certainty that Paul Lennox killed Dr. Schaedel in error for Alex Bruce. And if there is no other possible explanation for such a killing, I feel, on the time-honored Holmesian principle, that I was justified in treating my hypothesis almost as a fact.

"The events of the night of April 6th now become clear. Miss Wood (it is simpler to continue to use her maiden name) invited Mr. Bruce to call on her that evening, and then sent a hurried request to Mary Roberts to come over, in order that she might have a witness to her innocence. If Mr. Bruce had called, she would have found some pretext for sending him home at exactly eleven thirty; Miss Robert's presence would also help in avoiding a protracted farewell which might disrupt the time schedule. But Mr. Bruce, as I believe merely by chance, happened to forget the appointment and worked overtime at the laboratory, thereby saving his own life and, indirectly, causing the death of Dr. Schaedel.

"Paul Lennox had meanwhile invited Mr. Lamb to his room and

brought the conversation, at the proper time, around to some notes which he wished to discuss, but which needed to be typed. Then, after calling attention to the time, he dismissed Mr. Lamb, set his phonograph alibi going, and slipped out of the room, with a new and quite unidentifiable ice pick. He lay in wait in front of Miss Wood's house, having arrived just after the innocent Dr. Schaedel had stopped to ask the time and his way to International House. Seeing a man of ordinary height and build, dressed in a gray suit, come from the door at the time stipulated in the schedule, Lennox naturally took the man for Mr. Bruce. You too, Mr. Ross, admitted to making the same mistake momentarily when you saw your uncle enter Miss Wood's house."

Kurt nodded silently.

"We shall pass over the next few moments quickly. They are not pleasant. Lennox stabbed his victim, dropped beside him a symbol (which was at that time absolutely meaningless and intended simply as a red herring), and suddenly felt himself seized by Mr. Ross. He slipped away, however, unrecognized, made his way quickly back to International House, and carried out the rest of his alibi procedure, without realizing as yet the terrible mistake that he had made.

"In the meantime, Miss Wood and Miss Roberts had heard the one brief cry of Dr. Schaedel, but had been prevented from reaching the scene of the crime quickly enough by reason of Miss Wood's fortunate stumble—a point which, together with the obvious necessity of a careful time schedule, helped make me positive of her complicity. The rest is for the newspapers.

"You have often told me, Mr. Lamb, how much impressed you were with Mr. Lennox as an actor—how he seemed, despite lack of training, to have that natural genius which makes for great acting. And surely few greater performances have ever been given than that of Mr. Lennox on the night of the murder. He had just finished establishing his alibi, everything was secure . . . when into your room walks the man whom he had just murdered. He did give way to one sudden start, which all but upset your precious bourbon; but from then on, to judge by your narrative, he was superb. I doubt if he drank much; in his place I should have been afraid to, for fear of accidental self-revelation. But he entered fully into the spirit of the binge, seemed as magnificently intoxicated as any of you, and sang one of the greatest bawdy ballads in the language, while all the time the question tormented him: *Whom have I killed?*

"When he did learn the identity of his victim, a brilliant idea occurred to him. The symbol had had no meaning when first he invented it; he had simply left it because it seemed to indicate the crime of a more flamboyant person than he was thought to be. In actual fact, I believe Mr. Lennox to have been as intensely theatrical as the Fonseca drama in which he starred; but among his better acting performances was that of the quiet, sardonic, pipe-smoking young scholar. And this hidden theatrical flair, combined with a very practical desire to create a convincing false trail, led him to invent the Vignards.

"And this, gentlemen, is where I underestimated his ingenuity. When he rolled off such resounding authorities as Werner Kurbrand's *Volksmythologie der Schweiz* and Ludwig Urmayer's *Nachgeschichte des gnostischen Glaubens* —books of which I had never heard in any of my researches—I confidently expected them to prove fruits of his admirable imagination. I wrote to the University of Chicago library, where he claimed to have encountered them, and was amazed to receive, not a letter of disclaimer, but the books themselves. It was another touch worthy of the cautious Mr. Lennox. I read the volumes through carefully; and while they contain nothing definitely substantiating the Vignard legend, there are odd hints and unexplained references which probably would dovetail smoothly with the material in the destroyed notebook. Doubtless Mr. Lennox had come across these works in his researches at Chicago; and the memory of these ambiguous passages aided him when he came to concoct his mighty myth.

"It was a good piece of invention, and I admire him for it. He knew enough of similar curious sects to invent one which was just sufficiently fantastic to be completely plausible. He told his yarn under a pledge of utter secrecy, but with an inner conviction that at least one member of the group would feel it his duty to give the story to the police and to the newspapers. Richard Worthing was the perfect person to do so; and his resultant predicaments have been among the few glimpses of humour in this whole case.

"There, gentlemen, are my reasonings on the first murder; and allow me, before I proceed, to point out to you that all the facts upon which I base them were known to Mr. Bruce, as was also my theory of the erroneous murder." Dr. Ashwin paused.

"Why did not you do something?" Kurt cried. "My uncle was dead and you knew who had killed him; yet you do nothing. I cannot understand it."

"It seems to me," Dr. Griswold interposed, "that there was nothing that he could do. The chain of reasoning is all highly ingenious; and I, for one, find it completely convincing. But there is very little evidence which could appear in a court of law."

"That I admit," sighed Ashwin reluctantly. "All that I can definitely prove is that Paul Lennox's Vignard story is, in essence, unsubstantiated, as my reply from Chicago demonstrates, and that he did have in his possession, on the night of April 6th, a sound-effect record such as his alibi required. Mr. Lamb, perhaps you had best relate what you discovered in San Francisco?"

Martin told briefly his experience with the clay-smoking old clerk, including the identification of Alex as an earlier inquirer.

"You do get around, Martin," was Alex's only comment.

"Last Sunday," Ashwin resumed, "I gave Mr. Lamb a little list of the points which he should consider in order to reach my conclusions. With the permission of the rest, I shall explain them henceforth as I go along, lest Mr. Lamb accuse me of cryptic charlatanry. To date we have covered the first three—that is:

A: THE POINT OF THE FATHER'S RELIGION.
B: THE POINT OF THE SUPERFLUOUS ALIBI
(*which is two points*).
and C: THE POINT OF THE FORTUNATE STUMBLE

—all of which, I hope, are now clear.

"Thus we have finished with the first murder, which is, I firmly believe, solved as fully as ever it will be, even though legal proof is incomplete. Before you raise objections, allow me to discuss the remaining appearances of the Seven of Calvary. But first I should like to suggest a brief rest—preferably wordless. . . ."

"I think you might resume your discussion," Dr. Griswold suggested after some five minutes of restful silence.

"Very well." Dr. Ashwin finished off his glass and turned again to face his guests, who roused themselves anew to sharp attentiveness. "I have now brought my résumé up to Thursday, April 19th—the night of the dress rehearsal of *Don Juan Returns*. At that point I was completely checkmated; I felt sure that I had solved the murder of Dr. Schaedel, and I felt almost equally sure that another attempt would soon be made on the life of Mr. Bruce; and yet I could do nothing but ask Mr. Lamb to watch carefully the two men involved.

"And then came the poisoning of Paul Lennox. You were all present on that occasion; I need not refresh your memories. With this event, I failed lamentably, for once, to perceive the obvious. Instead my mind leaped to what might be called the pseudo-obvious—to the thought that here at last was the real murder, for which the other had been in the nature of a miscued rehearsal. This would mean that Paul Lennox had been the intended victim of the first killing, and that the murderer of Dr. Schaedel must be sought among those who had a motive for killing Lennox. It was this, I may add, that led me into futile speculations concerning the previously mentioned professor and his wife.

"I confess even to have entertained briefly the theory that the story of the Vignards might be true, and that Mr. Lennox had indeed been killed because of his knowledge of the sect. But this theory was disposed of finally when the real killer of Lennox rifled his room—left unlocked in its owner's excitement on the previous evening—and tore from a certain notebook those pages dealing with the Vignards, leaving on a previous page enough to show what had been stolen. As I explained at some length to Mr. Lamb, a true Vignard would have stolen the entire notebook. But since later events agree in exposing the Vignards as a myth, there is no use in elaborating this point here. I may merely add that Mr. Lennox had doubtless written up this matter of the Vignards in an old notebook (the preceding pages on Jean Stauffacher and the history of Lausanne are probably genuine) in case he should be called upon to substantiate his story.

"But there were many objections to considering Mr. Lennox as the originally intended victim. For one thing, there was no indication that he had proposed going to Miss Wood's on the night of April 6th. But most important, I could find no flaw in the case which I had built up against him as the likely murderer—a case now fully substantiated by the answer from Chicago and by the evidence of Mr. Lamb's clay-smoking old gentleman.

"I resolved for the moment simply to try to find Mr. Lennox's killer without reference to the first murder, and considered the classic trinity of Motive, Means, and Opportunity. Motive, because of the complex emotional situation I have already outlined, gave me a plethora of suspects, all of whom also had opportunity. Means pointed chiefly, although not necessarily exclusively, to the chemical student Alex Bruce. And a comparison of memory between Mr. Lamb and Dr. Griswold showed us further that it was Mr. Bruce who had broken the glass of stage wine, and therefore almost certainly Mr. Bruce who had earlier prepared the other glass.

"The next three points which I suggested to Mr. Lamb are those which led me out of this impasse to the solution which must already be clear to the rest of you. The first was Mr. Lamb's description of a brief bit of dialogue overheard by him at the 'Morris party.' Mr. Bruce, impressed by my theory of the erroneous murder, was expounding it to Mr. Lennox, who seemed disproportionately anxious to dissuade Mr. Bruce from such a belief. This is

D: THE POINT OF THE DISPUTED THEORY.

"The second was the great diversity in means between the two murders, a diversity so great as to imply either different agents or some striking necessity for change. This point

E: THE POINT OF THE VARYING WEAPONS

led me directly into the next as I asked myself, 'Why did Paul Lennox have to die at that moment of that play?' I found the answer on reading Mr. Lamb's translation. You must all remember the speech during which the poison was entering Mr. Lennox's system. I shall forbear reading it aloud to you; I fear that my declamatory style is ill suited to sixteenth century rodomontade. But its essence is this: Don Juan knows that he is about to die at the hands of the avenging Don Félix. He says, in effect, 'I know that this is, from your point of view, a just killing; I have seduced, I have murdered, I have gloried in my crimes. But rather than perform abject penance and beg you for my life, I prefer to die in my full glory as lecher and murderer.' And these, gentlemen, were the last coherent words of Paul Lennox."

As Dr. Ashwin paused, the silence of the room grew loud. Martin himself had not realized the dread appropriateness of that speech, nor why that scene had been chosen for a killing. Now it was too clear, and he shuddered. Alex sat unmoved.

"Thus," Ashwin resumed, it was

F: THE POINT OF THE SEVILLIAN TIRADE

which brought me closest to the truth. And it was the murderous attack upon Mr. Bruce which confirmed me in my new belief, and led me to pin my faith on

G: THE POINT OF THE EYE AND THE TOOTH.

I had fallen into the grievous error, fostered no doubt by my fondness for mystery novels, of believing that a series of murders involving a strange symbol must all be traced to one murderer. Now I saw that each attack was simply a logical consequence of the previous one.

"I have explained how I had reasoned that Paul Lennox must be the murderer of Dr. Schaedel. I now believe that Mr. Bruce, knowing my theory that the first murder was a mistake and having his interest stirred by Mr. Lennox's obvious unwillingness to have him believe in that theory, proceeded to form the same conclusions as I. He had the same facts to work with, and I do not know what corroborative details. His opinion was probably confirmed beyond doubt when he learned that Paul Lennox had indeed rented the typewriter record needed for his alibi. He felt, as did I, that the scheduled killing, with himself as victim, would in time still take place; and he resolved to forestall it by killing Lennox first.

"The symbol of the Seven of Calvary he left under the poisoned glass probably to indicate that Lennox was the source of the symbol; and he chose that moment of your play, Mr. Lamb, in order to provide Paul Lennox with a most appropriate dying utterance—a grim piece of humor. Afterwards, not only to clear himself but also, I hope, to clear possible innocent suspects, he laid two false trails leading to the Vignards—one, the notebook; the other, the sign on Richard Worthing's door. But, clever though the crime was, one person other than I saw through it. That person, needless to say, was Paul Lennox's accomplice in the first murder, Cynthia Wood Bruce, who knew that one person and only one had a motive for killing her lover and leaving the Seven beside him—his intended victim. So she, in turn, sought an eye for an eye and a tooth for a tooth by shooting Mr. Bruce and hurling at him that damnable symbol, thereby rounding out

G: THE POINT OF THE EYE AND THE TOOTH."

Again Dr. Ashwin paused and filled his glass. "Gentlemen," he said, "I believe that that concludes my exposition."

The group sat in silence for a full minute. Then Alex spoke. "Dr. Griswold's first objection still holds; you know that very well. You've no proof."

"I know that, Mr. Bruce. For my part, I want no proof. Self-defense has always seemed to me the strongest of justifications."

Alex smiled slowly. "I admit nothing, you understand."

"I understand."

"But since you are so ingenious, Dr. Ashwin, at perceiving the obvious, allow me to remind you that the case is not yet closed. The third attack was a failure, and I am still alive."

"And, you wish to imply, in peril of your life? True."

"Well?" Alex spread his hands and looked questioningly at Dr. Ashwin.

"Well . . . I understand that you admit nothing, Mr. Bruce, but, if my theories were correct, this is the advice that I should give: Make out a complete statement of all you know concerning the case. Add to it the evidence of the old man at Zolotoy's and, if you wish, the corroborating evidence which I received from Chicago. Make clear beyond a doubt why you killed Paul Lennox (granting always my suppositions) and why he had wished to kill you and with whose aid. Seal this statement and turn it over to someone whom you trust—I offer myself as a candidate for the position—with instructions to hand the contents over to the police and the newspapers in case of your sudden death. Inform your assailant of what you have done. I think she will realize that the publication of such a document, even though its statements are incapable of legal proof, would be sufficient to ruin her forever in the eyes of the world and, even more important, in the eyes of her father. However much she loved her lover, however much she wishes to avenge his death, I cannot help believing that she loves her own life and her financial security even more."

Alex thought a moment and then nodded. "Thanks," he said. "That seems like good advice—of course, granted the premises. Anything else?"

"Yes," Dr. Ashwin replied emphatically. "For God's sake get a divorce!"

The ensuing half-hour was anticlimactically pleasant. Aided ably by Dr. Griswold, Ashwin turned the conversation to general literary topics, and the evening ended as a quiet and cultured symposium.

At last Alex Bruce rose. "I'm afraid I must be getting home," he said. "I want to do a good bit of writing this evening. Thank you for your hospitality, Dr. Ashwin; I think I shall drop into your classroom tomorrow. I may have something to give you."

Kurt also rose. "I shall walk home with you, Alex," he offered. "I should ever regret it were anything to happen." His words were ordinary enough, but in his voice Martin read an intense feeling of gratitude toward the man who had avenged his uncle.

Martin lingered for one more glass of scotch, after first fetching a second glass of water for Dr. Griswold, who had sat in blinking silence during the farewells. At last, sipping his chaste drink, he spoke. "It was an admirable exposition, Ashwin," he said. "I should describe it, however, as a piece of criticism rather than of scholarship. You have offered conviction rather than proof."

"It is probably just as well." Ashwin settled back in his swivel chair. "If I had had definite proof, my conscience might have rebuked me for not going to the police—as I assuredly should not have done. I am not a sentimentalist who condones murder, but I feel that Mr. Bruce had quite as much right as the State—more, if anything—to execute the murderer of Dr. Schaedel."

Dr. Griswold nodded. "And you, Martin, as a loyal Watson, are you completely satisfied with your master's exposition of the case?"

Martin roused himself. "All but one thing. Dr. Ashwin, you mentioned all of your supposedly helpful little points but the last—

H. THE POINT OF THE SEVEN OF CALVARY."

"Mr. Lamb, you are a slave-driver. For this I shall punish you mercilessly when we commence reading the *Hitopadeça* on Friday. The Seven of Calvary was at first a completely meaningless symbol—a pointless red herring, to mix metaphors. Thanks to Mr. Lennox, it assumed a false meaning as the symbol of a non-existent sect. And thanks to Mr. Bruce and Miss Wood, it assumed an even more confusing meaning as a symbol of private vengeance.

"On each appearance, the Seven of Calvary had a different meaning. The first, or Schaedel-Seven, meant nothing. The second, or Lennox-Seven, meant '*Here lies the murderer of Dr. Schaedel.*' The third, or Worthing-Seven, meant '*Boogie, boogie, boogie! Here come the Vignards!*' And the fourth, or Bruce-Seven, meant '*Paul Lennox can still strike, even from beyond the grave.*' "

"Then the point . . . ?"

"The Point of the Seven of Calvary, Mr. Lamb, is that it had no point." With which Dr. Ashwin poured the last drops from his bottle of Highland Cream.

POSTLUDE

I poured the last of the coffee as Martin finished his narrative.

"Well Tony," he asked lightly, "are you content?"

"Content with Ashwin's explanations? Quite, and rather inclined to kick myself around a block or two. But I would like some footnotes."

"Footnotes?"

"A little of the what-became-of-who business."

Martin settled back in a manner which reminded me of his descriptions of Ashwin in the swivel chair. Their corruptions had apparently been mutual. "Alex," he began, "apparently carried out Dr. Ashwin's suggestion. At least I know that he gave him a large sealed envelope and that the Seven of Calvary never appeared again. He got his divorce in Reno, and I think that Robert R. Wood knew as little of his daughter's divorce as he did of her marriage. Alex has a decent job now with a chemical firm, and is engaged to a pleasant sweet girl. I introduced them—I always do—rates on request. The rest of Cynthia's life story is too long to go into now; I'll tell it to you some other time. Suffice it that she's quite lived up to her early promise."

"And the others?"

"The Leshins returned to Europe in May and never came back to Berkeley, although I heard that a very good offer had been made him. He was an excellent lecturer. Associations, I suppose. . . . For the same reason, I refused when Drexel wanted to try *Don Juan Returns* again the next semester. It was produced eventually by the Federal Theatre Project in Los Angeles, with quite astounding criminological results. Maybe it really is a jinx play . . . but that's another story, and an even longer one."

"And Kurt?"

"The illness of General Pompilio Sanchez proved fatal, which effectively removed the necessity of Lupe's marrying her father's choice. She and Kurt are married now and living in Los Angeles—very happy when last I saw them, with an amazing infant which has Kurt's features and Lupe's complexion. Don't ask me what became of Boritsin and Worthing—I haven't the least idea, and don't much care."

"Two more questions, Martin. I am a strict host who exacts payment in full for French toast and bacon."

"And worth it at that. What are they?"

"Has Ashwin had any further chances of proving his detective ability?"

"Tony," Martin smiled, "I begin to suspect your motives . . . But I tell you what—We'll both call on him some night soon and you can get all the fascinating facts. The Maskeleyne cipher ought to appeal to you, and that odd business about the Angel's Flight—a problem that really should belong to Dr. Fell. But the other question?"

"What's become of the entrancing Mona?"

"Oh," a little too carelessly, "she's still in Berkeley. And that reminds me, Tony—mind if I use your phone?"

I nodded, and Martin stepped eagerly into the next room. As I lit a cigarette and began in my mind to frame Martin's narrative into possible shape for a novel, I could hear his voice.

"Hello. International House? . . . May I speak to Miss Morales, please?"

Well, I thought, a love story needn't necessarily spoil the novel.

EXPLICIT

Nine Times Nine

This locked room is dedicated to
JOHN DICKSON CARR
facile princeps and prince of facility

The characters in this book are completely fictitious. There is no religious order called the Sisters of Martha of Bethany. There is, at the time of writing, no cult in Los Angeles called the Temple of Light, though Lord knows what there may be before publication date. The description of wet weather in Los Angeles on Friday, March 29, 1940, is a base canard; the rain held off that week-end until Saturday.

ONE

Long after the power of the Nine Times Nine had been destroyed forever, Matt Duncan was checking through back files of Los Angeles newspapers, making notes for a feature article on the fitful and futile censorship of burlesque. The subject had good possibilities; you could illustrate it with newsphotos of vice squad investigators giving demonstrations. . . . Matt grinned over his work and even forgot, for minutes at a time, to be annoyed by the library's no-smoking regulation.

But as he went through the plump edition of Easter Sunday, 1940, he began to forget burlesque. One small item after another sprang from the page in purposeful montage. Matt supposed that he had read the paper the morning it appeared. He must have; but he could not recall having read these squibs. They had been meaningless then; his eyes had glanced bluntly off the names of Harrigan and Marshall and Ahasver. But he could see it now; this was the case in miniature—a dossier of foreboding.

The first piece of this collection had clearly been written by a young reporter who hoped some day to be a columnist:

EASTER POSTPONED A WEEK

Thanksgiving may have come a week early in 1939, but here's some consolation to make up for it. In 1940 Easter comes a week late.

But don't let this influence your vote in the presidential primaries. This is one shock to tradition that doesn't come from Washington.

In fact, according to Ahasver, the religious leader of the Children of Light, it isn't a shock to tradition at all. It is tradition. Ahasver knows. He was there.

Because Ahasver, you see, is the Wandering Jew. At least that's what he says, and when you sit in the Temple of Light and watch the neon shining on his famous yellow robe, you somehow don't feel inclined to argue about a little point like that.

"The gospels are in error," Ahasver announced to the world yesterday. "The only true Gospel is the Gospel of Joseph of Arimathea, which I found three years ago in a Tibetan lamasery; and there you will read that Christ was crucified on the Friday following the Passover, as I too remember.

"Therefore we Children of Light will make this small beginning here in Los Angeles to celebrate the true date of Easter. In time all Christianity shall join us."

Your reporter was so impressed with this first-hand testimony that he forgot to ask the Man in the Yellow Robe if anyone had bothered to notify the Easter Bunny.

The Children of Light, Matt thought as he read, did sound funny then. They were fair game for any cub who could type gags faster than he could think. Matt wondered if this same reporter had written any of the later stories, when all Los Angeles debated about Ahasver, when many saw the Light and more talked of lynching—but nobody laughed.

The next item had its humorous side, perhaps, but in this case the reporter had chosen to ignore it:

LAWYER RESUMES PUBLIC ACTIVITY

"Silence is good for a man's soul."

This was the explanation vouchsafed last night by R. Joseph Harrigan, eminent Los Angeles attorney, for his forty-day absence from political activity.

"In the present state of the nation," Harrigan said at the post-Lenten banquet of the Knights of Columbus, "no man can trust himself to open speech without danger of falling into the deadly sin of Anger. For this reason, I have abstained from all public speaking during Lent.

"But a man owes a duty to his country as well as to his soul, and I rejoice that my time of silence is past. I ask grace to keep me from anger, but I pray that I may never lose the power of righteous indignation."

As usual, Harrigan's speaking schedule is once more crowded. This week he will address the League of Women Voters, the Young Republicans, the Associated Farmers, and the Holy Name Society.

The next was a small notice hidden in a corner:

CHAPEL DEDICATED

Tomorrow, Easter Monday, the new chapel of the Sisters of Martha of Bethany will be consecrated by Archbishop John J. Cantwell. The chapel is the gift of Ellen Harrigan and is dedicated to the memory of Rufus Harrigan, pioneer Angeleno.

The third Harrigan item was on the book page:

Fleece My Sheep, by A. Wolfe Harrigan. *Revised edition.* Venture House. New edition of the standard work on phony religious rackets. Indispensable reading—especially in Los Angeles.—M. L.

These four fragments, Matt supposed, the ideal armchair reasoner could have pieced together as early as that Easter Sunday. Wolfe Harrigan's name would have linked him with the charitable Ellen and the oratorical R. Joseph, and the subject of his book might have indicated some connection with Ahasver. But not even Mycroft Holmes, in the stilly recesses of the Diogenes Club, could have connected these four notices with the fifth:

BODY IDENTIFIED

The mangled body found last Wednesday on the tracks near the Union Depot has been identified as J. J. Madison, 51, retired taxidermist, of 2234 Palermo drive, it was learned today. Identification was established by Detective Lieutenant Terence Marshall, who traced the serial number on the battered pair of spectacles found beside the body.

The inquest, postponed pending identification, will be held tomorrow.

Good work, that identification, thought Matt; but, of course, he would expect that of Marshall now. He wondered how that inquest had come out, and what the retired taxidermist would think of being involved, even so indirectly as this, with what the papers were to call the Astral Body Murder.

The next item the hypothetical Mycroft might have fitted in more readily:

JURY SPLITS ON "SCRYER"

Hermann Sussmaul, better known as the Swami Mahopadhyaya Virasenanda, was free to scry again yesterday, when Judge Warren Hill discharged the jury which had failed to reach a verdict in his trial for obtaining money under false pretenses.

Sussmaul received the nickname of "The Town Scryer" from a local columnist when he was indicted by the grand jury on charges of reading the future for lonely ladies in pools of different colored ink. The color used was said to vary according to the price paid.

Hall of Justice gossips put the vote at 11 to 1 for conviction.

The last of the items had, of course, no direct bearing on the question of the yellow robe, save as it accounted for Matt's own entrance into the case. It read simply:

22 WRITERS DROPPED FROM PROJECT

Necessary retrenchments in WPA expenditures, together with difficulties in securing the required local sponsorship, occasioned the dismissal as of the end of this month of 22 members of the local writers' project, it was announced yesterday.

That was the one of those six items which Matt had read carefully on that Easter Sunday morning.

The story, he learned at the office Monday (while the Harrigan Memorial Chapel of the Sisters of Martha of Bethany was being consecrated), had slipped into print prematurely. Personnel wasn't handing out the pink slips yet—wouldn't even announce who was to get them until the end of the week. The idea probably was that a man who knew he was being fired anyway might scamp his work in the interim—the sort of thing a bright-eyed efficiency boy might think up, in inhuman ignorance of the effect on the whole staff of not knowing where the ax would fall.

And if it fell—well, it had fallen on him often enough before in private industry. You were taken on last, so you're the first to be dropped. Maybe you get another job, the firm retrenches, you're a new man again, and so back to the old routine—daytimes hunting a job, night times turning out pulps—sometimes selling them and more often not. Matt was still young, but he had developed a certain resentful resignation by now. He only smiled now if he thought of the days when he used to have money enough to take a girl out and she'd burble, "So you're a writer! My, that must be exciting!"

Matt tried not to think about the ax. He sweated valiantly at the history of the so-called mission church of Our Lady of the Angels just as though he was going to stay on and finish the job. But sometimes, underneath his industry, there came a sneaking hopeless wish that he believed the things he was reading about, so that he could at least ease his mind by a brief prayer to avert that pink slip.

Not that it would have done any good. As Sister Ursula often told him later, prayers are answered if it is best for us; and if he hadn't been one of the twenty-two, he would (to produce a masterful understatement) have missed some interesting experiences.

Anyone who told him this, however, on that dismal last Friday in March would have been inviting destruction. That was when the slips came out, and Matt knew that he was one of the twenty-two.

A week before, on Good Friday, he had gone down to the mission church by the Plaza, subject of his research, and listened to as much as he could take of the Three Hours' service. He had felt no religious emotions, but he had been oddly impressed by the phenomenon of a day of sorrow—twenty-four hours chosen out of the bright cycle of the sun and neatly vested in black. A sort of spiritual eclipse. He could not understand it at the time—an hour is an hour; what happens in that hour determines its color, not the day on which it chances to fall. But now, as he walked along the garishness of Main Street on the evening of this second and darker Friday, he began to understand.

It wasn't that he'd thought of the Writers' Project as anything permanent. There was youthful arrogance and scorn in his feelings for some of the older men of the project—career men, as he termed them diplomatically. But he had wanted to leave at his own time—when his own unsubsidized writing could support him. It hadn't been easy—doing eight hours of research at the office or the library and then coming home to hammer out a hopefully slanted short short or (with more pleasure but less hope) another chapter of that endlessly sprawling novel which might sometime take recognizable shape. But there had been a certain security about it. No matter how many rejections piled up in the bureau drawer, there was still the check from the project. And now . . .

He had thought that a burlesque show might relieve him. But now, in the unreserved top of the balcony, he felt a certain sense of sacrilege at allowing such roundly foul buffoonery to obtrude upon his black mood. He walked out in the midst of a promising strip number and found the nearest bar.

"Want to buy me a drink?" asked the girl in the second-hand evening gown.

"No," said Matt.

"Go on. A nice-looking man like you hadn't ought to be lonely." She pushed her stool closer to his.

"I cannot buy you a drink," Matt said carefully, "because you are a phantom. The City Council and the State Board of Equalization have announced that you are no more. Main Street is cleaned up, they have told us; there is no such thing as a B-girl. So even if I buy you a drink, how can you drink it? You aren't here."

"You could try."

"No."

"All right. If that's the way you feel about it. . . ."

Matt stared into the mirror behind the bar. It would take a B-girl, he decided, to call him nice-looking. Basically, perhaps, his wasn't a bad face; but the scar didn't do it any real good. The scar ran from his left temple clear across his cheek almost to the corner of his mouth. It hadn't healed badly, considering the hasty and secret measures that had been taken when the fraternity initiation went wrong; but it did produce a certain puckering disproportion. And the unaccountable streak of white that ran through his shaggy black hair looked neither striking nor distinguished; it just made him something of a freak. He frowned into the mirror. This wasn't helping Black Friday any. Maudlin self-pity, that's what it was.

He finished the rye and pushed the small glass across the bar with a dime, a nickel, and no wasted words. While he waited for its return he watched in the mirror the B-girl's newest victim. Now this one she could call nice-looking and it would be sheer understatement. Everything was perfect from the just-high-enough forehead to the just-large-enough mustache. Even the carefully groomed hair was just-not-quite-too-slick. Well-dressed, too, for Main Street—running a terrible risk of ending the evening by being rolled.

There was something else about him, too. Something familiar. Then his long-lashed eyes met Matt's in the mirror.

"Gregory!" Matt exclaimed, and "Matt!" cried the other.

"I guess you boys want to be alone," said the B-girl, and stalked away.

If Matt had paused to think, he might have remembered that he and Gregory Randall had never exactly liked each other. In fact Gregory, a junior when Matt was a pledge, had been indirectly responsible for that scar. Even more important was the distinction of class or, to speak more accurately, the difference in the amount of money they had to spend. As a freshman in 1929, Matt had enjoyed a financial freedom which seemed fabulous to him in 1940; but even then he had not been in a class with a Randall, son of one of the half-dozen biggest brokers in Los Angeles.

But it was almost eight years since Matt had even seen Greg Randall, and such a chance reunion called for good feelings and good cheer. Besides, it might help. So the two shook hands vigorously and called each other the most warmly obscene names and asked each other what's become of Old Hungadunga until it was time for another round.

Gregory gulped his Manhattan and looked at Matt's glass. "What's that?"

"Rye."

"Drink it up and I'll join you in another. Cocktails are slow." His eye took in at once Matt's hesitation and his frayed cuffs. "This one is on me," he added, in a tone which made Matt at once grateful and resentful.

Greg took his straight rye with the gasping splutter of a man spoiled by mixed drinks. "I feel low," he said at last.

"So do I."

"Too bad." But he didn't ask why. "Yes, Matt, old man, I feel low. Low as a snake's belly or a policeman's arch or all the other bright cracks. I'm on a spot, I am."

"T. F. Randall's son on a spot? What's the System coming to?"

Greg looked puzzled. "Look here, Matt, that's a funny thing to say. You haven't gone Red or anything, have you?"

Matt grinned. "Hadn't you heard? Comes the revolution, I'm slated to be a commissar."

Randall thought about it. "I see," he said. "You're joking. But I really am in a mess, Matt."

Matt drew on his memory for the most likely explanation. "What's the matter? Have you got to marry the girl?"

"No. That's just it."

"What do you mean, that's just it?"

"I mean that's it. I don't have to. I mean, I have not to. It's the other way round. And speaking of rounds—" He gestured to the bartender.

"The other . . . Oh. You mean she won't marry you."

"Yes," sighed Gregory Randall. He caught a glimpse of himself in the mirror and took out a comb.

"I've seen your name in the gossip columns from time to time, Greg. I like to see how the other half of one per cent lives. I thought you were the catch of the season—the last several seasons in fact. Who is this coy damsel?"

"She's such a child, that's it." Gregory ended his hair-combing with a dab at each end of his mustache. "She doesn't know her own mind."

"Cradle-snatching? You're too young for that."

"You mean too old, don't you?"

"Skip it. But where's the rub?"

"Poverty, chastity, and obedience!" Greg snorted.

"I beg your pardon?"

"I said poverty, chastity, and obedience. The hell with them."

"The hell with them," Matt agreed. "They pretty much sum up the past year of my life. And the next year probably, too, if I can find anything to obey. But I never heard of a man objecting to them in a wife excepting maybe the first—and you can remedy that."

"But she won't be a wife. She wants to be a sister."

"I've heard that one before."

"No, you haven't. She doesn't want to be a sister to me. She wants to be a Sister of Martha of Bethany."

"And who might—? Oh. . . . You mean a *Sister!*"

"Yes. That's it. A sister. A nun."

"Oh." The full horror of the situation began to hit Matt in unison with the last rye. "You mean that this child wants to lock herself away from the world to become a nun?"

"That," said Gregory Randall desolately, "is exactly what I mean."

"Look." Matt fingered the dimes in his pocket. "Let's have another on me and you tell me all about this. This is serious. I mean, I thought I was on a spot but, hell, it's just what everybody's going through who isn't—if you won't start thinking I'm a Red again—who isn't a Randall. But this is different. It isn't right somehow. It's like some dark arm of the past reaching into our modern life. I want to know how things like this happen. Tell me about it. Who is this infant?"

"Infant's a bit strong, old man, but still . . . She's Concha Harrigan. Her uncle is Dad's attorney. But don't get me wrong. This isn't any of your family-arranged affairs. We met at a party and were going swell before we even knew who each other were . . . was."

"You mean she's one of *the* Harrigans?"

"You know them?" Greg seemed doubtful.

"I know about them, of course, and I've read Wolfe's books on the screwball cults that bless our fair city. Swell stuff. But Concha? That's no Irish name."

"Her mother was a Pelayo. Aristocratic old Spanish family—dons and land-grants and such. Rancho Pelayo, that they made all the subdivisions out of. Only it was old Rufus Harrigan that made the money on that. Her name's really María Concepción Harrigan Pelayo. Sometimes she even signs herself that way. She is such a kid."

"Hold on. This is going too fast. She's called Concha because her grandfather made subdivisions?"

"Sort of. It's a nickname for Concepción. I wanted to call her Mary, but she likes Concha. She says she's as much a Pelayo as a Harrigan. I don't know. One thing's sure anyway. She's not going to be a Randall."

"But why? How did she—?"

"We were engaged. Six weeks after I met her we were engaged. I know she's young, but eleven years isn't so much difference. Lots of people work out all right that way. And then her aunt . . . Well, you see, Aunt Ellen is religious. I mean they all are, the Harrigans and the Pelayos, all but Arthur, only Ellen's more so. She does good works and goes to church every day and won't eat meat on Wednesdays. You get the picture?"

"I get it."

"So Aunt Ellen decided to give the Sisters of Martha of Bethany a memorial chapel in honor of Rufus Harrigan, that eminent and sainted land-pirate."

Matt smiled. "You haven't gone Red, have you, Greg?"

"No," said Greg seriously. "What makes you think that? Anyway, this Sister Ursula starts coming around to see Aunt Ellen about arrangements, only she sees Concha, too. And you could just see her licking her chops. Such a nice girl and such a good wealthy family. Mmm! So she and Aunt Ellen go to work. Uncle Joseph and her father probably had a hand in it, too. We will give our daughter to the honor and glory of God. Poverty, chastity, and obedience!" He set his glass down with a startling thump which drowned out his monosyllable. The bartender chose to misinterpret the thump, and that was all right with everybody.

"You mean they've—they've framed this poor kid into this thing?"

"I guess you'd call it that. I never thought much about the power of the Church. I mean, you read about Jesuits and Inquisitions and such; but you think about all that as past and gone. Only when it comes into your own life like this . . . well, it's different."

"It's a damned crime, that's what it is," Matt announced vigorously. "To bust up your life to lure the Harrigan heiress into a convent. . . . Well, Greg?"

"Well?"

"Well, what the hell are you going to do about it?"

"Do about it? What can I do about it? She won't be eighteen till next month—she can't marry without her father's consent. And I'm no young Lochinvar anyway, Matt. I can't see myself carrying her off from it all."

Matt seized the fresh drink enthusiastically. "Can't you? That's just too bad."

"Why?"

"Because that's just what you're going to do."

"Look here, Matt, old man—"

Matt's voice approached exaltation. "Are you going to let this Concha child of yours be walled up for life like a heroine in a Gothic novel? The sweet hell you are. You're going to go out there and confront the Harrigan family and tell them what's what. You're going to grab Concha and tell her you love her and she's going to marry you. And what you're going to tell Sister Ursula I blush to mention. This is 1940. A girl leads her own life now without family or superstition. Are you going to let her slip through your hands?"

"But, Matt . . . " said Gregory Randall feebly.

"Have you got your car? Good. I'll drive you out; I haven't had my hand on a steering wheel in months. Make a new man of me. And we'll show the Harrigans—*and* the Pelayos—a thing or many. Come on."

It wasn't so much that Matt was tight. All the rye had done was loosen him up a little—put him on a splendid peak from which he could see the troubles of others and free himself from his own concern by godlike intervention. And so he plunged himself headlong into the lives of the Harrigans—and the tragic events that followed the Nine Times Nine.

TWO

When they came out of the bar, it had begun to rain. Nothing serious, but a persistent March drizzle.

"I think I'll stop in this drugstore," Gregory Randall said as they walked to the parking lot. He came out with a glugging parcel tucked under his arm.

"Cold medicine?" Matt asked.

"No, I don't believe in syrups. I always—Oh, I see. You mean—Yes. It is that kind of cold medicine."

"Go easy on it. We've had enough already. Remember you've got to make a good impression on the family."

As Matt slid behind the steering wheel, Greg tucked himself into the corner and unwrapped the parcel. He tore the foil off the bottle and handed it over.

"No, thanks. I think maybe I'm through drinking tonight. I'm having fun without it."

Randall took a long draught. "You understand, Matt, old man, I'm not really what you'd call a drinking man. It's just that . . . Well, I was a lot younger when you knew me. Almost as young as Concha. Things that were all very well then . . . I've got a position now, you understand. Dad's office—I wouldn't have you think that I'm just the boss's son. I'm someone in my own right."

"Who?" Matt asked.

"Who? Why—I mean, I count for something. That's why I feel it's time I got married. A man in my position. And that's why I feel I really need this. I'm not used to this sort of thing. Dashing around at night in the rain. . . ."

"Remember about the course of true love? What did you expect? Just find a girl, say. 'Look here, I think it'd be nice if we got married,' so then you marry her and settle down in your position? It isn't so simple. Hell, Greg, if you want something you've got to fight for it."

"I wouldn't like you to think I'm not a fighting man, Matt."

Glug. "Remind me to tell you about the way I handled the Warden-McKinley bond issue. But this is different. This is so—so personal."

"She's worth it, isn't she?"

"Concha," said Gregory Randall, with broad and glugging simplicity, "is worth anything."

"All right then."

It was a long drive from Main Street to the hills just west of Hollywood, but they said little more. Matt was too busy enjoying his sudden and exhilarating release from self-preoccupation and the smooth pleasure of a fine car, glidingly responsive to his touch; and Greg seemed to find the cough medicine sufficient in itself.

The rain was worse now. The neon of the city glistened with a wet radiance when they hit that splendid stretch on Sunset where the south side of the boulevard seems to fall away like a dissolving curtain and reveal the city in gleaming miniature.

Matt felt almost sober now, but his exalted mood persisted. "One thing I do understand in the Bible," he said, "is the temptation on the mountain. To see the kingdoms of the earth spread out before you. . . . That was before electricity, too. If Satan had had neon, he might have won."

Gregory Randall said nothing.

A block farther on, following the directions Greg had given him, Matt turned north and drove up a winding road with infrequent streetlights and no sign of house numbers. At the end of the road loomed an imposing building, not so vast in size (probably a mere six bedrooms, Matt calculated), but still with something of old-fashioned massiveness about it. Definitely not a house—a mansion.

Matt slowed down and turned to his companion. "Is that the place?"

The only answer was a snore.

Matt pulled up to the curb, then leaned over and shook his passenger. From Greg's lap rolled the bottle, now nearly glugless. The next snore was louder and more resonant.

"Damn," said Matt. This was a nice howdyedo. Quite obviously Gregory had been indulging in purest truth when he said he was not a drinking man. Even a man with a position should recognize the parlous borderline between stimulating the nerves and passing out.

But Greg or no Greg, Matt had come here on a mission. Childe Rowland to the dark tower came and things. There was a maiden in distress—

Matt had started out without an overcoat—not that his threadbare remnant would have made much difference in this downpour. Greg was wearing a beautiful camel's hair coat, which he obviously did not need in the seclusion of the closed coupé. Matt's earlier

unconscious prophecy was coming true; Gregory Randall was doomed to end the evening by being rolled.
It was not easy to remove an overcoat from an inert snoring mass. Twice Matt found himself slapped in the face by a flabby hand, and once, as he was being rolled about, Gregory opened his lips, though not his eyes.
"Think nothing of it," he said genially, and relapsed into chaos.
Matt wrapped the sumptuous coat around himself and started out to the dark tower.

There was a butler. There would be. It is rumoured that the middle class of other countries takes servants calmly, as a matter of course; but no American under the rank of economic royalist is happy in the presence of a man whose occupation and manner combine to murmur politely, "I am, sir, your inferior." When this same manner is accompanied, as in this case, by an eyebrow quirk which adds the qualification, "In a pig's eye," the difficulties of the situation are intensified.
Matt's fine fervor was fading. Childe Rowland may have faced an ogre, but never a butler. "I should like," he said as bravely as he could, "to see Miss Harrigan."
It was probably the camel's hair coat that did the trick. Obviously no one completely beneath notice could possess such a garment.
"Is she expecting you?" the butler went so far as to say.
"I—well, I have an important message for her."
"And what is the name?"
"Matthew Duncan."
"Please step in here. I shall inquire if she will see you."
He retired. The British spirit of compromise had triumphed; he had admitted the intruder, but had not said sir.
The full tide of chivalry had pretty thoroughly ebbed from Matt's bosom. He was well on the way to deciding that he had made a damned fool of himself. If the butler had returned twenty seconds later, he might have found an empty hallway.
"This way, please," the man enunciated—there was no other word for it. "Miss Harrigan will see you."
Matt wondered what she would be like. Almost all he knew specifically was her age and her mixed lineage. An Iberian Hibernian of seventeen, however, was promising enough. A brunette she would be—that much was more than likely. A good deal of temper probably—temper that would certainly be vented full on his hapless head. If he had only had the sense to turn around and drive Greg home. . . .
"Mr. Duncan," the butler announced, opening a door.
Matt smelled incense as he came in. That puzzled him. He somehow hadn't pictured her as the exotic type. Then he saw the

odd-looking sort of madonna opposite the door and the candles burning in front of it. This was worse yet. The devout type. Maybe after all she belonged in a—

"Yes, Mr. Duncan?" said a quietly sharp voice.

He looked away from the shrine. In a carved oak chair, resembling an individual-size pew, sat a small elderly woman, dressed in formless black. Her right hand, resting on the arm of the chair, dangled a long chain of brown wooden beads, which seemed only slightly smaller replicas of her intense little eyes.

"You find me at my evening devotions," she said. There was no tone of explanation or apology—simply a statement of fact and an implied hope that she would not be long interrupted.

"I . . . I asked to see Miss Harrigan," Matt ventured.

"I am Miss Harrigan."

Then Matt remembered. The religious Aunt Ellen, the source of all this trouble—naturally, she was Miss Harrigan. The butler would interpret literally according to formal usage: the girl would be Miss Concha—no, you couldn't say that. Miss Mary, perhaps? Miss Concepción?

Aunt Ellen also understood. "From your confusion, young man, I take it that you wished to see my niece?"

"Yes, I did. I'm sorry I interrupted you at your prayers. If you'll tell me where I can find her . . . ?"

"I am afraid she is busy at the moment. You could not see her. If there is some message that I—"

This had all gone hopelessly wrong. More than anything else, Matt simply wanted to get the hell out of there. Silence was strong in the chapel. From the next room came the sound of typing.

"I'll come back some other time," Matt said. "Sorry to have bothered you."

The door from the hall opened and a round pink face appeared. "Ellen," it said, "has Mary come down yet?"

"No, Joseph. She is still with Sister Ursula."

"It's taking a long time, isn't it? I hope she'll be able to make the child see the proper path to follow—Hello! Company at your prayers, Ellen?"

"Come in, Joseph," said Miss Harrigan. "This is Mr. Duncan—my brother, Mr. Harrigan. He came with some sort of message for Mary."

R. Joseph Harrigan stepped into the room. He was tall and solid, just this side of corpulence. His cheeks had the sleek smoothness of the well-barbered man-about-town, and his lips fell easily into the smile of one who must meet too many people. His suit was unobtrusively excellent. His lapel was empty, but you felt he must have just put the gardenia in the icebox.

"I am always glad to meet one of Mary's friends," he announced in rounded tones. "A man mustn't let himself get out of touch with the younger generation, you know."

"You say," Matt hesitated, "that Miss Harrigan is with Sister Ursula?"

"Why, yes," said Miss Ellen. "Though I—"

The lawyer withdrew his extended hand. "Exactly, young man. We fail to see what concern it is of yours if my niece chooses—"

"Oh, no concern of mine, sir. But as I said, I'm here as an envoy, so to speak; and I certainly think it is a concern of Gregory Randall's."

"Randall? He sent you here?" Joseph was patently incredulous.

"Yes." It was not an exact statement, but it would serve. "He sent me here with a message to his fiancée, and I feel that I should deliver it. Will you let me see Miss Harrigan, or is she being held incommunicado?"

This taunting phrase slipped out unpremeditated. Matt himself was amazed to hear it, and instantly more regretful than ever that he had involved himself in this embassy. R. Joseph Harrigan swelled visibly. "Young man," he puffed, "I cannot believe that any friend of Gregory Randall's would have the brazen effrontery to come here and insult us in our own home. Frankly, sir, I think this is some trick, and I must request you—"

"Please," said Ellen Harrigan. "This is a chapel."

Harrigan lowered his voice. "Quite true, Ellen. And that is all the more reason why this fellow should display some trace of common decency."

There was a pause. The typing went on in the next room, and one of the candles spluttered.

"Look," said Matt. "This is a h—a frightful mess. It's just sort of happened. I don't know how I got into it or how to get out. Let's just say quits and wash the whole thing up. I'm sorry I've offended you, and please don't hold it against Greg. There. Goodby."

He stepped to the door and tried to turn the knob. It was locked. For an instant absurdly melodramatic thoughts flashed through his mind, to be dispelled by Ellen Harrigan's calm, "That's the wrong door."

"Who's there?" said a voice on the other side, as the typing halted.

"No one, Wolfe. Just a mistake."

So the unseen typist would be A. Wolfe Harrigan, author of those excellent books on bogus cults. Matt should have liked to meet him—he imagined a quiet but brilliant scholar, so wrapped up perhaps in his researches that he did not even notice the fate which was being forced on his daughter. But there was no hope now of a social meeting with any Harrigan.

No one spoke, as Matt, feeling more completely humiliated than he had ever before felt in his life, found the right door and went out. As he reached the hall he heard Joseph Harrigan's dulcet voice.

"Ellen, that young man has been drinking."

The butler, thank God, was nowhere in sight. Matt reached the door unobserved and tightened the camel's hair coat about him before facing the wet night. Damn it all, he didn't have even intoxication to fall back on as an excuse. He had simply made a complete idiot of himself, upset an old lady at her prayers, infuriated a leading citizen, and possibly done unmeasured harm to Greg Randall's cause. And all not even for Hecuba—just for some wild quixotic notion.

He stood in the rain and looked back at the house. One thing he had not liked, and that was the smug complacency with which R. Joseph Harrigan had hoped that the nun would show the girl the proper path to follow. Perhaps he should have tried harder to see her. It wasn't pretty to think of a young girl being bludgeoned into . . .

Someone else was watching the Harrigan mansion. Matt noticed it abruptly—the sheen of a wet raincoat in the light from a window. Over at the left toward the back of the house, about (as best he could figure) where the chapel was. But the chapel had no windows at body-level—only two squares for ventilation high in the wall.

Was the house being guarded? Was that part of the plan? No, that didn't make sense. If there were guards, he himself would have been challenged before he reached the butler. Then it must be . . .

Matt's caution checked his expulsive sigh of relief. Here was something to do—no standing around chapels making a fool of yourself, but good solid direct action—to atone to the family for your stupid crassness, you told yourself in words; to compensate for your own frustration, you knew without words.

The figure had vanished now. The crack of light was a small one; it had hit the raincoat only by chance. But it might do so again; Matt kept his eyes fixed on that little beam of light as he edged his way along the wall. He could hear the typing again now; it must come from the same room as the light.

Then he saw it. A smooth plump hand reaching into the beam. The hand fumbled, as though with a catch, then seemed to push the window ever so slightly. The narrow band of light widened almost imperceptibly. The typing had stopped.

He couldn't see the body in the rain and the darkness—only the hand. A woman's—no, on second thought more probably a man's hand, despite the ornate ring, but soft and effeminate. If—

Then from the darkness came a squeal of pain. The hand vanished. For an instant the beam shone on the raincoated figure, running rapidly straight at Matt. It shone, too, on something metallic in the other hand.

And now came action, sudden, unpremeditated, and immeasurably relieving. In the wet darkness the wearer of the raincoat hurtled plump into Matt. He gasped a choking oath, and for a moment Matt felt a steel cylinder pressed against his ribs. Then something caught his foot and the two went down together onto the sodden grass.

A fight is one thing. You feel freedom and pain and exultation all at once. But this was something else. As a fighter Raincoat was beneath contempt, weak and pudgy. But his hand held a little tool which could still the sturdiest fighter.

Twice the end of that tool pressed against Matt's body. Twice, his spine shaken with a chill quivering which he might have recognized as fear if he had had time for such reflections, he jerked himself to safety. Then, with a hastily improvised twist which he could never have repeated, Matt straddled safely on Raincoat's cushiony belly, leaning forward to press down on the struggling wrist of the armed hand.

"Drop it," he said with a calm that astonished him. "There's a good Raincoat." To emphasize the request, he bounced a bit on the rubbery stomach. "Papa says to drop it."

Raincoat was pouring forth a steady flood of vigorous words in some language strange to Matt. His only other answer was to try harder than ever to free his wrist. On his other hand Matt could feel a liquid which was warmer than rain.

"I'd advise you," said a deep voice from the darkness, "to knock him out and take it away. He won't play nice."

Wherever the advice came from, it was sound. For a second Matt released the man's flaying left and drove his own right home efficiently just behind the ear. The struggles stopped abruptly.

"Neat work," said the voice. "Let's go inside."

Matt rose dripping to his feet, the small automatic now in his hand. "Who are you?" he demanded.

"Isn't that my question? After all, I live here."

"Oh. Then you're Wolfe Harrigan?"

"Courtesies later; first we'll get this hulk inside. Can't leave him to rot out here—might ruin the croquet lawn. Oh, yes, that is a croquet lawn you've been rolling about on. Come on—give a hand."

Once inside the study, Matt looked at Wolfe Harrigan in open admiration. This was no quietly brilliant scholar such as he had expected from his writings. Harrigan's height topped Matt's own six feet by a good two inches, and his whole body was built on that scale. He moved about the room—adjusting Raincoat on the sofa, closing the French windows, pouring drinks—with that easy litheness which comes only of complete and conscious muscular control. Even his steel-gray hair seemed a mark of strength rather than of age. Matt was never to see him save in this house or at the Temple of Light; but somehow his mind showed him Wolfe Harrigan on a cloud-topping mountain trail or at the wheel of a skimming sailboat.

"Here," said Wolfe. "You need a drink. And even if you don't, you probably want one." He stripped off his sopping shirt and threw it at Raincoat. "I shan't bother the family for a clean one now. The fireplace'll dry me off." He stood astraddle before the open flames. "Now, if you care to add another service to what you've already done, you might gratify my curiosity. Who the devil are you?"

"My name is Duncan—Matt Duncan."

"I didn't ask your name. I said who are you. Names tell nothing—or at most what sort of taste your parents had. The only names that mean anything are phonies—like our friend's there. The Swami Mahopadhyaya Virasenanda. . . ." He made a noise of disgust. "But he can wait. Your name, I take it, is real?"

"Yes."

"And therefore meaningless. Go on. Who are you?"

"I plead the rights of hospitality, Mr. Harrigan. My question first, before I deliver an autobiography."

"Your question, no less?" Wolfe Harrigan smiled indulgently.

But it wasn't easy to bring out. You can't simply ask a man, under such extraordinary circumstances, if he knows what is being done to his daughter. While Matt still fumbled with his beginning, a rap came on the door to the chapel.

Harrigan crossed and turned the knob. (It was one of those you lock by pressing a button from the inside.)

The young man who slouched in looked like a cheaply made reprint of Wolfe Harrigan—the same general format, but lacking the strength and beauty of the original. He seemed to lean against an invisible support as he stood, and he spoke without bothering to take the cigarette from his mouth.

"Thought you might like to know they were coming down," he said.

Harrigan hastily pulled a knit jacket over his bare torso. "And what's the decision?" he asked sharply.

"I don't know yet." The youth's eyes took in the room—the stranger in the muddy camel's hair, the unconscious body in the raincoat. "What goes on?" he wanted to know.

Wolfe Harrigan seemed to wipe away the two figures with a quick gesture. "That's not important. What does Concha say? Has Sister Ursula finally persuaded her to—"

Matt rose. "Look here, Mr. Harrigan. That's what I've come to talk about, and I'm going to. If you think—"

The young man looked him up and down. "Knight errant," he said with quiet scorn. Taking the half-smoked cigarette from his mouth, he doubled it up and tossed it at the fireplace.

"Mr. Harrigan, you've got to listen to me. Of all the people I've met in this house, you're the only one I feel I can talk to. You—"

There were voices in the chapel. "Hush," said Harrigan.

His sister Ellen moved softly into the room. She was smiling, and there were happy tears in her eyes. "Wolfe," she said. "Wolfe. She did it. Mary has agreed—"

"No!" Wolfe Harrigan let out a bellow of delight. "Ellen! It's splendid!"

Matt took a step forward. "Sir! You can't—"

In the chapel doorway stood a nun in unearthly garb. Behind her you could see another nun and R. Joseph Harrigan. The gathering of the vultures, Matt thought.

"Sister Ursula," cried Wolfe, "you're magnificent. You actually—?"

"Yes," said Sister Ursula. "Yes, I have finally talked that silly child out of becoming a nun."

THREE

Matt's heroic world turned several somersaults, ended with a neat double flip-up, and stood still.

"It was a struggle," Sister Ursula went on. "The poor girl is so young. At that age it's so easy to let your personal discontent masquerade as God's will."

"Did you . . . " Wolfe Harrigan spoke with a hesitancy in marked contrast to his former brusque self-possession. "Did you learn why she—"

Sister Ursula was grave. "We aren't priests; you know. But there was something a little like the confessional about this. So if you please—"

Wolfe turned away. "You're right, Sister."

"But I promise you, it's gone now. And we must go, too. We should have been back hours ago, but I had special dispensation from the Mother Superior. My!" she smiled. "You read about the saints sitting up with some poor sinner and struggling with the devil. I tell you it's nothing to sitting up with a poor child who wants to be a saint and struggling with what she thinks is God!"

"Arthur will drive you back," said Wolfe Harrigan.

"Thank you!" She raised her voice. "Sister Felicitas! We're going home!" She turned as she spoke, revealing Matt's presence to the indignant eyes of R. Joseph Harrigan.

"Good heavens" the lawyer spluttered. "It's the young drunk! Wolfe, what is the meaning of this?"

The elder Harrigan frowned at Matt. "You know my brother?"

"Does he know me! Listen, Wolfe. This young man broke in on Ellen at her devotions this evening and launched into the most insulting remarks about Mary. He seemed to believe that we were driving the girl into a convent against her will, and that he was the white-plumed knight who would rescue her."

"And what did you do?"

"Do? What should a man do? I threw him out." Joseph raised his chin and straightened his sleeves as though he had attended to the matter personally.

"Whereupon," Wolfe added, "he lingers around the house just long enough to save my life. Young man, I think you are assuming the status of an enigmatic figure. A little explaining mightn't be out of order."

"Your job, pop," the young Harrigan muttered through a fresh cigarette. "Screwballs are your specialty."

Matt had been watching Sister Ursula. You couldn't tell what she looked like. She might be anything. The dark blue gown hid the lines of her body, and the pale blue headdress made her face simply a pink blob gleaming above the starched white neckpiece. The skin looked smooth—almost as smooth as Joseph's—but there was no way of fixing her age. Only one thing about her was definite and personal—her blue eyes, kind and wise and understanding. The Harrigans, even Wolfe, had intimidated Matt; but in front of Sister Ursula he felt that he could tell his absurd story, with one slight bit of censorship.

"All right," he said. "I'll wash up the mystery. I'm a friend of Greg Randall's, or was. I saw him tonight for the first time in years, and we got to talking about his broken engagement. It sounded—though I can see now how foolish that was—as though there were a family conspiracy against him."

"Ridiculous!" Joseph Harrigan pronounced. "Nothing could please me more than to welcome old T. F.'s son into the family. But when a mere child is so absurdly self-willed—"

"I know. We just got the wrong picture. So we came out here to make a protest—try to break up this imagined conspiracy. Only Greg was taken ill on the way out here, and I had to drop him off and call a doctor. Then I got to thinking I should maybe go on with the plan myself—be his ambassador like. You see what it got me. So now I offer my humblest apologies—and I mean it—to all the Harrigans and most especially to you, Sister Ursula, for the strange ideas I had about you."

Arthur Harrigan crumpled another cigarette and said, "Nuts."

Sister Ursula seemed not to hear him. She smiled at Matt and said, "There's a road paved with good intentions."

"I know." Matt was shamefaced.

"But I don't agree," she added, "with the popular idea of where it leads. Come, Sister Felicitas."

At a glance from his father, Arthur shambled off after the two nuns. As he passed Matt, he gave him a look, with more pity than contempt in it.

"I'll go now, too," said Matt. "I hope—"

"Just a minute, young man," Joseph was commanding. "There's more to explain. What's all this about saving my brother's life?"

"And what," said Ellen, "is this?" She pointed at the still unconscious Raincoat.

Wolfe chuckled. "We've been having fun and games tonight children. Sit down and you shall hear all." Matt started to edge away. "You too, Duncan. Lord, man, you played a lead in this melodrama. You can't walk out on it now." Wolfe seated himself behind the desk and took up a handful of small darts. Facing him across the room hung a painted wooden target. As he spoke, he punctuated his remarks with sudden deft tosses of unvarying accuracy.

"Helpful thing, these darts," he observed. "Better than solitaire for resting the mind, and not unuseful for other purposes. If it weren't for these and Mr. Duncan, we might have had an even more exciting evening. Mary come down, by the way?"

"She's still upstairs," said Ellen. "Sister Ursula thought it would be best to leave her alone for a while."

"Good. You needn't repeat all this harrowing episode to her then. She may have been acting a bit strangely of late; but I still don't think she'd relish a threat against her father's life."

"Good heavens, Wolfe," Joseph boomed. "You don't mean that this fellow actually—"

"Show it to them, Duncan."

Matt reached into the pocket of the camel's hair and silently drew out Raincoat's automatic.

"They aren't being carried just for sport this season," Wolfe commented. "And by the way, Duncan, why not take off that mudbedaubed coat? It's warm enough in here by the fire."

Matt thought of the clothes under the coat and shook his head.

"But who is this man?" Joseph demanded. "Why should he sneak around here with a gun? And where does Duncan come in?"

"Remember the Sussmaul case that I was preparing evidence

on? The Swami who read the future in colored inks and who was turned loose last week by a hung jury?"

"Of course. And I've heard some nasty rumors around the Hall of Justice about that jury."

"Naturally, he'll come up for trial again and my evidence is still essential. Well, tonight I was working on my dossier on the Children of Light. Slow going, some of it. I have to be careful about facts and even more careful about my conclusions. At one point I was stuck; the paragraph simply would not come out the way it should. So I reared back in this chair and began tossing darts." He illustrated the action as he spoke. "Outer circle—inner circle—*and* a bull's-eye. Just like that. And my thoughts started flowing just as smoothly.

"Then I saw the hand out of the corner of my eye. See that ring on his finger? I had a good description of that from the operative I had set on him. I knew it was Sussmaul all right—or the Swami, as he prefers—and I knew he wasn't feeling too friendly towards me. I had two more darts in my hand. I used one in a possibly rather foolish manner, then turned in my chair and let the other fly plop into his hand. I don't think he liked it.

"He let out one squeal and started running. I slipped around the back way instead of straight out through the windows—I didn't want to make too good a target. I thought he'd either have vanished by then or be lurking in ambush. Fancy my delight when I found him spreadeagled on the ground with our young friend here on top of him."

"Good work, young man," the lawyer nodded grudgingly. "Though how you happened to be there I'm hanged if I can see. However, we thank you. And now, Wolfe, I suppose you intend to call the police?"

"Why?" asked Wolfe simply.

"Why?" Good heavens, can there be any question of why? Breaking and entering, carrying a concealed weapon, loitering with intent to commit a felony—and you ask why? This man is a public menace—a danger to society."

"Exactly. And that is why I shall do nothing of the kind. Our raincoated friend was discharged last week after a jury disagreed on the charges of obtaining money under false pretenses—charges largely based on evidence which I had assembled. Since then I've learned why, and you've probably guessed as much from your rumors, Joseph. One of the jurors, though he firmly swore to the contrary, was a devout follower of this man."

"Outrageous! You can have the man up for perjury."

"And again I decline. Because whatever steps I take against this man or his followers he will use as evidence of persecution. He will become a martyred leader, and more dangerous than ever. I don't want him picked up for loitering or breaking or anything else but the one charge: obtaining money under false pretenses. If I can prove to the hilt that this whole Swami business is one stinking racket, then I'll have done my work. Meanwhile I let him alone. Duncan has drawn his fangs for tonight. I doubt if he'll feel in the mood to make another attempt very soon. Before long he'll be back on trial; and this time the jury won't disagree."

"If you won't think of yourself," his brother protested, "think of Ellen and Mary. You should have a police guard on this house day and night while this dangerous lunatic is at large."

Wolfe Harrigan laughed. "I've got my darts," he said, and threw one deftly into the bull's-eye.

Joseph Harrigan rose, with an ease surprising for a man of his weight. "There's no drilling any sense into you, Wolfe. I'd best be getting home. Can I give you a lift, young man?"

Matt realized that this was a gesture of all-is-forgiven, and appreciated it. "I've got a car," he said. "Thanks all the same."

"Good night, then." The lawyer extended his hand and Matt took it. His handclasp was good—firm and sound, with nothing oily or flabby about it. Matt was beginning to realize, as had many an attorney in court, that it was easy to underestimate R. Joseph Harrigan.

"Good night, Ellen. Wolfe. I'll find my way out."

Ellen rose, too. "There's been so much happening tonight that I still have another decade to say, and if I stay up too late I might oversleep for mass. Good night, Wolfe. And Mr. Duncan."

She went with quiet dignity toward the chapel. Matt noticed that the rosary was still in her hand.

"Sit down," said Wolfe Harrigan. "No need for you to run off. Don't play darts, do you? Shame. Nobody does." He rose, plucked the darts from the target, and resumed his seat. "Now we'll go back to the inquisition. If I remember where we left off, you were about to answer my 'Who are you?' "

So Matt told him—about the comfortable middle-class childhood with a widowed mother, the mother's death halfway through his college course, the abrupt 1930 cessation of the Duncan income, the need to quit school and go to work, and the endless series of jobs: assembly lines, service stations, chain groceries, finally newspapers; and eventually the recession, no jobs at all, and the Writers' Project.

It was the newspaper work that interested Wolfe Harrigan. Between dart-tosses he slipped in shrewd questions about the extent and nature of that work, and seemed satisfied with the replies. When Matt had finished the whole story, he nodded.

"Yes," he said slowly. "It's a nice piece of luck all around. You've done more than save my life, Duncan."

"I haven't even done that," Matt objected. "A guy bumped into me, and I landed on top. That's all."

"Have it your own way. But you're going to be much more useful than that. You know my books?"

"I've read *Signs and Wonders* and *Fleece My Sheep.*"

"Then you know my style. It's a good style. But it's not good for my purposes. I'm read by scholars and literati, and that isn't what I want. Such men are in no danger from fake religions. It's the plain, ordinary lower-middle-class that I've got to reach. The people who have retired with a small home and a little money and a kind heart and no sense. Those are the ones I have to save. And what do they read? Certainly not scholarly works published in exquisite format by Venture House at $3.50. I've tried to write for magazines and newspapers, but it's no go. The editors say my articles are excellent, but what do I think I'm writing for. So how about it?"

Matt hesitated. "Do you mean that I—"

"That's it, Duncan. You're to take over the Harrigan Crusade, Department of Popularizing. Or at least you're to make a stab at it. I guarantee nothing. If I don't like your work or if the editors turn it down, out on your ear you go. If it sells, the whole check is yours and you get your own by-line. My files are open to you at any time. This isn't even a ghost-writing proposition. All I do is furnish the raw material. Yours are the labor and the glory."

Matt gulped. "Inarticulate," he said, "is one of the few things I've never been called, but that's what I am now. A break like this—"

Wolfe waved his hand. "That's that. No gratitude. This is purely business. I think you're the man I want. Don't spoil it by going soft."

Matt grinned and whistled *Who's Afraid of the Big Bad Wolf.*

"And I don't like puns," said Harrigan. "even when they're whistled. Now, are you free tomorrow night?"

"I'm free," said Matt ruefully, "just about every night."

"Good. We're going spying."

"Spying?"

"Right into the enemy's camp. Ever hear of the Children of Light?"

"Only when you mentioned them just now."

"Hm. A memory for details. Good—handy thing to have in this game. Ever hear of Ahasver—the Man in the Yellow Robe—claims to be the Wandering Jew?"

"Good Lord! No, I haven't."

"You'll hear plenty tomorrow night." Harrigan rose again to retrieve his darts. On his way back to the desk he paused and stood in front of Matt, looking down. "One thing more," he said. "Your slant on this, I expect, will be purely commercial. It's good copy and that's that. But if we're to work together, I want you to understand me.

"I'm a Harrigan. All right, that means I've a much larger than necessary income for life, and I'm free to devote myself to a career that doesn't make money. I picked on this one—exposing religious rackets—and I've worked hard at it for thirty years. I think I've done some good. But my motives aren't quite the same as those of the usual trust-buster or muck-raker. They go a little deeper."

The fire was getting low now, and cast dying flickerings over Wolfe Harrigan's tall form. "Religion runs in the Harrigans, and to us religion means the Catholic Church. It comes out in different forms. Ellen believes in charity and intense private devotion. Joseph likes to think he's the Church Militant in Public Life. And you know how the family religion hit Concha in an adolescent crisis.

"Well, my career is religious, too. I'm a lay crusader. I'm not fighting rackets alone, I'm fighting heresy. I don't expect you to look at it that way, but now you know where I stand." He seated himself again at the desk. "Any questions?"

"Yes. One. But it isn't about what you just said. I'm all for your work, I want to work with you, and your exact motives are no business of mine. But my question goes back further—memory for detail again, I guess."

"Good." Wolfe leaned forward. "What is it?"

"You said before you hit the Swami's hand you used the other dart 'possibly in a rather foolish manner.' How?"

Wolfe laughed. "It will sound idiotic, Duncan. You see, I sometimes read detective fiction."

"So?"

"And I have a marked weakness for the dying message—the last clew by which the murdered man, in extremis, leaves a cryptic token of his murderer's identity. The sort of thing Ellery Queen has so much fun with. And the idea occurred to me that if my other dart failed and the Swami fulfilled his doubtless lethal purpose, I might leave such a clew."

"But how?"

"Look over there."

Matt obeyed the pointing hand. Under the dart target stood two bookcases. One was filled with historical works. The other held a series of letter files, each with a large hand-printed label. A dart transfixed the label which read:

HERMANN SUSSMAUL
(SWAMI MAHOPADHYAYA VIRASENANDA)

Matt turned around with a smile. "Nice," he said. "Now I'll know what to look for when we find the corpse."

Wolfe Harrigan rose. "Afraid it's time to say good night. I want to finish these notes for the Ahasver dossier. That's where you'll find the dart, by the way. He's the one who's really dangerous—and who finds me dangerous, too. But I'll tell you all that tomorrow night. The big show starts at eight. Come here for dinner at six thirty. That will give us time enough."

"Thanks," said Matt. "But I don't know—"

"If it's clothes that's worrying you, we don't dress. Ellen is so used to my own slovenly wardrobe that she probably thinks it's a sign of vast affluence. So come."

"I will. But how about Raincoat?"

"He's stirring by now. You did a nice lasting job, Duncan. Give me his plaything and I'll see he gets out of here all right. Go on. Don't worry. I'd sooner he didn't see you. You might be useful sometime if he doesn't know you're my friend."

Matt looked from the dart to the automatic. "Clews are all very well," he said seriously. "But if you hold on to this mascot you won't need to leave them."

Only a true scryer could have told him how wrong he was.

FOUR

"The name," Matt said, "is still Duncan, only this time I'm expected. I'm afraid I'm early, though."

Hardly a muscle moved, but the butler managed to express his opinion of Matt's own overcoat and incidentally of Matt and of Mr. Harrigan's strange acquaintances in general. All he said, however, was, "Mr. Harrigan will be down shortly. He requests you to wait in his study."

Today, Saturday, was dry but still cold. The fire was blazing, and Matt took advantage of the waiting period to warm himself and to make sure that he looked relatively presentable in the more nearly new and decent of his two suits—the double-breasted Oxford blue with the almost invisible lighter pattern. Nice suit, once.

Satisfied that the coat did not reveal that he had lost ten pounds since buying it and that the shirt collar did not look as though it had been turned (SING HOY—*Shirts 8c—Mending Free*), he found himself marveling once more at the twist of fortune which found him here dining with the Harrigans.

Fortune's private in this case, Gregory Randall, had not been in the least interested. Last night, of course, talking to him had been out of the question; Matt had simply driven him home, poured him into the arms of the Randall butler (who added sleepy crossness to his professional disdain), left the car, and waited forty-five minutes (overcoatless) for an owl streetcar into town. His appearance had hardly been prepossessing enough for hitch-hiking.

Today he had called Greg four times until at last, around three in the afternoon, the butler admitted that Mr. Gregory might be induced to come to the phone.

Matt could feel the agony of a major hangover vibrating over the wires. "Hello, Greg," he began. "Matt Duncan speaking."

"Who?"

"Matt. Matt Duncan."

"Oh," said Gregory. After a moment's reflection, he added, "Hello."

"How are you this afternoon?"

"I'm not a drinking man," said Gregory plaintively. That seemed to answer the question.

"Look. A lot happened last night. You don't know what you missed. A Swami tried to kill Harrigan. He's trying me out as a writing assistant. *And* Concha isn't going to be a nun."

"So." The voice was dull. "Well, well."

"Didn't you hear, Greg? I said Concha isn't going to be a nun."

"Please. Don't shout. If you knew what my head was like and then those noises go through it . . . "

Matt had hung up as soon as possible. He would talk to Greg about it later, when memory and perception were sharper. He was surprised, though, that not even the news of Concha's release had penetrated the fog of the hangover. He himself, in such a case . . .

He broke off these random musings as a girl came into the room. Her face was turned away; he could see only that she was slim and dark and wearing a housedress which looked so simple that it must have cost real folding money. Carrying a large volume, she was heading for the bookcase—not the small cases with the history works and letter files, but the large and wonderfully miscellaneous case that covered a whole wall.

"Hello," Matt said.

The girl dropped the book and whirled about, poised as though for instant flight. All Matt could see was her eyes—large black eyes, with fear glinting in their depths.

"I'm harmless," he added. He walked over to her, feeling absurdly like a naturalist trying not to startle the wild fauna, and picked up the book. This was a Materia Medica, and it had fallen open to a page headed *Hyoscyamus*.

The girl looked up at him. "It always falls open to that page," she said. There was something in her voice very like terror.

Matt closed the book, found the sizable gap in the case, and pushed it home. "Books do that," he said casually.

"Do they? So conveniently?"

Resolutely Matt refused to notice anything out of the way. "I suppose you must be Miss Harrigan? Or should we wait for somebody to introduce us?"

She had turned away from him again. "No," she said.

"All right then. I'm Matt Duncan. Maybe your father mentioned me?"

When she faced him now, it was hard to credit what he had just seen. The dread, the apprehension of unnamed terror were gone. Shyness remained, but it was only the shyness of a young girl confronted with a strange guest. "Oh, yes," she smiled. "Father told me all about last night. That was keen of you."

Now he could see her real face, and not a sketch to be labeled "Emotion No. 7: Fear." It was an odd face: the black hair, olive skin, and deep eyes of her mother's race, contrasted with an almost rugged modeling of features which more than suggested her father. In a photograph you might have taken it for the face of a young man, but in the warming glow of her presence you knew her intense femininity.

She was being the Compleat Young Hostess now. "Cigarette, Mr. Duncan? There must be—Oh, you have your own? Then won't you sit down? Shall I ring for a drink?"

"If you'd join me."

"No, thanks."

"Then I won't bother."

"It's nice again today, isn't it? Of course, it's cold but I don't mind that so much, not with a nice fireplace like this. But yesterday was nasty."

"Greg sends you his love," Matt invented politely.

"Oh. Does he?" There was an all but imperceptible pause. "Tell me, Mr. Duncan, where did you go to school?"

"University, you mean? Southern California. That is, I—"

"That's where I go now, too. Isn't that funny? I like it, too. It's awfully exciting being out with people and meeting all sorts. I mean, after so many years in that convent school, not that I didn't like that, too, but it's keen getting out into the world. Uncle Joseph thinks I ought to join a good sorority, but Father isn't so strong on the idea. He says you should make your friends for yourself and not just take them all in one certified bunch."

"I think your father's right. I was a fraternity man myself, but I'm not sure I gained anything from it. Except that I mightn't be here tonight if—"

"Did you see the Rose Bowl game? I was in the rooting section. I was at every game in the Coliseum and I even went up North for the Berkeley game. It's so exciting, isn't it? I mean the bands and the cheering and everything. The spring semester isn't nearly so much fun."

Greg was right, Matt was reflecting. She was young, terribly young. But there had been no youth in that first glimpse of her; then she had been ageless with terror. There was more to this girl, much more, than all her childish prattle revealed. He wondered how one might reach it. . . .

Matt reached over to the desk for a matchbox.

"Some of my friends say I don't know a safety from a dropkick," Concha was babbling, "but if anybody has as much fun at a game as I have I don't see that that really matters, do you? I mean, think of all the people that go to symphony concerts and don't even—"

Matt opened the matchbox. The suddenness of the explosion made them both leap to their feet. The sharp noise still rang in their ears, and the smell of powder was in the air.

For an instant the ageless look hovered on Concha's face. Then she grinned, all child again. "That's just Arthur," she explained. "My brother—have you met him?"

"I met him."

"I know what you mean. But he's all right really—well, almost. Only he's always pulling jokes like that. It runs in the family, I guess; Aunt Ellen says Uncle Joseph used to be just like that only he outgrew it so maybe Arthur will, too. Only I'm glad you bit instead of Father; he doesn't like it."

Matt looked at the trigger arrangement which detonated the blank cartridge when the matchbox was opened. Neat little contrivance—good mechanical ingenuity in the vacant-looking Arthur.

"I shouldn't say I've really met your brother yet. Just saw him for a moment last night, in the midst of all the confusion. Will he be at dinner?"

"Arthur at home on a Saturday night? Don't be silly. He's out some place having fun. He always is. But maybe you'll see more of him some other time. Father says you may be around a lot."

"I hope so. If I live up to specifications. That still leaves your mother I haven't met yet. I hope—"

"Mr. Duncan. My mother is dead." Her eyes involuntarily glanced towards the bookcase and the heavy volume which opened at *Hyoscyamus*. They were not a child's eyes.

Before Matt could speak, the door from the hall opened and Wolfe Harrigan strode in.

"I heard a shot," he said levelly.

Matt handed him the matchbox. "You have a playful son, sir."

Wolfe looked at it, relaxed, and smiled. "Sorry, Duncan. But after last night, I can't say I fancy the sound of a shot around here. You've met my daughter?"

"We took matters into our own hands."

"Then if that's all settled," said Wolfe Harrigan sensibly, "let's go eat."

"You have an excellent cook, sir," said Matt as they drove off to the Temple of Light.

"I have, and I thank you in her name. But don't call me sir. Wolfe will be better if we hit it off, and if we don't there's no call for servility."

Matt smiled to himself. This was such a fine crust of brusqueness that Wolfe Harrigan assumed to hide his eager friendliness. "Now," he said, "you might give me a few footnotes before we get there."

"All right." Somehow Wolfe Harrigan managed to talk, light a pipe, and drive skillfully all at the same time. "Here's the picture. Some two years ago I began noticing a new series of ads on the religious pages of the Sunday papers. Brief little notices that gave merely an hour and an address and said, 'Ahasver will speak on The Seven Vials,' or 'Are the Four Horsemen here? Ahasver will tell you.' The usual apocalyptic stuff. I mightn't have paid much attention if it hadn't been for the name Ahasver. Naturally that interested me."

"Why?"

"Because it's the name of the Wandering Jew. Of course, he's been known under a dozen others; but in the Leiden pamphlet of 1602, which started the whole thing, he is *'ein Jude mit Namen Ahasverus.'* I'd never heard the name in any other connection; so I felt that this called for some investigation.

"I went to a meeting. Nothing much happened. I thought he was skillful—knew how to handle an audience—but he said nothing exciting, and the crowd was small and poor. I had a look at the collection plate; there can't have been over ten dollars in it. There was no telling him then from any other wandering evangelist, aside from his odd name and the yellow robe which he wore.

"Later I began hearing more and more about him. He had soon gathered a solid little group of supporters, and before long he started to make 'revelations' to them. They spread the word, and the crowds began coming. It wasn't long before he'd taken in enough to build the Temple of Light. And then things really started. Now he's one of the half-dozen biggest cult leaders in Los Angeles—which you realize is no small distinction."

"But what does he teach? What are his—what-do-you-call-'ems—doctrines?"

Wolfe smiled. "You're being naive, Duncan. A heresy, I'll admit, used to have distinctive doctrines. It made some appeal to reason and to scholarship. But now all it needs is a leader with a good personality, a sense of stage effect, and a few catch phrases. Oh, Ahasver does have some tenets of belief, but I doubt if all his followers accept them, any more than most American Presbyterians believed in predestination even while it was still an article of faith. Any more, for the matter of that, than many supposed Catholics believe in original sin, or limbo, or possibly even transubstantiation."

"I think I see. It's the same set-up as the political world—a leader and a slogan and you're set. But what are his doctrines?"

"Briefly, they run something like this: That modern Christianity results from a conspiracy of Paul and Luke, who twisted the true facts of Christ's life to suit their own purposes. That the only true Gospel is the Gospel of Joseph of Arimathea, which Ahasver claims to have found in Tibet and himself translated from the ancient manuscripts. That Christ, Joseph of Arimathea, and Ahasver were all members of the ascetic Jewish order known as the Essenes. And that Ahasver's immortality—for he does lay literal claim to being the Wandering Jew—was imposed on him by Christ, not as a punishment, but so that he could carry the spark of truth on through all the ages when the false Christianity of Paul and Luke would be in the ascendant.

"He asserts—and makes out a fair case for it—that Paul-Luke Christianity is in a bad way today. The time has come at last, after these nineteen centuries, for him to step forward and teach the truth. The old order is on the way out—

> *et antiquum documentum*
> *novo cedat ritui,*

as we sing at Benediction. So Ahasver is giving people The Truth, and making a very good thing of it."

"Sounds harmless enough," said Matt.

Wolfe snorted. "Watch him tonight. Listen to him, and watch his audience. Watch the collection baskets, too. Listen to the people on their way out. Then tell me if you think this man in the yellow robe is harmless."

Ten blocks away they could see the neon sign, clear white against the sky:

LIGHT

it flashed—first the whole word, then each letter separately, then the whole word again.

Six blocks away they began to notice the traffic. Three blocks away Wolfe Harrigan turned off into a parking lot.

"That goes to Ahasver, too," he said to Matt, as he paid the attendant.

The Temple of Light was a plain white frame building on a once quiet side street, a structure rather reminiscent of the old style of country courthouse. Apart from its size it would have been inconspicuous, if it were not for the patterns of neon tubing which writhed glowingly over all the façade.

"Light," Wolfe explained. "Sometimes I think Ahasver has himself a bit mixed up with Ahura Mazda. Every possible color, you'll notice. If it can't be obtained from gas he uses tinted glass. All but one—yellow. He himself wears yellow as a symbol of his past degradation, but none of his followers is allowed to. Can't even read a book bound in it, or eat yellow food. They love it."

There was nothing spectacular or picturesque about the followers entering the building. They looked like any random group at a revival meeting or a municipal band concert or a neighborhood movie house. There was only one unusual feature about the crowd—the absence of youth. Matt saw no one else under forty, and a good half of those present seemed to be at least sixty.

In each of the three large doorways to the auditorium stood two greeters—a woman in flowing white and a man dressed, despite the weather, in a white summer suit. Each wore a badge of white ribbon and a fixed but neighborly smile. The man who greeted Wolfe Harrigan was surprisingly young, not long past his twenty-first birthday, but the other two were elderly, sedate, and on the paunchy side. The women looked like officers of the Sawyers Corners Sewing Guild and Literary Society.

The young man beamed—Wolfe's was evidently a familiar face. "Glad you're here tonight. We have something very special." He sounded a little like a floorwalker; you expected him to add, "On aisle three."

"Special?"

"Oh, yes. We're going to give the Nine Times Nine." His smile became intensified. Cherubic was the word, Matt decided. It was more of a beam than a smile, and it lit up the round face until automatically you looked down at the shoulders to watch the wings sprout. "You'll find the best seats in the balcony," he added.

"And what," said Matt as they climbed the stairs, "may the Nine Times Nine be?"

"So I said to Bessie," a voice drifted past them, " 'It's no wonder,' I said. 'You can't have curiosity and good dumplings, too.' "

"You'll see," Wolfe replied. "In fact, I wouldn't be surprised if . . . Well, we'll see."

"Keep us out of it, that's all I say. If they want to raise ned over in Europe, let 'em raise ned, but keep us out of it."

"I've voted the straight Democratic ticket for forty years now, but if two terms was enough for George Washington, it's enough for any man."

"Oh, but, Carrie, just wait till you see her in this! Like I said to Aunt Mabel, that's just what my Lillian . . . "

Matt was feeling disappointed. This was all too ordinary. This was what he heard every day in his ramshackle hotel up on Bunker Hill. Even the astounding play of lighting over the large auditorium could not make this assemblage anything but a good solid lot of transplanted Middle-Westerners, honest and plain and American.

The organist was quietly improvising around *Trees* and *At Dawning*. Matt was enjoying the beautific smile on the face of a two-hundred-pound woman with bleached hair and a faded housedress when he felt a hand on his arm and turned.

"Thought I recognized you, young feller," said the thin old man on his right.

Matt grinned and shook hands. Fred Simmons was one of the oldest permanent residents of the Angels' Flight Hotel, and Matt had often passed the time of day with him in the lobby. A retired grocer from Sioux City, Iowa, he had about him a certain Abe Martin mixture of kindliness and hoss sense.

"Glad to see you here," Simmons went on. "We don't get enough of the young people. To busy jittering, I guess —and them that don't jitter go organizing Youth Congresses. But it's good to see young folk taking an interest in something like this. You come here often?"

"This is my first time."

"You picked a good one, son. I hear He's going to have us give the Nine Times Nine. That'll show 'em."

"What is this—?"

"Hush," Simmons warned him. The organist was now playing *Sweet Mystery of Life*—apparently a cue that things were starting, for relative quiet began to spread over the audience. Then behind the curtain a high tenor voice joined in the tune.

On the last note the rainbow curtains parted. The stage was bare, but, from the flies, shifting and varicolored lights were projected onto its whitewashed walls. Downstage left was a small table, with a chair and the usual water pitcher. Here sat a plump elderly man who looked like the retired head of a small bank. And upstage center sat Ahasver.

"That's Him," Fred Simmons whispered needlessly. There was no mistaking him, even for Matt who had never seen him before. He dominated the stage and the whole auditorium. But it was even harder to guess what he actually looked like than it had been with Sister Ursula. His face was obscured by a black, spade-shaped beard, along the Assyrian style. And his body was completely enveloped by the famous Yellow Robe.

There was nothing of gold or saffron or lemon or chrome about the robe. It was absolutely and blatantly yellow, a pure, simple, and hideous declaration of a primary color. It displayed no embroidery, no cabalistic signs, no sense of style in its designing. It was just that—a yellow robe.

The sleeves were full length, and yellow gloves made them seem to extend even over the fingers. The shoulders were sloping and unpadded, and there was no gathering at the waist to hamper the robe in its full cascade to the ground. Above the shoulders it continued into a hood which completed the concealment of Ahasver's body. All that you could see of him for beard and robe was the nose, which certainly substantiated at least his racial claim, and the deep-set eyes with the black hollows beneath them.

The man by the water pitcher rose. "Dear followers of the Ancients," he addressed the audience. "As some of you may have heard, this is to be a very special night in the Temple of Light, and I know you don't want to waste time listening to me talk. So I won't take up any of your time beyond stopping to greet the many new faces that I see here tonight. I tell you, friends, you don't know how right you were to come here. And I want all of you who are new to turn around and shake hands with your brother or sister on the right because we're all Children of Light, aren't we, and so we're all bretheren and sisteren."

Dutifully Matt turned and again shook hands with Fred Simmons. This was enough to dispel the momentary excitement he had felt at the sight of the man in the yellow robe with his dominating personality. The proceedings here might be strange, grotesque, ludicrous; but there could be nothing dangerous about them when they rested on a congregation of ordinary, wholesome, salt-of-the-earth Fred Simmonses.

"And now," the ex-banker announced, "before we hear from the man from whom you're all waiting to hear from, I know he'd like us to sing one verse of *Old Christianity*. Come on now, everybody. Let's make this good."

The play of light faded on the white wall back of the stage, and in its stead appeared the lines of the song flashed from a projection machine above the stage. The organist began to play *John Brown's Body*, and the audience joined in piecemeal:

> The Ancients teach us truly how to be at one with them,
> How to win the star-crowned garland and the royal diadem,
> And ascend in joy eternal to the New Jerusalem,
>   As we go marching on.

So far only about half the audience was singing. Some of them—including Fred Simmons, who made a sort of humming grunt—looked as though the words were hard. But now the whole auditorium shook with happy and tuneless bellows as the familiar refrain appeared:

> Old Christianity is mold'ring in the grave,
> Old Christianity is mold'ring in the grave,
> Old Christianity is mold'ring in the grave,
>   While we go marching on.

Matt had doubted that the singing could grow louder, but now it did. Fred Simmons' face grew red with exultant puffing, and Matt found himself joining in with a vigor which rarely characterized his sober vocalism. He could even hear Wolfe Harrigan's voice raised in the chorus. For these were words that everybody had known forever, long before they had heard of Ahasver and the Ancients—words that are a part of the American race:

> Glory! Glory! Hallelujah!
> Glory! Glory! Hallelujah!
> Glory! Glory! Hallelujah!
> WHILE WE GO MARCH ING ON!!!

At that final, tremendous ON!!! Ahasver rose from his seat and advanced to center stage. The vast sound perished in instant silence, like one of those trick effects in Russian choirs. At an almost invisible gesture from one yellow arm, a white-suited attendant wheeled a sturdy lectern out from the wings. On it a heavy leather-bound book lay open. From the balcony you could see that its pages were blank.

Matt glanced at the men on either side of him. Wolfe Harrigan sat tense and curious, like a surgeon about to watch the film of an unusual operation. Fred Simmons was leaning forward, the tip of his tongue protruding between his thin lips. His breath was rapid, and there was a glint in his eyes which Matt had never seen before.

Ahasver wasted no time on polite greetings. That was the business of the man with the water pitcher. Instead he plunged straight into his discourse. "You all do know this book," he said. It was a good voice: deep and vibrant, rich and well-trained, yet somehow avoiding any suggestion of staginess. There was a slight accent, but not that of any living tongue. "You all do know how I have recourse to it in times of tribulation—yea, and of lamentation. For is it not written in the fifth chapter of the Gospel according to Joseph:

And Jesus said unto his disciples: Seek and ye shall find. Open and ye shall read. For unto them that know the Ancients shall be given the power that they may read where to other eyes is parchment only.

Thus have I opened, and thus now do I read."

And thus Ahasver went on, in his quasi-Biblical style. What he said, Matt concluded, was equal parts Christianity and Theosophy, with liberal dashes of Dale Carnegie and the Republican National Committee. It was a platitudinous sermon on knowing one's self and fusing one's self with some nebulous higher powers known as the Ancients. But the rewards it held out were no vague promises of future bliss; they were pointed and documented assurances that the man who knew the Ancients could win friends and influence people no end.

As he spoke, Ahasver constantly scanned the blank pages before him as though he were reading from a teletype machine. Suddenly he paused, seemed to reread a message, and resumed: "I have just received a communication of great interest to us all." (Fred Simmons shifted eagerly.) "The new long-range Communist bombing plane left Siberia yesterday on a test flight to Alaska. Its real intention was not a test, but a bombing raid upon the city of Nome." (Matt heard a sharp gasp of horror from Simmons.) "But fear not. I have received intelligence from Joseph himself that he perceived the approach of this danger and destroyed the plane in mid-ocean. You will not read of this in your newspapers; the Tass agency of the Red Government has resolved to suppress the fact. But remember this when you hear Communistic doctrines preached abroad, and learn to recognize these devils for what they are. By their fruits ye shall know them." (Fred Simmons nodded fervid agreement.)

"Some there are who think to make friends and allies of these enemies. To them I can only say, as the Ancient Jesus said before me, and as it is written in the seventh chapter of the Gospel according to Joseph: 'Make unto yourselves friends of the mammon of iniquity, but see that ye realize the price of that friendship.' "

Suddenly Wolfe Harrigan seized Matt's arm. His face glistened with excitement. "Remember that!" he said. "It doesn't settle things, but it helps. I don't know how I missed it when I read the Gospel. But remember!"

"But—" Matt started.

"Explain later."

So Matt fished out a pencil and paper, jotted down the quotation from the Gospel according to Joseph as best he could remember it, and tried to follow the rest of the sermon.

There wasn't much more. Almost abruptly Ahasver stopped his

imaginary reading and announced, "The Ancients have concluded. Now I must rest a moment to regain strength. Then I have a most important request to make of you."

As the man in the yellow robe resumed his seat, the organ began the intermezzo from *Cavalleria Rusticana*. Fred Simmons turned to Matt. "Isn't he great? He sure wakes you up. Makes you see what's going on all around you."

With the first notes of the organ, white-suited men started along the aisles with baskets. There had been no ardent exhortations to Give; but the people gave none the less freely. As a basket passed along their row, Matt (dropping in a dime; the show was worth it) noticed that it was filled mostly with paper money, and not all ones by a long shot. Fred Simmons contributed two dollars, which Matt was certain he could not possibly afford.

The organ stopped at last, and there was only the rustle of the collection. Even that ceased as Ahasver came forward again.

"You have heard me speak," he said, "of the Nine Times Nine." He paused. All through the house ran that wordless noise of expectation which a concert audience gives on recognizing the opening bars of a song. Fred Simmons' lips were parted, and his bony old hands trembled.

"You have heard," Ahasver went on, "how a lama refused to permit me to transcribe the Gospel according to Joseph, and how the Nine Times Nine was set upon him, and how lo! he was no more. And other stories likewise have you heard of the Nine Times Nine, but never have you been called upon to set the Nine Times Nine. Tonight . . . " He let the resonance of his voice die softly away in the death-still auditorium. "Tonight ye shall do so."

Only the faintest hushed murmurs sounded as the lights in the auditorium dimmed. Then the colors on the stage died, too. For an instant there was absolute darkness. Then from above came a spot of the forbidden yellow, bathing Ahasver.

"By the strength of this hated color," he half chanted, "by the yellow gabardine which I wore in the ghetto, by the yellow priests who sought to keep truth from the world, by all sereness and rot, by all hatred and death that is embodied in this color, I call upon the Ancients. Do ye call also. Say after me: O Ancients!"

The sound arose, hesitant, muffled, twanging, and tumultuous: "O ANCIENTS!"

"Ye know, O Ancients, him who would destroy us. Ye know how he denies our truth, scorns our ideals, ridicules our heritage, mocks at our beliefs, and undermines our teachings. Ye know the plans that ripen within his evil brain and the disaster that those plans would bring upon us. Yea, and upon you as well, O Masters of Light!

"Therefore I call upon the Nine! Upon Jesus, upon Gautama,

upon Confucius. Upon Elijah, upon Daniel, upon Saint Germain. Upon Joseph, upon Plato, upon Krishna. All of you say after me: I call upon the Nine!"

"I CALL UPON THE NINE!"

"Now call I upon the Nine who serve the Nine: Upon Cherubim, upon Seraphim, upon Thrones. Upon Dominions, upon Virtues, upon Powers. Upon Principalities, upon Arch-angels, upon Angels! I call upon the Nine Times Nine! Say ye after me: I call upon the Nine Times Nine!"

"I CALL UPON THE NINE TIMES NINE!"

"Hearken unto us as we cry for deliverance. Free us from this evil man, O Nine Times Nine! Destroy him utterly! Now do ye all lift your voices with mine and cry to the Nine Times Nine: Destroy him!"

"DESTROY HIM!"

Matt was drowning in vast billows of sound that hurtled from wall to wall of the auditorium. His eyes at last accustomed to the darkness, he looked at his neighbors. They were no ordinary Southern Californians now. They were participants in a mystery of hate—eyes burning, lips parted, teeth gleaming. The placid fat woman with the bleached hair was a Midwest Maenad, ready to render her enemies. Even the homely face of Fred Simmons was a distorted mask of mean fury. Matt could no longer smile at the ritual, no matter how absurd, that could transform plain and good people into the vessels of mad hatred.

The yellow-gloved hand moved ever so lightly, and the audience took the cue.

"DESTROY HIM!" they roared again, and once more, "DESTROY HIM!"

Then the light came on, suddenly and without warning. Matt saw the people blink at each other under the many colors and seem to wonder what they had said. Fred Simmons avoided his eye.

Ahasver spoke now in a more ordinary tone. "It is not given to us to know when the Nine Times Nine may be fulfilled. It cannot be in less than twelve hours, nor in more than a month. And that any who doubt may be convinced, I must needs tell you the name of this devil of yellow hate, this fiend who would destroy us. Watch your papers, and know the power of the Ancients when ye read of the death of Wolfe Harrigan."

Matt looked at Wolfe. He was grinning contentedly.

FIVE

When Matt awoke that Low Sunday (Easter, according to the Children of Light), he had a moment's difficulty placing himself. Then he saw the dart-board and remembered. He was lying on the couch which had received Raincoat, and somebody had thoughtfully thrown a blanket over him.

He lit a cigarette and began to reconstruct the evening—the drab meeting which had turned into such wild fantasy with the setting of the Nine Times Nine, then the return to this house and the long hours of solid work while Wolfe Harrigan, glowing with enthusiasm, had taken his new assistant through all the notes and files and shown him the raw materials for his work. Matt remembered fascination slowly giving place to pure weariness. The last he recalled was sitting on this couch while Wolfe read excerpts from the Gospel according to Joseph—mad stuff, about how Christ spent seven years in India and Tibet learning the secrets of the Ancients as an ambassador to the Essene sect.

That must have finished him. He looked at his watch. Good Lord! Two o'clock. But it must have been well on toward five when he had fallen helplessly asleep.

The hall door opened and Arthur Harrigan slouched in. "Where's Pop?" he asked.

"I don't know. I just woke up."

"Jeez." Arthur looked at him with admiration. "Did you drag Pop out on a bender? Nobody's done that in ten years."

"We were working."

"Working, huh?" Arthur delivered a man-to-man leer.

"Cigarette?"

"Thanks. I ran out, and the drugstore's a long ways." Arthur flopped into a chair and let the cigarette dangle from his lower lip. "You're a strange one in this family," he drawled.

"Why?"

"You look like maybe you'd been around. You're human. The rest of us here—the Harrigan tribe—we've got too much money to be good and too much religion to be bad. We just hover. Watch out for us, though. Especially for Concha."

"Why for her?"

"Maybe you're just what she needs only she doesn't know it yet. Day before yesterday she was going to be a saint. She's on the rebound now, and here you are. You dress like hell and you're ugly as sin; but hell and sin have their points, particularly when you're her age. So watch out."

Matt frowned. "I don't know as I like that, Harrigan. It's a hell of a way to talk about your sister."

"Is it?"

The chapel door opened softly and Wolfe Harrigan's gray head peered in. "Oh, you're up, Duncan. Good. Want some breakfast?"

"Look, Pop," Arthur broke in. "I've got to talk to you."

"The answer," said Wolfe, "is still no. What do you usually start the day with?"

"So Duncan's breakfast counts for more than my life?"

"Don't be melodramatic."

"What are you trying to make out of me? Do you think I want to sit around on my fanny all my life and be the son of the Harrigans?" He crumpled his cigarette and tossed it away. "I want to do something on my own. And these guys'll cut me in for five gr—thousand. Ten'd be better, but they'll take five. You wouldn't even notice it, Pop."

"I'd notice you using it."

"But look, Pop—"

"No."

Arthur hesitated in irresolute fury, so irate that he stood almost straight. "All right. That's that. I'll see them tonight and tell them I'm Papa's little angel and the hell with them. But we're through, Pop, you and me. I mean that. You may be a 'good man,' but you're hard as hell. And if anybody wants to put another curse on you—well, they can count me in."

He left the room suddenly.

" 'Do something on his own'!" Wolfe Harrigan snorted. "Do you know what this is he wants to be cut in on? A gambling joint. He's been a patron there. I knew about it, but what could I do? Finally, the proprietors decided they could get more money out of him another way. They want to take him 'into partnership,' and they'll clean him and me, too, if they can. And he prates about the right to lead his own life!"

"So the Nine Times Nine got into the papers? Swell publicity."

"No. It didn't. Not a word. But what makes you think so?"

"Arthur's grand speech. 'If anybody wants to put another curse on you.' I thought you'd decided not to tell the family about last night's curse."

"I didn't. I was afraid they'd worry, after the Swami."

"Then how did Arthur find out about the Nine Times Nine?"

"I don't know," said Wolfe Harrigan slowly.

"Have some more toast?" Concha urged.

Matt shook his head and mumbled "O, ank ou," through a mouth filled with the remains of his fifth slice.

"Nobody eats much toast around here and I do like to watch it jump. Please, let me make you another."

His mouth was clear again. "If I don't have to eat it."

"You're nice." She sliced off a fresh piece of bread, put it in the toaster, and pulled down the lever.

Matt supposed that she must have gone to mass that morning, but she couldn't have worn her present costume of black slacks and a bright red sweater. Particularly not that sweater. She was being quite different from yesterday—neither a child nor a wraith, but a delightful blend of girl and woman.

"Tell me," she said, "are you going to live here?"

"Good Lord, no. Why should I?"

"You've sort of been around this weekend. And it might be nice."

Matt finished his tomato juice. "Madame is so kind."

"No, really it might. I mean, having somebody young around the house besides Arthur. He's such a droop."

"How about Gregory?"

"A different kind of droop. But you—you're something else again. You're alive and real the way—" her voice altered subtly—"the way Father is."

"Your father," Matt shifted the subject, "is just about the swellest person I've met in lo these long years. He does something to you. He makes you want to feel and act and work as intensely as he does. And it's grand work he's doing. At first I thought of it as just a job, but now I'm beginning to see. . . . "

The girl half-pouted. "Don't let's talk about Father. Let's talk about you."

"Want to go slumming, Miss Harrigan? Life in the raw—"

She made a face. "Don't be sill. And please call me Concha. I like that. Do you know what my name really is? It's María Concepción Harrigán Pelayo, and I love it." Even *Harrigan* became a liquid Spanish word as she uttered it.

Matt smiled. "You're a sweet child, Concha."

She stood up suddenly, her eyes fierce and her high breasts trembling. "Don't say that. I'm not either a child. I'm almost eighteen. Do I look like a child? I can see your eyes; I know you don't think so. And I don't feel like a child, either. I know things—awful things—things a child couldn't bear. And I'm holding them in me, like a woman, and they hurt. But I won't be a child. I won't!"

With a little pop, the toast shot up out of the machine. The scene was punctured. Concha stood there for a moment, her red lips twisting. Then she turned and ran out of the room. Matt didn't know whether she was laughing or crying.

Often thereafter Matt tried to reconstruct that Sunday afternoon, but it was hard to fix people and their movements exactly in his mind. Concha disappeared after that breakfast scene; where she went he did not know. Arthur, obedient for all his fine show of rebellion, was sent off to fetch Sister Ursula and Sister Felicitas. Aunt Ellen, it appeared, had caught a cold over the rainy weekend and was unable to go to the convent for a necessary business interview about some charitable arrangements, so special permission had been secured. . . . (The Sisters of Martha of Bethany, Matt thought, seemed to lead a singularly free life for nuns. He had thought that all religious women were strictly cloistered and you talked to them through iron grilles.) Then at some point R. Joseph had come (apparently he regularly took Sunday dinner with the family), found no one free to talk to but Arthur, and wandered about disconsolately.

And most of this time Matt was locked up in the study with Wolfe Harrigan, going over more details that had not been covered the night before. The word "locked" is used literally.

"Afraid," Wolfe explained, half-smiling, "that Friday night worried me more than I liked to admit. It was too easy for the Swami to push open those French windows. They're bolted now, top and bottom. And the doors are locked, too. Concha says I'll perish for fresh air, but I point out the hardihood of the continental races."

At last Wolfe decided that their preliminary work was over. "I think you've got a rough idea now of what we're doing. The important thing on the present agenda, as you must realize, is the Children of Light. There's something purposive about that organization. It's gathering power and it plans to use it. That business last night about the Communist bombing plane was absurd but indicative. Political allusions, and frequently far more direct ones, are creeping more and more often into the messages of the Ancients. What we need to know now is the identity of this Ahasver, and who's running the shebang."

"Haven't you any idea yet?"

"I wouldn't say that. I have an idea, but—well, to be frank, Duncan, I'm not telling even you. There are a few notes I haven't shown you. You'll read them eventually—and I hope it's I who'll give them to you."

"What do you mean? Who else would?"

Wolfe was tossing darts again. "I merely meant this: Last night, after I'd tucked you in on the couch, I wrote out a holograph codicil to my will, naming you my literary executor."

"Me?"

"You. After two days you know more about my work than my whole family put together. Yes, and I think you care more. At my death all my notes and papers will be handed over to you, to make what use of you please. Unless my judgment is slipping badly, it will be a good use. And I've warned you," he added heavily as Matt started to speak, "how I feel about effusions of gratitude. See who that is at the hall door."

Matt turned the knob of the bolt and opened the door. The caller was Concha. She had changed again, this time to a bright plaid dress with a demure black velvet bodice. It made her look roughly fourteen.

"Look," said Matt. "Do me a favor? Stay one person long enough for me to get used to it."

" 'A woman is a sometime thing,' " she half-sang. "You'll get used to it, all right. Won't he, Father?"

"I suppose he'll have to if we're to lead a peaceful existence around here. What did you want, Concha?"

She pointed. "Him."

"Is that all? Very well, darling. I'm through with him for the time being. You can have him."

"Hey," said Matt. "Haven't you people heard about the thirteenth amendment? Am I just property?"

Concha frowned at him in the manner of one appraising an offering on the auction block. "He looks strong, Massa Harrigan, powerful strong. Kin he tote and carry?"

"Sho nuff, Missy," said Wolfe.

"Kin he pick cotton and plant taters?"

"Sho nuff, Missy."

"And kin he play croquet?"

"Sho nuff," said Matt.

"Don't bother to wrap him. I'll just take him this way." She slipped her arm through Matt's and led him gaily off.

Concha was being very resolutely gay now; and Matt, struggling constantly to adjust himself to the mercurial moods of her youth, began to feel far older than his twenty-seven years could possibly justify. He realized further that people who have not played croquet for many years should not blithely answer "Sho nuff" when asked if they play it.

But the game was fun all the same. The croquet lawn, scene of Matt's struggle with Raincoat, lay just beyond the French windows of the study. The day had turned warm, and the late sun beat hotly back from these west-facing windows. It was good to be outdoors in that sun with a lovely, if exceedingly unsettling, girl. For lovely, Matt had decided upon mature reflection, she emphatically was.

Matt was hopelessly beaten from the start. Concha's pleasure in knocking his ball to far corners of the earth was positively devilish; and she would generally coast comfortably up against the home post before he was halfway round. But, incompetent loser though he was, he was sorry when R. Joseph Harrigan descended upon them.

Joseph, it was obvious, was lonely. He had had no one to talk to all afternoon (Arthur could not be said to count as a responsive audience), and he was a man who had to talk. Matt must have looked like a promising auditor, for the lawyer bore down upon him eagerly.

The verb "bore" soon began to acquire a final d. Concha stood for a bit, tapping her mallet restlessly, and finally gave up and slipped around the back way into the house, unnoticed by Joseph, who was explaining the sort of man really needed on the Supreme Court.

The two men were sitting on a bench, across the croquet lawn from the French windows. Wolfe hadn't turned on his light, Matt noticed idly, though it was getting near sunset. The last rays were now glaring against the uncurtained glass with blinding intensity.

Matt spurned a croquet ball with his foot and turned his attention back to Joseph. The man's talk, he was slowly coming to realize, was honestly worth listening to. You can disagree completely with a speaker's position, and still enjoy and respect the acuteness with which he presents it. So Matt felt now. Most of Joseph's opinions he would have dismissed, coming from another, as sheer reactionary drivel; but he sensed in this exponent a certain rockbound integrity which impressed him. He began to listen more closely, to answer, even occasionally, to his surprise, to agree. Despite the manner and appearance of the plutocratic politician, there was in R. Joseph Harrigan something of the same strength and purposiveness which Matt so admired in his brother.

"You can say what you like, sir," he was protesting, "about inefficiency and bad administration on the WPA arts projects. I worked on one; I could probably tell more stories of that sort than you've ever heard. But in spite of all that, you must admit the necessity and the value of—" He stopped dead.

"Go on, young man." R. Joseph was interested.

The sun had left the French windows. Now you could see the study behind them dimly outlined in the glow of a plentiful fire. And you could see something more.

"I'm sorry, sir. But look at those windows."

Joseph looked. The glow revealed the front of Wolfe's desk. Wolfe's own chair was invisible in shadow, but bending over the desk was a strange figure. The face was hidden, but the costume was clearly visible. Leaning over Wolfe Harrigan's desk was a man in a yellow robe.

"Young man," said Joseph tensely, "we're going inside."

Matt was with him on that. There was only one conceivable reason why Ahasver should come to Wolfe Harrigan's study. He never doubted for an instant that the man was Ahasver. The face might be invisible, but that robe, that hood, were identification enough.

Matt started toward the windows, but R. Joseph, alert and efficient in the emergency, laid a hand on his arm. "They're locked, remember. Besides, he can see us coming if we go that way. Come around back." And the lawyer set off at a trot around the corner of the house to the back door. But Joseph was not built for physical agility; his heroic ride to the rescue began with a tumble over a wicket.

Matt didn't even pause to help him to his feet. The more he thought of the Yellow Robe in the study, the more he knew that he was needed there. His ears rang with the tumultuous triple shout of "DESTROY HIM!" Wolfe may have scoffed at the menace of the Ancients; but the physical threat of the presence of Ahasver himself was another matter.

As he reached the back door he looked around. R. Joseph had turned the corner at a great rate, only to come a cropper and just miss braining himself against the stone back of the fireplace. Despite the urgency of the moment, it was hard to keep back a snort. Toppled dignity is ludicrous even in the shadow of danger. But Matt controlled himself, slipped into the hall, and rapped loudly on the study door.

There had been no answer when Joseph, not so impeccably neat as usual, joined him. "Try the knob," he suggested.

"I tried. The latch is on."

"Then the chapel door. That might—"

Miss Ellen Harrigan looked up in amazement from her rosary as her brother and that strange young man dashed into the chapel and began to pound on the door of the study, rattling the knob and shoving at the wood with their shoulders.

"What on earth are you doing?"

"We saw . . . man in there . . . yellow robe . . . Wolfe . . . might be danger . . . " Joseph panted.

"Might be?" said Matt. "Something's wrong, God knows. He doesn't answer."

"Do you think we could break it down?"

"We can try. I'll count to three, and we'll both hit it at once. Between us we ought to—"

"Just a moment." Matt recognized the cool voice of Sister Ursula, and turned to see the two nuns in the other doorway of the chapel. "Did I understand that you think something has happened to Mr. Harrigan?"

"You did."

"I devoutly hope that nothing has happened." She crossed herself and glanced at the picture of the Virgin. "But if anything has, don't you think it would be better to make sure?"

"How?"

"Go around and look in the French windows."

The complete sensibility of this suggestion cooled Matt off. Of course. See what's happened and then if—well, you might as well face it—if you have to call the police, they can do whatever's necessary themselves. Much more sensible.

Matt kept muttering these scattered thoughts to himself as he went around again to the croquet ground. Now that he was close to the windows he could see the room clearly in the firelight. And he could see—he stopped swallowing for a minute and his throat got dry—he could see the body of Wolfe Harrigan lying on the floor by the desk, with the face shot half away.

He could also see that there was no one else at all in the room.

SIX

Ten years ago Terence Marshall was a familiar name to American newspaper readers. He was one of those freak combinations that make such good copy; a Phi Beta Kappa man, a Rhodes scholar, and an All-American football player. His young opinions on this and that received nation-wide publicity, a fact most distressing to him now in his more serious and soberer thirties.

Then he went to Oxford on his scholarship, and the feature writers found another anomaly to publicize. Marshall's public career was at an end; but a chance friendship brought him to his true life-work. The young man who sat next to him at a Rugger game and kindly explained the peculiar features of British football to the dazed American turned out to be the son of an Assistant Commissioner at Scotland Yard; and Terence Marshall had his eyes opened to the inside aspects of law enforcement and detection.

On his return to Los Angeles he declined with impartiality offers of teaching positions and contracts in professional sports. Starting from the bottom, he had become a patrolman on the Los Angeles police force. His rise had been sure, if not spectacular. The taxidermist episode already referred to was the closest approach to an important case which he had handled; but he had not muffed any of the lesser routine which came his way. He was now a Detective Lieutenant, and beloved of the D.A.'s office as the one detective on the force whom you could trust to round off a case that would stand up unassailably in court.

Now Terence Marshall stood in the drawing room of the Harrigan home, undertaking what might well prove to be the first major case of his career. He was an impressive figure: six-feet-two in height, a hundred and ninety pounds in weight, ruggedly homely in features, and already a trifle gray in hair.

"Officer Drake," he was saying, "took down your preliminary statements when he came in the squad car, but I'd like to go over them with you again, while the medical officer is getting his report ready. First, let's settle the time element. When did any of you last see Wolfe Harrigan?"

After a little pause, Concha spoke. Her voice showed a resolute effort to be calm and helpful, but her emotion betrayed itself in a wavering pitch, ludicrously like a boy's changing voice. "I went into the study late in the afternoon. Mr. Duncan was there, and I took him away to play croquet with me."

"Time?"

"I—I really don't know. I think about five o'clock."

"Duncan?"

"About that, near as I can estimate."

"So. Now did anyone see Harrigan after five o'clock?"

"I cannot say," Joseph announced, "that I *saw* my poor brother, but . . ."

"Well?"

"I spoke with him. I rapped on the door, but he shouted out that he was working and told me to go away."

"What time was this?"

"Shortly before six. I remember thinking that there was over an hour before dinner. It was just after that that I joined the two young people on the croquet lawn."

"When was that, Duncan?"

Matt had been thinking. "The way I work it out is like this, Lieutenant. When I—when I looked in through those French windows, I checked the time. It was just 6:15. That'd make it about two minutes earlier when we saw the figure in the yellow robe. I think Miss Harrigan came into the house about ten minutes before that, and Mr. Harrigan—Mr. Joseph Harrigan, that is—had joined us on the lawn about five minutes earlier."

Concha and Joseph nodded their agreement.

"All right," said Marshall. "Then at 5:55, roughly, Mr. Harrigan shouted at his brother. At 6:13, Duncan and Joseph Harrigan see a man in his study and try to get in. At 6:15, Duncan sees the body. Can anybody fill in the time gap there?"

Silence.

"Now then. You'll understand I have to go through with the routine no matter how open-and-shut a case may seem. I'll have to ask each of you to account for himself during those twenty minutes. Miss Harrigan?"

Aunt Ellen was quiet and submissive. Her eyes were doubly red from weeping and from her cold. "Let me see. I went into the chapel a little after six. The sisters and I had been discussing a plan for a new wing to the orphanage, and I wanted to say a private prayer for its success. I was there until—until Joseph and Mr. Duncan came in."

"And before six?"

"I was with the sisters in my sitting room upstairs."

"Do you ladies agree on the time?"

It was Sister Ursula who spoke. Matt reflected that he had not yet heard one sound from Sister Felicitas. "I couldn't swear to it, Lieutenant, but it was something like that."

"And where were you after six?"

"Miss Harrigan was kind enough to ask us to have a glass of port and a slice of fruitcake before we left. She rang for the butler, who brought the repast up to the sitting room. We were still there when we heard all the commotion and came down."

"Duncan and Harrigan we've heard. You, Mr. Harrigan?" He directed the question at Arthur, who was sitting atilt in his chair, seemingly more preoccupied with whether he dared smoke than with the tragedy.

"I was in my room," he mumbled.

"Doing what?"

"Reading. Waiting for the nuns to leave."

"Why for that?"

"Because I had to chauffeur them."

"And how long were you there?"

"About an hour, I guess, before I heard all the thumping."

"That leaves only you, Miss Harrigan. Where did you go when you left the croquet lawn?"

"To the kitchen."

"The kitchen?"

"Sometimes Janet lets me help. She says, you never can tell, I might marry a poor man. I like it."

The Lieutenant smiled for the first time since his arrival. "And you were there until the noise at 6:15?"

"Yes."

"All right. Now, did anybody, during these twenty minutes, hear the shot fired? No one? Miss Harrigan, you were in the chapel next door. Didn't you—?"

"I heard nothing."

"And none of you saw anyone else—I mean anyone who had no right to be here? All right. Will you please all wait here? I want to talk to the servants and have a good look at the study."

The presence of the Lieutenant had kept them all drawn up to the standards of formal behaviour. Now the tension relaxed. Aunt Ellen fell to sniffling, and Concha suddenly flung herself to her knees, buried her face in Sister Ursula's dark-blue habit, and began sobbing terribly.

"The Lieutenant," Joseph passed judgment, "seems a sound young man. Courteous, too. Nothing of the rubber hose about him."

Arthur sniffed. "He knows you're a big shot, Uncle Joe. It'd cost him his badge."

R. Joseph Harrigan frowned. "This is neither the time nor the place for such sarcasm, Arthur. I think, furthermore, that you might have the decency to refrain from smoking."

Matt guiltily tucked back the packet he had started to take out. The group sat in silence.

An officer stuck his head into the room. "Which of you is Duncan?"

Matt rose. "I am."

"Lieutenant wants to see you in the study."

The body was gone; that helped. A photographer was folding up his tripod, and a scrawny middle-aged man with a black bag sat on the couch. The Lieutenant stood, unconsciously in one of Wolfe Harrigan's favorite attitudes, in front of the fireplace. The fire was dead now, apparently put out with water.

"All right, Duncan," Marshall said as Matt entered the room. "Where do you fit into this?"

"What do you mean, where do I fit in?"

"I mean what are you doing here? You don't belong with the Harrigans. You aren't their kind of people. So where do you fit in?"

Matt felt himself on the defensive. "I've been working with Mr. Harrigan."

"Working? What on?"

"He took me on as a—I guess you might call it an assistant —a sort of combination laboratory-worker and ghost-writer."

"Been with him long?"

"Only since Friday."

"How long have you known him?"

"Since Friday."

"So. You meet him and right like that you're his assistant. Nice work, and you got it. Maybe you better tell me a little more."

Matt told him, sketchily and uncomfortably.

"Writers' Project," Marshall repeated. "So. I know your head there; I'll have a word with him. And things start happening in this household as soon as you get here. Interesting. Very. But that isn't what I called you in here for. Sit down."

Matt sat down on the couch beside the middle-aged man, who nodded in affable silence.

"You," the Lieutenant went on, "were the last person, according to all the testimony, who was in this room for any length of time. Miss Harrigan came in only briefly, and the brother didn't even get past the door. Now when you were here, was the room all barricaded?"

"Yes. As I told you, there'd been an attack on Mr. Harrigan Friday night. He wasn't taking any more chances."

"All right. Now I'm asking you to look over this room and tell us if everything is the way it was when you were last in here. Especially the exits and entrances. Don't worry about touching things; we've been all over the place."

As Matt went around the room, his amazement mounted. The French windows were securely bolted at top and bottom. The small high windows on either side of the fireplace were fixed and immovable anyway. The hall door, broken down by the police, was now propped up against the wall, its bolt still shot into the locking position. That left only the chapel door with the push button lock. You could go out that way and pull it shut and locked behind you; but Aunt Ellen had been sitting out there.

He paused in his tour. "This is crazy."

"You're telling me," Lieutenant Marshall snorted. "But you're sure this is the way it was?"

"Yes."

"All right. Anything else wrong?"

Matt looked about. "The papers on the desk have been rearranged since I last saw them, I think; but that's what you'd expect if he was working there. The fire's out. It was going good when I was in here."

The middle-aged man spoke for the first time. "Don't mention that damned fire to me."

"The doc's sore and I don't blame him. That fire was blazing like a furnace—played hell with his job. The body was so warm it might have just finished dying that minute."

"But why put it out?"

"Somebody might have been burning something. If they were, they succeeded. All we found was that."

Marshall gestured at a small piece of metal on the table.

"A silencer. Then no wonder nobody heard the shot."

"Right. Now take a look at the automatic. Ever see it before?"

Matt examined it. "I can't say for sure. I don't remember any identifying marks. But it's just like the one I took away from the Swami."

"So. Thought that might be it. And was the silencer on it then?"

"I can't quite . . . Yes, I remember now. It was."

"I expected as much. Great help the weapon's going to be in this. Notice anything else?"

"That scratch on the desk. I'm positive that wasn't there this afternoon."

"Any ideas what might have caused it?"

Matt examined the scratch closely. It was about two inches wide and ran some six inches in from the edge of the flat-topped desk. Not a deep scratch—just enough to take off some of the varnish. "No," he said at last. "Afraid I haven't."

"And just why," demanded the Lieutenant, "do you keep darting eager glances at that bookcase?"

"Darting is good."

"I don't get it. What are you looking for?"

"There's one thing I'd hoped for, and don't find."

"Something that was here before?"

"No. Something I hoped might be. A dart in a filing case."

The Lieutenant and the doctor exchanged puzzled glances. "Did you indeed? And why might you have expected that?"

Matt told him of Wolfe Harrigan's idea of leaving a clew, and of the dart in the Swami's file. "So I had hoped," he finished, "that there might be a dart in the Ahasver file. It could have helped."

"Look at the file," said Marshall tersely.

Matt looked. In the back of the file labeled AHASVER he could make out a small pricked hole. "Then it was—?"

"We found it there. Took it out for fingerprints. Smudgy, but only Harrigan's own."

"Then doesn't that settle it?"

"Does it? Come on. We're going back to the family. You can go whenever you're ready, Doc. I'll get your full report in the morning."

The family group looked as though no one had spoken a word since Matt left it. Sister Felicitas and Aunt Ellen were telling their rosaries. Sister Ursula's hand was stroking Concha's black hair. The girl's shoulders had stopped shaking. Arthur was dissecting a cigarette with uncertain fingers. Joseph was doing nothing, majestically.

"All right," said the Lieutenant. "I've had men at the Temple of Light ever since I heard this story. Tonight's their big Easter service; Ahasver can't get away. In a few minutes I'm taking you, Mr. Harrigan, and Duncan over there to see if you can identify Ahasver as the figure you saw."

Concha looked up. Her face was sad and tear-streaked; but it lacked the terror which Matt had seen there before. "Then it was—that man?"

The Lieutenant did not answer directly. "Your father was planning to break up his racket; that's motive enough. He put the curse of death on your father last night—there's premeditation. Your uncle and Duncan saw a man in his fancy-dress costume in the study. And your father left a strange sort of dying message pointing to him as the murderer."

"Isn't that enough?" Joseph demanded. "I'll confess that I never took Wolfe's crusading seriously enough; but now I plan to follow in his footsteps myself. That such dangerous maniacs should be allowed at large—"

"Oh, sure, that's enough, I guess. But . . . Miss Harrigan, how long were you in that chapel?"

"Around ten minutes, I think, Lieutenant."

"You're sure of that? People can guess at time very inaccurately. Mightn't it have been more like one minute, or two at the most?"

"No." Aunt Ellen was firm. "I was just meditating on the fifth mystery. I remember distinctly."

"On the what?"

"When we say the rosary," Sister Ursula put in, "we meditate on a mystery—some aspect of Our Lady's life—for each decade, or set of ten beads. Miss Harrigan means that she had almost finished the rosary."

"And how long does that take?"

"It generally takes me," said Aunt Ellen, "about ten minutes. So I must have been in the chapel at least that long."

"And who did you see come out of the study?"

"Why, no one, Lieutenant."

"In all those ten minutes you didn't see anyone go in or out of your brother's study?"

"Not a soul."

"All right," said Marshall patiently. "At 6:13 Duncan and Harrigan saw a man in a yellow robe in the study. At 6:15 Duncan looks in again and he isn't there. So. Now every door and window was locked securely from the inside except the door to the chapel, which could have been locked from outside. And in front of that door Miss Harrigan had been sitting for ten minutes and had not seen a soul."

Sister Ursula frowned. "But that's not possible."

"Miracles," said Marshall with a trace of professional bitterness, "are in your line, aren't they?"

"To God," Sister Ursula reproved him, "all things are indeed possible. But I find it hard to discern the hand of God in this. There must be some mistake in the evidence."

"There's no mistake," the Lieutenant groaned wearily. "A nice, pretty open-and-shut case. Only one possible suspect. And the trouble is, the whole thing just plain couldn't have happened. Well . . . ! Come on, Mr. Harrigan. Duncan. We're going to talk to this Ahasver. And in the meantime, I'm afraid I'm going to have to leave a couple of men here."

Joseph seemed about to protest, then apparently changed his mind. "A wise precaution, Lieutenant. We cannot be too careful with such dangers at large."

"That's the way to look at it."

"Oh, Lieutenant."

"Yes, Sister?"

"Do you want us here, or may we go back to the convent?"

"I'll have a police car take you back."

"Oh. Thank you very much."

"It isn't funny."

"No. But it is funny to think of the Mother Superior when we drive up in the police car."

Aunt Ellen left with her brother and the Lieutenant. Matt lingered a moment, feeling that there was something he could say to Concha, some little word that might help; but he could think of nothing.

As he turned to go, he could barely overhear a whispered dialogue:

"Mary, my dear."

"Yes, Sister Ursula?"

"I want you to do something very important for me."

"Yes? What is it?"

"I want you to stay with your aunt every minute from now until after mass tomorrow morning. Particularly you must go to mass with her."

"Why—why, yes."

Concha sounded puzzled. Matt, going off to join the Lieutenant, was no less so.

SEVEN

"I wonder," said R. Joseph Harrigan, "if it might be better if I stayed in the background during our visit to the Temple of Light." Even in the police car he looked like a Public Figure; you expected him to tip his hat to invisible multitudes along the street.

"Why?" Lieutenant Marshall asked, practically.

"Need you ask, Lieutenant? After all, my face is not unknown.

These miscreants will recognize me as the brother of their victim; it will put them on their guard."

Marshall thought it over. "No," he said slowly. "I had considered trying a surprise attack, but on second thought it isn't such a good idea. We'll just confront them with the facts."

"You know your own business, of course," said Joseph in tones which implied an exactly opposite opinion.

"Question I wanted to ask you," said Marshall after a brief pause. "Couldn't very well in front of the family. How about women?"

Joseph bridled noticeably. "I'm not sure that I understand your question. If you mean what I think you do, I resent it strongly. I am sure that since Marta—since his wife's death a year ago, my brother had led a strictly celibate existence."

"All right. I'm not on the vice squad any more, thank God; but it wouldn't have to be that necessarily. Any close woman friends; any possibility, maybe, of remarriage?"

"*Close* friends? I should say no—and certainly no thought of remarriage. He saw Mrs. Randall, of course, and Ellen's fellow-members in the Altar and Rosary Guild, and the nuns, and the mothers of some of Mary's school friends; but Ellen and Mary were the only women at all close to him. Wolfe was in many ways a very lonely man, Lieutenant."

"He's got plenty of company now," said Marshall drily.

"Doctor Magruder!"

The lean and mild-mannered police surgeon stopped in the hallway and stared at the nun. "Sister Ursula!" he exclaimed at last. "Good Heavens! I haven't seen you since the good old days at the clinic. Don't tell me you're mixed up in this business?"

"The Harrigans are very dear friends of mine."

"Frightful, isn't it?" Dr. Magruder shook his head pityingly. "Splendid man, Mr. Harrigan, to be taken off like this. You know, Sister, try as I will, I cannot accustom myself to sudden and violent death. If I could only get enough money ahead to retire to private practice. . . . Ah, well, we all have our dreams."

Sister Ursula smiled. "I'll pray for that intention. But could I ask you two questions?"

Magruder frowned. "Most unofficial, you know. If the Lieutenant wanted anything told, he'd tell it."

"I know police routine," said the nun surprisingly. "But these are very harmless questions."

"In that case . . . Well, you may ask them. I don't say I'll answer, mind now."

Sister Ursula fingered the beads hanging from her waist and

seemed to gain confidence from them. "The first is this: Were you able to determine the time of death?"

Dr. Magruder ventured a timid smile. "You say that much more cold-bloodedly than I could, Sister."

"Death isn't so horrible after you've worked in a charity ward, Doctor. And besides, I'm so much more certain than you are that death is swallowed up in victory. But I mustn't proselytize now. Can you answer that question?"

"No, I can't. But not out of official censorship. I simply don't know. Presumably, of course, during the twenty minutes between the time his brother spoke to him and the time the young man saw him dead, but that's not medical evidence. The heat from the fire in that room makes it impossible to draw any exact conclusions."

"Thank you," the nun replied gravely. "And the other question is this: The Lieutenant said that Mr. Harrigan had left a strange sort of dying message. Could you tell me what that was?"

"Hm. I suppose that really . . . After all, it will be in tomorrow's papers, and no harm done. Very well." And he explained about the dart.

"Thank you. Thank you and God bless you, Doctor Magruder. And let me know if ever you leave the force. We might find a patient or two for you."

With rapid deftness, despite the encumbering volume of her habit, Sister Ursula went to the telephone stand in the hall, wrote a brief message on the pad, tore off the sheet, folded it, and inscribed in a neat, well-formed hand: FOR LIEUTENANT MARSHALL.

As she left to join Sister Felicitas in the waiting police car, she handed the note to the guard at the door. "Please," she said. "Give this to the Lieutenant when he gets back. It is most important."

At Marshall's command, the police chauffeur contemptuously parked the car in the yellow zone in front of the Temple of Light. No contributions to Ahasver's parking system were going to go on the department's expense account.

The only Child of Light on duty in the vestibule was the cherubic youth who had greeted Matt and Wolfe the night before. At the sight of this invasion, the boy frowned and looked perturbed.

Matt wondered why. The Lieutenant was in plainclothes; there was nothing noticeably official about him. Was Joseph's face indeed so well known that the youth recognized him instantly? Or had the greeter known last night who Wolfe was, and remembered Matt as his companion?

By the time the three had crossed the vestibule, the cherub's face had settled back into its usual smile of greeting. "Good evening, friends," he chirped cheerily. "I'm afraid you're late for the service. It's almost over."

"Good," Marshall announced briefly. "We want to see the head man."

Inside the auditorium they could hear the hypnotic voice of Ahasver droning on in unintelligible syllables.

"You mean . . . " (reverence crept into the young voice) "you mean Ahasver?"

"As he's known here, yes."

"Lieutenant," Joseph broke in, "do you mean that you know who—?"

"That's enough," said Marshall curtly. "Where can we see him?"

The sound of the voice inside ceased, and the organ struck up *Old Christianity.*

"That's the end," the cherub informed them. "The people will be coming out now. If you wait a minute, I'll take you backstage—I mean, back to the Chamber of Contemplation."

"The words aren't the same," the Lieutenant complained as he listened to this new version of the great hymn.

"Aren't they *beautiful*? Ahasver read them once in his book. They come from the Ancients."

Marshall made no comment aloud.

The last "ON!!!" rang out with such volume that Matt expected the doors to burst open. "There," said the youth. "Now I'll take you around. Follow me."

He led them into the auditorium and down a side aisle. It was hard work swimming against the current of outpouring Children of Light. Matt heard voices around him.

"Wasn't he wonderful tonight?"

"It's so nice to really know when Easter is, isn't it? When you think how much he brings us from the Ancients . . . "

"He certainly makes you think. Something's got to be done about this country, and we're the ones to do it."

"Remember last night? My, that was exciting."

"And I surely would like to know what's going to happen to that dreadful man after we put the Nine Times Nine on him."

They were such harmless people, Matt thought, such poor innocents. But he remembered their faces last night when they uttered the Nine Times Nine, and he remembered the size of the bills which had come from these shabby pockets; and he felt an eager desire to get back to Wolfe Harrigan's study and get on with the work.

"Here we are," the cherub said, pausing before the door of a room built into the wings of the auditorium's stage . "Master," he announced, tapping on the door and falling into Ahasver's own archaic idiom, "here are some would speak with you."

The voice rang deep from inside. "I am free, and I deny myself to none. Let them enter."

The cherub opened the door, and the three men stepped into a small yellow cubicle. The sheer yellowness of it overwhelmed them all for a moment. The wallpaper, the carpet, the couch, and the hassock upon which Ahasver sat cross-legged were all of the same pure yellow as his robe, forming in all such a unified mass of color that the leader's figure was nearly invisible against it, and he seemed to be only a beard hanging in space.

"Degradation," he pronounced, as though guessing their thoughts, "and contemplation are one. This ye must learn. And therefore is my Chamber of Contemplation bedizened in the hue of my degradation." If the faces of Matt, Joseph, or the Lieutenant occasioned any surprise in him, he concealed it magnificently. They might have been any three devout followers who chose to visit the Master. "You may go," he added calmly to the cherub.

"But, Master," the youth protested, "these men are—"

"What is it to me or to thee who they are? They have come to me, and that is sufficient. Go."

Reluctantly the cherub went. "Now," Ahasver turned to his guests and waved courteously at the couch, "what is it ye would know?"

"I would know," said Lieutenant Terence Marshall, "where the hell you were at six o'clock this afternoon."

Ellen Harrigan was reading a chapter in *The Imitation of Christ* when Concha came into her room. Silver-backed hairbrush in hand, the child was punctiliously giving her short black hair its nightly hundred strokes.

"Aunt Ellen," she ventured.

"Yes, Mary?"

"I'm sorry to bother you, but would you mind . . . What I mean is, could I . . . Can I sleep in here with you tonight?"

"Certainly, child. I must admit I shan't mind company myself. But take care you don't catch my cold."

"Colds! How can we talk like this about colds—No. I'm sorry. Don't let me make you stop reading."

Ellen closed her book. "God gave us more than our own souls to look out for. If you need someone to talk to, Mary . . . "

Concha sat down on the bed. "I don't know what I need. I do need something. I need it terribly." Mechanically she went on brushing.

"I know, dear. But don't worry about your father. We know what he was, and we know that all is well with him. We shall have masses said, of course, but I can't think that your father will stay in purgatory for long."

"Can I go to mass with you tomorrow, Aunt Ellen?"

Ellen Harrigan's dry old face glowed with pleasure. "Of course, my dear. Whenever you want to."

"I can't—I don't think I ought to take communion, like you, but I do want to go. . . . Aunt Ellen."

"Yes, dear?"

"When did Father go to confession last?"

Aunt Ellen frowned. "A week ago last Wednesday. He went to communion on Holy Thursday, just as he always—did. But why?"

"Then that's all right. I'd hate to have to think—"

"Think what, dear?"

"Nothing. . . . Aunt Ellen?"

"Yes?"

The hand holding the brush hung inactive. "You know about these things maybe . . . if anybody does. Tell me. Is it a sin to want something awful?"

"It isn't wrong to want something very badly, unless of course that something belongs to somebody else. That would be against the tenth commandment."

"No, no. I mean to want something to happen—something awful." Concha's voice was earnest and terrible.

Ellen sat on the bed beside the girl and took her free hand. "Thoughts aren't sins unless we entertain them willfully and dwell on them. No one can be responsible for the temptations that come into his mind, if he doesn't yield to them. Our Lord himself was tempted."

"But if you do dwell on a thought—if you hate it, but just can't help it—if you keep wanting this awful thing—is that a sin?"

"You'd better talk to Father O'Toole next time you go to confession. Tell him all about it. But in the meantime, don't let it worry you, child. I'm sure it isn't anything so very dreadful."

"But it *is*." Her young voice was pleading.

"Don't take on so, dear. Try to cast out these thoughts. Simply don't think about this awful thing any more."

"But I have to, Aunt Ellen. Really I have to. I mean because—well, because it's happened."

Ellen Harrigan drew her hand away with a little start. Wearily Concha raised her brush and resumed stroking her hair.

In the overpowering Chamber of Contemplation, Ahasver plucked at his beard (most contemplatively) with one yellow-gloved hand. "Where I was at six o'clock this afternoon? What is that to you, and by what right do you ask it of me?"

Marshall showed his badge silently.

"Verily?" Ahasver smiled. "And these gentlemen?"

"Witnesses."

"And whereunto may they bear witness?"

"You're answering the questions."

"Very well. It is not my place to obstruct the forces ruling this country—as yet. At six, you say?"

"Yes."

"At six . . . As you know, officer, this is Easter Sunday. No, do not interrupt me, I pray you. You, too, are bound to the old superstitions; in time even you shall recognize the new truths, of which this is one of the smallest. Today is Easter Sunday; and to commemorate this glorious day of the ascension of one of the Ancients to the Ancient of Ancients, I called a meeting of the innermost group: the Twelve of the Nine.

"For ye must know," he explained with a trace of condescension, "that there have been nine great Ancients, and that each of these has had twelve apostles. For this reason my closest circle of initiates numbers one hundred and eight, in honor of those twelve of the Nine who stood closest to the Ancients."

"When I want a lecture I'll come to the regular service. Let's hear about six o'clock."

"This closed meeting," Ahasver went on imperturbably, "lasted from five o'clock until seven. It was held in the Auditorium here. I spoke for almost the full two hours."

"You mean you can produce a hundred and eight witnesses to swear you were in this building from 5:55 to 6:15 today?"

"I can, though I see as yet no reason why it should be necessary. Will you tell me, officer, why I should do so?"

Instead of answering him, Marshall turned to Matt. "How about it?" he asked.

Matt shook his head. "I couldn't swear. It's the same costume all right—that much I'm sure of. But I couldn't swear to the man."

"And you, Mr. Harrigan?"

Joseph glared at the religious leader. "There stands the man who murdered my brother!" he declared dramatically.

"Come now, Mr. Harrigan. I don't want conclusions and opinions. I want to know if you, as a lawyer, would go into court and swear that that is the man you saw."

Joseph Harrigan cleared his throat and made the noise sound significant. "As a man, Lieutenant, I am morally positive of this rogue's guilt. But if you put it to me as a lawyer, with all due regard for the rules of evidence and the credibility of the testimony of eyewitnesses, the answer—Well, Lieutenant, I regret that the answer is no. I can swear only to the costume."

A slow smile had spread over the cultist's face as Joseph spoke. "Why so timorous, Mr. Harrigan? Your brother would not have permitted a trifling doubt so to confuse him. Why not go further and swear that I was the man? For I was, you know."

Harrigan sprang from the couch. "How dare you!" he bellowed.

"Have you the brazen insolence to squat there and tell me to my nose that you thrust an automatic into my brother's face and foully did him to death? By God, I'll—"

"Easy there," Marshall muttered. "Hold him, Duncan; he's a-rearin'. Now look here, you; do I understand that you're making a confession?"

Ahasver still smiled, poised and self-assured. "You do, officer."

"All right. But what becomes of the Twelve of the Nine and the hundred and eight witnesses you were going to give me?"

"That, officer, is precisely why I am making this confession. I killed Wolfe Harrigan this afternoon, *and* I addressed the Twelve of the Nine. For is it not written in the eleventh chapter of the Gospel according to Joseph:

> Know ye therefore that there be truth in all things, even where man discerneth falsehood; but it must sometimes chance that truth doth weigh against truth in even balance, and neither shall be believed.

In this case, however, the balance is not even. Despite my reputation for truth, I fear that you will accept one hundred and eight sworn statements against my single word; and even if you should not, surely a court of law will. And this is well, because I must continue my work in freedom. That work should not cease even for that minute of eternity which the state might occupy in a vain attempt to execute me."

A new power seemed to have flowed into Ahasver as he made his strange confession. He was no longer merely a self-confident showman. Now he seemed an arbiter of life and death, calmly and smilingly passing immortal judgment. Lieutenant Marshall tried hard to suppress an involuntary tone of awe as he asked, "Are you trying to suggest that you were in both places at once?"

"I am not suggesting, officer; I am stating the truth."

Marshall seemed near strangulation. He was red in the face as he blurted, "Go ahead. Tell us about it."

"Mr. Harrigan," Ahasver went on coolly, "was a dangerous and evil man."

"Am I to stand here," shouted Joseph, "and listen to such vile words about my poor brother?"

"Sit down," Marshall grunted. "Objection overruled. Go on."

"He was evil, you must understand, because he believed only in the evil superstitions of the old order. His brain and his soul were filled with the perversions of Paul and Luke, rendered still more perverse by generations of popes and cardinals. He was dangerous because he sought to destroy the Light! and it was needful that the Light should destroy him. I was the agent of that Light.

"Last night all of us, all the children of the Light, set upon Wolfe Harrigan the Nine Times Nine, as was commanded of me by the Ancients. From that setting came my strength, I am not an Ancient, though some of my followers flatter me by thinking so. I am not the Light, but am to bear witness of the Light. In myself I am but a poor Jew lost in the maze of immortality, and I cannot release my astral body at will unless strength be given me from otherwhere. Through the Nine Times Nine, this strength was given me, and I fulfilled my mission."

Marshall was conquering the hypnotic spell of Ahasver's words. "How?" he asked skeptically.

"While part of me preached here to the Twelve of the Nine, the other and more vital part went—"

"This is poisonous rot!" R. Joseph interrupted. "I refuse to countenance an astral body, no matter how well it explains that devilish locked study. My brother was killed by a man, not a spirit. I saw that man, and it was this charlatan. If he hopes to delude us with tales of astral bodies—"

"May I continue, officer?"

"Go ahead. I understand your feelings, Mr. Harrigan, and God knows you've got my sympathy; but let's hear this out."

"Thank you, officer. I am not certain of the exact time, but it was shortly after six o'clock when I went to Mr. Harrigan's home. He was locked in his study. Apparently he had feared the Nine Times Nine, but he did not realize how futile his precautions were to prove. Weapons . . ." (Ahasver seemed to be picking his words cautiously) "weapons, I need hardly tell you, cannot be carried on the astral body. I had intended using the psychic powers of the Ancients, as I had once been compelled to do in Tibet, but when I saw the automatic on his . . . desk, I resolved on that means instead to conserve my psychic energy. I shot him in the face, that his lying mouth might be wiped out forever. For is it not written—"

"All right. Where did he fall?"

"Have I not told you enough? I shall continue my story when you have charged me."

Marshall rose. "That'd be ducky, wouldn't it? Just the publicity you need. Sorry, brother. Thanks for a good show."

Outside the temple a plainclothes-man stepped up to the Lieutenant, exchanged a few words, and went back to his post. Evidently Marshall, for all his patent scorn, was not taking any chances.

"May I return to my own home?" R. Joseph Harrigan demanded. "If even that contemptible murderous heretic is free to follow his own devices, surely I—"

"Wait a minute. Don't get on your high horse before I can even answer you. Sure, you can go home. Were you your brother's lawyer?"

"In private affairs, yes. His professional work, of course, was carried on in collaboration with the District Attorney's office."

"I'll get in touch with you tomorrow about his will. So long, and watch out for astral bodies. Like a police escort home?"

"I'll take a cab over on the boulevard." R. Joseph looked disappointed, as though this courteous treatment had done him out of a chance to be indignant.

"How about me?" Matt asked.

"You're coming back to the house and help me go over Harrigan's papers. If he was training you for an assistant, you ought to be more help to me than any of the others."

"So you really think," Matt wondered as they drove off in the police car, "that Ahasver's in the clear?"

"Who said that? I refused to arrest him because that was what he wanted. He'd have had a lawyer there with a writ and a hundred and eight depositions first thing tomorrow morning, and been out and free again like a nice pretty martyr. Just what the doctor ordered."

"Then you think—"

"I think," said Lieutenant Marshall heavily, "that a beard and a robe prove almighty little."

EIGHT

"Wait here," Lieutenant Marshall ordered, and Matt dutifully waited in the dark hallway while the officer disappeared into the study. From inside came the clicks of a telephone dial and then the Lieutenant's voice, unusually subdued.

The house was otherwise silent, not with the stilly hush of death, but with the quite ordinary silence of a home whose inhabitants have all gone to sleep. It was hard to believe that violence and terror had invaded this calm place only a few hours before.

Matt lit a cigarette and tried to devote his mind to the problem of that study, where something in a yellow robe had come and been seen and killed and vanished as though it had never been. He had got no further than the rankly fantastic notion of a secret passageway when the Lieutenant reopened the door, which had been restored during their absence to some semblance of working order by an anonymous carpenter on the force.

"Come in," Marshall commanded. He paused, as though judging

how much to say. "That was Mike Jordan I was talking to," he said at last. "I've known him for years, known him well, too; and if he says a man is to be trusted, I'll take his word for it. You seem to have clicked with him on the Project, pink slip or no pink slip."

"He was swell to work with."

"Don't get me wrong," the Lieutenant added hastily. "This doesn't put you out in the clear with wings sprouting and a nice little halo labeled 'Innocent.' It just means that I can use you for what I want without worrying too much about it."

"And what do you want?"

Marshall took up his stance again in front of the fireplace. "Families," he announced didactically, "known damn little about themselves. If you want a phony picture of a man, faked and hoked out of all recognition, just go to his nearest and dearest ones. Any case I've ever walked into, after a week I could tell you more about each person involved than any one of them could have told about another. We see them raw. We see the essence, without all the prettifactions that ordinary life builds up around them.

"But all that takes a little time. As I said, about a week. Now in this case, you've got all the advantages of the police: you come into the family cold, you see them under tension and excitement, you get the outside viewpoint; but you've got a head start on us by two days. You haven't been here long enough to start in taking everybody at the family evaluation; but you have seen enough to know a little more than I do.

"So, frankly, I'd like you to stick around. I want to talk out loud to you, and I want you to talk. You can be damned useful if you want to." He paused again, then looked straight at Matt. "Is it a deal?"

"It's a deal."

"All right. Let's have us a little open forum. I'm not asking you for a statement. I just want to talk. Tell me anything you think of, ask me what you want to know within reason, and let me do the sifting. If we hit on something vital, you can make a formal statement later. This is strictly off the record."

"Look. I'll lead with a question. Does this approach mean you think this is a family crime?"

"Hell, Duncan, I don't know. To answer that I'd have to start my own talking out loud."

"It's not a nice thought," said Matt reflectively.

"Is murder ever a nice thought? Does it make murder any the more pleasant, any the cleaner, if the murderer has nothing to do with the victim, or at most a strict business relationship? Is the pervert who picks a stranger for experiment, the business-man who gets rid of his partner for the benefit of his pocket, a decenter sort of chap than the daughter who kills her father because living with him is hell?

"No, Duncan; if we're going to talk about this case, you've got to realize that a murderer is a murderer. There are no degrees of murder save those the law recognizes, and I mean the law, and not the arrogant whims of a bemused jury. Murder—" Marshall broke off and looked somewhat abashed. "Sorry, Duncan. I did debating at Oxford; it seems to stick in the blood."

"Go on," Matt grinned. "I think I like this better than your official style."

Marshall laughed. "If you knew how hard I sweat all day to hide the fact that I used to be—God help me!—a Phi Bete . . . ! All right. I won't worry about you. I'll say what I feel like saying, and not give a damn whether it seems to come from the detective lieutenant or from the Rhodes scholar."

"But do you," Matt persisted, "think that this is a private and personal crime, rooted in this house?"

"As I said, I don't know. It's this way: No matter how much scientific criminology may accomplish, no matter how many clews point in what directions, the first thing a police detective wants to know is: Who wanted him dead? Motive is a stronger indication than any proof of means or opportunity. It all comes around to the good old *Cui bono?* And if Captain Harding heard Latin dropping from my fair lips he'd have my badge.

"Now in this case we've got a man whose very life provides us with two completely separate sets of motives. He was (a) a rich man, who (b) exposed criminals. And there you are. His richness means—I think we're safe in assuming till we've read the will—that anybody in the family had a motive."

"Come now," Matt broke in. "That's nonsense. I'll admit people might kill a distant relative for inheritance, but your own brother, your father . . . "

Marshall sighed. "The trouble with you is, you believe in humanity. If you'd ever known a woman—and a charming woman she was, too—who'd insured her three children and then poisoned them one by one so she could keep her fancy man in the proper style . . . "

Matt gave in. "As you please. I still don't believe it, but go ahead."

"All right. That's one group of motives: anyone who might get money from his death. The other group is the criminals, the religious racketeers. Any one of them might have killed him, either to avenge past exposures or to forestall future ones. This could be either of two kinds of crime—and your guess is as good as mine as to which it is."

"If motive lets you down, how about the means and opportunity that you mentioned so scornfully?"

"A lot of help means is. Wolfe Harrigan was shot with the automatic you took from the Swami. Yes, we've checked its number; it was sold, quite openly, to Hermann Sussmaul about a year ago. He claimed he was being persecuted—threats against his life—managed to get a permit. I suspect some palm-greasing somewhere. The ballistic check-up has come through, too. There's no question that that was the means.

"All right. So what? You gave that gun to Harrigan Friday night. Nobody admits having seen it since. He probably kept it in his desk here. He might have taken it out for any reason—perhaps telling the story of Friday night. No, means is no good."

"There's another possibility."

"I think I know what you mean. That he gave it back to Sussmaul Friday night after you left, and so it does mean Sussmaul. All right. Can you see Harrigan, can you see any man, under the circumstances, saying, 'Here. You forgot your pistol. Drop around again, and better luck next time'? Can you imagine that?"

"No."

"Then we'll take it that the automatic was here, probably right in this room, over the weekend; and that anyone who had access to Wolfe Harrigan also had access to the gun. In other words, Opportunity provides Means. The two points are one."

"And how about Opportunity?"

"You know as much about that as anybody. Let's postpone for a moment the question of how the murderer got out of this room; and we're left with the fact that anybody could have got in. Anybody, that is, that Wolfe Harrigan wanted to let in. Miss Harrigan was with the nuns earlier, but she had come down here alone. Joseph was wandering around. The cook is uncertain on time, there might have been a gap between the time the girl left you and the time when she showed up in the kitchen. Arthur was alone in his room.

"And nobody was where he could see this hall door. Anyone from outside who knew about the back entrance could have slipped in that way—if, of course, Wolfe was willing to admit him. Opportunity doesn't even serve to tie things down to the family, though at first glance you might think so. To be sure, nobody, not even the servants, recalls seeing anybody suspicious around here; but murderers are apt to be sort of shy about being seen."

"So where are we?" Matt asked.

"Exactly nowhere."

"We do know, though, of one person who had definite intent upon the life of Wolfe Harrigan."

"Two," Marshall corrected, "if you count Ahasver and the Nine

Times Nine. But you still like Sussmaul the Swami, don't you? All right. We'll see. He's being dragged in tonight. I'll see what I can get out of him tomorrow."

Matt jumped. "What was that?"

The light rapping on the door was repeated. Cautiously, his right hand resting on his service pistol, Marshall opened the door.

One of the officers on duty stood there, holding out a note. "Almost forgot this sir. That nun left it for you."

At about this time Detective Sergeant Krauter stood in the midst of a disarrayed and disgusting apartment. The windows had been open to the cold night ever since the detective's entrance, but the sickening smell of stale cheap incense still poisoned the room.

There had been no need for such a thorough search. Either the Swami Mahopadhyaya Virasenanda was in his customary abode or he was not. But the Sergeant's wife liked fortune-tellers (though happily of a less expensive class), and Sergeant Krauter had taken a malicious and unofficial pleasure in playing hell with the joint.

Now he turned beaming and surveyed the havoc which he had wrought with the hyperdeluxe furnishings. "I guess he ain't here," he said satisfied.

The manager pulled her dressing gown even tighter around ner. "I told you that five times already," she insisted. "Nobody's seen him here since Friday night. He went out then and he hasn't come back." She caught a disturbing glimpse of herself in the gold-framed mirror and saw flecks of cold cream which her hasty wiping had missed. "Now will you get out?"

"But how do you know he ain't been here?" Krauter was being persistent. "You can't see everybody that comes and goes."

"I—I was watching for him," the manager admitted defiantly.

"So!" Krauter pounced. "Behind in his rent, was he? Making trouble around the house?"

"The Swami," she retorted indignantly, "is as fine a tenant as ever I had. Never a breath of trouble from him. And not only does he pay his rent on the dot, but he used to give me free scryings—even the purple ones. If you only knew, officer, how much happiness a man like the Swami can bring into a woman's life, you wouldn't be persecuting him in this absurd manner."

"Happiness!" the Sergeant snorted. "Lady, if you only knew—" He broke off; his wife's notions, heavy though they weighed on him, were not official business. "Why were you watching for him?"

The manager turned her head away and tried unsuccessfully to dab at the cold cream with a corner of her sleeve.

"Come on. What made you suspicious? Let's have it."

"Oh, well. I'm sure the Swami must have had some very good

reason for it, but all the same I was a little worried. After all this is a respectable house, and—"

"Out with it, lady."

"He . . . I saw him in the hall and he was tightening his belt only he didn't think anybody was looking and he—he was Carrying a Gun."

The Sergeant groaned. All that work to learn just what they knew to start with. "O.K.," he said. "I'll be going. But you remember if that rat shows up and you don't phone headquarters, you'll be liable for . . . " He paused and then found a legal phrase of just the right impressiveness. "For harboring a fugitive."

The manager opened the door with impatient relief. But the Sergeant had halted on his way out. "When was this apartment cleaned last?"

"Friday morning."

The Sergeant looked reflectively down at the ashtray. One half of the cigarettes in it were ordinary half-inch stubs. The others were almost two inches long, and bent double.

Lieutenant Marshall unfolded the nun's note, read it rapidly, and passed it to Matt. It ran:

MY DEAR LIEUTENANT:

> Please do not think this a frivolous request. The Harrigans or Dr. Magruder can assure you that I am not given to whims.
>
> I am asking you to ascertain whether any files or books other than the Ahasver file show signs of having been pricked by a dart.
>
> I shall not affront your professional intelligence by giving reasons for this request. In fact, I fear it is presumptuous of me to make it, since such a search has doubtless been conducted already.
>
> Sincerely yours,
MARY URSULA, O.M.B.

"What does she mean?" Matt demanded.

"She mean's that I'm a damned fool, but she's too polite to say so. She's right too; I am. Even after I heard your story, I never thought of looking for another dart-prick. Well, Duncan, here's your chance to do some police work. We're going hunting."

It was long slow work. The Lieutenant produced a magnifying glass from his pocket and Matt found one on the desk. Carefully they scrutinized the backs of each file under the dart board. They had not been at it long when the Lieutenant let out a premature cry of gleeful discovery, only to grunt disgust and shove the file back into its place.

"What's up?" Matt asked.

"Thought I had something there. Hole pricked in the back of the Swami Sussmaul file. But then I remembered your story of Friday. Of course there would have to be."

"And there's only one hole?"

"Only one."

Matt made the next discovery—oddly enough not among the files, but in one of the volumes of history in the case with them. The Lieutenant looked at the book and tossed it aside with a snort.

But after the most thorough search, that volume was the only one which bore the telling mark. "It would have to be in this bookcase," Marshall reflected. "The others are too far away for him to aim straight, and the angle would be next to impossible. And yet all we can find is this." He flipped the volume open to its title page and read:

THE REIGN OF
WILLIAM THE SECOND
KING OF ENGLAND
together with
Some Particulars of the Effect
upon
THE CHURCH IN ENGLAND
of
THE FIRST CRUSADE

"That's a help, that is. He must have been practicing—seeing if he could aim at a book and make the dart stick."

"Now," said Matt, "that I've finished my first job of police work, would you mind telling me just what I've been doing? Why should there be another volume here with a dart-prick in it?"

"That's obvious. I should have seen it myself. Supposing somebody was framing Ahasver. In other words, that you were deliberately allowed to see that yellow robe. All right. That means the dart is a frame too, stuck in the Ahasver file by the murderer. But it's still possible that Harrigan did throw the dart where it had its true meaning. If, for instance, we'd found a second mark in the Swami's file, that would mean that Harrigan had actually thrown the dart there to leave us a clew to the Swami, but that Sussmaul had pulled it out and stuck it in the Ahasver volume."

"Do you think Ahasver was framed?"

"You ask more questions. I think this much: He was either framed or guilty. There was no reason on God's earth for anybody to wear the yellow robe unless he either was Ahasver or was trying like hell to implicate him. Same goes for the dart."

"But Ahasver's alibi—"

"All right. One hundred and eight people saw a man in a yellow robe at the Temple. You saw a man in a yellow robe here. Who saw Ahasver? Who has ever seen Ahasver? All anybody sees is a robe and a beard."

"We didn't even see a beard."

"What? Was this a clean-shaven astral body that you saw hovering?"

"I don't know. The head was turned away from the window, and that lama-ish hood obscured it. All we saw was the robe."

"So. I don't know whether that helps or complicates. . . . You know, Duncan, that Temple alibi is easier to see through and harder to crack than anything else I've ever run into. Every one of those hundred and eight disciples will swear on the Gospel according to Joseph that he saw Ahasver this afternoon. All he actually saw is somebody in Ahasver's get-up, but try and prove that. If I could only learn who Ahasver really is . . . "

"If you arrest the man, you can strip him or do what you like."

"Can we? Leave our rights out of the question; he'd have a lawyer there so quick we'd never get him past the booking desk. . . . You can't help me on this, can you, Duncan?"

"Me? Why?"

Marshall took a sheet of typescript from the desk. "Have you seen this?"

Matt glanced at it. "No. This must be what he was working on this afternoon."

"Read it."

Matt read:

The personal identity of this charlatan Ahasver and the nature of the forces operating behind and through him is still a mystery. The strong bias of his teachings against established religions and against all liberal philosophies (for Ahasver can outdo the Honorable Martin Dies or even the Reverend Father Coughlin) indicates that his movement may have a political purpose.

Ahasver is such an excellent platform performer that one tends to suspect that he has been hired for just that purpose, and that some other Child of Light stands behind him as a guiding power. My own surmise as to the identity of that Child is so startling and, I regretfully confess, so unsupported by factual evidence, that it must remain for the moment known only to me.

"He had some idea," said Marshall. "And you were his confidential assistant. How about it?"

"This was on his mind today. He made some cryptic remarks this afternoon—Lord! I remember now. He said there were some secret notes which he hadn't shown even me."

"What are we waiting for?" And Marshall pointed sternly at the paper-laden desk.

NINE

Two long hours later Matt looked up logily from the outspread mass of papers. "You know," he muttered, "I work late in this room. This is my third night here, and already I'm beginning to remember sleep as something far off and beautiful—just a fond and shimmering memory."

"At least," Marshall grunted, "you're a bachelor."

Matt shoved the papers away and leaned back in the chair, the same chair from which Wolfe Harrigan had so often tossed his darts and in which he must have sat that very afternoon as he received his last visitor. "One thing's sure. Those secret notes aren't here. Not a trace of them. But the time wasn't wasted; you've got a complete list now of every iron Harrigan had in the fire."

"Small-time stuff. We'll give it a routine check-up and that'll be that. Ahasver and the Swami are still the only ones in the lot important enough to worry about. These two-for-a-nickel fortune-tellers aren't going to risk a murder rap for the sake of their businesses."

Matt rose and stretched. "And maybe now I could go home? You've no idea how good even that foul bedroom of mine is going to look tonight."

The Lieutenant had risen, too. "Don't tempt me, Duncan. If I start thinking of Leona, I'm apt to scrap the whole damned thing and scram for home myself. But we've got one more job."

Matt groaned. "And what might that be?"

"We're going over this room. Aside from you, nobody but the police has been in here since the body was found. Let it go a day, and there's no telling what false leads might be planted. Now we're going to find out, here and now, how this locked-room business was hocused. Sit down again; I want to do some talking first.

"The first thing is to define this seemingly impossible situation. All right. A man is shot in a room from which, apparently, no one could have made an exit. Now what's the first rational possibility that strikes you?"

"But somebody must have made an exit. Joseph and I saw—"

"I know. But forget that for a minute. How would you explain it otherwise?"

"Suicide?"

"Right. Possibility number one: Suicide. Now how does that check with the known facts? Direction of bullet, O.K. Presence of weapon, O.K. Motive, missing. Still, you could make out a pretty good case if it wasn't for one thing. The paraffin test shows that neither of Harrigan's hands has fired a gun recently; and since he must have died instantaneously, he can't very well have had time to remove gloves. He died barehanded, and his hands are innocent. That lets out suicide."

"How about some mechanical contrivance for pulling the trigger so that his hands wouldn't be marked?"

"Why? Just to be nasty? But even if he had, what became of the contrivance? The squad went over this room like a plague of locusts. No, suicide's out. Now how else can a man be shot in a room nobody left?"

"He could," Matt ventured hesitantly, "have been shot from outside and the weapon tossed in."

"Good enough. Possibility number two: Shot from outside. But there's no more room for a bullet to get in, much less the automatic itself, than there is for the murderer to get out. And to clinch it, there are powder burns on what's left of Harrigan's face. He was shot in this room, and the murderer was physically present in the room with him."

"Hell," said Matt, "that's just what Joseph and I told you to start with. Why this roundabout chain to prove it?"

"Because it had to be proved. Don't you see? Ever since you told me about the lighting effects at the Temple, I've been worried. Remember? Ahasver uses a projector to throw colors on the back wall of the stage. There was a possibility that the yellow figure you saw was just a projected image; we had to prove that somebody was really here."

Matt grinned. "Sorry, Lieutenant, but I could have disproved your projection theory without all that fuss. Remember—we were in the dusk outside and could see in here because the fire was bright. If an image had been projected from outside against the windows, we couldn't have seen it because of the light behind it. If it was projected from inside here onto a screen or a wall, the same argument goes as for a suicide device: your plague of locusts would have found it."

Marshall thought this over and nodded. "All right. Projection is out on all counts. No optical illusions here. The murderer was in this room. Therefore, in some manner, the murderer left this room, and left it all locked up behind him. How?

"We'll take all the exits one by one. Item, one door to hall, broken down by police and partially restored by Officer Lundgren. This door was bolted from inside. Now look at that bolt. All that shows on this side is a round knob. You turn it to the right, and a good solid bolt shoots into the jamb. To the left, and the door is free again. Point: It has to be turned *from this side*. You can't simply slip a catch, walk out, and let it lock behind you. And it can't be jiggered from the other side. It isn't a question of just sliding a bolt across with a piece of string; this is a knob, that has to be turned by actual pressure. It's stiff, too—needs oiling badly." Marshall paused and looked at Matt. "Satisfied?"

Matt nodded. "He didn't get out through there."

Marshall walked over to the north wall. "Item, one small window set high in wall. Does not open. Putty in cracks at least a year old. Satisfied?"

"Satisfied."

"Item, one fireplace. Wide but exceedingly sooty chimney. Probably could be climbed if necessary. But the top of the chimney is covered with fine wire mesh to keep ashes from blowing over the croquet lawn, and the dust and soot up there has not been disturbed. Satisfied?"

"Satisfied."

"Item, another small window, same as hereinbefore described. Item, one pair of large French windows, bolted at top and bottom. Also in need of oiling. Satisfied?"

"No." Matt paused in their tour of inspection and knelt down to examine the lower bolt. "I'll admit it's stiff," he said after testing it, "but wouldn't it be possible to slam the window in such a way that this bolt would fall into place?"

Marshall shook his head. "Barely possible, I grant, though so damned unlikely as not to be worth bothering about. But even if you do that, how do you fix the upper bolt? I confess you can slam a thing hard enough to make it drop, but how can you make it shoot up?"

"String," Matt answered promptly. "Look. This'll work. You loop a piece of string around the upper bolt and let the ends hang outside. Then you go out and slam the window so that the lower bolt falls into place. Then pull down on both ends of the string, pulley-like, and jerk the upper bolt into place. Result: One room you couldn't possibly have got out of."

Marshall frowned. "Did you hear a window slam?"

"We were hammering on the door; we couldn't have heard it."

"Well, there's maybe one way to check this bright idea." The Lieutenant pulled a chair over to the windows, stood on its seat, and opened both frames. Carefully he looked along the top edges, then stood down.

"Sorry. There's a solid undisturbed layer of dust all over the frames, and I'm damned if I see how you could have pulled any string trick without disturbing it. Now are you satisfied?"

"Yes," Matt admitted.

"Then we've covered every aperture of this room but one—the chapel door. And that is the one way out of this room that you can lock behind you. I may add, for your edification, that the room has been checked thoroughly for all secret passages, sliding panels, Priest's Holes, and other nefarious contraptions. This search resulted in the discovery of item, one abandoned rat hole in the corner behind the big bookcase, diameter three inches, and item, one hole in the back of the fireplace where the cement had fallen out between rocks, diameter two inches. So we're left with the chapel door."

"And in front of that chapel door Ellen Harrigan had been sitting for ten minutes, and swears no one went in or out."

"Exactly." Lieutenant Marshall's tone was now hard and serious. "So what does that mean?"

"It means we've overlooked something somewhere."

"Does it? Or does it mean that Ellen Harrigan is either shielding someone—which definitely limits the murderer to this family—or else—"

Again there was a rap on the door, this time a more excited and peremptory rap.

Marshall broke off his conjecture. This visitor was the other officer on guard, and in a rare state of excitement. "Lieutenant! We've found it!"

"You don't have to wake up the house. Found what?"

"Come on out in back."

At a signal from Marshall, Matt followed along, out the back entrance and alongside the rear extension of the house which held the kitchen and the servants' quarters.

"I heard a noise out back here," the officer was explaining. "A prowler, I says to myself. Let's see what goes on. So I come back out here, only I don't see nobody. I think it was maybe a cat or something so I start to come back, only I smell something. And then I see there's a fire going in the incinerator. Seems like I remember it was out earlier tonight so I decide to check up. And when I see what it is, I just leave it there and go get you. 'This is important,' I says to myself. 'The Lieutenant better see this for himself.'"

They were in the back yard now, a dingy and utilitarian-looking area for so fine an establishment. Here were washlines and ashcans and boxes filled with old tins and bottles. And in the center of the yard stood the incinerator, giving out stifled puffs of acrid smoke.

Lieutenant Marshall strode across the yard and yanked out the smoldering mass. "Give us your flash, Rafferty."

The object was already partially consumed, but there was no mistaking its nature. It was a yellow robe, cut to the design of Ahasver's.

Matt had returned to his dingy little hotel at such hours before, but never, as now, cold sober. At other times he had always passed through the lobby in unheeding haste; but now all its drabness stabbed through his exhaustion. The two dusty bare light bulbs were like unwinking old eyes set in a sagging face. The droning snore of the night clerk was the only human sound that would not have seemed out of place.

With a shock Matt realized, as he climbed the rickety stairs, that he too stood to benefit by Wolfe Harrigan's death. Or did he? Did a literary executor profit at all from the royalties of his work; or was it all a labor of love, the revenues of which flowed direct into the estate? At any rate, the post should give him some reputation with Harrigan's publishers, a certain position which might make the acceptance of his own work more likely. He might not always be living in hotels like this.

He was finding, to his exasperation, that these surroundings became more than ever intolerable after he had been at the Harrigan home. A house of death that mansion might be; but it was also a house of comfort, with filling food and hot water and good plumbing. Death is not so terrible among the rich, he thought; with them it only balances the account, while from the poor it takes their last possession.

Matt shook himself. Only in such a state of sleepless exhaustion could he be so deeply platitudinous. He unlocked the door of his room, reached his hand into the darkness, and clicked the light switch.

Nothing happened.

Foolishly he clicked again and yet again. The room was still black. He swore quietly and closed the door behind him.

"Do not lock it," a soft voice advised.

Matt started. "What the hell—"

"I said, do not lock it. No, do not strike a match, either. Feel your way to the bed; you must know the room well enough. Then sit down, so that we can talk."

Matt hesitated. "Do as I say," the voice persisted. "I do not need to tell you that I should not be making these threatening commands unless I was armed."

Being a hero is all very well in its way, but sometimes rather pointless. Matt obediently felt his way to the bed and sat down. He had left the window-blind up, he remembered; now it was pulled down to leave the room in full obscurity.

"It is true, is it not," the voice went on calmly, "that the late and regretted Wolfe Harrigan made of you his literary executor?"

"His will hasn't been read yet."

"Please. Let us not be at cross purposes. Men know things that have not yet been read, even without psychic aid. Is it true?"

A lie, Matt decided, would probably not be believed; moreover, only through the truth could he play along and learn the purpose of this visit. "Yes," he said.

"Good. Then my vigil has not been wasted. And if you knew with what difficulty I located this vile room, you would feel highly flattered by my perseverance." The voice was silent for a moment, then resumed in more businesslike tones. "Mr. Duncan, at what price do you value your integrity?"

"I don't know. I've never had an offer."

"Please. I am not here to banter cross talk. If we are not smart, we shall understand each other better. Is it your resolve to use everything which you find among those papers which fall into your hands?"

"It is."

"And is it your further resolve to cooperate with the District Attorney's office, as was the wont of Mr. Harrigan?"

"I hadn't thought about that. I suppose it is."

The voice made a clucking noise. "Very well, Mr. Duncan. I must inform you that you have your choice between two courses, both passive in nature. You are going to be either bribed or killed."

In the silence Matt strained his eyes toward the spot from which the voice seemed to come. He could barely make out the shape of the chair, but not the figure seated in it. "There doesn't seem to be much choice, does there?" he said at last.

"Good. I am pleased to see, Mr. Duncan, that I am dealing with a man of sense. Now to the terms of the offer: would five thousand dollars be of interest to you?"

If only, Matt thought, he could keep the conversation going long enough to grasp some clew to this man's identity. There was a faintly accented flavor to his speech, but it was not the same as Ahasver's. The voice, moreover, was pitched somewhat higher than the cultist's. "That's a poor price for integrity," he said.

"Hardly for the integrity of anyone living in this hotel. However, I am a generous man. Seventy-five hundred?"

"That's better."

"Then you agree?"

"I'm not saying. What do I have to do?"

"Give to me a certain file from Mr. Harrigan's collection, and forget all knowledge of its contents when the District Attorney's office asks you about it. It is a simple task."

"Which file?"

"You are eager, Mr. Duncan. I shall tell you which file when you have given your definite assent."

Soundlessly Matt stretched forth his arm into the vacant darkness. The gesture seemed to pass unnoticed; no reproving comment came from the voice.

"Come, Mr. Duncan. It will be a great pity if it should become necessary to assign to you the other passive rôle. Believe me, I should regret it; and I dare go so far as to believe that you should do likewise. And do not think that I should be afraid to shoot in the hallowed precincts of a public hotel. Your dresser, if I remember, is beside your bed. Listen."

Matt heard the plop of a silenced shot and then the thud of a bullet burrowing into wood. Silently he placed both out-stretched hands before his nose and wiggled the fingers. Even this derisive action drew no comment from the voice.

"I must urge you to hasten your decision," it went on implacably. "Your snoring night clerk did not see me enter. No one knows of my presence here. I should feel no compunction . . ."

As the voice spoke on in level deadliness, Matt stretched forth his arm again, but this time with a purpose. He was sure now that the owner of the voice could not see in the dark and had fired only from memory. And he knew the peculiar habits of the window-blind. Without moving his body—that would have made the bed creak—he could just touch the edge of the blind with the tips of his fingers. But that was enough.

With those tips he gently tweaked the edge. Suddenly, with a tumultuous clatter, the blind flew upward. Instantly the man in the chair had sprung to his feet, faced the window, and fired. Glass clinked into the street below.

Before the man could recover his guard, Matt was behind him, pinning his arms tautly against his sides. It was Friday night's struggle over again, without the mud, but with the same cast. For the voice, as Matt saw in the first light from the window, belonged to the Swami Mahopadhyaya Virasenanda, otherwise known as Hermann Sussmaul.

The silenced automatic fell to the floor as Matt wrenched at the man's wrist, and a swift thrust of Matt's foot sent the weapon scuttling under the bed. "Go on," Matt urged. "Make more noise. The sooner somebody comes up to investigate the better I'll like it."

The Swami was swearing again in that language unknown to Matt which was his present help in time of struggle. And on this occasion whatever strange gods he invoked were kinder than on Friday. A terrific jerk, which must have come near throwing his shoulder out of joint, freed him for an instant. Matt stepped back toward the bed to guard the approach to the automatic. But the Swami's thoughts were no longer centered on destruction. He had seen the fire escape outside the window, and before Matt could intercept him, he had flung up the window, swung himself over the ledge and was halfway down the iron ladder.

Regretfully Matt screwed back the bulb which Sussmaul had loosened. The room was a mess, not only from the struggle but also apparently from a thorough and (as it must have been) fruitless search during his absence.

He crawled down into the musty space beneath the bed and emerged sneezing, with the automatic. He stood for a moment balancing it in his hand. "That guy," he thought, "is damned careless where he leaves his accessories."

When Lieutenant Marshall finally got home that night, he entered neither the pampering comfort of the Harrigan mansion nor the dispiriting shoddiness of Matt's hotel. He simply walked into the living room of an ordinary Southern California five-room bungalow and fell flat on his face.

Sleepily he struggled to his feet, picked up young Terry's quacking Donald Duck pull-toy, threw it at the sofa, missed, and tiptoed to the bedroom.

Leona switched on the light on her side of the double bed as he came in to the room. Marshall paused in the doorway, beaming on her, rejoicing even through his sleep-starved stupor that he was one man whose wife went to bed with a clean face and greeted you looking like a human being, and a damned lovely one at that.

"Hard night?" Leona whispered.

"As hell. Tell you in the morning. I'm dead." He dropped his coat casually across a chair and didn't even notice Leona's frown. "How did you amuse yourself?"

"Read until I was sleepy."

"Another mystery?" There was only a little professional scorn in his voice.

"Yes, and it was marvelous. All about a locked-room problem. I love those. Got a cigarette? I ran out."

"Don't—!" Marshall thundered.

"You'll wake Terry."

"Don't," he resumed in a strained whisper, "say locked-room to me."

"The socks," Leona observed, "go in the laundry bag, not the waste basket. But this is wonderful. It has a whole chapter called 'The Locked-Room Lecture.' "

"I told you not to—!"

"Sh," Leona yawned. "It goes all over everything and it tells you every possible solution is to a locked-room situation. It's marvelous."

Lieutenant Marshall stood for a moment in drowsy nakedness. Then he pulled himself up and vigorously blinked the sleep from his eyes. "Where is that book?" he demanded.

TEN

Matt woke up toward noon with a feeling something like the prime ancestor of all hangovers. He looked around the room and didn't feel any better. It is not a comforting sensation, upon first awaking, to see a bullet hole in your dresser and to feel the cold draught from a shot-shattered window.

Even the day's first smoke brought no peace to his spirit. The most nearly comforting item was the hard feel of the Swami's automatic under his pillow—though that reassuring weapon, he reflected, should be turned over to the police at once.

As he pulled on old slacks and a patched polo shirt, he tried to decide on a program for the day. He supposed that he should get in touch with the Harrigans; but his position in that household, now that Wolfe had left it, was decidedly anomalous. He should certainly see Lieutenant Marshall, if only to report last night's invasion; but how did you go about seeing a detective lieutenant? Where did you find him?

But when he breakfasted at a counter joint (where better employed individuals were already gulping lunch), he forgot these problems in his absorption in the morning papers. Wars and politics were lucky to appear on the front page at all, so strongly had the Harrigan case appealed to every editor. The sheer impossibility of the crime was hardly mentioned; Marshall had apparently played down the locked-room angle in his announcements to the press. What made the story headline material was not the murder itself, but the sublime claim of Ahasver. "THE ASTRAL BODY MURDER," most of the papers called it.

There were interviews with Ahasver, interviews with dozens of other occult leaders (for they grow by the dozen in Los Angeles), an interview with the eminent mystic authority Manly P. Hall (who seemed to find nothing surprising in such a claim), and even an interview with Boris Karloff, who had, by a fortunate coincidence, committed just such a crime in a Universal picture shortly to be released.

The rival occultists were divided in their opinions. The less imaginative condemned Ahasver as a rank charlatan, while the more ingenious pointed out that they could easily have performed such a deed themselves, but were law-abiding citizens.

Then there were photographs: of Ahasver, of the Temple, of Ahasver again, and once, anticlimactically, of R. Joseph Harrigan (a flashlight snapped at a banquet). Aside from that one picture, the Harrigan family was neglected, for which Matt was thankful. They had enough to face without news photographers.

He read the stories carefully and learned nothing. The impression that a reader would gather from the papers was that Wolfe Harrigan had been accidentally killed by a stray prowler, that Ahasver had jumped at the chance to seize the credit, and that some impressionable witness had then decided that he did see a yellow robe. This theory required a complete chronological reversal of the facts; but in itself it possessed a certain plausibility. Matt half suspected that it was Lieutenant Marshall's own shrewd contribution, a pacifying bone for the press to gnaw on while the police continued its investigation unimpeded.

When Matt returned to the hotel, his plans for the day still undecided, Fred Simmons sat on the sagging couch in the lobby, surrounded by a complete assortment of the morning's extras.

"Hello," said Matt.

The gaunt ex-grocer usually responded to the younger man's greeting with homely affability; but this morning he looked up hard and hostile. "So that's why you were at the Temple. And I talked about how good it was to see young people there! Spying, you and your precious Wolfe Harrigan! Don't bother to lie, young fellow; your name's down here as a witness, and if you're a friend of that man, you were up to no good at the Temple. But now you know; you saw, with your own eyes, what the Nine Times Nine can do."

"Did I? That's what I keep asking myself. What did I see with my own eyes?"

"Smart, ain't you? But the Nine Times Nine can do a darned sight more than you've seen yet, and you'd better remember it. Do you know that the Governor of this state is a Communist? Put that in your pipe and smoke it."

Matt started to laugh, then looked at Fred Simmons' eyes and stopped. He had no fears of a successful Nine-Times-Nine offensive against the Governor of California; but he remembered Wolfe Harrigan's fear of a powerful political intent hidden behind the Children of Light. And if the teachings of Ahasver could bring that gleam of lusting hatred into men's eyes . . .

"Hey!" the ancient desk clerk shouted. "Duncan! There's a lady phoned and wants you should call her. Ellen Harrigan. Here's the number."

Matt walked away from Fred Simmons and took the slip of paper. "Thanks."

"Ain't that the sister of the man that got murdered yesterday?" The old eyes glistened behind their five-and-dime spectacles, but this was the relatively clean light of normal sadistic curiosity, the ordinary casual thirst of the race, which likes blood impersonally, but has no special desire to spill it.

The butler answered Matt's call, sounding quite unperturbed by the mere murder of a master, and put him through to Ellen Harrigan's extension.

"This is Matt Duncan, Miss Harrigan. You wanted to speak to me?"

"Yes." Aunt Ellen went right to the point. "I want to offer you our guest bedroom. Now please, Mr. Duncan, don't interrupt me with polite protestations. My brother had spoken of, if I may say it crudely, installing you here to help him with his work; and I think that in this sad time of stress your presence is even more needed. Please say that you will come."

"I'm afraid I'd only be a trouble to you. A stranger at such a time as this . . . "

"At such a time as this, as you say, Mr. Duncan, a stranger might be rather helpful. My brother Joseph agrees that this is advisable, particularly if you are to handle my brother's papers, and I have spoken to Lieutenant Marshall. He thinks the arrangement convenient from his point of view as well."

Matt's protestations were only perfunctory. The thought of good breakfasts and smooth linen triumphed over any compunctions.

The unpleasant moment had been with the butler. Only with the greatest reluctance did Matt surrender to him his shabby suitcase. To be sure, he had carefully packed only his most nearly presentable clothes (discovering as he did so that the Swami's demonstration bullet had ruined one of his three almost decent shirts); but even these were hardly fit for the austere inspection of a butler.

"Miss Harrigan is expecting you on the croquet lawn," the dignitary informed him. "Shall I show you out?"

"No, thanks. I can find it." As Matt followed his memory, he caught a glimpse of the butler carrying the suitcase upstairs, at arm's length.

The lawn was bright in the sun. Wickets and posts glinted like a neckpiece of gay costume jewelry spread out on a background of green velvet. And on the bench from which Matt and Joseph had looked in at the French windows sat Miss Harrigan—Miss Concha Harrigan.

"It's you," Matt said foolishly.

"It is?" Concha inspected herself. "Why, so it is! What did you expect?"

"The butler said 'Miss Harrigan'—all I thought of was your aunt."

"I should be annoyed."

"Please don't. By the way, what is the butler's name? He must have one. It seems stupid always to think of him as The Butler. It's like those symbolic plays—The Man, The Woman, The Policeman."

Concha looked at him. "You see," she said.

"See what?"

"You're embarrassed to see me because my father died yesterday. You're too tongue-tied for condolences, so you try to be bright and meaningless. And right off you say Policeman. We can't get away."

"Smart child."

"I'm not a child," said Concha gravely. "I told you that. And the butler's name," she added with a slow smile, "is Bunyan."

Matt laughed. "John or Paul?"

"It is a funny name, isn't it? Arthur says it's corny."

"This, Miss Harrigan, is a cruel comment to make to any sister, but I must confess that that is just what I should expect your brother to say."

"You don't like Arthur?"

"Not wildly."

"He doesn't like you, either. He says that all this trouble started after you came here."

"Well . . . didn't it?"

"Uh-huh. Sorry you came?"

"No."

"Neither am I." She held out her hand. "Shake."

Matt sat on the bench beside her, stretched out his long legs, closed his eyes, and threw back his head. "Sun feels good," he murmured.

"Can I be a smart child again?"

"Sure. Go ahead."

"You're thinking: 'This is all very nice. It's very nice here and she's a sweet little girl and everything else; but she isn't acting like a daughter whose father was murdered last night.' "

Her voice cracked a little. Matt opened his eyes and saw that she was standing now. "But what can I do?" she went on pleadingly. "We aren't the same, not any of us. I can't spend all my time praying for him like Aunt Ellen, or Throw Myself Into My Work like Uncle Joseph, or even go around moping and making nasty stupid remarks like Arthur. And I won't cry. That's childish."

"You can sit down and talk to me and stop worrying about what I'm thinking, that's what you can do. Or we could play croquet."

"I think maybe I'd sooner talk. . . . I cut school today." She was still young enough so that it sounded like the confession of some dreadful guilt.

"As who wouldn't?"

"But this was different. I didn't just up and cut school. You see, Sister Ursula told me to."

"Fine advice from a nun. Undermining our American institutions, that's what she's doing. Mind if I smoke?"

"Go ahead. You know, it was funny. She told me to stay with Aunt Ellen all last night and go to mass with her this morning—sounds almost like a penance, doesn't it? But I suppose you wouldn't know."

"I thought penances were what you paid when you went to confession."

"*Paid!*" For an instant the Hispano-Irish temper blazed up. "Oh," she added more calmly, "people do believe the silliest things. Nobody ever has to pay anything for confession. A penance is what you do to atone—usually a few prayers." She laughed reminiscently. "I remember when Arthur was eighteen. He came home one Saturday from confession and he went up to my room—I was having a tea party for my dolls—and he said, 'You know what I have to say for a penance? I guessed five our fathers and five hail marys; that was the worst I'd ever had. Then he laughed and said, 'No. *Three rosaries.* I'm a man now!'"

"I'm afraid I'm just a non-Catholic dullard. I don't see anything funny about that."

"I was afraid you wouldn't." She sighed a little.

"But why should Sister Ursula ask you to do that? Or is that something else beyond my understanding?"

"It's beyond mine, too. I don't know. It bothers me. When we got back from church, I called her and told her everything that Aunt Ellen did. She specially wanted to know did she go to confession and communion."

"And did she?"

"Just to communion. You see, Aunt Ellen's a daily communicant and I don't think she's ever out of the state of grace anyway. But I suppose that's something else you wouldn't understand."

"I'm afraid I wouldn't."

Concha looked at him fixedly. "You don't like Catholics, do you?"

"I've nothing against them." Matt was embarrassed. "It's a free country. But my mother was an agnostic of the old school—you know, Thomas Paine and Robert Ingersoll. 'Let Man be free from the tyranny of the priesthood!' I'm afraid I never quite got over it."

"And my mother," said Concha softly, "believed in God and loved Him and served Him. And she had bad eyesight and she died."

This was a strange remark. In the silence that followed it, Matt kept turning it over in his mind and trying to shape some sense out of it. "She had bad eyesight and she died. . . ." For some reason he could see the study again and a frightened girl and a book that fell open at *Hyoscyamus*.

Bunyan was standing by the French windows. "Mr. Gregory Randall wishes to see you, Miss."

"Oh, bother. Tell him—tell him I'm prostrated."

"Prostrated? Very well, Miss. But might not a simple headache be more plausible?"

"Go on," Matt urged. "See him. Greg's a good guy, and I think you've pretty much played hell with him."

"How?"

"Oh, first all this nunnery business. You've no notion how hard that hit him. He wasn't himself. And if you turn him out now . . ."

"All right. Bunyan, show Mr. Randall out here."

"He expressed a desire, Miss, to see you alone."

Matt rose. "I'll be in the study. Might as well be looking over some of those papers."

"No," said Concha firmly. "You stay here."

Gregory Randall was obviously surprised to see Matt. His greeting was affable enough; but he had clearly forgotten completely what Matt had tried to force through the penumbra of his hangover on Saturday.

The conventional phrases disposed of, Gregory turned to Concha and took her hand in his. "This has been a very terrible thing," he said earnestly.

"Yes," said Concha, and left it at that.

"I know how you must be feeling. For a while I even wondered if I dared to intrude on your sorrow at a time like this; but I felt at least that my place was by your side. A woman needs a shoulder to weep on." The effect aimed at was that of jocose sympathy.

"I've got a shoulder." Concha freed her hand and gestured toward Matt. "Feel. It's sopping."

Gregory gave his friend something close to a glare. "Of course, I am glad that you had someone to—to cheer you up. But after all, no stranger is quite the same as the man one is to marry."

"I'm afraid," said Concha, "I wouldn't know about that."

"A terrible thing." Greg reverted to his earlier theme. "Your father was a splendid man, my dear—a great man, if I may say so. His loss leaves a gap that will not be readily filled. Few men knew

Wolfe Harrigan, but those of us who did know what his passing means. And above all what it must mean to you—to his family."

"Please."

"He was your shelter and your protection," Gregory went on. "And now you are left exposed to the storms and buffets of the world."

Concha smiled maliciously. "I could still go into a convent."

"Good heavens! Do you still entertain that fantastic notion? Even now, when you—"

"No. No, a lot's happened since Friday. Hasn't it, Matt?"

"That's one way of putting it," said Matt drily.

Gregory was looking at him suspiciously. "Then you have given up the absurd idea of devoting yourself to God?"

"No. It's just that Sister Ursula has shown me that there's more than one way of doing that."

"Sister Ursula? But I thought she—"

"Please. Let's not talk about it. It's over and that's that. Now—Why did you come out here?"

Gregory was completely taken aback. "Why? Why, indeed! What is a man to do when his fiancée is in trouble? What could I do but—"

"Fly to my side?" Concha prompted.

"Fly to your side," Greg repeated in all seriousness. "Exactly. My place is at your side, my dear, now and forever."

"I think," said Matt, "I'd better check over those papers."

"Must you?" Greg asked hastily. "I don't like to drive you away, old man."

"I know. But work is work." He started toward the window.

Concha put out a restraining hand. "No," she said softly.

"Surely, my dear," Greg protested, "if Duncan has work to do, we have no right to interfere. Of course, his company would be pleasant, but when the voice of duty calls—"

"He's been working too hard lately. He should stay."

"Working? Here?"

"Yes. Mr. Harrigan took me on as an assistant. I tried to tell you all about it Saturday, but I don't think you were up to listening."

"No. A frightful headache," Greg explained to the girl. "Migraine. I have it occasionally. Then," he resumed, his eyes resting speculatively on Matt, "you were working out here on Sunday?"

"Yes."

"Then you're—in the thick of things, so to speak?"

There was an overtone of implication which Matt resented, but decided to ignore. "Oh, yes. Hadn't you heard? The Lieutenant's swearing out a warrant for my arrest today."

"Good heavens!" Randall sounded torn between shock and

delight. "But in that case, old man—I mean to say, why are you still here? Why haven't you tried to—"

"Mr. Duncan," said Concha coolly, "is being sardonic. He thinks it goes well with his scarred face."

"Oh! For a moment I thought you were serious. I suppose I should have known better. But heavens! to think of your having actually been here when it . . . And to think that I was at Mrs. Upton's garden party quietly enjoying myself and never realizing—"

"Look." said Concha. "Yes, I know a lady doesn't start her speeches so abruptly. Mr. Duncan's directness is spoiling my convent manners. But look. For the second time, why did you come here? You didn't leave your beloved office just to say how sorry you were or look into my fair eyes or tell us about Mrs. Upton's garden party. Why did you come here?"

"I had hoped to explain that," said Gregory stiffly, "when Duncan went to work on his papers."

"Which he is not going to do. Now will you tell me?"

"Look," said Matt. "I really—"

"No! Now, Gregory . . . ?"

"Very well. I came here, Concha, to ask you to fix a day for our wedding."

Concha laughed. "Come now! Is that seemly? Is that suitable to your position? Does a Randall fix the wedding date before even the funeral is held? Or is it thrift, Horatio? I doubt if we'll have baked meats."

"I don't know what you're talking about, Concha. All I can see is that you are alone in the world now—"

"Surrounded by nothing but an uncle, an aunt, and a brother."

"And you need a man to rely on. I am asking for the privilege, my dear, of sheltering you."

"How too exciting!"

"How can you laugh at me like this? I am offering you a home and comfort and security and you—you stand there and laugh at me to my face. Yes, and grin at my friend while you're doing it! It isn't right, my dear."

Gregory Randall was dull. Gregory Randall was pompous and literal and good-looking beyond the tolerance of humanity; but at the moment Matt felt deeply moved by him. This disquieting child was indeed playing hell with him; and it wasn't a pleasant spectacle to watch.

"Look here, Concha," Matt tried to interpose.

"You keep out of this, Duncan" Greg snapped. "What are you doing here anyway, I'd like to know. Looking over papers, indeed! A likely story!"

At that moment anything might have happened. There was a

petty but nonetheless menacing tension in the air. Matt flexed his right arm in readiness as Gregory glared and shouted.

But then came a booming, "Well, well, well," and R. Joseph Harrigan was upon them.

"Gregory!" he cried. "Good to see you, my boy!"

With a visible struggle, Gregory brought himself under control. "Good afternoon, sir. Dad asked me to express his sympathy to you."

"That's good of him. And good of you to come out here."

"Not at all, sir. This is a frightful business. I can't tell you—"

"Let's not talk about it, my boy."

"I feel that I should have been here. I know it's a foolish thought; but I can't help thinking that if I had only been here instead of at Mrs. Upton's garden party—"

"Nonsense. Nonsense, Gregory. What could you have done? What could we do, Duncan and I? We saw that villainous fakir—saw him through those windows there—but what could we do? However, I'm afraid Mary would rather talk about something else."

"I don't know, Uncle Joe. There are even less pleasant topics."

Joseph frowned, but probed no deeper. "Could you stay for dinner, my boy? I'm sure Ellen would be delighted to have you. There's something of a family conference tonight; but we know that you wouldn't be out of place. After all—"

"Gregory has a business engagement for dinner," said Concha.

Greg stared at her and started to contradict, then changed his mind and glanced at his wristwatch. "Yes, that's true. I'm glad you reminded me. I'm afraid I'll have to dash, sir. Goodby, Concha." He did not speak to Matt.

Joseph gazed after him, rubbing his tonsure-like bald spot. "Something's the matter with that young man," he announced. "Are you sure he came out here merely to offer his sympathy?" He bestowed upon Concha a coyly avuncular leer.

"Oh, no," she smiled. "He came here to tell us about Mrs. Upton's garden party."

A sudden misgiving struck Matt. It was barely possible that that might be true.

ELEVEN

Dinner was admirable if uneventful. The cook was seemingly as uneffected as Bunyan by all that went on around her. The entire household, in fact, had assumed an excellant façade of imperturbability. The conversation at table was nowise suggestive of a house of death; it consisted solely and normally of the oratorical rotundity of Joseph, the cheap cynicism of Arthur, the quiet and pious comments of Ellen, and a few jangling discords from the unpredictable Concha.

After dinner, R. Joseph clapped Matt jovially on the shoulder. "I'm sure you'll understand, young man. A little family conclave. We'll be through in no time."

Matt nodded his understanding and wandered off. He would have liked to be present at that conclave. There were interesting possibilities to it, particularly if, as he surmised, Joseph was to reveal the will. But he resigned himself to absence, and looked about for company.

He found it in the kitchen, where Officer Rafferty was enjoying a plentiful cold supper and easing its passage with a tall glass of dark and glowing bock.

The officer was evidently in a friendly mood. "Good evening, my lad," he said expansively. "You're the one was with the Lieutenant last night, ain't you?"

"I am," said Matt. "Just now nobody loves me. Can I sit here with you, or should I go out to the garden and eat worms?"

"Janet!" Rafferty called to the cook. "Another bottle of beer for the gentleman! They set a good table here," he went on appreciatively. "My sister's in service in Beverly Hills, and you'd be surprised how stingy some of these rich folk are about their food."

Janet was a plump and comely woman with pure white hair but a youngish face. As she set down the beer, she stared at Matt with overt curiosity. "You're the one that saw him, aren't you—along with Mr. Joseph?"

"Yes," Matt admitted. "At least we saw something."

"You saw *him* all right. When a man's a devil it doesn't matter how many witnesses swear he was somewheres else. And a man'd have to be a devil to kill Mr. Harrigan."

"I don't suppose," Matt ventured, "that you saw anyone strange around here that day?"

"How could I and me with a Sunday dinner to get that nobody ever ate at all and that dear child coming in here to pester me to teach her how to cook?"

"Miss Harrigan was here with you when you heard us pounding on the door?"

"Indeed and she was. 'What's that, Janet?' she said. 'More'n likely Mr. Arthur playing some fool trick,' I said. Ah, little do we know . . ."

"True for you, Janet," said Rafferty as chorus.

"Did—" Matt hardly knew what he was groping for, but some

inner curiosity drove him on. "Did Miss Harrigan talk to you about anything but cooking when she was in here with you?"

Janet wrinkled her brows. "It's funny you should be asking that. She did indeed, and I've been wondering why. It's like as if she had some notion of death in the air, as you might say."

"What did she talk about?"

"About her mother. Oh, the questions she asked me—not that I could tell her much."

"About her mother's death, you mean?"

"Yes. You see, she was away at the convent then. She never knew, poor lamb, what her mother was like those last weeks—half blind she was, and that put out about it. She was proud, was Mrs. Harrigan—proud the way it takes a Spaniard to be. She couldn't give up the sight of the world and her strength to get about in it. It hurt her, that it did."

"How did Mrs. Harrigan die?"

"Now that I don't rightly know. Her heart, I guess. It was of a Wednesday—my day off, that is. I left in the morning, and she was all right. Moody and sad, but well enough if it wasn't for her eyes. When I came back that night she was dead, poor thing. Ah, well, she was well out of it. She could never have abided being blind and helpless; it was God's mercy to take her."

"True for you," said Rafferty. "And, Janet—another beer?"

Matt noticed that his cigarette was the focus of the officer's sharpest attention. It made him nervous.

"You're the one that caught the Swami, too, ain't you?" Rafferty asked with somewhat overdone casualness.

"Last Friday, you mean? Yes."

"They can't locate him. He's got away clean. Sergeant Krauter was up to his apartment last night. Couldn't find hide nor hair of him." Still he was watching the cigarette.

"Will the Lieutenant be out here tonight? I've got some news for him about the Swami."

"Have you now? But you might like to know that Sergeant Krauter did find something interesting in the apartment."

Matt took a final puff and crushed out the short stub of his cigarette. "What was that?"

Officer Rafferty sighed relief and disappointment. "He found some cigarettes bent a funny way. I've seen a couple around in this house too; but I haven't seen anybody do it yet. I thought maybe . . ."

"You mean smoked only about an inch or less and then bent in two?"

"Yes. You know who does that?"

"Sure. Arthur."

The swing-door to the dining room opened to admit Lieutenant

Terence Marshall. "I had an idea I'd find you here, Rafferty," he said.

Rafferty rose to attention and relapsed into his seat at a gesture from his superior. "A man's got to eat, Lieutenant."

"Did I say no?" He pointed at the beer. "Is there more where that came from?"

"Sure. But listen, Lieutenant. Have I got a clew! You know who left them cigarettes in the Swami's apartment like Krauter said? *Arthur Harrigan!*"

"And what does that prove?"

"Why, it proves . . . it proves . . . Well, hell, Lieutenant, it must prove *something.*"

"Sure. Now go back to your post and figure out what."

Rafferty gulped the last of his bock and retired regretfully.

The Lieutenant sat in moody silence until Matt at last ventured, "Can I offer a clew, or will I get sent out of the room, too?"

Marshall laughed. "Try it and see. I know I'm not being sweetness and light just now; but I don't what you'd call take to this whole damned set-up. All right, what's your clew?"

So Matt told him of the voice in the darkness of the hotel room. At the end of the story he pulled the automatic out of his holster (an ingenious improvisation from an old pair of suspenders) and handed it over.

"Same model as the other," Marshall mused. "Our friend's consistent. Good thing you moved out here, isn't it?"

"Why?"

"I won't have to put a separate guard on you. He'll try it again, of course. We may get him that way."

"Do you think he . . . ?"

"Hell, no. That's obvious on the face of it. He had nothing to do with Harrigan's murder—his attack on you proves that."

"Because he tries to shoot me it's a proof that he didn't shoot my employer? You'll pardon me, Lieutenant, if I fail to follow these brilliant deductions."

"Good God, man, an imbecile could see that!—Sorry. A bad temper is not a professional asset."

"There's a classic phrase for this state of affairs: 'The police are baffled.' "

Marshall drained his glass. "It isn't funny. And since I've elevated you to the rank of semi-official Watson, the least you could do is show some respect."

Matt grinned. "O.K. by me. Tell me all, Master, and I shall listen rapt."

"No time now. As soon as that family conference is over, I've got work to do. Tell you what: tomorrow's my day off, unless something sudden breaks. If the case goes on at this pace, they can handle routine without me. So come to dinner. You'll like my wife and you'll like her cooking and you might even like our kid. Then we can settle down afterwards and thrash this damned thing out."

"Glad to."

"Fine. Here's the address." He scribbled it down.

Bunyan entered through the swing-door. "Mr. Harrigan asks both of you gentlemen to step into the study."

The family conclave had apparently not been a peaceful one. Joseph's ordinarily pink face was bright red. Arthur slouched in a corner, resolutely sulking. Concha was ominously quiet, with the stillness of repressed emotion. Only Ellen seemed serene and normal, if somewhat sniffling.

"Good evening, gentlemen!" Joseph greeted them in his best after-dinner manner (which seemed to require something of an effort at the moment). "Will you find seats for yourselves? Good. We have decided, Lieutenant, that there is no reason why we should delay in communicating to you the terms of my poor brother's will. In so many homicide cases, as I know from professional experience, a will is of prime importance; and though that importance, as you will see, does not exist here, we appreciate the necessity of your carrying out the usual routine.

"I may add that this reading has been hardly in the nature of a surprise. Wolfe never made any secret of his testamentary dispositions—"

"Oh, yeah?" There was a snarl in Arthur's voice.

"In principle, that is. Naturally, a few details . . ."

"I understand," said Marshall. "Go on."

"To begin with, of course, there are the usual bequests to servants and several to charitable and religious institutions, including the Sisters of Martha of Bethany. Do you wish the detailed list of these?"

"No."

"You are a direct and efficient man, Lieutenant." Joseph beamed. "The residuary legatees are naturally the deceased's children—in other words, Mary and Arthur here."

Marshall frowned. "That's all?"

"Yes. If it seems strange to you that my sister and I are overlooked, let me point out that we shared the family fortune with Wolfe equally many years ago. There is no reason why any part of his share should now revert to us."

"How much will this residue amount to?"

"That it is impossible to say exactly at the moment. I am certain, however, that each share will run well into six figures."

The Lieutenant whistled. "On a policeman's salary, that sounds like plenty. How's it to be administered?"

Arthur made an undefinable but certainly not friendly noise.

Joseph chose not to heed him. "The residue is to be divided into two equal trust funds. One of these is to be held for my niece until her twenty-first birthday or her marriage, if that should take place with the consent of the trustees after her eighteenth birthday. After the twenty-first, of course, she is free to marry as she chooses."

"Who are the trustees?"

"Myself and T. F. Randall—the broker, you know. A client of mine and an old family friend."

"And the other half?"

"That is to be held, under the same trustees, for my nephew until his twenty-fifth birthday. At that time, he is to receive the whole of the capital if either trustee thinks it wise. If, however, both trustees deem it inadvisable to give him the full sum, he will receive the half thereof, the rest continuing in the trust fund. This judgment of fitness is to be held thereafter, if need be, every five years. At the end of each such interval, he is to receive the half or the whole, as the trustees see fit, until his fortieth birthday, when the entire capital shall be his without questions."

"It isn't just," Arthur burst out. "It's a hell of a way to treat your own son!"

"Arthur!" Aunt Ellen reproved.

"Well, it is. If he didn't have any faith in me, why couldn't he just disinherit me or cut me off with a shilling or something? Why keep me dangling around Uncle Joe and sucking up to him so I'd get the full capital? And why make me wait four years to touch a cent of the principal? Doesn't he think I want to make anything of my life?"

"Maybe," said Concha, "that's just what he did think."

"You can talk. As soon as you're eighteen you can marry Greg Randall and get your whole capital, while I'll have to come around to you begging for crumbs."

"I'm afraid," said Marshall drily, "I can't waste much sympathy on a young man who's starving on the income from a six-figure trust fund. Maybe we don't look at these things the same way—Those are all the provisions, Mr. Harrigan?"

"Yes. . . ."

Marshall noticed the hesitancy. "Something else?"

"There was . . . that is, I believe I heard Mr. Duncan mention a codicil appointing him as literary executor?"

"Yes," said Matt. "Mr. Harrigan made it out late Saturday night."

"Did you see it for yourself?"

"No. He told me about it."

"Hmm. It was not given to me to deposit with the will, but

then, of course . . . Lieutenant, perhaps you found it among these papers?"

"No. Did you come across it, Duncan?"

Matt shook his head. "No personal papers in this lot—just notes on the work."

"Then I fail to see what can be done about this reported appointment. There is no provision in the will as it stands for a specific literary executor; my position as executor of the estate would naturally embrace those duties as well. However, I should be glad, young man, of any assistance which you could give me in this difficult task, concerning which you doubtless know more than I do. Probably a salary for your efforts can be arranged from the estate."

"It's funny," Marshall wondered aloud. "Nothing else seems to have been taken from this room, except possibly one set of notes. And if that codicil vanished between the time Duncan left your brother and the time of the police search, then it must have been taken by—"

"Come in," said Ellen in answer to a rap.

For the first time Matt saw Bunyan perturbed. "There is an exceedingly strange individual here to see you, sir," he informed Joseph. "He also asked particularly for you, officer."

"We can't be disturbed at a time like this," said Joseph. "Who is this fellow?"

"He says," Bunyan announced hesitantly, "that his name is Ahasver."

The man in the yellow robe entered the room with a quiet effect of underplayed power. His muscles were well-trained; his body movements displayed a minimum of effort and a maximum of grace. Pausing by the door, he bowed to each of the company in turn: first to Ellen, then to her niece, then to Joseph, Arthur, and so at last to Matt and the Lieutenant. The bow was simple, but seemed in effect ceremonial.

"Will you kindly," Joseph exploded, "cease this mumbo-jumbo, sir, and tell us why the devil you have come to plague this household again?"

Ahasver looked around the room and smiled. "I should hardly recognize the place, Lieutenant, after your squad has been so thorough."

"As though," Marshall snorted, "you'd have recognized it anyway!"

"You are still skeptical? How much must a man suffer from the arrogant incredulity of the modern mind! For is it not written in the eleventh chapter of the Gospel according to Joseph:

Seeing, they shall see not; and hearing, they shall hear not.
Yea, from all their senses shall no sense enter into them.

And even so it is."

"All right," said the Lieutenant. "When you were in here before our search, how many piles of papers were on the desk?"

"Three."

There was no hesitation. Ahasver gave the answer as coolly and directly as though he had been asked, "What's one plus two?" Matt and the Lieutenant exchanged a glance; three was right.

"And where," asked Matt, "was the box of darts—before the search?" Ahasver smiled. "You think to trap me so easily? Well do ye know that it was even where now it is: on the desk near the edge at the right hand of the chair."

"You're wasting time, Lieutenant," Joseph snapped. "Can you still have any doubt that this man is my brother's murderer? Stop worrying as to *whether* he did it. The question is *how?*"

"A little eager, aren't you, Uncle Joe?" Arthur murmured.

"And a little eager to point out the eagerness, aren't you?" Marshall countered.

"One moment," Aunt Ellen interposed. "It would seem to me that the question before us at the moment is not what this man may have done in the past, but why he has dared to come here now. Come, sir, what is your reason for this affront?"

"Affront? My dear madam, you do me an injustice. I have simply come here to make my most sincere apologies for my necessary act. Out of all good must come sorrow, even as sorrow itself ever brings forth good. This we learn from the Ancients. And thus the good accomplished for Truth by your brother's death brings with it the concomitant sadness of your loss. For that I wish to extend to you my sympathy."

This was a little different from Ahasver in his own Temple. He was no longer dominating, rousing, hypnotic; but this quiet suavity, this perfectly finished performance, carried its own peculiar conviction. So rich was his voice, so persuasive were his intonations, that for a moment Matt found himself all but believing in the sincerity of this nonsensical apology.

Concha rose. "Lieutenant," she announced, "ever since childhood I have had a phobia about beards. No, if I must be technical, a fetishism might be better. My nurse used to have to slap my little pink hands, because they just *would* reach out and grab a nice beaver. I haven't had a spell like that in years, but I feel one coming on now. And I wonder if you'd stand by the door while I indulge myself?"

The Lieutenant chuckled. "Gladly, Miss Harrigan. I belong to the modern school: No Repressions; Never Let a Fetish Fester.

And if your idiosyncrasies should drive you on to such perverse acts as pulling off gloves and playing with ink-pads (you'll find one there on the desk), I'd be much interested in the results."

Still grinning, he moved to the door. Matt rose and covered the French windows. The family sat complacent while Concha advanced slowly upon the man in the yellow robe, her fingers twitching.

Ahasver stood still until she had nearly reached him. Then he spoke, softly but forcefully. "I should advise you, Lieutenant, to restrain this young lady."

"And why?"

"Because I drove out to this house under police guard. Naturally a man in my position must take precautions against unthinking revenge, even upon such a mission of mercy as this. Certain friends of mine at the City Hall arranged for an escort, which is now waiting outside and doubtless chatting with your own guards. If, under these circumstances, they were to report that I was manhandled by this family under your very eye, I fear that the report would not greatly improve your standing on the force."

Marshall stood for a moment irresolute, then advanced and took Concha by the arm. "Your round," he muttered, gently thrusting the girl away. "And now, my beloved Master, will you kindly get the hell out of here? Or will your guard report me for using language unbecoming an officer?"

"There is no trust in mankind," sighed Ahasver plaintively. "I come here with more-than-Christian love in my heart—the love of the Ancients—and I meet only with resentment, threats, and abuse. But I accept them even as I accept this yellow symbol of degradation. For is it not—"

"You heard the Lieutenant!" Joseph barked. "And whether my sister likes my language or not, I am going to repeat his order: Get the hell out of here!"

Slowly and regretfully Ahasver repeated his ceremonial bow, this time in reverse order ending with Ellen. With dignity he departed, moving as smoothly as he had entered.

"Nuts!" observed Arthur indolently.

"For once," said Marshall, "I'm with you. But there's something about this visit that isn't strictly kosher. He didn't come here just to . . . May I use the phone?"

At Ellen's nod, the Lieutenant sat at the desk and snapped off rapid orders. The nearest radio car was to establish contact at once with one of the guards at the Temple and have him phone this number immediately.

"I knew," said Joseph heavily, "that such rapscallions usually had political connections, but I had never dreamed that they extended so far as to such wanton corruption of the police force."

"I don't know," said Marshall. "You can't blame whoever gave him that escort; in a way it was a reasonable request. But it certainly played hell with your niece's bright idea." He gazed at Concha with open admiration. "Smart child, Miss Harrigan."

Concha seemed not to resent the term from him. "I just thought you'd like to know," she said.

Ellen shuddered and rose. "The presence of that man will not depart from me. I tell you he is evil. There is something not of this world about him, nor of God's world either."

"Come, my dear," Joseph bumbled. "He is evil, I grant you; but thank God, it is no evil beyond the power of the Lieutenant and myself to combat."

"I hope you are right, Joseph; I pray that you are right. . . . You will excuse me?" She went into the chapel.

"The solution of all woes," Arthur sneered. "A little wear-and-tear on the knees, a spot of polite mumbling while your thoughts stray free, and there you are. Pretty, isn't it?"

Joseph did not explode this time. He spoke levelly and coldly. "Arthur, if nothing else in your stupidly misguided life has taught you any reverence or respect for your elders, I must at least ask you to keep in mind the terms of the trust which you have heard tonight."

Arthur rose. "The hell with that. And the sweetest hell, my most revered uncle, with you. I can look after myself." He crumpled his cigarette, tossed it into the fireplace, and sauntered out of the room. As he spoke his defiance, Matt thought (or was he imagining things?), his eyes flicked for one instant to the case of files.

Marshall hastily answered the ringing of the phone, asked a terse question or two, and listened to the report. Then he slowly replaced the instrument and turned to the others.

"Ahasver," he announced, "has not left the Temple tonight. Moreover, he is at this moment personally conducting a service, which has been going on in his presence for the past hour."

Involuntarily Joseph crossed himself. Concha sniffed the air.

"Lieutenant," she asked, "do you smell brimstone?"

TWELVE

Despite the invitations of the Harrigan family, Matt did not attend the requiem mass on Tuesday morning. This was not, as he gathered, the actual funeral mass; burial could not take place until after the inquest, which had been postponed till the latter part of the week. (He imagined that Marshall was reluctant to lay before a coroner's jury such a tangled mess of improbabilities, and optimistically hoped that a few days' more work might show him a way out.)

He would only feel embarrassed, Matt decided, in the midst of family mourning and incomprehensible ritual; he could best show the very real sadness which he felt at Wolfe Harrigan's death by staying home and carrying on Wolfe's work. So while the *Dies Irae* was chanted and the censers were swung in a solemn high mass, Matt stayed at his dead employer's desk and labored in a fashion which he hoped was not too unworthy of its former occupant.

The file on Ahasver particularly engrossed his attention. It was taking shape excellently; he had already at least enough material for a feature article which should prove at once destructive and non-libelous. But he was exasperated by one gap and one superfluity. The gap, of course, was Wolfe's lost conjecture as to the identity of Ahasver and of the power behind him. The superfluity was Matt's own note, hastily jotted down in the Temple of Light, concerning the mammon of iniquity. How that phrase fitted into the picture he could not determine; and yet it had seemed somehow to strengthen Wolfe in whatever his hypothesis had been.

Throughout this work he examined carefully every last scrap of paper, far more thoroughly than he had been able to do in the rapid going-over with the Lieutenant. Hopefully he searched for two things: the codicil to the will, and those most secret notes on the identity of Ahasver's backer. In both matters, he was forced to confess ruefully, his search was absolutely futile.

At last, weary of this persistent futility, he leaned back in the chair and picked up a dart. His first toss went wild, hit the wall, and clattered on the floor. The second struck the edge of the board and hung there quivering. Matt felt encouraged. A few more tries . . . Perhaps Wolfe was right about this dart business as a relaxation in the midst of work. Matt himself, unimaginatively, had always used solitaire.

The third dart was no better and no worse than the second, and the fourth repeated the fiasco of the first. Matt held the fifth poised for what he swore would be a really perfect toss, when a light rap at the door interrupted him.

It was Concha who obeyed his shouted command to come in. "Hello," he began cheerfully, then paused and looked at her. "What's the matter?"

She sat down on the couch. "I've been crying. Isn't that silly?"

"I don't know. Sometimes it helps."

"I knew you'd say that. Men always think that no matter what's wrong with a woman, a good cry will fix things."

"And doesn't it?"

"That's the worst thing about it—you're perfectly right. Only usually I can't cry. It sticks here, and I can't breathe or feel anything, but I can't cry. Only today at mass . . . Oh, I must be wrong. I must be, Matt. Please tell me I'm wrong."

"About the theory of crying? I'm hardly an expert, of course, but—"

"Don't treat me like a child. You know what I . . . No. You don't. Of course you don't. I'm sorry. You must think me very foolish."

"Not at all."

"Now you're being indulgent. Goodby!"

The door slammed behind her. Matt shrugged and tossed the fifth dart, which barely touched the outer rim of the paint. That was better. As he rose to collect the darts for another try, the door opened again.

"What I came in here to say was," Concha announced, as formally as Bunyan, "Sister Ursula came back from church with the family and she wants to know if you're too busy or can she speak with you."

"With me? What on earth for?"

"I didn't presume to ask. Will you see her?"

"Of course."

"I'll tell her." Concha paused in the doorway. "Please. Do you think I'm an idiot?"

"Yes," said Matt flatly.

She smiled—a smile as bright as it was unexpected. "Good," she said.

It was odd, Matt reflected, that you always thought of Sister Ursula in the singular but she existed, so to speak, in the plural. You never saw her alone; there was inevitably Sister Felicitas, who did nothing, who said nothing, but whose presence presumably satisfied some regulation of the order.

Matt rose as the nuns entered and seated themselves on the couch. "Please sit down, Mr. Duncan," Sister Ursula began. "I take it you are wondering why I should so expressly want to see you?"

"I'll admit I am."

"Then let us waste no time on courtesies. I want to see you because I understand from the family that you are acting as a sort of unofficial aide to Lieutenant Marshall. Is that true?"

"If you lay plenty of stress on the unofficial, yes."

"Good. I should have liked to approach the Lieutenant himself, but I fear that the Mother Superior might not consider that a suitable mission. However, it was natural that we should attend the funeral, and if I can talk with you on the same visit . . .

You see, Mr. Duncan, I am going to find the murderer of Wolfe Harrigan."

Matt smiled. "That's nice."

Beneath the headdress gleamed a responsive smile. "I don't blame you for sounding doubtful. But you see I am not inexperienced at detection. The Mother Superior was quite astounded when I proved what had been happening to the sacramental wine. And then there was that little business of vandalism when someone slashed the missal which Sister Perpetua was illuminating. In fact, Sister Immaculata always calls me—" She stopped short, her cheeks reddening. "Oh, dear me!" she said.

"What's the matter?"

"I think," she said slowly, "that everyone has a particular Deadly Sin—one out of the Seven to which his moral self is peculiarly susceptible. Mine is Pride. As Saint Paul says, 'There was given me a sting of my flesh, an angel of Satan, to buffet me.' And I'm afraid I cannot even glory in my infirmity, because to glory would be the infirmity itself. So please, Mr. Duncan—accept me, and don't force me to indulge in my sin."

"Very well, Sister. I accept you—if my acceptance means anything. Now what?"

"I should add—and console my conscience by claiming that it is simply a statement of fact—that I know a good deal about police methods and criminology."

"I suppose you're a great reader of mystery novels and always solve them in chapter two?"

"You're making fun of me. No, I am not too fond of mystery novels; but my father was a police captain, and when I was twenty I was going to be a policewoman. That was before my health broke, and that long convalescence showed me the other way I could take."

"It's funny to think of you planning to be a policewoman. I imagine we generally think of nuns as just being and always having been nuns. If I tried to think of you as a little girl, I'd see you about so high, but still in your habit, and still meek and mild."

"And you think nuns are meek and mild?" Sister Ursula laughed quietly. "Some are, of course; look at Sister Felicitas. (Don't think I'm embarrassing her—she's deaf, poor thing.) But on the other hand—no, I won't say any names; they wouldn't mean anything to you and besides I shouldn't. But there are nuns who could make the staunchest policewoman quail in her regulation boots."

"Very well. I stand rebuked. I shall henceforth look upon nuns as holy terrors until proved otherwise. And now, Sister Ursula, what do you want from me?"

"Information. As much as you can tell me about the case without violating the Lieutenant's confidence."

"Mm. I don't see why not. But first, would you tell me why you are so anxious to solve this case?"

"That is hard, Mr. Duncan. Partly because I love Wolfe Harrigan and his family, partly because our order is deeply indebted to them, partly out of an absolute desire for justice, partly to destroy a still-menacing danger, partly, I confess, because of the sting of my flesh, but most of all, I think—yes, this is the chief reason: I do not want what now seems a miracle of evil to go unsolved."

Matt was delighted and impressed by Sister Ursula's alert response to his narrative and by her shrewdly interposed questions. He began to feel that her pride might be deadly and sinful, but was certainly not unjustified. This was no otherworldly innocence before him, but a lively, sensible, and wise woman.

Especially was her interest aroused by "the mammon of iniquity." "I see what he meant," she murmured half to herself. "It is not impossible, of course—but it is not a happy thought."

"What did he mean?"

"Mr. Duncan, have you ever read the translation of the New Testament made at Rheims—often loosely called the Douay version?"

One other time she fobbed him off without an answer. That was when he had concluded the exposition of the locked room with, "The Lieutenant seems driven to the conclusion that Ellen Harrigan must be shielding someone."

"Oh, no, Mr. Duncan." Sister Ursula was positive. "Miss Harrigan is telling the strictest truth. That we know and must rely on in solving this problem."

"But how can you be so sure?"

"Did Mary—No, I suppose you call her Concha. The child is so proud, poor thing, of her Spanish blood. Did Concha tell you of my sending her to mass?"

"Yes."

"And of all that happened there?"

"Yes."

"Then you know why we must believe Miss Harrigan. Go on, please."

When he had finished, Sister Ursula sat for a moment in reflection. Sister Felicitas, Matt noticed with amusement, had fallen sound asleep. "There are little questions," Sister Ursula roused herself to say. "Why was the codicil stolen? Who tried to burn the yellow robe? Why did Arthur visit the Swami? Such things as these. But they will probably become clear of themselves if only we can solve the major questions."

"And those are?"

"Let me speak like a memorandum:

A: Is this crime rooted in Wolfe Harrigan's work or in his family?
B: In either category, who is the murderer?
C: Who is Ahasver, and who, if anyone, is behind him? (though this may well prove irrelevant to the case).
D: Why did the murderer wear the yellow robe?
E: How did he leave this room?

Is that a satisfactory list?"

"Yes. Answer those and—"

"Just a moment. You forgot to tell me, Mr. Duncan, if Lieutenant Marshall received my note Sunday night?"

"He did."

"And did you hunt for another pricked book?"

"He said he was a fool not to have done that in the first place. Score one for you, Sister."

"And," her voice was excited, "did you find one?"

"Yes. But it was no good."

"What was it?"

"Not one of the files at all. A book about the crusades. Mr. Harrigan must have been practicing."

"Perhaps. But please—may I see it?"

Matt fetched the volume from the shelf and handed it over. Sister Ursula glanced at the title page, then all but dropped the book. She sat back on the couch trying to catch her breath, an expression of pure physical pain on her face. "No!" she gasped. "Jesus, Mary, and Joseph!" It was not an oath, but a prayer for deliverance. Her hand sought the comforting beads of her rosary and her lips moved silently.

At last she rose. "I am going to the chapel," she said. Her voice was calm again, but horror was only half hid in her eyes.

Matt frowned. "Do you mean that—"

"I mean that now only the last question remains, and I am afraid."

"But how—"

"Tell the Lieutenant," she forced herself to say, "tell him to remember the name of our memorial chapel."

Sister Felicitas was still placidly sleeping. Matt opened the French windows, stepped out onto the croquet lawn, and lit a cigarette. He wished—in fact, he came as near as he was able to praying—that he knew what that title page had conveyed to Sister Ursula. She was obviously not a woman easily frightened, but fear had been her dominant reaction to that harmless inscription.

But even she had confessed that the last question still remained unanswered. Matt strolled across the lawn to the bench and sat there staring at the windows. There was no doubt that he had seen something actual in that room, something that had no longer been there when the police broke in. It was difficult to see into the room now; but then, with the fire blazing . . .

He broke off his puzzling. There was something moving in the room now. He could not see it clearly, but well enough to know that it was not a nun. He threw the cigarette away, dashed across the lawn (as best as one can dash across a space sprinkled with wickets), and burst into the room.

Arthur Harrigan stood in front of the case of letter-files, his hand outstretched. He froze in that position as Matt entered the room. Slowly his dull eyes turned.

"Well?" he drawled.

"What the devil do you think you're up to?"

Arthur smiled a lackluster smile. "Sentiment, you know. My father's room. Natural enough act on returning from his requiem, isn't it?"

"Touching as all hell. Now get out of it and stay out."

"Of course," said Arthur slowly, "I'm only his son. You're the Lord God Almighty surrounded by seven hundred seraphim."

"I'm the man who's looking after this room. So get out."

"Are you? Seems to me that codicil you talked so much about never showed up. Funny anybody should take that—if it ever existed."

"I'm warning you—"

"You've got no more right here than I have. A damned sight less, in fact. And what are you so jittery about, Duncan? What is there in this room that you're so afraid I might find? Do you think I might guess how you left it locked after you had—"

"Another crack like that, Arthur my pet, and you get what's coming to you. If you don't want trouble, you'll leave this room now."

"Urgent, aren't you? No, I don't believe you think I'm clever enough to work out your locked room. That wouldn't be worrying you. What else could it be? A clew to what? Not something my sister left here after you'd—"

"I warned you," said Matt.

It was a neat punch, intended to stun rather than to annihilate, and it did its job neatly. Arthur was still on the floor, shaking his head in groggy incredulity, as Sister Ursula reentered.

"I'm sorry," Matt told her. "It had to be done."

"And nicely done, too," she observed calmly. "You didn't even wake Sister Felicitas."

Arthur lurched to his feet and held on to the desk. "Nuns!" he muttered, and staggered off through the French windows.

"I don't doubt," said Sister Ursula, "that that was necessary. But please let me warn you against needless violence in this house.

Remember what has happened here. There are already passions enough warring about us; do not add to them."

As she went over to rouse Sister Felicitas, Concha came in. "I was hunting for Arthur to drive you home," she said, "but I can't find him."

Sister Ursula smiled. "We'll get back all right. Oh, and by the way, Mary—who in this family plays croquet?"

"Are you spoiling for a game, Sister? I'll play you."

"I'm not certain that this habit would allow of such activity. No. I simply wanted to know."

Concha looked toward Matt for enlightenment, but received none. "Well, there's me of course. I think I like it the most. Mr. Duncan isn't bad—no, really you're not. Aunt Ellen doesn't play at all, I don't think. Arthur can, but he won't unless we play for money and I think that spoils the fun. Uncle Joseph plays sometimes if he can forget his dignity."

"Thank you." Sister Ursula was grave out of all proportion to the subject. "Is your aunt in her sitting room?"

"Yes."

"We're going to see Miss Harrigan!" she shouted at Sister Felicitas, and led the older nun to the door. As they were leaving, she turned back for an instant. "Thank you, Mr. Duncan," she said. "If I want to see you again, I can find you here?"

"For a while anyway, Sister. And I hope—"

Her glance warned him against saying more in front of Concha. "Again thank you," and she was gone.

"What was she thanking you for?"

"Wouldn't you like to know?"

Concha perched on the desk and dangled her slim bare legs. "Greg called me today. I had Bunyan tell him I wasn't home."

Matt crossed to the French windows, closed them, and started shooting the bolts in place. "You're a fool, darling."

"Does that mean I'm a darling fool? All right, *don't* answer. What are you doing now?"

He went back to the hall door and turned its knob. "Locking up."

"Locking . . . " Abruptly Concha stopped and shuddered. "You mean, the way it was . . . "

"I'm not reconstructing the crime, if that's what you mean. I'm just plain old locking up. People seem to want to get in here."

"What people?"

"Your darling brother for one, and a friend of mine with a funny name who keeps dropping his automatics in the damnedest places. Who has the key to the chapel door?"

"Uncle Joe, I guess."

"I'll stop by his office this afternoon and get it. Come on." He took her by the arm and led her out into the chapel.

"You're going out?"

"Dinner engagement." He pushed the button of the spring-lock, drew the door to, and rattled it. It was reassuringly solid.

"Oh . . . " She sounded downcast.

Matt checked over the entrances in his mind, gave one last jerk to the chapel door, and was satisfied. "And I just hope," he said, "somebody tries that trick again."

THIRTEEN

It was probably the subconscious awareness of Ahasver that made Matt notice the beard. Not that it was anything like the Master's Assyrian spade—this one was a luxuriantly flowing mass of deep reddish brown. But Matt had become what advertising jargon might call beard-conscious; and even such a different form of beaver attracted his attention.

This was in the elevator as he rode up to R. Joseph Harrigan's law office; and that magnificently odd beard provided matter for amused reflection while Matt, having been told that Mr. Harrigan would see him in a minute, waited a quarter hour in the sumptuously chaste ante-room. He was about to lay his case for admission before the receptionist once more when a near bellow resounded from inside R. Joseph's private office.

It was the Harrigan voice—there was no mistaking it—but now no longer suave and politic. the pink of Joseph's face must have turned bright red to accompany such a roar. And, like the projectile hurtled forth by this detonation, Gregory Randall shot out of the door.

Matt rose and extended his hand; but Gregory sped past him, whether deliberately cutting him or simply blinded by his own tense preoccupation, Matt could not tell. He had only a glimpse of Greg's too handsome features twisted by a blend of rage and chagrin; and then R. Joseph, almost his usual bland and formal self, was standing in the doorway inviting him into the office.

The business about the key was simply transacted, with no reference to the scene just past. Joseph agreed that locking the room was a sensible precaution (even though Matt thought it tactful not to mention Arthur's snooping) and that Matt, despite the absence of the codicil, was the logical custodian.

As he unsnapped the key from his ring, R. Joseph Harrigan fixed

Matt with a glance he might bestow on the opposition's star witness. "You are a friend of Gregory Randall's?"

"Yes. Though I haven't seen much of him for years till just recently."

"Would you know . . . I realize that this is a personal question which you might not care to answer, but would you know anything of his present financial status?"

"Not a thing, I'm afraid. But after all, a Randall . . . "

"Yes, yes, Of course. But this is a perverse world, young man. Even Randalls and Harrigans are not above the reverses of fortune. . . . Perhaps I had best be frank. You saw that unfortunate scene, and you are entitled to an explanation."

"I assure you, sir, there's no need . . . "

"I can understand now why Mary was so cool to young Randall yesterday. There is something positively indecent in this pressing haste for marriage which he displays."

Matt tried to come to his friend's defense. "Your niece is a charming girl; there isn't necessarily any hidden motive in being eager to marry her."

"Even in view of the will? And in view—I tell you this in confidence, Duncan—in view of the fact that my brother, if not actually opposed to the marriage, was at least strongly in favor of putting it off for several years? Now that he is gone, young Randall, presuming on my friendship for his father, seems to think that he can bludgeon me as trustee into giving my consent to an instant wedding. He has much to learn, that lad, much to learn."

R. Joseph nodded sagaciously to himself, like Polonius in modern dress. Then rousing himself, he handed over the key. "Forget my ruminations, young man," he advised brusquely.

When Matt stepped out into the hall, there, waiting for the elevator, was the beard again. This time Matt looked at him more closely, noticed the dark glasses, the turned-down hat brim, and began to wonder and to smile.

There was still a half-hour to kill before he needed to leave for the Marshalls'; and there is no better place to kill a half-hour in downtown Los Angeles than Pershing Square. Matt hoped the beard might enjoy it, too.

Pershing Square has sometimes been called the Hyde Park of Los Angeles. This is a well-intentioned metaphor, but almost as inaccurate as it would be to describe Aimee Semple McPherson's Angelus Temple as the Los Angeles Westminster. England, to be sure, is fertile in eccentrics, in characters; but the denizens of Pershing Square need newer and more vivid words to describe them—sound American words like screwball and crackpot.

There is no formal speaking in the square, no official addressing of the populace from stands. In fact, there are even signs (completely disregarded by all) warning you that any blocking of the walks is strictly forbidden. If you feel the urge to exercise your right of free speech, you have simply to buttonhole any passing stranger and begin speaking loudly. In five minutes you will have an audience of at least two dozen, audibly representing some three dozen conflicting views.

Usually Matt could find battles raging on a half dozen or so different fronts—one group debating Roosevelt, another the Communist party line, another fundamental religion, and at least a group apiece on the Townsend plan and Ham-&-Eggs. But today Pershing Square was dominated by a strange unanimity. Every topic broached came back to one single theme:

Fascism: "Sure, that's what the upper classes want—we should worry so much about fascism in Europe we don't even see it here in our own country. What do you think this Ahasver is? A little Hitler, that's what he is; and it's time somebody stepped on him."

Communism: "Whatever else they say about this guy in the yellow robe, he's got one good idea: Wipe out the Communists. If they don't like it here in America . . . "

Religion: "It's a Gospel, ain't it, same as the others? All right then, if you believe in the other Gospels, why not in that? And in the Gospel according to Joseph it says clear's day . . . "

Pensions: "All right, who put him in the Senate? Ham-&-Eggs, that's who put him there. And what does he do to us? He betrays us, sells us out. Now this Ahasver is really for us. He knows we've got a right to live and by God we're agoing to fight for it."

Sensation: "He's a menace to society, he is. Going around killing people like that is witchcraft, and what does it say in the Good Book? Go on, what does it say? 'Thou shalt not suffer a witch to live'!"

Matt looked down at a newspaper lying on a bench. The headline read:

NEAR RIOT AVERTED

ANGRY MOB STORMS
TEMPLE OF LIGHT

This was the macrocosm of the Harrigan case, this hurly-burly of crisscrossed excitement. But it was the microcosm that perturbed Matt. He could not forget Joseph's ruminations so easily as the lawyer had commanded. He could not forget that Gregory Randall was indecently avid to bring about a marriage which the living Wolfe Harrigan had obstructed; nor could he forget that R. Joseph had stepped surprisingly out of character in order to inform him, unofficial confidant of the investigating Lieutenant, of that suspicious fact.

The streetcar was so crowded that Matt, wedged in between a corpulent businessman and a dear old lady with seventy-nine bundles, was unable to verify his suspicions of the beard; but when he got off, he waited at the corner until he saw the now familiar flamboyant figure retracing its way from the car's next stop. He loitered until he was sure that the beaver had a chance to rediscover him, and then set out for the Marshalls' home.

The Lieutenant answered the bell himself. He was wearing a frilly rubber apron and holding a red-headed two-year-old in his arms. He looked foolish, knew it, and didn't think much of the idea.

"I was helping Leona," he said (in a tone which seemed to add, "Want to make something of it?") "Come on in."

Matt glanced over his shoulder, saw that the beard was safely ensconced behind a tree across the street, and entered the house.

"Nice place."

"We like it. This, as you might guess, is Terry."

"Hello, Terry." Matt sounded grave and a little uneasy.

"Say hello like a big boy. What shall we call the man, huh? Mr. Duncan? Uncle Matt?"

"Scatch," said Terry, pointing with great interest at Matt's scar. Matt laughed. "Scatch'll do."

"Which reminds me." Marshall set Terry down on the sofa. "Maybe a little scatch and soda before dinner?"

"Swell—only make mine straight."

"Mine, too. I just put in the soda to point the gag. My mistake."

Marshall went off to the kitchen, and Matt found himself alone and helpless before the big eyes of Terry. Tentatively he made a face, but Terry was not interested. Then he noticed the Donald Duck in a corner, fetched it out, and began to pull it along the rug, trying his best to produce appropriate quacks.

"No," said Terry decisively. "*He* quacks. Don't *you* quack."

Abashed, Matt stopped his noises and heard that the duck was indeed quacking very nicely on its own. Terry watched it for a bit, then climbed down from the sofa, reached underneath, found a large rubber ball with Pinocchio on it, and handed it to Matt. "So," he said.

Matt looked at the ball. "So?"

"So." Terry was emphatic.

"So . . . " said Matt reflectively. "Well, well."

Terry reached up his small fist, tapped the ball in Matt's hand, and stamped his foot. "SO!"

Matt's eyes lit up with relief as Marshall returned with a tray, a bottle, and three small glasses. "I'm afraid I need an interpreter."

Terry, too, appealed to his father. "Da," he pleaded, "make Scatch so."

"You learn these things," said Marshall philosophically as he poured the drinks. " 'So' means 'throw'—as in ball."

Matt got it. He backed off a little and threw the Pinocchio ball softly to Terry, who crowed with pleasure.

Marshall handed Matt his glass. "Thanks. But why the third? Don't tell me you're weaning the infant on this?"

"Terry was weaned," said Marshall, with the father's pitying contempt for the bachelor, "fourteen months ago. Don't you think my wife wants any refreshment?"

Matt raised his glass. "Well, to Terry and your wife! That'll do for a starter."

"So!" said Terry, and threw (or soo) the ball back with a perfection of aim that knocked the glass from Matt's hand and spread a nice puddle of whisky on the rug.

"Terry!" came a voice from the kitchen door. Leona Marshall, her hair even redder than her son's, hurried into the room and with what seemed like one motion scooped Terry up in her arms, shook a reprimanding finger at him, tossed the ball onto the couch, replaced the glass on the tray, produced a cloth from nowhere, mopped up the puddle, wiped her hand, and extended it to Matt. "Good evening, Mr. Duncan. Nice to meet you."

"Kind of you to invite me."

"No kindness of mine. I'm just an obedient slave. Though it was," she smiled, "kind of Terence to tell me this morning. He usually gives me about an hour's notice at best." She looked down at her son. "Time for bed now, Terry. Say good night."

"Scatch so some more," Terry protested.

Leona frowned. "Scatch?"

"That's me," said Matt. "The scar."

"Oh. No, darling, Scatch'll throw some more some other time. You go to sleep now. He's so good about going to bed," she explained to Matt, and added hastily, "I hope."

And good he was, apparently to Leona's own amazement. "Dinner's as soon as I get back," she announced as she bore Terry off. "Ask Mr. Duncan if he wants to wash."

"Do you want to wash?" the Lieutenant asked dutifully. "Or do you think a refill might pass the time better?"

For answer Matt held out his glass.

"Duncan, you have sound ideas. But let me warn you to wash at some point in the evening. Leona's never happy unless somebody uses her guest towels."

In a surprisingly short time Leona was back. "You must be a

good influence, Mr. Duncan," she said, untying her apron. "He was an angel. You should see him now, all tucked in with his panda. Would you like to peek in?" she suggested eagerly.

"I'm afraid," Matt hastily replied, "I might disturb him."

Marshall grinned. "You'll get used to it sometime." He held out the third glass. "Leona?"

"Look," said Matt. "Haven't I seen you somewhere before?"

"Duncan," the Lieutenant laughed, "that line creaks anywhere, and right in front of a woman's husband it's rank."

"No. I mean it. I—" He set down his glass and stared incredulously at Mrs. Marshall. "Good God, you're *Leona!*"

Leona nodded calmly and took another sip. "Uh-huh. You see, darling, my Dread Past catches up with me. Yes, Mr. Duncan, I'm Leona. The Flame Girl."

Matt burst out in hearty howls. "This is marvelous. When I think of the time I've sat up in the gallery of the Follies Burlesque and watched Leona do the Flame Dance! The Red-Headed Passion Flower—wasn't that what they called you?"

"That," said Marshall drily, "was one of the printable epithets."

"I even used to get ideas. I'd think if maybe sometime I could ever meet Leona—" He caught Marshall's eye and stopped the sentence there. "And now at last I do meet Leona and find the Compleat Housewife."

Leona finished her drink. "Isn't it shocking? That was way back when Terence was on the vice squad. They raided the show and dragged all of us off to jail, only I got a life sentence. A good life, too, in its way." She touched Marshall's hand lightly with hers—a casual-seeming gesture, but Matt felt the enduring love and warmth which it expressed.

"No hankering for the old life?"

"Heavens, no! Besides, I'm afraid Terry fixed that. He didn't really help my chief professional asset. But now come on to dinner. The roast'll dry out if we get going on my past."

"And Leona's roasts," said Marshall proudly, "are something to savor." He started to lead the way to the dining room.

"Terence!" said the one-time pride of the Follies. "Are you going in to dinner looking like that?"

"No, dear." The Lieutenant of Detectives sheepishly removed his rubber apron.

"I never," Matt confessed a half hour later, "tasted a leg of lamb quite like that. What does it? The touch of your fair hands?"

"It's a Persian seasoning, of all things. You wouldn't believe the name if I told you. You mix it to a paste with olive oil and coat the roast with it. Like it?"

"Like it?" Matt exclaimed reverently. "If I ever get married" (he gave two sharp raps on the wood of the table) "you can give my bride a package for her wedding present."

"More?"

"By all means."

Leona beamed with that contentment peculiar to a cook who is serving a second helping to a well-pleased guest. "I like to try things," she said. "I get ideas and I try them on myself when Terence is working, and then if they're any good he gets them."

"And they're always good," Marshall maintained.

"Not always. You should taste some of my lunches."

The street lights went on just then. Through the dining room window Matt could see his bearded shadow still at his post. "Look, Marshall," he interrupted. "Am I being tailed?"

Lieutenant Marshall leaned back and expansively undid a vest button. "Yes," he admitted. "Does that surprise you?"

"No. No, I suppose not. But must it be done so badly?"

"You mean you spotted the man? That is bad. There's a passage I remember in one of the Holmes stories—"

"I thought you didn't like mysteries," said Leona.

"Hell, darling, Sherlock Holmes isn't just mysteries, any more than *Macbeth* is just a play or *Bist du bei mir* is just a tune. The Holmes chronicles are something wonderful and superhuman and apart. I grew up on them, and I worship at the shrine."

"I'll agree they aren't mysteries," said Leona, with a noticeable absence of her husband's enthusiasm. "Anybody that'll hold out clews on you like that—"

"This passage, now . . . " Matt suggested.

"Yes. I think it's in *The Lion's Mane*. The explorer says, 'I saw no one,' and Holmes replies, 'That is what you may expect to see when I follow you.' Well, that's the ideal of all shadowing. We aren't all Holmeses in the police force, but nobody should let a man notice he's being followed. What made you realize it?"

"I couldn't help it. He's got a big bushy red beard and dark glasses."

Marshall laughed. "The police force pleads not guilty. Some of us may be bad; but dear God, not that bad."

"But he is shadowing me," Matt insisted.

The Lieutenant looked more sober. "That's interesting. Now who else would want you tailed? One thing—if he's as obvious as all that, your own tail will spot him and somebody else will be set to tail *him*. Pretty picture, isn't it?"

"I love it," said Leona. "It's a nice game. Couldn't I play, too? And I'm sure Terry'd be just wild about it. You know," she confided to Matt, "the more I learn about the Serious Aspects of Police Work, the more it reminds me of Terry. Finished?"

Matt nodded regretfully. "If I had any more room . . . "

Leona had risen and was clearing the table. "You'd better have some room, because for dessert there's blueberry pie. Do you like blueberries?"

"There's room," said Matt.

FOURTEEN

"As Leona said," Marshall began, "I don't like mystery stories."

The two men were seated in front of the fireplace, with the bottle and glasses between them on a table from a nest. From the kitchen they could hear the clatter of Leona washing up the dinner dishes. Matt had offered to help, but his hostess had persuaded him that she was quite unused to masculine assistance. "Terence always says, 'The more you keep your man out of the kitchen, the sooner he'll get you out of it.' It hasn't worked yet," she added, "but I'm still hoping." Matt had remembered the rubber apron, and decided that Marshall's masculine independence was somewhat less strong when there wasn't company.

"But this book," the Lieutenant went on, "has something. Apparently this damned locked-room business is old stuff to mystery novelists, even though it's new in my police experience. And this novelist has an entire chapter in which he analyzes every possible solution of the situation. Now what I want to do is read these solutions to you, and we'll try and see which of them can possibly fit our case. I never thought I'd see the day when I tried to solve a case with a mystery novel; but damn it all, this is a mystery-novel case. Ordinary routine just doesn't apply."

"Who wrote this book?"

"A guy named John Dickson Carr, and he damned near makes me change my mind about mystery novels. I'll confess" (he sounded almost belligerent about it) "that I read the whole damned novel last night, sleepy as I was; and it's first-rate writing. If mystery novels are as good as this nowadays, maybe I'd better give them another try. But that's beside the point. We aren't interested in the literary excellence of Mr. Carr's *Three Coffins**; we want to know how a murderer gets out of a locked room." He began to fill a corncob.

"Now Carr's detective, Dr. Gideon Fell—a splendidly ponderous old man who sounds like G. K. Chesterton with a drop of walrus blood—starts out by specifying that you must have a validly locked

---

* New York, Harper Bros., 1935.

room, 'hermetically sealed', as he calls it. Early novelists, it seems, used to shirk the problem with secret passages, which Dr. Fell finds disgusting. I'm not so worried about the esthetic aspect, but we know from expert testimony that there are no secret passages in that room nor any other holes or apertures large enough to admit a weapon or a hand. That is fact, and we're with the Doctor so far. Now for his theories of classification:

" 'First!' he says. 'There is the crime committed in a hermetically sealed room which really is hermetically sealed, and from which no murderer escaped because no murderer was actually in the room.' "

"But," Matt protested, "Joseph and I saw the murderer."

"A guy named Stuart Mills 'saw the murderer' in this book, too, and still the explanation fitted under this head. Let's go on to the more detailed listings:

1. It is not murder, but a series of coincidences ending in an accident which looks like murder.

What's wrong with that for our case?"

"Everything. Accident is completely out of the question. If Wolfe Harrigan had shot himself accidentally, his fingerprints would be on the gun. Unless . . . Could the automatic have been dropped and gone off in no one's hands?"

"Dropped after Harrigan had obligingly wiped the handle clean and then stooped over so that he received powder burns? No go. Then Point Number One, Accident, is out. Next:

2. It is murder, but the victim is impelled to kill himself or crash into an accidental death.

This, it appears, involves either the power of suggestion or a poisonous gas that drives the man mad. Any comments?"

"Same as before. If the situation doesn't fit suicide, it can't fit murder by suggestion. Wolfe Harrigan didn't pull that trigger."

"I agree. Point Number Two, Suggestion, out. Next:

3. It is murder, by a mechanical device already planted in the room, and hidden undetectably in some innocent-looking piece of furniture.

I don't like that 'undetectably.' It doesn't sound what you'd call flattering to the police search. But imagine something 'undetectably hidden,' and go on from there."

"I don't know as I can. That's saying, 'Imagine the impossible is possible and still prove why it couldn't happen.' "

"All right. I'll take this one myself. If a contraption did exist for firing that automatic, it must have been attached to the weapon in some way. If so, then somebody must have detached it before the police broke in; and if you're going to put a man in that room anyway for detaching, he might as well be the murderer. That's no help. Point Number Three, Mechanical Device, out.

4. It is suicide, which is intended to look like murder.

All the variations on this involve getting rid of the weapon, so that the police find, say, a stabbed corpse with no knife at hand—conclusion: murder. But our problem is the exact opposite. We have a corpse and a weapon, but we can prove that the corpse did not use the weapon. Point Number Four, Suicide, out.

"The next one is tricky:

5. It is a murder which derives its problem from illusion and impersonation."

"I don't follow that."

"I'm not sure I quite get the example he gives here myself. It involves the murderer pretending to be the victim, so that the victim seems to have entered the room the instant before it is locked whereas he's actually been lying inside murdered for some time. Of course that couldn't apply in our case, but . . . "

"I think I know what's tempting you. That word 'illusion.' You're back at the projected scenery. I tell you there's no possibility of a magic lantern show. Try for yourself projecting a picture on glass with a fire back of it."

The Lieutenant puffed slowly. "I know. But this figure you saw . . . Did it do anything? Did it even move?"

"We looked at it only a second and then started inside. I don't think it moved in that time, but I couldn't swear to it."

"Then if it wasn't a person . . . ?"

"If it wasn't a person, it was a statue as big as a man. How did *that* get out of the room? Is that any easier?"

"No. But I still like this illusion business. Tell me—think back. Was there anything about that yellow figure that you saw that was—well, wrong?"

Matt looked down at the glowing tip of his cigarette and tried to see again the thing in the yellow robe. At last he said, "Yes. One thing, though I don't see where it helps. He didn't have on his gloves."

Matt had finished the cigarette when the Lieutenant stopped swearing. "Didn't have on his gloves!" he concluded. "It's preposterous! It's fantastic! You mean those yellow gloves that Ahasver always wears?"

"Yes."

"But they're an intrinsic part of his costume. Whether it was Ahasver or somebody made up like him, still . . . God alone knows how many times a murderer has put on gloves to commit his crime, but this will echo down the casebooks of the future as the first murder on record in which the murderer took off his gloves!"

"I'm sorry. But as I think back that's what I see—a flesh-colored hand resting on the desk."

Marshall snorted. "I try to straighten this mess out, and I just get in deeper. I try to find a hint of an illusion that will smooth out everything, and instead I discover a gloveless murderer who leaves no fingerprints. Well, then, the light arrangement kills visual illusion; and if the illusion was anything solid, we're up against the same problem as with a murderer. So Point Number Five, Impersonation and/or Illusion, out. Next:

6. It is a murder which, although committed by somebody outside the room at the time, nevertheless seems to have been committed by somebody who must have been inside.

This one is tricky as all hell, and some of the gags propounded as examples might well work. At least I know they'd worry the hell out of a medical examiner. But most of them are stabbings or bludgeonings and irrelevant to our case. Now why couldn't this crime have been committed by someone outside of the room?"

"Two reasons. A, the powder burns on Harrigan's face establish that the murderer must have been close to him. B, the gun ballistically proved to have fired the bullet was in the room. I'll admit you could maybe work out some fantastic idea of the shot having been fired in at an incredible angle through the rat hole or the crack in the fireplace, but neither of those holes is conceivably large enough to admit the gun itself."

"All right. Point Number Six, Murder from Outside, out.

7. This is a murder depending on an effect exactly the reverse of number 5. That is, the victim is presumed to be dead long before he actually is.

In other words, the victim is only unconscious—say, drugged —while all the battering on the locked door goes on. The door is broken in, and the actual murder takes place in all the attendant confusion. Objections?"

"No one but the police was in that room between the breaking down of the door and the finding of the corpse. Besides, I saw Wolfe lying dead before we broke in."

"That might have been the unconscious stage."

"But I saw his face . . . Still, even discounting that, if we accept this idea the murderer must have been one of the officers summoned by chance, which, as we used to say in geometry, is absurd."

"Right. Point Number Seven, Murder After the Fact, out. And that, my dear Watson, ends the list of situations in which no murderer was actually in the room. Are you quite satisfied that none of them applies?"

"I was to start with. We know the murderer was in the room."

"All right. Now the grumpy and splendiferous Dr. Fell gives us his list of the ways a murderer can hocus a door after his escape, to make us think it was locked on the inside. He starts:

1. Tampering with the key which is still in the lock.

Several pretty examples with pliers and string."

"But none of the openings to the study had a key in its lock."

"Right. That's out. Next:

2. Simply removing the hinges of the door without disturbing lock or bolt.

What have you got against that?"

"It couldn't be done on the French windows. Those are bolted top and bottom, so that even if you removed the hinges they'd still be firmly fixed. It couldn't be done with the chapel door, because that entrance is closed not only by a lock but by a witness."

"That leaves the hall door. Why not that?"

"Time. The murderer would have had to come out into the hall, remove the hinges, go back into the room, turn the bolt, squeeze out into the hall again, and replace the hinges. And between the time I was hammering on the hall door and the time I came out of the chapel into the hall again—well, I can't say exactly, but it couldn't possibly be over a minute."

"I don't know. If the hinges are clean—that could be prepared beforehand—you can take them apart in about three seconds flat. I wouldn't be too sure on the time element alone. But there's another point that queers it: the hinges on that door are on the inside of the room. So Point Number Two, Hinges, is out. The next two are:

3. Tampering with the bolt. String again.
4. Tampering with a falling bar or latch.

We went over all the bolts and latches in that room and disproved those possibilities. There remains:

> 5. An illusion, simple but effective. The murderer, after committing his crime, has locked the door from the outside and kept the key.

He then reintroduces the key to the room after it's been broken into, in such a way that we police, who seem to swallow anything, think that it's been there all along. Objection?"

"Keys don't interest us. They've no bearing on the situation."

"Exactly. Well, my friend, there, according to what Leona assures me is the foremost fictional authority on the subject, is your list of all the possible solutions to a locked room. And where are we?"

Matt took another drink without bothering to answer the rhetorical question. From the kitchen came the sound of Leona's approaching footsteps.

Hastily Lieutenant Marshall drew a small metal lid from his pocket and clamped it on his pipe. "Keeps the coals in," he explained. "Leona doesn't like holes in the furniture or my suits."

"But you've been smoking all this time without it."

"I know. But Leona doesn't know that." The Lieutenant picked up *The Three Coffins* again and stared at it as though illumination were bound somehow to filter out of its covers.

"Now me," said Leona a little later, when the two men had given her an outline of their fruitless efforts, "I *like* a locked room. I've got the advantage over both of you. I'm not tied up with the people involved, and my job doesn't depend on solving it."

"I might remind you, darling," said Marshall gently, "that your livelihood does."

"I know, but that doesn't seem so immediate, somehow. I can just look at your locked room as though it were a puzzle in a Carr book; and from that point of view, let me tell you it's a honey. Now locked rooms are my special weakness in mysteries. I don't care about terrific alibis that take a two-page timetable to explain, or brilliant murder-devices that need machine-shop diagrams or involve the latest scientific developments in the use of insulin; but give me a locked room and I'm happy."

"Not that I grudge you your happiness," said her husband, "but if, out of your vast experience with locked rooms, you might give us humble mortals some small hint . . . "

"Isn't he ponderous when he's sarcastic, Mr. Duncan? You can hear the floor creak.—You surely can't expect me to help you, darling, if that Carr chapter doesn't turn the trick. That's the last and definitive word on the subject. But I could suggest a different classification."

"Go on. Anything to give me a lead."

"All right. The Locked Room (my, I wish I could bumble like Dr. Fell) falls into three categories:

A: The murder was committed before the room was locked.

B: The murder was committed while the room was locked.

C: The murder was committed after the room was broken into.

Does that help?"

"It's a start," Marshall grunted. "Go on."

"Now in your case we can strike out C right away. The only persons who had a chance to commit murder after the room was broken into are the men from the radio car."

"Check."

"B means murder from a distance, murder by mechanical device, or murder by suggestion."

"We've gone into each of those," said Matt. "They're no good."

"All right then. You're left with A. The murder was committed before the room was locked. Why shouldn't it have been? You don't know the exact time of death, do you?"

"That damned fire spoiled our chances on that. It could have been any time."

"Well? What's wrong with it? Isn't it a logical conclusion by elimination? There's a start for you."

"I hate to discourage my wife when she's being helpful, but that's out too. That room was actually 'locked,' as you say—'sealed' might be better—when Ellen Harrigan went into the chapel. At least five minutes thereafter, Duncan and Joseph saw the robed figure in the study. I'll admit that the murder *an sich,* the murder *qua* murder—"

"Oxford," Leona whispered to Matt. "It happens sometimes —like a tic."

"All right. The just plain old murder then, if you like that better, may have happened before the room was sealed. Quite possibly it did. But someone in a yellow robe was in that room afterwards; and the problem of how he got out is the same whether the murder took place when Duncan saw him or half an hour earlier."

"I've got a wonderful husband," Leona sighed. "He has just finished proving to his complete satisfaction that his locked-room crime did not take place before, during, or after the time the room was sealed. Isn't it marvelous?"

"What's marvelous," the Lieutenant growled, "is that you've got me all excited about this locked-room business. The obvious answer, to any common or garden cop, is that Miss Harrigan did see somebody come out of that room and is keeping quiet about it."

"But—" Matt started.

"But nothing. That somebody can't have been Ahasver or the Swami or any other cult faker, or Ellen wouldn't be protecting him. It can't have been you, Duncan, or Joseph, because you two were together. So. What's left? It was either Arthur or Concha Harrigan. The whole damned problem is as simple as that if you look at it right."

"But, Terence!" Leona protested. "That isn't cricket. Mr. Carr wouldn't like it. You build up a sealed room and then just say, 'Aha! It wasn't sealed at all. Fooled you!' It's worse than a secret passageway."

"The ethics of mystery novels are no concern of mine. Haven't we just got through proving that your locked-room conventions can't possibly apply here? But, hell, if I only knew some way of tackling the Harrigan woman . . . You can't just up and grill her the way you would a burglary suspect or a gunman's moll."

"But Sister Ursula claims," Matt insisted, "that Miss Harrigan's evidence is the one certain thing in the whole set-up."

"She does, does she? And what does Sister Ursula know about it?"

"I forgot to tell you. She's going to solve the case." And Matt, half-smiling and half-serious, told of Sister Ursula's ideas and ambitions.

"Hm," Marshall reflected. "Could be. Stranger things have happened. A fellow lieutenant of mine had a case solved for him last summer by the dumbest sergeant on the force, and if our own sergeants are going to solve cases I wouldn't put it past a nun. And that was a good tip she gave me about the dart, even though nothing came of it."

"I don't know about that. She looked at that crusade book and it seemed to mean a lot to her. She was horrified—stricken dumb for a minute. Then she said the only remaining problem was how the murderer got out."

"Good Lord! What did she mean?"

"She wouldn't say. Just told me that you should remember the name of the nuns' new memorial chapel."

"Their new memorial chapel? God in heaven, how should I remember that? I never even heard it."

"Neither had I; so I asked Miss Harrigan. She donated it, you know. It's the Rufus Harrigan Memorial Chapel."

"Good old Rufus," said Marshall. "The pride of Los Angeles. Came out here on an Irish work-crew building the Union Pacific. Tended bar till he'd made enough money to start buying real estate—and God did he buy it! Married late in life, when he'd become a respectable City Father, and reared this family—all just to give me a headache."

"I know about Rufus," said Leona quietly. "One of his deathbed acts was to pull a neat little trick which drove my father out of business. That's what makes Flame Girls."

"But what the sweet hell has that got to do with books on English history and locked rooms? I think that precious Sister of yours is damned well pulling my leg."

"I don't," Matt maintained. "I don't know why, but I don't."

"So?" Marshall rose, stood in front of the false fireplace, and stretched. "But Sister or no Sister, Rufus or no Rufus, sealed room or no sealed room, I've already done too damned much thinking for a man on his day off. I move we call it a day. No, don't go home, Duncan; I didn't mean that. But let's just drink and talk and the hell with the murder."

"You look very manly straddling the fireplace, darling," said Leona, "But we like heat, too."

Two hours later, when Matt knew more about detection, burlesque houses, and the feeding of two-year-olds than he had ever imagined there was to learn, he finally started home.

"Come again," Leona insisted. "Even if Terence doesn't need a stooge, you're welcome. Come in the afternoon sometime and you can play with Terry."

"I will if I can stay for dinner and you'll have lamb."

"Terence, the man loves me only for my cooking. I'm hurt."

"Remember, honey, he saw the Flame Dance. Even your lamb couldn't wipe out that memory. Better make it an evening, Duncan, when she has a man to protect her."

Matt had forgotten the beard. His only thoughts as he strolled along the tree-sheltered side street were of warmth and comfort—good food, good whisky, and the vicarious happiness of domesticity. A man could even put up with a brat, he thought; maybe they grow on you.

The abrupt noise of a scuffle behind him shattered this pretty revery. He whirled about to see two figures scuffling on the ground. Two others jumped from a car parked up the street and hastened to the scene of the rumpus. So did Matt. As he drew near he saw a sudden flash and an instant later heard the shot.

FIFTEEN

The struggle was over when Matt reached the spot. One of the combatants—a tall and husky individual—was supporting in his arms the limp and sagging form of the other—Matt's beaver-shadow.

The men from the car had come up, too. "Drop that gun!" one of them snapped. "We've got you covered!"

"So," said the tall figure. "It's you, Ragland. Give me a hand with this dope. We'll take him into the house till the ambulance comes."

"My God, it's the Lieutenant! Where did you come from?"

"Don't mind me," said Marshall. "I just live here. Come on. Lend a hand."

The other officer confronted Matt, gun drawn. "Well?" he snarled. "What do you want?"

"Don't get tough," said the Lieutenant over his shoulder, as he and Ragland carried off the unconscious beaver. "That's the guy you were tailing. Remember? You might need him. Come along, Matt—and you might pick up that automatic. He's been dropping them again."

Leona's housewifely efficiency extended even to this situation. She helped settle the beard on a sofa and then vanished, to return almost instantly with hot water and bandages. "There," she said after a minute's deft work. "That'll do. Hasty sort of job, but you've called the ambulance, haven't you, dear?"

"Yes, dear."

(The two other officers exchanged a malicious grin.)

"Now" (she wiped her hands on a remaining fragment of bandage) "what on earth happened?"

"I wouldn't mind knowing myself," said Matt.

"All right. Have a drink, boys? I won't report you."

They didn't mind if they did.

"I was curious about Duncan's bearded shadow. I watched when Duncan left and saw this man emerge from behind a tree over there and start out after him. So I joined the procession. Then I saw something in the beaver's hand that didn't look healthy, so I snuck up behind and jumped him. We had a little tussle, and the damned fool shot himself through the shoulder. How does it look?"

"Nothing serious," said Leona.

"Here's his automatic." Matt handed it over. "You said he's dropping them again. Then you mean that he's . . . ?"

"Sure. I could stage a spectacular act and rip the whiskers off, but I'll leave that for the emergency hospital. I'd like them to see their patient first in his full beauty. That's your Swami, all right. Who the hell else would want to shadow you? And do it so atrociously? And if you want further proof, he started swearing in the struggle, just as you've described before."

"In some strange language? What the devil is that?"

"It's a mixture, just like the Swami himself. I've looked up his record. He's half Jew and half Gypsy, for all his Hindu pretensions, and a libel on both races. And this pet language of his seems to be a mixture of Romany and Yiddish."

"Nice guy," said Ragland philosophically.

"I still don't quite get his part in all this. I'd like to—"

"He's coming around," said Leona.

The Swami Mahopadhyaya Virasenanda cocked open one glassy eye and stared up at the Lieutenant. "Who are you?"

"Lieutenant Marshall, homicide. That make you any happier, toots?"

"You . . . you shot me," the Swami faltered, horrified.

"Snap out of it. You shot yourself. Moral: Never pull the trigger when you're in a clinch. It isn't healthy. Marshall's Rules for Longevity: Number Six. Now suppose you tell us a couple of things."

"I am not talking." The Swami's voice was weak but resolute.

"All right. So you're not talking. But you're sick. You're hurt bad. And you're going to a hospital—a police hospital, Sussmaul. If you play ball, they'll patch you up fine. If not—well, I'd hate to see you when you come out. I've got a weak stomach."

"That is nonsense." But the man's eyes lent no conviction to the statement.

"Nonsense? All right. You can think what you like. You'll change your mind when it's too late."

"Shall I persuade him, Lieutenant?" asked Leona.

Marshall saw the iodine bottle in her hand and repressed a smile. "You can try."

She lifted the bandage and applied cotton liberally doused in iodine. The Swami let out a sharp squeal of pain; his whole plump body twitched with the torment.

"That," said Marshall, "will give you a rough idea. It's too bad you aren't talking. It won't make much difference after this whether the second jury acquits you or not. You won't care."

"Another dose, Lieutenant?" Leona looked efficiently grim.

"Very well," the Swami gasped. "Perhaps I shall talk. A little. I am not afraid, you understand. It is only that I wish to repay your kindness in sending me to the hospital."

"Sure. You're not afraid. Why have you been tailing Duncan here? Why did you hide in his room and threaten him?"

"I shall be frank, Lieutenant. I wish him to give me certain papers of the late Mr. Harrigan so that the District Attorney will find even greater difficulty in convicting me again. There is nothing against the law in asking a man for papers, is there?"

"There's a law about getting them at the point of a gun."

"The gun? Oh, Lieutenant, you mean that I intended to shoot him?" He tried to laugh, but choked. "Water, please."

"When you finish talking."

"The gun—that is only for effect. That is a stage setting, like a crystal ball. It calls up the atmosphere to induce him to give. That is all."

"The charge," said Marshall drily, "will probably be intent to commit assault with a deadly weapon. You can tell the judge about stage-settings. Now tell us about Arthur Harrigan."

"That fool!" Swami Sussmaul exploded. "That imbecile! If ever I—" He quieted down suddenly. "I beg your pardon, Lieutenant. You mean Arthur Harrigan, the son?"

"I do."

"I do not know him. I was thinking of the father. His full name, you know, was Arthur Wolfe Harrigan. No, the son I have never seen."

"All right. Take the father. You think he's an imbecile, you hate him, and he was killed last Sunday. Where were you then?"

"I do not know where I was all day. One cannot always remember. At what time, Lieutenant?"

"Say from five o'clock on."

"Oh, that I can tell you. I can prove to you where I was."

"Some mugs," said Ragland, "will swear to anything." His tone was bitter; presumably a recent case still rankled.

"But this is not a mug, officer. No, indeed. On Sunday last from five until after seven I was at the convent of the Sisters of Martha of Bethany."

"You never used that word in front of me before," said Leona reproachfully.

"Do you blame me?"

"On due reflection, no. Shall I give him some more treatment?"

"But this is the truth I tell you, Lieutenant. You see, I was concerned for my soul. I thought almost that Mr. Harrigan might be right and that I was not following the true occult light." His speech began to sound formal, almost memorized. "So I went out to the convent and talked to one sister who sent me to another and then to another until I saw Sister Immaculata, who seems to be their chief theological authority."

"Their what?" said Ragland plaintively. Nobody noticed him.

"She talked with me for an hour and more, but at the end I

remained unconvinced. I think now that both she and Harrigan have deluded themselves and that I am closer to Truth, which is why I have tried to persuade Mr. Duncan to cease from this Harrigan-inspired persecution of me. But that, Lieutenant, is where I was when Mr. Harrigan was killed."

The sound of the ambulance drawing up outside kept Marshall from another outburst. Leona hurried to the door. "If they ring the bell," she said, "it'll wake Terry."

When the Swami Mahopadhyaya Virasenanda had been carried off to the emergency hospital, Marshall was still muttering to himself in picturesque phrases.

"Maybe you should learn the Swami's language, darling," Leona suggested. "English doesn't seem to be adequate—if you can call it English."

"One thing is certain," said Marshall. "We'll check that alibi, of course, but I've no doubt it'll stand up. It sounds foolproof. But it does mean this much: The Swami had no more religious qualms than Terry has. What this proves is that he knew something was going to happen that he'd want an alibi for."

"Well," said Matt, "I think I'll start home again. We'll see what comes out from behind trees this time."

"Ragland," said Marshall, "you've got to tail this lad out to West Hollywood anyway. Why not simplify things and take him along in the car? God knows you're no secret to him by now."

"Sure, Lieutenant. Anything goes."

Marshall slipped one arm around his wife, turned her face up to his, and kissed her lightly. "This has been one sweet day off, hasn't it, honey?"

"You know," said Leona, "I think I've enjoyed it."

As Matt took out the latchkey which Ellen had given him, he noticed on his ring the other key from Joseph, and a nonsensical but nonetheless persistent curiosity began to plague him. He slipped off his shoes, left them by the staircase, and tiptoed down the dark passage and into the chapel, lit by the red flicker of the vigil lights before the Virgin.

He felt the door to the study. It was secure. Quietly he unlocked it and entered the room, that room that was the focus of the whole mad case. He paused a moment, listening he had no idea for what, then switched on the light.

The instant that his eyes were used to the brightness he saw the gap in the file-case. He crossed the room, looked more closely, then went on a swift and silent tour of the openings. Every lock and bolt was in place, and the key to the one other door was on his ring.

But someone had stolen—not any of the invaluable files; that would have been an amazing, but still a plausibly motivated feat—but the history of the Church in England under William the Second.

Matt's questions the next morning did no good. Not that he'd expected them to; but there was the offhand chance that someone had borrowed the book for a legitimate reason before the sealing up, and that he simply hadn't noticed its absence earlier. So he asked each member of the household separately if he had happened to see a volume on William the Second—he needed to check a reference to certain English heresies during that reign and thought he remembered seeing such a book in Wolfe Harrigan's library.

The results were absolutely negative. He got no information whatsoever, and not even any interesting reactions. He made two other tries, equally unproductive: a phone call to Joseph, who assured him that, so far as he knew, there were no other copies of that chapel door key at large; and a search of the incinerator. But the method of disposal had varied this time, if indeed the thief was the same person who had tried to burn the yellow robe. The most careful probing of the ashes yielded nothing that might have been part of a book.

The motive for the theft was obvious: The thief must have been the murderer. Sister Ursula's conjecture about the dart was right. Wolfe himself had tossed at the English church history, and the murderer had removed the dart and thrust it in the Ahasver file. Now belatedly he had thought that the police might examine the other books for a possible dart-prick. He concluded that they had not done so already (or at least had failed to understand their find) because no action had been taken. So he simply removed the book.

Flaw, thought Matt. Wouldn't stealing a book simply call official attention to it? But then he realized that no one save Wolfe Harrigan himself could have looked at a gap in that shelf and said which book was missing. Supposing it had been any of the others—say that book with the long German title about survivals of Gnostic beliefs—Matt knew that he would have had no idea what had been taken. No, the reasoning was all right: the murderer had stolen the book, and stolen it because he did not know that Sister Ursula had seen it, and had understood.

But how had he done this? One of three things must be true: A, and most likely, there was another key to that door. B, and most tempting, there was some incredible way in and out of a sealed room not covered in last night's elaborate discussion. C, and most fantastic, books can be stolen by an astral body.

But—Matt suddenly paused in his musing and let out a hearty chortle of sheer delight—the book was stolen because the murderer-thief wished to incriminate Ahasver. If the first visit to the locked room had been by supernatural means, there was no conceivable reason for this second one. If Ahasver were to steal anything, he would take his own file, not the pricked volume which pointed elsewhere. Therefore the first escape had been rational, and this one as well. It was something, at least, to be able to disprove the astral-body hypothesis on other grounds than pure disbelief and ridicule.

"What are you laughing at?"

"Oh! Good morning, Concha. I didn't hear you come in."

"Sorry. Father always threatened to use violence if I walked into the study without knocking. I didn't know if you'd be so strict."

"I shall be in the future. Violence it is. But since you're in here now . . . "

"What were you laughing at?"

"If you're going to insist on not being a child, you should stop asking questions like that. There's a certain Why-Daddy? tone about your voice. And you're so damned persistent."

"If I'm a child you can't swear at me. So there. But what—"

"All right. I was laughing because at least I don't have to worry about astral bodies. There—are you happy now?"

"Nice word, happy." Concha was looking at the gap in the case. "It's gone, isn't it?"

"Isn't what gone?"

"The book on William the Second that you kept asking about. You didn't sound so casual as you meant to, you know. I did a little asking myself, and found out you'd been questioning everybody about it."

"Mislaid somewhere, probably. I simply wanted to check a reference in your father's notes, and I thought I remembered seeing some such volume around here."

"Please, Matt. Don't let's play games. Things are still happening, aren't they? And I have to know about them—I have to."

"Why? Your father is dead. That's terrible for you, I know, but it's over. Marshall's a smart man. He'll figure it all out. That's his business. Justice will be done and the dead can rest in peace; but it's not for you to eat your heart out over."

"The wisdom of being ten years older," Concha sighed. "You're at a silly age, Matt. When you're my age you can feel the truth; when you're Sister Ursula's you can know it. But at your age or Greg's or maybe even the Lieutenant's, you just go fumbling around pretending to know with the young and feel with the old and claiming advantage over either."

Matt smiled. "Profound. And what truth are you feeling now?"

"That death ends things only for the one that's dead. I don't know what can end them for the rest of us. My father is dead: *treason has done his worst: nor steel, nor poison, malice domestic, foreign levy, nothing can touch him further.* . . . We studied

Macbeth at the convent last year," she added, all child again for an instant.

"Cheery play. You know what actors think of people who quote it?"

"Malice domestic," she went on. "That's it. Nothing can touch him further, but things can touch us. And that's the worst. It's all through the house—suspicion, fear, maybe even something worse. And I know what suspicion can do."

"Suspicion," said Matt, "of hyoscine?"

Her face changed again into that ageless mask of terror. "Oh, Matt," she gasped. "If I could only tell you . . . But I can't. No. Not even you." She pressed her hand to her mouth and turned away for a moment.

"Sorry. I'm afraid I was trying to be brilliant. I shan't again."

She faced him once more. The back of her knuckles showed the white welts of teeth marks, but her face was composed. "You're keen, you know. Really you are. You're swell. But why don't you tell me things?"

"What things?"

She pointed at the gap. "That."

"I told you. I needed the book and I couldn't find it. It's probably been mislaid."

"Don't try to shelter me! I was here with you last night when you locked up. Remember? I saw that case then and there wasn't any gap in it—I'm sure. So it can't have been mislaid. It must have been taken, and taken after you locked up. Don't you see now why I'm afraid? Don't you even see why I came in here after you this morning? This room isn't safe. Things happen in this room."

"You're all worked up over nothing. All because you think you remember something. That gap was there last night. I hadn't hunted for the book before simply because I didn't need it. Isn't it nearly lunchtime?"

"Yes. But Matt—"

"What's for lunch, do you know?"

"All right. I'll play nice. I'll be the little flower by the great oak tree. I'll weep with delight if you give me a smile and tremble with fear at your frown. Want to lace my stays sometime? La, sir, you've no notion what a woman suffers. And for lunch, milord, we'll have eggs. Possibly fish, conceivably cheese, but probably eggs."

"This isn't Friday."

"It might as well be. You see, it's Janet's day out and Aunt Ellen takes over the household. And she abstains on Wednesdays—not just Lent, but all year round. I'm not sure it's really nice to inflict your holiness on other people like that."

"You don't like fish and things?"

"I wasn't born to be a Catholic. I want my meat."

"Then look—if dinner's going to be so lenten, how's about us going out to dinner someplace tonight?"

"Of course," she smiled, "I wasn't hinting or anything like that, but it's keen of you to take me up on it. It's a date. And because you're so nice, I'll tell you something."

"What?"

Her voice was serious again. "Why I'm afraid. Part of why I'm afraid, anyway."

"You shouldn't be."

"I know. You want me to think that all this is something outside of us—something that finished with Father's death. But that's only part of it—it's all around us and we can't get out."

"You're feeling truth again?"

"Partly. But seeing it, too. Yesterday I was loose-endish. I know I ought to go back to school. I don't know what'll happen to my grades if I stay away like this and mid-terms coming up. But I can't go back right now. I can't have people watching me in class and nudging each other and saying, 'See? That's her! Her father was murdered!' I've got to stay out a few days—give them a chance to forget."

"Don't count on that. I've been a newspaperman; I know. You'll never get a chance to forget it. Fifty years from now they'll dig it out again for a caption: DAUGHTER OF MURDERED MAN BECOMES GREAT-GRANDMOTHER."

"In only fifty years? My, the children didn't lose any time, did they?"

"The Latin blood, you know. Matures young."

"I'm glad you're admitting that at least. But anyhoo—that's why I've been staying home. And it's almost even worse here. I don't have anything to do. Janet's sick of having me around the kitchen, and I can't read. Sometimes I talk to Mr. Rafferty. He has a daughter my age. I think maybe I'd like to meet her. But he gets tired of me, too. So I decided to do Arthur a favor."

"Arthur?"

"Oh, I know he's a droop, and I suppose if you come right down to it I don't like him very much. But he is my brother. And when you do favors for people it isn't so much because you like the people as because you like the way it makes you feel. That's why you're taking me out to dinner. You feel how magnanimous you are to tie yourself down to a child all evening just because she's leading a hell of a life, only you wonder if you have enough money because she's probably spoiled."

"Look here," Matt began.

"That's all right. I have it all planned, and dinner will be seventy cents for both of us including the tip and you'll love it. But Arthur—I decided I'd straighten out his room for him. It always gets into such an icky mess, and he hates to have anybody touch it, but he never does anything about it himself. And whenever I clean it up he gets mad as anything and then later on he decides it was a good idea and says Thank you. He was out, so I went up there and set to work.

"It was a job. Are all men like that? I know Father was almost as bad. Uncle Joe's apartment always looks nice, but then he has a Filipino houseboy. Is your room a mess, too?"

Matt thought of shattered panes and bullet holes in dressers. "I think it's the life I lead."

"So I straightened it all up nice and polished the ashtrays and washed his comb and brush and took some clothes that needed mending and found some books that I'm sure Aunt Ellen doesn't know are in the house."

"And what did you do with them?"

"Read them. I had to have some fun, didn't I? And my education, sir, has been neglected. Nobody tells me things." She paused. "I don't suppose you might—"

"Look," said Matt. "You know how it is with the birds and the bees?"

"Yes."

"Well, it's different with us."

"So I gather. We're much more inventive—at least in Arthur's books. But that wasn't all I discovered in those books. I found a bookmark."

"A bookmark?"

"Yes. Want to see?"

Matt nodded. Concha turned away and pulled down the zipper of her blouse. "Old-fashioned, isn't it?" she observed. "But until designers give us sensible breast-pockets, we'll—well, we'll just have to do without the pockets. One of the girls at the convent used to call it the First National Bank. Then we'd tease her about the phenomenal growth of her branches."

"Fine chit-chat for young ladies, I must say. I thought you went to school with nice girls."

"I know. Men never realize how nice girls talk when they're among themselves. But here. Look what I found in Arthur's book. Then wonder why I'm afraid. Wonder why I have to be bright and chipper and silly for fear of—" She broke off before the catch in her voice could grow to the full dimensions of a sob.

Matt held the object in his hand. It was still warm from Concha's breasts—a natural fact which he found unaccountably disturbing. But the object itself was disturbing enough, in a terribly different manner—a swatch of yellow cloth, exactly matching the robe taken from the incinerator.

SIXTEEN

Lieutenant Marshall's interview with Sister Immaculata had gone smoothly—too damned smoothly, the Lieutenant thought. Sussmaul had been extraordinarily clever for a man who could be so asinine at shadowing. He had not even mentioned his name, attempted nothing to force himself on the attention of the nuns and indicate that the alibi was deliberately planted. Instead he had come to the convent simply as an anonymous seeker of guidance.

Of course, the nuns remembered him. Such requests, as he had doubtless realized, are uncommon enough in themselves without any forced effort to make them memorable. And though he had given no name, Sister Immaculata identified his photograph positively. There was no doubt whatsoever that the Swami Mahopadhyaya Virasenanda had been at the Convent of the Sisters of Martha of Bethany when Wolfe Harrigan was killed.

Why he had so dearly wanted an alibi was another question. The answer could probably be sweated out of him in time; but in the meanwhile it was one more unsolved factor in the problem. And this was a case whose solution Marshall had no desire to entrust to time and routine. He knew that it is only in novels that you live in dread of the murderer's striking again; your average sane murderer is a sensible and businesslike individual, who commits the crime that seems necessary to him and then gracefully retires from the avocation of murder. And if this was a family crime, with the Harrigan money as motive, there was no cause to suspect any further violence. But if Harrigan had been killed for revenge or to prevent him from giving out information, then young Duncan or, in fact, almost any member of the family still stood in serious peril. This damned business had to be washed up, and that soon.

Frowning, Marshall took a wrong turn and found himself in a bright patio, filled with greenly growing things whose names were as unknown to the Lieutenant as their presence was delightful. He sat down on one of the sunny benches and wondered (a) if you could smoke in a convent, and (b) if there was a phone anywheres about.

The whole convent had been a surprise to him. He had expected an austere cluster of cells, where you stood in front of gratings and whispered to the immured inmates in stilly darkness. Instead it was more like—he hunted for a simile for the neatness, the simplicity, the clean airiness and order of the place. A cross, perhaps, between a hospital and a good private school.

A nun was crossing the patio, carrying a banner of gold-embroidered silk hanging from a heavy wooden pole. It was a cumbersome burden.

Marshall put away his pipe, still unlit. "Could I help you, Sister? You seem to be having trouble."

"Thank you. That is kind of—But aren't you Lieutenant Marshall?"

"Then you must be Sister Ursula. I beg your pardon. One nun, I'm afraid, still looks like another to me. But I'm sure no one else here would know me."

"What brings you out here, Lieutenant? Has Mr. Duncan told you of my ambitions?"

"Yes, but that's not the cause of my visit. Much more prosaic. Checking up an alibi."

"Here?"

Marshall explained Sussmaul's curious preoccupation with his soul at the exact hour of a murder.

"Dear me!" said Sister Ursula. "Won't you sit down again, Lieutenant—or can you spare the time?"

"A few minutes—more, if you need, Sister."

"Thank you. And you can smoke, of course. In monasteries they say the flowers don't grow right without tobacco smoke, though ours seem to prosper well enough. Brother Hilary used to call it 'the gardener's incense.' So go right ahead.—You see what this visit of the Swami's means, Lieutenant?"

"I'd like to hear what you think it means," said Marshall noncommittally.

"That the robbery of Mr. Harrigan's study was set for that hour. We know that the Swami was not the murderer nor even an accomplice because of his threats against Mr. Duncan. If he had had anything to do with the killing, he would have taken his own file or had his agent take it. His later crimes exonerate him for the first."

"That's what I tried to tell Duncan. He didn't seem to see it."

"Well, then—he wanted an alibi for something. It must be something for which he would be officially investigated, because no private acquaintance of his would come around the convent checking up on him—is that the right phrase? And no other official investigation has involved an event last Sunday that might concern him, has it?"

"No."

"Then whatever event he expected to need the alibi for did not take place. Doesn't it seem likely that that event was a robbery of Wolfe Harrigan's study, the plans for which were frustrated by the murder?"

Marshall smiled. "Sister, when Duncan told me about your ambitions, I was inclined to be most irreverently panicked. But now I think maybe it's not such a wild idea after all. That's pretty much the way I had things doped myself. Now carry on from there. Have you any ideas as to his accomplice in this projected robbery that never came off?"

"I think I'd rather not say about that."

"Duncan told you Sergeant Krauter's story about the Swami's apartment and the cigarettes?"

"Yes."

"I see. All right. We'll skip that. Who's the lady?" He gestured at the face of an elderly woman, wearing the headdress of the order, embroidered on the banner.

"That is our founder—Blessed Mother La Roche. Sister Perpetua just finished embroidering this. It's to stand by the altar Saturday—her feast day, you know."

"Is she a saint?"

"No. Not yet. Of course, we are prosecuting her cause most vigorously. It is the dearest hope of our lives to live to see Mother La Roche canonized. But so far she has only attained the rank of Blessed. That is," she groped for a comparison that would be clear to the Lieutenant, "a little like a non-commissioned officer, I suppose."

"This is a strange order of yours, Sister. I didn't know that nuns could have so much freedom—wander about so much and do so many things. You do hospital work and teaching, too, don't you? A little of everything, I've heard."

"Even housework." Sister Ursula smiled "When poor women are sick or in childbed, they can often find a charitable agency to supply them with nursing care, but meanwhile the household goes to pieces. There's no one to do the housework and look after the other children. That's one of our jobs. That is why we're called the Sisters of Martha of Bethany. You remember perhaps? Lazarus had two sisters, and Martha complained because Mary spent too much time listening to Our Lord and too little running the house. Mother La Roche thought there was a good deal to be said for Martha."

"But other convents are stricter, aren't they?"

"In some ways. We take the usual triple vow of poverty, chastity, and obedience; but we aren't subject to canon law. You see, we've never asked approbation from the Holy See. Mother La Roche wished this community to be a lay one, with only private vows. In the strictest technical sense, I suppose, we're not nuns at all."

"I don't quite follow."

"People don't. It's chiefly a technical distinction, but it does give us a somewhat freer hand in our work. And Friday we're completely free."

"Every Friday?"

"Heavens, no. I mean this Friday. Day after tomorrow. You see, we take our vows for only a year at a time, and there is a one-day gap just before the feast of Mother La Roche. For twenty-four hours we are theoretically free from all vows. Of course, no one ever does anything about it, but it's nice to think that you could if you wanted to."

Marshall rose. "This is strange and fascinating stuff, Sister. I'd like to hear more, but I've got work to do. Mind if I come out again sometime?"

"That might be soon. If you're willing, I'd like to speak to you in day or two—and very seriously."

"You mean about . . . ?"

"Yes. We have to clear this frightful matter up, Lieutenant."

He did not smile at the "we."

"Don't I know, Sister!"

"It's far more important than just solving a case. It means the happiness of that family. They're good people, Lieutenant. They don't deserve to live in the valley of darkness and fear like this. And the girl is at such a transitional age—this could force her whole life one way or another."

"Tell me, Sister," said Marshall slowly, "what did William the Second mean to you?"

Sister Ursula rose and stood firm. The banner of Mother La Roche fluttered in a light breeze. "That I cannot tell you, Lieutenant. Until I can prove how the murderer left that room, my accusation would be meaningless. I know now who killed Wolfe Harrigan, but of what use is my knowledge when I can prove nothing? And now, Lieutenant, if you would be so kind as to help me with this banner before you go . . . ?"

"Certainly. And then if you could tell me where there's a phone . . ."

The phone rang while Matt was examining the swatch of yellow cloth. After a minute in which Matt said little but listened intently, he replaced the phone in its cradle and turned to Concha. "The Lieutenant," he said shortly, "wants me to help him in a plan. I'd better get a coat." He started for the door.

"But . . ." Concha gestured at the cloth in his hand.

"Oh, this. Tuck it back in its hiding place." He smiled to himself. "It's probably the only clew in history that could have inspired Robert Herrick."

She didn't answer the smile. "But doesn't it . . . isn't . . . ?"

"Don't fret, Concha. Yellow's a common enough color; we're just obsessed by it. Probably this is just something he was trying to match for a present to a girl-friend." He opened the door. "So now I'll be missing Aunt Ellen's egg-luncheon. See you at dinner."

"What did the Lieutenant want? He isn't—you aren't going into any danger, are you?"

"I thought you felt all the danger concentrated in this room? No, this is safe enough. He has a bright idea about who wore the yellow robe Monday night and wants me to help prove it."

Concha turned away to restore the swatch to its cache. "Go with God," she said softly. "That sounds silly in English, doesn't it?"

Matt closed the door and turned down the hall, so preoccupied with a confused mixture of thought and emotion that he just escaped collision with Bunyan.

That dignitary paused and for the first time addressed Matt courteously and respectfully. "Mr. Duncan, please do not consider me an eavesdropper; but I could not help overhearing your last remark. Do I gather correctly that the Lieutenant assumes that it was not Ahasver who visited here on Monday evening?"

"An information bureau, that's what I'm becoming. Ask Mr. Duncan!"

"I do not wish to intrude upon official secrets, but if indeed that is the case . . . "

"Supposing we say it's a possibility. What then?"

"Then I fear that I must ask for this evening off and attend the Temple of Light. Thank you, Mr. Duncan."

Matt stared after the smoothly retreating form of the butler, then shook himself. "No," he said aloud. "That's too damned corny."

"Robin Cooper," said Marshall feelingly, as he and Matt drove away from the Harrigan home. "Isn't that a cute name? Just ducky, that is. I'm damned if I can see a dope with a name like that putting over such a trick, but that's the way it looks from here."

"What put you on his trail?"

"Checked with our men about any of the Temple staff coming or going during the service Monday night while Ahasver was paying his little call on us. This Cooper left and came back at times that would about fit. If anybody was doubling for Ahasver, it looks like him."

"But how can I testify to that?"

"I'm not asking you for an out-and-out false statement. There's probably a smart lawyer mixed up with the Children of Light somewheres, and they could make trouble for us. All I'm asking you to do is to agree when I say, 'Is that the man?' Sure it's the man—it's some man, anyway."

Matt shrugged. "O.K. by me, Lieutenant."

"All right. So if we can prove that this Cooper can pass himself off as the Master, that doesn't look so good for the alibi with a hundred and eight witnesses."

"But Ahasver can't have been the murderer, or he'd have carried off his file. Whoever killed Harrigan left me enough material on Ahasver for a set of feature articles to blast hell out of him."

"Consoling thought for you, isn't it? The murderer must have taken whatever affected him when he killed Harrigan; and therefore you, carrying on Harrigan's work, aren't in any danger."

"But nothing was taken, so far as we can positively tell. At least none of the files. There's nothing missing but the codicil to the will, possibly the secret notes, and the book that was taken last night."

"What book? Holding out on me, Matt? Come on—tell papa everything."

Matt told everything.

"So. Things get messier and messier, don't they? But at least Miss Harrigan wasn't saying her beads in the chapel this time. And I like your point about eliminating the supernatural. Sort of comforting, isn't it? By the way, for fair exchange of information—the Swami's alibi checks. It's letter-perfect and iron-clad."

The Lieutenant lit his pipe and drove in silence for a while. "This should be the place," he said at last. It was an old and large rooming house on a Hollywood side street near Sunset and Vine. "Now we'll see what our precious Robin has to say for himself. What kind of parents, in God's name, would call their kid Robin?"

"Just ordinary parents," said Matt. "Run-of-the-Milne, so to speak.—Look. Do you see what I see?"

Lieutenant Marshall looked and saw. Descending the steps of Robin Cooper's rooming house was the portly and dignified form of R. Joseph Harrigan.

Joseph noticed them at once and came over to the car, fuming with indignation and viciously puffing a freshly lit cigar. "Confound it, sirs," he shouted, "have you hit on this rascal's trail, too? I only hope you can get more out of him than I did."

"Helping us out with our detecting?" Marshall smiled.

"Can you pretend that you don't need help? My brother has been dead for three days, and have you so much as made an arrest? Have you even called an inquest so that we can lay away his body in Christian burial? I don't approve of a man's taking the law into his own hands. The institutions of society are sacred, and the police force is, I suppose, one of those institutions. But what is a man to do when faced with such rank incomp—"

"Hold on there, Mr. Harrigan. Three days isn't a lifetime. A twenty-four hour solution may be a pretty ideal, but things don't always work out that way. We're following up certain leads now, and I think that I can assure you—"

"Damn it, Lieutenant, you sound like a newspaper report! 'The police have matters well in hand and promise an early arrest!' For once only my nephew's language can express what I feel. My comment on your assurance, Lieutenant Marshall, is 'Nuts!' "

"Having fun, aren't you? You know you've got so damned much political pull in this man's town that I've got to sit here and take whatever you say. So go ahead. Go right ahead. But while you're about it, you might explain just what the hell you're doing here."

"Doing your work for you, Lieutenant. Checking up on this Cooper individual."

"And why on him?"

"Because—though how we can ever prove it, Heaven only knows—because he is the 'Ahasver' who called on Monday night!"

"Fascinating. And what leads you to that conclusion?"

"I recognized him. There was something familiar about that man—something different from the Ahasver we had seen before, and still familiar. Finally, I put my finger on it: the young man who had escorted us to the yellow dressing room Sunday night."

"So? And how did you know that young man's name and address?"

R. Joseph expanded with pride. "I called the Temple and explained that I had lost a purse at the service on Sunday, that an obliging young usher had found it for me, and that I wished to send him a token of my gratitude. I described our cherubic friend, and they gave me the name of Robin Cooper and this address."

"Nice work, sir; my professional congratulations. And just what did you find out by it?"

"Hang it all, Lieutenant, I'll not stand here and be badgered. You came to see this man yourself. Very well. Go see him, and much good may it do you. I have work to do—and I could only wish that you attended to yours as assiduously." With which R. Joseph Harrigan stamped off down the street to his parked automobile.

"There's nothing like a big-shot lawyer," sighed Marshall. "He thinks he owns the world, with a nice band of legal tape wrapped around the middle. Still that was smart, his tracking down Robin. Might have helped us if we hadn't had the report on him. Well, come on."

"First door to the right on the second floor," the landlady told them. The cherub answered their knock with a flustered expression on his face and a damp floor-cloth in his hand.

"*More* company? My. Well, what is it this time? Oh! You're the friends of that *furious* old gentleman, aren't you? I remember you were with him Sunday night."

"Aren't you going to ask us in?" said Marshall. "Or do I have to get official?"

"Oh, come in. Come in, by all means. The room's a *frightful* mess already. Look at that stain." He knelt down and finished mopping up the floor as he spoke. "Want some coffee? I simply *have* to have a room with housekeeping privileges. I just *live* on coffee. Won't you have some?"

"Thanks," said Marshall. "We wouldn't mind. What did the old man do? Spill your brew?"

"He started waving and stamping around and finally knocked over my cup. Silly, *brutish* way to behave. Never trust a man with a temper, Lieutenant."

"And how did you know my rank?"

"The old man called you that Sunday night. I remember things. A doorkeeper has to, you know."

"You didn't hear about it Monday night, by any chance?"

"Monday night? How should I hear anything about *you* on Monday night? Oh, you mean that *stupid* idea of the old man's—that I was somewhere pretending to be Ahasver. That's just *ridiculous.*—Cream or sugar?"

"Neither, thanks."

"My, how *Spartan!* Well . . . " The cherubic Robin Cooper perched on his bed, leaving the chairs to his guests. "What can I do for you?"

"Tell us a few things about yourself. What made you leave Little Theater work for the greater glory of Ahasver?"

"Lieutenant!" Robin Cooper was all aflutter. "You *are* a detective! How did you know I used to be an actor?"

"Well, now, I don't know," said Marshall heavily. "For a while I thought maybe you were an ex-heavyweight, but somehow I changed my mind."

"Aren't you *dreadful!*"

Marshall made a sour face. "Sure. I'm the Big Bad Wolf. What else have you done?"

"Well," said Cooper proudly, "I was a Communist."

"Were you now?" Marshall was more interested. "You wouldn't have been one of those nice boys that joined the Young Communists' League on a salary from the Red Squad?"

"Lieutenant! What makes you *think* such a thing?" (But Matt, watching him, felt that the guess had hit the mark.) "I was searching for Truth. At first I thought I might find it in Art, and then I plunged into the Social Struggle. But now I know that all that was pure Error, and that Truth is in the words of the Ancients."

"How'd you land your job with Ahasver?"

"I went to one of his little meetings before he was well known, and I was simply carried *away* by the man! Such sincerity, such *strength!* I think I might say," he simpered modestly, "that I was one of his first Disciples. Naturally, the positions of trust, such as doorkeeper, would go to his earliest followers."

"You mean you believe all this stuff about the Ancients?"

"*Believe* it? My dear Lieutenant, I *live* it!" And Robin Cooper launched forth into a five-minute dissertation on the Beauties of the Teachings of the Ancients, fruitcake-crammed with Capitals and *italics*. Matt strolled over to the window and watched the uneventful incidents of the neighborhood—a child on its tricycle, a woman with a heavy shopping bag, an old man taking his pipe and beard for a constitutional. These were normal and pleasant and real; a happy contrast to the metaphysical blethering of the cherub. But the people at the Temple of Light had been normal, too, and the Ahasver-advocates in Pershing Square; normal and ordinary until that yellow-drenched spell had fallen upon them.

"So how," Robin Cooper concluded, "can one *help* but believe? Surely even you, Lieutenant, could find peace and solace if you would really *study* these Teachings instead of *mocking* them."

"I've got peace and solace, thank you," said Marshall. "I'll stack my wife and kid up against your Ancients any day."

Matt drew out a pack of cigarettes and offered them to his host.

"Heavens, no!" Cooper squealed. "Those dreadful *things!* Don't you know that Man must do without these stimulants of the Flesh if he ever *hopes* to reach a Higher Plane?"

"The followers of Ahasver aren't allowed tobacco?"

"Oh, my, no! Nor *liquor,* either, of course."

"How about coffee?"

"Ahasver doesn't really *like* us to use that, either. But I feel I cannot divorce myself from the Flesh completely as yet. In *time* I hope—"

"Where," Marshall snapped abruptly, "did you go when you left the Temple Monday night?"

"Where did I . . . ? Oh! You're back at that *silly* notion, aren't you? Now let me see, did I leave the Temple Monday? Oh, yes, of course. I had to go see the printer. He'd sent us a *frightfully* messy proof of the weekly Letter of Light, and I simply *had* to explain all the corrections myself."

"So. This printer do much for you?"

"Oodles. All our books and pamphlets—"

"I get it. Come on, Matt. I think we've done all we can here."

"Going, Lieutenant? I *wish* you'd stay—both of you. I'm sure if I could only *talk* with you a little, I could make you see—"

"Thanks for the coffee. You brew a good strong cup. We may see you again."

"Oh, I *hope* so. Real *men* like you are needed in our organization. But, Lieutenant . . . "

"Yes?"

"It's all very *well,* of course, to go about investigating murders, but shouldn't one know where to stop?"

"And just what does that crack mean?"

"I mean, Mr. Harrigan had such a lot of *silly* ideas about Ahasver being somebody else and finding out who controlled the Temple—as though anything human could control the Ancients. And now here you are investigating Mr. Harrigan's murder. That should have its effect, shouldn't it? A sort of object lesson?"

"Are you trying to—?"

"In short, Lieutenant, if I were you, I'd leave the Temple alone." The cherub's voice was still light, but no longer fluttery. There was cold earnest in it now.

"Cops that scare easy," said Marshall levelly, "don't get to be Lieutenants. Forget about being a bogeyman; you're cuter the other way. And don't stamp your foot at me, you gweat big dweadful mans!"

"You *will* misunderstand me, Lieutenant," said Robin in sweet despair.

"But why the hell," Matt demanded as they got into the car, "didn't you pitch into our fair feathered friend?"

"What'd be the use?"

"And I didn't even have to say, 'Thou art the man!' "

"Harrigan spoiled that for us. Robin had had time to think up a story for where he was Monday; and if the printer gets that much business from the Temple, he'll back up any yarn they want to spin. But Mr. Cooper still interests me. I'll go further—I am fascinated by our sweet little Robin."

"Why, *Lieutenant!*" Matt imitated the cherub's birdlike cadences.

"It's a good act. It's a honey of an act. But it is an act, and it slipped at the end. He's no ecstatic hanger-on of the Ancients. He knows what he's about; and unless my guess is way off, he's probably about as influential as any member of the Temple."

"You think so? Him?"

"The stupid tendency of the normal male is to discount everything said or done by one who seems effeminate. You think, 'Nuts, he's a swish—the hell with him.' It's about as clever a front as you can pick. Smart lad, our Robin."

"Do you think he's this power-behind-the-throne that Wolfe Harrigan was trying to trace?"

"Could be. Or he could be the contact-man between that power and Ahasver.—You noticed the ashtray, of course?"

Matt nodded. The cherub did not smoke. Joseph, who had just come from the room, smoked cigars. But in the ashtray, along with a cigar butt and some heavy ash, had been several cigarettes, briefly smoked and doubled over.

SEVENTEEN

Concha Harrigan paused before the memorial cross that marks the entrance to Olvera Street. "Is this where we're going to eat?" Matt demanded.

Her face fell. "Don't you like it?"

"I used to. When it started, it was a swell idea—build up a little Mexican street in the midst of the city, keep flourishing the traditions of our native minority—sure, it was fine. But since then it's got so damned over-ridden with tourism and artiness . . . Look at it. One great big Gift Shoppe, and quaint as all hell. A few Mexes run shops and make money out of it, yes; but what's the rest of the floating population? A bunch of Iowa tourists and long-haired pretty-boys, mixed in equal proportions."

"In other words," said Concha, "the only kind of tourists it should cater to is your own kind."

"Child, you have the damnedest way of saying the truth in the most balloon-pricking manner. All right, so the Iowans and the pretty-boys have as much right here as I have. But that doesn't make me like it."

Concha looked down the street of cluttered quaintness. "In some ways I suppose you're right. It certainly hasn't turned out the way it was planned. Mother was on the planning committee, you know—representative of the Pelayo family. I guess that's why I like it so much. Here I'm not a Harrigan at all; I'm a Pelayo. That fits better. But if you want to go somewhere else . . . "

Matt touched her gloved hand. "This'll do fine if I have a Pelayo to show me around."

"Thanks. You're sweet."

They started down the street, its rough paving barred to traffic and littered with countless souvenir booths. Matt looked at an unending row of sombrero-shaped ashtrays, each inscribed *A Memory of Old Los Angeles*. "They'll have Popeyes here next," he said.

"This is where we're going." Concha stopped in front of an open tent on the right of the street. The interior was crowded with crude oilcloth-covered tables, backless stools and benches, a charcoal-heated stove, and flocks of cooking utensils. The walls were decorated by two lithographs—one of the Virgin of Guadalupe and one of Franklin D. Roosevelt. By the entrance a blind man let his fingers run idly over the strings of a harp, and in a corner three paisanos sat with beer and tacos.

With Concha's appearance things came alive. The proprietress bustled over joyously, the old lady turning tortillas on the charcoal griddle let out a Latin hoot of greeting, the paisanos lifted their glasses in a toast, and the blind man, hearing the name Pelayo, began playing a slow, sad waltz.

For here, evidently, Concha was Señorita Pelayo in name as well as in spirit. In appearance, too, for as she jabbered eagerly with the plump and comely proprietress, all trace of Harrigan fell away and she was, save for her quietly smart clothes, just another Mexican girl.

Matt felt like visiting royalty as they were professionally escorted to a table in the rear. But visiting royalty is usually provided with an interpreter or addressed in its own language; he was lost in this torrential Spanish.

"She wants to know," Concha turned to him, seeming to find some difficulty in forcing herself back into English, "if you want coffee. I thought maybe you'd sooner have beer."

"There's an understanding woman for you! Beer it is. But don't I have any say on the rest of the meal?"

"I ordered the combinación—it's a little of everything. You do like Mexican food, don't you?"

"Love it. What's that the blind man's playing?"

Concha bit her lip. "It's what my mother always used to request. A sad song it is—all about how this poor man used to have a grand rancho and now all that's left is these four cornfields. All the happiness he knew is gone. *Ya todo acabó. Acabó*—Ichabod—the glory is departed. See! I can make bilingual puns. Just like Mr. Joyce or something."

"Don't be bright. I was just beginning to see you."

"See me?"

"Yes. You fit here. You're the right age. You're a human being—or were until you started to be gay and clever for my benefit."

"Now who's pricking balloons? But what kind of a human being am I?"

"A pretty good kind, I think. The kind that warms without burning and cools without freezing. And you're complete. You don't have the gaps you have at home—the inconsistencies, the jerks. Here you're rounded and whole."

She made no answer, but began to sing softly to the harp's accompaniment. It wasn't much of a voice, but light and sweet and clear—like Gracie Allen's, Matt thought incongruously. The paisanos looked up from their beer, grinned, and joined in with sustaining harmony. The tent was full of soothing melancholy.

"So here you are!" said a harsh voice.

Matt tore his gaze from Concha and looked up at Gregory Randall, whose incredibly handsome wax-model features were now distorted with something very close to rage. "This is a fine thing!" Randall continued. "To find you deceiving me here in front of these—these peasants!"

"Hello, Greg," said Matt.

"Don't you Greg me. I might have known there was something behind all your sudden desire to help me, Duncan. Nobody ever does anything for nothing in this world, I've learned that. But I thought I could trust you, old man—a fraternity brother!" he added, as though this were the depth of tragic horror.

"Look! Can I help it if your girl doesn't like fish?"

"Fish? What has fish got to do with it? Oh, I see all your plans now. As soon as I told you about her, you made your decision. A beautiful girl with lots of money and no mind of her own—a foolish rich child. Right up your alley, wasn't it? And you even used my car to get out there and got me so drunk that I was helpless. Smart work, Duncan. Sucking up to the old man and getting in his good graces; swallowing all that stupid rant from him that I could never stomach; probably telling him plenty about me, too, while you feathered yourself a pretty nest."

"Gregory," said Concha, "don't you think you've said enough?"

"I haven't begun to say enough. I've heard about your carryings on, the two of you; but I'm willing to forgive you, Concha. You're young, you don't understand how things look. But I can't have those sort of rumors going around about my fiancée."

"I can overlook the grammar of that sentence," said Concha, "but not its inaccuracy. Now will you please go?"

"If you'll come with me. Concha, my dear, cut yourself loose from this man once and for all, and I'll never reproach you for what you've done. I—"

"For what I've done!" Concha rose, her black eyes blazing. "Watch out, Gregory. It isn't safe to brave me on my home grounds like this—you might get your foul mouth scratched off your pretty face. Now get out of here!" She pointed at the entrance with a sweeping gesture and added a few comments in vigorous Spanish—doubtless instructions as to just where he was to go.

The three paisanos interchanged a look and rose in a body to the defense of Señorita Pelayo. They left their laziness at the table with their beer and advanced, a lithe and menacing bodyguard.

"Call off the Marines, honey," said Matt. "I can take care of this." He followed the retreating Gregory out into the street. A pine-nut vendor caught the smell of battle and yelled to his compañeros in gleeful expectancy.

Gregory halted with his back to a booth of gourd-ware and plaited straw. "Come on," he taunted. "Be the big he-man for the fair lady. You know you're stronger than I am. That's why you dared try such a contemptible trick to start with."

"And you know you're weaker than I am, so you think you can say anything and get away with it. Well, here's where you learn different. I don't so much mind what your little bond-selling rat-brain thinks of me, but when you start throwing around cracks about Concha and her father, that's another matter."

"I dare you to come a step nearer!"

"And you call Concha a child! You haven't grown up that far yet—you puling baby. Let's see what this does to that profile."

It was then that Matt saw Arthur on the edge of the gathering crowd. He should have guessed that Gregory had never tracked them down nor thought up all those calumnies by himself. But before Matt was fully aware of his presence, young Harrigan had thrust out a thin leg and tripped him neatly. He came down hard on the rough stones of the street and felt Arthur and Gregory land on top of him with one thud.

The next minute might be covered by film montage, but never by straight prose narrative. Concha's three loyal slaves plunged promptly into the battle and pulled his enemies off Matt's back. Then two other loungers, seeing the odds uneven, joined in on the Randall-Harrigan team. Two passing sailors abandoned their girls and joined in the fight, magnificently indifferent as to which side they slugged.

It was probably one of the sailors who knocked over the gourd-and-straw-stand and brought its proprietor into the fray, but Matt never did learn who pulled the knife which sketched a fresh design on his scarred cheek. He was too busy fighting off Gregory for that.

For while the other combatants were content simply to revel in the fight, Gregory had gone unexpectedly and completely wild, with the hysteria of an eddic warrior who had just assumed his bear sark. For a while, his chief ambition was strangulation; but a broken gourd entered his hand somehow, after which he seemed more interested in a little eye-gouging.

A fight is one thing; but handling a maniac is another, especially when the maniac is abetted by a friend with a grudge to pay. As the gourd missed his eye for the third time by a matter of millimeters, Matt began to long for the peaceful company of the Swami Sussmaul and his homely habit of scattering automatics. He even began to long for one of those automatics.

Then the police whistle sounded.

Matt felt Concha's hand in his and heard her whisper, "Come on!" The next instant they were in a picturesque basement shop with every inch of wall covered by candles and a tallow vat simmering in the center.

"We didn't come through here, Jesús," said Concha.

Jesús grinned broadly and made an expressive gesture of thumb and middle finger. "Hokay, Señorita Pelayo."

Then they were out the back door of the shop and crawling through a maze of water pipes and out a minute wooden door into an alley. There Concha paused a second to wipe the blood from Matt's face, then tucked her arm under his and led him out onto Main Street. She dragged him along, as fast as one unsuspiciously could, past the Plaza, across the street, and into the church of Our Lady Queen of the Angels.

The interior of the old church was a dark setting for the white radiance of the main altar. No service was going on now, but the blaze from the altar shone on quiet forms huddled in kneeling devotion about the dim pews.

"Sanctuary," Concha whispered. "Ancient and honorable tradition." She dipped her hand in the font by the entrance, crossed herself, and went on to the main aisle, where she knelt on both knees and was still for a moment. Matt stood beside her awkwardly, not knowing what was expected of him.

"It's all right," she murmured as she rose. "You don't have to do anything."

Matt said nothing but followed her down the aisle. She knelt again at the altar rail. Matt slipped into an empty pew and sat there looking around. There was a certain peace, a dim quietude about this old church—old, that is, as the West reckons age. He was beginning to understand something indefinable, something that he had not gathered in all his historical research on the church for the Project or even from his visit here on Good Friday.

Concha rose at last from the rail. Before the picture of Our Lady of Guadalupe, she paused and lit a vigil light. Her lips barely moved. Her face was grave as she turned away.

"Do we go now?" said Matt.

Concha's feet loitered toward the door. "I guess so. They won't be looking for you any more. We can get to the car. . . ." She paused, her hand suspended halfway to the font. "No. Please. Sit down. Back there."

Puzzled but obedient, Matt took the pew underneath Saint Emigdius. Concha knelt in the aisle, then slipped in beside him. There was no one else in this dark back part of the church.

She took his hand and held it in a clasp warm even through her glove; but there was nothing amorous about the gesture. It was rather one of ease and trust. "There's peace here," she said. "I'm not in the world any more. I can feel the things that count, and the things that don't count I can just look at and not have to feel."

"And what counts?"

She nodded toward the altar. "That. That and the way it makes me feel. And you a little—knowing I can talk to you. You're all right here, Matt. I hadn't expected that. I thought bringing you here would tear me, but it all fits together. And so now I can talk."

Matt stroked her hand in encouraging silence.

"Oh, God," she said (and it was not an oath), "let my father's soul rest in peace." Then she was silent for a long time.

"I've been trying," she said at last, "to build it up gradually so that you could see why, but there's no making sense of it. It gets even worse when you try to be logical about it. So I'll just have to blurt it out. It's the why of everything—why I wanted to go into a convent and why I'm all jerky, as you said, and why I have to know who was in that room and why. It's . . . Oh, you won't believe me, but . . . You see, Matt, I think maybe my father killed my mother."

There was nothing you could say to that. Matt sat numb, still holding her tense hand and waiting for her to go on—for some cue to come that a man could answer. The sense of the statement hardly reached him; it was too sudden, too shocking for quick comprehension.

It was Concha who broke the silence with a sharp, high, instantly stifled laugh. "It sounds so funny when you say it like that and all of a sudden I know I'm wrong. You can't say it here and believe it. You say it and you know you were mad ever to think it. But still . . . "

"What made you think it?"

"I was away when she died—you knew that? I hadn't seen her for months, and then I had the wire and I came home and she was dead. And they never told me what she died of—just how sick she'd been, her eyes and all, but never anything certain. So I worried. I loved my mother, Matt. You don't know how much she meant to me, how much more than all the others, even Father. And then one day I was looking for a book in Father's study and I accidentally knocked down that book about drugs and it opened at—where you saw. At about hyoscine. I was just curious. That was all then. I read about hyoscine and how you can poison people by dropping it in their eyes and I remember how Mother had eyedrops. You could put things in eyedrops if you knew what to put, and then there wouldn't be any suspicion and you wouldn't have to be even around when it happened."

"But your father! How could you think that he . . . ?"

"They weren't happy. I wasn't supposed to know that, but I did. Children know things. They loved each other and they were both wonderful people and they weren't happy. Abuelita—that's Mother's mother—she hated the Harrigans and everything about them. Grandfather Rufus was hard and cruel, and all his fortune came because he was smart and made money that should have been the Pelayos'. While Abuelita was alive, Mother used to defend Father and say he couldn't be blamed for what Grandfather Rufus did; but after Abuelita died, Mother began to talk that way herself. It was as though her mother's spirit had gone into her. She couldn't help it. She loved my father, but sometimes she hated the Harrigans. And so they weren't happy, even if Father was very patient, and I thought that if sometime she had goaded him too far . . .

"It was an awful thought. I didn't want to think about it, but I couldn't help it. It grew like a cancer or something. It just went through me and it was part of me and there I was thinking that my father was a murderer. And I began to feel—oh, I don't know—like Hamlet, I guess. That was the same thing you know. I mean juice of deadly hebanon in a vial—that's henbane, hyoscine. Oh, I looked it all up, everything, only you couldn't through the ear, it would have to be the eye and that's where you could with her."

"But couldn't you have found out for sure?"

"How? Whenever I tried to ask more about Mother's death, everybody shushed me. It was one thing even Arthur wouldn't talk about. And that was Janet's day off so she didn't know anything and that made it look even worse. It was terrible, Matt. I even began to wish . . . No, I didn't really wish my father would die. I only wished that if my thought was right he would be punished. And things weren't the same with us any more. Even before I had the thought. It was as though he had a wall just high enough so I couldn't peek over and he'd look out over it and smile at me but I knew it was there and it was hiding something from me. And then when he did die . . . It was almost as though I was responsible. You see, I'd wanted it . . . almost; and then when it happened . . . Don't you see?"

She gave up talking and burrowed her face into Matt's shoulder, her whole body given over to sobs. He patted her back and looked at the monstrance on the altar and up at Saint Emigdius and knew that he would never find the words he needed.

Two ancient Mexican women, dressed in shapeless black with black shawls over their heads, paused in crossing themselves at the entrance and looked back toward the sobs. "*Habrán perdido a su niñito,*" said one, compassionately regarding the young couple.

"*¡Dios los tenga en su bondad!*" murmured the other.

Concha straightened up and made dabs at her eyes. "There. Now you know why I'm funny. No. Don't try to say anything. There isn't anything to say. Take me home now, please."

"Take him back to his cell," said Lieutenant Marshall.

The Swami Mahopadhyaya Virasenanda, limp and sweating, smiled with mock courtesy. "You are most kind, Lieutenant."

"Take him away."

They took him away.

"I know," said Marshall to the police stenographer, "that I'm right on this burglary angle, but what the hell can I do about it? He's got the wind up so bad about the murder that there's no getting a word out of him. It ties up—no question about that. But who was his accomplice?"

The stenographer shrugged. "He'll wear down in time. They all do."

"Time. . . . Sure, time. But I'd like to know."

Sergeant Krauter came in with a sheaf of papers. "Here's the last of the reports, Lieutenant."

"No soap?"

"Not a bubble."

Marshall leafed through the papers. "This covers every man and woman that Harrigan was investigating?"

"Everyone, and all accounted for. All nice, ordinary accountings, too—no phony business in the whole lot but Ahasver and the Swami. If you ask me, it's between them.

"In their class. Krauter, this case is a toss-up between the amateur and the professional. There's motive either way—the estate or silence. Now our professional group has narrowed down to Ahasver (whoever he is), his sweet little Robin, and Sussmaul; and the will seems to limit the family to Arthur and the girl."

"My money's on the Swami," said Krauter feelingly. "I know these fortunetellers."

Marshall read the reports through more carefully and laid them down. "Routine. It wouldn't make good reading, but it had to be done. Now that's out of the way."

"What do we do next?"

"You might try to figure out how a man in a yellow robe slips through a rat hole; or alternatively how you can make a pillar of the church break down and admit perjury. If you can solve either of those problems, Krauter, I'll pin my Lieutenant's badge on you."

"The Civil Service Commission wouldn't let you," said Krauter practically. "But what are you going to do tomorrow?"

The Lieutenant stood up and stretched. "God, I'm tired. Never try to catch up on your sleep with a two-year-old in the house. As for tomorrow—for my own poor part, look you, I'm going to get me to a nunnery."

"Huh?" said Sergeant Krauter.

"You wouldn't like to stop off someplace?" Matt asked as they crossed Vine Street.

"No, thanks."

They were at Highland before Concha spoke again. "I'm glad Greg showed up."

"Glad? Of all the low tricks!"

"Yes, I know it was nasty of Arthur to set him spying on us—it must have been Arthur, mustn't it?—but still it was a good thing. It made us go into the church to get away, and that made me come out right somehow."

"All is for the best," said Matt. "And so forth."

"And so the evening didn't go the way I'd planned."

"What had you planned? Fun and games with your friends on the Pelayo side?"

"No." Her voice was small and she kept her face turned away. "I had different plans, Matt, before we—went in the church."

"So?"

"We were going to go some place to dance and you were going to have some drinks."

"Sound thought. It isn't too late for that now."

"Yes, it is. Much too late. We were going to dance and you were going to drink and then—then you weren't going to take me home."

"A fine escort! Expect me to pass out on you or—Whoa! What do you mean, not take you home? Where should I take you?"

"Some place. You know. Some place where you take" (she choked a little) "a woman."

Matt slowed up and turned to stare at the girl. "You mean that you . . . ?"

She looked up at him defensively. "It's the way I felt. Everything's gone to pieces. My mother, my father, the newspapers, all the suspicion and hatred in the house . . . I felt I had to . . . "

"To go to hell," Matt exploded. "Look, honey. You're a sweet child. You're a lot more than that sometimes. But if you think that I'd be such a heel as to—"

"I know. That's why you were going to drink."

Suddenly Matt burst out into loud laughter. "God, it's marvellous! Weaken my resistance? Render me helpless in my innocence and simplicity and then—Damn it, Concha, I ought to stop this car here and now and spank some sense into you. What on earth made you think of such a wild idea?"

She said nothing.

"What's the matter? Say something!" She was still silent. "Mad because I threatened to spank you? If somebody'd started in doing that a long time ago, life would be simpler at Harrigans'."

She made no reply.

They rode in silence out Sunset and turned onto the side street. Matt stopped in front of the house. "Want to get out here? I'll take the car around to the garage. Or are you speaking to me yet?"

Concha lifted her face, and he saw that she had been silently crying all this time. "You . . . you laughed at me."

He looked at her red eyes and streaked cheeks, at the puckering of her mouth which twitched her face into a grotesque fright. "You'd laugh now," he said gently, "if you could see yourself."

She leaned forward, caught his lapels, and dissolved on his shoulder. For what seemed like hours he tried to comfort her, with no idea of what random phrases he muttered. At last she looked up, sniffing but improved.

"That wasn't nice, was it? Twice in one evening. Men shouldn't ever see women cry. It's pretty in pictures, but when it's real it's just something awful." She opened her handbag and tried to repair as best she could in the little light from the dashboard.

"And there's nothing," said Matt, "that makes a man feel so goddamned helpless. Feel better now?"

"I guess so. But please—you won't laugh at me any more?"

"I'll try not to."

"Arthur always laughs at me, and Uncle Joe, and sometimes even Aunt Ellen. I thought you'd be different."

"Maybe I can be."

"'Cause you are so different from them. You're real and strong, like out of another world. I've never known anybody like you."

"Guys like me are a dime a dozen, honey. You just don't shop at the right counters."

"You see what I told you—what you laughed at—it wasn't really true. But I didn't tell you the truth because it would only make you laugh worse, I thought. I thought if I tried to be—oh, you know—sophisticated and worldly about it you wouldn't think it was funny."

"I don't know as I quite get it."

"I mean, if I said I wanted you to take me just because I was tired of it all . . . Well, I mean—people do things like that, don't they? You read about it."

"Not people like you, Concha."

"I know. I see that now. But I thought a man might react that way when he'd just be mad if I told him the real reason."

"Which is?"

"Don't you know?" She put away her bag and twisted sideways on the seat, half-kneeling and looking fixedly into his eyes. "Don't you, darling?"

"I know we'd better be getting inside, or Aunt Ellen—"

"Oh, Matt, I love you something terrible. It hurts. It hurts worse than death and hate and everything. I—"

She leaned forward and pressed her lips against Matt's, awkwardly, innocently, tenderly. Against his will he felt his arm press her warm body close to him. Whatever else of her was child, he realized with a shock, that body was all woman.

"Look." He was arguing as much with himself as with her. "Don't let's make damn fools of ourselves. This isn't natural. We're thrown together under tension. Things happen all around us. Things happen to us, too. We've got to keep our heads—sleep on it."

"I don't suppose you'll believe me," said Concha softly, "but that was my first kiss. Oh, I mean people have pecked at me; but I never *felt* kissed before." Her eyes had a new light all their own in the dimness of the car.

Gently Matt thrust her into the opposite corner. "As far as I'm concerned, it's your last."

"But darling!"

"It's a good thing," he said, "you didn't try out your little scheme. I'm suddenly realizing it might have worked."

EIGHTEEN

Matt was on the phone early the next morning. Luck was with him; he found Lieutenant Marshall still at home.

"Duncan speaking."

"O? Ah ah oo ah?" remarked the Lieutenant.

"I'm afraid I didn't get that."

Gulp. "If you will call a man at breakfast, you have to put up with his talking through food. I said, What's on your mind?"

Matt thought of churches and fresh scars and tear-damp shoulders. "Plenty. But not all official. What I want at the moment is the answer to one question."

"Terry!" he heard Leona's voice. "Don't throw mush at your father when he's telephoning."

"Sure," said Marshall. "Any other time's O.K. Well, what's the question?"

"Look. Do you know anything about the death of Mrs. Wolfe Harrigan?"

All at once Marshall sounded distant and anything but friendly and confiding. "A little. Why?"

"I can't tell you—not yet, anyway. I may be some kinds of rat, but not all. But tell me this much—"

"Sorry, Duncan, but I'm not an open information bureau. Frankly, I've told you things when I've thought you could help me—not just to satisfy your curiosity."

"Terry! Leave your father alone. He's looking mad enough without your help."

"All right. But I'll ask one question just the same. Is there any possibility that her death might have been a murder?"

"No possibility whatsoever."

"You're certain?"

"Positive."

"Thanks. Give my love to Leona and Terry."

Concha joined Matt halfway through his own breakfast. Aunt Ellen was at mass, and Arthur was sleeping off whatever revelry he and Greg Randall had indulged in after the Battle of Olvera Street.

The girl was silent this morning: no reference to the night before, no attempts at bright chitchat, no sport with leaping toast. When she did look at Matt, it was with the sad eyes of a dog that has been rebuffed by its master.

"Is your cheek all right?" she asked at last.

"Fine. Thanks for washing and dressing it last night. Janet fixed it up again this morning and said what a neat job you'd done."

"I wonder how she thought you got it."

"She didn't ask. No nonsense about Janet. Strange things happen, but she has her job and she does it."

Silence.

"Well," said Concha, "that covers Janet, doesn't it?"

"Look," said Matt abruptly. "I want you to do something."

"What?"

"Tell the Lieutenant about—about your idea. If anything was wrong, surely he'd at least have heard something. He can set you right."

"I am set right. I told you that. I got rid of it last night. For a minute I was free. But you can't stay free, can you? One thing goes away and another comes. Like the man with the evil spirit only it doesn't have to be seven others. One's enough."

"Tell him anyway. You know the thought's still there hidden away in back somewheres; you can't get rid of things so simply as that. Try it."

"Maybe . . . " She broke a crisp slice of bacon into little pieces. "I want a favor, too, Matt."

"Yes?"

"Drive me out to the convent this morning. I want to talk to Sister Ursula, and I'd sort of like to have you along, too. Do you mind?"

Bunyan came in just then, a certain plus-value of self-satisfaction added to his usual smug sufficiency. "I beg your pardon, Miss Mary. I had not intended to intrude."

"That's all right. Go ahead."

"I merely wished to inquire of Mr. Duncan if he knew whether the police lieutenant would be calling here in the course of the day?"

"I'm not sure," said Matt. "I wouldn't be surprised. Did you get your night off last night?"

"Indeed I did, sir. But if I may be so bold, would you communicate to the Lieutenant that I have some information of prime importance to his case and should be glad to see him at his earliest opportunity?"

Concha clapped her hands. "Why, Bunyan! I bet you're a detective in disguise! What's your secret?"

"That, Miss Mary, you must learn from the Lieutenant." He bowed and withdrew suavely.

Lieutenant Marshall was refreshing the flowers of the patio with gardener's incense. "Frankly, Sister," he was saying, "what I really want from you is a little unofficial police work."

"I don't see what I can do," Sister Ursula protested gently, with a cautious glance at Sister Felicitas, who dozed near them in the sun. "I'm perfectly willing to try to reason and talk, but what I could do practically . . . " She seemed, however, not unflattered by the idea.

"There's one thing you can do, that I'm helpless to even try. You can break down Ellen Harrigan's story."

"Lieutenant!"

"I know. She's sort of your patroness here, isn't she? But I thought that you, Sister, might put justice above even the advantage of your order."

"You misunderstand me, Lieutenant. I was not being indignant—merely astonished. Please go on."

"This sealed-room business isn't just locked; it's dead-locked. There's no possible way in or out of that room save through the chapel door. And Ellen Harrigan was at that door. Obvious conclusion: She's protecting someone. And I can't use third-degree methods on her, or I'd have all her brother's political influence on my neck and probably the Archbishop to boot."

"But I thought you understood that—"

"I know. I can't ask you to violate any confidence she might place in you. But I had a situation like this in the Rafetti case. The whole force was certain Big Mike had killed him, but there was no evidence. Nobody knew positively but Big Mike's confessor, and of course I couldn't get a word out of him. But I did drop a hint, and he worked on Big Mike until the lug confessed."

"That was his duty even without your hint, Lieutenant."

"Was it? But that's what I mean you could do. Not worm confidences out of Miss Harrigan, but persuade her that the best thing she can do is to tell the truth to the police."

"But there's no sense to that. She has told the truth."

"Nonsense. The only solution to this case lies in making her tell what she saw."

"You know all that she saw. Her evidence is the one reliable fact you have: that no one came out of that chapel door for ten minutes before Matt Duncan saw Mr. Harrigan's body."

"But how can you—?"

"You will find her out here, Miss Harrigan," came a nun's voice, and Concha entered the patio, followed by Matt.

"Lieutenant! It's Fate, Matt, isn't it?"

"Fate? I'm a married man, Miss Harrigan."

"No. Matt wanted me to ask you something, and I didn't want to, so I came out here just in case you went to the house. And now . . ."

"Fate," said Sister Ursula, "is a pagan concept for a Harrigan. God's will counts for something, too."

"Very well, Miss Harrigan. If Fate and God and the duties of a policeman all combine to bring me here, you might as well ask your question. What is it?"

"Lieutenant, do you know . . . Oh, no! I can't. Really, Matt, I just can't."

"Is it—what you told me about last Friday?" Sister Ursula asked gently.

Concha nodded without a word.

"Go on then. Ask it. Terror vanishes when you take it out and look at it."

"First principles of psychoanalysis," Marshall smiled.

"You've no idea, Lieutenant, how many of those principles had already been known to the Church for nineteen centuries. But go on, Mary."

"All right. Lieutenant Marshall—do you know how my mother died?"

Marshall looked reflectively at Matt. "She died," he said easily, "a natural death. Heart clot. Probably precipitated by strain and worry over her blindness."

"How do you know?"

"Do you think I'd approach a case without checking up on any other recent deaths in the same family? One of the first things I did was to look up the record and get a full report on your mother. Nothing out of the way at all."

Concha stretched her arms out high. "I'm in the sun," she said. "It's warm and it's good. Thanks, Matt. Sister. You were sweet to make me ask."

"I'm glad you came out today," said Sister Ursula. "Sister Perpetua was asking after you. She wants you to see her illuminated missal; she's finished it now."

"Has she? Oh, how keen! I'd love to see it."

"She's in the library now. Would you like to go see her? You know where it is."

"Why? Aren't you coming?"

"My dear, that missal is the most beautiful material thing ever created in this convent, but I've quite run out of comments on it. There's only so much one can say about beauty, and I have said it. But you go."

"All right. I shan't be long."

"This is an astounding and wonderful labor of Sister Perpetua's. She is attempting to re-create medieval effects using modern methods and materials; and I feel that she has been markedly . . ." Concha's footsteps died away down the arcade, and the nun's voice changed abruptly. "Now, Lieutenant, will you please tell us what you really know about Mrs. Harrigan's death."

"Why, Sister, what makes you think that I—"

"You were a little too glib, Lieutenant. Please tell me the truth. I am sure you would have difficulty in finding anyone more devoted to that poor child than I am, or Mr. Duncan here. I think that we deserve to know."

"All right. Everybody but Miss Harrigan knows anyway, though Joseph did a brilliant job of hushing it up."

Sister Ursula shuddered. "Suicide?"

"Yes. I guess she couldn't stand the thought of blindness. Terrible thing, this old Spanish pride. And after her mother's death she seems to have felt the whole burden of the race on her shoulders—the last of the Pelayos. Messy death, too. Stabbed herself with an heirloom knife—finest Toledo steel. There was an inquest—I saw the transcript—but it was held behind closed doors, and nothing got into the papers. Wonderful what pulling the right strings can do. I gather that she was even buried with the full rites of the church. You could quote *Hamlet* on that:

>   Her death was doubtful;
> And, but that great command o'ersways the order,
> She should in ground unsanctified have lodg'd . . . "

"The Church gave her the benefit of the doubt, then. It's very rare to forbid a suicide burial. There is always the possibility of some momentary aberration that drove the poor victim to his act; and your own story indicates that the death of her mother and the obsession of family pride had combined to drive the half-blind woman to a state where she might forget the canon which (if I too may quote *Hamlet*) the Everlasting has fixed 'gainst self-slaughter. And is such mercy in burial any worse than your telling a kind lie to her daughter?"

It all fell into place now, Matt thought. All the hugger-mugger and secrecy about Mrs. Harrigan's death to prevent a scandal that would blot the fair name of Harrigan and also (to give the devil his due) to spare her daughter that bitter knowledge. Then the memory of her parents' unhappiness and the cruel chance of that book which fell open at *Hyoscine,* and all Concha's adolescent self-torture growing out of that caprice of Fate—or would Sister Ursula think that, too, the will of God?

"And what gave the girl the idea of murder?" said Marshall.

Sister Ursula stared at him innocently. "What on earth do you mean?"

"Now who's too glib? Why else should she be so eager and yet so afraid to know, and so infinitely relieved by natural death? Come on, Sister; what gave her the idea?"

Sister Ursula shook her head. "I don't know what you're talking about, Lieutenant."

"All right. Have it your way. But I can't help my wicked thoughts, can I? Thoughts like, for instance, supposing she suspected her father? That could be a new motive—open up a whole fresh line of . . . "

"And William the Second?" Sister Ursula interposed hastily. "How does that indicate her?"

"How the sweet—How does it indicate anybody?"

"If only I knew the *how,*" Sister Ursula murmured. "The *who* is so obvious, unless . . . " She started suddenly. "Lieutenant! I know the Harrigan family. The two young people are dark, and the two older ones are gray. But does anyone—anyone at all connected with this case—have red hair?"

"Hey!" said Marshall.

"Please. I am not being cryptic. At least, not wantonly so. But these other suspects of yours—the ones outside the family—do they?"

"No."

"Nor anyone else at all connected?"

"Nobody but my wife and son. The only redheads in the whole cast."

Sister Ursula seemed relieved. "Then I am right. But how stupid of me to have overlooked such a possibility. I cannot help wondering what other stupidities we may have committed among us. Please: has anything new come up, anything I should know about?"

"Bunyan has a secret," said Matt. "I'm supposed to give you that message, Lieutenant. He wants to see you today. He went to a Temple of Light meeting last night, and today he looks as self-satisfied as a canary who's just disposed of the biggest tom in the neighborhood."

"The Temple?" Marshall repeated. "So. The more I think about that Temple angle, the less I like it. I'll see Bunyan this afternoon, but nothing he could tell me about the Temple would interest me so much as a way out of that sealed room. We spent a whole night on that room," he added plaintively to Sister Ursula. "We went over every possible angle and all the impossible ones. I kept hoping that somewhere we'd hit on what made sense, but all we did was run up against one more impossibility."

"And what was that?" the nun demanded eagerly.

"Sister, you sound as though you *wanted* another impossibility."

"I think perhaps I do. Two pieces of wood may be asymmetrical and almost shapeless. Fit them together, and you have a perfect geometrical figure. Impossibilities can be like that, too. What is this one?"

"All right. You asked for it. Yellow gloves are a part of the Ahasver costume—a fixed adjunct to the yellow robe. The murderer left no fingerprints anywhere. But when Duncan saw him through the window, *he had taken off his gloves!*"

She turned to Matt. "You mean you saw a bare hand?"

"Yes. I couldn't see the face, but I do remember that bare flesh against the desk."

"And why," Marshall lamented, "any murderer, however cockeyed, should peel off his gloves to—"

"Lieutenant!" Sister Ursula's voice was sharp and efficient. "Will you please be at the Harrigan home tomorrow afternoon?"

"Probably. This is my job. But why so urgent?"

"I am beginning to see a way out. No, please don't ask me to explain now; but I think tomorrow, on the ground, I can show you how the man in the yellow robe left the room."

"And who the man is?" asked Marshall. "After all, that helps too."

"I have known that for too long. Unless," she added as an afterthought, "Ahasver's hair should prove as false as his beard. And now, if I could beg you both to tell me everything that has happened since Mr. Duncan gave me his outline of events on Tuesday . . ."

"In any standard whodunit," Marshall had remarked in the car, "Bunyan would have been rubbed out by now. The Man Who Knew Too Much."

But an unscathed butler greeted them at the door. "Well," said the Lieutenant, after Concha had somewhat reluctantly excused herself, "here I am."

"Ah," Bunyan smiled. "If you gentlemen will be so kind as to step into the study where we may be unobserved, I shall be more than happy to divulge to you the true identity of Ahasver."

NINETEEN

It was a strange group of five men who sat together in the balcony of the Temple that Thursday night. Attending the Temple of Light, Matt reflected, was getting to be like going to the theater or a football game—there was no telling what acquaintances you might pick up.

He had started in with R. Joseph Harrigan. The full details of the secret and the resultant plan Bunyan had reserved for the Lieutenant's private ear; all Matt knew was that there was to be an extraordinary revelation this night and that R. Joseph had been invited as the most interested and least excitable representative of the family.

No sooner were they in the foyer (where Matt looked in vain for the cherubic countenance of Robin Cooper among the greeters) than the lawyer exclaimed, "Arthur! What on earth are you doing here?"

Arthur shambled over to them reluctantly. "When you hear your butler making a date with a cop, you get curious."

"And, Gregory!" Joseph boomed. "Glad to see you, young man!"

Gregory Randall looked anything but glad. "Arthur said he wanted company," he muttered half-defensively.

"I know," Joseph nodded. "You feel embarrassed at meeting me after that foolish scene on Tuesday. Tush, boy! We all are carried away at times. No hard feelings."

Gregory drew Matt back from the others as they started up the stairs. "I hope you understand about last night, old man."

"I guess I do." Matt's voice was not too warm.

"After all, when all's said and done—what I mean is—"

"A man in your position," Matt prompted.

"Exactly. I'm glad you understood. A man in my position has, after all, a certain—well, a certain position to uphold. I know it was absurd of me to lose my temper so, but in view of everything . . . " He noticed the fresh scar and broke off. "Did I—?"

"You should have seen it fresh," said Matt cheerfully. "Five stitches and a blood transfusion. Of course, it's pretty much healed up by now."

Greg, accepting the statement with his usual literal faith, fell into shocked silence, and Matt turned his attention to the talk of the two old men with thin tight lips and turkey-gobbler necks who were ascending the stairs ahead of them.

"The Nine Times Nine sure did the work," said one. "We showed that Harrigan, all right." There was relish in his dry voice.

The other chuckled harshly. "And that ain't all we're going to do. You wait. That was just one enemy. You wait till we really start cleaning up. You wait and see where the Reds and the Cath'lics and the dirty Jews get off then."

The first one scratched his bald spot. "But Ahasver's a Jew himself, ain't he?"

"That don't prove nothing. So was Jesus, wasn't he? Well?"

The first seemed content with this form of logic. "I'd like to see anybody stop us," he said grimly.

At the top of the stairs Matt ran plump into Fred Simmons. That retired storekeeper seemed cruelly torn between his natural good-hearted friendliness and his enmity for any Harrigan spy. He said "Hello," in an exact state of balance between the two feelings.

"Hello," Matt replied, then added on a chance, "This is Mr. Randall, Mr. Simmons. Randall's been trying to persuade me I'm all wrong about the Temple—persuaded me to come back tonight and listen again."

Fred Simmons expanded and eagerly shook the hand of the badly confused Greg Randall. "Fine work, Randall. I've tried to tell Duncan here that young men like him and you are just what we need. Maybe you can help get him out of those tomfool ideas of Harrigan's. Mind if I sit with you?"

Matt found himself sitting between R. Joseph and Fred Simmons, with Arthur and Greg at opposite ends of the party. All through the organ voluntary on stickily familiar themes, he could hear the lawyer berating his nephew on his unseemly conduct of the past week and the ex-storekeeper eagerly, if monologously, debating articles of faith with his new-found comrade in the Ancients.

"I'm right glad Randall brought you of a Thursday," Simmons said, turning to Matt. "That's Special Study Night. Tonight Ahasver always tells us about the perils threatening America, so we'll know what to do when . . . "

"When what?"

"Hush." The high tenor had begun *Sweet Mystery of Life*. The service started as before: the parting of the curtains to reveal Ahasver in yellow splendor on a bare stage, the service-club welcome from the man by the water pitcher (Matt enjoyed seeing Gregory wince as Simmons wrung his hand), and the communal singing of *Old Christianity*. If possible, this last was even louder and more vigorous than on Saturday; the congregation seemed to have been infused with new strength and devotion.

"You see, Duncan," Fred Simmons explained, "we know now it's all real. Some people maybe doubted a little before. Not me, of course. No, sir. But some people maybe thought it was all kind of—well, unlikely, like. But since we set the Nine Times Nine and it worked—well, now we know where we are."

Now there was dead silence as Ahasver rose and came to the front center of the stage. "Ye all do know," he began softly, "why we are met together tonight. It is that I may teach ye the truth, and that the truth may make ye free, and free our great and glorious land as well. But before I tell ye these things which it is meet and fitting that ye know, I must cast mine eye upon the book, that from its pages I may glean what messages the Ancients have for us."

Matt looked at his companions. Arthur was masking an alert curiosity with his habitual pose of boredom. R. Joseph, his head cocked studiously to one side, seemed to be studying the leader's platform manner from the professional angle. Fred Simmons awaited the words of the Ancients in rapt tension. And Gregory was just plain bewildered.

Ahasver beckoned to the wings, and a white-clad page wheeled on the volume of blank sheets. "For is it not written," the rich voice asked, "In the eighth chapter of the Gospel according to Joseph:

> Knowledge sought availeth much; but knowledge given shall be all in all.

Therefore let us learn what knowledge is given unto us." He lowered his eyes and scanned the blank pages.

Suddenly the yellow figure stiffened. "No . . . !" he gasped half-audibly, and read more intently—so intently that Matt was almost convinced that the pages did bear a message. There had been dead silence while Ahasver paused, but now a little rustling murmur began to slither over the audience. Fred Simmons leaned forward, deeply perturbed.

Then Ahasver closed the book, and the thud cut through the murmur and reduced it to silence. "I have read," he announced slowly and clearly, "my last message from this stage. No—be ye not affrighted. Raise not your voices in the murmuration of wonder. But hear and attend.

"It is the Will of the Ancients that I follow, and that alone that rules my life. First, the command imposed upon me by the Ancient Jesus in Jerusalem, and then, as I grew wiser in the great Wisdom of the Ancients, the commands of all the Nine. It was at Their behest that I came here to the City of the Angels and sought to give unto you what Truth I might. It is now at Their behest that I leave you, and whither I go no man knoweth.

"Hear ye now the parting words of Ahasver."

Matt turned to Simmons, but the faithful disciple had no eyes or ears for things of this world. All his attention was fixed on the

Master who had just uttered these incredible words of farewell. R. Joseph looked as astounded, though hardly with the same emotions; and Gregory seemed, if anything, more amazed than ever.

It was an astonishing sermon, this speech of farewell, filled with a humanity and a tolerance foreign to anything else in Ahasver's career. He bade the people to forget hatred in his memory, to leave to that which is good, to defend the democracy of the land, but not to let that defense become in itself the worst enemy of democracy through intolerance. The audience stirred restlessly at first, cheated perhaps of the sport of its regular Thursday night denunciations, but slowly seemed won over to at least passive comprehension of this new line.

Finally, Ahasver paused and retired, with slow dignity, to the back of the stage. The houselights dimmed to blackness, and the multicolored play on the rear wall followed them into the dark. There was visible only the yellow spot beating down from above upon the yellow figure of Ahasver.

"The blessings of the Nine," pronounced the man in the yellow robe, "yea, and of the Nine Times Nine, be upon you forever. For is it not written in the last chapter of the Gospel according to Joseph:

> Man serveth the Ancients that They may love him; and They in Their turn serve him that They may hold his love. These two are all—love and service. And lo, these two are one.

Farewell!"

With this even the yellow spot went out. For an instant the auditorium was completely black. Then the lights went on in full brilliance. Momentarily they showed the stage, empty save for a somewhat bewildered man by the water pitcher. Then the curtain descended, and the organist struck up an exit march.

"Well!" said Fred Simmons, and then, as though the event had reduced his vocabulary to one helpless monosyllable, "Well!"

The Lieutenant had told Matt and Joseph to meet him backstage in the Chamber of Contemplation for full footnotes. He had said nothing about Arthur and Gregory, but those two young men tagged along anyway.

"Astounding," Joseph declared roundly. "Truly astounding! How could Marshall have persuaded that rascal to give up his demagoguery so completely?"

"Wonderful man, the Lieutenant," said Arthur. "Maybe he could even get you to give up politics."

The group paused outside the yellow chamber. "You can't do this to me!" a voice was protesting vehemently.

Matt opened the door. Sergeant Krauter was standing pleased guard over the man in the yellow robe and observing, "Can't we? Now ain't that just too bad?"

"Hello," said Matt hesitantly.

"Hello, Mr. Duncan. Come on in—all of you—if you can fit. The Lieutenant'll be here in a minute. How'd it go?"

"Swell. They don't know what hit them."

The Sergeant jerked a thumb at Ahasver. "Neither does he. Jeez," he added wistfully, "I wisht my wife was here."

"In here," said Marshall's voice outside. The Lieutenant strode in, followed by the impeccable Bunyan and—Matt's eyes popped—a man in a yellow robe.

The other under Krauter's guard jumped to his feet. "Judas!" he hissed.

"What the hell, Mason," said the second Ahasver quietly. "The game's up and this was the best way out."

"You rat!"

"Sure. Sure I'm a rat. So what? The ship's sinking—that's enough to make a rat out of anybody."

"Look," said Matt. "Let's get this straight? What the hell goes on?"

"Exactly, sir," Joseph rumbled. "How many men in yellow robes are there?"

Marshall pointed at the one who had just come in. "You know this one, both of you, though you may not recognize him when he isn't camping. Take off the whiskers, Jack Dalton, and let the gentlemen feast on your beautiful puss."

The man in the yellow robe obliged.

"The Cherub!" Matt whistled.

"Good heavens!" said Joseph. "It's that young man!"

"What young man?" said Gregory, feebly and unheeded.

"Surprise?" asked Robin Cooper. "I thought you two were so certain that you'd recognized me in these robes before. Just to keep the record straight," he added, "you were right—probably without knowing it."

"Then who in heaven's name, Lieutenant, is this?"

"Take the floor, Bunyan," said Marshall. "This is your show."

The butler stepped forward, as unmoved and self-sufficient as ever. "I fear," he began, "that I must preface my remarks with a small apology to the Harrigan family, who, with the exception of Mr. Wolfe, have known me under what might be considered false pretenses."

"I know," said Arthur. "You're Inspector Bunyan of Scotland Yard."

Ahasver's face (the Krauter-watched Ahasver's, that is), usually impassive, was going through a lively little routine of recognition and amazement. "Bannister!" he cried.

Bunyan bowed. "At your service. My real name, if I may be permitted a moment of autobiographical revelation, is Dominic Wyndham Bannister, formerly Bishop—self-ordained, I may add—of the Episcopal Church of Established Spiritualism. That was a pleasing and profitable profession until Mr. Harrigan chose to expose certain of my manifestations. When I protested that the untrained and disinherited son of an aristocratic family must earn his bread as best he may, he pointed out that my qualifications might make me an excellent butler. I have come to believe that he was right."

"Fascinating," snorted Joseph. "But what has your past record to do with Ahasver?"

"Although, sir, I have given up the commercial practices of my misguided youth, I still take a certain professional interest in the development of spiritualist devices, and often visit with my former colleagues. From them I had recently heard two rumors, one that Ahasver was said to be a member of our old Chicago group, and the other that Glenn Mason was in town.

"Now I had known Mason moderately well in Chicago, when my see was situated there. He was a stock actor, then, who augmented his income on his free Sunday evenings by playing a leading rôle in the rituals of the Church of Christ Spiritualist. He was a versatile gentleman; in one evening I saw him in the spiritual characters of George Washington, Robert Ingersoll, and the Emperor Caligula. He left Chicago, however, rather hurriedly. In his offstage activities he had apparently assumed the rôle of Giovanni Casanova, with a singular ignorance of the laws governing the age of consent. Criminal charges had been brought against him.

"From what I knew of Mason's style, I thought it not unlikely that he might be this mysterious Ahasver, though I had postponed mentioning the matter to Mr. Harrigan until I could be more certain. When I saw an 'Ahasver' on Monday who certainly was not Mason, I thought no more of the affair until I overheard the Lieutenant's suspicion that the Monday-Ahasver was not the genuine article. Immediately I attended a service, convinced myself of his identity, and reported my discovery to the Lieutenant."

"So," Marshall took up the narrative, "I wired to Chicago, got the Mason records, had a little talk with Ahasver here, and persuaded him that maybe it might save scandal if he didn't go on tonight. I'd been sure already that Cooper doubled for him on Monday, so I tackled him for this job. Once he was persuaded that the ship was sinking, it was easy."

"But why," Joseph blustered, "all this rigmarole about being called by the Ancients? Why not simply arrest the rascal and expose him?"

"This was Bunyan's suggestion. He knows the tricks of the trade. If we'd arrested Ahasver, you can guess what would happen. He'd have been 'framed'. He'd be a persecuted martyr. The Children of Light would fight on to clear his good name. He'd become the Mooney of the crackpots. But after this recall-effect, the church will just plain dissolve. It isn't strong enough to carry on without his personality."

"Shrewd," said Joseph grudgingly.

"All right. We've carried out Harrigan's work. We've broken up the Children of Light. And now, for my own work, comes the question of who was back of it? Mason, are you talking? Who did you take orders from?"

Ahasver-Mason pointed at Cooper-Ahasver. "As rat to rat, there's the guy. He doped out the lighting effects and everything. He gave me my speeches and I memorized them."

"Is that true, Cooper?"

Robin Cooper smiled with a superior self-satisfaction to top Bunyan's. "Why, yes, Lieutenant. You might say that I was really Ahasver all the time. This lout simply wore the clothes."

"And who," Marshall snapped, "wore the clothes Sunday afternoon?"

"Sunday . . . ? Heavens! Are you back at that Harrigan business again? I've told you we know nothing about that. It was a good chance for publicity and we took it. That's all. It's obvious, of course, that someone deliberately tried to frame us, but" (his eyes brushed leisurely over the men in the room) "I have no idea who it could have been."

"And who told you to set the Nine Times Nine on Harrigan?"

"Told me? I don't take orders, Lieutenant. I give them."

"Gave them."

"Give them. Despite this evening, I feel that my power is not completely at an end. It might be inadvisable for others if they thought it was."

"So. Well, one thing's certain. We saw this evening that every member of this congregation accepts you readily as Ahasver. And that means that one of you two has no alibi at all for Sunday afternoon."

"My," said Robin Cooper. "How dreadful!"

"And for whom, sir, is the third glass?" asked the butler, as he brought a tray into the study to Matt and the Lieutenant.

"For you, Bunyan, if you can forget your dignity long enough to set down that tray and join us. Or do you prefer Bannister?"

"I think, sir, that I have by now so completely accustomed myself to Bunyan that—"

"All right." Marshall lifted his glass. "To Bunyan! Nice spot of work you did tonight."

"Thank you, sir."

"But God knows what I did. Matt, I feel like Pandora. I've lifted the lid on mischief and it's flying all over the place."

"Closed the lid, you mean—or am I just being literal like my dear friend Greg?"

"You are. I've closed the lid on the Temple, but I've lifted it on something else. Tonight wasn't wise. It wasn't safe, with a murderer still at large. Robby-wobby's asking for something—and I'm not too sure that he'll be the one to get it."

"Well, it's done now."

"It is, and nothing I can do but be careful. I feel like Mark Antony, too."

"On one drink?"

"The end of the funeral oration scene. You know:

Now let it work. Mischief, thou art afoot,
Take thou what course thou wilt!"

"My small experience with the police" Bunyan observed, "has hardly led me to expect from them allusions to Pandora and correct quotations in blank verse."

"Oxford," said Marshall tersely.

"Indeed, sir?" Over Bunyan's face passed the closest approximation to surprise which he had displayed in the entire case. But his cool superiority quickly reassured itself. "I was Cambridge myself."

Matt smiled and picked up the phone. He was uncertain of convent regulations, but it was early yet—only about nine.

Sister Ursula was not only available, she was eager and proved an enthralled audience to his narrative of the evening's events.

"That give you any new ideas?" he concluded.

"New? No, not new ideas, Mr. Duncan, but it does help me in carrying out my old ones. I can't tell you how grateful I am to you for calling me—almost as grateful as I am (though this sounds shocking) to Blessed Mother La Roche for dying on the date she did."

"Any questions or messages?"

"Yes." Sister Ursula sounded reflective. "One question—did you see the color of Mr. Mason-Ahasver's real hair?"

"It was black, like the beard. But why—?"

"Patience, Mr. Duncan, is one of the cardinal virtues. And I have one message—for the Lieutenant."

"Yes?"

"Please urge him to put a heavy guard around all members of the Harrigan family and above all around Robin Cooper, unless he wants another murder. I earnestly entreat him to do this—as earnestly as I pray God to forgive my presumption in meddling with such matters."

"Any other message?"

"No—yes. Ask Miss Harrigan to pray for me. You might even try it yourself, Mr. Duncan. I need every prayer I can get." Her tone was nowise jesting.

TWENTY

Friday morning.

The man said, "Who are you?"

The woman said, "Don't you even know that?"

The man said, "I've never seen you before in my life."

The woman said, "Are you so sure of that?"

The man said, "Of course I'm sure. I never forget a face. But that's enough of that. What the devil are you here for?"

The woman neatly folded a crease in her bright flowered print. "I'll answer your other question instead. Do you know Robin Cooper?"

The man frowned. "I've seen him, yes. What's that to you? Are you a friend of his?"

The woman said nothing.

The man said, "Did he send you here?"

The woman said, "Robin Cooper has funny ideas. He thinks somebody tried to murder him and then got cold feet."

The man said, "Absurd. We're wasting time."

The woman said, "He's talking."

The man said, "What's that to you?"

The woman kept her eyes on the open toe of her shoe. "I thought there might be something in it for the person who warned you."

The man said, "Nonsense. I know he talked. It doesn't affect me."

The woman said, "That was before he thought about the murderer with cold feet. He's deciding maybe he should talk some more and make himself safe. If you've told all you know, you're safe."

The man said, "And how much do *you* know?"

The woman said, "Enough to come here."

The man said, "And with all Cooper's ideas that doesn't frighten you?"

The woman said, "Not here. You wouldn't dare. And I shan't see you any place but here."

The man said, "Go peddle your warnings somewhere else. I'm not in the market."

The woman said, "All right. It was worth the chance. No harm done."

The man said, "No. No harm done."

When the woman was gone, he said to himself, "No cold feet this time."

Friday afternoon.

Matt looked around the study. This wasn't quite the conventional omnium-gatherum of suspects, tremulously awaiting the final lecture. At least five candidates were missing. The Swami Sussmaul was in jail. So was Ahasver, or Glenn Mason now, pending the arrival of extradition warrants from Illinois. Robin Cooper was probably at his home—wherever he was, he was under unobtrusive but vigilant police guard. R. Joseph Harrigan was detained at this office by an important appointment. And Sister Ursula had decided, in view of Concha's narrative of Wednesday night on Olvera Street, that inviting Gregory Randall to the Harrigans' just now would be an unwise move no matter how grave the cause.

So the nun's audience consisted only of three Harrigans—Ellen, Arthur, and Concha—Bunyan-Bannister (promoted for the occasion from servant to professionally interested spectator), Lieutenant Marshall, Matt himself, and of course Sister Felicitas dozing in a corner.

"Start in, Sister," said Marshall. "I've got a crawling in my spine tells me something's about due to pop, and not in this room, either; but what can I do? So on with the dance; let Rome burn where it may."

"You will forgive me," Sister Ursula began, "if I seem didactic. It is difficult to face an audience like this and not fall into a preaching manner. But please feel free to interrupt me whenever you think necessary.

"As Lieutenant Marshall has warned you, this is an unofficial session. The Lieutenant was flattering enough to ask me certain questions about this case and to give me some important bits of information. As a result, I think that I have solved this locked-room problem; and I want you, all so closely involved with the case, to hear me present my solution.

"Now the Lieutenant, after cudgeling his brain for days with every possible trick aspect of the problem, has come to the simple conclusion that there is no problem at all. He wants not merely to cut the Gordian knot, but to claim that no such knot ever existed. And he does this by disbelieving Miss Harrigan's testimony. No, please, Miss Harrigan; do not look so angrily upon the poor man. It is his official duty to let no respect for persons interfere with his suspicions; and the reasoning that leads him to this suspicion is perfectly sound—for a Protestant."

"For a Protestant!" Marshall echoed. "My dear Sister Ursula, I have all the respect in the world for your church, but I cannot believe that it is the sole font of human reason. Logic is logic, even for a Protestant."

"I beg your pardon, Lieutenant. Logic is one thing; the interpretation of facts is another. Look at this sequence of facts: On Sunday evening Miss Harrigan told you that no one had come out of that door while she was in the chapel. For the rest of that evening and the next morning, her niece was constantly with her. They went to mass together and there Miss Harrigan, never having left her niece's side for a moment, received communion. What is your interpretation of those facts, Lieutenant?"

"That Miss Harrigan is a devout and good woman—which is no earthly obstacle to believing that she'd tell a lie to shield a member of her family."

"True. I admit—if you will pardon me, Miss Harrigan—that such a lie from her would not be inconceivable. But her later actions, on that hypothesis, become quite beyond belief. A Catholic knows that a lie is a sin; and a lie in so serious an instance as this would be no venial, but a mortal sin. To receive the sacrament of communion in a state of mortal sin is the most grievous sacrilege which a Catholic can commit. If Miss Harrigan had lied, she had two courses open to her: to abstain from her daily communion or to confess her sin and receive absolution. She did neither; therefore, she told the truth."

"If I may speak, sir, as a fellow Protestant," Bunyan deigned to say, "I can assure you that Sister Ursula's reasoning is quite sound. It might not apply perhaps to those demi-apostates who style themselves 'practical' Catholics; but a truly devout Roman such as Miss Harrigan could more easily commit murder than such a sacrilege."

"All right," said Marshall. "You have now wiped out the only possible solution. So. Would you mind telling us just what is left?"

"Certainly," Sister Ursula smiled. "Now let us consider the problem again from the beginning. I wish that Joseph Harrigan were here so that we might compare eyewitness accounts; but we shall have to content ourselves with Mr. Duncan. Now, Mr. Duncan—when you first looked through this window Sunday afternoon at sunset, what did you see?"

"A man in a yellow robe."

"And when you looked through for the second time, what did you see?"

"The body of Wolfe Harrigan."

"What, then, had vanished from the room in the interval?"

"A man in a yellow robe."

"And there," she turned to the Lieutenant, "is where we have gone wrong from the beginning. Let us take it again: What was seen first? A man in a yellow robe. What was seen later? A man. What had vanished?"

It was Concha who cried out, "A yellow robe!" and then looked amazed at her own conclusion. The others in the room leaned forward with such a sudden expression of interest that they seemed like marionettes jerked by a single string. All, that is, save Sister Felicitas, who went right on napping, and Arthur Harrigan, who leaned back and said, "Nuts!"

The coffee had perked long enough. Robin Cooper poured himself a cup and drank it scalding hot, then turned his attention again to the rough draft before him. ". . . in view of all that has happened . . . it would surely be obvious even to the official mind . . . in order to assure my invaluable silence. . . ."

He felt no pride in his handiwork. It was a clumsy approach, not at all worthy of his usual skill. He crumpled the note and drank another cup of coffee. A personal interview, to be sure, would be more dangerous, but also far more likely to be productive. And the danger could be readily counterbalanced—forestalled, if necessary.

He took the heavy .45 from its drawer. (Pawnbrokers could be obligingly unsuspicious if you knew the right ones.) There would be no slip-up this time. And though the risk was great, the possible benefits quite outweighed it.

Rats leave the sinking ship, yes. But suppose a rat knows that the ship has gone down with a mass of bullion still in her hold—bullion that can be retrieved and turned to clear profit if rattish ingenuity functions smartly enough?

There was a noise outside the door. Robin Cooper frowned at the interruption of his plans. Or was it an interruption? Were the plans coming to meet him? He slipped back the safety catch and stood ready.

Lieutenant Marshall had taken a moment to assimilate this new idea. "You mean," he said slowly, "that Harrigan was wearing that yellow robe?"

"I am not sure of the verb, Lieutenant. The robe was on him, yes; but do we say that a corpse *wears* its winding-sheet?"

"He was already dead?"

"Yes. The fire, you remember, made the room too hot for any accurate fixing of the time of death. What you saw, Mr. Duncan, was the body of Wolfe Harrigan, its legs probably pressed against the desk by a chair and its torso propped up by a stick of wood which left that scratch on the surface of the desk. When he was killed it is not possible to say exactly, but certainly after his brother had spoken to him."

"But why? What earthly sense . . . "

"The murderer knew that the setting sun would blind anyone looking into that window before six-fifteen. At that time, the glare gone, the light from the fire would reveal the man in the yellow robe to anyone on the croquet lawn, thereby giving apparent direct evidence of who the murderer had been."

"But what good did that do? If the idea was to make Duncan and Joseph think they'd seen the murderer, why frame the situation so that the man in yellow couldn't have got out?"

"Some murderers, Lieutenant, may plan locked rooms; but if they do, the death is made to seem natural, accidental, or suicidal. This death was patently none of those things; this murderer had the locked room thrust upon him. You were supposed to think that the man in yellow had left by the chapel door. It was pure chance that after my interview with her, Miss Harrigan had decided to go into the chapel to pray. If it had not been for that chance, we should have been certain, as the murderer intended us to be, that the crime was committed either by Ahasver or by a man disguised to look like him."

Vesuvian clouds were billowing up from Marshall's corn-cob. "No, Sister Ursula," he protested. "It won't do. It's ingenious—damned ingenious—but it doesn't turn the trick. It's all very well to say that the murderer left the room earlier; but we're still faced with an impossibility. If the yellow robe was draped around Wolfe Harrigan, what became of it?"

"Of course. I left that out. I'm sorry; I am not really accustomed to this sort of thing. Have you forgotten, Lieutenant, that there is a hole in your sealed room?"

"The rat hole? That leads nowhere—just into a space between floor and cellar. And the hole in the back of the fireplace is far too small to get a robe through."

"But it is large enough," said Sister Ursula, "for a wire."

"A wire?"

"Why do you keep thinking that the robe left the room?"

"Because it wasn't there any more. Or is that Protestant logic again?"

"No. Protestants, I believe, are especially emphatic concerning the destructive properties of fire."

"Fire? Sister Ursula, you're going mad. We sifted the ashes of that fire. No cloth robe could have burned up so fully in that time that we wouldn't have found some traces of it."

"And who," asked Sister Ursula, "says it was cloth?"

"Why—well, hang it all, Sister—"

"Remember that that robe was not for wear, but solely for the purpose of being seen at sunset from the croquet lawn. Paper would do quite as well, and could be much more easily destroyed.

"Let me recapitulate. Sometime between five fifty-five and, to be precise, six thirteen, the murderer was admitted by Mr. Harrigan to his study and there shot him. He then draped the body in the yellow robe and propped it up as I have described, ready to be seen at sunset. A long piece of wire was then attached to the paper robe and connected with a short string to the wooden prop. The other end of the wire was thrust through the hole in the back of the fireplace. All was ready, and the murderer left by the chapel door, locking it behind him.

"After the alarm was raised, in the brief interval between Mr. Duncan's two glimpses of the body, the murderer went behind the fireplace and pulled the wire, dragging the robe off the body and the prop from under it, so that it fell to the floor and became merely the body of Wolfe Harrigan, instead of a yellow-robed visitant. Another tug on the wire pulled both the stick and the paper robe into the fire. The robe and the string would go up in flames at once, and a stick in a fireplace is as unnoticeable as was Chesterton's corpse on a battlefield. All this would take only a matter of seconds. In the later confusion, the wire could be tossed into the backyard, where it too would be inconspicuous."

Marshall puffed. "That's certainly the only idea propounded so far that would account for the situation. I must say, Sister, I like it. When did you hit on it?"

"When Mr. Duncan told me about the missing gloves."

"Gloves? How—No, hold on a minute. Let me try to be brilliant, too. After all, it's only my profession. The murderer did wear gloves; we know that from the fact that he left no prints and that the dart, with Harrigan's prints, was smudged but not wiped. Also anyone disguised as Ahasver would wear gloves; it's part of the costume. Therefore the figure in the yellow robe was neither the murderer nor a masquerader. And from there—"

"Quite so, Lieutenant. A robe, you see, can be readily disposed of; gloves could not. So the hands were left bare."

"Nice," said Marshall. "Very nice. But I don't suppose you'd care to go on now and tell us who this murderer was?"

The audience in the study stirred restlessly. This time even Arthur looked interested.

"Oh, dear," sighed Sister Ursula. "You still haven't understood William the Second?"

The telephone rang.

"I'll take that," said the Lieutenant. "Marshall speaking.—Oh, hello, Krauter.—Yes.—Yes.—No! My dear God!—Yes. Right. I'll be there in—let's see—make it twenty minutes. Keep everything under control." He hung up and turned back to Sister Ursula. "All right. My spine wasn't crawling for nothing. I've got to clear out in a minute. Come on—what's the meaning of William the Second?"

Sister Ursula was hesitant and confused. Her eyes remained on the phone. "That wasn't . . . ?"

"Cooper's alive, if that's what you mean. Go on."

"Oh, thank God!" She touched the rosary at her belt, and her lips moved silently. "Now," she resumed at last, "you agree that that dart-prick was intentional? That Wolfe Harrigan intended that book, rather than any of his files, as a clew to his murderer?"

"Yes."

"Mary, you are closer to your history lessons than any of the rest of us. Who was William the Second?"

"He was the son of William the Conqueror, wasn't he? Ruled England in the late eleventh century and was killed by an arrow in a forest. That's all I can remember."

"But what was his name—his nickname, rather?"

"Oh!" Concha sat very still; her answer was hardly audible. "He was called William *Rufus*."

"Exactly. And what, Miss Harrigan, is your brother's full name?"

Ellen's voice shook. "Rufus Joseph Harrigan."

"You should have guessed that, Lieutenant," Sister Ursula went on. "It was natural that Rufus Harrigan's firstborn son should be named Rufus, and equally natural that he should drop the name and use only the initial *R.* to establish himself in public life on his own merits, rather than as his famous father's namesake."

Arthur whistled. Speechlessly Concha sought her aunt's hand and held it fast.

"But he was with—" Matt started, and then paused.

"True, Mr. Duncan. He was with you. And there could be no more damning fact. The essence of the whole plan was that the murderer must have an alibi at six thirteen. Of those in this house, only Joseph Harrigan and Mary had accounted for themselves at that time; and Mary's alibi had to be true because it also covered the period between six thirteen and six fifteen, when the wire must have been pulled.

"But Joseph was with me from six thirteen to six fifteen. How could he have pulled that wire?"

"Didn't he stumble and fall to the ground when you were hurrying into the house? And didn't he fall exactly behind the fireplace? Even without the book, his guilt could be proved. He was the only person who both profited by the false time scheme and had the chance to pull the wire."

"I suppose," Matt reflected, "that's why you asked who played croquet. In case no witnesses were already on the croquet lawn, he had to have an excuse for getting somebody out there before sunset."

"But if all this was so clear to you, Sister," Marshall asked, "why did you keep probing around for a redheaded murderer?"

"William's nickname of Rufus means simply redhead. If there had been a pre-eminently redheaded suspect, it would have been possible that all my conclusions were wrong and that the dart pointed at him or her. But since of all those connected with the case, only your wife and child are redhaired—"

"It was all like a horrible practical joke, wasn't it?" said Concha. "Like those stupid tricks Arthur plays. And Aunt Ellen tells us so often how Uncle Joseph used to be like that. All that mechanical ingenuity for cruel gags, and then . . . this."

"I should have thought of that," said the nun. "It is indicative."

"No! I cannot believe it, Sister Ursula." Ellen Harrigan's voice was suddenly old. "That my own brother should kill my own brother . . . Why?" The "Why?" was a plaintive cry of incredulous despair.

"Because he was back of Ahasver. Or to be more exact, he was back of Robin Cooper. Here I can make only conjectures, but they are supported by the facts. I have shown that Joseph must have killed his brother. He had no personal or financial motive for doing so. We know that Wolfe Harrigan had a suspicion of the identity of Ahasver's backer—a suspicion too horrible for him to voice even to his confidential assistant. And there are certain other indications. You, Mr. Duncan, told me of Robin Cooper's shocked surprise when the three of you entered the Temple. The Lieutenant was in plain clothes, and your scar is surely not so terrifying as all that. That shock was probably occasioned by the unexpected sight of the power behind the robe walking into the Temple. Then it is too much to believe that the setting of the Nine Times Nine the night before the murder was mere coincidence. That ceremony must have been ordered, and ordered by the man who knew that its threat would be fulfilled.

"And then there is the attempted murder of Robin Cooper."

"What?" cried Matt. "When?"

"The first attempt was made on that afternoon when you and the Lieutenant called on Cooper. Joseph's excuse for being there was very thin indeed. When you entered Cooper's room you found that Joseph had spilled his host's coffee and that someone had left cigarette butts apparently incriminating Arthur. Now Joseph rages with his voice; it is not like him to stamp about the room and knock over cups. I suggest that the cup was upset because it was poisoned."

"I can understand," said Marshall, "why Joseph might decide to rub out Robin; that makes sense. But why should he poison a cup and then carefully upset it? That's nonsense."

"Not at all. The plan, as I imagine it to have been, was that Cooper should be found dead, with evidence that he had been serving coffee for two and that his companion had been Arthur. But Joseph saw you two drive up (you told me that the window overlooked the street), knew that he would be trapped on the scene of the crime, and upset the cup."

"But my brother couldn't be the founder of such a cult, Sister Ursula. He was a good man and a devout Catholic."

"I regret," said Sister Ursula, "that membership in the Church is no guarantee of godliness."

"But how could a man leave the True Church to—"

"I doubt if the religious aspect concerned Joseph. It was simply necessary background. The Children of Light were building slowly into a strong political unit. I shan't call Joseph a fascist—the word is used too freely now to mean anything. But he is a demagogue, avid for political power. If he had fallen in with a priest of the Coughlin stripe, he might have tried to build up his following within the Church; but happily such priests are rarer than our detractors might have you believe."

"Jeez!" said Arthur. "Uncle Joe giving me fine moral lectures on my gambling, and meanwhile planning to frame me for murder! But what can you prove, Sister? I'd love to see you pin it on him, but this is all guesswork."

"Not all. There are indications, clews to support my theory. A very small one is the phrase Wolfe Harrigan noticed in the Gospel according to Joseph—the phrase 'mammon of iniquity.' "

"What does that mean?" Matt demanded. "It's been plaguing the life out of me."

"A phrase from one of the parables, is it not?" said Bunyan. "Anyone might quote it, save possibly the godless younger generation. Though if I remember correctly it reads 'mammon of unrighteousness.' "

"Exactly. So it does in the King James version. The phrase 'mammon of iniquity' is from the Rheims translation, the Catholic version; no Protestant could have thought of it. This showed that a Catholic was involved somewhere in the preparation of the Gospel according to Joseph, which is the basis of Ahasverism. More indicative is the quickness with which Ahasver picked up cues and made his false confession; it seems as though Joseph, in his apparent denunciation of his brother's murderer, was actually feeding information to Ahasver to enable him to make his publicity claim.

"Most significant of all: Nothing was taken from this room save Wolfe Harrigan's secret notes on Ahasver's backer and the codicil appointing Mr. Duncan as literary executor. No one could have taken these things but the murderer, and I have shown that the murderer must have been Joseph Harrigan. He would have taken those notes only if they directly concerned him; if he had merely wanted to lay a false trail of theft, the file would have suited his purpose far better. And destroying the codicil made Mr. Duncan's work directly subject to Joseph Harrigan's supervision, so that he could refuse to allow publication of any material that he might think dangerous."

"Just a minute," said Matt. "Go back, please, to the attempt on the Cherub's life. You said *first* attempt."

Sister Ursula looked at the telephone and then at the Lieutenant.

"Good guess, Sister," said Marshall. "Or was it a guess? Yes—that was Krauter. They've just caught R. Joseph Harrigan in his second attempt on Cooper."

TWENTY-ONE

After that things moved rapidly. Joseph Harrigan was taken into custody on Friday. On Saturday the inquest was held, and a verdict of murder returned naming Joseph Harrigan. On Sunday the delayed funeral took place at last in Calvary Cemetery. On Monday the District Attorney went before the Grand Jury and asked for and received the indictment of Joseph Harrigan on two counts of attempted murder and one of murder in the first degree.

It was all rounded off now, as Lieutenant Marshall said to Matt Duncan on Tuesday night. They were seated once more in masculine comfort before the fireplace, while Leona showed the delighted Concha what a darling Terry was when he was asleep.

"Of course," the Lieutenant added, "Harrigan is pleading not guilty, but he won't have a chance."

"Won't he?" Matt questioned. "You've got him cold on at least one of the counts of attempted murder, but there's still a lot of loose ends on the main charge."

"I don't think so. I've checked over everything carefully—with Sister Ursula's help, I'm not ashamed to admit—and I think we've got it sewed up. What puzzles you?"

"For one thing, the theft of that William the Second book."

"Joseph, of course. Of all possible people, he had the best opportunity to have a copy made of that key. What else?"

"Lots of things. Arthur's cigarettes at the Swami's—was that another attempt to frame him? And the Swami's alibi, and the yellow robe in the incinerator."

"All that's straightened out now. We finally made Sussmaul talk. He'd been prying around for facts about the Harrigans—anything to give him a toe-hold—and he'd learned about Arthur's need for ready money. He got in touch with the little rat and persuaded him to sell out his own father and steal that file. The theft was scheduled for Sunday afternoon; hence the Swami's alibi. But after the murder Arthur got cold feet, and Sussmaul tried to put pressure on you instead."

"And the extra yellow robe? If the robe we saw was paper, where did the cloth robe come from and how did it get into the incinerator?"

"Remember Arthur's weakness for practical jokes? Well, the murder was on March thirty-first. What was the next day?"

"April first."

"Exactly. All Fools' Day. Arthur had planned a hoax on his father—probably was going to show up as Ahasver and spill all sorts of phony information. That's how he knew about the Nine Times Nine—he'd been at the Temple studying his part. But after the murder a yellow robe was a damned dangerous thing to have in your possession; so he got rid of it as quickly as possible."

"But I still can't follow motive. If Joseph was backing the Temple of Light, why should he try so hard to involve Ahasver in the murder?"

"Partly, of course, because the yellow robe was the essential part of the trick he played on you for an alibi. And partly because he knew the Temple was doomed. Rats and ships again. Even Wolfe's death couldn't save the Ahasver organization from exposure, particularly after you came on the scene. But Wolfe had to die because he was too close to exposing, not only Ahasver's racket, but Joseph's connection with it. There was no saving the Temple; the best Joseph could hope was to save himself. And he's failed even there. If nothing else cooks his goose, Cooper's testimony will; it appears that Robby doesn't like big bad men who try to murder him."

"I wish," said Matt, "for Con . . . for the family's sake that Joseph could be persuaded to plead guilty. You're right; he hasn't got a chance. And it would save a hell of a lot of scandal and notoriety. Isn't there any way of—"

"Here come the girls," Marshall broke in. "I think the less Miss Harrigan hears about this case now, the better."

"Hello," said Leona. "Concha thinks Terry is wonderful and I told her how to make those cheese biscuits and she wishes they had rubber trays in their icebox. And what have you two been up to all this time?"

"Swapping limericks," said Lieutenant Marshall.

"Oh," said Concha. "Tell us some!"

"Wait till you're married, Miss Harrigan," said Marshall cheerfully, and then wondered why this innocent remark should cause such an embarrassed pause.

The woman said, "It was my fault. I confess that to you. I thought it was a thirst for justice, a desire to help the family; but there is no use in deceiving myself. It was my pride, too—my devil, the sting of my flesh. And I had to make certain. So that part of your sin was my responsibility."

The man said, "God! I never knew you."

The woman said, "I trusted that you wouldn't. The habit makes such a difference. And Friday was the vigil of Mother La Roche when we are free of our vows and can wear street clothes. But being free of my vows doesn't lessen the badness of what I did. That is why I got Lieutenant Marshall's permission to come here. Telling you is part of my penance."

The man said, "But why did you do it?"

The woman said, "Reason can be a faulty thing. But after I had seen your face when I said Robin Cooper . . . Can you forgive me?"

The man smiled bitterly. He said, "I can forgive you."

The woman was grave. "Thank you. Sins fester when they're not told. First, they must be told to God through the priest's ear; but it helps too if you can tell them to man and make atonement for what has happened—spare the living even if you cannot restore the dead."

The man said, "You can never make atonement for what has happened."

The woman said, "No. But *you* can."

The man was silent and then said, "Pray for me, Sister. And when you go out, tell that keeper—turnkey—whatever you call him—that I want to speak to him."

When the officer came, the man said, "I want to see a priest. And tell the District Attorney that I want to change my plea."

Leona had remembered that they were out of bacon for breakfast, and the Lieutenant had driven her off to a distant all-night market.

"I think," said Matt, "that the Marshalls are being tactful."

"I'm glad," said Concha frankly. "We haven't been really alone since—since last Wednesday."

"I know."

She drew in her lower lip. "I thought so. Why do you try to keep away from me, Matt?"

"Why not?"

"You do like me, don't you?" He didn't answer—just sat watching the fire. "They're happy here, aren't they?" she said.

"They are. Leona's profession may have been a strange one, but she was a woiking goil—not an heiress."

"So that's it. But Matt darling—"

"Part of it. Besides you're so damned young and you change your mind so much. In two weeks you've been engaged to Greg, ready to enter a convent, and now—"

"That's not fair. I wasn't in love with Gregory. I never even thought I was. And now Arthur's done the one good deed of his life and told me why he helped Gregory find us the other night. Gregory wanted to marry me as soon as I was eighteen because his father's firm is wobbly and my share would tide things over."

"And Arthur was supposed to get a cut? There's another reason. Think of having that for a brother-in-law."

"Don't joke Matt. Tonight's been awful for me. To see two people loving each other and being so happy . . . "

"Nice young men who've just been kicked off relief don't marry Harrigans."

"But you've got your job with the estate."

"For how long?"

"And besides if I . . . " This was hard to say, but finally she forced it out. "If I marry without the trustees' consent, I shan't be an heiress."

Deliberately Matt kept from looking at her and poured himself another drink. "Don't be noble. You'll have me in tears."

"Who's being noble? You are. You're trying to be harsh just so as to make me give up."

Matt swallowed a double shot straight and still felt jittery. "Look honey," he said. "Let's just wait and see what happens. OK?"

Concha rose and stood by the fire. "OK," she said. She was half smiling and half on the verge of dissolving. "I do like this house. How much do you suppose it costs?"

"Less than you'd ever pay and more than I'd ever have."

"Don't they have loans and things—with initials?" She crossed over and sat on the arm of his chair. "At least," she said, "you might kiss me."

"Why not?" said Matt. "Though God knows I could think up some swell answers to that one."

Rocket To The Morgue

For
The Manana Literary Society
and in particular for
ROBERT HEINLEIN
and
CLEVE CARTMILL

ONE

THE FIRST DAY:
Thursday, October 30, 1941

Leona Marshall stretched her long legs out on the bed and clasped her hands comfortably behind her red head. "Isn't it nice I couldn't nurse her?" she murmured. "Think how awkward it would be for you to take over a feeding."

Her husband took the bottle from the electric warmer and tested the milk on the inside of his wrist. "Handy-like," he agreed. He seemed satisfied with the milk and wrapped the bottle in a cloth. Then he lifted his three-month-old daughter from her bassinet and held her up high. The two beamed fatuously and gloriously at each other.

"No games," Leona warned him. "She has to learn that meal times are strictly business."

"We aren't playing games," Terence Marshall protested unconvincingly, settling his daughter into the crook of his arm and tenderly poking her plump stomach.

"No?" Leona's voice was suspicious.

"No. You know what, Leona; this is a fat little wench you've got here. Think she'll ever grow up to have her mother's figure?"

"Such as it is now . . . " Leona surveyed herself ruefully.

"It'll do. Come on, darling, open your mouth. This is milk. Nice milk. You remember." The little pink lips parted reluctantly, then clasped avidly on the rubber nipple.

"Anything interesting happen today?" Leona wondered.

The baby released the nipple and turned her head vaguely toward the voice. Her father said, "Damn it, Leona, if I'm going to take feedings you might at least let me give them in peace."

"But did anything?"

"Here, darling. Nice nipple . . . Oh, nothing special. Just a murder. No," he cut his wife off hastily before she could speak. "Nothing up your alley. And why a lieutenant on Homicide should be cursed with a wife who loves mystery novels is one example of the ways of God to man that Milton forgot to justify. Nothing at all pretty about this one. No locked room, no mysterious weapons, no unbreakable alibis—the last mainly because we haven't even got a suspect yet."

"Still . . . " said Leona.

"All right—if you'll stay hushed. I'll tell you about it. She doesn't mind my talking. See: it kind of lulls her. No, this was just a bum in a Main Street rooming house. A floater. Name, according to the register, Jonathan Tarbell. Nothing on him to check that one way or the other. Been there a fortnight, according to the clerk. Just slept there, never around in the daytime. One visitor who called a couple of times—description too vague to help.

"Shot through the heart at close range. Thirty-five automatic. Weapon smartly, if extravagantly, left right beside the body. No prints, which together with the man's bare hands rules out suicide. Somebody, presumably the murderer, had searched the room, but hadn't bothered to take over three hundred dollars in cash.

"So it shapes up like this: Tarbell's clothes were new and fairly good, and he had plenty of cash—far too much for a man living in the lower depths. The murderer wanted something in the room, but not money. So in all likelihood Tarbell was tied up with some kind of a racket (blackmail, at a guess), pushed it too far, and got taken care of.

"That much is clear, and the obvious next step—"

"Aren't you ever going to burp her?" Leona asked.

"Now look. If I don't tell you about what I'm doing, you plague us with questions. If I do try to tell you, you start interrupting me and—"

"Go ahead and burp her."

"All right."

"And don't forget the burp cloth. We can't go having your suit cleaned every day."

"All right. And anyway I hadn't forgotten it." Lieutenant Marshall spread a diaper over his shoulder and hoisted his daughter up. "The trouble with you, madam," he went on, patting the infant's rump, "is that you haven't any real interest in crime itself. All you care about is the fancy frills and furbelows of romanticism that the whodunit writers trick it out in. Crime itself is essentially flat, dull, drab, and infinitely important." He spoke in the grave orotund tone into which his usual colloquialism occasionally lapsed, and his daughter answered him with a burp equally grave and even more orotund.

"I know," Leona chortled. "She's going to grow up to be a critic."

Marshall grinned at the baby. "Let's throw your mother a bone, huh?" With his free hand he fished out of his pocket a string of beads and a scrap of paper and tossed them over to the bed. "See what you make of those while we finish our dinner."

"Clews!" Leona cried gleefully.

"No, Ursula." Marshall resolutely turned his daughter's face away from her mother. "You can play with clews when you're a big girl. Right now you drink your milk."

"She took the whole bottle," he announced proudly ten minutes later. "Now you can talk."

"Where did you find these? Is she wet?"

"To the second question, what do you think? To the first, that bit of paper was in among the unstolen currency. The rosary had slipped down through a hole in the lining of his pocket. Indicates the body was searched by an amateur—always beware torn linings. And those two items are the sole damned leads we've got to go on."

Leona looked at the two letters and five figures scrawled on the paper. "A phone number and a rosary . . . I suppose you've checked the number?"

"It's an apartment hotel out on Rossmore near Wilshire. Veddy veddy swank. Not what you'd expect to be in communication with a corpse on Skid Row. Some twenty-odd apartments, though. It's going to be a job checking 'em all." He folded back Ursula's nightgown and began taking out safety pins.

"And a rosary . . . Just what does that prove? Supposing a blackmailer does have his religious moments—how does that give you a lead?"

Marshall stuck the pins in a cake of soap and went to work deftly on the diaper problem. Ursula decided she was being tickled and liked it. "Look at the rosary closer."

"It's nicely carved, probably quite an expensive one. Hand work, and good. Aside from that . . ."

"A zero on today's recitation, my sweet. You're the clew-addict, but on this you flop badly. How many sets of beads are there?"

"One . . . two . . . Seven."

"Exactly. And that's all wrong. I've noticed the rosaries that the nuns carry. There should be five sets. So there's something strange about this one, and I've got to check up on it." He finished pinning the extra diaper for night wear, pulled the baby's gown down, and fastened the drawstring.

"With Sister Ursula?"

"Uh huh." Marshall looked not too happy. "The last time I was mixed up in a case with Catholic religious clews, the goddamnedest things happened I've ever heard of in the history of homicide. Since then life's been peaceful. Just nice ordinary routine restful murders. And now this rosary crops up . . ."

Leona rose. "It's been swell having a few minutes' rest. Thanks, Terence. And now I've got to finish getting dinner ready. The Duncans'll be here any minute."

Lieutenant Marshall held his daughter in one arm and put the other around his wife. "I love you," he said.

"Which of us?"

"Both of you. And Terry too." He jerked his head toward the next room. "Is he asleep?"

"Probably not." Leona leaned over and made a face at the baby, who appreciated it. Then she put her lips firmly and warmly against her husband's. "I'm lucky," she said.

While Leona bustled competently about the kitchen, Terence Marshall assembled whisky and soda and glasses on a tray. He glanced at the clock and at the door, and then settled down for a moment with Dudley Fitts' latest volume of translations from the Greek Anthology. Occasionally he referred to his worn volume of the original and nodded with pleasure at the translation.

It had been agreeable, in the cool walks of Oxford, for Rhodes Scholar Marshall to speculate on the possibilities of continuing the scholarly life—the contemplation of chaste and ordered beauty, the strict rigor and infinite flexibility of the scholastic mind. Then had come his chance acquaintance with young Southey and his introduction, through Assistant Commissioner Southey, to the methodical wonders of Scotland Yard.

Here, he realized, in the police work so damned and scorned by the man in the street, was the one perfect career for the individual who combined good will, a well-trained mind, and a body which had brought him All-America honors for two years running. And he had succeeded in the career, though only by dint of keeping his mind and his good will as much under wraps as possible. If any of the boys were to see him now, his eyes coursing over Greek minuscules and his lips curved in quiet contentment, nothing but fear of his athletic prowess could prevent mayhem.

The doorbell rang, and he set the Greek Anthology aside.

"Be there in a minute," Leona called from the kitchen.

Lieutenant Marshall opened the door to admit the Duncans. He had met them on the Harrigan case (that case of the Nine Times Nine in which "the goddamnedest things happened" and through which he had met the amazing nun whose name he had given his daughter), and their hesitant and confused romance had been the one note of happiness in that murderous business.

Six months of marriage had changed them. Concha (María de la Concepción, to give the full name bestowed on her by her Spanish mother) was no longer a frightened and groping child, but a young woman beginning to feel for the first time sure of her place in life. And Matt Duncan was losing his bitter touchiness and slowly becoming willing to admit that people sometimes did like him and might even mean well by him.

"Sorry we're late," Matt said. "Believe it or not, we were waiting for a streetcar."

Concha nodded. "And we have, by the latest statistics, the coldest corner in Los Angeles to wait on. I'm frozen."

"Until you're twenty-one," said Lieutenant Marshall, "I am strictly violating the California law by giving you a drink; but that makes it medicinal. I don't think I'll report myself."

Concha handed her host her coat and accepted a high-ball. "If we only had a car . . ." she murmured.

Matt Duncan downed a quick straight one and refilled his glass. "If Stuart likes this novel I'm working on, we'll see what can be arranged. Though if we get into the war, God knows if they'll be selling cars. Or novels either."

"If?" said Marshall quietly.

"Only I don't see," Concha insisted, "why we have to wait for any old novel. If you'd only—"

Matt set down his glass. "Look. We are *not* going into that again."

"I only said—"

"Let it go."

Marshall grinned. "Children . . . !" he said chidingly.

Matt Duncan turned to him. "Terence, I like the touching story of your marriage. Arresting a girl in a vice-squad raid on a burleycue, and proposing to her while she was serving her jail sentence. You were a smart man to marry a woman with no money of her own."

"I don't know about that. I'm certain neither Terry nor Ursula would object too strongly to having a mother who was an heiress."

"And it isn't my own," Concha argued. "It's ours now, and why you shouldn't use it to buy a car if you wanted to—"

"Mary!" Matt's voice was quietly grim.

Concha shuddered. "You're going to have to shelter me, Lieutenant. He never uses my real name unless he's mad as anything."

"And I've got a right to be mad. Here I—"

Terence Marshall sighed relief as his wife came in.

"I won't ask you do you want to see the children sleeping," she greeted the guests, "because you've always been such perfect lambs about it that I feel you ought to be let off for once. And besides dinner's ready."

The Duncans looked pleased at both announcements.

"I want you to do me a favor, Concha," said Lieutenant Marshall as he served seconds of the rabbit.

"Do it," Matt advised his wife. "There isn't any favor could repay Leona's cooking."

"I'm jealous," Concha pouted. "What I cook he just sits down and eats and never says anything about. Only maybe that's just as well . . . What's the favor, Lieutenant?"

"I do wish you'd get around to calling me Terence. I hate to seem official off-duty. But this is an official favor at that. I need Sister Ursula's advice on something, and I want you to drive out to the convent with me."

"Why?"

"Why? Hell, I don't quite know. But I can invade the Stately Mansions of the Rich with the greatest aplomb, and I can even manage not to look too out of place in a queer dive; but the one place in the city of Los Angeles where I feel like a peculiarly sore thumb is that convent. Come along and hold my hand."

"On one condition: Leona has to give me the recipe for this rabbit."

"Fair enough. Mind if I steal your wife tomorrow afternoon, Matt?"

"He won't even notice. He's in labor with a fantasy novel."

"Oh. More rabbit, Matt? Sympathetic magic for fertility?"

Matt Duncan looked up startled and brooding.

"Thanks. Look, Terence. From all your experience, what is the one safe and certain way of committing murder?"

"At an offhand guess, the only sure way I know is to take your victim to Washington. I think it's fifteen years now since the capital police got a conviction on murder. Would that fit your plans? Only of course if it was a woman they could get you on the Mann act. I suppose murder is an immoral purpose."

"It's a man," said Matt darkly. "A male at least."

"Fun," observed Leona. "We have murder at the dinner table all the time, but it's always after the fact. This is a new approach. Who's the victim?"

"My darling dearest Hilary. Hilary St. John Foulkes, to you."

"Foulkes?"

"The only son and heir of the late great Fowler Foulkes, whose demise is mourned by none so much as by the poor bastards who have anything to do with his son."

"But who is Fowler Foulkes?" Leona asked.

Marshall laughed. "My wife! She loves mysteries, but get her on the truly important matters of reading . . . Hell yes, I grew up on the Dr. Derringer stories, and there's never been anything to touch them. Sacred, that's what they are. By why murder Hilary?"

"Meet him," said Matt. "Just meet him once. That's all. You don't need any extra motives. In fact, I haven't even got that far, and look at me."

"Murder in the absolute and altruistic?"

"Not quite. But what's your recommendation on method?"

"Introduce me to him some time and I'll diagnose. You've got to pick the method for the individual. Artistry in Crime; that's the Marshall motto."

"Let them talk," Concha conceded tolerantly. "But Leona, about this rabbit—"

"Oh yes. It's simple as anything, that's the nice part of it. Have your rabbit all cut up and jointed and put in a baking pan. Over it you slice up onions and green pepper and salt pork, and sprinkle it with paprika. No salt, remember; the pork takes care of that."

"Our wives can exchange recipes far more easily than we can," Marshall went on to Matt. "Murder doesn't reduce itself to formula so readily. You have to grasp the inexorably right but fleeting instant."

"Pour a cup of boiling water over it and bake it in a medium oven for an hour (that's usually enough) or maybe an hour and a half. About half way through you can take off some of the liquid; the rabbit sort of melts. And make your gravy with that and what's left in the pan when you're through."

"That's the easiest way to cook rabbit I ever heard of, and" Concha set down the bone she had been gnawing and wiped her fingers, "far and away the best. Got a pencil, Matt?"

Matt fumbled for his pencil and looked across at the Lieutenant. "About that murder, Terence. You think I'm kidding, don't you?" His smile was set and harsh.

II

With lightning decision Captain Comet switched off the televisor and pressed the synchrosynthetic selenichromium mesh on his space-tanned wrist.

Adam Fink, the androgynous robot, clanked into the room.

"Quick!" snapped the lithe but brawny Captain. "The *Centauri III* is even now leaving the space port with a cargo of contraband xurghil weed for Venus. Take Gah-Djet, the mechanical brain, and travel at once to X-763, the maneuverable asteroid. Intercept the *Centauri* at the point marked Q prime on this orbit."

The electronic pattern-grooves of Adam Fink's metal mind recorded his master's orders. He turned clanking to go.

"And remember that Princess Zurilla of Neptune is aboard. No harm must befall her!"

The robot's head clanked in a jerking nod, and he left the room. Captain Comet's tense muscles flexed as he switched the televisor on again and beheld the central control room of the Interspacial Patrol.

"Z-999," he barked.

Suddenly the machine faded and went dead. A pulsing arc of purple light grew in the middle of the room and forth from it stepped a green-bearded Centaurian.

"Xix!" Captain Comet gasped. "Xix, the xurghil-smuggler!"

Joe Henderson jerked the copy from his typewriter and looked at the stack of blank paper-and-carbon sandwiches beside him. "I've got the Captain in an awful fix now," he said.

The little man on the couch yawned. "Grensham wants that copy end of this week."

"He'll get it. I'm darned if I know quite what happens next, but he'll get it."

"In the last ten minutes," said the little man reflectively, "your typewriter pinged twenty-five times. It averages ten words to a line. That makes two hundred and fifty words. From Grensham that's two fifty. So in ten minutes of lying here on the couch, I've made a quarter. Life could be worse."

Joe Henderson's face in repose had an almost adolescent blankness. His slow shy smile gave it warmth and charm. "I know, you old horse thief. All the time I'm typing, I think, 'Every ping, a penny for Phyn.' "

"Life could be worse," the agent repeated. "Like for instance there could be more than one Hilary Foulkes."

Henderson frowned at the pile of unused paper. "What's wrong with Hilary? I met him once with Vance, and he seemed harmless."

"Didn't I tell you about the deal I arranged with MacNamara?"

Henderson made a distasteful face. "MacNamara? I don't think so."

"We were going to launch a reprint mag called *Galactic Stories*. Signed up with the Foulkes estate for a Dr. Derringer reprint in each issue. All announced and everything. But that sonofabitch Hilary slips over a clause I don't read. It says at the rates we pay we've got to print *reprinted from* blank *copyright* blank *by* blank *by permission of Hilary Foulkes,* in type just as big as the title. Otherwise we pay five hundred smackers per story."

"I don't know as I'm any too sympathetic there. You know what a racket this reprint stuff is."

"How come a racket? We give the public good reading matter cheaper than it could ever buy it first hand."

"Sure, and cut the throats of us poor dopes that write it."

"Stuff and nonsense, Joe. You don't understand business. Writers never do . . . But who the hell's going to read a reprint story if it says *Reprint* on it? Not that I mean we sail under false pretences, but you don't have to go reminding them like that. And who can pay five hundred sinkers for pulp rights? So that's how come *Galactic Stories* folded."

Henderson nodded, not listening. "Look! Gah-Djet the mechanical brain'll spot those androids of Xix's with his detecto-tendrils and then . . . " He fed fresh paper into the typewriter, poised his fingers for an instant, and set to work.

M. Halstead Phyn (Author's Representative—Fantasy and

Science Fiction Our Exclusive Specialty) heard the first ping with pleasure and felt the round copper coin jangle into his pocket. "All the same," he muttered, "some day I'm going to take that Hilary bastard. And not for pennies."

III

Austin Carter was waiting for the phone to ring. He sat in a chair and resolutely refused to pace. Calmly indifferent, that's what he was. He reread a paragraph for the fifth time and suddenly found himself wondering what book he was reading.

He looked at the spine. *Memories of a Useful Life,* by Nehemiah Atchison. He threw it down and shouted, "Where the hell did we acquire Nehemiah Atchison?"

Bernice Carter looked up from the portable typewriter. When her husband was working, he used the office model in the study and embedded himself into the cottonwool of a sternly enforced silence. Bernice had composed her first saleable story in the office of a weekly news-sheet, answering questions about local politics between sentences. Sometimes now her stories refused to go right unless she was shouted at occasionally.

"He's some sort of great-second-uncle of Matt Duncan's. Those memoirs were privately printed as an inspiration to his family."

Austin Carter pitilessly kicked Nehemiah across the floor. "Damned if that's the kind of inspiration I need right now."

"They're pretty funny, in a nice stuffy way." Bernice's voice was as cool and fresh as her skin and her eyes. "I read them the other night."

Carter grunted and stared around. "Where's my solitaire cards?"

"In the study, I guess. Look, sweet: you know everything about the market. How much sex will Don stand for?"

"In a word, none." Carter half smiled. "Remember that story where my mathematical genius liked to watch women's breasts because they were such beautiful fifth-order curves?"

"I remember. Don changed it to heads. But that sounded all right."

"The hell it did. Head's aren't fifth-order curves. I don't mind his improving my morals, but I do object to his bolloxing my mathematics. What sly obscenity are you planning to put over on the poor man?"

"No; I guess I'd better behave. But this one's an inter-planetary romance, and I just couldn't help wondering about the physiological aspect. Pity . . ."

Carter had risen to hunt for his cards, but now he contented himself with merely pacing. "Something will happen," he muttered. "I know it. It can't help but go wrong. There's a jinx on this novel, and that jinx is our darling Hilary."

"But Hilary hasn't got anything to do with this now."

"He'll find some way. And all because I refused to pay him a hundred dollars. Can you tie that? So I wanted to use quotations from the Derringer stories for chapter-head quotes in the novel. God knows that's not infringing on his territory. It wouldn't cut in on his sales. If anything, it's just another free plug. But would Hilary see it that way? One hundred dollars to use that handful of quotes, and the most I could hope to get on royalties out of the damned book would be four, five hundred."

"Never mind," said Bernice soothingly. "If this film sale goes through, you'll be practically in Hilary's class yourself."

"In a class with *that*? Madam!" He glared at the phone. "Bixon says the trend is all of a sudden toward fantasy pictures now, and Weinberg at Metropolis is hot as hell on this."

"He says."

"They must be through conference by now. Bixon said he'd call me as soon as—What shall we do with our ill-gotten gains, Berni?"

"Pay income tax."

"There'll be some left. Every time you hear people complaining about how much they paid in taxes, just stop and figure out how much must be left if they had that big an income. We'll have some left; and what shall we do?"

"Save it for me to live on while you go to war."

"No. I don't doubt we'll be at war soon enough. But let's be mayflies and carp the diem before it dies. Anyway, you're practically self-supporting. You know what I'd like to do?"

"Charter a space ship."

"Of course. But failing that I'd like to take you around to the National Parks and Monuments. Especially the Monuments, and above all Canyon de Chelly. I don't know another spot that has the combination of absolute beauty and historical impact that that Canyon has. The sheer titanic walls and the peaceful green—"

"You're like Macbeth, sweet," said Bernice. "When you get to an emotional peak of tension, you go all lyrical. You—"

The telephone rang.

Austin Carter answered it. "Hello.—Oh yes, Bixon. Yes.—Yes.—I see.—Of course." His voice was trailing down from hope to resignation. "Yes.—Well, there's always another time.—Sure, let me know. 'Bye."

"They didn't like it," Bernice translated.

Carter's brown eyes glowed with fury. "They liked it all right. Weinberg was nuts about it, in fact."

"They just liked it too well to buy it?"

"No. It's—"

"It couldn't be Hilary?"

"It is. Metropolis is planning to produce a series of Dr. Derringer pictures. Hilary whispered that they'd never clear the rights if they bought that dreadful Carter novel."

Bernice looked him up and down. "The whisky's in the kitchen, sweet. And while you go and get manfully drunk, I'd better get ahead with this novelet."

"Hilary . . ." said Austin Carter between clenched teeth.

IV

Veronica Foulkes stroked the ears of her Pekinese with one languid hand and rang for tea with the other.

"Of course, my dear, I don't expect you to understand fully. You aren't a Wimpole."

The slim English girl smiled. "After all, I'm engaged to one. And I think I understand Vance a little."

"Yes," Veronica Foulkes conceded. "You can understand me somewhat through my brother. But is that kind of understanding enough? You're so different from us, my dear. So earthbound. And even understanding Vance wouldn't help. He is a man. He's free to roam as he will while I . . . I need something and I'm not even sure what it is. You never feel like that, do you, Jenny? Do you ever—I don't know—yearn?"

Jenny Green shamelessly cribbed a line from *Patience*. "I yearn my living," she said. "At least, I hope I do. Hilary's so generous to me as his secretary."

"Hilary!" In anyone less gracefully voluptuous, the noise that followed would have been a snort. "Oh, yes. Hilary understands how to take care of himself and his family. But what does all this mean?" Her sweeping gesture included everything in the quietly luxurious apartment, from her own rose hostess-gown to the maid bringing in the silver tea service. "What does all this pampering of the body mean when the soul—Just set it here, Alice."

Jenny Green spread marmalade on toast. "I think 'all this' is very pleasant."

"Ah, éclairs! No, Jenny, it's just that you're not sensitive. You don't realize how Hilary—Oh, well, I often wonder if other women are really as sensitive as I am. If only Vance were here!"

"May I join you in that wish?"

Veronica Foulkes shuddered gracefully. "Don't ever marry, Jenny. Not even Vance. Marriage means the end of everything. Marriage is the destruction of the free individual. Marriage is—"

"You mean you'd like to divorce Hilary?"

Veronica gasped. "Heavens, no. I couldn't *stand* the scandal of a divorce. And you know the views of the Church."

"Why should they affect you, Ron? To hear Vance talk, I've always thought the Wimpoles were one of the oldest established families of atheists in America."

"I don't know . . . Atheism is pretty thin rations. Sometimes I think I have a vocation. If I could leave all this behind and devote myself to the life of a nun—the beauty, the purity, the simplicity of it . . ." Her words issued mushily through her third éclair.

"And Hilary?"

"Well, you can see I couldn't divorce him. I wouldn't think of it. But now if he were to die . . ." she added brightly.

Jenny Green stared at her with something like shock. "I *do* wish Vance were in town," she said soberly.

V

"No, Vance." The woman shoved away his hand. "We've got to talk this out. A romp in the hay isn't going to solve the problem."

"I don't know." The man smiled. He had an oddly narrow and pallid face, which bushy crimson hair enlivened. His eyes were a pale blue, with a watery keenness to them. "I think fine that way. Best plot idea I ever had hit me in bed with an octoroon in São Paolo."

The woman said, "Ha, ha. You're fun, Vance, while it's all still fun. Now it's gone damned serious on us. He wants five hundred dollars, or he'll turn over the whole report to my husband."

Vance Wimpole frowned. "I don't see yet how he got on our track. I've been so careful. Nobody knows I'm in Los Angeles. Even my sister thinks I'm still wandering the seven seas."

"He did get on our trail. That's the point. I don't care how. And can you get the money?"

"I can get it in . . . " he calculated mentally ". . . a week. I've got two hundred on me. I can do a novelet worth three hundred in four or five days. Send it off airmail, and Stuart always mails my checks airmail . . . A week from today you'll have the five hundred."

"By which time," said the woman bitterly, "you'll have found somebody else to spend the two hundred on that you have."

Wimpole poured himself a stiff drink. "I've never been one of the rejection slip boys. I've always made money easy, even if it never sticks around very long. But to loll back and have a sweet regular income pouring in . . ."

"If only he'll stop at this," the woman said. "If we can somehow keep him from coming back for more . . ."

"One plump and worthless brother-in-law," Wimpole mused, "stands between me and the administratorship of the wealthiest literary estate in America." He lifted his glass in a wordless toast.

VI

Sister Mary Patientia, O.M.B., laid down her stylus and contemplated an immaculately punched sheet of Braille. This portion of her day's work was ended. She bowed her head and offered a brief prayer of thanks to the Virgin because there had been no mistakes in her transcription.

Then, alone out of all the people in Los Angeles and probably in the world, she prayed for Hilary Foulkes.

For Christ said on the mount: Love your enemies, do good to those who hate you, and pray for those who persecute you.

Hilary Foulkes had earned many prayers in his life.

VII

Among the readers of this narrative there may be a few of those pitiable people who have never read the Dr. Derringer stories, of that benighted handful whom Alexander Woollcott has called "as lamentable as a child who never saw a Christmas tree."

For those few, a word or two of explanation may be necessary. You others, who know *The Purple Light* and *Beneath the Abyss* as firmly and loyally as you know *Through the Looking-Glass* or *A Study in Scarlet* or *Treasure Island,* may be patient with the author's attempt to frame wonders in words.

Fantasy fiction is a loose term to cover a broad field. It embraces everything from *The Lost World* to *The Sword in the Stone,* from *She* to *Caleb Catlum's America.* But it has its aficionados, as intense and devoted as the audience for mysteries or westerns or hammock-romances. And the most loyal, the most fanatical of these followers of fantasy are the devotees of the fiction of science—scientification to its fans, or more simply stf.

Like the detective story, science fiction can be traced back to dim and ancient origins. And also like the detective story, it blossomed in the nineteenth century into the form in which we know it now. Edgar Allan Poe was very nearly as influential in one field as in the other. But the true Poe of science fiction, and the Wilkie Collins too, was Jules Verne.

Neither Poe nor Collins, however, is responsible for the living popularity of the detective story. That honor belongs to Conan Doyle, who added nothing to the form itself, contributed no feature that was not inherent in the work of the pioneers, but created a character of such superhuman proportions that he transcended the bounds of any one of literature and became part of the consciousness of the world.

What Doyle performed with Sherlock Holmes, Fowler Foulkes achieved a decade or so later with Dr. Derringer. The scion of an old San Francisco family, Foulkes dabbled for a time in the Bohemian literary efforts so popular in that city at the turn of the century. He contributed to *The Lark* and was an intimate of Gellett Burgess and of Amrose Bierce. He wrote pageants for the Bohemian Club and had a volume of verses published by Paul Elder.

And then he hit upon Dr. Derringer.

Foulkes' verses (which some critics prefer to those of George Stirling, finding in them an interesting anticipation of Jeffers' awareness of the meaning of the California landscape) are forgotten. His two plays, once successfully presented by Henry Miller, are as dead in the repertory as are those of Clyde Fitch. His series of historical novels, from the founding of the Mission Dolores to the earthquake of 1906, are known only to collectors of Californiana.

But there is not a corner of the world that does not know the stumpy, bull-chested, spade-bearded figure of Dr. Derringer, with his roaring voice, his silver-headed cane, and his devastating mind. Leland Stanford University still receives letters begging scientific advice and addressed to

Garth Derringer, Ph.D.
Department of Physics

and whimsical scholars delight in visiting the Foulkes Memorial Library of that University to confound each other with variorum readings from the earlier texts.

The story is told of a seismographic expedition which attained after arduous months the supposedly unattainable upper reaches of the Kulopangu. The chief of the Ngutlumbi was entranced by the elaborate apparatus set up to record earthquake shocks. He inspected it from all angles and at last inquired, confident of the answer, "Dokka Derinja, him make?"

This particular tale may display a touch of fanciful exaggeration, but it nonetheless typifies the esteem which the world has wisely accorded to the masterly creation of Fowler Foulkes.

Of Foulkes' other creation, his son Hilary, you have already heard somewhat and are to hear much more. Indeed, you will be in at the death.

TWO

THE SECOND DAY:
Friday, October 31, 1941

"And what," Lieutenant Marshall asked Concha Duncan as they drove west through the fall sunshine, "what is Matt's particular grudge against Hilary?"

The girl frowned. "I don't blame him really. Only it isn't funny to talk about murder."

"Murder's like suicide. Or writing. The more you talk about it, the less apt you are to do it. Release mechanism. But what's the motive?"

"It was a nasty trick . . . I don't suppose you know who Don Stuart is? Anyway he was an important science fiction writer and now he's editor of *Surprising Stories* (that's science) and *The Worlds Beyond* (that's pure fantasy). He's bought some of Matt's stuff and seems to think he's a comer. So Stuart got the bright idea wouldn't it be fun to have some contemporary Dr. Derringer stories."

Marshall nodded. "That's an idea. Foulkes died over ten years ago, didn't he? And he was even then a little behind the times. There are whole fields of modern science the magnificent doctor never touched. Think what he could do with atom-smashing or Dunne's time theories. Let's see—how old is Dr. Derringer now?"

"You mean how long ago were the stories?"

"I mean how old is that great man. The first stories were around the turn of the century and he was then about forty . . . That'd make him eightyish now. He could still be going strong."

"You talk as though he were a real man."

"Isn't he? I mean, doesn't one feel that he is? But go on with your story."

"That's what Stuart said. About how people think he's real. So he wrote to Austin Carter and outlined this idea and said that if he didn't want it he should farm it out to somebody else in the M.L.S., and so—"

"Whoa! Just to keep things straight, who's Austin Carter?"

"He's the biggest name in all Stuart's stable of writers. In fact, he's I think three of the biggest names. He's nice, too; he got Matt started in the field."

"And the M.L.S.?"

"That's the Mañana Literary Society. Austin Carter started calling it that because people always talk about the terrific honey of a story they're going to write tomorrow. Like you said about . . . murder. Only lots of them do really write them. The M.L.S. is all the people around here who work at fantasy and science fiction, and Carter is sort of a contact between them here and Stuart in New York."

"I follow. Though I've got a feeling I'm on the edges of a strange new world. Go on."

"So Carter farmed out this Derringer idea to Matt. Of course Matt was all excited because he says the three greatest men ever written are Dr. Derringer, Sherlock Holmes, and the Scarecrow of Oz. So he worked out synopses for six stories and Stuart okayed them, and he wrote to the Foulkes estate and they gave permission for a nominal fee to be arranged upon completion, and he worked like anything and turned out the set.

"Only then Hilary announced the fee. It was fifty dollars a story, and you couldn't do any 'arranging' about it. Matt was getting a bonus rate of a cent and a quarter from Stuart on these, so that made it about sixty-two fifty a story for him. And by the time he gets through paying Hilary, that'll leave him a total profit of seventy-five dollars for six stories. And he's not through paying yet because we spent the money from Stuart most of it, and says he's damned if he'll touch any of my money to pay his business debts."

Marshall grunted. "I don't much blame him myself. I mean for the murderous gleam. Hilary sounds sweet."

"And I haven't told you the worst. The very day that Matt got Hilary's letter and hit the ceiling, we read in a gossip column where Mrs. Hilary Foulkes had just bought a fifty-dollar fur jacket for her dog. Honest, Lieutenant, if I ever see that dog . . . Matt says he wouldn't mind so much if his honest sweat had bought Mrs. Foulkes a dress or champagne or anything humanly reasonable; but a fur jacket for a dog . . ."

"And I bet it's a Peke at that."

"It probably—Oh, you turn to the right here."

The convent of the Sisters of Martha of Bethany had originally been laid out as a rich and formal estate in the Westwood Hills. At the depth of the depression, it was munificently bestowed upon the nuns by a wealthy and generous layman who could no longer afford the taxes and assessments.

To the nuns it was a beautiful white elephant, a never-ending source of worry and delight. The sun, the view of the ocean from the hilltop, and the unspoken but patent envy of the Mothers Superior of other orders made partial atonement for the mile-and-a-half walk to the bus line and the constant cares of upkeep. And the ornate swimming pool furnished a splendid treat for the Mexican children who came weekly in school buses from the north end of town.

The sister portress lowered suspiciously at Lieutenant Marshall (she enjoyed her own slightly heretical views concerning the importance of men, tending to visualize Heaven as a noble matriarchy where the Virgin generously conceded a certain position to her Son), but smiled at Concha, whose aunt was one of the most loyal supporters of the convent.

"You can wait in the patio," she told them. "Though there's another lady there already waiting for Sister Ursula."

Even on overcast days, this patio seemed greenly bright with that peculiar submarine greenness of growing things. Today, in vivid autumn sunlight, it was verdantly aglow.

"I like this place," Marshall confessed, "even if I don't feel I fit. I used to have strange ideas of a convent. Maria Monk stuff. Dank and dismal and silent, save for an occasional wail from a newly bricked wall. But all this is so fresh and clean. It's . . . it's like a hospital without pain."

"It is a hospital," said Concha. "And it cures the other kind of pain."

Marshall paused in filling his pipe. "What a solemn thought from you, Concha! And why do Catholics always like to talk in paradoxes?"

She blushed a little. "I didn't think that up myself. I heard Sister Ursula say it once. But you won't tell me what we're here for? What are you going to ask her?"

The Lieutenant lit his pipe reflectively. "Nothing spectacular. Unfortunately, I just need some technical information." He took the seven-decade rosary from his pocket. "Ever see anything like this?"

Concha frowned. "That's a funny one. No. I thought Aunt Ellen had every kind of rosary and scapular and medal that ever existed, but I never saw one before with seven decades. Does that—is it a clew?"

"Maybe. I don't know yet. That's why I'm here."

"Sir!" a woman's voice demanded imperatively.

Marshall turned. The woman was not what one might expect to find in a convent. Her body was ripe with a fullness which comes from neither of those two ideals of the Church, virginity or motherhood. And her smart fall outfit must have cost—well, he knew nothing precisely about such things; but if he saw it on Leona, he'd certainly worry about their bank account.

"Must you, sir?" she said.

Marshall looked blank. "I beg your pardon. Must I what?"

"Must you smoke a pipe here in this holy spot?"

He grinned relief. "Sorry if it offends you, madam. But the nuns rather like it. Sister Ursula says the monks call pipe smoke 'the gardener's incense.' "

The woman raised well-plucked eyebrows. "But such levity! Even if I smoked myself, I should no more think of smoking here than—"

"Did I keep you waiting?" The robes of an order make most women seem to move either with undue bustle or with equally undue majesty. On Sister Ursula, however, they always seemed the only possible garments for her at once quiet and vigorous movements. Her voice, too, had neither hushed piety nor disciplinary sternness; it was simply a good and pleasing voice.

"I was helping Sister Patientia shellac Braille pages. You'll forgive me?" She smiled at Marshall, kissed Concha lightly, and glanced curiously at the strange woman.

"This lady was here ahead of us," Marshall said.

"Dear me, Lieutenant! You make me sound like a butcher shop."

"I do not wish to intrude." The woman dripped offended hauteur. "I shall wait in the chapel. Where the only incense," she added emphatically, "is that offered to the honor and glory of God." She swept away. Her walk was at once devout and dignified; but still you noticed the curving sway of her full hips.

"My!" Concha gasped. "Who is she?"

"I don't know, my dear. I don't even know her name. She simply came and told the portress that she was suffering and that she wanted to talk with a Bride of Christ. I think Reverend Mother was a little startled by such devout language, but she asked me to talk with her. After all, if she's in any sort of trouble and we can help her . . ."

"And," Concha added with kindly malice, "you are having trouble with funds for that baby clinic out by the Lockheed plant."

Sister Ursula smiled. When she smiled, she looked not much older than Concha. When she was serious, she was completely ageless. Lieutenant Marshall, and even his shrewdly feminine wife, had never dared venture a guess as to her actual age. "I am sure," she said reprovingly, "that no such unworthy thought ever crossed Reverend Mother's mind. At least, not consciously."

Marshall relit his briar. "She thought I was being sacrilegious to smoke here."

"Oh dear. I foresee troubles with her. It's hard enough as a rule to try to make people holy at all. But when they set themselves up to be far more holy than God or His Church ever intended them to be, then it's a really dreadful problem to bring them down to humanity again." She led the way to a sunny stone bench. "Is this your day off, Lieutenant, or are you calling on duty?"

"On duty, I'm afraid."

"You mean you want me to—" Sister Ursula had leaned forward, an almost imperceptible sparkle in her eyes. But abruptly she broke off and sat back. "Oh dear, there I go again," she sighed. "We Brides of Christ, as the lady rightly calls us (though I must say I find the expression far more comfortable in a devotional poem than in ordinary conversation), do have our faults. And you know mine and you keep pandering to it. But first tell me: how is Ursula?"

"She smiles now, and you know she's human. And she weighs two ounces more than Terry did at her age. Come and see her."

"I will try." She smiled as Marshall reached into his pocket. "Snapshots already?"

"No."

The smile changed to a perplexed frown as she saw what he brought out. "Lieutenant! I thought you were the staunchest of agnostics."

"I'm afraid I'm not carrying this rosary for devotional purposes. I just want to know what you can tell me about it."

Sister Ursula puzzled over the skillfully and elaborately carved beads. "Where did you get this?" she asked at last.

"What is it?" Marshall countered.

"It is a rosary," she said slowly. "But it is not the Rosary. That is, it is not the conventional set of beads with which one meditates on the mysteries of the redemption in devotion to our Blessed Mother."

"So? I thought a rosary was a rosary."

"Oh dear, no. The popular devotion revealed to the monk Dominic is certainly the most widespread of rosaries, but there are others. I know, for instance, of a rosary of the Infant of Prague; and I believe that there are indeed Tibetan and other non-Christian rosaries. The number and arrangement of beads varies naturally with the prayers intended to be recited, and this has seven sets. The crucifix, of course, eliminates anything like a lamaic rosary. But what might seven symbolize. The seven sacraments . . . The seven dolors . . ."

"Or it might be a multiple of seven," Concha suggested. "The regular rosary has five decades, and you say it three times round for the fifteen mysteries."

"A multiple . . . Yes, thank you, Mary. I remember now."

"You know what this is."

"Yes. It is a rosary of the Stations of the Cross. There are fourteen of those, and you say this twice, meditating on a station with each decade."

"I never heard of that," said Concha.

"I am not surprised. A priest in San Fransisco started the devotion some forty years ago, so that many Californians who then lived near no church might still make the stations. But Father Harris was killed in the earthquake, and the devotion died out. I believe that it was never formally approved by the Holy See. Not, of course, that that means it's to be condemned. Any individual is free to say the proper prayers in the devotional form that most appeals to him."

Marshall looked disappointed. "You mean, then, that this is perfectly all right? It's orthodoxly Catholic?"

"Not precisely orthodox, perhaps, but certainly not heretical."

"Hang it. If it had belonged to some strange minor off-shoot of a sect, it could have been a great help to me in narrowing things down."

"I should think you could narrow things down a good deal even from this. The devotion flourished for only a few years and almost entirely in one city. The wood is unusual, and the carving is exceptionally fine; this rosary was probably made to order and cost a good deal. It doubtless belonged to one of Father Harris' wealthy patronesses."

Marshall nodded. "That sounds logical. And if the rosary's worth something on its own as an object of art, that might account for . . ."

"May I make a suggestion? Leave it with me, and I'll show it to Sister Perpetua, who knows more about religious art than I should ever have thought possible. I wouldn't be surprised if she could even tell you the name of the carver and in fact the period of his work to which it belongs."

"Thanks. We'll try that." He handed over the rosary.

"And Lieutenant . . . You wouldn't care to tell me anything about the . . . the circumstances?" There was that sparkle in her eyes again.

"Certainly. But there's nothing interesting about them. Not worthy of you, Sister. Just a matter of trying to trace a floater who got himself killed. This rosary's about the only lead we've got to check his identity.

"Go on . . . No! Oh, Lieutenant, I'm ashamed of myself. I've been good for a year now, haven't I? We've been good friends and I love your children and I've never once tried to interfere and solve your cases for you. I even shut my ears that night you tried to tell me about the Magruder poisoning affair, and look how beautifully you solved it yourself."

"In three weeks," said Marshall, "and I'll swear you wouldn't have taken five minutes to spot the point of that unused match folder."

"Please. Don't try to flatter me. It's your business to solve crimes, and it's not mine. I want to be good. But I've been good so long that I—I've begun to itch."

"Madam, after the job you did a year ago, you're more than welcome to solve my cases any time you want to. If you itch so, why shouldn't you scratch it?"

"It's hard to explain . . . But look at it this way. You've met Sister Felicitas. She has a vice; it's loving sleep too much. You'd be—well, you might almost say an occasion of sin if you proffered her a nice feather bed. Or Sister—no, I shan't name names; but I can think of two or three that only the Devil himself should leave a box of chocolates beside.

"You see, the rules of the order, to say nothing of our own religious devotion, don't leave much scope in our lives for what the world thinks major and serious vices. So we come to realize the importance of the rest of the Seven Deadly Sins. Everyone admits the evil of Lust and most people include Avarice, at least on principle; but there are dangers to the soul in Gluttony too, and in Sloth. And in Pride.

"Before, when you were kind enough to say that I helped you—No, that's false modesty, which is the worst emblem of Pride. When I helped you, I took great pride in how clever I was being. I felt power. I even," she lowered her eyes, "I even exercised power over a man's life. And I won't do it again. I'll do all I can to find out what you need about this rosary, but I don't want to know any more. Or rather I want not to want to."

"All right. But I've got a confession to make too. For the past year I've been hoping somehow to tempt you back where I think you belong. I needed the dope on this rosary, yes; but I welcomed that need because it gave me a chance to present you with a criminal case needing your specialized knowledge. It isn't much of a case, but if you'd hear me out and tell me—"

"No," said Sister Ursula firmly. For a moment they sat, the policeman and the nun, looking at each other as earnestly as unhappy lovers.

Then Marshall grinned. "All right. But if the Devil ever rides you unbearably hard, I'll always stand ready to take his side. The force lost a wonderful policewoman when you decided to take the veil."

"Thank you. And now I must try to console Sister Patientia—or no, there's that strange woman waiting in the chapel."

"What's the matter with Sister Patientia?" Concha demanded. To her the nuns, who had known her from childhood, were like so many aunts.

"I'm afraid she's rather vexed, and understandably so."

"What happened?"

"She was engaged in a Braille transcription of one of the Dr. Derringer novels and wrote to the Foulkes estate to clear copyright. You know that such consent is always given free automatically; you simply have to secure permission as a matter of form. Well, the heir replied that he would be delighted to have the blind read his father's work, and that the standard commercial reprint fees would apply."

Lieutenant Marshall whistled. "That Hilary! I'm going to be investigating his murder yet."

II

The chapel—the chaste new white-and-gold Rufus Harrigan Memorial Chapel, gift of Concha's Aunt Ellen—was empty save for the smartly dressed woman who knelt at the communion rail. As she heard the nun's footsteps she rose and crossed herself, slowly, as one for whom the gesture still has to be thought out step by step.

Sister Ursula genuflected before the altar. "You wished to talk with me?" she asked quietly.

"If you will be so kind to one who has suffered."

"We can go out in the patio. The irreverent man with the pipe has gone now."

"Thank you, Sister."

"What was it you wanted?" Sister Ursula asked as they walked along the corridor.

"I want to know all about what it is like to be a Bride of Christ."

The nun's hand toyed unthinkingly with the strange rosary. "That isn't an easy question to answer, you know. Sister Immaculata is working on a biography of Blessed Mother La Roche, the founder of our order. She says that any one who would attempt to put the true meaning of a nun's life into words must be either Saint Theresa or a simpleton."

"Saint Theresa!" the woman sighed. "That dear sweet little thing!"

Sister Ursula smiled. "I mean the other Theresa, of Avila, who—"

But the woman interrupted her. "I beg your pardon, Sister, but that rosary—"

"Yes?"

"Where did you get it?" For a moment her devotional manner had vanished, and she seemed alertly interested. "Where did it come from?"

"I don't know," Sister Ursula answered truthfully. "Why? Do you know anything about it?"

"Know anything? Why, I'm sure it's my—" The woman paused. She raised her clasped hands to her full breasts and let her head sink pensively. "But we must not think of such things now, must we? No, Sister, it makes no difference. Tell me what you can of your life."

Sister Ursula bit her lip. That rosary came from a murdered man. If this woman knew anything about it . . . Though what connection there could be between such an expensive article as this and what the Lieutenant had called a "floater" . . . Still if she could try to find out . . .

The angel of Satan had rarely buffeted her so strongly. But she said only, "I think the best way I can explain is to show you a little of our work. We are called, as you know, the Sisters of Martha of Bethany, because Mother La Roche believed . . ."

III

In the early days of Olsen and Johnson, long before Hell zapopped, they had a skit which took place in a hotel room. Among the manifold and wondrous inconveniences of this room was a drunk who wandered in from time to time trying to find the bathroom.

On his fifth entrance he looked at the two unhappy comedians and moaned desolately, "Are you in *all* the rooms?"

So Lieutenant Marshall felt now. He had dropped Concha off at the Duncan's apartment, refusing to interrupt Matt's work even for the laudable project of splitting a beer, and driven on to the very different and opulent apartment hotel whose phone number he had found on the Tarbell corpse.

On the way to the convent he had heard about Hilary Foulkes from Concha. At the convent he had heard more about Hilary Foulkes from Sister Ursula. And here the first name that caught his eye on the mailboxes was

HILARY ST. J. FOULKES

". . . in all the rooms . . ." Lieutenant Marshall muttered.

A uniformed maid answered the door. To Marshall's, "I want to speak to Mr. Foulkes," she replied, "I will take in your card, sir."

"I'm afraid I haven't one on me. Just tell him it's the police." He was about to add some reassuring phrase to ward off the usual civilian terror of police authority, but the girl's face instantly brightened.

"Oh yes, Inspector, I'll tell him. He'll be delighted."

Marshall did not scratch his head. He was not given to the gesture, and in fact had never known anyone who was; but he understood the emotion which novelists mean when they write, "He scratched his head." He had never before encountered any individual who welcomed the police so eagerly; and he certainly should have expected Hilary St. John Foulkes, from all he had heard so far, to be the last to do so.

He seated himself gingerly on an exquisite and spindly chair. This living-room was a woman's room. There was no solid comfortable chair for leg-stretching and pipe-smoking. The entire room was daintily and painfully neat. No trace of ashes or glasses or magazines or other normal signs of human enjoyment. The only reading matter was a small bookcase filled with admirably tooled leatherbound volumes. Marshall felt sure, even before he examined them, that they were the complete works of Fowler Foulkes.

He lit his pipe, looked about for an ashtray, and ended hopelessly by tucking the match into the cuff of his trousers. He was here, he admitted to himself frankly, because he was curious to see what the hell this Hilary was like. There was not a chance in a hundred—or to be more precise, there was just one chance in twenty-four—that Hilary had anything to do with the Tarbell corpse on Main Street. But, he assuaged his conscience, you had to start someplace in this apartment hotel.

"Inspector! But this is splendid!"

The voice surprised Marshall. He hardly knew why, but he had expected an effeminate piping. This voice, deeper and clearer and more rounded even than his own had been at the height of his debating career, hardly fitted his first rough concept of Hilary.

The man fitted better visually than aurally. He was a little under average height and a little over average weight. Not that he was fat; just that one might have preferred cheeks a trifle less plump and a neck that did not roll over the collar. He wore a beautiful red-and-gold dressing gown, which Marshall instantly coveted, over too tightly cut pin-stripe trousers and a shirt of delicate pink with stiff white collar, all of which Marshall wouldn't have worn to a masquerade.

There was a penguinish waddle to his walk, and the officer half expected a flipper instead of the soft hand that eagerly took his.

"The name," he said, "is Marshall. And the rank is just Lieutenant."

"Delighted, Lieutenant, delighted. Do sit down. Shall I ring for tea?"

"No thanks. I won't take up much of your time. I merely want to ask a couple of questions."

Hilary Foulkes sat leaning forward politely, his hand pinching the lobe of his right ear. Marshall faintly remembered a widespread publicity still of his father in the same pose. "Naturally, naturally. But I am amazed, Lieutenant, at such prompt service."

"Service?"

A tone of hurt doubt was apparent in Hilary's voice. "You *are* from Homicide, aren't you?"

"Yes, but—"

Hilary settled back relieved. "Go ahead. Go ahead. It was only that it seemed so rapid. It can't be an hour since I phoned."

"You phoned to Homicide?"

"Of course. Wouldn't you if someone were trying to murder you?"

Marshall preserved impassivity behind his pipe. "Of course, Mr. Foulkes. I only wish that more citizens had your civic conscience." If a notable visitor was going to think wonders of the department for its rapid service, why disillusion him? Actually, Marshall reflected, the call had probably been routed through to poor old Halloran, who had a way with cranks, and who might get around here some time in the next week or two.

"Now I don't know quite how to commence, Lieutenant. Perhaps if you were to ask me the usual formula questions—or do you have a formula for a man who's being murdered?"

"We're more used to dealing with him after the fact, I'm afraid; but it's a pleasure to get ahead of time for once. First of all, Mr. Foulkes, who is trying to murder you?"

"Heavens! Heavens, Lieutenant, if I knew that, do you think I'd have sent for you? This is all a mystery to me so far. And naturally I'm curious."

"Then what was the nature of the attempt?"

"The attempts, Lieutenant. The attempts. There have been several. Let me see . . . The first was the car—or was it the brick? But both of those are so uncertain."

"Let me hear them anyway."

"Well now, the car. The car. That would be a week ago, more or less. I was taking Pitti Sing for her walk. We were crossing Wilshire Boulevard when a car made a left turn through a stop sign, going I should guess a good forty miles an hour, and bore down on us. We escaped only by the skin of our teeth. Skins of our teeth? No matter."

"That could have been an accident. Our Los Angeles drivers, I'm afraid, are notorious."

"I know. Once could be an accident, I know. So could the brick that fell so near me the next day, from an unfinished building where no workmen were in sight."

"You take these walks regularly?"

"Regularly? Frequently, at least. Yes, frequently. Usually about seven in the evening I take Pitti Sing for a walk."

"Pitti Sing is your dog?"

"My wife's, Lieutenant. A Pekinese."

Marshall managed not to smile, remembering the fur jacket and his now verified guess. "Notice anything about the car?"

"It was a convertible—I believe a Mercury, though I would not swear to the fact. I didn't notice the license, nor even who was driving. It all happened so suddenly . . ."

"Of course. Any further details on the brick episode?"

"Nothing."

Marshall puffed at his pipe. I don't know that you need worry yourself, Mr. Foulkes. I realize that two such episodes on successive evenings are enough to perturb one, but don't you think—?"

"Oh, but I haven't told you about the chocolates. The chocolates. I had a birthday last week, and among various other gifts I received a box of chocolates by mail. There was no card, but I thought nothing of that. Stores do make mistakes in wrapping you know. But when I took the first piece—how I thank Heaven that my wife was not with me then! If she had tasted first . . . But fortunately as I lifted this chocolate cherry, I noticed a tiny mark like a pinprick in the bottom. I had only recently read a novel concerning poisoned chocolates, and I must confess I trembled.

"Call me foolishly apprehensive if you will, Lieutenant. But the combination of the car, the brick, the missing card, and the novel frightened me. I took the chocolates to a chemist for analysis.

Each of them contained quite enough cyanide to kill half a dozen people—providing, of course, that a half dozen people could eat one chocolate."

Marshall grunted. He had expected nothing but the recital of a pampered neurotic with a persecution complex, and the car and the brick fitted that pattern beautifully. The chocolates were different. He took the copy of the analyst's report which Hilary handed him. He knew the firm. Irreproachable standing. Damn it, he'd really happened on to something.

"I'll confess," he said, "that this puts a different complexion on things. Do you have the wrappings of that candy box?"

"No," Hilary admitted ruefully. "The maid had burned all the birthday wrappings before I made my discovery."

"You have the box itself?"

"It is still at the analyst's with the chocolates. I shall give you a note to him."

"Did you happen to notice where it was from?"

"Here in Los Angeles. It was one of the standard two-pound boxes of the Doris Dainty Shoppes, though I have of course no idea from which branch."

Marshall sighed. Try tracing the purchase of a box of standard mixture from any of thirty-odd branches! "So," he said. "All right. Maybe we better approach this from the other end. Who would have any interest, Mr. Foulkes, in killing you?"

"Me? In killing me?" Hilary Foulkes spread his plump hands in the blandest of innocence. "That's what worries me. Who on earth could possibly want to kill me?"

Before Marshall could quite choke at this charming effrontery, a girl came into the room. She was slim and long-legged and carried herself with an easy and unobtrusive grace. "Cousin Hilary—" she began. "Oh, I'm sorry. I didn't realize you had—"

Marshall rose, but Hilary did not. He waved one hand languidly and said, "Yes, my dear?"

"I don't like to interrupt, but Alice wants to know if Veronica is going to be home to dinner. I don't even know where she's gone."

"Neither do I, my dear. Neither do I. But she will doubtless be home. You may tell Alice so." His eyes lit on the still uncomfortably standing police officer. "Oh, Jenny, this is Lieutenant Marshall. My cousin, Miss Green."

The girl's voice was light and friendly, with a trace of an English accent. "How do you do, Lieutenant. I hope Cousin Hilary is showing you proper hospitality. We can't do too much for those who may so soon have to defend us."

Marshall smiled. "Not that kind of Lieutenant, I'm afraid. Just police."

"Oh!" Her eyes widened. "Hilary, what on earth have you been up to?"

Hilary wriggled. "Nothing of importance, my dear. Nothing of importance. The Lieutenant was merely . . . was merely . . ."

Marshall took up the sentence. "I merely wanted to know if your cousin had ever heard of a man named Tarbell. Part of a routine check-up."

Hilary and the girl looked equally blank.

"Jonathan Tarbell," Marshall added. "Or," he went on, "whether a rosary with seven decades meant anything to him."

"That's sets of beads?" the girl asked. "Seven sets? Wasn't that—" There was no perceptible movement from Hilary, or at most a slight flicker of his eyes, but the girl broke off. "No," she said. "I'm thinking of something else."

Hilary smiled blandly and said, "And I fear the Lieutenant is not finding me very helpful. Mr. Tarbrush and the rosary are equally unfamiliar to me."

"I won't ask counter-questions," Jenny Green smiled. "I'll just leave you to plague Hilary. Oh." She paused. "Are you the Lieutenant Marshall who solved the Harrigan case last year?"

Marshall nodded.

"My! We were in New York then, but even there the papers were full of it. That was wonderful and don't try to say anything because I know I'm only embarrassing you. Sorry, and goodbye."

Hilary glanced after the girl as Marshall reseated himself. "You understand I didn't wish to mention these murder attempts in front of her. It would only worry her."

"Of course."

"And I'd like to congratulate you, Lieutenant, on the rapidity with which you picked up my hint. Most ingenious, those questions about the rosary and Mr. Tarpon. Most ingenious."

Marshall let it go at that. Those leads could be followed up later to better advantage. "But to return to our motives—" he began.

"And I am most fortunate," Hilary went on, "to have drawn the man who solved the Harrigan case. Most fortunate. That was a curious business, wasn't it? Locked room affair, as I remember."

"Yes," said Marshall tersely. "But to get back to our own case: It's nonsense, Mr. Foulkes, to say that there's no one who might want to murder you. There's never been a living human being of whom that was true. Surely you can make some nominations?"

Hilary puzzled. "Frankly, Lieutenant, no. Frankly. I lead a quiet, peaceful, and unobtrusive life. I have no close friends, and therefore no close enemies. My wife is faithful to me, and I to her."

"And you are a wealthy man."

"True. But need the fact necessarily mean that anyone wishes to kill me?"

"I'm afraid so. Sex and money are the two all-dominant motives for murder, and of the two I'll lay odds on money every time. So let me ask: Who is your heir?"

"My wife, of course. We have no children. Miss Green, whom you just met, will receive a comfortable income for life from a trust fund. Otherwise my wife inherits the whole of the estate."

"That includes your father's estate?"

"Naturally."

"And who will act as literary executor of the Foulkes properties?"

"My wife's brother, D. Vance Wimpole. He seemed a logical choice for the post since his father was something of a self-appointed Boswell to mine. Moreover he is himself a writer, though for the pulps," Hilary uttered the horrid word with ineffable disdain, "and is so very much part of the family. Not only is he my brother-in-law; he is soon to marry my cousin."

"Then by your death this Mr. Wimpole would secure a wife with a comfortable life income and the control over an exceedingly valuable literary estate?"

Hilary looked uncomfortable. "Nonsense, my dear Lieutenant. Utter nonsense. Vance is an eccentric, a madman if you will, but a murderer—Heavens! Besides, he is at present in Kamchatka or Kalamazoo or some such outlandish place. The chocolates were mailed in Los Angeles."

Marshall looked about hopelessly for someplace to knock out his pipe. "Mr. Foulkes, if you insist that you're being attacked, as this analyst's report certainly confirms, you must admit that someone has a reason for doing so. Obviously, your wife, your cousin, and your brother-in-law stand to gain markedly by your death. What about others? Have you . . . Have you ever made any business enemies? Say through your administration of the Foulkes estate?"

Hilary resumed the lobe-pulling pose. "You seem a sympathetic man, Lieutenant. So many people will not understand the difficulties of my position."

"Yes?"

"If my father had invented Mr. Emerson's mousetrap, no one would question my right to collect fees from those who followed the beaten path to his door. If my father had built up some great and world-embracing business enterprise, no one but a Communist would begrudge me the income from it. But because my father enriched the world with a great character and a number of immortal narratives, some men sneer at me and assert that I have no right to this income.

"As you are well aware, I have every legal right. Our copyright laws protect an author's offspring quite as thoroughly as they do the author himself. And I have moral right too. In fact a moral duty. A moral duty to see that my father's work is respected, that it does not enter the public domain where any insignificant dolt may do as he will with it, that the works of Fowler Foulkes are as carefully guarded now as he would have guarded them were he still alive."

"In short," Marshall summarized, "you do think you might have made some enemies in administering the estate."

"It is possible. Possible, although it seems ludicrous that such petty enemies might lead to murder. But if you pin me down, Lieutenant, I can think of no one who might wish to kill me, Hilary Foulkes, an individual. These attacks must be directed against the son of Fowler Foulkes, against the administrator of the Foulkes estate."

"One point though. Your birthday. Timing it for that day made sure you'd open a box you might otherwise have regarded with suspicion. Wouldn't that point at some intimate?"

"My birthday is mentioned in my father's autobiography. In Wimpole's memoir too, I imagine"

"So," Marshall frowned and drew out his notebook. "All right. Now, Mr. Foulkes, if you could give me the names of any individuals who—"

The maid came in just then with a bulky package. "Excuse me, sir. This came by special messenger and it's marked RUSH. I thought perhaps—"

Hilary waved it away. "Set it down there. Well, Lieutenant, it's naturally impossible for me to remember the names of all those whose unreasonable requests I have at one time or another seen fit to reject. Possibly—"

"That package," Marshall interrupted. "Something you ordered?"

"No. I've no notion what it is. No notion. But that can wait. The most recent of these—"

Marshall leaned over the package and held up his hand for silence. The peremptory authority of the gesture hushed Hilary instantly.

In the silent room the ticking was clearly audible.

IV

"Where's your phone?" Marshall snapped.

"It ticks," Hilary observed. "How curious! It ticks . . ."

"Where's the phone?"

"It . . . Oh my heavens! Lieutenant! It's a bomb!"

"There is," Marshall admitted dryly, "that possibility. Now where's a phone?"

For the first time Hilary moved with rapidity. He leaped at the package, and Marshall had to counter swiftly to ward him off.

"But Lieutenant! We've got to go put it in the bath-tub! We've got to—" His voice had gone up an octave.

Marshall held him by the arm and spoke firmly. "You called the police. All right. The police are here and in charge, and you're doing what I say. Leave that box alone and show me a phone."

"Leave it alone and show you the phone." Hilary giggled. "You rime, Lieutenant. You rime."

"The phone!" Marshall snapped.

"Right here." Still on the verge of hysterical giggles, Hilary removed the decorative flounces that had hid the instrument.

"Playing with possible bombs isn't healthy," Marshall explained as he dialed, automatically noting that Hilary's phone had a different number from the number of the building found on Tarbell. "And popping them in water is a popular fallacy. The only safe medium is lubricating oil, and I doubt if you've got a tubful of that handy.—Hello, Marshall speaking, Homicide. Give me the Emergency Squad.—No Mr. Foulkes, we'll leave it to the experts. You can clear out if you want to and—Hello. Lieutenant Marshall speaking. I want to report a possible bomb. I—"

His attention had been distracted from his host, and Hilary Foulkes seized the opportunity to make a dash for the package. What his intentions might have been was never to be learned. Marshall's long legs shot out across his path, and Hilary came down with a crash and lay still.

"No," Marshall went calmly on into the phone. "That wasn't the bomb. Just interference."

He gave the address, received the usual warning to do nothing until the squad got there, and hung up. He bent over Hilary, worried for a moment, but found nothing seriously wrong. Bump on the back of the head from hitting one of the spindly chairs. No damage, and Hilary would probably be less trouble if simply left on ice for a bit.

Marshall frowned, then nodded. Through two corridors he found his way into the kitchen. The maid, who apparently doubled in aluminium, was peeling potatoes. "Hello," he said. "Mr. Foulkes is expecting some visitors on very secret business. They don't want to take any chances in being seen. Would you please go for a walk?" He handed her a dollar bill. "Have a soda or see a newsreel or something."

"But I've got to get dinner and if it isn't ready on time Mrs. Foulkes'll—" she paused. "You're the police, aren't you?"

"Yes."

"I'll go."

"Please tell Miss Green too. Is there anyone else in the apartment?"

"Only Pitti Sing, and she's asleep."

"She can stay," said Marshall grimly. "And who's in the apartment under us?"

"It's vacant, sir."

"Good,"

The Foulkes apartment was large and multiple. The turning and the door that Marshall was sure would bring him back to the living-room led him instead into a chastely furnished bedroom.

"I'm blind as a bat without my glasses," he announced loudly. "Is that you, Mr. Foulkes?"

Jenny Green laughed, a laugh that was half embarrassment and half youthful pleasure: "You're a gentleman, Lieutenant." Her fresh pink and white skin disappeared into a faded wrapper.

"At times I regret it," Marshall confessed. "But look: Your cousin has secret affairs coming up and wants you should clear out for half an hour."

"Are you joking?"

"No. He seems to mean it."

"Oh. And when Hilary means something . . . I know. Thanks."

The second try worked and he reached the living-room. Hilary was still unconscious. And the package still ticked.

Marshall lifted a corner of the rug, shook out his pipe, and dropped the rug back over the ashes. He lit up a fresh pipeful and stared at the box. The temptation to investigate it was strong, but he remembered the cheering stories taught in the police training school of what happened to smart coppers who decided they were as good as the Emergency Squad. He copied down in his notebook the name of the messenger service and the cryptic numerals which presumably could help trace the order.

The box went on ticking.

He heard the maid leave, and a little later Miss Green. The apartment below was vacant. The ceiling was high. If the bomb did go off in the next ten minutes, it could injure no one—except, of course, Hilary Foulkes and the Lieutenant. He could probably arouse Hilary and carry him downstairs. But at the same time he should stay here and stand guard over the bomb. Mrs. Foulkes would probably be home soon. If she should come in and decide to investigate the package . . .

He puffed and tried to sort out what he knew so far. A car, a brick, poisoned chocolates, and a bomb. Somebody was decidedly in earnest, and at the same time curiously inefficient about it. And somewhere there tied into this a rosary and a phone number and a Main Street corpse. They had to fit in; there had been a marked reaction on that rosary question.

The box went on ticking.

The discrepancy of the phone numbers was easy to explain. This was probably an unlisted phone. Anyone trying to get in touch with Hilary would be unable to get it from the company and forced to content himself with the apartment house phone. But why should Jonathan Tarbell . . .

The ticking was louder now.

Louder than a jukebox at midnight, louder than a radio serial, louder than an air raid siren, louder than the world.

It was the world, that ticking.

Marshall thought of the Tell-Tale Heart. But that was proof of Death Past. This ticking was proof of Death to Come, of . . .

He swore at himself, looked around the room, found a radio, and switched it on full blast. He never noticed what the sound was once it came over. He knew only that it drowned out the ticking.

It also drowned out the entrance of Veronica Foulkes. The first that Marshall knew of her presence was a loud scream, loud enough to top ticking and radio and all.

". . . to keep the loveliness of your hands soft and white in the hardest water . . ." a dripping voice was booming.

Marshall switched off the radio.

"You!" Veronica cried. "You're the man with the pipe in the garden!"

The Lieutenant bowed. "How nice to meet again. Now, madam, if you would kindly—"

"Hilary! What have you done to Hilary! He won't speak to me! He . . . he just lies there . . ."

"Your husband, Mrs. Foulkes, has had a slight accident. Everything will be all right. I represent the police and am in charge. Now if you will just—"

"I don't believe it. You're not a policeman!" Her bosom heaved, and she was just the guy to do it. "You've attacked Hilary, and I—"

"Please!" Marshall protested. "I'm trying to warn you. Will you kindly leave this apartment?"

"Warn me? So you admit you're a criminal! I knew it. Policemen don't smoke pipes in convents. Get out of here! And at once, or I'll call the real police!"

"But Mrs. Foulkes, I'm trying to tell you, since I must. There's a bomb—"

"Bomb! Oh! You're trying to kill us all. You—"

With that, she flung herself upon him. The phrase "tooth and nail" suddenly assumed a fresh and vivid meaning for Lieutenant Marshall. He felt blood coursing from the gouge in his cheek as he vainly tried to pinion her wrists to her sides. The long spiked heels of her shoes dug viciously into his shanks, and she poured out words that seemed scarcely apposite in so punctilious a critic of conventual etiquette.

At last he secured a firm and clenching grip on her wrists and managed to wrap his long leg around her threshing ankles. "Now, madam," he panted, "will you be good?"

Her next move left him speechless. She looked up, murmured, "You *so* strong," and kissed him with full and parted lips.

It was, of course, at this moment that the Emergency Squad arrived.

The Squad seemed more interested in this tableau than in the bomb. With a deceptive appearance of ease and carelessness two of the men transferred the ticking package to a metal container full of lubricating oil. Sergeant Borigian said, "There's an undeveloped lot next door; we'll take 'er apart there." With the same routined indifference the two men lifted the container and carried away the oil and the ticking. And all this time their eyes seemed never to leave the red-faced Lieutenant, the buxom and gasping woman, and the unconscious man on the floor.

When the men had gone, Sergeant Borigian grinned and observed, "Looks like you've done a little taking apart yourself, Lieutenant."

Marshall started to speak, but Veronica Foulkes cut across him with, "My husband! Aren't you going to do anything about him?"

"Looks like he's done plenty," the Sergeant ventured.

Hilary groaned. In an instant Veronica was beside him, stroking his forehead and murmuring phrases that might have been better suited to Pitti Sing. Slowly Hilary opened his eyes and seemed astounded to behold himself and the room still in one piece.

"It ticked . . ." he faltered. "Where is it?"

"There," Veronica murmured. "He won't hurt ums again. There's a real policeman here now. With a uniform."

"Lieutenant," said Sergeant Borigian, "what worries me is I can't decide whether to report your conduct to headquarters or to your wife."

Hilary sat up, "Where did you come from, Ron? But that doesn't matter. Where's the bomb, Lieutenant? Where's the bomb?"

"Mr. Foulkes," said Marshall, "this is Sergeant Borigian of the Emergency Squad. His men are looking after the bomb. Everything's under control, and you're perfectly safe."

Veronica gazed from one man to the other. "What is happening here?"

Hilary wavered onto his feet. "There, my dear, there. I'll explain later. And you will find out who, Lieutenant?"

I've got damned little to go on, Mr. Foulkes, as you very well know, and I'll have to have another session with you tomorrow. But right now what I've got to do is check up on the delivery of this parcel." He hesitated and glanced at Veronica. "One thing
"

"You may speak freely before my wife, Lieutenant. It will be hopeless now to try to keep things from her. Hopeless."

"Do you want us to put a guard on your apartment? It can easily be arranged."

Hilary shook his head fuzzily. "I think not. You see, Lieutenant, I want to know who this is. If we frighten him away with a guard, we may never manage to learn his identity."

"Think it over. I'd sooner not know who tried to murder you than prove positively who succeeded. I'll give you a ring in the morning. Coming, Sergeant?"

As they waited for the elevator, Sergeant Borigian suggested, "Want to watch the investigation? From a distance of course; we don't want no amateurs from Homicide cluttering things up."

"No thanks. I've got to check this delivery while the trail's warm. Let the clerk sleep on it and he'll forget everything. I'll phone into Headquarters for your report in about—will an hour be all right?"

"For a preliminary, sure." The heavy-set Sergeant fell broodingly silent. Then he burst out, "Look, Lieutenant. My job's to keep bombs from going off and find out what they're made of. It's nothing to me who sent 'em to who or why. But when I walk in and find a detective Lieutenant . . . Will you tell me what the hell's going on up there?"

"Brother," said Marshall feelingly, "I wish you'd tell me."

V

Tracing an order is a job that Marshall hates. It always means much brandishing of credentials and the assumption of the heavy policeman role. Executives seem to fear that every inquirer is the sinister agent of some foreign power, or worse yet, of a competitor.

After a great deal of this official brow-beating, Marshall had prevailed upon the central office of the Angelus Parcel Delivery Service to divulge that the package whose number he gave had been sent from the Hollywood branch, and upon the manager of the Hollywood branch to admit that Q73X4 meant our Miss Jones.

Our Miss Jones would have been markedly pretty if she had not been made up on the chance that a casting director might sometime want to send a parcel. "Sure," she said cheerfully, "I remember the guy sent that package." She checked back in her records. "That was at ten thirty-five this morning, only he said we shouldn't make delivery till three this afternoon. I remember him swell."

"You must take quite a few orders in a day," Marshall ventured cautiously. "Was there anything to make you remember this man especially?"

"Sure. First of all I thought it was kind of screwy marking a package RUSH and then leaving instructions not to deliver if for four and a half hours. And then I noticed the name it was going to. Hilary Saint John Foulkes."

". . . all the rooms . . ." thought Marshall. "And why should you notice that name in particular?"

"On account of last night me and my boyfriend were looking at a magazine and there was an ad for men's talcum powder with a lot of signatures-like—you know, endorsements—and they were all big shots only I didn't know who was this one so I said to my boyfriend, I said 'Who's this Hilary?' and he said 'That's the son of Fowler Foulkes' and I said 'But who is he?' and he said 'Just that, far's I know' and I said 'So just because you're somebody's son you get dough for endorsing stuff?' and he said '*Somebody's* son? But he's the son of Fowler Foulkes!' and I said 'So who's he?' so then we had a fight. So that's how come I noticed the name."

Marshall nodded satisfied. "All right." Witnesses can be like overhelpful natives who tell the explorer exactly what he most wants to hear, true or not; and such witnesses never survive cross-examination; but this sounded circumstantial and convincing. "Now, Miss Jones, can you describe the person who sent this package?"

"Sure. He was a funny old boy."

"Old?"

"Yeah. He must've been all of fifty if he was a day. He wasn't so very tall, but he was built big, if you know what I mean. He had a big barrel of a chest on him, like a gorilla or something. His nose was big and kind of hooked—Roman, I guess you'd call it. And he had a great big black beard. You wouldn't forget him very easy. Oh yes, and he carried a cane, with a silver head on it."

Our Miss Jones wondered why the detective should first look so blankly incredulous and then burst out into an admiring guffaw.

He was, Marshall realized, up against a murderer with a peculiarly outrageous gag sense. The girl had just given a perfect description of Dr. Derringer.

VI

"There's nothing like beer when you knock off from a day's work." Matt Duncan popped the top off and handed the foaming bottle to Lieutenant Marshall.

"Don't you want a glass?" Concha suggested.

"If I can't have a stein," said Marshall, "right straight from the bottle is next best. And besides, why make more dishes for you to wash?"

"Thank you, kind sir."

"Aren't you having any?"

"Uh uh. I don't like beer, and I'm not going to be one of these girls who go around pretending they do."

Matt exhaled loudly after a mighty draft. "Hits the spot, that does. Now what are you on the trail of, Terence?"

Lieutenant Marshall looked mournful. "Curse of the profession. Nobody ever suspects you of just a friendly call in passing."

"This is non-professional?"

"Well . . ."

"It is not," said Concha. "I can see that gleam in your eye. I'll bet it's still that floater with the rosary you were asking Sister Ursula about."

"What's that?" Matt asked idly.

"Nothing important. Fellow named Tarbell got bumped off down on Main Street. But that isn't what I—"

Matt wrinkled his brow. "Tarbell . . . I met a Tarbell somewhere recently. It's not a common name. Jonathan Tarbell . . ."

Marshall leaned forward. "So. Maybe this is a professional call after all. Where? When?"

"Damn, I can't remember. It was just casual . . . I know. It was at Austin Carter's."

"You remember," Concha put in. "The man I was telling you about with the Mañana Literary Society."

Marshall nodded. "Friend of Carter's then, this Tarbell?"

"No, I think he'd come with somebody."

"Who?"

"I can't remember. Nobody I know well. Runcible maybe, or Chantrelle."

"So." Marshall nodded slowly to himself. "Matt, I'm going to ask you a favor, and I'm not going to explain any of my reasons. You'll have to take me on trust."

A buzzer buzzed. Concha said, "Phone. I'll take it," and vanished.

"O.K.," Matt conceded. "Tentatively granted. What goes?"

"I want you to take me out to Carter's for the next meeting of the Mañana Literary Society. Don't introduce me as Lieutenant; I'll be just another tomorrower."

"I ask you no questions and you tell me no lies, is that it?"

"That's about the size of it."

"Well for one thing, Terence, you've got a wrong idea of the M.L.S. It isn't a matter of regular meetings. It's just when some of the boys happen to get together, usually at Carter's. And for another, I don't know as I like furnishing the sheep's clothing for a wolf like you in our quiet flock."

Marshall set down his beer. "Matt, if I talked I could make you see how important this might be. There's a damned good chance it could solve one murder and forestall another. And if you insist, I'll talk. But I don't want to. Not yet."

Matt started to speak, then sat glaring into his beer. "Friendship's one thing," he said at last, "and police duty's another. I don't know as I'm willing to—"

It was just then that Concha returned. "The phone's for you, Lieutenant, and it's Sister Ursula of all people. Oh and look, while I think of it: we're going out to Carter's tonight, and he always likes to meet people. Why don't you and Leona come along? You'll like fantasy writers. They're nuts."

Matt shrugged resignedly. "You can't win."

Marshall was smiling to himself as he answered the phone. "Yes, Sister?"

"Leona told me you weren't home yet, so I thought I'd try here. It might be important."

"Yes?"

"That rosary, you know. Sister Perpetua says it's a very famous piece of carving which was thought to be lost. She says it was done by Domenico Saltimbanco, which is apparently a most eminent name from the way she pronounces it, and was carved to order for the first Mrs. Fowler Foulkes."

Marshall expressed himself, and then hastily apologized.

"Don't apologize, Lieutenant. It is surprising, isn't it, when we were speaking of Hilary Foulkes only this afternoon? But this isn't Hilary's mother; I think he was born of the second marriage. The first Mrs. Foulkes was a most prominent laywoman, you know."

"I don't know how I can thank you, Sister."

"If you really wanted to thank me . . . But no. I won't even ask it. I do try to be good, you know. Goodbye, Lieutenant."

VII

The sign said:

! ! ! DANGER ! ! !
NITROSYNCRETIC LABORATORY
! KEEP OUT !

Marshall paused and stared. "So," he observed. "And what the hell is a nitrosyncretic laboratory?"

Matt Duncan smiled. "Nice gag, isn't it? You see, the way this house is situated on a hill, people come to this door before the proper main door. This is Austin's work-room, and he used to have a hell of a time with *Liberty* salesmen. Poundings on the door are distracting-like when you're working on the collapse of an interstellar empire. But since he put up that sign, salesmen take one look, shudder, and get the hell out."

Leona laughed. "I'll have to try something like that for when the children take naps."

"The children . . ." Concha repeated. "It must be nice to say that so casually."

"Do I really sound casual? I know I try to, but I still go sort of warm all over."

Marshall coughed. "The children are home and asleep and there's a competent girl in charge of them. For the moment they're hers, and we're just people. Come on, darling. Let's see the science fiction menagerie."

Bernice Carter met them at the proper door. "Austin's holding forth," she said softly. "We'll postpone introductions till he's done."

"These people," Matt told her, "are Marshalls. They just want to listen."

"They'll have the chance," said Bernice.

The menagerie was meager this evening. In the large living-room were only five men. The tall thin one established in the heavy chair under the reading lamp Marshall rightly took for his host. Of the others, one was somewhat plump and somewhat short—rather like a poor man's edition of Hilary without that almost unconscious assumption of self-importance which only being born heir to the Foulkes fortune could give. One was a stocky individual with a goatee (and no mustache) and a serious air. One was an open-faced youth who might well be a college sophomore. The fourth was a small sharp-faced man whose little eyes conveyed an odd mixture of boredom and complete absorption.

"And that," Austin Carter was saying, "is just the trouble with his stuff. It's too damned galactic. Science fiction can be interesting only so long as you preserve the human frame of reference. Of course the reader should think, 'Golly, this is wonderful! Space ships and blasters and stuff!' But he should also think 'After all, maybe that's just the way I'd feel if I rode on a space ship.' If your concepts become too grandiose, you've left the reader a thousand parsecs behind."

"Still," the sharp-faced man protested, "his stuff sells. And his fans yowl for more."

"I'm laying a bet they won't much longer. You can distend a reader's mind with new concepts only so far. Eventually he says 'Phooey!' and goes back to the more homely commonplaces of Joe here, or me, who modestly consider the destruction of a solar system or maybe just a planet as colossal enough, without annihilating galaxies left and right."

The sophomore opened his mouth, considered, and said hesitantly, "Stapledon."

"Olaf Stapledon's a special case. For one thing, he's a great writer, which most of us haven't much hope of being. For another, he's not hitting the magazine market. But most of all, he's got the amazing faculty of leading you on so gradually that you're willing to accept his vasty concepts as familiar."

"And that," said the goatee, "is one of the greatest services that science fiction can render to science. In which respect Stapledon is surely the most notable talent to enter the field since Fowler Foulkes."

Austin Carter frowned at the name of the Master. The sharp-faced man snorted. Bernice took advantage of the silence to become hostess.

"These people seem to be listening raptly, but they might as well know who they're listening to. Or whom, just in case they're that kind of people. Matt, I think you know everybody, and probably you do too, Concha. And these, Matt informs me, are Marshalls. My husband, Austin Carter, Mr. Runcible," (the plumpish one) "Mr. Phyn," (the sharp-faced one) "Mr. Chantrelle," (the goatee) "and Joe Henderson."

Marshall and Leona duly gave and received greetings.

"They're novices," Matt explained. "Don't expect them to show due reverence for a great name. And I don't mean you, Austin."

"So?" Marshall glanced inquiringly at the poor man's Hilary. Runcible, if not a great name, was at least a delightfully freakish one.

Runcible shook his head and waved an indefinite gesture of disclaimer. Austin Carter laughed. "No. Runcible so far is just a name signed to letters to the editor. Though you might mark it down for future reference; some first-rate men have come up from the fan ranks. But the name that struck Matt dumb with awe when he first heard it was Joe Henderson."

The sophomore shuffled and hung his head. "I write a little."

"By which," Bernice Carter translated, "he means that he's the oldest name in science fiction that's still big-time. When he can find the time between hacking out Captain Comet, he can still turn out stuff that puts young upstarts like Austin and me right in our places. He's been leading the field for fifteen years, and he still looks nineteen and if only I had a goose handy I could offer a very pretty demonstration of Joe not saying boo to it."

Joe Henderson's grin spread over his face as slowly as that of the Cheshire Cat and far more warmly. "Get along with you, Berni," he drawled.

Carter slapped him on the back. "The modesty of true genius," he announced. "Which makes me just as glad that I've never laid claim to either quality. But as I was saying to Joe when you folks came in—"

"One more minute of being hostess," Bernice interrupted. "Then you can go on." She collected wraps, took orders for drinks, and vanished.

"Anybody else coming?" Matt asked. "I'd like these poor innocents to see the M.L.S. in full swing."

"Anson Macdonald and Lyle Monroe may be around, and possibly Tony Boucher. Tell me, Matt, what'd you think of that last opus of Tony's?"

"Nuts. He wrote it with his eyes shut and one hand tied behind him. Same old stuff. Mutiny on a space ship, the uncharted asteroid loaded with uranium ore, and Martians trying to steal it on a time warp. Hell, it's routine."

Marshall blinked. "It's a little hard for an innocent, as Matt rightly calls me, to take that all in one gulp. I can't quite think of space ships and uranium and Martians as being drably commonplace."

"You get to think that way," said Austin Carter. "Supposing in real life you broke down a locked door and found a corpse bleeding from twenty wounds with no possible weapon any place. You'd maybe think it a trifle peculiar. But the mystery fan would say—"

Leona, being a mystery fan, picked up her cue. "Just another locked room."

"Exactly. So to us it's 'just another space ship' or 'just another time warp' or—"

"And what," Marshall asked, "is a time warp?"

"Mostly," Carter confessed, "a handy device. The term refers of course to the theory of the curvature of the Space-Time continuum. A warp in that framework could produce most curious results—possibly send you off, not on ordinary time travel, but completely out of this continuum."

"I like 'ordinary time travel,' " said Leona. "So prosaic."

"You can have fun with a time warp," Joe Henderson contributed.

Concha laughed. "The first time I came across one was in a story of yours, Joe. There was a reference to a character in an earlier episode who had gone off on a time warp and never been seen again. I thought it was a new kind of binge."

"Time warps," Carter went on, "are handy. They're part of the patter, like subspace, which don't ask me to explain. They let you do the damnedest things and make them sound scientific. As indeed they quite possibly are. Ask Chantrelle here; he's from Caltech."

"To my mind, Mr. Marshall," the goatee observed somewhat ponderously, "the free imagination of these writers is of more scientific value to the progress of mankind than ninety per cent of the theses written for the doctorate."

"And this imagination is absolutely free? You must get away with murder."

Carter shook his head. "Not any longer. Or at least not in the better markets. Good science fiction requires more self-consistency, more plausibility than any conceivable realism. Your world of the future can't exist in any high-fantastic vacuum. It's got to be real and detailed and inhabited by real people. With all due apologies to Captain Comet, Joe, the days of the pure gadget story and the interplanetary horse opera are over."

Marshall gratefully accepted beer from his hostess. "I'm not sure I follow those terms."

Carter looked about the group. "With two new victims, I'm afraid I'm about to repeat my famous lecture on science fiction. Runcible won't mind because there's nothing a fan loves like listening, and Phyn here is always hopeful I may say something worth stealing. To the others I apologize, but here goes:

"Science fiction is essentially a magazine field. Outside of Fowler Foulkes and H. G. Wells, practically no contemporary imaginative writer has been commercially successful in book form. So its development has to be studied in the mags. And these, way back in the early days, were possibly, to the non-fan outsider, not so good. They had, to be sure, scope and imagination, an originality and a vigor that few other pulps could equal; and neither quality had ever been markedly prized in the slick field.

"But they also had a sort of cold inhumanity. The science was the thing, and the hell with the people involved. On the one hand you had what I call the inter-planetary horse operas, which were sometimes pretty weak even on their science. These were pure Westerns translated into cosmic terms. Instead of fighting off bands of hostile red-skins, you fought off bands of hostile Martians, and as you pulled out your trusty blaster, they regularly bit the stardust.

"The gadget stories were more interesting. They frequently made honest attempts at forecasting scientific developments. Atomic power, stratosphere exploration, the rocket flight that so absorbs Chantrelle, all the features that may revolutionize the second half of this century as thoroughly as radio and the airplane have transformed this half—all these became familiar, workable things.

"But the writers stopped there. Interest lay in the gadget itself. And science fiction was headed for a blind alley until the realization came that even science fiction must remain fiction, and fiction is basically about people, not subatomic blasters nor time warps.

"So there's a new school now, and I suppose Don Stuart, the editor of *Surprising,* is as responsible as anybody. Don's idea was this, and it was revolutionary: Grant your gadgets, and start your story from there.

"In other words, assume certain advances in civilization, then work out convincingly just how those would affect the lives of ordinary individuals like you and me.

"For instance, in one story of René Lafayette's there is a noble amount of whisky-drinking, and the name of the whisky is Old Space Ranger. And that one phrase paints an entire picture of a civilization in which interplanetary travel is the merest commonplace. No amount of gadgetary description could make the fact of space ships so simply convincing.

"In other words, to sum it all up in a phrase of Don's: 'I want a story that would be published in a magazine of the twenty-fifth century.'"

VIII

After this lecture, the conversation grew general. Matt and the Carters talked shop, the thin-faced Phyn interjected an occasional word of wry commercialism, and Mr. Chantrelle spoke of the coming test run of his latest rocket car.

Marshall sat back and drank his beer. It was indeed a strange new world, and a fascinating one. But he could not give it his whole attention. The policeman's mind kept reverting to duty, and in the midst of phrases about klystrons and space orbits and the positronic brain tracks of Asimov's robots he tried to sum up these people in connection with the attempts on Hilary Foulkes' life.

They didn't fit. Not at all well. Despite the high-flown fantasy of their conversation, they were as quietly ordinary people as he ever encountered. Or where they? Were not their very ordinary traits the possible marks of murder?

Motives he could not know yet; but it seemed not too unlikely that anyone in this field might at some time have had a run-in with Hilary. And granting motive, how could these individuals react?

Bernice Carter was coolly efficient as a hostess and as a conversationalist. Might that efficiency extend to the calm performance of a necessary elimination?

Austin Carter was, in a far more intelligent way, as self-sufficient and self-important as Hilary. Might two such dominances conflict fatally?

Phyn (apparently an agent specializing in this field of fiction) was shrewd and acquisitive. Might he not find personal gain a sufficient motive for any action?

Joe Henderson was inarticulate and repressed. Might repressions gathered too long burst forth lethally?

Chantrelle . . .

But this was random guesswork, unworthy of a detective lieutenant even when off duty. Marshall waited for the next passing of an angel and said, "I met somebody the other day might interest people in your field. Hilary Foulkes—the great Fowler's son."

"Oh," said Austin Carter. "Hilary." His voice was absolutely expressionless.

"You know him?"

"I know his brother-in-law, D. Vance Wimpole. There, sir, is one of the damnedest and most fabulous figures in the whole pulp field, and he tackles most of it. Fair on science fiction and excellent on fantasy. But what I mean by fabulous: One night in New York Don Stuart and I were seeing him off to Chicago. He got talking and outlined a fantasy short ad lib from hook to tag. Don liked it, but said, 'The trouble is, now you'll never write it. You never do write what you've talked out first.' And Vance said, 'Oh, won't I?'

"He left by train for Chicago around eight. The next morning the story was on Don's desk, air-mail special delivery from Chi. I won't say it was a masterpiece, but it was publishable as it stood and it drew good fan mail."

Joe Henderson nodded. "That's Vance for you."

"Where is he now?" Bernice asked.

"I had a letter from him yesterday," Chantrelle said. "Postmarked from Victoria. He's on his way back from Alaska and should be here in a week or so. I'm postponing the test run until he arrives."

"Sure of that?" the agent demanded. "I thought—"

"Yes?"

"Nothing."

"I'd like to meet this prodigy," said Marshall. "But about—"

"Oh," Carter picked up his story, "Vance is something. He uses an especially geared electric typewriter because he composes faster than any ordinary machine can go. He works only six months out of the year and spends the other six hunting anything from polar bears to blondes. He—"

Marshall reluctantly listened to all the unbelievable saga of D. Vance Wimpole. The subject of Hilary had been deftly killed, but not before he had caught a sharp glitter in the little eyes of Phyn and an expression of relief on the face of Bernice Carter as her husband maneuvered away.

Around eleven Leona interrupted a fascinating discussion (on whether you could construct a robot werewolf) to say, "This is fun, but we've got a girl staying with the children and she has to go home sometime."

The Carters' sorrow sounded most sincere. "You too, Matt?" Austin added.

"Afraid so. I want to get some work done in the morning."

"Just a minute then. I want to show you those pictures of the Denvention. I keep forgetting."

As Carter went downstairs to the Nitrosyncretic Laboratory, Marshall asked, "I'm still innocent. What's a Denvention?"

Bernice explained. "The science fiction fans are highly organized, and they have Annual World Conventions. The last one was in Denver, so the fans, ever incorrigible neologists, called it the Denvention. The next one's here in Los Angeles, and I'm afraid it's called the Pacificon."

There followed ten minutes of looking at pictures of people

of whom Marshall knew nothing. Carter, he gathered, was an enthusiastic camera fiend with every known photographic gadget and even an adjunct to the Nitro Lab in which he did his own developing and printing. The pictures were good, particularly the nude which had wandered in by mistake. It reminded him of Leona in her unreformed days. He said as much, and the men thereafter accorded her a certain respect which they had not displayed to the mother of two wonderful children.

"And what," he asked at last, "is this weird display?"

"That?" They had a costume party on the last night. Come as Your Favorite Stf Character. Berni wanted to go as Dale Arden, but I'm afraid it was an overambitious project."

"And who's this lad with the beard and the stick?"

"That's Austin," said Bernice. "I took this picture."

"So. And what did you finally go as?"

"The Wicked Queen of Ixion in Joe's *Cosmic Legion* stories. It was fun."

IX

"It was fun," Leona echoed as they went down the stairs. "I think I'll lay off mysteries for a while and try this strange stuff. It sounds appetizing. How about you? How about you?" she repeated after a silence.

"Uh? Oh. Sorry dear." Lieutenant Marshall was wondering if he should tell Hilary Foulkes how shrewd a guess he had suddenly made as to the identity of his so far fumbling murderer.

THREE

THE THIRD DAY:
Saturday, November 1, 1941

A photograph and the knowledge that one of the individuals depicted had himself developed the picture.

It was little enough to go on, Marshall reflected as he sat at his desk and went over the latest routine reports on Jonathan Tarbell, which told him precisely nothing.

And what tied the two cases together? A phone number and a rosary.

Any of his colleagues would hoot at him, or at best smile derisively. But Marshall could not help believing that the two cases were one, and that his prime duty at the moment was not so much to crack the murder of the floater Tarbell as to prevent the murder of Hilary Foulkes.

"Let him get himself murdered," Leona had protested sleepily after they were in bed last night. "Then it'll be a big case and there'll be headlines about Heir to Foulkes Estate and you can solve it and be famous. And who cares if Hilary lives or dies?"

Then Marshall had tried to explain the basic sanctity and importance of human life, any life (which was a curious concept to expound in the 1940's), and the significance of the preventive over the punitive in a policeman's duties until Leona said that having debated at Oxford was swell only at this hour it might wake the children. So he slept, but in his dreams he kept pursuing and trying to frustrate a barrel-chested, black-bearded man who was seeking to garotte with a rosary that oddly named fan who resembled Hilary.

There was something about a rocket too, and an old volume of *Who's What,* though he couldn't remember in the morning where they fitted in. (A complete record of this dream would have been of the greatest interest to Austin Carter or Hugo Chantrelle, both of whom were disciples of J. W. Dunne.)

The dream reminded him. He set aside the Tarbell reports, took up the phone, dialed an inter-office number, and gave instructions for a thorough canvassing of all theatrical costumers to trace the rental of a large black spade beard of the Derringer model. Probably unnecessary, but worth a try.

He hesitated, phone in hand. Then he nodded resolutely to himself, got an outside line, and dialed Hilary Foulkes' unlisted number.

Veronica Foulkes' "Hello" was rich with indefinite emotional overtones. Marshall could imagine her investing a grocery order, if she ever stooped to so plebeian a task, with the quality of a Borgia laying in the month's supply of acqua tofana.

"May I speak to Mr. Foulkes?"

"Who is this please?"

"The fiend with the pipe," said Marshall perversely, and wondered if she would hang up.

She didn't. In a moment Hilary's smooth deep voice was asking, "Yes? Yes?"

"Marshall speaking, Mr. Foulkes."

"Oh. Hold on a minute. I'll take this on the extension in my study. Hold on."

Marshall held on and wondered why Hilary always repeated everything. It was like a stammer or a tic, and probably a psychoanalyst could have fun with it.

"Yes," Hilary resumed after a few seconds. "Didn't want to disturb my wife, Lieutenant. She's been terribly nervous since that bomb episode. Terribly. And what did you find out about that? What sort of bomb was it?"

"Very common type. No creative imagination. Anyone with underworld connections could pick one up easily."

"Underworld connections? But Lieutenant . . . You can't mean I'm being threatened by a gang?"

"Don't jump to conclusions, Mr. Foulkes. The damnedest people can have some underworld connections. Especially with the political setup in this town. I'll lay odds that even a stranger in town like you, if he had as much as you have, could get hold of such a machine after a little nosing about and palm-greasing. Our only hope of tracing it is through a stool, and that's not too likely."

"Oh," said Hilary sadly.

"But why I called: Have you thought of any more—shall I say, candidates?"

"No, Lieutenant. Heavens no. Excepting that as I said—"

"Yes. The various people you may have offended as executor of the estate. So tell me: Have you ever offended one Austin Carter?"

"Carter? Carter? Let me see . . . Oh yes. That was the man who wanted to quote all sorts of things from my father's works and wouldn't pay for them. I was firm about it; so then he cut out the quotations rather than pay me anything."

"Was that all?"

"Yes, Lieutenant. Yes, excepting . . . Well," Hilary chuckled, "I confess I may have played some small part in causing Metropolis Pictures to decide against Mr. Carter's last novel. I naturally felt that a man who has displayed such shocking irreverence toward my father hardly belonged in the same studio that has done such fine work in producing Dr. Derringer films. Naturally."

"Naturally," Marshall echoed, admiring the ingenuous ingenuity with which Hilary presented his case.

"But Lieutenant—"

"Yes?"

"Do you mean to imply that you . . . that you have any evidence against this Mr. Carter?"

Marshall hesitated. "Will you be home this afternoon?"

"Yes."

"Good, I'll be out to see you. I want to ask you a few more questions and give you some idea of what evidence I have. Then we can see if you wish to prefer charges."

"My!" Hilary gasped. "This is such prompt work, Lieutenant. So very prompt. I never expected . . ."

There was a long silence. Marshall said "Yes?" twice. There was no answer. He said "Mr. Foulkes!" loudly, and he heard a groan and a sort of thudding crash. Then there was only silence on the line. He jiggled the phone cradle fruitlessly, then hung up and dialed again. He got the busy signal; the Foulkes' receiver was still off.

Marshall got an inter-office number, gave certain instructions, hung up, and reached for his hat.

Then, on an afterthought, he dialed the number found on Jonathan Tarbell.

II

There was no excitement in front of the apartment hotel. No crowds, no patrol car.

"Stable doors, maybe," Marshall said to Sergeant Ragland. "But you stay here in front of the entrance. There shouldn't be much mid-morning traffic. Get the names of everybody that comes out and his reason for being here."

His first stop was at the manager's apartment.

Her greeting was reserved. "Yes, I did go up to the Foulkeses'. But Mrs. Foulkes herself answered the door and assured me that her husband was working in his study as usual. I couldn't very well force my way in, could I? And since you didn't choose to tell me what was the matter . . ."

"All right," Marshall said. "Thanks."

"I hope you realize," she went on, "that this apartment house is not accustomed to having the police—"

"Sorry. But we go where we're needed. Thank you."

He rode up in the elevator half-relieved. If Veronica Foulkes, in the same apartment, was not aware that anything was wrong . . . He paused in his thoughts. Unless, of course, Mrs. Foulkes herself . . .

The maid Alice answered the bell at the Foulkes apartment.

"I'd like to speak to Mr. Foulkes."

"He's in his study, sir, and I'm afraid he won't want to be disturbed."

"It's most important. I—"

"I remember, sir. You're the police. But even for the police I don't like to interrupt Mr. Foulkes. He's very particular, sir."

"What is it, Alice?" Veronica Foulkes, in a negligee too impressively sumptuous to be seductive, came up behind the maid. Her eyes gleamed as she saw the visitor. "You again!"

"Sorry, Mrs. Foulkes. But it's highly important that I speak with your husband at once."

She seemed to repress a whole anthology of remarks as she glanced at the servant. "You were talking to him on the phone not half an hour ago."

"Have you seen him since then?"

"No. He's still in his study."

"Then I'm afraid I must ask you to let me in. Or," Marshall added as she hesitated, "must I use official persuasion?"

Veronica made a gesture of resignation. "Very well. Come in."

She crossed the living-room and knocked on the door of the study. She repeated the knock twice, then opened the door.

As Marshall followed her into the living-room, a gentle voice said, "Good morning, Lieutenant."

Marshall looked about and started. He was so amazed to behold Sister Ursula in this apartment that he had still found no words of greeting when Veronica Foulkes' sharp scream shrilled through the room.

"He's dead!" Veronica gasped. There seemed to be terror and genuine sorrow in her voice. She stood rooted in the doorway, unable to make her body follow her gaze to what lay on the floor.

Marshall pushed past her and bent over Hilary Foulkes. There was almost no blood; but only the ornate metal handle of the weapon was visible between the plumply fleshed shoulder-blades. The knife itself was buried. The telephone lay sprawled on the floor as inert and voiceless as its owner.

"You!" Veronica went on intensely. "Until I met you, nothing ever happened. Life was all right then. And what do you do? First you insult me, then you beat poor Hilary into unconsciousness, then you attack me, and now . . ."

Marshall rose. Some of the tension had faded from his face. "I'm sorry to be anticlimactic, Mrs. Foulkes, but your husband is still alive. And medical aid is more important right now than disrupting your version of the facts." He went past her again into the living-room and turned to Sister Ursula. Sister Felicitas, he noticed, was there too, and as usual, asleep.

"Sister," he said sincerely, "I don't know how in the name of your favorite saint you got here, but I've never been gladder to see anyone. I'm going to ask you to be useful. If I were a sheriff I'd swear you in as deputy. Watch these women and don't let anyone, for any reason, enter that study till the doctor comes."

Sister Ursula nodded and said "Certainly." The maid goggled, and the cousin whom Marshall had met before hesitated in the hall doorway, looking questioningly at Veronica.

"My husband's dying!" Mrs. Foulkes exclaimed. "And you forbid me to—"

"I'm afraid I do."

"I'd like to see you stop me!"

She saw. As she started toward Hilary's body, Marshall's hand clamped down on her wrist and a quick jerk brought her across the room and deposited her on the sofa beside the nuns. "And stay there!" he said tersely.

Marshall used the manager's phone downstairs. To use the Foulkes phone would mean replacing the fallen apparatus, and he wanted an exact photograph of that. While the dowager-like manager dithered about murmuring prayers that the name of the house could be kept out of the papers, he requested an ambulance, a doctor, a fingerprint man, and a photographer, and thanked his stars for the foresight which had made sure before he left headquarters that such a request could be instantly filled.

Sergeant Ragland stood in the lobby, still guarding the door. "There wasn't anybody tried to get out," he said.

"Sorry, Rags. Come on upstairs. May be something for you there."

"D.O.A., Lieutenant?" Ragland brightened.

"Not quite. Keep your fingers crossed."

The Lieutenant stationed his disappointed Sergeant at the door leading into the study and confronted the assembled witnesses. Five of them, and all women. He groaned a little, but the thought of the astute Sister Ursula on the scene of the crime consoled him.

"All right," he begán. "At ten thirty-five I telephoned Mr. Foulkes. You, Mrs. Foulkes, answered the call and brought him to this phone here. He wanted to talk privately and went off to the extension phone in the study. I take it he shut the door after him?"

Veronica nodded.

"All right. Go on from there."

"Then the manager rang the bell and wanted to see my husband, heaven knows why. I told her he was working."

"My doing, I'm afraid. I thought that if anything had happened she might get needed help to him before I could get here. And then?"

"Then," said Veronica Foulkes with deadly restraint, "you came."

"But that's a half hour later, and what happened from then on I know myself. What I want to find out now is the in-between."

Sister Ursula spoke up. "But Mrs. Foulkes is quite correct. So far as we in this room knew, nothing happened —that is, nothing concerning Mr. Foulkes—between the time he took your call and your own arrival here."

"You were here all that time, Sister?"

"Here in this room, with Mrs. Foulkes and Sister Felicitas."

He turned to the maid. "And where were you?"

"In the kitchen, sir, baking. That's why I didn't answer the phone when you called. I'd just finished my work when you rang the doorbell, sir."

"And you, Miss—?"

"Green," said the cousin. "And may I hope you forget other things as easily as my name?"

Marshall blushed and felt Sister Ursula's curious eyes upon him.

"You . . . you did send for a doctor?" the girl went on eagerly.

"Of course, Miss Green. And there's nothing we can do for your cousin meanwhile. Any amateur attempt to shift him or to remove the knife might be exceedingly dangerous."

"But he—?" Her voice shook a little.

"I don't think there's any danger. And the best way you can help him is by helping me to prevent another such attack." His voice was surprisingly gentle. It was pleasantly unusual to find somebody who seemed really to give a damn about Hilary. "So if you'll tell me where you were from ten thirty-five until my arrival here?"

"In my room, typing some letters that Cousin Hilary had dictated."

"So." Marshall frowned. "I'm not very certain of the groundplan of this apartment."

"I know." The girl half laughed, and Marshall reddened again. "But it's simple enough, at least as far as you're concerned now. East of this living-room—on that side, that is—there's only Hilary's study and a bath opening off it. To the west there's the rest of the apartment: two bedrooms and the kitchen and dinette and the maid's room."

Marshall digested the description. "So. Then anyone—say either you or Alice—coming from the rest of the apartment to the study would have to come through this room?"

"Yes. Or of course we could go out into the hall and around. The study has its own separate entrance."

Marshall nodded. "All right. Now, Sister, what time did you get here?"

"A little after ten, Lieutenant."

"You were here in this room when Mr. Foulkes took my call?"

"Yes. He was in the dinette finishing breakfast. He came in here (I must say he looked rather surprised to see Sister Felicitas and me) and went on into the study."

"And you stayed here . . .?"

"All the rest of the time until you arrived. And if I may anticipate your next question: No one went through this door to the study after Mr. Foulkes."

"Neither in nor out?"

"Neither."

"And Mrs. Foulkes was with you all that time?"

"This is too much!" Veronica exploded. "Not only must you ask my guests and my dependants all the questions that you should rightfully ask me, but now you go as far as to imply—"

"Please, Mrs. Foulkes," Sister Ursula interposed gently. "The Lieutenant has only been performing his routine duties. I hope," she added, with what might, from any one else, almost have been a wink.

"Thank you, Sister. And Mrs. Foulkes was with you?"

"Yes."

"Did you hear any noise from the study?"

"I confess that I didn't. Did you, Mrs. Foulkes?"

"No," Veronica was careful to speak to the nun rather than to the officer.

"But then she and I were deeply engrossed in conversation, and Sister Felicitas, as you know, is rather deaf. I think it would have had to be a serious struggle to make itself heard."

"So. Then it's clear that Mr. Foulkes' assailant came in through the hall door to the study and struck him down silently without any scuffle. All right. I think that's all I need to ask you at the moment. Please remain here, however, until after I've talked with the doctor, who should be here any minute." He rose, made a slight bow, and went into the study.

Hilary sprawled there undignifiedly in his shirt sleeves. (Today's shirt was a delicate mauve.) The splendid red-and-gold dressing gown was draped over a chair across the room. He was still unconscious. A good thing, that. Movement before the arrival of doctor and ambulance would simply entail needless pain and danger. Marshall contemplated the hilt and its angle, and calculated that the worst damage possible would be slight. He hoped.

He fumbled in his pocket, drew out a piece of chalk, bent down, and outlined the position of the body, worrying a little about the effect of chalk marks on a Persian rug. Leona, he was sure, would raise hell.

"Lieutenant!"

He stared up. "Sister! How did you get in here? Ragland!"

The Sergeant looked abashed. "She come in right after you, Lieutenant. I thought she was with you."

"All right. Well, Sister, since you're here—?"

Sister Ursula stood by the hall door. "Look at this."

Marshall looked. Not only was the button pressed which indicated that the door was locked. You could easily enough lock it behind you that way. But the night chain was on.

He said nothing. Holding the knob gently in a handkerchief, he turned it to release the lock and opened the door. With the chain on, it opened about an inch. Not conceivably far enough for a hand to reach in and hocus it.

Obstinate annoyance settled on his face. "Somebody put the latch on afterwards."

"Who? When? Remember, Lieutenant, that no one but Mr.

Foulkes went into this room before your arrival. After that, Mrs. Foulkes went only as far as the threshold. When she tried to go farther, you jerked her back. While you were gone, I obeyed your instructions and saw that no one came in here. Since then, Sergeant Ragland has been at the door."

"So?"

So . . . Please don't let my presence restrain you, Lieutenant. Express yourself as freely as you please. But I'm afraid you're confronted again with what Leona calls a locked room problem."

III

The doctor rose from his examination. "Nasty," he observed. "But I'll pull him through all right. O.K., boys!" He gestured to the ambulance attendants with the stretcher.

"Can't you wait till the photographer get's here?" Marshall protested.

"Sorry, my boy." He was younger than Marshall, but the phrase seemed part of his professional equipment. "Which would you sooner do: photograph a corpse or interview a healthy victim? Get along with it there."

"Hold on. We'll need his prints at least if we're to learn anything from this room. If this desk yields a stamping pad . . ." It did, and Marshall busied himself with Hilary's limp hands. "When can I talk to him?" he asked as he worked.

"Do I know? This afternoon possibly. Come around late and see. May have to put him under opiates though. Near thing, that. From where it went in, you'd expect it to have struck the heart. But the blow was directed toward the right. Odd."

Marshall set aside the printed paper. "You can load him now. You'll be careful of the hilt when you remove the knife?"

"Prints? I know my business, my boy, and if the murderer knew his it won't matter anyway. See you tonight."

"Just a minute," Sister Ursula interposed.

"Yes, Sister?"

"Could that wound possibly have been self-inflicted?"

The doctor gave a superior snort. "Look." He grabbed the Lieutenant, whirled him around, and jabbed a long finger at a point between the spine and the left clavicle. "Try stabbing yourself there. Just try it."

"I'm afraid my habit is rather hampering." Sister Ursula tried. "But it does seem as though if I had no sleeves I might reach there."

"Reach there, certainly." The doctor demonstrated. "Strain on the shoulder muscles, but you can reach. Possibly even strike. But you reach from below. So even if you struck with enough force to penetrate, which I doubt, the blow would be directed upwards. This wound points down."

"You couldn't reach there the other way?" Marshall asked. "From above?"

"Physical impossibility," the doctor snapped dogmatically.

The stretcher-bearers had passed into the next room. Veronica Foulkes was making inarticulate little moans as her unconscious husband passed by.

"Then he positively was attacked," said Marshall.

The doctor snorted again and stalked out wordlessly, in a sort of Groucho Marx crouch.

"So." Marshall whistled. "Thanks for specifying that point, Sister. I'd taken it for granted—always a bad thing to do. But now we know for certain, and where does it get us?" He walked over and opened the door of the bathroom. There was one small window. A midget might conceivably have squeezed through it, but even a midget must have disarranged the neat row of shaving things arranged on its sill. (They did not include, Marshall noticed, the talc which Hilary St. J. Foulkes had nationally endorsed.)

He pushed the shower curtain all the way back. The stall was empty.

He returned to the study. One of the large windows was open. Both had screens which were hooked on the inside. He unlatched one screen and leaned out. The wall here was absolutely blank save for windows. No cornices, nothing but window sills a good fifteen feet away in any direction. Three stories below was a bare cement area.

He turned around. "The problem" he stated, "isn't getting in. There's nothing to show that the assailant mightn't have been waiting in here, possibly hidden in the bathroom, when Hilary came to answer my call. But as for getting out . . . I can give you three possible descriptions, Sister, of this would-be murderer."

"Yes, Lieutenant?"

"All right. A, he is the Invisible Man in person and walked right past you out there. B, he has suction pads on his feet like a gecko, and hung on to the wall out there while he worked some sort of string-trick on the screens, then clambered to the ground or to the roof, still by suction. C, he has a pseudopodal finger that he inserted through the one-inch crack in the door to maneuver the chain into locking position. There you are; take your pick."

"I like the first one best," said Sister Ursula seriously. "The Invisible Man."

"And why?"

"Remember, Lieutenant, that that is the title, not only of a novel by Wells, but also of a short story by Chesterton. As a Catholic, I naturally prefer the latter."

Lieutenant Marshall shrugged resignedly. But before he could pursue this cryptic hint, the photographer and the fingerprint expert had arrived. The next twenty minutes were crowded.

When the experts were through, Marshall's patience was near an end and he knew no more than he had to start with. The prints in the room were almost exclusively Hilary's or the maid's, with here and there a random and plausible specimen of Miss Green's or of Mrs. Foulkes' (and securing the specimen prints of the latter had been one of the major nightmares in the expert's life). The hall door had only Hilary's prints on both inner and outer knobs, and no trace of gloved smudges. The telephone also had only his.

Marshall himself lay in the chalked outline for a photograph of the crime. That is, he lay in it as well as his six foot two could fit into the outline of Hilary's five foot nine. Then he experimented with falls from various positions, and concluded that Hilary must (as had indeed seemed obvious all along) have been struck down while he was seated at the desk telephoning. Sister Ursula checked that in the next room, with voices talking, the sounds even of Marshall's heavier body were audible but not strikingly noticeable. You heard them only if you were listening for them.

At last the Lieutenant again confronted the women in the livingroom. "I've done all I can here now," he said, "and there's nothing further I need to ask you until I've talked with Mr. Foulkes. You'll be doing the police a favor if you don't pester the hospital with attempts to see him until I notify you that he's receiving. In the meantime, you can all be trying to remember any events of this morning or earlier that might throw light on the matter, and especially any individuals you think likely to have made such an attempt. Of course, Mr. Foulkes may, and we trust he will, be able to tell us his assailant's identity without further ado. But we must be ready in case he can't. Sister, may I drive you home?"

"Certainly, Lieutenant. And you have room for Sister Felicitas too?"

He had forgotten the other nun completely. One always did.

IV

Sister Ursula occupied the front seat of the sedan with the Lieutenant. Sergeant Ragland climbed in back with Sister Felicitas and felt embarrassed by the combination of back seats and nuns until he decided that he might as well take a little snooze too.

"All right," said Marshall at last. "Now tell me why you were there."

Sister Ursula hesitated the least trifle. "You remember what I told you about Sister Patientia and her brailling *Beneath the Abyss*?"

"Yes."

"Well, she did want that work to get into the hands of the blind readers, and Mr. Foulkes' refusal made a terrible legal obstacle. She thought that if she appealed to him personally he might perhaps relent. But she is quite unused to dealing with the public; she lives almost as though she were in a cloistered order. And since I'm the one that Reverend Mother always uses for what you might call public relations work . . ."

"Was this Sister Patientia's own idea?"

"Well . . . I may have suggested to her that the personal approach often helps . . . "

"And how did you find out where Hilary lives?"

"I called the society gossip editor of the *Times*"

"So. And all because I was working on a murder case that somehow involved a rosary of the first Mrs. Foulkes."

"Lieutenant!" Sister Ursula frowned, but there was a smile half-hidden in her voice. "How can you accuse me of such a thing? You . . . you aren't angry with me, are you?"

"Angry?" Marshall grinned. "Sister, when I came to see you yesterday, my chief fear was that the Tarbell affair was too dull to tempt you. Things have changed now. If there ever was a case that demanded your peculiar perspicacity, this is it. And you don't have to worry about temptations any more. You're right in the middle of this. And you're going to hear all I know about it." So he told her, from Jonathan Tarbell through the attempts on Hilary's life on to his evening with the science fiction writers.

She nodded as he finished. "And you're suspicious of this Austin Carter?"

"Who could help being? He has a first-rate revenge motive, if Hilary queered a film sale for him. His photographic lab must contain some cyanide preparation, such as was used in the chocolates attempt, and he owns a Dr. Derringer disguise, which figured in the bomb episode."

"And does he," Sister Ursula asked gently, "have feet like a gecko or a pseudopodal finger?"

"Does anybody? Until we can crack the method of this attempt, the best thing to do is to ignore it and concentrate on the others. We saw once before, or rather you saw how an absolutely impossible situation can have a perfectly simple solution. And now tell me what happened when you went calling on Sister Patientia's behalf. Did you see Hilary?"

"He was just getting up when we arrived. I said we'd wait. And then imagine how amazed I was when our hostess came in to entertain us!"

Marshall chuckled. "Not nearly so amazed as she when she found me straddling her husband's body with a bomb ticking beside me. But what did she want with you that day at the convent anyway?"

"I think she wanted what every person wants at some time: peace and quiet, solace and solitude. Oh, I know she's a foolish, flamboyant, melodramatic woman, and quite possibly none too bright. But that's all the more reason why I think she was sincere. Her whole behavior is pointless, aimless. She has no foundation, nothing fixed to cling to. And she came there seeking something solid."

"She has a marriage. That's solid enough for Leona and me."

"She isn't Leona. And you aren't Hilary. In fact, Mrs. Foulkes seemed to have some romantic notion of breaking up that marriage and becoming a nun. 'Abandoning the carnal wedding bed for the spiritual' she called it, which I assured her was hardly a correct interpretation of the Church's attitude toward marriage."

"So. And do you think there's any danger of her doing that?"

"Only under the most unusual circumstances, say a very long desertion or the hopeless insanity of a husband, would there be even the remotest chance of a convent's accepting a married woman."

"Nothing but virgins?"

"Spinsters at least. And widows, of course."

Marshall jerked his head up. "Widows! There's a sweet thought. Do you suppose—Hell, this is nuts, but when religion goes fanatic no motivation is impossible. Do you suppose she could be so wrapped up in her Bride-of-Christ idea that she might make herself a widow?"

Sister Ursula smiled. "Beautiful, Lieutenant. I congratulate you on as admirably perverse a motive for murder as I have ever heard. But I'm afraid it couldn't apply here. Mrs. Foulkes is a self-indulgent emotionalist rather than a fanatic. I can't imagine her having the intense, the (if I may use the word in all seriousness) damnable wrong-headedness to pursue such a course. And besides, I think I cured her of her desire to join our order."

"How?"

"Simply by showing her what we do. You know why we're called the Sisters of Martha of Bethany. Our founder, Blessed Mother La Roche, was willing to admit that Mary had chosen the better part only because after all Our Lord said so; but she thought there was much to be said for Martha, who did all the housework while her sister was devotedly spiritual. So ours is an order that does the dirty work.

"Some of us nurse, some work with the blind, many of us simply do menial housework for poor invalid mothers. We salvage clothes, we help to establish hostels for youth and what you call floaters . . . Oh, we keep ourselves busy, Lieutenant. We glorify God by doing even unto the least of these all the good that we can. And

I'm afraid Mrs. Foulkes' vision of being a nun was composed solely of song and incense and beautiful white garments."

Marshall grinned. "I guess that'll hold her. And what did you talk about this morning?"

"Mostly more of the same. Though she didn't quite out and say it, what she wanted to know was if there were any religious orders in which one could be ecstatically holy by doing nothing whatsoever."

"And did this religious tête-à-tête happen to verge upon, say, rosaries?"

"Oddly enough, yes. But I don't think I learned anything. She brought the matter up herself. She said that she had read a pious memoir of her father-in-law's first wife which mentioned that unusual devotion of the Stations, and she wondered if it was such a rosary that she had seen in my hand. I said it was, and she wanted to know where it came from; but I managed to evade the question. I asked if perhaps her husband had such a rosary as a family relic, but she did a little evading herself and left us with the score tied."

"Love all. Nice Christian result. And goose-eggs seem to be what this case runs to . . ."

"It was nice of you to drive us home," Sister Ursula said after the car had stopped at the convent and she had waked Sister Felicitas. "And your next step?"

"To find out where Austin Carter was at ten-thirty this morning."

"Good luck. And," she added, "watch out for that pseudopod."

V

There was a sound of rapid typing behind the door of the Nitrosyncretic Laboratory. Marshall knocked.

Over the typing came a casual, "Go to hell!"

Marshall opened the door.

Half the room was filled with mysterious apparatus which he took to be for the developing and printing of pictures. The rest of the room contained a couch, a desk, and bookcases, filled chiefly with pulps. On one wall hung a vivid picture of a space ship being engulfed by what was presumably a space octopus. On the far wall, too distant to read distinctly, was a hand-drawn chronological chart.

Austin Carter typed three lines without looking up. Then he jerked the paper from his machine, laid it on a pile of manuscript, and said, "If I had any conscience, Marshall, I should firmly tell you to go to hell and stay there. But I've reached a good stopping place and I could stand a moment's rest and some beer. Join me?"

"Thanks." Marshall sat on the couch. "The room's a let-down after that admirable sign."

Carter went to a small refrigerator, such as usually serves for infant formula, withdrew two cans of beer, punctured them, and handed one to his guest. "Your health, sir!"

He was tall, this Carter, even a little taller than the Lieutenant, and of one same even slenderness from shoulders to hips. He held himself rather stiffly and moved with precision. Marshall groped for what the man reminded him of, and finally decided that it was Phileas Fogg, who went around the world in eighty days.

"I had an interesting time last night," he said. "Afraid Matt has seduced me into a new field of pleasure."

"Good. Always glad to make converts. Have you read any of Matt's stuff?"

"Not yet."

"He's a comer. Bit weak on the science side, but first-rate on fantasy."

Marshall glanced at the typewriter. "What did I break in in the midst of?"

"That? I think maybe that's going to be fun. Wheels-of-If sort of thing, you know."

"I'm afraid I don't know. Remember I'm an innocent."

"Well, it's—You know a little about modern time theory? J. W. Dunne, or maybe Priestley's popularizations of his work? But we needn't go into the details of that. To put it simply, let's say that every alternate implies its own future. In other words, whenever anything either could happen or not happen, it both does and does not happen, and two different world-lines go on from there."

Marshall thought a moment. "You mean that, say at this point in history, there will be one world if Hitler goes on unchecked or another if he is defeated?"

"Not exactly. That's old and obvious. What I mean is that there will be one world in which he goes on unchecked *and* another in which he is defeated. Each world exists as completely as the other. And so in the past. We are in a world in which the American revolution was a success. There is a world in which it was a failure.

"Now for instance in this story: I'm writing about a world in which Upton Sinclair won the EPIC campaign here in California, but Landon beat Roosevelt in '36. As a result California drifts more to the left and the nation to the extreme right until there is civil war, ending in the establishment on the west coast of the first English-speaking socialist republic. From there on . . . but I'm not too sure yet myself of all the details. You'd better wait and read it."

Marshall whistled. "You boys think of the goddamnedest things."

"Oh, the concept's not original with me. Just this application. I think Stanley Weinbaum was the first to play with it seriously in his *Worlds of If* in the old *Amazing*. Then there's de Camp's brilliant *Wheels of If,* and a Broadway turkey called *If Booth Had Missed,* and an excellent short story of Stephen Vincent Benét's about if Napoleon had been born twenty years earlier. And of course there's *If, or History Rewritten,* by Belloc and Chesterton and Guedalla and a dozen others—noble book! —or on a less cosmic plane, just the *if*'s of a human life, there's the Dunsany play *If* or Priestley's beautiful intellectual thriller, *Dangerous Corner.*" He reeled off this comprehensive bibliography as casually as he drank his beer.

"I'll try some of those," said Marshall.

"The best thing in that book of collected *If* essays is one called *If Lee Had Lost at Gettysburg.* You read that title and do a double take and say, 'But he *did* lose.' Then as you read on, you realize that the essay is written as by a professor living in the world in which Gettysburg was a great Southern victory, speculating on the possibilities of an *if*-world in which it was a defeat (that is, of course, our world) and thereby revealing the nature of his own. Dazzling job, and you know who wrote it? Winston Churchill, no less. There's a certain satisfaction in claiming him as a brother fantasy writer."

"I'll watch out for this story of yours," Marshall said, and meant it. "What's its name?"

"*EPIC.* Don Stuart likes one word titles, and that has a good double meaning in this case. Only it won't be under my name; it'll be by Robert Hadley."

"Why?"

"Because all the Austin Carter stories have to fit that chart over there. They're all interdependent—running characters and a consistent scheme of the future. That is, the events of story A are part of the background to story N happening a thousand years later. Sort of a millennial and galactic *comédie humaine,* and hard as hell to keep track of without that chart. And even with it. So whatever's outside the series is by Robert Hadley—that is, in a one-cent market or better. I don't like to hurt the commercial value of those names, so whenever I sell a reject for under a cent it's by Clyde Summers."

Marshall found himself fascinated, almost against his will. Austin Carter was possibly a trifle too fond of hearing himself talk, but he talked well. Another man's shop talk, if the man is intelligent, is the most interesting listening to be found; and this particular brand of shop talk was exceptionally so.

Nevertheless, the Lieutenant was there on duty. "What are your working hours?" he asked.

"I get up around eight-thirty as a rule, and I'm down here pounding by nine-thirty. Grab lunch whenever I feel like knocking off, and then if it's going good work on till three or four. Some men, I know, work best at night; but I like daytimes unless I'm rushing against a deadline."

"You've been working all day on this?"

"Yes, except for a sandwich a little while ago, and doing pretty nicely. It flows today."

"And alone, of course?" Carter looked at him oddly, and Marshall shifted to, "I mean, I wonder if you have many intruders like me?"

"No, and frankly I'd add 'Thank God' if you hadn't happened to hit me just at a moment when I was glad to knock off. Like another beer?"

"Thanks, I think I will. Tell me, Carter. You have a nice speculative mind. Do you ever apply it to other problems than science and fantasy?"

Austin Carter handed over the beer. "You mean like murder?"

"Why do you ask that?"

"I remembered your wife was a fan. Thought maybe she'd been springing some problem on you."

"As a matter of fact, that's just the case. She's trying her hand at a whodunit herself, and she's written herself into a locked room that she can't get out of. I thought maybe you'd like to play."

Carter nodded. "Go ahead. I'll try anything. Kick an idea around enough and sometimes you get places."

"All right: You've got a man with a knife plunged into his back at such an angle that the doctor swears the wound can't possibly be self-inflicted. He's in the study of his apartment, a room that has three doors. One of these leads to a dead end in a bathroom. One has three absolutely reliable witnesses in front of it who swear that no one has used it. The third is chained from the inside, and opens only an inch so that no hand could conceivably have reached in to fasten that chain. The window screens are latched on the inside, and the wall outside the windows, which are three stories from the ground, is absolutely sheer. She was trying a locked room to end all locked rooms, and I'm afraid she's over-reached herself."

Marshall was watching his host carefully throughout this recital, but he failed to detect the slightest flicker of guilty knowledge. Instead a growing grin of amusement spread over Carter's lean face. He took a long swig of beer and announced, "Simplicity itself, my dear Watson."

"That's nice," Marshall observed dryly. "So how did the murderer get out?"

"Well, I can think of three possible methods: A, he never got out because he never was there. The dagger was conveyed through space and plunged into the victim's heart by teleportation. See Charles Fort and don't laugh too hastily. If stones can fall from the ceiling in a closed room, if people can burn to death on unburnt beds, teleporting a dagger should be simple. Not that I'm certain of the angle of the direction on a teleported stab; but aside from that, do you like it?"

"Go on."

"B, the murderer dissembled his component atoms on one side of the wall, filtered through by osmosis, and reassembled them on the other side. Not that I think much of that one. I'm inclined to believe the conscious or sub-conscious rearrangement of the corporeal atoms accounts for the change of a werewolf and for the vampire's ability to pass through locked doors; but I doubt if any normal, non-supernatural being has mastered the power."

Marshall entered into the spirit of the thing. "Is there any guarantee that the murderer is normal and non-supernatural?"

"In a whodunit, yes. Rules of the game. In life, of course, you couldn't be so sure, could you? But C, and far more likely, the murderer simply entered and left through the fourth dimension of space. Remember that to a dweller in two-dimensional space, the problem of how to enter a square bounded on all four sides is a fantastic and insoluble one. To us, there's nothing to it; we simply enter through the third dimension. For instance—"

His deft fingers arranged four matches in a square on the desk. "Our friend Ignatius Q. Flatman" (who was a paper clip) "wants to get in there. He tries each wall of the square. *Im*-possible. But I can simply lift up Ignatius . . . so . . . and put him plumb square in the middle of his impossible situation. Just so your murderer could leave the locked room by means of another dimension perpendicular to all three of those we know. Or maybe prettier yet: maybe Something lifted him up and out of that room, just as I now lift up Ignatius, and maybe Something will eventually, in Its whimsical mood, drop him . . . so . . . right into your lap."

Marshall picked up Ignatius Q. Flatman and began twisting him cruelly. "That's all?"

"Did I say three? Well, here's a fourth, and this I like best. D, the murderer entered the room by perfectly ordinary methods and left it equally ordinarily, probably by the living-room door."

"But the evidence states—"

"I know. Only you see, the murderer did this at—What time did the murder occur?"

"Between ten-thirty and eleven."

"Then the murderer left around say nine o'clock."

"*Before* the murder?"

"Of course. He committed the murder, set the dials of his trusty time machine back an hour or so, and left the room. He could lock every conceivable exit from the inside and then calmly go back and leave by one of those exits *before* he had locked it. And better yet, to the Impossible Situation he could add the Perfect Alibi. He could then call on the detective in charge of the case and be visiting with him at the exact hour when the murder was being committed."

"I'm groggy," said Marshall.

"You see why we can't have detective stories in science fiction? It's the one impossible form for Don's hypothetical magazine of the twenty-fifth century. So many maneuverings are logically possible that you could never conceivably exclude the guilt of anyone. So you understand now how childishly simple your locked room is to a science fictioneer?"

"I understand." Marshall sounded a little grim.

"And now, Lieutenant, maybe you'll be so kind as to tell me if you have any idea who killed Hilary?"

Marshall was drinking beer when this grenade was so lightly tossed at him. His spluttering did not do his suit any good, and it was the one that had just come back from the cleaners. Now he was on his feet, and towering over the seated Carter.

"Unless," he said slowly, "you can offer me some convincing explanation of that remark, you're going to take a little trip downtown."

"I believe I am supposed at this point to light a cigaret nonchalantly? Very well, I hereby do so." The flame of the match was steady in his hand. "Of course I knew who you were Lieutenant. No, Matt didn't betray you; but I remembered your name faintly from accounts of the Rheem business and the Harrigan case, and I knew that Concha Duncan was a Harrigan. So when you, a homicide detective presumably on duty, come here and listen obligingly to my ravings until you get a chance to ask where I was this morning, I begin to have my suspicions. Then you propound in detail a 'hypothetical' murder case supposedly written by your wife. That was too much, Lieutenant. My own wife writes, I know, and very well indeed thank you; but I doubt if she'd do much with two children to look after. No, you miscast your wife so grievously that I became sure I was being Grilled for my Guilty Knowledge of a true murder."

"And why Hilary?" Marshall insisted quietly.

"Then it was? You don't mind if I emit a small *Yippee!*, do you?"

"You admit that you'd be glad to see him dead?"

"Of course. That's why I guessed that your visit concerned him. You'd mentioned him last night, and he was the only person I could think of that I might possibly have a motive for murdering."

For a moment the two men contemplated each other in silence. Then Austin Carter said, "Another beer?"

Marshall relaxed. "No, thanks."

"I've heard sinister rumors that the police won't accept the hospitality of murderers."

"That's the British for you. We're not so ritualistic. But I've got to go talk with Hilary."

Carter raised an eyebrow. "Lieutenant! Spiritualism yet?"

Marshall smiled. "No. You see, Carter, the attack failed. Hilary Foulkes is still very much alive."

Carter was startled and displeased. "Oh well," he said after a pause. "Half a loaf . . ."

"Of course."

"And I'm not under arrest?"

"We'll see what Hilary has to say. Thanks for the beer." Marshall paused in the doorway. "By the bye, confidential-like, which of those methods *did* you use?"

"The time machine, of course. Care for a demonstration?"

"Some other time. Soon."

The typing was resumed almost as soon as Marshall had shut the door behind him.

VI

Marshall mounted the impressive steps leading to the Cedars of Lebanon Hospital. At the Emergency Hospital they had told him, "He was well enough to move all right, and he insisted he wanted to recover in comfort." And the Cedars, which is *the* hospital in Hollywood, was of course far more fitting for a Foulkes scion than the Emergency.

"I'd like to see Mr. Foulkes," he said at the desk.

"Are you from the press?"

"Lord, no. I'm from the police."

"Oh. Just a moment. I'll see if he can see you."

Marshall frowned. "He's all right, isn't he?"

"Yes, but—"

A young man with buck teeth said, "What room's Hilary Foulkes?"

"Are you from the press?" the girl repeated.

"Sure thing, baby?" The youth waved a card.

"Go right on up. Third floor. The floor desk will direct you."

Marshall gasped. "Look!" he expostulated. "You keep the police waiting while you send that pup—"

"I'm sorry, sir. Mr. Foulkes left orders to admit only the press. If you'll wait a—"

But Marshall was already in the elevator. He didn't bother to be polite at the third floor desk. He showed his badge and said "Foulkes?" in a derby-hat voice.

There were five men in Hilary's room, all with pencils and pads. There was a pneumatic nurse deftly arranging flowers. And there was Hilary, propped up in bed, leaning forward to ease the wound in his back but looking otherwise as good as new. "D-e-r," he was saying, "r-i-n, g-e-r. Oh, Lieutenant, glad to see you. Very glad. Can you imagine it? Some of these youths haven't read the Dr. Derringer stories."

"A corrupt generation," Marshall observed. "As soon as the limelight begins to tire your eyes, Mr. Foulkes, there are a few matters I'd like to take up with you."

"Lieutenant," one of the reporters echoed. "Say! You wouldn't be from Homicide, would you?"

"It's an honorary commission from the Swiss navy," said Marshall, and watched the nurse abstractedly while Hilary made certain that every significant detail of his father's career went into the reporters' notebooks. Two books, presumably rushed from home for the occasion, stood by the bedside: *Life and Dr. Derringer: An Autobiography* by Fowler Foulkes, and *Foulkes the Man* by Darrell Wimpole. But Hilary never found the need to refer to them. He knew his subject as thoroughly as an actor in *Tobacco Road* must have known his lines toward the end of the run, or perhaps more appropriately, as thoroughly as a priest knows the words of the daily sacrifice of the Mass. The ritual words had their ritual gesture too. Instead of the gnawing of a turnip or the sign of the Cross, this was the pulling of a lobe. And with this echoing tug at the ear, Hilary seemed to recapture a little of the domineering dignity so characteristic of his father's publicity photographs.

"By the time," Marshall said when the last of the pressmen had left, "that all that goes out over the A.P. and the U.P., it ought to sell a few thousand more Foulkes items."

"You mean . . .?" Hilary laughed. "Why, Lieutenant, I do believe you think me guilty of playing this up simply to stimulate the influx of royalties. Heavens, I am shocked at such an idea. Shocked. It's simply that I owe so much to my father. Everything, you might say."

"You might."

"So naturally I feel that it is incumbent upon me to keep his memory green. I could hardly pass up the one pleasant aspect of this most astonishing occurrence."

"You're cool, Mr. Foulkes, aren't you?"

"I'm alive," said Hilary simply. "Alive. And that in itself is such a sheer and beautiful relief that I don't care to contemplate how close to death I was."

Marshall turned to the nurse. "Could you go have a beer or something? I'm afraid this conference is confidential official business."

The nurse looked from the badge to the Lieutenant's face. "I like Dick Tracy's jaw better," she said, but she left.

Hilary leaned farther forward. "Tell me, Lieutenant, have you arrested him?"

Marshall nearly sighed with relief. "Then you did see who it was. And I suppose the press learned it before I did. Well, come on. There'll be a warrant out for him in nothing flat."

"Oh, no, Lieutenant. You misunderstand me. I thought that by now *you'd* know."

Marshall swore. "I not only don't know Who, but I haven't the remotest idea of How. But start in at the beginning; maybe your story will give me some sort of a lead."

"I was talking to you," Hilary said slowly. "You remember. You were asking me about Austin Carter—" He broke off sharply. "Did he do it? Austin Carter, I mean?"

"Sure," said Marshall sourly. "He confessed. He did it with his little gadget."

"I don't understand."

"Do I? But go ahead. We'll catch up on Mr. Carter later."

"Very well. I was talking to you, as I say, when suddenly I heard a light footfall behind me. I started to turn, but before I could do so I felt a terrible pain between my shoulder-blades. A terrible pain. It was accompanied by a blow so strong that it knocked me forward against the desk. I tried to rise, but I lost my balance and fell to the floor. And that is the last that I remember until I was in the Emergency Hospital."

"You saw nothing, and you heard only a 'light footfall?' "

"Correct, Lieutenant."

"Could you gage anything by that footfall? Male or female? Large or small?"

"I'm afraid not. I didn't have time to listen carefully."

"It surprised you?"

"Very much."

"Then wouldn't that perhaps indicate male and heavy? If the sound could possibly have meant the not abnormal presence of your wife or the maid, you mightn't have been so startled."

Hilary beamed. "Beautiful, Lieutenant, beautiful. I am convinced that you will have apprehended this villain in no time. No time at all."

"Now tell me: When you went into the study, was the night chain fastened on the hall door?"

"I don't know. I'm sure I don't know. It usually is."

"And were the windows open or closed?"

"Closed."

"All of them?"

"I open one window when I go in to settle down for my morning's work on the estate accounts. But this morning I had come directly from the breakfast table to the phone."

Marshall grunted. "Gecko," he said.

Hilary peered at him curiously. "Yes, Lieutenant?"

"Hell, I might as well tell you. Even if a window was God knows why opened, nobody could get in or out through those windows."

"No. Of course not."

"Your wife and two visiting nuns were watching the door to the living-room. No one came out between the phone call and when I found you. And the night chain was on the hall door."

"My . . .!" said Hilary in an awed voice. "My . . .!"

"In short, if it weren't for the medical evidence on your wound, I'd suspect you of staging the whole thing for the sake of that press conference you just had—all purely to keep your father's memory green, of course."

"Lieutenant! Then this . . . Why, it's a locked room! Heavens, I am fortunate!"

"Fortunate?"

"Because it's you on the case. That Harrigan business was a locked room too, and look how neatly you disposed of that. So neatly. Why, you're the ideal man for this. And it's the ideal case for you."

"That's nice."

"And there must be some way of telling who was in there and attacked me. Fingerprints?" he suggested with the layman's blind confidence.

"Only yours and the maid's. Even yours alone on the dagger, with superimposed smudges, some of which were doubtless made in extracting it from you. Which while we're at it . . ." He reached into his breast pocket and produced a murderously beautiful piece of Persian metal work. "Do you know this?"

"Why, of course! That's my paper cutter. It was my father's. The Zemindar of Kota Guti presented it to him after reading *The Purple Light*. So many people think that was my father's best book, although he himself always preferred *The Missions in Twilight*. What do you think, Lieutenant?"

"I'll take up esthetics with you later, Mr. Foulkes. God knows there's nothing I like better than talking about Dr. Derringer; but right now I want to know if this back-stabbing paper cutter was on your desk this morning?"

"Frankly, Lieutenant, I don't know. Frankly, I was hurrying to answer the phone. I didn't notice my desk."

"It's unlikely that the murderer reached over your shoulder to snatch up the weapon. It was probably taken earlier, which would indicate . . . Was it there yesterday?"

"Yesterday? Yes. Yes, I'm sure. I used it to open my mail."

"At what time?"

"About three."

"Then at some time between three yesterday and ten-thirty this morning, this knife was stolen. Or even if the murderer somehow snaffled it right from under your nose, its use still implies familiarity with your study." Marshall ran his thumb along the blade. "See how short that is? That's what you probably owe your life to. The same wound with a longer blade could have been fatal."

"But Lieutenant . . ." Hilary's round face was puzzled.

"Yes?"

"There isn't anyone familiar with my study. Oh, of course Ron and Jenny and Alice. But all these others that we've spoken of, the people whom I may have offended as executor—that's all been by mail."

"So. And your brother-in-law?"

"Vance? But he's I don't know where and anyway . . ."

Marshall rose. "Just the same, I'd like to have a complete list of all your potential business enemies."

"I think Jenny could give you that more easily than I could. Miss Green, that is. She sometimes acts as my secretary, you know. She understands all about files and things."

"I'll speak to her. And I want you to know, for your own comfort, Mr. Foulkes, that there's going to be a police guard in the corridor of this hospital until you leave and another at your home thereafter. And I'd advise you not to see any newspapermen except in groups, and even then not without checking their credentials. I would advise you not to see them at all, but one impossible problem is enough to tackle at a time."

"Thank you, Lieutenant. Thank you. And you'll let me know when you catch my murderer, won't you?"

That last request was so touchingly childish that it set Marshall off on a new train of thought. Perhaps that was the key to Hilary: his infinite childishness. Like a child he avidly hoarded his treasures, like a child he marveled adoringly at the perfection of his wonderful father, like a child . . . Marshall thought of the ripe-fleshed Veronica Foulkes. What would it be like to be married to a child?

A telephone booth reminded him of a distasteful but necessary piece of routine work. He stepped in, dropped his nickel, and dialed the Duncans' number. They lived in the apartment house across the street, but he preferred the impersonality of a phone for this purpose.

He was glad that Concha answered. "Terence Marshall speaking," he said, "and don't tell Matt. Is he in earshot?"

"He went out for a walk. But what is this, Lieutenant? I suppose I ought to feel flattered when a handsome officer asks me to keep secrets from my husband, but I'm just plain puzzled."

"Only this: Where was Matt this morning?"

"Working, of course."

"You were in the apartment too?"

"I was ironing and mending. All but when I went out to shop."

"How long were you gone?"

"A half hour or more. Maybe almost an hour."

"And this was when?"

"Between ten and eleven. But Lieutenant, you sound like an alibi. I mean, like trying to check one. Are you—?"

"Please, Concha. You'll understand soon enough what this is all about. And you'll see why I insist you don't say a word to Matt about this. For the sake of routine, I had to check up on him; but there's no use worrying him."

"And he's in the clear?" Concha's voice was breathless.

"He's in the clear," Marshall lied, and hung up.

VII

The newspapers did well by the event. Even in the midst of wars and rumors of wars, the mysterious stabbing of a celebrity is always welcome, and Hilary had gladly provided further details of bombs and poisoned chocolates. The story was enriched by a brief biography of Fowler Foulkes and a condensed bibliography of his best known works; and all in all neither Hilary nor his publishers had the slightest cause for complaint.

Bernice Carter was reading the evening paper when her husband emerged from the Nitrosyncretic Laboratory. "Fate, milord, is just," she observed.

"Hilary?" Austin Carter asked casually.

"Uh huh. Somebody tried to carve him up under highly unlikely circumstances. That'll teach him to frustrate film sales. Here's the paper; you can—But hold on a minute!"

Carter struck a match on the stone fireplace and lit a cigarette. "Yes?"

"How did you know I meant Hilary?"

"People," he sighed, "keep asking me how I know things. Haven't they any faith in E.S.P.? Don't they realize my latent potentialities as a telepath?"

"But how did you know?"

"My trusting helpmate . . . That Lieutenant Marshall dropped in this afternoon and, as I believe the proper phrase goes, grilled me. Oh, very unobtrusively, you understand."

"And what did you do?"

"What should I do? I confessed, of course. Worked out a magnificent scheme for committing murder with a time machine. I think it'll make a good novelet for Don."

Bernice smiled. "Scavenger! Here I try to frame my imaginings out of whole cloth, but you simply grab everything that happens and twist it into scientifiction. Thank God at least for Don's strict standards of censorship. They're all that prevents my most intimate secrets from being broadcast to every newsstand at a cent a word."

"A cent and a half, I think," Austin Carter said judiciously. "They'd surely rate a bonus."

"But, sweet . . ." Bernice's cool voice was for once a trifle perturbed.

"Yes, madam?"

"If the Lieutenant thought you were worth grilling . . . You haven't—you aren't tied up with this in any way, are you? You didn't . . . do anything to Hilary?"

"No, madam." His voice was level and convincing.

Bernice smiled again. "Then why the hell didn't you?"

VIII

Veronica Foulkes threw down the paper. Her teacup rattled ominously as she stirred it. "Not a word about me! Why, Hilary might not even have a wife for all that . . . that rag says."

"Come now, Veronica," Jenny Green protested. "How can you worry about a trifle like that when Hilary's lying there in that hospital—"

"—in perfect ease and comfort with a beautiful nurse and reporters simply flocking around him. No, Jenny, I haven't much sympathy to waste on Hilary. Heaven knows how he got into this trouble, but I think he's come out of it very luckily. Hilary doesn't know what nerves are, any more than you do."

"But is he out of it? If they've made all these attempts, they aren't going to stop now, are they?"

Veronica set down the cup she was lifting. "My God, Jenny! That's true. They might come back and . . . Oh but no. That dreadful Lieutenant has given him a police guard and it's coming home with him and we're perfectly safe. So do relax, dear. Can't you see how I need soothing? A woman with my nerves can stand only so much."

Jenny Green left a fresh cup untouched and rose. "I see. You know, Ron, I can stand only so much too."

"You can stand . . .! Oh but my dear! And what concern is it of yours, I'd like to know? Oh, I know Hilary is your cousin, and very fortunate you've been having such a lovely home here with us, and that's all the more reason you should show a little consideration for me. How many wives, I ask you, would let their husbands bring relatives into their own house to live with them?"

"Come off it, Veronica." Jenny Green was not quite smiling. "If you hadn't tolerated me in your lovely home, Hilary would have had to have a typist. And how many wives would let their husband et cetera as above?"

Veronica laughed. "Now that, my dear Jenny, is simply nonsense. Do you think for a moment that I could be *jealous* of Hilary? Do you think I don't know . . . " She stopped herself. "All I can say is, if any woman could ever lure Hilary into being unfaithful to me, she'd be welcome to what she got. And what do you think that means to a woman of my—"

"Veronica." Jenny's voice was cold. "Sometimes I think it would be better for everyone, and certainly for Hilary, if you would simply stop talking and go ahead and take either a lover or the veil. But I'm afraid the trouble is you'd want to do both."

"How dare . . .!" Veronica's ordinarily throaty voice grew speechlessly shrill. "If Hilary ever—Where are you going?"

"To my room. I need to do some typing for Hilary."

Veronica Foulkes, left alone, bit her lips, stamped her foot, and squeezed from her eyes the start of a spate of tears. Then abruptly she reconsidered, wiped her eyes, and examined her face in a compact mirror. It was possible that reporters might call.

IX

The green-furred, six-legged corpse of the blasted thryx slung across his brawny shoulders, Captain Comet made his laborious way over the endless Martian desert. For two days he had seen no sign of life, save for the thryx, whose murderous attack he had foiled at the last minute by the decompo-rays of his blaster.

Now even the blaster was no longer of use. It needed recharging, and that must wait until he found the space ship again. His emergency sythetic rations were dwindling too. Gah-Djet, the mechanical brain, was in the hands of the xurghil smugglers. Adam Fink was a clanking prisoner in the power of the mad priests of Ctarbuj. And the Princess Zurilla . . .

Captain Comet shook his weary head to clear it of these dismal thoughts. The bright orange blood of the thryx dripped down his shoulders as he mounted yet another of the endless dunes of rosy Martian sand. Might the space ship lie beyond this one? His radio-sensitive indicator gave clear evidence of a source of atomic power somewhere nearby.

He topped the dune. And there, spread out before in the shadow of evening, gleamed . . .

Was it a typical Martio-mirage? Or was it . . . his heart stopped . . . was it the fabulously Lost City of Xanatopsis?

Joe Henderson jerked the paper from the typewriter. "Now I wonder," he said quietly in answer to his own question. Then he looked at the couch. "Still counting ping-pennies?"

M. Halstead Phyn grunted a negative. "Reading the paper." He was silent for a minute, then let out a loud *Kee-rist!* "But in spades!" he added feelingly.

"What is it?"

"Look at this. Just look at this, will you?"

Joe Henderson read the article. "My!" was all he said.

The agent was aflame. "But look, Joe. It's perfect. See, it says here this is only the latest of a series of attempts. All right, so if anybody's working on a series he's not going to stop with this installment. He's going to carry right on, and the tag's going to put the quietus on Hilary."

"But why should you be so hepped up about it?"

"Why? Remember the deal with *Galactic* about the reprints? So now Hilary gets polished off, and who'll be the executor of the estate? I don't know for sure, you understand, but it's odds on that it'll be Vance Wimpole. All right, so Vance is executor. We can talk to him. He's in the business. And after publicity like this, a Dr. Derringer reprint series'll clean up. We won't be able to turn 'em out fast enough. They'll melt away from the stands, but melt! It's perfect, Joey boy, if you ever prayed, do some tall praying for me now!"

"I don't know," Joe Henderson drawled. "I don't know as I could pray for a man's death. Not even," he added after mature reflection, "for Hilary's."

"It's dog eat dog in this racket, Joe. The hell with a conscience."

"Besides," Henderson added practically, "how can you be so sure Vance'll kick through?"

"I'm sure enough. Oh, I'm sure all right." A new and even brighter light began to glint in Phyn's little eyes. "You know what, Joe? Vance never uses an agent, does he? Always sells direct?"

"Far's I know."

"I think . . . Yes, I think I'm going to handle all D. Vance Wimpole's sales after this. He doesn't know it yet; but he's going to be glad to do it. Glad." Phyn relaxed on the couch, grinning to himself.

X

Concha Duncan set the steak on the table at once proudly and ruefully. "I'll have to learn to be a better cook, Matt. I can broil a good steak, but . . ."

Matt whetted the carving knife, with a gleam in his eyes betokening an already whetted appetite. "Steak's all right by me. Show me the man that doesn't welcome it."

"I know. But you keep saying I ought to shop within the budget and I keep getting good advice from Leona on what to do with cheap cuts and they go all wrong so I get some more steak, and look what it does to the budget. If you'd only let me . . . "

Matt cut through crisp brown into succulent red and watched rich warm juice flow onto the platter. "Now, darling. We won't go into that again. We are living on my income. Such, God help us, as it is."

"All right." Concha seated herself and began to serve the peas and the mashed potatoes. "I think they're good this time for once. No lumps. Maybe I'll reach up to Leona's standards yet."

"Leona," Matt stated, "is probably the most admirable wife man ever had. And I wouldn't swap you for her, not even with Terry and Ursula and the Lieutenant's salary thrown in."

Concha blew a kiss across the table and said, "Sweet."

"And the potatoes are wonderful."

"The man said they were an extra good shipment. Oh, when I was out shopping I ran into Doris Clyde. You wouldn't know her, but she was at school with me. Awfully nice girl. And first thing I thought when I saw her was, 'Maybe here's a girl for Joe.' Only it turns out she's married. He's a draftsman out at Douglas and doing ever so well."

"Everybody we meet outside of the M.L.S. is either in aircraft or in social service. They're the two great professions of the day. And the draft coming up for tomorrow. I bet you could get some symbolism out of that if you worked on it . . . But why is it you women are always trying to find a girl for Joe? Bernice is just as bad. Why not leave the poor boy alone?"

"Because he's . . . I don't know . . . he's so kind of sweet and helpless. You go all over motherly and you think the poor lamb needs a Good Woman."

"He wouldn't want a Good Woman if he had her. I think what Joe really wants is an honest-to-god bitch unhung, like his villainesses. Good women bore him terribly—or at any rate, that's his story."

"But the . . . the other sort'd be so bad for him. He's so kind and gentle."

"Then leave well enough alone. I'm glad your girl friend was married. Any other exciting adventures while marketing?"

"No . . . Matt . . .?"

"Yes?"

"Were you home all the time I was gone?"

"Sure. Why? Expecting a delivery or something?"

"No, it's just . . . Oh, I just wondered." They ate in silence for a moment. "Matt . . . do you think you really ought to talk that way you did the other night at the Marshalls? I mean about . . . you know."

"About murdering Hilary?" Matt asked cheerfully. "Darling,

was that shiver what is technically known as a wince? I've always wondered what one looked like."

Concha laughed. "Don't be silly. A wince is what you pull buckets out of wells with."

"Oh, I thought it was something you made jelly out of."

"Or of course," Concha suggested, "it could be what you start a bedtime story with. Wince upon a time . . ."

Matt looked into her eyes. "All right. Bright gay nonsense dialog. Swell. Only something's worrying you. What's wrong about Hilary?"

"I . . . I heard it on the radio while I was working in the kitchen this afternoon. Matt: Somebody did try to kill Hilary."

Her husband stared at her. "Well shut my big mouth!" he said softly.

XI

In the lounge car of the Lark, pullman train from San Francisco to Los Angeles, a tall thin man with a pale face and flaming hair sat contentedly with two high-balls and a blonde.

". . . and just as I fired," he was saying, "the jaguar sprang between us. The force of the rifle bullet was so great that it carried him right on into the gaping jaws of the lion, so violently that the lion choked to death. Thereby saving me one bullet."

"I don't believe it," said the blonde.

D. Vance Wimpole smiled to himself. "I'll try another one. This evening I read in the paper, much to my astonishment, that a murderous attack had been made on my brother-in-law. He was stabbed almost to death in a room that was locked or watched at every entrance. No one could have got in or out, and there in the middle of the room lay my brother-in-law with a dagger in his back. Do you believe that?"

"No," said the blonde.

"I don't blame you." Wimpole twirled his drink meditatively. "I don't blame you at all. That's why I'm going to Los Angeles, you know. If anybody's really set on murdering my brother-in-law, I wouldn't think of missing the fun for worlds. But meanwhile—"

"Hn?" said the blonde.

"Meanwhile the night is young and first we're going to have another drink and then there's no telling what may develop."

"I believe that," said the blonde.

XII

Sister Ursula had learned nothing fresh from the newspaper accounts, but the facts of Hilary's locked room continued to plague and distract her as she aided Sister Rose in arranging the altar for tomorrow's Mass.

Tomorrow would be November second, All Souls' Day, the day that the church consecrates especially to the memory of the dead. Hilary would recover from this wound; that seemed certain. But murderers are a notoriously persistent breed. By another All Souls' Day, would there be his departed soul to pray for? And perhaps another, a soul that had departed this body in a small chamber filled with gas?

And there was the floater Tarbell, so nebulous a character, whose soul had already gone to the private judgment. *Animula vagula nebula,* Sister Ursula thought wryly, and then shifted to more appropriate church Latin: *Requiescat in pace.*

And is not that, she mused, a fitting prayer for the living too? Let them rest in peace. Those who suffer and struggle and strive to kill, let them rest in peace. Let us rest in peace.

FOUR

INTERLUDE:
Sunday, November 2 to
Thursday, November 6, 1941

Ursula Marshall, happily full of formula, kicked her chubby legs. It was a friendly and joyful gesture, but it did not help the process of changing her diaper.

Her four-year-old brother looked on wide-eyed. "That looks like fun maybe, daddy. Is it?"

Lieutenant Marshall said, "What do you think?"

Terry gave the problem due attention. "Maybe yes," he announced. "Can I do it sometime, daddy?"

Marshall's large hands moved with surprising deftness. "By the time you can reach on top of a bathinet, I hope your sister won't be needing it."

"Then could I have another sister maybe?"

"We'll see about that. Perhaps we ought to get you practised up for when you have one of your own. And when you do, Terry, remember these words of fatherly advice: The more you help your wife with being a mother, the more time and energy she'll have for being a wife."

"What's energy?"

"Breakfast!" Leona called from the kitchen, thereby sparing her husband the grievous semantic problem of defining a term with no visible reference.

"You see, Terry?" he elucidated as they sat to table. "Because I got up and gave Ursula her early bottle, your mother had time" (he omitted the confusing new word) "to whip me up a buckwheat batter."

"I want a buckwheat batter," Terry announced inevitably.

"There dear," said Leona soothingly. "You've got your nice mush."

"Leona." Marshall firmly overrode Terry's outspoken comments on the nice mush. "Did you get anywhere sleeping on it?"

"Nowhere at all. That does usually work with mystery novels. I read them up to where the detective says, 'All the clews are now in your hands, my dear Whozit,' and then I go to sleep and in the morning I know the answer. But this didn't work out. Maybe it's because all the clews aren't in our hands."

"That's just it. There aren't any clews but a rosary and a photograph. Everything's so god—"

Leona glanced sideways at their son. "Terence!"

"So terribly nebulous. And a corpse is a—a darn sight more cooperative than a living victim who sits calmly back swiddling his press notices and murmurs gently, 'All right. Now you tell me who did it.' "

To most children a corpse at the breakfast table would be unbearably exciting. But Terry was too young yet to realize how romantically thrilling his father's profession would seem to others. Murder and corpses were just funny things that his parents talked about a lot. He now barely heard the word and went right on with his mush, which he had remembered that he liked.

"What I keep coming back to," Leona reflected, "is Sister Ursula's reference to the Invisible Man. She doesn't say things at random. So I reread that Chesterton story last night."

"Does it help?"

"It's the same moral as so many of his, of course: the easy danger of overlooking the obvious. The Invisible Man is the postman. All the witnesses swear that no one came near the house, and of course they never think of the man who comes and goes all the time. But who's your Invisible Man here? You checked on the maid?"

"Naturally."

"And—I know this sounds funny, but still . . . and Sister Felicitas?"

Marshall laughed. "I see what you mean. She is the Invisible Woman right enough."

"I knew you'd laugh at me. But remember the Holmes dictum: Eliminate the impossible . . ."

"Dr. Derringer put it another way in one of his scientific researches: 'Eliminate the impossible. Then if nothing remains, some part of the "impossible" was possible.' I think that might be more helpful here. But to please you, darling, I'll check on the good Sister. Her motive, I suppose, was to avenge the insult to Sister Patientia in the Braille work?"

"How many times, Terence, have I heard you say, 'Juries convict on evidence, not on motives?' "

"All right. But I doubt if Sister Felicitas could stay awake long enough for a murder . . . And what are the chances on some more b-u-c-k—"

"Buckwheat batter!" Terry crowed.

II

Jenny Green received Marshall with a friendly, "Good morning, Lieutenant."

"And to you, Miss Green."

"Veronica's at the hospital," she explained.

Marshall repressed a sigh of relief. "It's chiefly you I wanted to see anyway. You and that room."

"Me? How can I help you? But I'd be so glad if I could."

"You were Mr. Foulkes' secretary, weren't you?"

The girl shuddered. "Please don't say *were,* Lieutenant. You make it sound as though—as though whoever it was had succeeded."

"Sorry. Professional habit, I guess. This living corpse situation is a trifle irregular. You are, then?"

"Yes"

"Then might I ask you to go through your files and make me a list of everyone Mr. Foulkes ever had any serious financial or literary disputes with?"

She half-smiled. "I'm afraid that will take a while."

"I'm not surprised. But meanwhile I'll see if I can prise some secret out of that devilish study."

There's a time-honored dictum, Marshall thought as he stared at the unresponsive walls, that the more complex a situation has been made, the easier it is to solve. The simply conceived crime is the brain-twister. Which is doubtless true enough. Most complexities unravel instantly once you get hold of the right end of the thread. But when there are no threads . . .

Now there has to be a reason for any locked room situation. Criminals do not create locked rooms out of sheer devilment. The simplest reason is to make the death look like suicide; but if that were the case here, Hilary would have been stabbed in the front or the side. That was out. So was a framed accident.

The reason might be to give the criminal an alibi. It had been in that Harrigan case. But of possible suspects so far, the only ones with alibis at all had such impeccable ones that they could not be questioned for an instant. Perhaps in Miss Green's list . . .

Or there is one kind of locked room without a reason. That is the accidental one, never planned by the criminal. Some little thing might have gone wrong by chance to produce this effect of apparent impossibility.

. . . and if nothing remains, some part of the "impossible" was possible . . .

Marshall clucked irritably, left the study, and followed the sound of typing. He found Jenny Green methodically hunting through files and copying down names with a line or two to identify the cause of trouble in each case.

She looked up and asked, "Yes, Lieutenant?"

"Did you, Miss Green, ever grab a stick by the wrong end and then find the end wasn't there?"

"Am I supposed to answer?"

"Rhetorical. It's what I've been doing. I'm grabbing at the factual clews and I don't know enough about the people. Maybe you can help me?"

Jenny waved a hand at the typewriter. "But I don't know anything about those people. To me they're just names to type at the heads of letters."

"I don't mean those people necessarily. I mean Mr. Foulkes, his wife, his brother-in-law—you."

"Lieutenant, surely you—"

"I don't suspect anybody yet. I don't unsuspect anybody either. But the whole thing focuses around Hilary Foulkes, and I've got to know this—this Foulkes focus. The Foulkes-lore, if you'll forgive me."

"I'll try. I mean, try to tell you; I don't think I can forgive you. But sit down. And you can light your pipe if you want."

The only furniture beside the chair at the typing table consisted of a bed and a low boudoir chair covered with flowered chintz. Marshall chose the latter and did not feel so out of place as one might have expected; it was almost identical with the chair in which he gave Ursula her bottles.

"I've gathered," Jenny Green began slowly, "how people feel about Cousin Hilary. Sometimes I can even understand it a little. But he's been so different with me that I . . . Well, it isn't only that I owe a lot to him. My mother was some sort of forty-second cousin of Fowler Foulkes. My father was killed in the last war, before I was born. Mother went back to grandfather and I was born at the vicarage. Mother wasn't ever really well after that, and when grandfather died . . . Oh, I'm not going to tell you the whole story, but before Hilary came to England and decided to track down his transatlantic relatives, there were days when we didn't eat. So I feel gratitude all right, but more than that too. Hilary is

". . . well, he's nice to me. Quite aside from being good to me, if you understand."

"I think I do."

"But to make you see him . . . You'll have to go back. You'll have to see Fowler Foulkes. Yes, and Darrell Wimpole too. I never knew them, but from their books, and from hearing their children talk—You must read those books, Lieutenant. Foulkes' autobiography and the Wimpole memoir. They might help."

"I shall. But if meanwhile you—?"

"Fowler Foulkes . . . well, he was a lot like Dr. Derringer except for his appearance. He looked very much like Hilary; but I suppose you remember pictures of him?"

"Yes."

"But he acted as though he did have a barrel chest and a black spade beard and a silver-headed cane. He boomed and he dominated and he crushed people with his trenchant wit. It wasn't a pose. He was the real thing; a major personality. And Darrell Wimpole—"

"That's Mrs. Foulkes' father?"

"Yes. He was . . . he was the same sort of thing gone wrong. He was a major personality that didn't come off. He'd started with a freak success in some strange mathematical theory that sounded brilliant and was later disproved. He wrote a little and kept being on the verge of success. He was great at dominating salons until any one of interest appeared. Then when he met Foulkes, he changed entirely and became just a Boswellian satellite. Do you understand it? Because he couldn't succeed in being what he wanted, he could write about its perfection in Foulkes, because he was simply a Foulkes manqué. Does it make sense?"

"I think so. And the children of these men?"

"It's as though there were only so much vital energy, so much perfection; and father and son had to split it between them. Hilary's father, you see, achieved himself completely."

"So Hilary lives simply on his father's energy and is nothing in himself?"

"I wasn't going to put it so cruelly, Lieutenant; but that's much what I meant."

"And Wimpole's son? What is his name . . . Vance?"

"Vance . . ." Jenny Green leaned back and clasped her hands around her knees. Her eyes blurred away from their usual alertness. "Now Vance—"

At that point the doorbell rang. "And Alice is still out marketing." She jumped to her feet. "We'll finish this later, Lieutenant."

Marshall looked at the sheet in the typewriter. Scads of names, many unfamiliar. Webb Marlowe, Cleve Cartmill . . . Austin Carter, but he knew that already . . . Matt too, of course.

Marshall listened and heard Miss Green's tentative "Yes?" as she greeted, obviously, a complete stranger. Then there was a voice, a voice he knew slightly, saying, "I'd like to speak to Mr. Foulkes' business manager."

"I'm afraid Mr. Foulkes is his own business manager."

And God knows that's true enough, thought Marshall, trying to place the not quite unfamiliar voice. Then it identified itself.

"My name is Phyn. M. Halstead Phyn."

There was a smile in the girl's voice. "Oh yes. I remember typing letters to you. In fact, I was just about to refer to that file."

So the little agent, too, had had his troubles with Hilary. Hardly surprising. But perhaps worth looking into.

Marshall stepped out into the living-room. There were two men at the door. The second was that deceptively young and callow-seeming individual who was, Matt had informed him, unexcelled at either hack or creative fantasy. Henderson, that was the name.

Phyn registered surprise. "Mr. Marshall!" he exclaimed.

"I'm afraid we met under false pretenses, Phyn. The handle is Lieutenant. Homicide. Miss Green, is it all right with you if I ask these gentlemen to step in?"

"Certainly, Lieutenant. I'll finish that list for you."

"Thank you. Please come in, gentlemen."

Phyn sidled in uneasily. Henderson seemed lankily unperturbed by the Lieutenant's status, but somewhat awed by the apartment.

"I want," Marshall explained, "to ask you boys a few questions. First let's get the name straight. What beside Phyn?"

"M. Halstead. And it's P-h-y-n."

"The M. stands for?"

Phyn hesitated, and Henderson laconically supplied, "Michael."

Marshall grinned. "And I'll bet the Phyn used to be F-i-n-n. Can't blame you for changing it. Micky Finn isn't a good name for a man in a position of trust like an agent."

"Does anybody," Phyn asked ruefully, "trust an agent?"

"That I can't say. But I'm willing to try. Now tell me just why you should choose this bright morning to visit the scene of the crime?"

Phyn wisely chose not to answer the implication. "I don't know how much you understand about the literary business, Lieutenant—"

"The pulp racket," said Joe Henderson.

"A little, Phyn. And by the time this case is over, I expect to be an authority. But what should I understand to account for your call?"

"You do at least know the standing of the Dr. Derringer opi? Of course. Well, you see—"

It was then that Veronica Foulkes threw open the hall door and caroled joyously, "Look who's here!" When she saw the Lieutenant, her voice fell and she repeated, in a markedly different tone, "Just *look* who's here . . .!"

But her reaction hardly mattered. The pale and wiry man behind her took over and dominated the scene. Jenny Green had abandoned her typing and come at Veronica's call. Now she ran eagerly into the thin man's arms and said "Vance," very simply and happily. And D. Vance Wimpole was kissing her and greeting Phyn and Henderson and getting introduced to Marshall and demanding unlimited rounds of drinks all at once.

The next half hour was something nightmarish for Marshall. He wanted to talk with this brother-in-law for at least two reasons: first, because he might have information, being in the trade, of Hilary's business relations with science fictionists, and being in the family, of Hilary's relations with his wife and cousin (Miss Green's family narrative, though clear and suggestive, could always bear checking against another source); and second, because Marshall was markedly interested in just where the hell Wimpole himself had been for the past several weeks.

But there was no opportunity for coherent questioning. Wimpole had welcomed Marshall eagerly enough (". . . delighted to meet the man who's going to unlock Hilary's locked room . . . rotten taste in a murderer to go out of his way to be difficult, isn't it?"), but then he was off on the narrative of his travels or trading shop talk with the agent and the other writer, whose presence here at the Foulkes apartment he seemed to accept with infinite casualness.

And sandwiched in between narrative and shop talk were fraternal kisses for Veronica, affianced kisses for Jenny, and a meticulous attention to the replenishing of glasses which suggested that Wimpole was host here rather than guest.

One unasked question he did in a way answer.

". . . and I'm having the polar bear mounted. Make a wonderful rug for you, Ron. Or should I save it till Jenny and I set up housekeeping? Which by the way, Joe. Beautiful idea hit me. What happens if you mount a werewolf skin as a rug? Does it keep changing so you every so often look down and find you're treading on human parchment? Don't think I'll use it. Too busy. You can have it if you want."

Veronica shuddered. "Grisly!"

"Isn't it? Almost as bad, good mother, as lock a room and in it stab my brother-in-law, of course, but that wouldn't rime. Which by the way, Lieutenant, where do I stand on the suspect list?"

"High," said Marshall. In the presence of Vance Wimpole, anyone tended to become as laconic as Joe Henderson.

"I thought so. They say you're a shrewd man. It wouldn't be hard to see what a pretty motive I have. Financially, I mean. You can disregard the incest angle. So here. This is what they left me of my ticket and Pullman stub. Proves I was in San Francisco yesterday. Just thought you might like to know. Keep them if you wish. Press them with your dance programs. And did I write you, Ron, about that amazing sect of christianized voodoo I found in Santo Domingo?"

Marshall slipped the stubs back in their envelope and tucked them into his wallet. He'd have them checked, of course; but he had a fairly precise estimation of their worth without that. He only half listened to the narrative, colorfully incredible as it was, while he surveyed the other listeners.

They were themselves not too attentive to the words; but with one exception they were raptly fixed on the speaker. Jenny Green looked devotedly glad at this reunion, which was to be expected. What was less expected was that Wimpole's sister gazed upon him quite as devotedly, quite as—hell, you might almost say amorously as his fiancée. Phyn's interest was harder to analyze; he regarded D. Vance Wimpole almost as he might an unanticipatedly favorable contract, and seemed to be studying him, forming in his shrewd mind the proper approach to extract the last drop of profit. But why? Was this purely some angle of the agency business, or did it somehow tie in with the Foulkes situation?

The one exception was Joe Henderson. Marshall had not seen him notice a woman before, not as a woman, that is. Miss Green, Mrs. Carter, Concha, even Leona he had hardly more than glanced at. But now his stare adhered fixedly to Veronica Foulkes.

Marshall would have liked to stay. There were possibilities that might develop here with another round or two. But the presence of a police official would simply act as whatever was the opposite of a catalyst and damn it he was beginning to think in the quasi-scientific jargon of these boys. And besides, there was plenty of routine, both Foulkes and Tarbell, waiting for him at headquarters.

At the point in Wimpole's narrative where the christianized voodoo sect had developed a schism on the question of whether it was valid to baptize zombies, Marshall rose.

"I've some other matters to check up on," he said regretfully. "But I want to see you later, Mr. Wimpole. Where are you staying?"

"Here, naturally." It was Veronica Foulkes who answered.

"I'll sleep in the study," Wimpole explained. "Let you know, Lieutenant, if anything says, 'Now we're locked in for the night.' "

"I'll phone you, then. And when is your husband expected home from the hospital, Mrs. Foulkes?"

"Tomorrow or next day. They say he's recovering wonderfully."

"Grand!" Wimpole cried. "We'll have a recovery party. And it fits magnificently. Chantrelle—you know my mad friend over at Caltech—"

"You have mad friends any place," Jenny murmured. "I know. Won't you have fun being hostess to them? But Chantrelle has his model rocket car all ready for a demonstration. He's been holding it up till I got here. How's about it? We'll make it Hilary's Saved-from-the-Jaws-of-Death party. You'll come, of course, Joe, and Phyn. I'll ask some of the other fantasy boys, the Carters and the Bouchers and who's that bright new protégé of Austin's? Matt Duncan. I know," he added maliciously, "they'll love to celebrate Hilary's good health. And by all means you, Lieutenant." He beamed all over his pale face, and drained his glass. "If only we could make the party complete! Invite the murderer. But maybe that can be arranged."

As indeed it was.

III

Sister Ursula had keep the Foulkes case from her mind during the day's services and her All Souls' Day visit to the cemetery in Long beach and the grave of her father, that stalwart Iowan Captain of Police. But now, as she read the office of Compline before retiring, it recurred to plague her.

Oddly enough it was the *Qui habitat* that set her off, the ninetieth psalm.* This noble hymn of confidence in the Lord seemed to accord so curiously with Hilary Foulkes' trust, apparently so well deserved, in something that protected him. *Scapulis suis obumbrabit tibi* . . .

> With His pinions will He shelter thee, and under His wings thou shalt be secure.
> Like a shield His truth shall guard thee; thou shalt not fear the terrors of night,
> Nor the arrow that flies by day, nor the plague that prowleth in the dark, nor the noonday attack of the demon . . . ,

It had been almost noon, the attack, hadn't it? And was this as reasonable an explanation as any?

> A thousand shall fall at thy side and ten thousand at thy right hand, yet no evil shall come nigh thee . . .

---

* The numbering is of course that of the Douay version. In the King James, this psalm is the ninety-first.

> He has given His angels charge over thee . . .

A favorite line of the Devil's this, Sister Ursula smiled to herself. He quoted it to Christ on the pinnacle of the temple, and was answered by a brilliantly twisted quotation which put him in his place as a scriptural authority. But was it chance that the Tempter chose this line? Was there not something dangerous in a certain kind of confidence?

There was something here, something in this confused mélange of reflections on psalms and angels and devils and Hilary and religion . . . Sister Ursula paused and tried to put her finger on it, but it slipped away mockingly. At last she turned back to her breviary and went on to the *Nunc dimittis*.

IV

Lieutenant Marshall was checking over the reports on the rentals and sales of beards. They were not helpful. No beard of the Dr. Derringer type had been out on rental at the time of the bomb episode, and of the eight sales in the past year, only one was to a private individual, Bernice Carter. The rest had been to amateur theatrical groups.

The damnable thing was that this did not even narrow it down to the Carters. The bomb-sender might have owned such a beard for years. He might have bought or rented it out of town. He might conceivably have improvised it himself.

There had been equally little luck on the cyanide. The poison register would be a great and valuable institution if there were any reasonable certainty that the individuals signing did not simply make up their names and purposes in the spirit of free improvisation. If you have a suspect, with a good case proved against him otherwise, you may be able to trap him on a falsified entry with the aid of a handwriting expert (whom the defense will, of course, match with one quite as eminent); but as a source of much-needed leads, the system is hopeless.

Marshall had checked over one or two registers himself, in moody restlessness, and had grown weary of the number of people in Los Angeles who were troubled with rats and wanted arsenic. He liked, however, the arsenic entry which was signed *George Spelvin* and read, not *Rats,* but *Mice.* He wondered what actor with a cruel gag sense had decided to dispose of his superfluous girls, and rather hoped that such a piquant case might fall to his lot in time. But there was no trace anywhere of any of the names so far involved with Hilary Foulkes, save of course the Carter cyanide. (This too had been bought by Bernice, who seemed effectively to shelter her husband from such distracting crudities as shopping.)

Marshall was growling into his own non-existent beard when the phone rang. "Borigian speaking," he heard when he picked up the receiver. "Think I've got a lead for you on that bomb of yours. Can you come to the jail now?"

"Be right over," Marshall promised. Any kind of fresh lead sounded good. He needed to clear his head.

"I got thinking it over," Borigian explained in welcome, "and it seemed to me like there was something familiar about the screwy way whoever made that bomb attached the fuses. Then last night I was drinking beer down at the Lucky Spot and that boogy-woogy-playing dinge they've got was going good and all of a sudden it hits me. Louie Schalk. Remember the Austerlitz case?"

Marshall nodded.

"That bomb was Louie's work, though a smart mouthpiece got him off. And it had the same fuse-fastenings. So I decided to have a talk with Mr. Schalk."

"How'd you get him to talk?"

"He's been branching out lately, Louie has. He's a good chemist, and there's pretty strong evidence he's been making counterfeiting inks. So we pulled him in and talked about how we'd turn him over to the Feds unless he came clean."

"And he came clean?"

Borigian frowned. "I don't know. You talk to him, Lieutenant."

A half hour later Marshall had learned little beyond an interesting study in how an addiction to cheap wine can turn a promising chemist into a sordid criminal. Louie Schalk was little and thin and white-haired. His pale blue eyes showed hardly any remaining trace of intelligence, but his hands were the deft skilled hands of a good artisan.

"Honest, Lieutenant," he repeated for the seventh time, "that's all I know."

"The letter contained nothing but a hundred dollar bill and the instructions?"

"That's all."

"Repeat them again."

"I should put the unset bomb and directions for setting it in a parcel locker in the P.E. station at Sixth and Main. Then I should mail the key to General Delivery. I'd get another hundred after. And I did too."

"No signature to the letter?"

"No."

"Anything you remember about the typing?"

"Should I? A typewriter's a typewriter, ain't it?"

Marshall shrugged hopelessly. "And you went ahead just on that?"

"Why shouldn't I? Most people want bombs, they don't want you should know who they are, do they?"

"You get orders like that often?"

Schalk's thin lips tightened. "You're booking me on this one charge."

"All right. I'll take it that means Yes, but you've got your constitutional rights. So. And how do people find out about your . . . profession?"

Schalk was silent. "Hell, Lieutenant," Sergeant Borigian broke in, "everybody knows about Louie."

"Yes, but not in the circles I'm concerned with. Well, one more try. Tell me, Schalk: What was the name at General Delivery?"

Borigian grunted disapproval. "Don't think he'd give his real name, do you?"

"No. But the phony a man chooses can be just as indicative as his true name. What was it, Schalk?"

Louie Schalk frowned, trying to remember. "Got it," he said at last. "It was Dr. Garth Derringer."

While Marshall expressed himself, his eyes rested on the card on which Schalk had been booked. Suddenly his self-expression ceased, and his face took on a look almost of pleasure. One lead. One thing that fitted:

Residence: Elite Hotel

In the Elite Hotel, Jonathan Tarbell had died.

V

The Princess Zurilla shrank back against the gem-encrusted wall, her golden tresses gleaming brighter than the gems. Changul, High Priest of Xanatopsis, drew yet nearer and extended a lean hand, all seven of its bony fingers avidly twitching.

"From this hidden space port," his harsh voice droned on exultantly, "our ships used to blast off for Atlantis, in those glorious days when Terra was but a fragment of our colonial empire. We have not lost our cunning through the millennia, as Terra will learn to its disaster."

The fleshless hand clutched the smooth arm of the Princess. Zurilla's firm warm flesh trembled. "And you shall behold all this with me, my dear. You shall reign with me . . ." He broke off and crackled a command in Xanatoptic to the three-armed Rigelian servant who stood in attendance.

"No!" Princess Zurilla implored him. "Let me go! Let me return to my own people!"

"To your lover, you mean," the High Priest snarled. "To that too clever Captain Comet who will yet learn that he has met his match in me. No, you shall not go! You shall be mine down through the eons of the triumph of Xanatopsis!"

An agonized scream burst from Zurilla's throat. "Is there no escape?" she moaned. "Will no one save me?"

The slavering lips of the mad High Priest neared hers—and then the Princess Zurilla beheld a strange thing. The third arm of the Rigelian servant fell to the ground. Another arm twitched the horn from his forehead . . .

"Captain Comet!" she cried joyously, and knew no more.

"That's what I call timing," Joe Henderson observed, "when people knock on the door just when I reach a tag line."

M. Halstead Phyn said "I'll answer it," and jumped up from the couch eagerly. He opened the door, saw the visitors, and grinned like a cat given the freedom of a fish cannery.

"We're on our way to bring Hilary home," Vance Wimpole announced as he and his sister entered the room. "Thought we'd stop off and remind you about Chantrelle's rocket party. It's this Friday."

"Fine," said Joe Henderson.

"You're the damnedest one, Joe. I've never seen you miss a party yet and I think you love them; but you never say a word and you drink maybe two beers."

"I have my fun," Joe said.

"I guess you must. How goes the Cosmic Captain?"

"All right."

Phyn broke the ensuing silence. "Have you got a minute to spare, Wimpole? Because if you have . . ."

"Yes. I've been wanting to talk further about that business you mentioned. Got another room here?"

"We could go in the kitchen."

"O.K. Ron, you mind entertaining Joe?"

Veronica Foulkes had not said a word since they came in. Her brother's presence seemed to subdue her. But now that he had vanished with Phyn, she came alive again. She crossed her legs (she knew they were good) and leaned forward (she knew they were good too).

"Don't you think Vance is stimulating, Mr. Henderson? He makes life so much more vivid, so much more real."

"He's a good joe," said Joe.

"He has so much fun and yet he does so much work too. I like a man who *does* something, who really *is* somebody and not . . . not just a filial ghost. A man like Vance who makes all his money from writings that he really writes himself. . . . You write too, don't you, Mr. Henderson?"

"Some." Joe Henderson seemed even more tongue-tied than usual, and he was having trouble keeping his eyes polite.

"Writers are so understanding. They know about people. They

understand how a woman like me ticks. You do understand, I think, don't you?"

"Uh . . . " said Joe Henderson sympathetically.

"I knew you would. You'd see how lonely I am, or was until Vance came. And soon he'll be off again to Lord knows where and I . . . Won't you come and have tea with me some afternoon, Mr. Henderson? Just you and me and Pitti Sing?"

"I'd like to very much, Mrs. Foulkes." There was eagerness behind Joe's stiffly formal phrase.

"Mrs. Foulkes! But you must call me—No, everybody calls me Ron. You . . . you shall call me Nikki . . . Joe."

"Nikki," said Joe Henderson. His voice sounded as though it were changing.

Then the room was full of D. Vance Wimpole. He glanced at Joe's manuscript, smiled and nodded, downed the drink he was still carrying, shook hands with Phyn, clapped his fellow author on the back, took his sister's arm affectionately, and steered her out the door, all the while recounting an anecdote concerning the habits of the Galápagos turtle, which was equally improbable and improper.

When quiet had returned, Phyn thrust his hand out at Henderson. "Congratulate me, Joey. From this time forth M. Halstead Phyn collects ten per cent of every D. Vance Wimpole check, including the Scandinavian and plus five pseudonyms."

The startling statement had to be repeated before Henderson took it in. When he did, he whistled. "That's good going. How did you do it? Do you know where the body's hidden?"

"Something like that," said Phyn smugly.

VI

"Cousin Hilary's taking his nap," said Jenny Green. "I know he's anxious to see you, Lieutenant, but the doctor was very strict about a properly sensible convalescence."

"Commendable. And Mrs. Foulkes?"

"She and Vance went out together."

Poor kid, Marshall thought. Your fiancé goes gallivanting with his sister while you stay home to tend to Hilary's correspondence. But a man like Vance Wimpole must have the irresistible appeal of color after the vicarage and poverty . . . "Well," he said aloud, "that's all to the good, Miss Green. You and I can resume that conversation we were having the other day. Unless you're too busy?"

"I should be catching up on—but then, I suppose this is really doing Hilary's work too, isn't it? Very well, Lieutenant. Come in and make yourself comfortable."

The latter injunction Marshall found it impossible to obey in that room; but he lit his pipe and settled down to listening.

"Let's see . . . How much had I told you when those pulp people interrupted us? That Mr. Henderson is an odd one, isn't he? But he seems . . . I don't know, rather sweet."

Marshall laughed. "It's hard for a man to see that adjective applied to another man, but you may be right. Well, you were telling me about Wimpole and Foulkes and how they affected their children."

"Oh, yes. One thing I don't think I'd mentioned about Mr. Wimpole: He was an atheist. I don't mean just the ordinary kind of atheist that so many people are or think they are. He was a crusading atheist, who took it for a religion. He was always quoting Tom Paine and Bob Ingersoll, though there was, I gather, more of Ingersoll than Paine in him. And that worked on his children, though in different ways. It gave Vance his independence, that fine rational self-reliance that he has. He found what he needed inside himself. But Ron didn't. She's the sort of person who needs something, because she—please don't think this is catty, but because she isn't anything in herself. So she gropes and fumbles and reacts to a situation the way she thinks someone might react only she isn't really anyone. Or is that clear at all?"

"I think it is, a little. Say that we all, even if we can't accept a capitalized God, still need a lower case god of some sort. Mr. Foulkes found it in his father and Mr. Wimpole in himself, but Mrs. Foulkes is still hunting. Or has she—isn't it true to some extent she finds it in her brother?"

Jenny Green hesitated. "Yes . . . A little, perhaps. But Vance is . . . He's a hard god to worship. He doesn't stay put on the altar. You never know quite where you are. He can give you excitement but not peace. He's a god for a maenad but not for a nun, if you follow."

"And Mr. Foulkes?"

"What about him?"

"For his wife's lower case god."

Jenny frowned. "I don't think Ron understands Cousin Hilary. I don't think they understand each other."

"Tell me, while we're at this: It seems an odd marital pairing. How . . . ?"

"I think Cousin Hilary married Ron because she was her father's daughter. I gather she was more like Darrell Wimpole when she was younger. His atheism was enough for her then, and she felt or seemed to feel much as he did about Fowler Foulkes. I think Hilary wanted—well, should we say a high priestess for his religion?"

"And she failed him?"

"You can get tired of anything, Lieutenant. Now Ron says all she needs for hell is a world where all the books are by Fowler Foulkes and all the films are about Dr. Derringer."

Marshall puffed slowly at his pipe. That perverse use of Dr. Derringer as the murderous bomb sender . . . would not that appeal to just such a resentment? To use the symbol to destroy the reality . . .

"I've been talking more than I should," said Jenny Green. "More than I ever do, in fact. But you can see how important this is to me? If any word I say can prevent some devil from killing Cousin Hilary . . . Have I said anything helpful?"

"I'm damned," said Marshall, "if I know."

VII

"That Miss Green," Marshall said, "thinks you're sweet."

Joe Henderson was sitting cross-legged on a cushion before the stone fireplace. "Miss Green?" He looked up innocently.

"Hilary's cousin-secretary."

"Oh. I was over there today, Lieutenant. I went to . . . well, Mrs. Foulkes asked me to have tea and I . . . Your policeman almost didn't let me in."

"That's as it should be."

"But am I a suspect?"

Austin Carter laughed. "Put Joe up on the top of your list, Lieutenant."

Marshall looked puzzled. "Why? We've just been over all the Hilary-complications of the Mañana Literary Society (and thanks, Carter, for your cooperation), but it seems to me Henderson is about the only one to emerge with a clean bill of health."

"Ah, but you see, Lieutenant, we agreed, did we not, that the locked room attempt was made with a time machine? And Joe is our greatest authority on gadgets like that. See *Time Tunnel* in the current *Surprising*."

Marshall smiled. "That is suspicious. And motive?"

"Mrs. Foulkes. You should have seen Joe just after that tea party."

Joe Henderson, though seated, seemed to give the effect of shuffling his feet embarrassedly.

"But he didn't meet Mrs. Foulkes until after the attack."

"Lieutenant! How prosaically literal you can be! If the whole business was hocused by a time machine, why shouldn't the motivation arise after the fact? All the more ingenious a crime—alibi yourself by going back to when you had no reason to kill."

"I'm afraid, Henderson, Carter has bared your dread secret. Better confess."

Joe Henderson shook his head. "I'm not that smart."

"But seriously, Lieutenant," Austin Carter went on, "you ought to read *Time Tunnel*. That's Joe being non-hack, and it's a beautiful job. One of the swellest novelets to hit scientifiction in years."

"You really think so?" Joe Henderson, Carter's professional senior by ten years, looked as beamishly pleased as an amateur actor who has just received a kind word from the Lunts.

"Indeed I do. Henderson is still the Old Master when he wants to be. And that Storm Darroway . . . dear God, what a wench! If I could meet a woman like that, a thousand imterplanetary civilizations could smash and much I'd care!"

"The heroine of *Time Tunnel*?" Marshall asked.

"Of course not. You don't know your Henderson, Lieutenant. The villainess. The heroine is duller than dishwater. You see, one of the Henderson trademarks is the Two Women. They're the same two that run through all of Rider Haggard too. One represents Virtue and is blonde and beautiful and good and dull. The other represents Vice and is black and beautiful and evil and marvelous. It's always puzzled me why Joe can write only wicked women."

"Could I play at amateur psychoanalyst? Perhaps he has a secret conviction that women are evil and can therefore write only an evil woman convincingly."

Carter nodded. "Pretty. What do you say to that, Joe?"

Joe Henderson hesitated. "I don't know," he drawled at last. "I guess it's just a subconscious belief that the human female has spider blood."

VIII

"Yes," said the clerk at the Elite Hotel, "it'd be easy enough for anybody hereabouts to pick up who Louie Schalk was. Of course he was acquitted on the Austerlitz business, but we all knew what his racket was."

"And do you think," Marshall asked, "that Tarbell knew?"

"I can't say. He didn't talk much to people. But he could have easily."

Marshall nodded. This fitted all right. Whoever had known Tarbell, visited him here, and killed him, could have learned where to order a bomb.

"Oh, and Lieutenant."

"Yes?"

"You told me to tell you if anybody was asking for Tarbell."

"So?"

"Well, there was somebody. Not exactly asking for him; but asking about him."

"Good man. Who?"

"It was one of those nuns that come around here on social work sometimes. We've got a poor lunger up on the fourth, and she was fixing up to get him sent away. So we got to talking about the murder and she asked questions about this man used to visit Tarbell occasionally, and she showed me a picture and said did that look like him, and damned if it didn't."

Marshall's eyes popped. He was not surprised that Sister Ursula's proud curiosity had led her to investigate the Elite; but where on earth could she have secured a picture of any of the suspects? "You were so vague in your description," he objected. "What was it like?"

"I'd almost forgotten," the clerk apologized. "So many people come and go. But when I saw the picture, it all came back to me. She left it with me to show you. It's around here somewheres . . . Oh, here it is."

He handed it over. It was a page torn from a movie fan magazine, a striking still of that admirable actor Norval Prichard in his great role of Dr. Derringer.

IX

"So there are all the latest pieces of the jigsaw," said Marshall as he whisked a brush over the coat of his best suit, "And tonight you'll meet the people."

Leona executed some complicated maneuvers before the dressing table. "With your next bonus you're going to have to buy me a full length mirror. Does my slip show?"

"Just a little."

"It's nice of Mr. Chantrelle to ask us to his party. And I am curious to see this Hilary of yours. I never get a chance to meet the victims in your cases while they're still warm."

"I don't know that warm's the word for Hilary."

"A rocket party . . . That should be fun. And a rocket could be symbolic for clearing up a case. A loud noise and a spreading light . . ."

"Beauty falls from the air," Marshall said, and added questioningly another quotation: "Beauty is truth? Well, we'll see."

Leona was listening to shouts and murmurs off. "Oh my . . . A howl. I'll bet it's a burp left over from that last bottle. Will you check, dear, while I . . ."

Lieutenant Marshall picked up his screaming daughter, put her against his shoulder, and patted her resolutely with no result. He sat down on the low chintz-covered chair, held her on his knee, and shook her gently. The internal rattle was deafening.

Ursula stared questioningly in her father's face and parted her lips as though to emit the desired burp, Then her gaze switched. There had been no extraneous sound to distract her. Nothing had moved. But something in the corner of the room demanded her attention.

She stared fixedly at the thing and followed its slow and hesitant movements. Her father shook her again. "Don't pay any attention to that, darling," he said. "Make with the burp. Be a good girl."

Just as Leona entered the room, the baby relaxed her attention and burped splendidly. "She saw a Thing," Marshall said. "I don't know how the child authorities account for that phenomenon, but it always gives me the creeps when she becomes so damned absorbed in something that isn't there."

"Maybe it's our Invisible Man," Leona suggested.

"Gives me gooseflesh," he insisted. "I'll bet some of our fantasy boys could work it into a very pretty omen."

"Of what?"

"Of what? That, my darling, is what we're going to this party to find out. Come on."

FIVE

THE NINTH DAY:
Friday, November 7, 1941

Hugo Chantrelle told the story of his rocket party so often to the police that he came to know it by heart, came even to believe that he had in fact felt a sensation of dread premonition from the start of the evening. This sensation he accounted for with manifold references to Extra Sensory Perception, the Serial Universe, the common reaction of I-have-been-here-before, and the free movement of the mind in dreams along either direction of the time stream. It was an impressive explanation, even though the premonition was strictly after the fact, and emphatically a characteristic one.

For Hugo Chantrelle was an eccentric scientist. In working hours at the California Institute of Technology he was an uninspired routine laboratory man; but on his own time he devoted himself to those peripheral aspects of science which the scientific purist damns as mumbo-jumbo, those new alchemies and astrologies out of which the race may in time construct unsurmised wonders of chemistry and astronomy.

The rocketry of Pendray, the time-dreams of Dunne, the extra sensory perception of Rhine, the sea serpents of Gould, all these held his interests far more than any research conducted by the Institute. He was inevitably a member of the Fortean Society of America, and had his own file of unbelievable incidents eventually to be published as a supplement to the works of Charles Fort. It must be added in his favor that his scientific training automatically preserved him from the errors of the Master. His file was carefully authenticated, and often embellished with first-hand reports. And this was one reason why he had so gladly acceded to D. Vance Wimpole's notion of turning the rocket launching into a party for Hilary.

For locked rooms fit into the Fort pattern, if pattern it can be called, and Hugo Chantrelle looked forward to meeting Hilary much as he might to an encounter with a survivor of the *Mary Celeste* or with Benjamin Bathurst, the British diplomat who once walked around a team of horses and was never seen again.

So expectancy was Chantrelle's dominant emotion that night, expectancy of the meeting with Hilary and the success of the demonstration of his model rocket. The premonition of disaster came later, in his account to Sergeant Kello of the Pasadena police.

Too great expectancy must always involve anticlimax, which is possibly only a pedantic way of rephrasing the idea of the song *I'm building up to an awful let-down*. Chantrelle's let-down was double: He never had a chance to talk with Hilary alone, and nobody seemed to give much of a damn about his beautiful rocket. It was turning into just another party, and the host began to regret that Wimpole had talked him into serving liquor, a disturbing element which ordinarily never entered his life.

There were some of his own friends present, of course: several faculty members from the Institute, where he seemed to get on better with representatives of the departments of English and mathematics than with his own colleagues. There were some of the fantasy writers whom he cultivated: Anson MacDonald and Austin Carter and that promising newcomer Matt Duncan and Anthony Boucher and their several wives and Joe Henderson inevitably wifeless.

Ordinarily these might have been tractable guests, who listened with absorbed interest and occasionally contributed stimulating ideas of their own, Chantrelle was wont to maintain that the company of fantasy writers is invaluable to a scientist; they are the prophets of the future even as Verne and Foulkes were the prophets of today. Only occasionally did he admit to himself that he enjoyed their company because they received his heterodox views on the borderlands of science far more courteously than did his laboratory associates.

But even they were not receptive tonight. There were too many others. There was Hilary Foulkes, who had invested his entrance with wife and cousin with the air of a potentate leading a cortege, and who had thenceforth held court, in the chair most nearly approaching his own body in comfortable plumpness, dispensing anecdotes of his Immortal Father and of his own providential escape from death.

There was Veronica Foulkes, who had prowled about commencing a tête-à-tête with each available unattached male. Yes, even with Chantrelle, though women interested him as little as did liquor, and the nebulous stupidity of her egocentric mysticism had disgusted him; for his mind though eccentric, was stringently logical.

There was the agent Phyn. He was unobtrusive enough save for his fruitless endeavors to wangle a private conference with Hilary Foulkes and for an oddly dominant, whip-hand quality in his attitude toward Vance Wimpole; but Hugo Chantrelle disliked the presence, even the existence of agents. They reminded him that writers (even, or perhaps especially, writers of science fantasy) are commercial workers, when he preferred to think of them as free souls, as soaringly independent as, thanks to the canny marriage of his grandmother, was he himself.

There were two people whom he faintly remembered meeting once at the Carters, but whom he could not successfully place. The man named Marshall seemed not to fit in anywhere. Five minutes' conversation showed him up as neither scientist nor science-fictionist; and his suit, though good enough and well pressed, certainly proved that he did not belong to the circles in which the Foulkes moved. And yet he seemed in some curious way closely attached to the Foulkeses; his alert eyes hardly ever left Hilary, even for his own attractive wife.

Then there was the odd little man named Truncheon or Runtle or something equally unlikely. A fan, Chantrelle decided; Austin Carter was apt to have such satellites. He felt sorry for the lonely little man at one point, and went over to him to enlighten him with some details about the by now almost forgotten rocket. But Vance Wimpole came up at the same time, and Trundle's eyes lit up with the true fan's glow in the presence of An Author.

Wimpole, of course, was everywhere. He tended bar, he told stories, he introduced to each other with the most intimate charm people whom he had himself met five minutes earlier, he heckled Hilary's levee, he plagued his sister, he made casual love to the cousin, who seemed to be his fiancée—in short, he had by now turned a serious gathering of odd-minded men of scientific interests into the start of a first-rate brawl.

If Hugo Chantrelle's Extra Sensory Perception (or his awareness of past phrases of seriotemporal existence; he had not definitely decided which) had been as keen as he liked later to suppose, he might indeed have had premonitions.

He might have had a premonition when young Duncan was introduced to the comfortably enthroned Hilary Foulkes.

"Ah yes," Hilary murmured. "Duncan. Duncan. Oh yes, the daring young man with the audacity to write new Dr. Derringer stories. Most daring of you, Duncan. Delighted to meet you. Delighted. You know, I feel that I've been most generous to you. I really should have refused permission for your series. Duty to my father's memory and all that, you know. But I'm not such an ogre as some people make me out. After all, you pulp writers have to live, don't you?"

Duncan's pretty, Spanish-looking little wife had drawn him away, though not before he had uttered an ugly and threatening phrase. The scowl on his face was blacker than her hair.

He might have had a premonition when Veronica Foulkes, after having had no more success with several of the guests than she had had with her host, disappeared into the garden for some time with Joe Henderson.

She does rather resemble one of Joe's villainesses physically, Chantrelle had thought; but their minds are always astutely evil. Hers is merely commonplace and silly.

He was rather surprised to notice that Henderson returned with lipstick smudged on his face, so badly that the cousin caught hold of him and drew him aside for repairs before he met Hilary's eyes.

He might have had a premonition when Wimpole eventually, being (as Chantrelle's Scots grandfather would have said) under drink taken, gradually ceased making casual love to his fiancée and began to bestow tentative but certainly not casual advances upon others.

He had an enviable field to choose from. Carter and Marshall and Boucher and Duncan were all men blessed beyond the average with attractive wives. And of them all it was the long-legged Leona Marshall, whose red hair blended so notably with Vance's own, who seemed most to attract him.

Chantrelle missed the climax of this development; but its nature was not hard to deduce from Wimpole's nose-bleed and the quiet, earnest, and somewhat apologetic conversation of the Marshalls in a corner.

He might most appositely of all have had a premonition when he went down to the shed to check up on preparations for the rocket test; for he was going to hold that test come hell or high water. Some few of his guests, he was sure, were still interested; and the others could . . . Well, after all, consider the shape of a rocket.

There were three figures standing by the workshed. They were on the edge of the pool of light cast by the shed's window, and they gave in the dark night a curious effect of optical illusion. The central figure was a woman. The others were men; or rather, and this was what was perturbing, they were the same man. It was as though the woman were being escorted by a man and his *Doppelgänger*.

There is a pleasure in being deceived by our eyes. Perhaps it provides us with the consolatory thought that our senses are not perfect and that therefore things need not be quite so terrible as they seem. Chantrelle watched this double apparition with the same uneasy satisfaction that he had once felt when he stared too long at a waterfall and the very earth and rocks began to move as though serenaded by Orpheus his lute.

Then at the same time Chantrelle's assistant Gribble opened the door of the shed and the tall and sturdy Marshall stepped from somewhere out of the shadows. In the light the three figures were simply Hilary Foulkes, abandoning his throne at last for a breath of air, his cousin Miss was it Green? and that Frangible individual.

"All ready any time you say, boss," Gribble announced.

And the extra sensitive and serial-living Hugo Chantrelle had still not felt a premonition.

II

Gribble turned a switch, and bright lights picked out the course which the rocket was to follow. This was a carefully constructed trench four feet deep and extending some hundred yards down the arroyo, making a slight arc twice in its meanderings and ending in a spring-backed shock cushion of raw cotton.

Leona Marshall let out a loud sigh of disappointment. "The rocket just goes along there? But that's no fun. I thought rockets went up in the air *boom!*"

"And maybe off to Mars," Concha added. "Or leastways to the moon."

"Hush," Matt advised. "Austin's going to make a speech; I think that'll clear up your confusions."

The party was gathered on either side of the trench in front of the workshed. They had split more or less involuntarily into two groups: those who were in some way connected with Hilary Foulkes and those who led carefree and innocent lives.

On the western lip of the trench were the Bouchers and the MacDonalds and the several Caltech men. On the eastern lip were the Marshalls and the Duncans, Henderson and Phyn, D. Vance Wimpole, and the Foulkes-Green family. Hugo Chantrelle was in the pit of the workshed beside the rocket, and the Carters stood in the doorway of the shed facing both groups of auditors.

"Let there be silence," said Austin Carter. "I will have hush." And the mumblings of the party slowly died down, leaving nothing but the voice of Vance Wimpole saying ". . . marry the chief's daughter. Of course she was attractive enough, in a lard-laden sort of . . ." He sensed the silence, and let the phrase trail off.

"Thank you," Carter smiled. "Ladies and gentlemen . . . scientists, writers, housewives, and detectives . . . Hugo has asked me to say a few dedicatory words on rockets. You don't expect me to resist that, do you?"*

The murderer shifted restlessly. There were other matters more pressing than rockets. The murderer began to regret ever having come to this party.

"Most people," Carter went on, "know that a rocket is fun to shoot off on the Fourth. A few know that it's useful for signal flares. And for a very few, our host and me among them, the rocket is something to which to pin our hopes for the human future.

"Its origin goes back into legend, and almost inevitably Chinese legend at that. It was first used in warfare, chiefly as a creator of panic, as at the battle of Pienking. The rocket became known in Europe late in the fourteenth century. By 1405 von Eichstädt was writing of its military value, and by 1420 Joanes de Fontana was constructing fantastically shaped rockets and drafting plans for a never-constructed rocket car. To Fontana belongs the honor of first realizing that the rocket was not an end, but a means."

A means . . . The murderer frowned down at the rocket in the pit. Could this creation of the eccentric Mr. Chantrelle conceivably be a means of necessary elimination?

"For the next four centuries, the development of the rocket was at a standstill, until Sir William Congreve had the genial notion of encasing the gunpowder, not in paper, but in iron. The success of this device set inventors everywhere to fretting over rockets as a motive power of flight.

"But the modern history of rocketry begins with Konstantin Eduardovich Ziolkovsky, who in 1903 made the first scientific application of the rocket principle to the problems of space travel.

"Man has always aspired to reach the stars. But when he finally sprouted wings, he knew that they would be futile as those of Icarus in interplanetary space. Wings must beat against air. So must propellers. In the vacuum of space they would be helpless. But the force of an explosion is as strong a motive power in a vacuum as in air."

Force . . . Force exerted, not in a vacuum, but against a . . . Yes . . . Yes.

---

* For much of the following material, Mr. Carter asks me to acknowledge his indebtedness to P.E. Cleator's *Rockets Through Space: The Dawn of Interplanetary Travel*, New York, Simon, 1936. (The British edition, London, Allen, 1936, has even more fascinating pictures.)

"It's a popular misconception that this force requires air for the exhaust gasses to push against. This is arrant nonsense. See Newton's third law of motion. A gun, for instance, fired in a vacuum, has the same recoil as in the air. And a rocket fired in space would, by the reaction from the explosion, propel a space ship, which nothing else known to us could do.

"This Ziolkovsky concept of rockets in space gave the necessary impetus at last to serious rocket research. I don't need to do more than mention the first great names in the field: Goddard, Oberth, Esnault-Pelterie; or refer to the the more important societies: the pioneer *Verein für Raumschiffahrt,* the British Interplanetry Society, the American Rocket Society, to remind you of the vast amount of practical work which has been going on especially in the past twenty years."

The murderer gazed from the rocket to the plump victim and back again to the rocket. The plans were ripening nicely.

"Among these workers is Hugo Chantrelle. If the name of Chantrelle does not ring down with the ages with those of G. Edward Pendray and Willy Ley, it will be because our heterodox host, even within this heterodox pursuit of rocketry, has followed his own doubly heterodox path. For what absorbs him is not the rocket ship, but the rocket car.

"For both theoretical and technical reasons, the rocket car has been neglected by the societies. But Chantrelle has persevered, because he believes in its value as an ice-breaker. Man rejects anything too new and startling. He would have rejected the miracle of radio if it had not snuck up on him gradually through the telegraph and the simple signaling of wireless telegraphy. He may reject the miracle of space travel unless he is first accustomed to the rocket as a means of terrestrial transport. Thus Chantrelle's first goal in rocket tubes connecting major cities, through which freight and mail may be sent even more rapidly and far more cheaply than by air. He envisions a network of such tubes, spidering all over the continent."

But has he, the murderer thought, envisioned the notably practical use to which this tube is about to be put?

"One main problem is the difficulty of steering these pilotless transports in tubes which can rarely be built in a straight line. To solve this, Chantrelle has contrived a robot governor based on the principle of the reflection of sound-waves, and this is what we are to see tried out tonight. You will notice that the walls of this trench curve twice. The rocket should, in theory, keep itself always a certain distance from each wall and thereby negotiate the curves readily. The rocket used for this test is a slow one. There has been no attempt to attain maximum exhaust velocity. It will move at only about fifty miles an hour. The final commercial rockets for the tubes will, of course, move at between two and three hundred miles per hour."

But fifty, the murderer thought, should do beautifully for this occasion. The murderer's eyes glistened, and a pink tongue licked dry lips. A certain pleasure can be derived from sheer necessity.

Austin Carter's normally assured voice grew a trifle hesitant. "There's just one point about rockets I'd like to venture on my own before we start the demonstration. I don't know if Hugo agrees with me on this; he probably hasn't even bothered himself about it. But it's this: That the rocket carries in its zooming path the hopes of all men of good will. By leaving this planet, man may become worthy of his dominion over it, and attain dominion over himself. The realization that there is something beyond this earth, if only in a purely physical sense, may unite this earth, may change men from a horde of wretchedly warring clans to a noble union of mankind.

"I may be deluded in my hopes. The discovery of new worlds may be as futile as the discovery of the New World. It may mean only further imperial wars of conquest, new chapters in the cruel exploitation of subject native races. But it may mean new unity, new vigor, new humanity, and the realization at last of all that is best in mankind. I hope so anyway," he ended, quietly and anticlimactically.

The murderer has heard little of this idealistic peroration. The murderer's eyes were fixed with a smiling glint upon Marshall. That detective, the murderer mused; this will give him to think.

III

Hugo Chantrelle had added a few words of his own, chiefly technical details which only his colleagues seemed to follow. He had spoken affectionately of his long months of work on the *Aspera IX*. All his model rockets, he explained, were named *Aspera*, for *per aspera,* eventually, *itur ad astra,* and he deplored the tendency of the facetious to refer to them as *Aspidistra.*

The group at the shed end of the trench crowded forward close to the lip and peered into the pit beneath the shed. The *Aspera IX* was some five feet long and a trifle under a foot in diameter. The gleam of light on her dull copper gave her the quality of a living thing forcibly holding itself back from motion. Chantrelle and Carter and the assistant Gribble conferred in the pit in voices too low to be heard. Then Chantrelle held up his hand.

There was silence. Gribble bent over the rocket. There was a flare of exhaust and a loud explosion. All eyes turned, tennis-wise to watch the rocket shoot past. But those eyes saw something else.

They saw a plump figure topple over the lip of the trench into the immediate path of the *Aspera IX*. The ears heard a crunch of bone and flesh, and sharp ringing screams.

The *Aspera IX* righted herself from the shock. She adjusted herself admirably to the curves in the trench and plunged undamaged into the cotton bales at the end. But no one heeded her epochal performance.

"Hilary!" Veronica Foulkes was screaming. "Hilary!" And Jenny Green was saying the same word softly and intensely.

"So they got him," Marshall swore with feeling. "Got him at last and right under my very exceedingly goddamned eyes . . ."

"Heavens!" a voice murmured. "Heavens!" The voice was shocked and trembling with terror and relief, but there was no mistaking its deep round tones.

Marshall whirled and stared at Hilary Foulkes. He followed Hilary's gaze down to the bleeding mass in the trench. "Then who . . .?" he demanded loudly.

No one answered him.

IV

From then on it was Lieutenant Marshall's party.

It was Marshall who ordered Chantrelle and Carter to let no one climb down into the trench. It was Marshall who sent Gribble to the house to phone the Pasadena police. It was Marshall who delegated his wife, aided by Concha Duncan, to minister to the women present and prevent hysterics. It was Marshall who himself descended into the trench, identified the plump pulp as that of the fan Runcible, made certain that it was dead (as though anyone beholding that impact could have had any doubt), and covered it with a tarpaulin (which is after all the same word as *pall*) from the shed.

Now it was Marshall who addressed the group gathered in Chantrelle's vast living-room. "The police," he began, "will be here in five or ten minutes."

"But Lieutenant," Hilary protested, "I thought you *were* the police."

"I am in Los Angeles. Here in Pasadena, I'm just another civilian. But a civilian with specialized knowledge and experience, and that I'm putting at your disposal now. We're going to spend those minutes before the Pasadena boys arrive in trying to get this business straight."

He looked about the group. They were sober enough now, in either meaning of the word. Nothing less like a triumphant rocket-launching party could be imagined. Social gaiety and scientific fervor were both obliterated by the sudden emergence of death.

But it was an impersonal sort of sobriety. As was, indeed, natural enough. No one here had known Runcible more than casually. He was an extra, a hanger-on, a speartoter. His death had been terrible to see, but it had stirred only physical response; there was no mourning, no personal sorrow at his passing. And with Hilary and his cousin, perhaps even with his wife, the emotion of relief so effectively drowned out any casual regret for Runcible's death that they looked almost jubilant.

It was one of the Caltech men who spoke up. "But why is there any need for the police? It was a most tragic accident, and there will doubtless be a highly unpleasant inquest; but the police . . ."

"Accident, hell," Marshall snorted. "Maybe some of you read the papers; but most of you must know that there has recently been a series of attempts on the life of Mr. Foulkes here. You also know, from your own observation, that Mr. Foulkes and the dead man were much of a build. In fact, both Mrs. Foulkes and I, seeing that body hurtle into the trench, thought at once that it was her husband. So. I think the conclusion's obvious."

"That poor man!" Hilary sighed, his sorrow serving as an inadequate mask for his relief. "To think that he laid down his life for mine!"

"Involuntarily, no doubt; but what Mr. Foulkes says is nonetheless true. The bright lights were focused on the trench. We on the edge were in half-darkness. And the curiously inefficient murderer who had previously made five unsuccessful attempts on Mr. Foulkes' life tonight made his sixth and most spectacularly unsuccessful."

There was another sigh of relief, this time from Hugo Chantrelle, who followed it with a fervent "Thank God."

"And why, sir?" Marshall demanded.

"Because, Lieutenant, if this is murder, there can be no public furor about the dangers of rocket experimentation. After Valier's sad death in 1930, there were shortsighted but rabid demands throughout Germany for the legal prohibition of all further work on rockets. But in this case . . . You can see why I thank God for your murderer."

"So, All right: Now did anyone see clearly what happened? I know that all of us (save one) had our attention firmly fixed on the *Aspera IX*. The murderer knew his principles of stage conjuring. I'm not expecting anybody to produce a diagram of just where each person was; but did anyone see any sudden movement that might have been the fatal shove?" Marshall paused, mentally biting his tongue for such a banal utterance as that last phrase.

There was silence.

"All right. I know how you might feel. You say to yourself, 'After all, I'm not too sure of what I saw, and I'm not going to send a man to the gas chamber on my guess.' But remember that this is a clumsy murderer, an ineffectual, frustrated murderer. He'll strike again when he gets the chance. And we've got to see that he never gets it. So come on. Tell anything that might help."

Matt Duncan rose, hesitantly, as one might to recite an unprepared lesson. He shoved his tousled black hair away from his brow, and the freakish white streak in it seemed to emphasize the bitter torsion of his features. "O.K., Terence," he said.

"So. Yes, Matt? You saw who shoved Runcible?"

Matt gulped audibly. "Saw, hell! I shoved him."

Concha's reaction was more a squeak than a scream. She put out one small hand as though to halt her husband's confession. Hilary was on his feet and booming something about Justice and At Last.

Marshall cut him short. "You shoved him, Matt?" he said gently.

"I couldn't help it. I was standing behind him. I'm a head taller than he is . . . was . . . so he didn't obstruct me. Then just as the rocket went off, I got a hell of a sharp jab in the back. I started to fall forward, so I put out my hands. You know how you do . . . I hit what's-his-name. I saw him stagger and then go forward and over and straight into . . ."

No one had noticed Leona slip away from the group, but now she stood beside Matt with a tumbler half full of whisky. "This'll help," she said.

He took it at a gulp and his body was unshaken. "Thanks," he nodded. "There. I've done it now. I've confessed. According to the notions of my wife's church, it ought to be clear sailing from here on in. But I still . . ."

"Lieutenant," Hilary demanded, "arrest this man! A sharp jab in the back, indeed! He's afraid someone else saw him, and he's trying to beat them to it. Arrest him, I say!"

"In the first place," said Marshall slowly, "I can't arrest anybody outside the city limits of Los Angles; and despite all gags as to their extent, we're outside them now. In the second place, I believe him. Go on, Matt. Can you tell us anything more about this jab?"

Matt's voice was unsure and wavering. "I can't, Terence. I didn't look around because all I could see was Whoozis falling and falling and then . . ." He shuddered and covered his face with his hands.

"Pull yourself together," said Marshall, feeling as futile as the phrase.

Matt lowered his hands. "Sure. Pull myself together. With these hands, no doubt. These hands that killed a man . . ."

A harsh dry voice spoke from the doorway, "Hot stuff!" it said. "A confession already!" Its uniformed owner grinned, then called over his shoulder, "Come on in, boys. We've got it all cleaned up."

The officer strode into the middle of the room. "Kello's the name folks. Sergeant Kello. K, e, l, l, O-O-O-O, like they sing on the radio. And it looks like we're going to have a short and easy time of it, don't it? All right, big boy," he addressed Matt, "what's your name and who'd you kill?"

"I'm afraid, Sergeant," Marshall interposed, "you're plunging in too fast. It isn't a question of handcuffs yet."

"Hell, brother, a confession's a confession, ain't it? And who're you anyway to tell me where I get off?"

Marshall showed his badge. "Marshall, Lieutenant, Homicide."

Sergeant Kello's round red face narrowed unpleasantly. "Marshall huh? Quite the big shot in L.A., ain't you? Well, brother, this is Pasadena. Keep your nose clean."

V

"Hell of a mess, ain't he, doc? Anyways there can't be much doubt about cause of death. Die right away?"

"Instantly."

"Never knew what hit him, huh? Serves the poor bastard right for playing around with rockets. The whole kit and caboodle of 'em's screwy if you ask me. Rockets . . . You identify this man, Mr. Carter?"

"As best I can from what's left of him. At any rate, that's the suit Runcible was wearing, you found his draft card in it, and he's the only member of the party not accounted for. His dentist can probably identify him more positively than I could."

"Don't teach your grandmother to suck eggs, Carter. Look at it this way: Would I try to tell you how to write a story?"

"Probably."

"Let's see: Runcible . . . First name, William? Address . . ."

"So this list, Mr. Chantrelle, is the people who were on the same side of the trench as Runcible, and these were on the other side?"

"Yes. My assistant Gribble, Mr. Carter and his wife, and I were in the pit."

"So it's just these ten who could've . . . But hell, what are we wasting time for? We know who did it."

"You ever have any trouble with this Duncan, Mr. Foulkes?"

"Trouble? I don't know that you'd call it trouble. But perhaps . . . One never knows how these pulp writers will react to the most ordinary business proposition. One never knows. We did have a . . . I suppose you might call it a financial disagreement. I referred to it casually this evening and Duncan burst forth into wild threats and gave me a look as though he . . . why, as though he wanted to murder me. And by Jove, he did!"

"Threats, huh? What kind of threats, Mr. Phyn?"

"You understand I wouldn't ordinarily talk like this about a friend, Sergeant, but under the circumstances . . ."

"Sure. Never does no harm to stand in good with the law. Shoot, brother."

"Before this evening, I mean. I think before he'd ever met Mr. Foulkes."

"What sort of threats?"

"Well, not threats exactly. Maybe just a lot of loose talk. But I do know that Duncan was all shot to hell when he learned about this financial finagling of Foulkes', and one night at Carter's when we were talking about the Perfect Crime he said he had at least the Perfect Victim. It sounded as though he meant it. He meant something anyway."

"You saw this push, Mr. Boucher?"

"I'm afraid so. Something bit me and I happened to jerk up my head just as the rocket started. I noticed Duncan because that odd white streak in his hair took the light. And it did look as though he himself was being shoved too."

"You saw him shoved?"

"I can't quite say that. He's tall, and whoever was behind him must have been shorter; I couldn't see anyone, But Duncan's body lurched forward as though—"

"You'd swear in court that you saw him shoved and that he didn't do the shoving himself?"

"I couldn't swear to that, no. But it's my firm impression that—"

"That's enough, Boucher."

"O.K., Marshall. We're smart in Pasadena too, but if somebody else does the spade work it's oke by us. You've been investigating these other attacks on Foulkes?"

"Yes."

"Duncan included among your suspects? Come on, brother. Talk, If you won't, I can go over your head and get an order from your chief for you to cooperate or else. Did you investigate Duncan?"

"Yes. Inevitable routine. He was one of the many business enemies that Hilary Foulkes had a habit of making."

"Find anything to tie him up with the attacks?"

"Nothing."

"But did you find anything that cleared him? It was possible for him to make every one of the other attacks on Foulkes, wasn't it?"

"It wasn't possible for anybody to make the last one."

"Yeah. I read about that. You boys just didn't go over the room careful enough. But Duncan hasn't got any alibis?"

"None."

"That's all I wanted to know, brother."

Sergeant Kello looked at his wrist watch. "We've been here an hour, boys. That's what I call making time. Sixty-minute Kello, that's me. And I didn't need that much. The more I talk to these dopes the surer I am of what I knew right the minute I came in that door. 'Somebody shoved me, officer . . .' Nuts! He knew somebody must've spotted him from across the trench, so he tried a fast one to clear himself. They can't get away with it, not with Kello on the job."

Hugo Chantrelle peered into the study which Kello was using. "I beg your pardon, Lieutenant—"

"Sergeant right now, brother. But you wait till the papers get hold of this. Pasadena Sergeant Frustrates Attacks on Celebrity after L.A. Police Star Fails. Lieutenant Kello . . . Sounds kind of good, don't it?"

"Yes indeed, Sergeant. But what I wanted to ask: My guests are getting exceedingly worried and tired. I simply can't put them all up for the night. And Mrs. Marshall and Mrs. Boucher are fretting about their children, who are in the charge of high school girls who apparently expect to go home long before this hour. And Mr. Wimpole—"

"Tell 'em they can go home now," said the future Lieutenant Kello expansively. "Tell 'em they can all go home. All but one." He jangled a pair of handcuffs playfully.

VI

Leona Marshall clicked on the light of her living room, crossed to the couch, and shook the shoulder of the sleeping high school girl. The girl sat up, rubbed her eyes, and said, "Oh. Have a nice party?"

Leona didn't try to answer that one. She just said, "I'm sorry we're so late, Doris. Here's your money, with the extra for the hours after midnight. Mr. Marshall's out in the car. He'll take you home."

"Sit down, Concha," she added when the girl had left, "I just want to take a look at the children to make doubly sure. Be right back."

Concha sat. It was easy to obey simple commands. This must be the way zombies feel, a sort of relief at just having to obey, after all the living problems of trying to shape life because now there isn't any life to shape any more. She sat and stared blankly in front of her until Leona returned.

Leona stood looking at her for a moment, then laid a gentle hand on her shoulder. "I prescribed whisky for Matt," she said quietly, "but I don't think it'd help you. Nothing could at the moment but maybe sleep. Here's some phenobarbital. Take another one later if you still toss, but one ought to do it."

"He didn't, Leona." Concha's voice was little and frightened.

"Of course he didn't. It's just that stupid Sergeant trying to do the job in record time and get a promotion."

"I know. That sounds so safe and simple. But first it's a Sergeant that wants a promotion. Then it could be a prosecutor that's coming up for reelection. Then it could be a jury that wanted to get home. It could all be so simple and commonplace only Matt . . . Matt'd be dead."

"Nonsense. They haven't got any kind of a case. Why, even Sergeant Kello only dared arrest him on a manslaughter charge. He admitted he'd have to have more evidence on the other attempts to prove premeditation before he could make it murder."

"But when they know what they're looking for they can find it even if it isn't there . . . Oh Leona . . ." The girl's sobs were dry and aching.

"There," Leona said soothingly. "You hear a lot about miscarriages of justice, convictions of innocent people. But they're one in a million. That's why you hear so much about them, just because they are so rare. He'll be all right."

Concha tried to choke back her sobs and force a smile. "You're sweet, Leona, trying to whistle in the dark for me. But how much of this do you believe yourself? Oh," she added with a gasp, before Leona could answer. "Hilary!"

"What about him?"

"He thinks Matt did it. And Hilary has money, ever so much money, and he can . . ."

"If it comes to fighting that way, you have money too, haven't you? And I'll tell you what you have to do with it first thing tomorrow. Go to your lawyer and have him get Matt out on bail. Since the present charge is only manslaughter, that'll be easy."

"But it'll be . . . murder as soon as that dreadful Sergeant . . ."

"Well," said Leona, "there's one certain and sure way of seeing to it that Matt is proved innocent. And that is to prove beyond any doubt who did it."

Marshall came in just then. "Applause," he observed. "And that, I promise you Concha, is what I'm out to do. Quite aside from the fact that it's the job I'm paid for."

Concha Duncan lifted a damp face. "Have you any ideas, Lieutenant? Any at all?"

Marshall grunted. "I did have one. And it stood in the pit beside Chantrelle. In this case we're strictly limited to the group on our side of the trench. Outside of the four Marshalls and Duncans, that leaves Mrs. Foulkes, the cousin, Vance Wimpole, Henderson, and the agent. And on the bomb," he mused aloud, "it has to be a man. No woman could get away with the Derringer get-up, especially feminine women. That leaves us Wimpole, Henderson, and Phyn. See how easy it is, Concha?"

The note of blithe confidence in his voice did not quite ring true.

SIX

THE LAST DAY:
Saturday, November 8, 1941

Early the next morning Marshall was at the rooming house on West Adams which had been the abode of William Runcible. Runcible, it seemed obvious, was a side-line; but as a corpse inevitably an important one. They knew nothing about this accident victim, Marshall reflected, not even how he made his living. And the Lieutenant's orderly mind rebelled against such lack of knowledge of the focal individual in a murder case.

The landlady looked paler than a woman of her build had any right to be. She held the morning paper clenched in a hand that shook slightly.

Marshall identified himself, and she gasped, "About Mr. Runcible? I saw it in here," she added hastily, brandishing the paper.

"A terrible thing," said Marshall gravely. "I wanted to ask a few questions about him and see his room."

"I'll be glad to tell you anything I can, officer."

"All right. How long had he been here with you?"

"Almost six months."

"And do you know where he came from?"

"He never said anything about that. He wasn't much of a one for talking about himself."

"Know anything of any family?"

"Not a thing, officer."

"Where did he work?"

"At the Safeway down the street. He was a grocery clerk there."

"A good tenant?"

"He was a nice-spoken young man and he paid his bills and he never made any trouble."

"Thank you." He considered her pale face and still trembling hand. "The news of his death seems to have been quite a shock to you."

"Yes . . . Yes, I guess it was. But it was coming on top of . . .

You see, we had a burglary here last night or early this morning I guess I should say. Mrs. Svoboda, she's a waitress in an all-night drive-in and when she came home she found this strange man prowling around in the halls and she screamed and woke me and I saw him leaving but when we called the police of course it was too late and we don't know if he took anything yet, but I was all upset and then this on top of it, why—"

"I can understand," said Marshall soothingly. "Now if I might have that key . . . ?"

Lieutenant Marshall had never gone over so unprofitable a room, unless perhaps it was the cheap cubicle in the Elite hotel where Jonathan Tarbell had died. You could learn from the room that its owner cared little for clothes and much for science fiction. And that was about all.

No letters save correspondence with other fans (Marshall automatically abstracted a couple of the least impersonal), no private papers, no note or address books. But infinite numbers of pulp paper scientifiction magazines and those curious mimeographed fan bulletins that are known by the portmanteau name of fanzines, a complete set of Fowler Foulkes, almost as reverently bound as Hilary's, a goodly lot of Shiel and Stapledon . . .

Nothing personal. Nothing at all. One curious item: a picture hook with no picture hanging from it and a blank space on the wall over the Foulkes collection. But this might be a relic from some earlier tenancy. Nothing . . .

Marshall was about to leave the room in disgust when his sharp eye caught a glint of white in one corner. He went over and investigated. There was a crack in the floorboards just beyond the wastepaper basket. This would be a note hurled at the basket, overshooting its target, and later trodden into the crack.

Marshall unfolded the paper and read:

He (or was it *H.?*) *says maybe. Keep hoping keed.*

J.T.

J. T. . . . No. That would be too much. Too pretty to be true. But now he suddenly remembered that Matt had mentioned meeting a Tarbell at Carter's. Runcible frequented Carter's . . .

Marshall felt in his coat pocket. His luck was in; he still had the morgue photograph of Jonathan Tarbell. He hurried downstairs to the landlady.

"Yes," she admitted. "He used to come to see Mr. Runcible right often. But he hasn't been around for a week or so. But what's this?"

This was the still of Norval Prichard as Dr. Derringer, which had fluttered out of Marshall's pocket as he took out the Tarbell photo.

"Why goodness me!" she gasped. "That's our burglar!"

II

In the quiet and sunny patio of the Sisters of Martha of Bethany, Concha Duncan struck a discordant note. She still wore the gay and flaunting scarlet gown which she had put on for the rocket party, and looked even more sorely out of place here than she had on the bus coming out.

But there was nothing gay and flaunting about her voice. "You've got to help us, Sister. You've simply got to. If anything happens to Matt . . . We haven't been married even a year yet, but we've been married all my life. All my life that counts is being married to Matt, and if anything happens to him, I . . . I'll have to die too."

"Life is God's gift, Mary," Sister Ursula said gently. "We can't toss it away at our own whims."

"I don't mean that. I just mean that if I haven't got Matt. I simply *can't* live any more. It'll stop inside me. So you must save him, Sister. You're so wise and good. You can do it."

"Lieutenant Marshall is an admirable man. Since Matt is innocent, and I cannot entertain the slightest doubt that he is, the Lieutenant will surely establish that fact in short order."

"But it's not his case, don't you see? It's that dreadful Sergeant from Pasadena. The Lieutenant can't do a thing; he hasn't any official standing."

"And you think that I, with even less standing, could succeed if he fails? The previous attempts on Mr. Foulkes' life are still in Lieutenant Marshall's domain. If he finds the man who is guilty of those, Sergeant Kello's case can never be made to stand up so long as he insists that Runcible was killed in error for Mr. Foulkes."

"Then you won't do anything?"

"I can't do anything. There's no need for me."

"All right." Concha rose smoothing her skirt. "I know what's the trouble. I've heard you talk to the Lieutenant like this. You're worrying about spiritual pride. You're worrying about the temptation of power over human life. You're worrying about your soul. All right. Save your soul. And pray for my husband's."

She turned to go. Sister Ursula rose and stood terribly still. One hand clutched the crucifix of her rosary, and her lips moved soundlessly. "Mary . . ." she said at last.

Concha was at the arcade leading out of the patio. She turned. "Yes?" she said bitterly.

"Tell me, Mary: How certain is the Lieutenant that Runcible was killed by mistake?"

Concha's face lit up. "Then you will help?"

"If asking questions will help for a start. Come back here and sit down with me on the bench. Now. Is he positive of that mistake?"

"You're a . . ." A laugh and a sob were contending in Concha's throat, "You're . . . I can't say it. I can't say anything."

"Blow your nose," Sister Ursula suggested softly. "Here. And don't try to say it. Just tell me about things."

"Well," (a gulp and a loud snuffle) "well, the Lieutenant's awfully certain on that. You see, the two men did look a lot alike. Hilary's maybe I'd guess ten years older than Runcible, but they're both the fleshy type that looks pretty much the same from twenty-five to fifty. And they both had on similar gray suits that night. Of course Hilary's must have cost about three times as much as Runcible's, but at night . . . The Lieutenant says it was funny when he saw them together with the Green girl; it looked as though she had the same man on each side of her."

Sister Ursula's eyes revealed a slight gleam. "The two of them together? Runcible and Mr. Foulkes? When was this?"

"It was just before the rocket test. The Lieutenant was keeping a close eye on Hilary of course. Hilary'd raised a fuss and said he couldn't go lugging bodyguards around to parties, so the Lieutenant pretended to agree only you see he was the bodyguard. So when Hilary went outside the Lieutenant followed him, and the cousin was with him, and they met this Runcible and talked for a while."

"And when the murder occurred, then, the Lieutenant was watching Mr. Foulkes instead of the rocket?"

"No. He admits he slipped up there pretty badly. Because there was a lot of shifting around so as to get a better view of the pit and he lost sight of Hilary just for a minute. But it wouldn't have made any difference anyway because it wasn't Hilary that got killed, it was Runcible, and we've got to find out who did it and now you will help us, won't you?"

Sister Ursula rose, smoothing down her robes. "Please ask Lieutenant Marshall to come to see me as soon as he can. And in the meantime . . . Where are you to meet Matt when he is released on bail?"

"At the lawyer's office. I couldn't stand going over to Pasadena and seeing where they . . . *keep* him. I want to see him free and try to think he's always going to be that way. And besides I wanted to come out here."

"Why don't you phone your lawyer's office and leave word for Matt to come here to meet you? If you wait downtown, you'll simply worry more; and I'm sure he won't want you to be all frowning and tear-stained when you meet him. Stay here in the good sun, or make a visit to the chapel. Ask our Lord and His blessed Mother to help you. For if I do succeed in freeing your husband, Mary, it will only be through Her intercession and His grace."

Concha nodded. "I will. It helps, prayer does. Even when it doesn't help from outside, it helps inside you."

"And you've helped me, Mary. You've shown me that my fear of pride was in itself a very special kind of pride. The soul saved at the expense of a brother's life can hardly be a cause for great rejoicing in heaven."

"But look. You said 'stay here.' Where are you going?"

Sister Ursula smiled. "The thought just crossed my mind that there was so much attendant confusion, that day when Mr. Foulkes was attacked in my presence, that I never had the opportunity of speaking with him about my real errand, clearing the copyright permission for Sister Patientia's braille work. I think, if Reverend Mother will allow me, that I shall go see him about that now."

III

Lieutenant Marshall read over again the note that he had taken from Runcible's room. He still didn't understand it. It involved chiefly the law of entropy, the paradoxes of Space-Time, and the theory of wave-mechanics, all couched in a jargon of technical erudition that made Austin Carter's conversation seem infantile. But the last paragraph was more personal, and seemed to imply that this Arthur Waring had known Runcible better than most of his correspondents.

An infant with pink and downy cheeks answered Marshall's ring. "I'd like to speak to Arthur Waring," the Lieutenant announced.

"That's me," the lad replied in a clear soprano.

"You—" Marshall checked himself; to ask if it mightn't be his father could simply antagonize the boy. He could remember his own youth, and how a boy's desire to seem older than his age is as strong as a woman's yearning to seem younger. But still, the precocity of that letter . . . "You're the Arthur Waring who was a friend of William Runcible's?"

The boy's face lit up. "Oh jeepers! Are you the police? I read about it in the paper."

Marshall nodded. "If I could talk to you a few minutes . . . ?"

The boy led the way to a small room. Marshall gasped as he entered. The entire wall was pictures. The same sort of pictures that he had seen in the Nitrosyncretic Lab, originals of illustrations for stf magazines, but hundreds, seemingly thousands of them.

Waring heard the gasp. "Aren't they swell? That's a Rogers cover over there, and I've got a half dozen Boks and three Finlays. And look over here; That's an original Cartier, and did that take some getting! When I'm illustrating for the mags I'm going to do like Rogers and just rent my originals and then I can be nice to the fans."

"You're an artist yourself?"

"Sort of. Only when you live on the West Coast you can't get a chance to do any commercial illustrating, but when I finish college I'm going back to New York and—Only you wanted to ask me questions, didn't you?"

Marshall, always willing (if sometimes reluctantly so) to spend long minutes buttering up a witness as a good investment, was pleased by this directness. "Yes. It seems hard to get any information at all about Runcible. If you were a friend of his, maybe you can help us."

"Well, I don't know if I was so awfully much of a *friend* of his. Of course we both belonged to the Califuturions (that's a fan club), and sometimes we'd swap mags or mostly he'd borrow mine because I had more. I've got some nice stuff here, officer."

Marshall looked about the room. No books here. Just an infinite number of pulp magazines, all carefully arranged by title and date; apparently almost complete files of a half dozen different publications, and assorted samples of others.

"I've got them all indexed too," Waring went on. "I made a complete index of all the best magazines from their start and I mimeographed it. Would you like to have a copy? Only you wanted me to tell you about Runcible. But what about him?"

"Well for instance: Did he have any family? We ought to notify them if he had, but I couldn't find any hint in his room."

"I don't think he had. He was a lot older'n most of us. He must've been . . . oh, almost thirty. I guess his folks were dead; he never talked about 'em. He never really talked about much of anything excepting science fiction. He was nuts about Fowler Foulkes. He had a big framed autographed picture of him in his room. He used to talk about him like he was god or something." There was a note of scorn in the high young voice.

"You don't like Foulkes?"

"Naw. He's a classic. I'm going to do an article for one of the fan-mags debunking the classics. Who cares about Foulkes or Poe or Verne? They're old stuff, and I'm going to show them up."

"Have you read them?" Marshall asked with quiet amusement.

"Well . . . no. Not much anyway. But all these people that rave about the classics, which maybe they were all right when *they* were young, but have they read what's being published now? You bet your life they haven't."

The point, Marshall was obliged to admit, had turned against him neatly. "So Runcible was all for the classics?"

"Especially Foulkes. He was funny other ways too. He was I guess what you might call a purist. He thought people ought to read books too besides all the mags only how could you have time? And he kept saying what fans ought to support was pro writing instead of fandom."

Apparently William Runcible, so silent in the presence of the Mañana Literary Society, had been voluble enough among the Califuturions. But his tastes and theories were hardly to the point. "What was he like?" Marshall wanted to know.

"That's hard to say now. He talked a lot and he used to write pieces for the fanzines—he wrote one for mine once—"

"You're a publisher?"

"Sure. Here." Waring crossed to a pile of mimeographed sheets and picked up a stapled magazine with a lithographed cover. It was called *Fandemonium*. "Take one. Only about Runcible. Somehow nobody ever got to know him very well. He did have a friend he brought around a couple of times; he seemed pretty close. Maybe you'd better try him, only I don't remember his name."

Resignedly Marshall brought out the picture of Tarbell.

Waring nodded eagerly. "That's the joe. Couldn't he tell you anything?"

"Not a thing," said Marshall truthfully.

"I think they were working on something together. They seemed thick as thieves. Maybe they were collaborating; Bill (that's Runcible) always said he wanted to write some time cause it was in the family. Only when he was doing the arm trick, this man said, 'Maybe that'll help too,' and how could it with writing?"

"The arm trick?"

"That was something Bill used to do at parties. It was a good trick only nobody else could ever do it. It looked awful, like something in a horror story illustrated by Cartier. He'd put his arm all around his neck and reach back to the ear on the same side as the arm if you see what I mean. And then he'd put both arms around his neck and clasp them under his chin. Wait a minute—I've got a picture I drew of it someplace here."

Marshall shuddered involuntarily as he looked at the pen-and-ink sketch. Not that it was so bad as that; it was, in fact, a surprisingly good piece of work. But it depicted a horrible apparition. It looked eerily like a severed head being borne by two unattached arms—John the Baptist displayed by a bodiless Salome. It was somehow more grisly, more dead than the crushed pulp of Runcible's factually dead head had been.

"You can have that too, if you want," Waring added. "Bill Runcible was funny maybe, but he was kind of a good guy. If I can help any, I want to."

"Thanks." Marshall failed to see how the macabre head could help, but it would be an unusually picturesque illustration for a dossier. "Anything else you can think of about Runcible? For instance, did he spend more money than he'd possibly make as a grocery clerk?"

"No. The only thing he spent much on was books. And he used

to say he liked his job fine only I don't see why, but then he was expecting to be drafted pretty soon anyways."

"You don't—" Marshall started to say, then stopped and stared at the boy. "Mr. Waring," he said gravely, "you have helped. Immeasurably. And I, sir, am an idiot."

IV

"Look at you!" Veronica Foulkes' throaty voice was scornful. "One thing at least you've spared me all these years. You've never been a drinking man. If you knew all I've gone through with Vance, and how terribly trying it is for a woman of my . . . And now look at you! Drinking even before lunch!"

Hilary poured himself another glass of straight scotch. "My dear!" he protested. "Surely one who talks as much as you do about her sensitivity must realize that others can be sensitive as well. Last night was a terrible shock for me. A terrible shock. That poor innocuous fan . . . And it might so easily have been me lying in the depths of that trench, crushed and mangled and pulped. So easily . . . " He gulped the glassful hastily and stared at his plump white hand. It still quivered slightly.

Veronica turned to the wall mirror and adjusted her hat. "I do hope," she observed tartly, "that I'll find you conscious when I get home. To think that I should learn at this late date that I married a drunkard!"

"One swallow," said Hilary seriously, "doesn't make a summer. Heavens! That's a pun, isn't it?" He seemed amazed.

"You can spare me your drunken wit."

"I didn't mean to. It just happened. It simply came up like . . . like . . . " A burp appositely ended his quest for a smile. "Like that. But seriously, Veronica, you can't call this a habit. After all, it's not every day that one has just escaped murder."

"It almost seems to be with you."

"Those other attempts . . . I can't explain it, but they didn't seem quite real. Even when I was stabbed. After all, nothing serious actually happened. It wasn't possible to realize fully what I had escaped. Not possible. But this time, when I could see that poor devil and have before my eyes what I should have been . . . I can't explain it, but—"

"Please! You might at least wait till I leave before you go on poisoning yourself."

Hilary set aside his freshly poured glass. "And what is this luncheon engagement?"

"I told you last night. But then you never hear a word I say anyway."

"I'm afraid last night I may have been a trifle preoccupied, my dear. Just a trifle."

"It's with that Henderson boy. You know, he's really a darling. I think he understands me. And you could never appreciate what a relief that is after the cold blank wall of indifference that I meet in my own house."

Hilary sighed and reached out for his glass. "Goodbye, my dear."

"You . . . you don't mind?" Veronica asked hopefully.

"Why should I? Why on earth should I?"

She shrugged. "Some husbands might be jealous. A little. A husband that was half a man himself . . . Hilary."

"Yes, my dear."

"You don't like me at all any more, do you?" Her voice was for once simple and direct.

"No, my dear."

"So," said Veronica. "That's that." Her voice rose cheerfully. "Now I simply must fly. I'm late as it is and—"

"Veronica."

"Yes . . . ?"

"Have you ever liked me?"

"I . . . I do have to hurry now, Hilary. I—"

"Have you?"

"I've tried. Honestly I've tried . . ."

"How typical of you, my dear." Hilary's voice was flat. "You always try. You tried music once, remember, and painting. Self-expression. You tried religion. You've tried lovers. Oh yes, I know. But whatever you try turns out to be too hard and you stop trying. You stop. You always try and you never do. You . . . " Hilary's voice stopped. For a moment he stared in silence at his wife.

"Goodbye . . . " she said hesitantly.

"Always trying and never succeeding," he repeated slowly. "And I am still alive . . . "

Without another word Veronica Foulkes snatched up her bag and left. Hilary laughed once, harshly. Then the room was still.

For five minutes he sat there motionless. Sometimes his eyes fixed speculatively on the study within which he had been so mysteriously wounded. Sometimes they gazed as though focused on a distant and invisible object, such as a rocket trench in Pasadena.

Finally he bestirred himself sufficiently to pour another whisky, and as he did so the doorbell rang. In a moment the maid ushered in two nuns. Hilary set the glass aside and reluctantly rose to his feet.

"Yes?" he asked, wavering almost imperceptibly.

The younger of the two (as best one can judge ages beneath the agelessness of religious habits) said, "We met briefly, Mr. Foulkes, on the day you were so mysteriously attacked. Just a murmured introduction in passing, and I can hardly blame you if later events drove it from your mind. I am Sister Mary Ursula and this is Sister Mary Felicitas, of the Order of Martha of Bethany."

Hilary made a polite acknowledgment and indicated chairs. The small old eyes of Sister Felicitas seemed to close the instant she was seated.

"Indeed I do recall you now, Sister. Indeed. The police lieutenant mentioned you as one of the witnesses who proved the apparent impossibility of . . . of what happened in there."

"May I congratulate you on your escape? You seem to have a singularly efficient guardian angel. And you are further fortunate in having Lieutenant Marshall on the case."

"Indeed I am. A most able officer. Most able."

"I did not refer simply to his ability. I can imagine how many of the police would be sarcastically scornful of such an 'impossible' situation; but since the Lieutenant had such an experience once before, he must be far more receptive."

Hilary smiled. "I had hardly thought that a woman of your order would have such an acquaintance with murder, or with police ways of thinking."

"My father was a policeman, and a good one. And I was planning to be a policewoman myself when my health broke down and I was forced to change my plans."

Hilary was politely sympathetic, but fidgety. He expressed due pleasure at the news that Sister Ursula's health for the past dozen years had been enviable and due appreciation of the fact that she had nonetheless never regretted the change of vocation. He accepted her further congratulations on his happy escape of the night before; but at last he said, with a trace of impatience, "But Sister, I am sure that you did not come here to discuss my fortunate avoidance of the Black angel."

"No indeed. When I met you before, I had come on business; and I fear I am persistent."

"Business? Business? But go on."

"You have possibly heard a little from your wife concerning the purposes and activities of our order—"

Hilary's manner visibly froze. "If you are soliciting donations, Sister, I think I should explain that the state of the book market in these uncertain times is far too parlous to leave me in a position where I should feel free to contemplate . . . Far too parlous," he concluded, leaving the overcomplicated sentence hanging in air.

Sister Ursula smiled. "In a way, I suppose, it is a donation that I am soliciting, but it will cost you nothing, Mr. Foulkes. I merely wish to ask you to reconsider your refusal of copyright to Sister Patientia, who wished to transcribe some of your father's work into Braille."

Hilary looked hurt. "But my dear Sister, I did not refuse her the copyright. By all means. She may transcribe those stories whenever she wishes. I simply asked for a conventional reprint fee."

"But this is voluntary, non-commercial work. The book will be read first by a few of the blind whom we look after. Then it will go to the State Library and from there circulate to all the blind of California. And no one will pay a cent for it."

"Books circulate freely from public libraries, my dear Sister, but the libraries pay the publishers and thereby indirectly the authors for the books. It is a necessary tribute to the literary profession. I owe it to my father's memory to collect what fees I can. And moreover, a man must live."

Sister Ursula glanced about the chastely expensive room. "Do you find bread alone a satisfactory diet, Mr. Foulkes?"

"I don't understand what you mean by that remark, Sister. I don't understand it. But I must make clear to you" (Hilary leaned forward, tugging impressively at the lobe of his ear) "that under no circumstances, for no matter how worthy a cause, will I countenance the wanton pirating of my father's works."

"I don't suppose it would affect your attitude to point out that every author or publisher that Sister Patientia has previously been in touch with has always given Braille rights free as a matter of course?"

"What an author chooses to do with his own work in a moment of caprice is no concern of mine. But this is not my own work. I hold it in sacred trust for my father, and I must be a good steward."

"There is another parable about a steward," Sister Ursula observed. "Perhaps its motivation is more—but please forgive me. That was an uncharitable thought. Even, perhaps, an inaccurate one. Please do not misunderstand me."

Hilary rose. His legs were perfectly steady now. "Not at all, Sister. Not at all. And I'm sure you'll find some generous patron who will enable you to meet my trifling fee. I would so gladly waive it myself, were it not for my duty to my father."

The hall door had opened and closed as he spoke. Now a thin pale face thrust itself into the room. "Hiya, Hilary! Oh, sorry. Company? Has Ron corrupted you? Are you going in for Spiritual Consolation too?"

Hilary beckoned his brother-in-law into the room. Jenny Green (a very smiling, happy and devoted Jenny Green) followed him. "Sister Ursula, may I present my brother-in-law, Vance Wimpole? And my cousin, Miss Green? Or did you meet her when I . . . ?"

"I did, but am happy to meet her again. And Mr. Wimpole."

"Glad to meet a nun, Sister. Variety. Which by the way," Wimpole jerked a thumb at the other nun, "who's the Seventh Sleeper?"

"My colleague, Sister Felicitas."

"Give me her address. I'll borrow her some time when a Good Girl wants a chaperone."

"Vance!" Jenny Green protested.

Sister Ursula smiled. "You seem very blithe for a household over which Death has been hovering for weeks."

"Why not?" Wimpole demanded. "They've got the guy that did it all, at the insignificant cost of the life of one fan. Of course no writer likes to lose even one fan, but I'm willing to get along without Runcible for Hilary's sake."

"Vance! That's no way to talk."

"You see, Sister? I'm henpecked already. I need a drink. Hilary! It can't have been you hitting that bottle before noon? Or did the good sisters need their schnapps?"

"Don't mind him," Jenny reassured the nun. "He's a boor and he loves it. But would you . . . do you . . . I mean, are you allowed . . . ?"

"I might take a small glass of port if you have it," said Sister Ursula.

The presence of the nuns had apparently restrained Hilary from his unwonted tippling. This avowal of tolerance sent him promptly back to the bottle. Vance Wimpole stared at him amazed.

"What, my dear brother-in-law, is the use of your being snatched from the hand of the assassin if you're going to plunge yourself into a drunkard's grave? Filthy stuff," he added, tucking it away.

"I think I can understand," Sister Ursula ventured. "The terrible relief of knowing that it's over, that you can breathe without wondering if it's your last breath. For I suppose you are sure that this young man who was arrested is the cause of it all?"

"Not a doubt in the world," said Wimpole broadly. "Hell—I beg your pardon, Sister—we've got witnesses saw him do it. He even admits it himself. Somebody pushed him, indeed! What Jury's going to believe that?"

"If that is true, I should imagine he would hate you more than ever now, Mr. Foulkes. Now that you've had him arrested and disgraced. If he were let out on bail, if he were free again now . . ."

Hilary's glass dropped from a shaking hand. "Hang it, Sister! You mean that devil would try it again?"

"It seems plausible, doesn't it? When a murderer has killed the wrong man, I should imagine that his passion to kill the right man would increase all the more. It would certainly seem strange if the death of this poor fan, may he rest in peace, should put an end to the attacks upon you."

Hilary picked up the glass and refilled it. He muttered "Thanks," apparently to no one in particular.

"Did you know this man who was killed, Mr. Foulkes? That would make it all the more painful for you."

"No. Never saw him before that night. Never."

"And did you become acquainted with him at all then? One is naturally curious as to what the poor victim was like, even though he is really unrelated to the case."

"What bloody tastes you've got, Sister!" Wimpole remarked.

Hilary answered the question. "No. Didn't see anything of him."

Vance Wimpole's eyes narrowed. "But you and Jenny were alone with him for a while, remember? Which by the way, that's been puzzling me. What went on?"

"Oh that," Hilary shrugged. "I went out for air. People can be most trying when one is something of a celebrity. Most trying. This fan followed us and pestered me with all sorts of questions about my father and his works. That was all, wasn't it, Jenny?"

"Yes," Jenny agreed after the slightest pause.

"I hardly had the opportunity to judge the man's character from—Excuse me. The telephone."

But Miss Green had already answered it. "It's for you, Cousin Hilary."

"Thanks. I'll take it in the study." He walked into the other room and shut the door behind him.

Jenny Green put a hand to her mouth. "Oh . . . " she gasped. "Not in there. Not in that room. That's where . . . "

"Nuts," said D. Vance Wimpole. "Duncan is in his cell. Nothing can touch Hilary further."

"But we still don't know how anything could ever have touched him. Maybe you could do it even from jail. We ought to seal up that room, lock it and never let anybody . . ."

Wimpole puts his arm around her. "Tush, toots. There's no boogyman in there. Nothing can happen."

But his eyes, like Jenny's and Sister Ursula's, remained fixed on the door.

It opened and Hilary came out intact. But it was a Hilary even more nervous and shaken than before. "You know who that call was from?" he demanded. "It was from him. Duncan. He's out on bail. He wants to come and see me. Says he wants to persuade me to drop charges, he's innocent. Innocent, he says, But he wants to come here . . . He'll kill me, I tell you. He'll kill me. He can go through locked walls and stab you with your own dagger and . . ."

His trembling hands could hardly hold the bottle.

V

Lieutenant Marshall had his troubles with the draft board. "But Lieutenant," the bald and elderly clerk kept insisting, "we simply cannot allow you to look at an enrollee's statement. These statements are strictly confidential. If we allowed them to be used for police purpose, we might as well install a Gestapo and be done with it."

"Look," Marshall pleaded. "The man's dead. I'm trying to catch his murderer. The American Civil Liberties Union isn't going to jump on your neck for helping me do that."

"I'm sorry, but rules are rules. You can see for yourself, Lieutenant—"

"I can see. But I cannot see that you're contributing much to defense or civil rights or the welfare of society or whathaveyou by holding up a man who's trying to prevent more murders."

The clerk relented a little. "If you told me what specific information you wanted, I might be able to help you. If it's a matter of indentification, say . . . ?"

"That's it chiefly. But it's hell to ask specific questions. What I want is just a gander at the whole thing to get a picture. There's something nebulously nibbling about in my mind that won't take shape. But what I mostly want to know is did he have any family? If he did, they can help me."

The clerk returned with the filled-in form and kept it carefully out of range of Marshall's eyes. "No. No family. Father and mother dead, and no claim for dependants. What else do you need to know?"

"Could you . . ." Marshall groped ". . . could you tell me when and where he was born?"

"August 5, 1915. Here in Los Angeles."

"Handy. That can be checked . . . And what'll it prove when I've checked it? All right. One important thing—if this isn't too much on the confidential anti-Gestapo side: What does it say under that question about Have you ever been known by any other name?" He smiled as he wondered what Austin Carter's draft board had made of his collection of names. Probably called in the F.B.I.

The clerk frowned. "I'm not sure if that is information I could rightly give out. But as it happens, there isn't anything. Funny . . . Looks as though he'd started to write something and changed his mind. Probably was filling in an answer on the wrong line. They will do that."

"So?" Marshall leaned forward. "Could I see that?"

"This . . . this squiggle? Just that?"

"Just that. All by itself."

The clerk sighed. "Very well." He placed blotters over the sheet so that nothing was visible but the one line, then laid it in front of the Lieutenant. "It looks like a capital J."

Marshall stared at it:

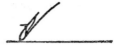

"Thanks," he said at last. "You've been a help. I'll try to return the favor some day."

"I wish you were a traffic officer then. I'm not expecting to commit a murder."

"Cheer up," said Marshall. "You never can tell."

The nebulous nibbling was stronger now. It was a crazy idea, too wild to mention yet to anyone on the force, too wild probably even for Leona's taste. Sister Ursula was the only person he could think of who wouldn't hoot impolitely at the notion.

He took out the delayed telegram from Chicago, which had so perplexed him when he received it an hour ago, and reread it. It began to make sense now. It fitted in with this other. And if he could only get any direct proof . . .

His first stop was the public library. He flipped through the card catalog, read the entries under

Foulkes, Fowler Harvey (1871–1930)

jotted down two call numbers, and went on into the history and biography department.

First he asked for a *Who's What* for 1928–1929. He read the entry there and nodded. Confirmation was nowise complete, but the idea was at least not disproved. He then settled down to a hasty leafing through two large books. The crazy notion looked better than ever.

His next stop was at the Bureau of Vital Statistics. When he emerged a half hour later he was beaming as brightly as he had after the birth of his son.

VI

Lieutenant Marshall was smoking his pipe in the patio when Sister Ursula returned to the convent. He sprang to his feet at her entrance and advanced eagerly toward her. "Sister," he cried, "I think I'm on to something! And if it works, we'll have Matt free and exonerated before that Pasadena halfwit can say 'Lieutenant Kello.' "

Sister Ursula smiled happily. "Tell me this great discovery," she urged. "But tell me other things first. Quickly, if you can, but do not skip too much. The patience of a saint and the ingenuity of a fiend could not have coaxed a coherent story out of Mary, poor child. Please give me all the background you can so that I can justly estimate your new find."

"Gladly. It helps get things straight in my own mind, Sister, to tell them to you. You ask the right questions, and you've got a sense of proportion. So here goes. Let's see; up through the locked room you know about. After that . . . "

Rapidly but fully he sketched over the later developments of this exasperating case, up through Matt's arrest. And as he spoke he kept marveling at the adroitly apposite quality of the nun's questions and the deft speed with which she took in all facts.

When he had concluded, she meditated in silence for a moment and then said, "It's all obvious enough, isn't it? All but one thing."

"That being the mere trifle of who's the murderer?"

"No. That locked room. The identity of the murderer is clear enough. But proving the case against him and freeing Matt will be exceedingly difficult with the 'impossibility' as an obstacle to overcome."

"And everything else is obvious? That's nice. Then listen to what I've been up to today: I'm on a trail that if it's right (and I'm praying it is) will prove that the death of William Runcible was no accident, but an essential detail of a well-conceived plot." He paused for sensation.

"But of course. That's been perfectly clear from the first. Tell me, though, how you intend to prove it."

Marshall gawped. "I'd sooner have you tell me why it's so allfired obvious."

"But of course it is. There's a perfect chain of probabilities, pointing directly to it. If you don't mind, however, I'd like to hold that back. It involves a serious accusation which I don't think it is quite time to make yet. Tell me your researches."

Marshall relit his pipe. "All right. It goes like this: How did this whole case start? With Jonathan Tarbell and a rosary. We had nothing at all on Tarbell—no connections, no previous police record, nothing."

"*Had* nothing, Lieutenant?"

"All right. I'll confess we have a little now, and it helps. But if you can hold out, so can I; that'll fit in better later. Let's go back to the beginning. We know nothing about Tarbell save that he had the phone number of the Foulkes' apartment house and a rosary which proved to be the property of the first Mrs. Foulkes Senior. Now if his death was an irrelevant subplot totally unconnected with the attacks on Hilary, then the caprices of fate are becoming uncommonly outrageous. It's where we start from, and it has to fit in."

"I agree, Lieutenant. I'll go further and say that if you had not investigated the death of Tarbell there never would have been a locked room."

"For the moment I'm not sure I follow that one. But to go on: Tarbell ties in at another point too. Matt Duncan once met him at

Carter's, probably with Runcible. A further checkup with Runcible's landlady and a fan friend of his shows that Tarbell was his most frequent and intimate companion. This pulls Runcible right into the middle of the case, as a protagonist and no innocent bystander. If Tarbell is connected with Hilary, and Runcible is closely connected with Tarbell, then no matter what all the Foulkeses swear there is a tie-up someplace."

"I agree."

"All right. So next I try to find out something about Runcible: who he is, where he comes from, what he does. The last is easy: he's a grocery clerk. The others are practically impossible. Nobody knows a thing about him except that he pays his bills regularly and is a purist in his tastes in fantasy. He lists no close relative for the draft board. But he does start to fill in the space about having gone under other names, and then changes his mind.

"Now getting confidential information out of a draft board is hell. Ask me, I'm an authority. But a draftee mightn't realize that. If it were at the moment exceedingly important to conceal his other name (true or false), if he were engaged on some enterprise that meant keeping that name secret, he might risk charges of falsifying his statement rather than make the information available."

"True, Lieutenant. And could you make anything out of what he started to write?"

Marshall drew out his notebook, found a blank page, and sketched the squiggle of William Runcible.

"It looks a little like a J," Sister Ursula mused. "Or it could be . . . yes, I think it is the start of a capital F."

"It is. I'm sure of that. And doubly sure because for once the murderer slipped. He went too far. Somebody had been in Runcible's room before I got there. It was unbelievably cleared of all personal papers, save for an overlooked note signed *J. T.* I'll come back to its contents later; at the moment it indicates just one more tie-in with Tarbell. No man could have lived in such an impersonal atmosphere. And last night the landlady saw a 'burglar,' who was wearing the good old familiar Dr. Derringer get-up."

"Curious," said Sister Ursula, "how that costume runs through this case. Is it simply macabre humor, or is there some psychological compulsion driving the murderer to use it?"

"I don't know. With Carter it could be a gag. But he's out now. With Veronica Foulkes it could be psychological; but could a woman get away with it? Which by the way, as Wimpole would say, that was smart work of yours at the Elite, Sister."

"I thought that a disguise used once might prove to be a habit. And now this burglar . . . you think the murderer searched Runcible's room?"

"He got there fastest," said Marshall sadly. "He did his best to destroy all evidence of who Runcible was. But in a way, he helped me. As I said, he went too far. He removed a picture from the wall.

"Now I learned later from the fan Waring that there was no secret about that picture. It was an autographed photo of Fowler Foulkes, a naturally treasured possession for any fantasy fan. If the picture had been left in place, I wouldn't have given it another look. But it was missing; and it could only be missing because the murderer thought it was, not part of a fan's collection, but an element in the evidence which he was destroying. Therefore that evidence concerned Fowler Foulkes."

"Excellent!" said Sister Ursula admiringly. "Lieutenant, why should you waste your time submitting such notable work to me for criticism?"

"Largely," Marshall admitted, "because it's coming out better now. It wasn't nearly this clear and logical in my mind when I started. So. Now how did that evidence concern Fowler Foulkes? I had an inkling, and I looked up the Foulkes biography in *Who's What*. And there it's been, staring us in the face all along.

"Hilary has built himself up in the public eye as The Son of Fowler Foulkes. We know that he's the son of a second marriage, but we automatically think of the first marriage as childless. I imagine it's because Hilary creates such a touching picture of the relationship between him and his father that you can imagine Fowler Foulkes leaning out from Abraham's bosom and proclaiming, 'This is my only-begotten son, in whom I am well pleased.' If you'll pardon the sacrilege."

"The sacrilege, I think, is Hilary's. He turns his father into God, after which it is only natural to think of himself as the Son of God. But the flaw, you mean to imply, lies in the 'only-begotten?' "

"Exactly. There was a child by the first marriage. Roger O'Donnell Foulkes, deceased. I checked it up further in Fowler Foulkes' autobiography. Roger was born in 1894. There are plenty of close and affectionate references to him, even after the second marriage and the birth of Hilary, up until 1914. Then there's not another word about him save for one allusion to World War I as 'this great struggle for humanity, to which I gladly surrendered my time, my self, and even the life of my son.' The Wimpole memoir isn't much help. It plays up Hilary, of course, because of his marriage to the Boswell's daughter, but it hardly mentions Roger. There is one cryptic mention of 'that deep sorrow of Fowler's life, which death did not heal.' What does all this add up to?"

"A serious quarrel which estranged father and son, and drove the son off to die in battle."

"And what would be apt to provoke such a quarrel at twenty? Can you think of anything more likely than an ill-considered marriage, with the Honorable Patricia St. John as stepmother doubtless having her say as to the girl's unsuitability? Standard formula. Cut off with a shilling, beyond doubt, and all the rest of it. And so off to volunteer in the Allied forces, to win death or glory on the battlefield, dashing off on his metaphorical white charger without waiting to discover that his poor wife was pregnant."

Sister Ursula nodded. "Then you think that your Runcible is the son of this ill-considered marriage of Roger Foulkes'?"

"I'm certain. I figured it this way: He may lie to the draft board about his name. But only a professionally adept deceiver makes up a false birthplace and birth date. Nine chances out of ten that much is correct, So I checked August 5, 1915, in our records here. No Runcible. But William Fowler Foulkes, eight pounds ten ounces, father Roger O'Donnell Foulkes, mother Eleanor Runcible Foulkes. It's easy to see what must have happened. Pressure brought to bear by the family to relinquish her claims and resume her maiden name in return for a lump sum.

"Now you know Hilary's family pride. Look how he has taken care of that distant English cousin. And a Foulkes working in a grocery store . . . This is guesswork, but I think there can't be much doubt that Runcible was gently putting the screws on Hilary. It can't have been a strong pressure, because he'd have no claim on the estate from a disinherited father. Just a sort of moral suasion and appeal to pride. And that's where Tarbell comes in."

"But how?"

Marshall took out the telegram from Chicago and handed it over. Sister Ursula read:

REGRET DELAY FILES MISLAID PRINTS MARKED TARBELL CORRESPOND HERMAN JARRETT HELD SUSPICION EXTORTION WEYRINGHAUSEN CASE RELEASED INSUFFICIENT EVIDENCE JUNE 1939.

"Do you remember the Weyringhausen case?" he asked.

"One of those missing-heir affairs, wasn't it? A meat-packing fortune and a son that was supposed to have been drowned at sea years ago and a claimant who was said to be that son. The Tichborne case repeating itself."

"Right. And this Jarrett was a backer of the claimant's. Which would seem to indicate that he specialized in finding heirs. They weren't able to prove fraud on him in the other case, and I doubt if there's fraud here. The pickings wouldn't be rewarding enough to justify it. But Tarbell-Jarrett hasn't been doing so well, to judge from where he was living, and he doubtless wanted to keep his hand in.

"The note signed *J. T.* that I found in Runcible's room corroborates this. It read *He says maybe. Keep hoping, keed.* Or possibly that *He* might be *H period.* That indicates Hilary was nibbling, and indicates too that they must have been able to present something of a case.

"What sort of evidence they had, we can't fully know. Most of it has probably been destroyed by now. But we do know that Runcible had his grandmother's rosary, which Tarbell was using as evidence, he had his marked physical resemblance to Hilary and to old Fowler himself, and he had the arm trick,"

"What on earth is that?"

Marshall explained and showed Waring's sketch. "Wimpole mentions it in the memoir, it was apparently the one good light parlor trick in Fowler Foulkes' dogmatic and dominant personality. Which is what Tarbell meant by saying it might be useful."

"These are amazing facts that you've uncovered, Lieutenant. But what sort of a pattern do you make out of them?"

Marshall paused before replying. "I've been looking at the works of that Charles Fort that Austin Carter and Matt loved to quote. It seems that a few years after the famous dissappearance of Ambrose Bierce there was another disappearance—that of one Ambrose Small. Mr. Fort suggests, and I honestly think only half in jest, that somebody was collecting Ambroses. Well, in this case, somebody's been collecting Foulkeses."

"Then why Tarbell?"

"Because only he knew that Runcible was a Foulkes. Don't you see: If Runcible's death seems a mistake, then the whole plot appears aimed at Hilary. Your whole question of motivation is in another light. Anyone whom Hilary has antagonized becomes a candidate; and that's a wide field. But if Runcible's death is deliberate, then the murderer must be a man who profits by the three deaths of Tarbell, Runcible, and Hilary. His motive can be only one thing. And there's only one man who has that motive."

"And one woman," Sister Ursula reminded him. "Perhaps even two."

"Can you see a woman visiting the Elite Hotel as Dr. Derringer? It's the man all right."

"But he had a series of most impressive alibis."

"Which topple over at the touch of a finger."

"And the locked room?"

"There is still that. God knows there is still that. Other things clear up. The bomb, for instance. I didn't see how anybody in this kind of circle would know about Louie Schalk; but it's evident now that Tarbell must have known, and might easily have mentioned the picturesque profession of his neighbor to a visitor—a visitor with whom he was dealing professionally and who later killed him. But that—" Marshall broke off, and his eyes lit up.

"Yes, Lieutenant?"

"That means the screws weren't on Hilary. Tarbell's visitor, according to the clerk, was Dr. Derringer—that is, the murderer. A shady dealer like Tarbell wouldn't object to a person of some fame and position disguising himself for visits to the Elite. And that phone number links Tarbell, not with Hilary personally, but with the Foulkes apartment. Say Tarbell was double-crossing Runcible, selling out to the two people who had the greatest interest in seeing Hilary maintained in status quo—"

"But you said that this was not blackmail proper. Just a gentle pressure appealing to Hilary's family pride."

"All right. Skip it. It's a sideline. It'll come straight, everything will come straight, when we break down that devilish locked room. And that's what I most need your help on, Sister. You unlocked a room once. Can't you do it again? If I can clear that up, I can make an arrest today on attempted murder, force Kello to withdraw his charges against Matt, and turn the murderer over to him on the capital charge. But how, in the name of all the words that should never shatter the peace of this patio, how was that locked room contrived?"

Sister Ursula pressed her hands together tightly over the cross of her rosary. "I hinted to you before what I thought was the nature of the solution."

"The Invisible Man? And a lot that helped, aside from Leona's brilliant theory that it might mean Sister Felicitas."

The nun laughed. But the laughter was nervous, strained, far from her usual free and full peal. "Sister Felicitas would be delighted by the joke, if I could make her hear it. But I can go further than a hint now. In this visit you have told me exactly how that room may be unlocked."

"I have?"

"And remember Dr. Derringer's dictum. Eliminate the impossible, and when nothing remains . . .'

"Sister!" Marshall's voice was harsh. "Are we playing games? Don't you realize that there may be a third murder while we—"

"No. There will not, there cannot be a third murder. Because, you see, you have neglected to mention yet another person who would profit by the death of a Foulkes."

Marshall emptied his pipe and filled it slowly. His expression changed from anger to doubt to amazement. "Sister," he said at last, "are you implying that . . . ?"

Another nun entered the patio. "Lieutenant Marshall?" she asked. "There's a telephone call for you."

Marshall's face was black when he returned. "So?" he grated. "That was Ragland. He's been phoning all over town for me. So there couldn't be another murder?"

"Lieutenant . . ." Sister Ursula's voice trembled a little.

"That was a bright suggestion of yours, that last. But I think this clears him. And," he added, heedless of the peace of the patio, "it's the same goddamned locked room."

VII

Veronica Foulkes stared at her brother curiously. "So it happened at last." She shut behind her the door to the study.

Vance Wimpole nodded his pale face. "It happened at last. They got Hilary."

"And it's the same as before?"

"The same as before. The night latch is on the hall door. Jenny here and I have been in this room ever since Hilary entered the study. No one has come or gone."

"You're very clever, Vance," Veronica said levelly.

"From one of your demonstrated ability, my dear, that is an impressive compliment."

"But possibly not quite so clever this time. Before, you had impartial witnesses. The two nuns. No one could suspect them. But who will pay attention to the evidence of your fiancée. And she is the only one who can prove that you did not enter that room."

"So that's how it's to be, Ron? I'm slated for the role of scapegoat this time? Come, that's hardly fair. Or necessary. You know that you've nothing to fear from my administration of the estate. You'll do better to keep me around."

"I don't know how you did it before. That was perfect. But this is too brazen, Vance. It's not that I want to turn you over to them. But they'll never believe this story."

"Marshall will. He's conditioned to locked rooms. That's probably what gave you the idea, isn't it?"

There was a tight circle drawn around these two as they stood there cold-bloodedly discussing the likelihood of their respective guilt. Vance's gay flamboyance had disappeared, and with it Veronica's rootless strivings for effect. They were naked now. The others with them, the brother's Jenny Green and the sister's newly acquired Joe Henderson, were silent and helpless and a thousand miles away.

"I wouldn't persist in that notion, Vance. I wouldn't mention it to Marshall. Or I might be moved to make some reference to airplane travel."

D. Vance Wimpole shrugged and reached for the bottle. When he had finished pouring two drinks, he was smiling. "Does it matter, Ron? Isn't it the main thing that Hilary is dead now? You are a free woman and I am the administrator of the Foulkes estate. If you care to pretend that you think me guilty of his death, well and good. It harms no one. They can never pin this crime on either of us. Come on, drink with me."

Veronica nodded silently and accepted a glass. They drank together.

Jenny Green shuddered. "I've never seen them like this before . . ." she murmured. "It's . . . they aren't human."

Joe Henderson blinked. "I know. It's . . ." He groped for words and found them in the only language in which he was truly articulate. "It's like watching something extraterrestrial, extragalactic even, across cold reaches of interstellar space . . ."

"And now," said Vance Wimpole, "now that that's settled, for the police." He looked up a number and dialed. "Police headquarters? I wish to report a murder. The murder of Hilary Foulkes."

The astonished voice of the desk sergeant crackled into the room. "What!" it exploded. "Again?"

"A total murder this time, officer. Please send your men at once." He added the address and hung up.

"Oh . . . !" Jenny Green gasped. "How can you be like this? Hilary's dead!"

Veronica paused in lighting a cigarette. "We know."

"But he was . . . He was so good to us all. He was so kind to me. And he was your husband, Veronica."

Wimpole leaned back against the table. "Don't be childish Jenny. Hilary was good to you, yes, out of an odd sort of family pride. You may possibly regret his death. But surely you have enough sense to see that no one else can."

"But you might at least have the decency to—"

"To play the crocodile? There'll be time for that later, with the police and the press. Now there are only you, so much a part of the family, and Joe, who probably sees all, possibly knows all, but certainly tells nothing prior to 2500 A.D. We cannot afford to waste these moments in tears, idle tears. We need to think, to map our campaign."

Veronica leaned forward eagerly. "How about suicide?"

Jenny gave a little stifled gasp.

Wimpole laughed. "No. no, my dear. Ron is not proposing a romantic suicide pact to obliterate our guilt. Hardly. You mean we might suggest that Hilary . . . How should it go? Say that he killed Runcible and then commited suicide out of remorse?"

"Yes," said Veronica tensely.

"Inadvisable of course from the point of view of insurance. And otherwise impossible. Marshall's no fool, even if Kello is. He's seen enough of Hilary to know that no crimes on earth, nor any other conceivable cause, could drive him to take his precious life. Physical impossibilities may be overcome, but not psychological. Hilary could never commit suicide. Besides, I have no doubt that the medical examiner will find that the angle of the blow is inconsistent. Or were you more careful this time?"

Jenny rose. "I'm going to my room. I can't stand this. You talk about Hilary as though he were a . . . a *thing* . . . a . . ."

". . . a prime bastard, which he was, and whose passing can have none but good effects."

"It's too cruel. I'm going."

Joe Henderson rose indecisively as though to follow her. Then the doorbell rang.

"Alice still out shopping?" Wimpole asked. "I'll take it. Mustn't keep the police waiting when they're so prompt."

Veronica Foulkes sprang to her feet as the visitors entered. They were not the police. They were Matt and Concha Duncan. Veronica extended a graceful arm, index finger pointing straight at Matt. "You dare to come back," she declaimed, "after the evil that you have wrought here!"

Vance Wimpole nodded approvingly. "Yes, Ron, I think that'll do as well as any. And we'll have Kello on our side. Duncan, my friend, you're elected."

VIII

Sister Ursula stood staring at the spot where Hilary's finally dead body had rested. "May God forgive me . . ." she murmured. "I never dreamed . . ."

Marshall paced about the room, glaring bitterly and abusing his pipe with hot and furious puffs. "There couldn't possibly be another murder. So you go off and leave Hilary here with his murderer."

"Yes," she confessed. "I did. I left him with his murderer . . . I wish that I could be a fatalist. I wish that I could shrug it off with a casual, 'It was written thus.' But I know that man operates through his free will, and that whatever end he may serve, he must bear the responsibility of his acts."

"The same damned business. Every detail repeated, down to the shirt sleeves. Pity the proud Hilary should die without his beautiful dressing gown . . . All the same but the knife."

"The knife?" Sister Ursula sounded distracted.

"Of course. The token of esteem from the Zemindar of Kota Guti is in our hands now. This time the murderer swiped a knife from the kitchen. Good idea, too; longer blade, more efficient. Everything the same—but at least this time we don't have to believe it. The locked room's out, thank God. We can discount the Green girl's testimony at once."

The nun's attention revived. "But no. You can't do that, Lieutenant. Then what becomes of the previous episode here in this same locked room?"

"Does that matter? If we've got him for murder, we're willing to waive a charge of attempted murder. I'll admit I would like to have all the threads tidily bunched up, but—"

"I waited too long to speak. And was it because it was necessary, as I convinced myself, or was it my devilish pride . . . ? At least save me from another mistake, and let me save you from yours. You must believe the Green girl's testimony, and you must let me show you how wrong you are."

Marshall hesitated. "I'll admit I've forced this case on you. I can't pull out without hearing what you've got to say . . . What do you want me to do?"

Sister Ursula frowned. "Simply this. Please, without any questions, call the surgeon who examined Mr. Foulkes' body and ask him to come out here again. Tell him . . . tell him you need fresh details that would be too hard to explain over the phone."

"Doc won't like that."

"It was the same dogmatic young man with the crouch whom we met before?"

"Yes."

"Please, Lieutenant. Bring him out here. Or do you wish to make a Kello of yourself?"

"All right." Marshall shrugged. "I'll take the chance." He used the study phone. Just as he was finishing, Sergeant Ragland came in.

"Hey, Lieutenant! There's a plain-clothes boy from Pasadena and he's got a warrant for one of the guys we're holding out there."

Marshall jammed down the mouthpiece noisily. "Kello!" he snorted, and made a peculiarly vicious swearword of the name.

It was indeed Sergeant Kello, and looking particularly pleased with himself. "Hiya, Marshall. This time I'm in your bailiwick, but it happens I've got authority with me. Look at this: bench warrant charging Matthew Duncan with murder. No more diddling around with manslaughter. We try to keep 'em safe in Pasadena, and your L.A. lawyers get 'em out to finish the job right under your nose. Soon's I got word of this, I talked the magistrate into changing the charge on the Runcible case. You can have him when we're through with him—us and the guy that runs the lethal gas chamber."

"I don't want him," said Marshall quietly. "He didn't kill Foulkes. He didn't kill Runcible either; but if you're set on making a fool of yourself, it's no skin off my nose."

"Thanks, Terence." Matt's voice was reasonably level. "I'd hate to see you fighting over me."

Vance Wimpole laughed. "Marshall's just jealous of your astuteness, Sergeant Kello. Carry off your prize and good luck to you. I'll be glad to see my brother-in-law avenged so promptly."

Marshall turned on him. "He'll be avenged. Don't worry about that. But not by Kello. You've got a few questions to answer first."

"I have? But Lieutenant! I admit that I have been present at a couple of the high points in this orgy of assassination, but the rest of the time I have been merely an offstage character."

"So? You didn't think you could keep Phyn's mouth shut forever, did you? Wouldn't it have been wiser to dispose of him too?"

"Vance!" Veronica cried out. "I told you that nasty little man couldn't be trusted. I warned you—"

"You idiot!" Wimpole snarled at his sister. "Can't you see this police dolt was groping in the dark? And now you—"

"Which by the way," said Marshall mockingly, "your sister's exclamation was no more of a give-away than your turning on her like that. So Phyn has been blackmailing you. And I'll lay odds on the subject matter. He saw you in Los Angeles while you were supposed to be at the ends of the earth. Very pretty, that train-stub alibi, but very futile. After the first locked room, you had more than time enough to fly to San Francisco and take that train back. And Mr. Phyn is going to stop and think when he weighs the profits of blackmail against the power of the police and a possible perjury charge."

D. Vance Wimpole poured himself a drink. His self-possession was beginning to return. "Lieutenant, I have just realized the motive behind these attacks upon me. You are still vexed because I found your delightful wife so attractive that evening at Chantrelle's."

"Huh?" Kello did a slow take and finally guffawed. "So that's it, Marshall? Out for a little private revenge? Well, pin this one on him if you can. All I want's the Runcible murderer, and I've got him right here. So long, boys."

"You won't need those handcuffs, Sergeant," said Matt firmly.

"So, I suppose you'd warn me in advance if I did? No, brother, you're going to wear the pretty bracelet and like it. We take good care of our murderers in Pasadena."

The sight of the flashing steel was too much for Concha. She had been standing beside Sister Ursula, sobbing dryly and quietly. Now she ran forward and threw her arms around her husband. "You can't!" she cried. "You can't take him away, Sergeant. I won't let you take him and kill him and be a Lieutenant. I'll—"

"Mary," said Matt warningly.

"He'll kill you, Matt. He's bad. He doesn't care about truth or anything but his old promotion. And he'll take you and—"

"Break it up, sister," said Sergeant Kello. "You can see him tomorrow—through the bars."

"Wait Sergeant," Sister Ursula stepped forward. "Please let me speak."

"And who the sweet h— I beg your pardon, Sister. But who might you be?"

"Who I am is not important. The Lieutenant will tell you later if you care. But I must not let you take this man back to prison. He did not kill William Runcible."

"Yeah? And I suppose you know who did?"

"Of course. It was Hilary Foulkes."

The reactions in the room were predominantly of scornful disbelief. Only Veronica Foulkes sounded receptive. "You mean then that Hilary killed himself after . . . ?"

There were loud protests. "But the medical evidence . . ." "But the psychology of the man . . . " "But the other attacks . . ."

Sister Ursula held up a hand. There was something so quietly imposing about her small erect figure in its archaic robes that even Sergeant Kello fell silent.

"No," she said. "No; Hilary Foulkes did not commit suicide. But please listen to what I know must be the truth."

IX

"The 'attacks' upon Hilary Foulkes," Sister Ursula began, "were suspicious from the first. They were too completely unsuccessful. The first two, the brick and the car, rest purely upon Mr. Foulkes' unsupported accounts. With the third, the chocolates, he 'happened' to notice a needle-prick in the coating and 'happened' to have been reading a novel which made him wary.

"The fourth, the bomb, was carefully timed for delivery at a certain hour; and Mr. Foulkes had made an appeal to the police for protection and expected an officer to be present at that hour. To be sure, coincidence helped here. The police were slow about answering what they took to be a routine crank complaint, but Lieutenant Marshall called at the right time on a then apparently unrelated matter. Even if he had not, the bomb was contrived to tick loudly; Mr. Foulkes himself could have noticed that ticking and called the Emergency Squad if no officer had been present.

"The fifth 'attack' the locked room, I shall pass by for the moment, observing only that it was obviously impossible for anyone but Mr. Foulkes to have engineered it."

"Hold on there," Sergeant Kello protested. "The medical evidence . . ."

"Please be patient, Sergeant. I shall set your mind at rest on that in a moment. But if all these 'attacks' were framed, what could be the purpose behind them? Two possible motives occurred to me: a chain of preparations to make a suicide seem like murder and defraud an insurance company, or a schizophrenic condition in which one part of the mind tries to produce physical evidence to justify the delusion of persecution which obsesses the other part.

"I did not know enough of Mr. Foulkes then to realize that neither of these hypotheses could conceivably fit him. He was sane, if a criminal can ever be called sane, and he was if anything abnormally tenacious of life. Neither mania nor suicide could possibly have motivated the feigned attacks.

"Not until it was too late did I see the third possibility: that the murderous attempts on Hilary Foulkes were preparation for the successful murder of another, apparently by mistake for Hilary Foulkes. There was only one person whose death could be contrived in that manner, and that was William Runcible."

"But why?" Matt Duncan protested. "God knows I want to believe this, Sister. I've got my reasons." He jangled his steel bracelet. "But why? Runcible was just a nebulous and negative fan. What should Hilary have against him?"

"Lieutenant Marshall, with an admirable persistence and refusal to accept the over-obvious, has established that Runcible was William Runcible Foulkes, son of Roger and grandson of Fowler Foulkes."

Veronica gasped. Her brother said slowly, "A lot of things are beginning to come clear now."

"But," Marshall protested, "the heir of a disinherited son couldn't have been any serious menace."

"Then manifestly, Lieutenant, Roger had not been disinherited. It will not do to say casually, 'Oh, Mr. Foulkes had no motive.' Only Mr. Foulkes could have planned the murder; only Runcible could have been the planned victim. Therefore Mr. Foulkes had a motive. Tell me, Mrs. Foulkes, did your father-in-law leave a will?"

"No." Veronica sounded puzzled and afraid. "No, he didn't."

"You know how old men feel about wills and death," Wimpole added. "And Hilary was all the family there was—we thought."

"Then William Runcible Foulkes had a claim, not only to the money in the estate, but to a share in its administration. The blow to Hilary Foulkes was more than merely financial, though that might have wounded him deeply enough. It was a blow to his prestige, to his position as his father's sole heir, custodian, and steward. No longer would his faintest whim be firmest law. From an autocratic despot he would become a mere shareholder in power. The threat was intolerable; it had to be removed.

"It is possible that Runcible himself did not realize the full extent of his claim on Hilary Foulkes. It is quite likely that Jonathan Tarbell had concealed Fowler Foulkes' intestacy from him, and was promising Runcible merely some aid as a member of the family, such as Miss Green has received, while he threatened Mr. Foulkes with the loss of half the estate. This notion is rendered more plausible by the fact that Runcible was not scared off by Tarbell's death. He did not see that the threat applied to him. If he knew anything of Tarbell's past, or even from what he knew of where the man lived, he might assume that he had been killed for quite other reasons.

"Mr Foulkes had strung Tarbell along with hopes, as the note found by the Lieutenant indicates, and killed him when his demands became too pressing, but the mistaken-identity murder of Runcible had to wait until Mr Wimpole's arrival. Mr. Foulkes knew that Runcible, as a fan, moved in the circles of what Austin Carter calls the Mañana Literary Society. Once Vance Wimpole had arrived, it would be simple to contrive some occasion of being accidentally in such a situation that the mistake might seem possible. Chantrelle's rocket party was the ideal opportunity, and Mr. Foulkes took full improvisatory advantage of it. Almost every individual present was a likely candidate for the role of intended murderer of Hilary Foulkes; it was probably only chance, Matthew, that made him pick on you. But tell me, Miss Green, was Hilary Foulkes' account of the meeting by the shed correct?"

Jenny Green swallowed hard. "I don't know . . . They did talk about Cousin Hilary's father. But Runcible didn't sound quite like a fan. It did seem more . . . somehow more intimate. As though he were trying to show Hilary how much he knew. And once he said, 'I've lost the rosary, but I still have enough,' So you must be right about that; but I still can't believe that Hilary . . ."

"About that rosary, Miss Green; did you know anything about it?"

"Why . . . It was odd. When Veronica was being interested in religion, she read a memoir of the first Mrs. Foulkes that praised her as a lay saint, and she told me about that queer rosary devotion and the famous specially carved one. When the Lieutenant asked us about seven-decade rosaries, I start to mention it, but Hilary signaled me to be quiet. Later I spoke to him about it, and he said that he didn't intend to have the name of his father's wife bandied about in a criminous conversation."

"And that didn't seem peculiar to you?"

"No," said Jenny Green stoutly. "It . . . it still doesn't. I can't believe any of this. And anyway, Cousin Hilary couldn't have stabbed himself. The doctor said so."

Sergeant Ragland had answered the door. Now he said, "Here's the doc, Lieutenant."

The police surgeon strode in with his habitual swooping stoop. "Well?" he demanded. "What's all the fuss, my boy?"

Sister Ursula spoke. "Is it possible, doctor, that on either this or the former occasion, Mr. Foulkes could have stabbed himself?"

"Bosh!" he snorted dogmatically. "Rank physical impossibility."

There were puzzled murmurs, half of relief, half of fear. "If

Hilary did kill him," Veronica Foulkes began haltingly. "Mind you, I'm not admitting it, but if he *did* kill that fan . . . "

"Your nephew, darling," said Vance Wimpole.

She said no more, but the unasked question was loud in the room.

"One other point," Sister Ursula went on. "May I have that sketch of Runcible, Lieutenant? Thank you. Now doctor, would you say, from the characteristics you can see here, that this man could be a close blood-relative of Hilary Foulkes'?"

The doctor contemplated the picture and looked annoyed. "Hard to say," he snapped. "Out of my line. Very little known anyway about exact genetic details of physiognomy. Now if this showed coloration . . . But in pen-and-ink, no. Could be, certainly. Marked resemblance."

"Thank you."

But he went on staring at the picture. "Ridiculous drawing," he observed testily. "Position of those arms. Both back around the neck clasping the chin. Rank physical impossibility." He swept out of the room in a fast crouch more than ever reminiscent of Groucho Marx.

X

"So you see?" said Sister Ursula quietly.

Marshall swore. He looked like a man whose solid earth has turned into quicksand.

"Remember the dictum of Dr. Derringer, Lieutenant. 'If nothing remains, some part of the "impossible" was possible.' Such dogmatic statements of physical impossibility apply to the normal man. But Hilary's father and his half-nephew were both double-jointed. Both were noted for this trick." She showed Kello and the others the grotesque sketch. "Your father, Mr. Wimpole, mentions in his memoir how those who had not seen the trick damned it as an impossibility. For Fowler Foulkes or for Runcible such a self-inflicted wound was perfectly possible. So we have no right to state flatly that it was impossible for Hilary Foulkes."

"Phooey!" Sergeant Kello snorted. "If a doctor says a wound can't be self-inflicted—"

The quiet Joe Henderson spoke up. "It's not just Foulkeses," he said. "Tony Boucher can do that too. I remember once he made an offer: Anybody could bring him a mystery novel where it was proved that death couldn't be suicide because of the direction of the wound, and if he couldn't get a knife or a gun into that position he'd pay out ten bucks. Nobody ever collected."

"We were all too ready," Sister Ursula went on, "to accept a verdict of 'impossible' as correct, when it really meant no more than 'unlikely'. In ninety-nine cases out of the hundred, such a self-inflicted wound would have been impossible. Perhaps the percentage is even higher than that. But here the evidence of the locked room clearly rendered any other solution even more unlikely—in fact this time quite truly impossible. That is what I meant by directing your attention, Lieutenant, to the Invisible Man, the man who is present but unnoticed: the victim."

"And I bit," said Vance Wimpole. "A good Fortean like me, and swallowing Science as gospel."

"The dressing gown," Marshall muttered. "That's why he was in shirt-sleeves both times. He had to take it off to get freedom of movement for his arm."

Sergeant Kello laughed heartily. "Nuts to L. A., Marshall. We may not be smart in Pasadena, but we don't swallow locked rooms like that. We'd've known right off that the only guy could've done it was the victim,"

"You are wise after the fact, Sergeant," Sister Ursula smiled. "But at that, what you say might be true of the average policeman who had never met with an apparently impossible situation. Remember, however, that this crime was designed to meet the inspection of Lieutenant Marshall, who was confronted only last year with a murder committed, at first glance, in quite as impossibly locked a room. He was, as one might say, conditioned to such a situation. I can imagine that one of the Harlem detectives who investigated the Fink case might have reacted similarly here. I am certain that Superintendent Hadley or Inspector Masters would have done so."

"I suppose that excuses me?" said Marshall sourly.

"And this brings us to the reasons for the 'impossible' situation, and none of them seemed to apply here. But the reason in this case, we can see now, was to gain time. You will notice that none of the 'attacks' was designed to implicate a specific attacker, although one did by chance lead the Lieutenant onto a false trail. Mr. Foulkes had to avoid an arrest while keeping the police interested. Any possible suspect must be still at large when the opportunity for the actual murder presented itself. So the locked room was deliberately contrived as a tough nut for the Lieutenant to try to crack, with the certainty that he would still be chipping his teeth on it when Runcible was finally murdered.

"The method had probably been evolving in his mind ever since he learned that the Lieutenant was the man who worked on the locked room Harrigan case. That morning, when he heard on the telephone that Lieutenant Marshall had located an accidentally perfect suspect and was almost ready for an arrest on suspicion, he realized that he had to act at once. He groaned and dropped the phone. Then in the time it took the Lieutenant to arrive and investigate, he had ample opportunity to stage his locked room attack, knowing that none of the household ever dared interrupt him when he was shut up in his study."

"O.K.," Kello grunted. "O.K. You make a good story out of it—up to today. But who the hell killed Hilary Foulkes?"

"Kello," said Marshall, "for once I'm with you. We're agreed, Sister, that Hilary could never have committed suicide. All right, so even granting that he made the phony attacks on himself and killed Tarbell and Runcible—who killed Hilary?"

Sister Ursula clasped tightly the crucifix of her rosary. For a moment her lips barely moved in silent prayer. "I'm afraid," she said at last, "that I did."

XI

Even Sergeant Kello was dumb. Concha stared from the nun to the study and back again incredulously. Lieutenant Marshall's pipe fell from his teeth, spilling coals on the rug, and not even Veronica Foulkes noticed it.

"I knew," Sister Ursula went on, "even before Lieutenant Marshall had established the motive, even before I had seen the sketch of William Runcible's arm trick, that Hilary Foulkes alone was responsible for all these crimes and seeming attempts at crime. But I knew also that legal proof would be a difficult matter. This morning I visited Mr. Foulkes about another matter, and I contrived to plant in his mind the idea that it would seem markedly queer to the authorities if the attempts on his life should cease after attaining a mistaken objective.

"It was apparent by the increasing complexity and audacity of the 'attempts' that the man's vanity was running away with him. No, vanity is not the right word. It was his overweening trust in fate, his confidence that nothing could fail him, since he was acting to uphold his sacred stewardship. It was, in fact, this almost religious assurance of his that gave me the first essential clew to his character and potentialities. I might almost say that I began to solve his crimes by reading a psalm in the office of Compline.

"I hoped that now, in the nervous reaction from his success, this self-assurance would carry him too far, that he would perpetrate an 'attempt' so patently fraudulent as to convince the police that the whole series was a hoax. But I over-reached myself. And so did Hilary Foulkes.

"He had not been drinking in my presence. I did not realize how much he had taken, nor how unaccustomed he was to liquor. His fuddled imagination failed him; he tried the locked room trick over again. But this time he was confused and shocked (successful murder had proved more of a strain than he had anticipated) and very drunk. His Persian dagger was in the hands of the police, and he was forced to use a hastily chosen kitchen knife, with a longer blade. The carefully planned wound, convincingly dangerous but actually safe, turned with the slip of a drunken hand into self-destruction.

"Suicide was impossible to Hilary Foulkes. But he killed himself, and the fault is mine."

There was silence in the room. Jenny Green sniffled quietly. Veronica Foulkes finally glared triumphantly at her brother and said, "See?" Vance Wimpole made a resigned grimace. Concha extended a hesitant hand toward her husband.

"Well, Kello?" Marshall demanded.

Sergeant Kello fingered his warrant. "A lot of talk . . ."

"All right. You bring Duncan to trial. So. The defense proves A: Hilary Foulkes had framed a series of faked attempts on his own life. B: Hilary Foulkes had the strongest of motives for killing Runcible. C: Hilary Foulkes died by his own hand. If we need to, we'll get Henderson's friend Boucher on the stand to demonstrate how it was done. We pile up all those items, and where are you? Hell, you won't even get an indictment."

Slowly Sergeant Kello's fingers shredded the warrant. "O.K., Lieutenant. Lieutenant . . ." he repeated, savoring the lost title wistfully.

Matt Duncan extended his hand (the steel links jerking Kello's up with it) and gripped Marshall's. "Thanks for the 'we,' Terence. It's the first time I've ever heard of a policeman presenting the case for the defense."

"It's a day for novelties," Vance Wimpole observed. "It's the first time that an action of Hilary's has ever saved any one trouble."

SEVEN

AFTERWORD:
Saturday, December 6, 1941

It was a Saturday night a month later, the last Saturday night of a nation nominally at peace. Lieutenant Marshall was hospitably mixing drinks for a company replete with one of Leona's noble dinners. There were present the Duncans and the Carters and Joe Henderson and Jenny Green.

"One thing," Marshall observed as he poured. "You've affected my taste in reading matter. You boys have got something here in this fantasy field." He gestured toward a bookshelf where two pulps stood beside the Greek Anthology. "At its best, it's fresh, vigorous, creative imagination, and the perfect escape literature. I never could find much escape myself in a mystery novel. Too close to home or too exasperatingly far from it. But in a space ship . . . God can I escape! Some of it, of course, can be pretty flat; but for instance in the two magazines that your friend Don Stuart edits, it's the McCoy."

The three writers bowed gratefully. "We'll prove that there's a market for fantasy yet," said Austin Carter. "Maybe even between book covers, though my novels so far haven't caused any particular worry for the fire wardens along the Thames. And wait till you see Matt's latest novelet. I kicked around that time machine alibi I sprang on you, but it wouldn't jell. So I generously turned it over to Matt and he did a sweet job. Don's always maintained that a scientifiction detective story was by definition impossible, but wait till you read that one."

"Thanks for the plug," said Matt. "I'll return it: How's your anthology coming?"

Carter made a face. "I'm doing an anthology of science fiction for Pocket Books," he explained. "And I've got the strictest instructions never to pay over fifty dollars for reprint rights on a story."

"So?" Marshall asked as he paused.

"So it doesn't contain any Fowler Foulkes. Vance wants a hundred or no dice."

Joe Henderson gaped. "Vance did that to you?"

"But," Matt objected, "I thought Metropolis reconsidered and bought your novel. Vance played ball on that."

"Sure. After I promised him a cut on the sale, or he'd repeat Hilary's trick of withholding the Derringer stories."

"Good God!" Marshall ejaculated. "All that trouble and what have we got in the end? Another Hilary."

"Please!" Jenny Green protested. "Oh, I know the things Cousin Hilary did. I know there's no excusing him. But he was good to me. Even in his will after he died. And I can't stand the way you all always talk about him . . ." There were the first wellings of tears in her eyes. Joe Henderson unobtrusively took her hand.

"Hilary's dead," said Austin Carter, "and the evil that he did lives after him very actively."

"A man is dead," said Marshall, "and the arrangement that allowed and all but compelled him to do wrong—in this case, the arbitrary administration of literary rights by a capricious individual—"

"Oxford," said Leona in a loud aside.

"All right. Anyway this arrangement allows and compels his successor to do likewise. A man dies, but nothing is changed unless the system dies too. You could work out some pretty metaphorical applications . . ."

"I don't know," Carter frowned. "I agree the system has worked badly on this estate; but what is one to do? When we eventually get into this war and the Navy calls me up for active duty, supposing I get killed? I certainly want Berni to enjoy whatever small income my stuff may still bring in."

"Thanks sweet," Bernice smiled. "But don't be in a hurry to leave me holding the royalties."

"The income," Marshall said. "Of course a writer's heirs should enjoy his income, unless one wishes to attack the whole problem of hereditary fortunes. But should they have wilful and unchecked control of his work? I can imagine something like a committee of the Authors' League of America which would pass on all applications for the use of material and fix a reasonable fee, which would of course be received by the estate. I—"

"You're getting out of your depth, dear, aren't you?" Leona suggested. "Tell these charming people your latest professional discovery."

"Oh." Marshall laughed. "Yes, this was one of my main reasons for having you over. Thought you'd all want to know. For my own satisfaction, you see, I've been checking up on loose ends on the Foulkes case. My report is in and done with, but there were things I wanted to know. Maybe they weren't my professional concern any longer, but I needed to know them.

"I went wrong from the start on this case. I'll admit that. I was too preoccupied with detail to see pattern. To Sister Ursula, it was clear from the start that the attacks originated with Hilary. Me, the bright industrious professional, I go snooping around on little trails of detail, and end up damned near arresting you, Mr. Carter."

Austin Carter grinned. "Some imp kept prompting me to try to goad you into that, Lieutenant."

"I know. And I kept trying to figure if that was a sign of malicious innocence or brilliant guilt."

"What was it put you on to Austin, Lieutenant?" Bernice Carter asked. "The Derringer costume?"

"But if you'd only asked me about that," said Jenny Green. "Or if I'd only thought to tell you . . . Hilary always had a Derringer costume, even long before I knew him. He used to wear it for family masquerades and such."

"Mr. MacLeish was right," Marshall sighed and quoted: " 'It is the questions that we do not know.' So I got beautifully lost on detail in those first attempts, and I got lost again toward the end. I got enough detailed facts to figure out two beautiful theories about Wimpole and Runcible, put them together, and thought I had everything. And all the time I kept worrying my eyes over these details, there was the grand pattern if I'd only step back a couple of feet and take it in.

"But even after we saw the big pattern, some of these details still bothered me until I realized that they were parts of incomplete sub-patterns. And I needed to fill in the rest."

"Skip the *mea culpa,* Terence," said Matt, "and tell us these sub-patterns."

"Well now, for instance, about Vance Wimpole. Most of my guess was right on that. He had been in Los Angeles from time to time during his supposed wanderings, and Phyn had seen him and was blackmailing him. But the whole set-up, including letters mailed by friends from distant points, was intended to circumvent detectives, not from homicide, but from a divorce-evidence agency. I managed to find out enough to set up in blackmail for myself; but I'll hold out the juicier details.

"And the other business is too bitterly good to be true. William Runcible Foulkes, I discovered by painstaking checking through records, was orphaned at an early age and brought up in an asylum. He learned a trade and grew up into a first-rate turret-lathe operator. He died in Chicago of natural causes in 1938."

The audience was duly and gogglingly petrified. "Then our Runcible . . . ?" Austin Carter ventured at last.

"Something we'll never know about this case is who did what and with which and to whom, or in less famous words, who was defrauding whom, in what manner. Did a false Runcible put himself over on Tarbell, that specialist in lost claimants? Were Runcible and Tarbell collaborators in fraud? Or did Tarbell convince a young innocent that he was the missing Foulkes heir and use him as a lever on Hilary?"

"Tune in to this station tomorrow and find out," Leona murmured.

"I wish this station knew. But it can make a guess that the last of those assumptions is correct. Tarbell was in Chicago building up his Weyringhausen case at the time the real Runcible died. And he did have the rosary, and God knows what else that was destroyed either at the Elite Hotel or at the rooming house on Adams. Say that he knew the young man was planning to press his claims when he up and dies. So Tarbell filches and preserves the evidence for future use. Finally fate is kind, and he runs on to a man with a marked physical resemblance to the Foulkes' even down to the arm trick. If this young man's own family background were hazy, it shouldn't be hard to persuade him that he was the descendant of the Fowler Foulkes whom he so idolizes."

"Then all Hilary's . . ." Jenny Green began. "It was all for nothing?"

"For nothing?" said Joe Henderson quietly.

"You and Bernice should be happy," Matt Duncan observed to his wife as they walked home from the streetcar. "It looks like you've finally got a nice girl for Joe."

"I like her."

"So do I. But she does seem mild for Joe's tastes. I'd have thought that bitch of a Foulkes woman was more his type."

"I think I know what happened there. Jenny says she and Joe were there when Mrs. Foulkes and her brother talked about Hilary's death, just before we came in. She says it was awful . . . like something inhuman. I think then Joe realized just how evil a woman can really be; and evil women sort of lost their fascination." Concha paused and removed a pebble from her shoe. "If we had a car . . ." she muttered.

"We're not going into that again!" Matt snapped.

"But I used my own money when . . . you know . . ."

"I know. Sorry, darling. I shouldn't have barked at you like that. You used your money, and it meant more than I ever thought money could mean. It meant that you loved me and needed me and wanted me free even when I was charged with killing a man. But still I . . . Damn it, my love, life is so confusedly much a matter of prides. Hilary had his own peculiar kind of pride. Sister Ursula has hers. Well, I have mine."

"I think," said Concha in a very little voice, "I've got a solution."

"Yes, dear?"

"I could spend the money on anything that was my own, couldn't I? I mean let's say I wanted to raise pedigreed chows. I could spend it on them couldn't I?"

"I guess so. I wouldn't stop you. But I don't know as how chows—"

"Silly. That was just for example like. I don't mean *chows*. But I could . . . oh I know I wouldn't be very good at it and not nearly so capable and admirable as Leona but then who is? and every time we go to the Marshalls' I get to thinking about it and . . . I could spend it raising my own baby, couldn't I?"

Matt Duncan did a very slow take. Then, though they were at that moment right under a bright street lamp, he took his wife in his arms. "Darling," he said a little later, "let's get home and make sure of that."

Thirty hours later, in the white-and-gold chapel of the Sisters of Martha of Bethany, the chaplain had just finished saying the requested month's mind Mass for the repose of the soul of Hilary Foulkes. A nun moved slowly about the chapel. As she paused in devotion before each station of the Cross, she fingered a curious rosary which should by rights have reposed in the Black Museum of the Los Angeles Police Department.

EIGHT

AFTERWORD:
By the Author

I've been interested in imaginative literature all my life, but twelve years ago science fiction, in particular, up and grabbed me by the scruff of the neck with an intensive grasp that shows no signs of weakening with time.

The causes were two: directly, my acquaintance with the Mañana Literary Society, which existed in fact precisely (aside from murders) as it is depicted in this book; indirectly, the fact that pulp science fiction had, at that time, just reached maturity both in thinking and in writing and was at a fine ripe stage to make converts easily.

One of the first results of my conversion (beyond immediately reading all the good pulp science fiction I could lay my hands on) was this novel, first published in 1942. In one way it was very badly timed: the readers of hardcover books had at that time never heard of science fiction, and the whole subject tended to seem a little unbelievable to them. In another way the timing was precisely right: I had the opportunity to present a first-hand picture of an important stage in the development of American popular entertainment—a phenomenon of which the book-readers have become conscious only at second hand in the last couple of years.

I'm surprised on rereading *Rocket to the Morgue* to see how little its statements about science fiction have dated. Pulp rates for stories in the better markets are now about twice what is mentioned here (but then so is the cost of everything else—and some magazines are still paying 1940 rates). Science fiction is no longer restricted to pulps; it now flourishes in slicks, in books, in films, radio, and television. There are more magazine markets for adult thought and prose: when this was written, there were only the two magazines edited by John W. Campbell, Jr. (known in *Rocket* as "Don Stuart"), but recently *Life* bracketed as "the aristocrats of science fiction": Campbell's *Astounding,* Horace Gold's *Galaxy,* and *The Magazine of Fantasy & Science Fiction,* edited by me and J. Francis McComas.

But the reprint racket is still a problem; the lowest level of space opera is still very much with us; mimeographed fanzines and National Science Fiction Conventions have not changed; the top "name" writers in the field are largely still the same; and all of Austin Carter's explanations of the nature and technique of science fiction are as true now as they were then—and as they would not have been a brief five years before.

Actually, science itself has dated the book more than any changes in science fiction. In 1942 atomic fission was another of the peculiar notions the s-f boys kicked around, like time warps and subspace; rockets were something that only eccentric monomaniacs experimented with. To supplement the out-dated section on rocketry herein, by all means get hold of Willy Ley's magnificently authoritative and readable *Rockets, Missiles, and Space Travel* (Viking, 1951).

I'm not only surprised but amused to see that, in the best science fiction tradition, I achieved some accurate on-the-nose prophecy. It looks as though I may have been tragically wrong in my hope that experiments for spaceflight would help world unity; but I did bring off two minor unconscious predictions. I used the title *Worlds Beyond* for a magazine (actually the unforgettable *Unknown Worlds*), and in 1950 there appeared on the stands a short-lived magazine with that title. I created a character called Captain Comet to parody all the inter-galactic supermen, and sure enough, there is now a comic book featuring the hyperspatial adventures of Captain Comet.

I think (as best anyone can judge his own work on rereading) that I've managed to capture a moment that has some interest as a historical footnote to popular literature. This is the way it was in Southern California just before the war, when science fiction was being given its present form by such authors as Robert A. Heinlein (still the undisputed Master), Cleve Cartmill, Jack Williamson, Edmond Hamilton, Henry Kuttner, C. L. Moore, and many others. (And this is as wise a place as any to add hastily that no character in this novel is based specifically on any actual writer—nor is any character quite devoid of some factual basis.)

I hope that some of the regular readers of whodunits may find this picture of the field provocative enough to make them investigate further—a much easier task now then when the novel was written. At that time there was no good anthology devoted to the best of science fiction—in fact, no such anthology, good or bad. Now you can start your investigations with the tastefully chosen collections of Groff Conklin, August Derleth, Raymond J. Healy (with or without J. Francis McComas), and Judith Merril; you can go on to sample the three "aristocrats" mentioned above; and from then on I trust you'll have as satisfying and stimulating a time varying your criminous diet with the wonders of logical imagination as I have enjoyed for the past dozen years—and expect to continue enjoying at least until my sons radio me their greetings from the moon.

Berkeley, California
December 12, 1951

The Case Of The Crumpled Knave

For

PHYLLIS WHITE

AT LAST

The characters, events, and institutions (with the exceptions of the United States Army and the Los Angeles Police Department) of this novel are completely fictional and have no reference to actual people or occurrences.

Characters

HUMPHREY GARNETT
retired research chemist

KAY GARNETT
his daughter

ARTHUR WILLOWE
his brother-in-law

WILL HARDING
his laboratory assistant

CAMILLA SALLICE
his protégée

COLONEL THEODORE RAND (U.S.A., retired)
his friend

RICHARD VINTON
film actor, engaged to Kay Garnett

MAX FARRINGTON
lawyer

MAURICE WARRINER
museum curator

DETECTIVE LIEUTENANT A. JACKSON
of the Los Angeles Police

FERGUS O'BREEN
private investigator

Le Pendu

It was quite literally a matter of life and death; and his own death was not a pleasant thing to contemplate. Clearly the next step was to send the telegram. The affair might not come to a head for several days yet, but the telegram must be sent now.

He broke off his incompleted game of patience (the knave of diamonds was hopelessly locked anyhow—a fact which pleased him ironically in view of what was to follow) and walked slowly around the room while he pondered the exact phrasing.

He was alone now in the study. Outside the window he could glimpse the Verdugo hills, calmly beautiful in the winter sunlight. But in here he was alone with the oddly assorted library, the cryptic chemical notes, the table for four-handed chess, the superb collection of playing cards. It was, he mused characteristically, a good setting.

He paused before a picture on the wall—an exquisite reproduction of one of the silver-gold tarot cards painted for Charles VI. They had always fascinated him, these tarots—dark symbols of an ancient mysticism, now lightly shuffled in a game of chance, but still strong with their old stark meaning. That was fitting for his plan—a daring, fantastic gamble with a core of desperate significance.

He had it now. Swiftly he crossed to the telephone while the perfect formula was still sharp in his mind. He dialed operator and asked for Western Union.

"I want to send a telegram," he said, "to Colonel Theodore Rand." He spelled out the name and added an address in a New York suburb.

"And what is the message?" the flat voice asked.

"COME TO LOS ANGELES AT ONCE STOP." He spoke slowly and clearly. "FLY IF NECESSARY STOP."

The voice interrupted mechanically. "You do not need to send the word STOP. Punctuation is now transmitted free of charge."

"Send it anyway." He smiled. "I like the effect."

"Very well, if you wish. It will count as a word. Is that all of the message?"

"No." His enunciation grew even sharper. "Add this. YOU MAY BE INVALUABLE WITNESS AT INQUEST ON MY BODY STOP." The voice emitted a noise of quite unprofessional surprise. "WATCH HECTOR—H, E, C, T, O, R

—CAREFULLY." He added the signature and hung up without bothering to hear the message read back.

He returned to the picture on the wall and allowed himself a moment of smiling pleasure. It was a curious omen to bless his telegram—the tarot known as Le Pendu . . . the Hanged Man.

Arthur Willowe Plays Solitaire

Arthur Willowe was the least clever person in the Garnett household. Everyone admitted that, including Willowe himself. Some of them were nice about it—Kay, for example, who loved him because he was her mother's brother, and never paused to remember that his lack of cleverness had killed her mother. Others were not so nice about it—for instance, the dominant ruler of the household, Humphrey Garnett himself, to whom forgiving and forgetting were as inalterably alien as an error in a chess game.

Thus lived or hated, Willowe always felt self-consciously unclever. He was out of place in this room, with its monuments to ingenuity—the cabinet of rare playing cards, the desk crammed with chemical formulae, the table especially designed for that arcane mystery known as four-handed chess. So he sat unobtrusively in a corner and played solitaire.

The Garnett household went in for solitaire extensively. In any of the rooms you were apt to come across a low table and a worn pack or two for the use of anyone who wished to think out a problem to paste-board accompaniment. But Arthur Willowe was unclever even in his choice of solitaires. Where the other men played the Zodiac or the Salic Law or La Nivernaise (elaborate involutions demanding two or more packs and a planned campaign as complex as a chess problem), Willowe contented himself with one pack and Klondike or Canfield, and lost even those with a persistence which would have cruelly disheartened anyone who laid a serious claim to an ingenious mind.

It was probably those two interrelated factors—devotion to solitaire and lack of cleverness—which made Arthur Willowe acutely aware of the impending murder.

He would not have put it so sharply as that himself. It was simply that there was a tension in the household, a tension so strong that it must inevitably be loosed by one hard moment of violence.

He noticed it first in the afternoon. He had tired of Canfield and was deciding to try Klondike for a change. He had just laid out the stock and the starter when his brother-in-law came in to telephone. Humphrey Garnett didn't look in the corner. People had a way of not looking at him, Willowe thought: he could commit a neat murder in a crowded room and afterwards twenty people would swear they hadn't seen him there. For a moment he sat wondering at himself for thinking of such a strange thing as murder; then he shrugged, and his weary old hands laid out the four cards across.

There was something of strength and efficiency in even the way Humphrey Garnett approached a telephone. There was not a waste movement of his compact muscles. The clicks of the dial were as sharp and regular as rifle practice. "Dr. White's office," Willowe heard him say.

There was a pause, and Willowe moved a card or two fitfully. Then his brother-in-law's vigorous voice cut across his thoughts. "White? Garnett speaking. Called to give you the weekly report. I'm still alive, and by God I love it." His laughter was free and rough. "I'll see you at your funeral, my fine threatening charlatan."

He hung up abruptly and dialed another number. "O'Breen?" There was a pause. "That you, O'Breen? Got that report for me?" A question at the other end seemed to interrupt him. "Damn it, man, what kind of a detective are you if you can't recognize a voice on the phone? This is Garnett speaking. Go ahead."

He was silent for a while. Silent, that is, verbally; Willowe could hear an occasional grunt of restrained joy and once an outburst of triumphant laughter. "Fine," Garnett said at last. "Good lad. Glad I took a chance on you. Call and see us sometime—as Kay's friend, of course. Not a word about this. Meanwhile send me a copy of that and your bill. And you needn't be too modest in your demands. God knows I couldn't overpay you for this."

He set down the receiver and stretched his wiry arms in a broad gesture of malicious glee. Then he saw Willowe. The quiet old man cringed a little. He felt what was coming.

Garnett walked slowly over to the table, contentedly rubbing a hairy wrist with an even hairier hand. "Don't be afraid, Arthur," he said with a curious harsh gentleness. "I'm not going to torment you. I'm not going to laugh at your piddling inefficiency. I'm not going to twit you for putting an eight on a ten. I'm not even going to mention automobiles or water hydrants."

Willowe's armor was thin. He winced at the last words (blood and water . . . they mixed then, and the blood was as thin as the water . . . Alicia's blood, thinly coursing . . .). He tried hopelessly to recover himself by moving the offending eight.

"Of course," Garnett meditated with tense humour, "we'll have to wait until Rand has come. We couldn't get rid of the bastard before then; the Colonel and I must have our four-handed chess, and small help you'd be, my dear Arthur, with your— But forgive me. I had intended not to waste my abuse on you. It's bigger game I'm after now."

He said the words lightly, but Willowe felt a menace hid in their careless tone.

"What do you think of Richard Vinton?" Garnett asked abruptly, with ironic stress on each syllable of the name.

Willowe saw the young Englishman in his mind; but he was not alone. There was a bright, redheaded girl with him, and their eyes were alive at each other's presence. "Kay loves him," he answered simply.

"Does she, Arthur? Does she now indeed? How I have underestimated you, Arthur! You're really a most entertaining conversationalist."

The old man looked after Garnett in confusion. It had been a true and an obvious remark; he failed to understand its hidden humor. Why should a father find his daughter's love so magnificently comic?

Garnett was gone; but the room was still a sounding box for his vibrant laughter. And as Willowe listened to it, he began to understand. It was not the laughter of comedy.

This odd episode, so meaningless and yet (to Willowe at least) so unnerving, forced the old man to observe Richard Vinton more carefully. He had never particularly noticed the young British actor before. In past years he had been alert to watch people and their oddities, and then talk them over with Alicia, to whom all things human were fascinating; but now . . .

He knew that Vinton was engaged to Kay Garnett, that he stayed at the house a great deal (there was even a room set aside for him), and that Humphrey Garnett, heretofore at least, had always seemed to relish his company as that of an equal in ingenuity. He thought he remembered vaguely that the young man's father, who bore some sort of British title, had been a crony of Garnett's during war days in Washington. Aside from that, Vinton was nothing to him but a pleasant young man who was building himself quite a reputation as a screen juvenile.

Now the young Briton seemed somehow more important. It was worth while distracting yourself from the cards to hear what he might say or what people might say to him.

Arthur Willowe was thinking these random thoughts on the sun porch. The study, for him, still rang with Garnett's throaty laughter; and the open air was a happier place. And so, because of these thoughts, he listened unseen when Kay and Vinton passed by him on their way from the garage to the front of the house.

"I've been thinking Richard, about what you told me the other night," Kay was saying in her clear young voice.

"Yes?" There was a painful hesitancy in that one clipped syllable.

"I— You know, darling, it would be foolish to say it doesn't matter to me. It does, of course. Everything about you has to matter, and matter terribly." Her voice paused, and her footsteps too.

"I understand," Vinton murmured, so low that Willowe could scarcely hear him.

"But it would be just as foolish to say that it made any real difference between us. I love you; and if you want to tell me things like that—why, it just proves how much you love me too. So thank you, dear—and that's all."

They went on in silence, and Willowe resumed his patience and his thoughts. More and more Vinton seemed focal; there was even a Secret now. Willowe capitalized the word in his thoughts. That made things more melodramatic and added fresh zest to this new game he had found to entertain him.

The next move in the game was on the part of Will Harding—the pale, sandy, earnest young man who was Garnett's laboratory assistant. He came out on the porch shortly after the voices ceased. He might even have seen the couple pass by; certainly his thoughts were fixed upon them.

He spoke jerkily, as though forced despite himself. "Mr. Willowe . . ."

Black seven on red eight. "Yes?" Fill the space from the stock. "What do you know about Richard Vinton?"

That, Willowe thought to himself, is what people call a guilty start. But he looked unconcerned and said, "No more than you do, I suppose." And he outlined what little he did know.

"You think he's—you know what I mean—all right?"

"I think so."

The young man's dull voice sounded troubled. "We don't really know much about him, do we? And you hear so much about actors and the things that happen in the colony—"

"If Kay trusts him, I imagine that we can. But why should it concern you so, Will?"

"Why, I just mean— After all, he's here so much, and he's going to— I just couldn't help wondering."

The words were so suspiciously indefinite that Willowe looked up from his game. For a moment he saw the young technician, whom he had always so envied for his unemotional efficiency, staring along the path by which the lovers had passed with something very close to fury in his gray eyes. It was only for a moment. Then he turned and regarded Willowe with so pacific and ordinary a gaze that the older man could scarcely trust that instant of memory.

But the memory lingered nonetheless; and when the last member of the Garnett household came onto the porch some minutes later, he could not refrain from probing there, too. This careworn but still darkly beautiful girl was Camilla Sallice; and with her nothing was associated in Willowe's mind—no facts, no feelings, only a dull resentment of her very presence. Who she was, where she came from, why she lived with them and called Garnett "Uncle Humphrey" (though Willowe knew the man had, apart from his daughter Kay, no living relatives)—none of these things was clear.

She smiled at him—that curious smile so characteristic of her in its blend of tragedy and gaiety. "Would you like a cushion from the swing, Mr. Willowe? That chair looks frightfully hard."

"No, thank you," he muttered ungraciously. That was one of the infuriating things about this girl. She wanted to be so much nicer to him than he had any intention of allowing her to be.

"You don't mind if I share the sun with you?"

"No." He waited a minute or two, while she settled herself on the chaise longue with a feline stretch of her supple body. Then he sprang his question, just as she seemed on the point of dozing. "And how well, Miss Sallice, do *you* know Richard Vinton?"

She sat up sharply, flushed and almost a little frightened. For the moment she was too taken aback to say anything. He regretted that; for when she did speak, she had regained control of herself.

"Quite as well as I care to," she said calmly. "After all, Mr. Willowe, he is Kay's."

Disgruntled, Willowe returned to the cards. But he had hardly dealt a fresh stock when Camilla Sallice added, with a quiet amusement which he failed to comprehend, "And what would you think of me as a blonde?"

As Willowe shaved for dinner, with the cherished straight razor which Alicia had given him for his birthday the very week before—before the accident—he thought all these little items through. He had long felt terror in this house; that was nothing new. But he had always thought its menace directed at himself. He was mortally (even—he toyed with the word—immortally) afraid of Humphrey Garnett. He knew how Garnett hated him for Alicia's accidental death (was it an accident? if he had not boastfully tried to drive when he knew he needed new glasses . . .) and he had gone in dread of impending revenge. It was a relief now to know that Garnett's enmity, for the moment at least, was directed at another object.

He knew a small trembling pleasure. He would be free for a little while of that oppressive dominance which Garnett exerted on him. He could think his own thoughts and plan his own plans, whether they pleased Humphrey Garnett or not. And it was reasonably certain that they would not please him.

Yes, this sudden tension of menace had its advantages. Smoke is in itself a stifling discomfort, but it is also a screen. Besides, this provided a new pleasure to distract him. In his petty respite, he found it markedly more entertaining to deal and arrange facts and emotions than to worry whether the ace was locked under the king (as it almost invariably was).

"All in all," he thought. "I should have quite a little collection for an investigator—if it should come to that." The thought was so absurd and yet (for even his quiet life had tender spots not formed for probing) so terrifyingly plausible that his old hand trembled just enough to produce a slight cut.

Humphrey Garnett Expounds A Parable

The conversation at dinner turned largely upon playing cards. This was not unusual; an interest which swayed Humphrey Garnett must inevitably affect the household which he dominated. But even Arthur Willowe, for all his unusually heightened perception, could not realize how vitally the lore of playing cards was to shape all their lives in the days to come.

The reactions of the group to cards were various. Kay, like a child, loved them for their beauty or oddity of design. Willowe's appreciation, too, was somewhat abstractly esthetic; but Camilla Sallice affected a preoccupation with the deeper occult meanings behind the now unheeded designs. Will Harding viewed the cards practically as tools with which to attain relaxation, and esteemed them highly as an aid to his work.

Richard Vinton, however, was the only one of the group to share their host's interest in the more scholarly and abstruse aspects of card history; and that, unfortunately, was the trend of tonight's conversation. This was presumably out of deference to their dinner guest —a gaunt, stooped, old gentleman named Warriner, whose exact identity Willowe failed to gather, but who seemed to have something professional to do with playing cards—curator of a museum collection or something of the sort.

At least the presence of this odd individual, who left his food almost untouched and subsisted largely on snuff taken between courses, served to dissipate for the moment the atmosphere of tension. There was only one awkward situation, and that was precipitated by the curator himself.

"Are you still engaged professionally, Mr. Garnett?" he asked, chiefly, it would seem, to cut short a heated controversy between the host and Vinton as to the relative priority of the German or Italian suit designs—a controversy which had been seething, as best

Willowe could remember, from the day of Vinton's entry into the house.

Garnett looked up with a quizzical frown. "Why, yes. You might say that I am, sir."

"Might one inquire the nature of your current researches?"

"One might not."

The family was inured to these abrupt answers; but Willowe feared lest their elderly guest might (and quite justly) feel some offense. However, he merely smiled and said, "A *secret*?"—adorning the word with an italicized emphasis which made it faintly ridiculous.

"A secret," Garnett retorted succinctly.

"Rather too much of a one, if you ask me." There was an inexplicable note of resentment in Will Harding's voice. Did he, perhaps, regret the secrecy which kept veiled his own part in these researches—whatever their nature might be?

"And how," the elderly scholar continued, "do you protect your deadly secrets against the unjustifiably curious? Do you, like Faustus' Covetousness, lock them up in your good chest?"

"I am quite capable of protecting myself." The words were simple, but Garnett's voice was rich in quiet menace. Willowe received the disquieting assurance that the man against whom Garnett protected himself would never live to disturb another victim.

The rest of the talk consisted chiefly of arguments on such topics as the relative origins of cards and chess, with much bandying about of Richard Brome and Isaac von Meckenen and other great names in the history of card design. This meant, of course, that Garnett, Vinton, and Warriner talked volubly, while the others respectfully ate and listened. It was all, Willowe thought, very ingenious and scholarly and impressive—and dull.

It was a relief when dinner was over and the men, as was their invariable nightly habit, retired to the study. Kay chose this time for going over household affairs with the cook who came in by the day; and Camilla Sallice, if the dinner had not tempted her too much, would settle down to a session of vocal practice. Her voice, Willowe granted reluctantly, was good—a somber, full-bodied contralto. Smoky, he thought, searching for the *mot juste,* and then winced self-consciously, remembering the purpose of smoke as it had presented itself to him earlier.

The old curator excused himself from joining the group in the study. He had, it appeared, an appointment to visit another eminent collector in Beverly Hills, and must depart at once, even when his host urged him to stay on for a game of vint—that curious Russian paraphrase of bridge which Garnett always upheld as a far subtler game than the American version. (That point Willowe could not judge; the science of cards eluded him. The only game which he fully enjoyed was rummy; there was a certain sense of power and compensation in scooping a fine fat fistful.)

Warriner too was seemingly not of the card-playing breed. "My dear sir," he explained. "I never touch playing cards save to relish their designs. 'Infinite riches' " he went on with punctuation from his snuff-box, " 'in a little room.' The perfection of a concise deck, yes; but the confusion of that beauty scattered in wanton play—no, my dear sir, no."

Now that the four men—Garnett, Vinton, Will Harding, and Willowe himself—were gathered in the study, that abnormal, irrational tension began to assert itself once more. "This is a prologue," Willowe thought almost involuntarily, "a prologue to something strong and terrible." He laid out his cards (he was back at Canfield now) with painful overdeliberation. "I must watch these people as though I had never seen them before—as though they were new characters whom I had to establish."

He looked at his brother-in-law. Humphrey Garnett's strong body was hunched over the great board of one hundred and sixty squares, while his long arms adjusted the chess pieces. There were red and green men in addition to the usual black and white—a full complement of each. His stubby fingers placed the exquisitely carved pieces with surprising delicacy.

Richard Vinton's hand abandoned the fascination of his wavy hair to pick up the green bishop. "It will be sport," he mused, admiring the intricate tracings of its miter, "to have a game of four-handed chess again." His rich voice had that slight trace of British accent which is sometimes so impressive to Hollywood producers. In Vinton's case, Willowe thought, it seemed to have served him very well indeed. "I haven't had a chance since the pater died."

Garnett shook back his shaggy hair and looked up. "I had some fine games with Sir Edward. I hope you live up to the family tradition, Richard. You'll find Colonel Rand a worthy opponent."

Richard Vinton smiled. "A sort of double family tradition now, isn't it, sir? I mean, it won't be many weeks before I'll be calling you father."

Garnett adjusted the white queen deliberately. "In chess," he said, "you can reckon your moves with certainty, provided you don't underestimate your adversary. But in other games—cards, for instance—chance plays a guiding part. Eh, Will?"

The dry young man with the sparse sandy hair and the rimless spectacles (how well that simple description characterized him, Willowe thought—if only it weren't for that moment on the porch . . .) looked up from a ponderous German work on chemistry. "What was that, Mr. Garnett?"

Garnett's stubby fingers massaged his firm chin. "I was merely developing a banal little parable, Will, to the effect that Richard cannot be quite sure of marrying Kay until the marriage has taken place. What do you think?"

"I think it's certain enough," Will Harding said in a flat hopeless voice, and went on reading.

Garnett, however, had hit his stride and was not to be stopped. He turned to his brother-in-law. "What is your opinion, Arthur? Which is the true symbol of life—chess or cards?"

Arthur Willowe paused while he decided which red nine to move, but not so much for the sake of the move as to give him time to mask his secret interest in the talk. He knew whichever nine he moved would be wrong anyway. Things were like that. His futile white hands abandoned the game of patience and wavered in the air while he sought the proper words for his answer. "I can scarcely say, Humphrey," was the best he could bring forth. "As you know, I have never been able to master even simple chess, let alone this complex four-handed affair. No, I fear I cannot judge your analogy." These were words. The truth was that he was afraid to judge the analogy—afraid of the purpose that might lie behind Garnett's verbal attack on Vinton.

Humphrey Garnett laughed loudly. There was something hairy even about his laughter. "That's one thing I'll say for you, Arthur. You're honest. You're not fit to do anything, and you admit it. You can't earn a cent, you can't play a game, you can't say a sentence worth hearing. You can, of course, play solitaire, if the moves are simple and only one pack is involved; and I can remember once thinking that you could drive a car."

There was something more than ordinarily vicious in Garnett's laughter this time. Arthur Willowe winced and drew into his shell of futility. For a moment he could not even be slyly observant. He could only see that street corner. The shattered glass and the blood and the water pouring out of the broken hydrant to wash it all away—all but the memory. He could see Alicia lying there so still, looking as though she were practicing some queer contortion act, like the shows they used to put on in the barn for two pins a head. He had lain there beside Alicia—his sister, Garnett's wife—thinking about the barn and wondering if he was dead too.

But of course he wasn't. He couldn't even die. He could do only one thing, and Garnett would despise him more than ever if he knew what that one thing was. Slowly he moved the wrong red nine, then forced his attention back to the others.

Garnett was still talking. "You can make a very pretty parable, for instance," he was saying to the dark young actor, "out of pinochle. Or do you happen to know that game?"

Vinton shook his head gracefully. "Unfortunately, no. It always makes me think of elderly and paunchy film executives."

"There are marriages in the game," Garnett went on. "That is to say, the king and queen of a suit. And it seems moral and laudable that you should score points for something so proper as a marriage. But there's much more profit in another sort of mating. A pinochle is a queen—and a knave. You see?"

Vinton shrugged. "I'm not sure I do."

"The knave," Garnett added emphatically, "of diamonds."

The room was silent. Will Harding read on in a strange new theory of atomic structure, Richard Vinton strolled over to examine the bookshelves, and Humphrey Garnett put the finishing touches to the great chess table. Arthur Willowe watched it all quietly—and, incidentally, lost another game of Canfield.

Then the two girls came into the study. With their coming, Willowe meditated, Humphrey Garnett's oddly assorted household was again complete. Kay Garnett, that dear daughter of so violent a father, was pre-eminently young—young, redheaded, and alive. She moved across the stuffy room with a grace that seemed to belong rather on the tennis court or on a high mountain path.

"Time for you all to get out," she said gaily. "I've got to see that Father keeps his hours." She moved over to Richard Vinton and frankly took the young actor's hand in hers.

The other girl stood near the doorway holding a glass. Camilla Sallice was several years older and some inches taller than Kay. Beside the younger girl's brightness she seemed worn and almost sullen.

"I brought you your nightcap this time, Uncle Humphrey," she said quietly. "I hope it's right. Scotch and plain water, no ice."

"You're a true Briton at heart, sir," Vinton observed.

Garnett smiled his thanks at the girl and set the glass aside. "Very well, gentlemen. My daughter's word is law here—especially when reinforced by Dr. White's. You may retire. I shall have my nightcap here in peace and then go to my rest. Are we ready for that experiment tomorrow, Will? That is, unless Colonel Rand's arrival postpones it."

The young laboratory assistant was placing his rimless spectacles in their case. "Everything's set, Mr. Garnett. Good night, sir." He nodded to the company.

"Good night, Will," Kay Garnett murmured. But he went out without answering her.

Garnett surveyed the chess table once more. "Thank God Rand is coming!" he exclaimed, stretching his long arms. "For six months I've had two other men in this house who could play four-handed chess, and now at last I have a fourth. I'll take the green men for myself," he went on dreamily. "They seem the most bizarre. You'll take the red, Richard—the color of youth and strength and vigor. White will suit Will—the poor, pale, efficient rabbit. That leaves the black pieces for Colonel Rand. That's as it should be. He's always liked black."

"I wouldn't." Kay shuddered a little. "It's such an ominous color—mourning and death and things."

"Omens don't bother me," Garnett laughed. "I've learned that fate can be shaped if you're strong enough to do it. And I am. Now at long last I am to have a game of four-handed chess, and death is the only agent that can keep me from it."

Camilla Sallice's voice was low and throbbing. "Please, Uncle Humphrey. Don't joke like that."

"And what, my dear," Garnett asked calmly, "makes you think that I'm joking?"

The Sallice girl had left the room; and Arthur Willowe, with an unobtrusive good night to the others, slipped out after her. If he waited for Kay and Vinton, they might feel they had to talk to him; and he knew that they wanted to be alone together. But in the hall he discovered that Vinton had followed him.

He looked up in surprise. The young actor was holding out a piece of paper covered with typing. He seemed to be trying hard not to smile.

"I found this under your balcony, sir," Vinton said respectfully. "It must have blown away. I thought perhaps you wouldn't want anyone else to see it."

Willowe stared at the sheet of paper with incredulous horror. "You—you read this, Richard?"

"I couldn't help noticing the name. It's not unknown." There was awkward embarrassment under the careful British reserve. "But I promise to respect your secret."

For a moment Arthur Willowe understood the hidden fury which he had seen briefly revealed in Will Harding's eyes. He wondered if he himself looked so abruptly altered as had the other. That would never do. Where there is fire, he thought confusedly, there must be smoke—smoke to hide the very glow of the fire. He laughed (the noise was shrill in his ears), mumbled some clumsy speech of thanks, and slipped up the stairs quietly.

In his own tidy room he felt better. It was amusing now to think that even he might be conceived to have a motive, if such a fantastically twisted one. But people had been killed for knowing what must not be known.

Yes, he thought, the net around Richard Vinton was drawing cruelly tight. He smiled as he phrased that; but the smile faded quickly. He was beginning to realize, in faint foreshadowing, that other net of strange compulsion which was drawn about Arthur Willowe.

Colonel Rand Rereads A Telegram

The trim little air-line hostess collected funny-looking passengers. That was why she liked Colonel Theodore Rand (U.S.A., retired). He was tall and well-set, with shoulders that looked padded and probably weren't. His hair was nearly white, and he had waxed mustaches. Even while he gazed out of the window at empty middle-western plains, he managed to be impressive, commanding, and just a little pompous. In short, he looked so exactly like a drawing by Peter Arno that she amused herself by wondering if he ever really said "harrumph."

The Colonel frowned imposingly and reached into his breast pocket. His long fingers drew out a folded piece of yellow paper. He read its message carefully:

COME TO LOS ANGELES AT ONCE STOP FLY IF NECESSARY STOP YOU MAY BE INVALUABLE WITNESS AT INQUEST ON MY BODY STOP WATCH HECTOR CAREFULLY

Colonel Rand had no idea how many times he had read that message since he had received it. He was a man of leisure living on a comfortable pension; there was no reason why he should not indulge a friend's strange whim. But all his military experience had not prepared him for an urgent invitation to an inquest, signed by the expectant victim.

And who in Heaven's name was Hector? The name meant nothing to Rand in any connection. The Colonel stared fiercely at the message, then slowly and with great deliberation he went "harrumph" to the intense glee of the little air-line hostess.

He looked again at the signature. That was what was so utterly incredible. You couldn't associate death with him, much less this calm acceptance of it. But there the name stood, in letters as clear and bold as the man himself:
HUMPHREY GARNETT

THE CASE

ONE

COLONEL RAND TAKES A TAXI

Colonel Rand took a taxi from the Burbank airport. The day was one of those brightly incredible samples of June in January which justify lyric-writers and All the Year Clubs even to the most tough-minded. The old soldier leaned back on the leather seat in stiff contentment, with no serious inkling, despite that perplexing and ominous telegram, of what awaited him at the end of his journey.

Then, without any warning, a voice began shouting, "*Yoo-oo-oo turn me inside out.*"

"I beg your pardon, sir!" the Colonel exclaimed.

"What's biting you, buddy?" the driver inquired in words largely drowned out by the voice, which was describing its further gyrations as "*Upside down and around about.*"

"Someone," Colonel Rand observed heavily, "seems to be comparing me to a blasted whirligig."

"Oh that." The driver seemed disappointed. "That's the radio."

The Colonel bristled. "My man, despite my years I am sufficiently aware of the wonders of modern science to realize that fact. But what can I do about it?"

"There's a knob in there," said the driver indifferently, and turned his attention to a traffic problem.

Colonel Rand had rarely gone "harrumph" with more vicious sincerity. He cast a trained glance over the interior of the cab and located the knob of the offending scientific marvel. The adenoidal voice was now comparing itself to a castoff glove, which seemed to the Colonel an unwarrantable slur on a worthy article of wearing apparel. He seized the knob and twisted.

It broke.

That was the beginning of the nightmare. In its way it was a good thing. Without this maddening introduction, the grave news that Colonel Rand was soon to learn would have wounded much more deeply. As it was, the whole business fused into wild fantasy. The song, now blaring forth at the instrument's top volume (which was considerable), apparently inspired the cab-driver. He put fresh spirit into his work. Traffic, even Southern California traffic, meant nothing to him. He seemed possessed of a delusion that all corners were banked, like the curves on a speedway. Colonel Rand came as near as possible to abandoning his fine military carriage as he was jolted from one side of the seat to the other, constantly reminded of the fact that he turned an anonymous young crooner upside down and inside out—which was, he thought, a consummation devoutly to be wished.

Even the narrow winding streets which led up into the bright Los Feliz hills did little to check the cab's progress. When the driver braked to a sudden stop before the Garnett home, he did so with a consummate jerk that threw the long-suffering Colonel flat on the floor and at the same time, apparently, started Young Adenoids announcing that everything was hotcha for his hot chickadee.

The cab door opened, and Colonel Rand lifted his embattled head, white mustaches gleaming against a surrealistically purple face, to tell the driver just what he thought of him—a plan which would have delayed his entering the house by at least fifteen minutes. But instead of the driver, he found himself glaring up at what must have been the biggest policeman in all Los Angeles.

"And just what do you think you're up to?" the officer demanded. While the Colonel puffed for breath, he repeated the question, shouting to drown out the crooner and adding a few colorful words which occurred rarely even in Rand's powerful vocabulary.

It is hard to be dignified when you are sprawled on the floor of a taxicab. Even the innate dignity of a retired army officer must suffer under such circumstances. "I have come to see Mr. Humphrey Garnett," the Colonel stated in precisely military syllables, and drew himself up to his full height.

Colonel Rand's full height, however, was one factor which had never crossed the mind of the designer of Los Angeles cabs. The Colonel sat down with an abrupt force which left his posterior as grievously wounded as his dignity.

"Drunk at this hour," the policeman observed.

Rand's face grew a deeper purple and he began to splutter.

"And at your age, too," the officer added reproachfully.

"*And my chickadee is hotcha for me,*" the crooner concluded.

Rand could never reconstruct, to his own satisfaction, how he got out of that cab. He recalled vague details of the process, which included knocking his forehead against the door, losing his hat, and pitching into the arms of the policeman, who seemed to take the whole matter much more calmly since he'd formed his drunk theory. The next clear moment came as Rand walked up the front steps of the house.

The crooner was only a noise in the distance now—still not exactly faint, but at least distant. The nightmare, Rand thought, was passing, even though it was annoying that this officer, evidently still suspicious, was accompanying him into the house. At first thought it seemed to him rather a small house for a man of Garnett's wealth; but he remembered his friend's hatred of pretense and of what he called doggishness. Despite that perturbing telegram, it would be fine to see his old friend again. Have a good sound game of four-handed chess perhaps, and see little Kay. Though she must be a good-sized young lady now. He smiled, with a quiet resumption of contentment.

"Say, buddy!"

He turned to see the cabdriver. The nightmare wasn't over yet.

"That'll be two bucks and a half you owe me."

He counted out the exact change, pointedly leaving no opportunity for a tip, and took up the bag the man scornfully proffered him.

The policeman looked at him pityingly. "So you'd even try to do a poor working man out of his money!"

Colonel Rand decided that it was high time to take a firm stand in this matter. "Officer," he said, "I do not know what strange ideas you seem to have formed concerning me, but I assure you that they are false. Any or all of them. I, sir, am a respectable citizen, a taxpayer, and a retired member of the military forces of this country."

"Now ain't that nice, General," the officer grinned, but the grin was not encouraging.

"What is more, I am a guest of Mr. Humphrey Garnett."

The officer squared himself. Rand was a large man, but he felt small beside this uniformed bulk. "And do you want to know what I think you are, with your taxicabs and your radios and your mustaches?" (There was something familiar about this official burst of fury. Rand could not place it at the time, but he later recalled its identity with the screen antics of one Edgar Kennedy.) "I think you're a crank, and I think you're drunk, and if you don't prove anything else, I'll be keeping you out of this door for the rest of this fine summer day."

The Colonel was past indignation. He assumed dignified silence in its stead. Quietly he reached into his breast pocket, took out the telegram, unfolded it, and passed it over.

The simple act of reading those twenty-five words took a good foot off the officer's height. He looked at the Colonel with a mixture of respect, awe, and incredulity. "Follow me," he said abruptly, and led the way into the house.

It seemed exceedingly odd to Colonel Rand that the policeman did not ring, but just walked in. It was even odder that a second policeman stood in the hallway near the door.

"Wait here," said Policeman Number One, and disappeared.

Colonel Rand opened his cigar case and took out a cigar. The whimsical thought crossed his mind that men in novels, under circumstances of similar confusion, always "select" a cigar. He wondered how they did that and why they'd bought the ones they didn't select.

As he struck a match, Policeman Number Two became vocal. "Hold it, pop," he said, and relapsed into silence.

Rand shook out the flame regretfully. " 'Drest in a little brief authority.' " he murmured, irritated by this meaningless officiousness. But he stood as silent as his uniformed companion, chewing hard on the unlit cigar. In a few moments, Number One appeared again.

"The Lieutenant says you should come right in," he announced. "This way."

There was still a nightmare quality to the proceedings, but its nature had changed. The first part had been mad and comical, even when it was most destructive of dignity. But there was a chill of earnestness about this second phase.

Colonel Rand followed Number One into a room which he recognized at a glance, even though he had never seen it before. It must be Humphrey Garnett's study. It was so exactly like the study of any house which Garnett had ever lived in. There was the strange miscellany of books, which seemed so random at first and later struck you as a complete, if cryptic, outline of the host's character. There was the littered desk, of course, and the huge cabinet which housed Garnett's invaluable collection of playing cards. And there was the exquisitely inlaid table designed especially for four-handed chess.

Rand began to feel a cruel conviction that that desired game of four-handed chess would never take place.

TWO

LIEUTENANT JACKSON TELLS OF A MURDER

Colonel Rand had examined the room in an instant. Now he looked at the two men in it. One, despite civilian clothes, he recognized at once as the Lieutenant of whom Number One had spoken, and obviously a Lieutenant of Detectives. He was young and rangy, but there was a professional directness and sharpness about him which stamped him unmistakably.

The other man was also young and equally obvious. At first glance, Rand decided against him. It was a type he didn't care for. Too good-looking, too well-dressed, too easy. Quite possibly, the Colonel's sense of fair play forced him to admit, this was a very decent chap; but he was definitely something in the artistic line, and that wasn't a man's work.

The young Lieutenant looked up and nodded as Rand entered, then turned back to the object of the Colonel's disaffection. "I'll want to speak to you again, Mr. Vinton. Will you wait outside with the others?" He spoke civilly enough, but Rand felt that his surface courtesy was no mask for the strict efficiency behind it.

Vinton agreed graciously. "Ever at your service, Lieutenant. Anything I can do for Miss Garnett—I think you understand. That sounds like a polite formula, but it means a great deal. I shall see you later." He smiled and turned to leave.

Rand had a better look at the fellow now. Suddenly he realized that this was no mere dislike of a type. Vinton wasn't the name he'd used then; but it was the same man, and a rotter from the word go. Too late the Colonel tried to suppress his automatic reaction. But he feared he was not successful.

Number One followed Vinton from the room. As soon as the two were gone, the Lieutenant asked, "You know that man?"

There was no use being secretive. Rand already suspected, with a dreadful sinking of his heart, the reason for the Lieutenant's presence; and any fact might now be of value. "Yes, I know him—blast him," he admitted.

"We'll take that up in a minute." The Lieutenant shoved some papers aside and took up a fresh pencil. "Won't you sit down, sir? My name is Jackson—Lieutenant of Detectives. And yours?"

"Rand. Theodore. Colonel. U.S.A., retired." The Colonel spoke sharply and clearly as the police officer jotted it down.

"You came here at Humphrey Garnett's invitation?"

"Yes."

"This telegram . . . " He fingered the yellow slip which Number One had brought him. "You received it—when?"

"Three days ago."

"Today's Monday. Sunday . . . Saturday . . . That would be Friday last?"

"Yes."

"What did you do?"

"Sent an answering wire announcing my arrival and left as soon as I could."

"Why?"

"Isn't that obvious? He was my friend. He needed me." Rand spoke with laconic sincerity.

"But although the message was such a strange one, you took no steps to check up on it?"

"Why should I?"

"You came all the way across the continent on what might easily have been a hoax of some sort?"

"To tell you the truth, Lieutenant, I did not care. I was sick to death of vegetating in a New York suburb—especially since my gardening efforts had taught me that nothing else was capable of vegetating there. So why should I? That message promised something interesting, whether it was truth or hoax. And if nothing more comes of it than a visit with an old friend, I shall be content."

"Hm." Jackson paused a minute, then seemed to accept, at least for the time being, the good faith of the Colonel's rash visit. "And who is this Hector?"

"Frankly, I have no idea."

"And who is the man who just left this room?"

The Colonel had by now recovered all his once imperiled dignity. He used it as he spoke. "Young man," he said, "you have asked enough questions. Now I am going to ask two. The first is: May I smoke?" He lit his cigar without waiting for a reply and went on between relieved puffs. "The second is: What, in God's name, is this all about?"

There was a sympathetic gravity on the young Lieutenant's face which answered the question without the need of words. Rand waved his cigar to brush aside futile phrases and sat smoking in silence for almost a minute. "So Garnett's dead," he said at last. "I shan't say anything about that. It means a lot to me, and I can't talk about what I feel. I wasn't made that way, and it's no use trying." There was another instant of silence, and then, with abrupt efficiency, the Colonel leaned forward, went "harrumph" and asked, "Murder?"

"I think so."

"Of course, or you wouldn't be here. Is he—have they—?"

"He's at the morgue, sir." The Lieutenant spoke respectfully and softly.

"Rotten luck. He was a good man. Well, Lieutenant, I'm yours now. Tell me what you think fit and ask your questions."

"There's not much to tell you, Colonel Rand. It's a simple case, and I'm in hopes that your arrival may make it even simpler. I'll put it as briefly as I can. You see, it's one of those times when circumstances are helpful and limit the investigation. You probably know that your friend didn't like house servants. He had a cook who came in by the day and a couple of Filipinos who cleaned once a week. So there was no one in this house last night except the family and their guests. The doors were all bolted on the inside this morning; and there's no reason to suspect any elaborate locked-room trickery.

"So that narrows it down to the five people in the house—Garnett's daughter Kay; his brother-in-law Arthur Willowe; his assistant, a young man named Harding; and two guests, Vinton, whom you just saw, and a Miss Sallice. Just what the Sallice girl's status in the family might be, I haven't been able to learn. Vinton is more or less a permanent member of the household; he even has his own room. He's Kay Garnett's fiancé."

Colonel Rand started. Jackson observed him a moment and went on. "Mr. Garnett stayed on in his study after the others had retired. They all went their separate ways, and any one of them might have come back to him, for all they can prove to the contrary—though, of course, they all deny it. Before they left, this Sallice girl had brought him a nightcap of whiskey and water, which he set aside to drink later. He drank only half of it. But that was enough."

"Poisoned?"

"Yes. Hydrocyanic acid—prussic, as most people call it. Death almost instantaneous. But he did manage to leave us a clue—the first time in actual experience that I've come across anything like that. And I'm not sure yet what it might mean. Apparently, as he lay dying, he deliberately crumpled one playing card."

Rand leaned forward with dignified eagerness. "If my guess proves right, sir, my arrival may indeed make the case simpler. Was this card a knave of diamonds?"

Jackson looked up sharply. "It was."

"And how do you interpret that, Lieutenant?"

"As I say, I don't quite know. If I remember anything about fortunetelling, it used to mean a blond young man; but there's only one such on our list, and he doesn't quite fit in. Then one of the men from the coroner's office was talking about a mystery novel he read that had a jack of diamonds in it, and it meant a pun on somebody's name in French. I don't see that that helps us much either."

"Hang your coroner's men and their mystery novels. Let me assure you, Lieutenant, that this knave of diamonds means a dark young man, and a darkhearted knave he is."

Jackson's interest was high. "Go on, Colonel."

Rand settled back and enjoyed his cigar for a moment. "Five years ago, sir, I was on a Cunarder returning home from a visit in England. I am a land man, and ocean travel has always seemed to me only a regrettable necessity. My one objection, despite all the mewlings of the pacifists, to the World War—my last active service—was that we had to cross an ocean to fight it. So instead of viewing the supposed beauties of the sea, I spent my time in the smoking room playing cards.

"There was a sound crowd of men on that voyage, mostly Britishers. I'd met a good few of them around the London clubs, and liked them. And then there was a young chap named Lawrence Massey. Nobody seemed to know anything about him; but several of the others had met him before, and we all accepted him."

Rand resumed his cigar while the Lieutenant looked impatient. "I think," he went on, "that it was this Massey who suggested we try pinochle. I'm not sure. None of us had ever tried it before—fact is, I never really thought it was a gentleman's game—but we were all tired of poker and contract, and pinochle proved interesting and challenging once we got into it—a truly first-rate game, with an admirable balance of chance and science. Massey won a good deal. At first we thought it was simply because he knew the game better—could play up to the really fine points—and we admired him for a deft player.

"Then old Vantage—Sir Herbert, you know—the War Office man—noticed that it was generally a double pinochle with which Massey made his big winnings. Those two queens of spades and two knaves of diamonds seemed to fall inevitably into his hand.

"Well, Lieutenant, I'll make a brief story out of it. It was a rotter's trick, and I'm frank to say I never quite caught the hang of it. There was sleight of hand involved, that I do know. Of course none of us would speak to him after that. Still, he'd made a fair killing already, and it didn't seem to worry him. But just snubbing him wasn't enough to satisfy old Vantage. That chap has a vicious sense of practical humor, and he had to carry on with it.

"It started with his merely dropping references to a knave of diamonds whenever Massey was within earshot. Then Vantage slipped down to Massey's stateroom and stuck a knave of diamonds on the door. It took the room steward some work to get it off. Next the old man bribed the bartender. He pasted a knave of diamonds on a glass, and every time Massey ordered a drink he got it in that glass.

"But the fellow took it damned well. I'll say that for him. He was a rotter, but he had guts. And he had his revenge on old Vantage the night of the masquerade ball. Vantage had got together a score of used decks and sorted out the diamond knaves. He'd sewn them into a kind of necklace, and his idea was to pop that over Massey's costume as soon as he appeared, so that everyone would think it was a part of his getup and ask him about it. But hanged if the plucky rascal didn't show up at the masquerade costumed as the knave of diamonds himself. And I'm damned if I didn't admire him for it."

Jackson spoke up as the Colonel paused with a reminiscent grin. "I take it that this Lawrence Massey is our Richard Vinton?"

"It is, sir."

"You are certain—it isn't just a resemblance?"

"Lieutenant, I will swear in any court you choose that Massey and Vinton are the same man."

"Did Humphrey Garnett know that?"

"That I can't tell you. He knew the Massey story, of course; he must have heard me tell it a dozen times. But I've no idea if he had identified Vinton."

"You didn't know, then, that he was about to marry into the Garnett family?"

"I never saw him from that time till today. I did know that little Kay was engaged—finding a suitable gift was a severe task for an elderly bachelor—but the name Richard Vinton naturally meant nothing to me."

Lieutenant Jackson rose with an officially definite air. "I think that will be all for the moment, Colonel Rand. Needless to say, we'll have more to talk about later." He glanced down at his notes and added, "By the way, when did you say you arrived in Los Angeles?"

"By the plane which reached Burbank airport about an hour ago." Rand smiled at the thought that his harmless movements would now be subjected to an official check.

"Thank you, Colonel. Now that this is over, I suppose you'll naturally want to see the family. You can ask the man at the door; he'll show you where they all are. And thank you, sir, very much indeed for your information; I feel strongly that this interview may prove to be the most important part of my case."

Colonel Rand left the study in a badly worried frame of mind. Had he said too much? The past isn't irrevocable; a young man with such spirit might well have changed for the better in five years. And if little Kay loved him . . .

He shrugged, went "harrumph", and started off to look for the family.

THREE

THE KNAVE OF DIAMONDS IS TAKEN PRISONER

Number Two had indicated the door in pantomime. Colonel Rand, still pondering the rightness of his action, was about to enter when a shrill voice from within made him pause.

"I tell you I'm afraid," the voice was crying. "I know you all think I'm not good for anything. He thought so too. And he was right, even if he didn't know about— But that doesn't make me any the less afraid to die."

Rand recognized the voice, charged as it was with terror. Poor futile old Willowe. The in-law hanger-on. But he was generally so quiet and unobtrusive. What could have brought him to this wild display of fear? Gently the Colonel opened the door.

The attention of the people in the room was so firmly fixed on Arthur Willowe that Rand's entrance went unnoticed. The vague little man sat in a large bright armchair which would ordinarily have effaced him completely. Now the stark terror of his face and voice made him for the moment the most vivid object in the room.

"It was all right when he was alive," Willowe chattered on. "I knew he couldn't do anything then because of all of you. Besides, I thought he was through with me. He wanted something else, I thought. But now he's dead and I was wrong and there's nothing to stop him. We'll all be dead together—Humphrey and Alicia and I. We'll have love and hate and death all for ourselves."

Kay Garnett leaned over him quietly. She had been crying, and her voice was still shaken. "Please, Uncle Arthur. Don't excite yourself so. It's time for your nap. You'd better rest."

"No! No! I don't want to rest. I might sleep, don't you see, and that would make it ever so much easier for *him*."

"Come now, old man." It was that plucky rotter, Massey or Vinton or whatever he called himself. "Don't take on so. We've all got to carry on, you know." He had indeed changed; there was a new strength and sincerity in Vinton which Rand had never observed in Massey.

The other young man in the room (a stranger to Rand—it must be the laboratory assistant, Harding, whom the Lieutenant had mentioned) thumbed a heavy book and tried to keep his eyes from the painful scene. Poor Willowe babbled on.

Then the dark girl (that, Rand supposed, would be the mysterious Miss Sallice) crossed softly to the old man's chair. "Please," she said gently. Her voice was rich and husky and sweet. "Please. Alicia wouldn't like you this way."

Arthur Willowe paused. "No. Of course. I'm sorry." He sounded like a little boy who had been scolded. Then he looked up in bewilderment. "Why do you talk about Alicia? What do you know about her? And what do we know about you? Who are you anyway?"

Before the girl could answer, Kay had seen Colonel Rand. Swiftly she darted across the room and threw herself into his arms. "Uncle Teddy! Oh, how good! How good!"

She cried a little and kissed him and laughed because the waxed mustaches tickled her and cried again. The old soldier held her close and was very happy.

Little Kay, bless her, had grown up just as he had hoped. She was fresh and lovely and clear and alive. She was her mother Alicia with a simple easiness added which had not been quite proper for young ladies when he and Alicia were—well, friends. It hadn't got further than that when she met Humphrey Garnett.

He stroked Kay's bright red hair and kissed the top of her head clumsily. She looked up, half smiled, and tossed her head as though to shake away the tears. Awkwardly the Colonel pulled the neat white handkerchief out of his breast pocket and wiped her blue-green eyes. Then, with automatic recollection of the past, he held the cloth to her nose.

She laughed nervously. "I'm a big girl now, Uncle Teddy. I worry about powdering my nose, not blowing it." Rand frowned; this forced gaiety was sadder than tears. "But I don't even worry about powder now," she went on. "I'm so glad you came. I need you."

She turned to face the room. "You'd better join the family group. We're waiting to hear what that nice young Lieutenant makes up his mind to do about . . . " (her voice quavered a little) ". . . about all this. He's been asking us questions all morning till we're reeling—we haven't even had time to think. It doesn't seem halfway real yet. It can't be true. It just can't." She broke off and took up the role of hostess. "You know Uncle Arthur, of course."

"Right. How are you, Willowe." The Colonel seized the weak hand sturdily. Pity Alicia's brother should have turned out so much what the young men would call a washout. Still he was in his way a likable sort of chap. Damned odd, that fit of hysteria just now . . .

"This is Miss Sallice—Colonel Rand. Camilla was a protégée of Father's." Was Rand imagining things, or did Kay's voice take on a trace of something harsh—almost of an unkindness quite foreign to her nature? He bowed formally to the young lady. Decidedly attractive, he observed, though the contrast to Kay made her seem somewhat full-blown and artificial. A subtle trace of exotic scent heightened the effect. He found himself looking at her again, more closely. Yes, for all the deft make-up, hers was a face of tragedy.

"And this is Will Harding, Father's lab assistant." The quiet young man set aside his weighty volume and rose politely. It was a good handshake—firm, without exaggeration. Rand decided, at a guess, that the man himself was like that.

"And this is Richard Vinton, my fiancé. You've certainly heard me talk about Uncle Teddy, Richard." The Englishman gave no sign of recognition, and Rand followed his lead. He even took the fellow's hand, with a warmth assumed for little Kay's sake.

The introductions were over, and there seemed to be nothing more to say. Obviously no one wanted to mention the one all-important topic, and no one could think of anything else worth mentioning in its place. Despite Kay's almost hysterical effort, this was no time for small talk.

Rand, seated uncomfortably in a corner, suddenly recalled that the Lieutenant had kept his telegram, and decided to busy himself seeing if he knew it from memory. One phrase worried him. WATCH HECTOR CAREFULLY. He looked about the silent room. Arthur Willowe, Will Harding, Richard Vinton—which of them . . . ? He wanted to blurt it out abruptly; it must be important.

The silence grew heavy. Willowe had picked up a deck of cards and was noiselessly dealing them onto the small table near him. Harding had returned to his ponderous book. Vinton was holding his fiancée's hand in surreptitious comfort. The Sallice girl was humming something indistinguishable and minor under her breath. The sun streamed into the room with oblivious cheerfulness.

Rand realized that his cigar had gone out, neglected; and his palate could never endure relighting a dead one. With a gesture of exasperation, he hurled the offending cigar at a large brass ash stand a few feet from him. His aim was too good. There was a crashing clatter, and stand and ashes were scattered over the floor.

Everyone started. It was as though someone had belched in the middle of the Armistice Day silence. Rand swore. Everything that happened to him was turning this tragedy into farce. Then he saw that this was his opportunity. They were all offguard—nerves on edge. He rose and bellowed, "All right then. Out with it. Who is Hector?"

And nothing happened. Nothing at all. There was no sign of any reaction but sheer bewilderment. If anyone there had suspicious knowledge, he was a genius at covering it up.

Kay stared at him as though he had suddenly gone mad. "Uncle Teddy!" she cried reproachfully.

Before he could explain himself, the door opened. The official forces came in—the Lieutenant and Numbers One and Two. Jackson strode sharp across the room to Vinton—a dramatic movement somewhat hampered by his tripping over the ash stand. But he recovered himself nimbly and said, "I'm afraid we'll have to take you along with us, Vinton."

Kay let out a little cry. She pressed a pale hand to her mouth and stood trembling. Arthur Willowe looked up from his solitaire long enough to say, "It's no use," and went on playing.

Rand advanced to the Lieutenant. After all, hang it, the fellow was Kay's fiancé. "Look here, sir," he said. "Merely because I told you what I did—"

"May I ask, Colonel, what that was?" Vinton inquired.

"It isn't only that, Colonel Rand," Jackson interposed. "You see, there were only his fingerprints on the glass. And there's even more to it than that."

Vinton shrugged. "I appreciate your position, Lieutenant," he said with easy confidence. "Under the apparent circumstances, I suppose I'd make the same arrest myself. There's very little use in my assuring you that you're wrong. But you are, of course, and you'll find that out if you continue your investigation. Meanwhile, I might as well go along with you."

Rand looked at the man with open admiration. It was the same fine bravado which he had displayed at the masquerade party—when, Rand reminded himself, he had been guilty beyond any possible doubt. But there was good in the fellow—courage, at least, which can mean a great deal. He found himself hoping sincerely that the chap was innocent this time.

FOUR

FERGUS IS SUMMONED

Some hours later, after an excellent lunch, efficiently prepared by the cook who came in by the day, had been swallowed untasted by a silent assemblage, Colonel Rand sat on the sun porch with Kay. He found comfort in the bright verdure of the hills which rolled before them. "From whence cometh help . . . " he murmured.

"He can't be guilty," Kay was insisting. "No matter if they find his fingerprints on everything in the room. I knew all that about the liner and the jack of diamonds. He told me two days ago; and I didn't care. It isn't what Richard used to be that matters. He's doing well as an actor now, and he's honest and clean. Of course I don't know what Father might have thought, but anyway he didn't know and so that proves he couldn't have meant Richard with that card, doesn't it?"

Rand essayed a comforting smile and patted her cold hand. "Of course, Kay. Of course."

"Kay!" It was Camilla Sallice, standing in the doorway. "There's a man here who wants to see you. He says Richard sent him."

Kay straightened up, with a conscious effort at recovering herself. "Oh. Thanks, Camilla. Please ask him to come out here. It's bright and clear; I feel better than in the house."

In a moment a small, sleek man came onto the porch. He was

dressed with quiet smartness and carried with him an air of deft efficiency. "Miss Garnett?" he asked.

"Yes." Kay hesitated.

"My name is Farrington—Max Farrington. You've probably heard Mr. Vinton speak of me. I'm his lawyer."

"Oh. Naturally. I should have thought to get in touch with you, but with Father . . . It all happened so suddenly. I've been wondering if I could do anything for Richard, and I just can't think straight."

"I understand, Miss Garnett. Mr. Vinton phoned me from the station. I talked a bit with him there, and he asked me to see you. If I could speak with you privately—"

Rand half rose, but Kay's hand restrained him. "I'm sorry," she said. "Colonel Rand, Mr. Farrington. Colonel Rand was my father's closest friend. I think I'd like to have him here while we talk."

Rand beamed. It was good to feel that the dear girl wanted him. Expansively he extended his cigar case to the lawyer.

"Sorry. I never smoke. Waste of valuable energy. But I'll be glad to have you with us, Colonel. You military men see straight to the core of things—no falderal—good men to have on a jury. Now you know the situation?"

Rand nodded. He had not as yet made up his mind about this suavely alert individual, and he wasn't going to commit himself verbally until he was sure.

"Very well." Farrington seated himself, with cautious regard for the crease of his trousers. "The police seem certain that they have the right man. We, I take it, are all equally certain that they have not. Now if the case comes to trial, I'll have my client make a straight plea of not guilty. That's inevitable; I shan't compromise his reputation with any fake business of 'not guilty by reason of insanity' or such tommyrot. And I'll probably get an acquittal. But in the meantime the newspapers will have done their work. A featured actor, well on his way to stardom, arrested for the murder of his fiancée's father—it's too good a story to neglect. They're bound to play it up for all it's worth. And so we—well, we want more than simply an acquittal."

"You mean, sir, that you—that is to say, that *we* want to prove beyond any doubt, not only that Richard Vinton is innocent, but that someone else is guilty?"

"Exactly. There you are, Colonel. What did I say about you military men? The direct approach every time. We want to prove that someone else is guilty. Now the police seem to be perfectly satisfied that their case is finished. They won't investigate much further. And work like that isn't in a lawyer's line; I'll defend him if he comes to trial, but I'd much rather that never happened. What we need, Miss Garnett, is a detective; and the man I always send such work to is laid up in the hospital at the moment as the result of a labor riot. Lawlessness," the lawyer muttered. "That's what it is. Merely because these men discovered that Larry was making reports of their activities to the company manager—as though he wasn't doing his job just the same as they were doing theirs. . . ."

Rand grunted. Conservative though he was, the use of spies in civilian industry had never seemed decent to him. He began to be a trifle dubious of this *Esquire*-garbed article.

"But what do you want us to do?" Kay asked.

Farrington cut off his resentment against labor. "What Mr. Vinton suggested was that you and I—and you too, of course, Colonel—might confer and select some private inquiry agent who'd take on the case. I know most of them by reputation and can give you advice. Some, naturally, would never do; they are tied up too closely with the police department and would be prejudiced against breaking down an offical case. Others—"

"Fergus!" Kay exclaimed.

"I beg your pardon, Miss Garnett?"

"Fergus O'Breen."

"And who is that?"

"You say you want somebody who's unprejudiced and fresh and not tied up with the police? Well, why not Fergus?"

"Excuse me, but is this Fergus a detective?"

"Of course. He's got a license and an office and everything. He's a crazy Irishman and young, but as smart as they make them. I went to school with his sister," she added, as though that explained everything.

"I don't know . . . " Farrington began.

Colonel Rand interrupted him. "There's something to Miss Garnett's idea, Farrington. A young man starting out on his career might be far more valuable in breaking down preconceived notions than would an older and more experienced person. We can at least interview the fellow and see what he promises."

"Of course, it's as Miss Garnett wishes. For myself and my client, I could prefer—"

"Then it's all settled." Kay rose. "I'll go call Fergus now. Come along, Uncle Teddy. You can listen in on the extension and see what he sounds like."

Colonel Rand felt embarrassingly like an eavesdropper as he stood with the extension to his ear. He had no notion then of how familiar the role of eavesdropper would become before he learned the truth of Humphrey Garnett's death.

He heard Kay dial the number and then a shrill voice which announced, "O'Breen Detective Agency."

"May I speak to Mr. O'Breen, please?"

"Just a moment. I'll see if he's in."

A pause, then a heavier voice which sounded suspiciously like the first one in a different register. "This is the O'Breen speaking."

"Fergus!"

"Kay sweetheart! And how are you this balmy afternoon?"

"Fergus," she faltered, "I want you to come over here right away. It's terribly important."

He hesitated. "You're speaking for yourself?"

"Yes." She was puzzled. "What do you mean?"

"I just thought— But it doesn't matter. Look. I'm supposed to see Mrs. Rittenthal in an hour and tell her who poisoned her darling itsybitsy Ming Toy. I could make it later—say around dinner time."

"Please, Fergus. Now. It's—it's professional," she added.

"In that case, darling, nothing could please me more. My business conscience is appeased, and Fergus of the Red Branch rides to your rescue. I didn't want to see Mrs. Rittenthal anyway. You see, it was her husband, and I'm damned if I blame him."

"Then you will come?"

"Of course. But what's the matter? Your voice sounds as though you were about to burst out keening."

"No questions now, Fergus. Please." Her voice was indeed dangerously shaky. "I'll tell you when you come."

"Which will be," he said firmly, "in roughly eleven shakes of a lamb's tail. 'By."

Rand hung up his extension. He was reserving judgment.

FIVE

FERGUS TAKES OVER

Colonel Rand had never before seen a detective in a tight-fitting yellow polo shirt. It was really not a good idea. It made the young man's lean face seem even leaner and clashed violently with his crimson hair—hair of so brilliant a shade that Rand wondered whether Kay was really entitled to be called a redhead after all. But then, the Colonel reflected, this was Southern California. If ever someone succeeded in establishing a Los Angeles Fascist organization, the mark of membership would indubitably be a polo shirt.

Rand had answered the doorbell, to see this red-and-yellow

apparition leaning against the jamb and hear him announce, with ancient Gaelic trumpets ringing in his crisp modern voice, "The O'Breen to see Miss Garnett." There had followed, with Farrington's technical assistance, a brief conference on the young man's qualifications.

These seemed auspicious enough. He had been in the private inquiry business for six months. He admitted frankly that this was his first murder case; but he had impressive references of clients satisfied by his solutions of several robberies and one arson. Rand was especially pleased with the account of how he had trapped a peculiarly obnoxious blackmailer by extra-legal means.

Farrington seemed highly satisfied—a trifle more readily, in fact, than Rand had anticipated. "Of course," the lawyer said, "I don't need to express how much I wish you luck. It isn't just your luck—it's mine and my client's and this young lady's as well. I feel I can safely leave the case in your hands now; I have the bail and other matters to see to." And with brisk politeness he took his leave.

Fergus uncoiled himself from his chair and began to pace the room softly but rapidly. "Now look, Kay," he began. "There isn't any use my saying how sorry I am this happened. I know how it's hit you, and I know it's going to hit you a lot worse, when you've had time to think about it. But we've got to be impersonal about the whole thing—and that's asking a hell of a lot from an Irishman. I've got to forget you used to spend weekends with my sister. I've got to forget the time you taught me to waltz and the time I gave you your first roller-coaster ride. In short, I've got to be serious and unsentimental—and so do you."

Kay managed a small smile. "All right, Fergus. I'll try. It isn't going to be easy, you know."

"Don't I know, darling." He stopped sharply. "Look at me now for a fine fatted fool. I start out being impersonal by calling my client *darling*. Even *Kay* is dangerous. I'll stick to *Miss Garnett*. Professional-like. And by the way, if my pacing bothers you, just tell me to quit."

"It's all right so far."

"Good. You see, there's two reasons for it. It helps me think, and then sometimes it gets people so nervous they say things they didn't mean to. Now for the questions. I know—I suppose you've had more than enough of 'em today already; but I've got to get it all straight."

"Go ahead—Mr. O'Breen."

"Thank you—Miss Garnett. Now tell me first of all about your father—what kind of a guy—I mean—well, tell me about him."

"Didn't you ever meet him?"

"I . . . " For a moment Fergus seemed not quite so self-possessed. "No, I can't say I did."

"I just thought—I was at your house so often, and Maureen used to come here."

Fergus squirmed quietly. "Well, I have talked with him on the telephone—but hardly in a social way."

Rand leaned forward. "Professional, then?"

"Yes, in a way, but— Look. Who's conducting this investigation? I'm supposed to be grilling, not being grilled. And I want to know what Humphrey Garnett was really like, not what he sounded like giving orders on the phone. Go on—Miss Garnett. Tell me things."

"I think Colonel Rand could do that better than I could. You see, to me Father was just—well, just my father. I mean, he was sweet and good and—I don't know; I always thought he was something marvelous."

Fergus whirled to Colonel Rand. "And was he?"

"Was he what?"

"Was he something marvelous?"

Rand went "harrumph". "Hang it, young fellow, you ought to know that a man doesn't think that way about another man. I liked Garnett. I liked him better than anyone else I've ever known. That's all I can say."

"When did you meet him?"

"I don't know exactly. It's hard to say; it seems as though you've always known the people who are close to you. Some time around 1910, I'd venture. I met him through this young lady's mother—Alicia Willowe then. We struck up a firm friendship and then we quarreled. I didn't see him again until just before the war—our work threw us together then. It seemed foolish to hold an ancient grudge, and we simply fell back into our old friendship. By that time he was married to Alicia and Kay was born. I was an unofficial member of the family until Garnett moved out here around eight years ago. Since then I've seen him once or twice a year on his trips east."

"Just a minute, Colonel," Fergus interrupted with a gesture something like a radio announcer shushing studio applause. "There's a lot in that brief statement of yours. Now comes questions. Why did you and Garnett quarrel?"

"I fail to see, sir, that that is any concern of yours."

Fergus shrugged. "That's the curse of being unofficial. No authority, no power. If I were a policeman, now, I could browbeat you—if I had the remotest idea how to browbeat. It just isn't in my character. Sweetness and light, that's what I am. All right, Colonel, so it's no concern of mine. I won't ever mention it again. Now then, after you had quarreled over Alicia Willowe—"

Rand thumped the arm of his chair vigorously. "Blast you, sir, do you mean to—"

Fergus once more waved him to silence. "We can't discuss that, can we, sir? I promised never to mention it again."

Rand subsided. For all the yellow polo shirt, he admitted grudgingly, the young man had a certain shrewdness. "Go on," he grunted.

"You say your work threw you together. What work was that?"

"I was attached to the General Staff. Garnett was doing research work in chemical warfare. We were both stationed in Washington."

"I see. When did Garnett retire from government service?"

"Immediately after the war. We very nearly had another quarrel then. He had suddenly become filled with some nebulous sort of weakling humanitarianism. He felt that the work he had been doing was wrong, and that he should devote himself henceforth to the causes of peace." Rand's voice was scornful.

"Wait a minute there, Colonel. What's wrong with peace? Me, I'm all for it, even if I am an Irishman. A good rousing fight with shillelaghs is one thing, but bombs and gas are another. I've yet to see why my fine head of red hair should be blown to shreds to make the world safe for plutocracy."

Rand shook his head sadly. "We didn't think like that when I was young. Perhaps that was because there were still some vestiges of honor left in war then. We still thought of Grant and Sherman and Lee—rebel though he was—of plumes and cavalry charges and glory. Men died, but they died honorably—and in one piece. Perhaps you young men are right now in your horror. I don't know."

"And what—coming back to our strayed muttons—did Garnett do for peace? Idealistic pacifism sounds a little out of his line from what I've heard of him."

"He spent ten years as a highly paid research technician for several large chemical companies and then retired. I may add that he found the service of peace much more profitable."

"Uncle Teddy!"

"I am not criticizing your father, my dear. I am simply doubting his humanitarian motives. Possibly I flatter him."

Fergus resumed his questions. "These regular trips east—what brought them about?"

"I don't know, exactly. He was carrying on some private researches—he had to keep his fine mind busy. These trips were probably connected with whatever he was doing on his own, but he never told me what that was."

"As intimate as you two were, he never told you?"

"Mr. O'Breen, you are young. When men are young, they share all their ambitions. They tell each other their newest hopes and ideas and perhaps work them out together. Garnett and I were like that once. But old men's friendships are different. They smoke together, they drink together, they play cards and chess and golf together; but all they tell each other are the newest versions of the oldest smoking-room stories. They respect each other's privacy. It's more comfortable—more dignified."

Fergus scratched his head and paced some more. "I never thought of it like that. You're right about young men. We shoot our mouths off about everything. But maybe you should keep your deepest self for yourself. It makes sense. . . . But at least you can tell me what kind of man Garnett was?"

"He had, sir, the most typically masculine mind which I have ever known. It was at once hard and intricate, strong and subtle. He could derive equal pleasure from climbing a mountain, solving an equation, catching a fish, inventing a new end game, or—if you will forgive me, Kay—making love to a beautiful woman. And he did them all exceedingly well."

"What was his temper like?"

"Vigorous. Whether good or bad, it was vigorous. He liked people and he hated them. I have never known him simply to tolerate a person—unless perhaps it was Arthur Willowe. Whatever he did, he strongly wanted to do. He never had whims. He went always in a straight, inflexible line."

"Would you call him a tolerant man?"

"No," said Rand simply.

"I begin to see him," Fergus said. "I'm sorry I never actually met him, even though I suppose he might well have decided to kick me out of the house. Maureen gave me pretty much the same idea from the times she visited you, Kay."

"I thought, Mr. O'Breen, that you'd decided on Miss Garnett?"

"Look, That's too much trouble. Suppose I just call you Client. That's easy, and still it's formal. Well, almost formal anyway."

"Very well . . . Detective." She tried hard to smile.

SIX

FERGUS HEARS THE FACTS

"All right." Fergus drew a sharp line in the air as though to mark the end of a section. "That's background. Fine. So much for that. But now for the facts in the case."

"I don't know quite how—" Kay began falteringly.

"Look. We'll take them, as the programs say, in the order of their appearance. That'll be simpler. And try to look at them as facts and not—not feel too much about them."

"I'll try."

"That's my fine wench. Now did anything happen before yesterday that could give us a sort of point of departure?"

"The telegram," Rand suggested, and went on to explain.

Fergus stopped pacing for a moment. "And the Lieutenant kept it. Helpful-like. Well, I don't blame him. Do you know if he checked the sending of it?"

"I asked him before he took Vinton away. He'd checked it by phone. It was sent from this telephone and charged to the phone bill. Beyond that, there wasn't any possible way of identifying the sender."

"Can you remember the exact words of the message?"

"Yes. Needless to say, it puzzled me, and I read it over a good many times. It went:

COME TO LOS ANGELES AT ONCE STOP FLY IF NECESSARY STOP YOU MAY BE INVALUABLE WITNESS AT INQUEST ON MY BODY STOP WATCH HECTOR CAREFULLY

And it was signed HUMPHREY GARNETT."

"Hmm. Do those sound like Mr. Garnett's words to you?"

"It's hard to say. Everyone's style sounds much the same in a telegram. But I'd say it was probably from him. It's direct and vigorous and a little cryptic. I would rather have expected him to sign himself simply GARNETT, but he used the full name occasionally."

"So that's why you asked that funny question," Kay put in.

"What funny question, Client?"

"He all of a sudden shouted out, 'Who is Hector?' I didn't know what to think."

"Very well. And who in the name of the sons of Usnech *is* Hector?"

"I haven't any idea."

"And you, sir?"

Rand shook his head. "It means nothing to me."

"At any rate, whoever Hector may be, this telegram seems to mean that Mr. Garnett expected an attempt on his life—and a successful one at that. Were you coming out here soon anyway, Colonel Rand?"

"Yes. My life in the east was growing regrettably dull, and I'd told Garnett I'd be out in a month or so. That's why this sudden urgency surprised me all the more"

"'YOU MAY BE INVALUABLE WITNESS,'" Fergus repeated. "How could you, if you didn't get here till after the crime? Or did he expect it wouldn't come off until after your arrival?"

"I was able to explain the knave of diamonds," Rand suggested.

"The knave of diamonds?"

"The crumpled knave," and Rand went on to retell the story of the Cunarder, old Vantage, and Lawrence Massey.

The young Irishman listened with keen interest. When the story was over he grunted unhappily. "So you knew all that. And I was staunchly upholding my professional honor, and all for what? Not even for Hecuba."

"I don't understand, Fergus."

"I mean this, Client. I almost let it slip when you asked me if I'd ever met your father. You see, this spot of work he had me do was concerned with Richard Vinton."

Kay gasped. "You mean that you told him—"

"Quiet there. Remember I haven't seen you for donkey's years. Maureen told me you were engaged, but I didn't remember the fellow's name. All I knew was that your father called me up at the office, said he'd heard about me from you as a promising young man—which I modestly assured him was a rank understatement—and told me to find out what I could about an actor calling himself Richard Vinton and claiming to be the son of Sir Edward Vinton.

"I didn't ask any questions—we don't, you know—All Work Strictly Confidential. I just went ahead and checked what I could myself here in town through his professional contacts—dug up some broken-down hams who'd known him years ago—got in touch with other sources in New York and London—your father had said not to spare expenses.

"Anyway, total upshot: Sir Edward Vinton's son is fighting in Spain—his conservative father's body must be leading the life of a corkscrew—and was recently reported missing; and this Vinton used to call himself Lawrence Massey and was reputedly a not-too-honest gambler."

"Did you come across this story about Massey and the knave of diamonds?" Rand asked.

"No. That yarn wasn't in my report, and that's what puzzles me. Because if the knave of diamonds did mean Vinton, how did Garnett know—unless he'd pieced together your story and mine . . ." He broke off sharply. "But after all, our purpose, if possible, is to save Vinton—not to tighten the chains around him. Let's get back to the telegram. Are there any other ways that you could prove invaluable?"

"None that I know of so far."

"All right. Let's get on with our reconstruction. Three days before the crime that telegram is sent. This is Monday. That would be last Friday. Now, Client, when did you learn the secrets of your fiancé's past?"

Kay hesitated. "That was Friday too. Richard took me to the preview of his latest picture. Afterwards we drove up in the hills and parked. It was a lovely night. . . . Suddenly he said, 'My dear, I can't go on like this any longer. If you're going to marry me, you must know all about me.'"

"And he told you—?"

"He told me that Vinton wasn't his real name and that he wasn't a son of Father's old friend in London and that he used to be a cardsharper who traveled on ocean liners. He tried to tell me details too, but I didn't want to hear any more. I've known him for almost a year, and I know that now he's as grand a man as any girl could want. To know that he's changed so much and made himself what he is—well, it just made me love him more."

She said all this very simply. Rand was watching her closely; she did love him—there was no possible doubt of that. And he resolved from that moment to do everything he could to help her and this strange young Irishman in their efforts to outwit the police.

Fergus had digested her story and was ready with more questions. "Did your father show any signs of displeasure with Vinton?"

"No. They got on well. You see, Richard's a very good chess player and he's interested in puzzles and cards the way Father is—was. They were quite congenial."

These details strengthened Rand's resolve. Artist or not, the young man apparently had a sound mental outlook.

"Good," Fergus observed. "Now as to the crime itself—"

Rand had heard, on all sides, so many references to the crime that he was by now somewhat confused. At last he was to hear a straight and simple account of as much as was known.

It boiled down to this: Garnett always ate breakfast regularly at seven, in order that he might have a long morning for his, so far, somewhat mysterious laboratory researches. The cook-by-the-day didn't arrive until eight; so Kay prepared the early breakfast for her father and his assistant, while the others ate later at their pleasure. This morning she had risen at six-thirty and set to work. Harding was in the kitchen at seven, and she served him, wondering what on earth could be keeping her generally punctual father. At about a quarter after, she went up to Garnett's room. The bed hadn't been slept in.

"And that worried you?" Fergus asked.

"No, it didn't really. You see, that had happened before. He always stayed up in the study after the rest of us went to bed. Dr. White said he should go to sleep early, but sometimes he'd get so engrossed in a problem that he'd stay up for hours and hours working on it and eventually just fall asleep there."

"You mean he did work at night on his own, besides the time he spent during the day with Harding?"

"I think so. I'm not sure. Sometimes it wasn't work, just—just being ingenious, you know." She smiled a little. "I remember once he tried to compose a five-deck solitaire. He used to play the Empress of India with four, but he wanted something even more involved. I came in the next morning and found him sound asleep. I couldn't even come into the room. There were cards piled every place."

"I remember," Rand nodded. "Garnett wrote me about that. He called it one of the few mental defeats of his life."

"So this time," Fergus picked up the thread, "you decided right off to look in the study?"

"Yes." Kay halted a moment. "I looked in the study . . . "

Humphrey Garnett was there. The lights were still burning, and he was lying face down in the middle of the floor. A few inches from his outstretched right hand lay a crumpled playing card. His hands had black gloves on them.

Fergus interrupted her again. "Why on earth should a man wear gloves to be murdered in? The black's a fetching notion for anticipated mourning, but still—"

"Oh, there's nothing surprising about that. When he stayed up alone like that, he often used to go over his collection of playing cards. Some of them are very rare and have to be handled carefully to keep them in good condition. He planned to leave them to a museum. So he wore gloves whenever he touched them."

"Was he wearing those gloves when you said good night to him?"

Kay thought back. "No. I think I could swear that he wasn't. Because he played with my hair when he kissed me good night, and I know I should have noticed it."

"Then look, Client. This business about fingerprints. Did the Lieutenant say definitely that he'd found only your fiancé's fingerprints on the glass?"

Again she pondered. "I think so."

Rand nodded. "Yes. He stated that quite clearly—it seemed his chief reason for the arrest."

Fergus paced more eagerly. "But if your father was ungloved when you left him, then he must have taken the glass in his fingers. Besides, there'd be Miss Sallice's prints if she brought it to him."

Kay looked up with pleased surprise. "Why yes. That's true. Then you mean—"

"I knew there was something cockeyed going on as soon as I heard about those fingerprints. Nowadays, when prints are talked about and written about so much, a man would have to be a damned fool to leave them planted so obviously."

"You think . . . ?"

"We'll just file that away for future reference. Go on."

Naturally, Kay had been frightened. She knew that her father had something the matter with his heart (a little questioning from Fergus made clear that it was an aortic aneurysm) and she felt dreadfully and unreasoningly sure that he was dead. She went over to him and touched him. He was cold. Then she saw that his face was twisted and she smelled the scent of bitter almonds and she knew what had happened.

She fainted then. She must have cried out first, although she couldn't remember it, because Will Harding came hurrying to her. He revived her, and reminded her that their first duty was to call the police. While they waited, she roused the rest of the household and gave them black coffee. It was something for her to do and kept her from having time to think.

"And how," Fergus asked, "did they react when you told them the news?"

"Let me see . . . I was too numb myself to notice very much. Camilla seemed more hurt than any of the others. Uncle Arthur was frightened rather than anything else—I don't know why. Richard was so good; he seemed to give me strength."

"Go on, Client."

There wasn't much more to tell. The police came and the men from the coroner's office and cameramen and fingerprint experts and reporters and everything. It was all a confused nightmare to Kay. She told them what she'd just told Fergus and they asked questions and they had interviews with everybody and then Uncle Teddy came and then all of a sudden Richard was arrested. And that was all.

Fergus had sprawled over a chair while she talked. Now he began to pace again. "I can see that they've got a good case against your Richard. I imagine they make out the motive something like this: He knew that Colonel Rand was coming out here soon and that his past would be disclosed as soon as the Colonel saw him. If your father knew what he had been, he'd forbid the marriage and disinherit you. Do you think he would have, Colonel?"

"Emphatically yes. Garnett had no tolerance for cheating or dishonesty of any sort. He prized mental strength and dexterity so highly that he loathed all shifts to get by without it. And yet, young man, according to you, Garnett already did know."

"It was only yesterday I gave him my report. He probably hadn't had a good chance to speak to Vinton yet. But even so, there was all the more need for action before Garnett could do anything rash. Either way you take it, he had to be disposed of promptly."

"Please!" Kay gasped sharply.

"There, Client. Don't look at me like that. I'm just saying what Jackson must be thinking. Abstractly, it makes a pretty good case, but just not good enough.

"It leaves too much unexplained. How did your father know Vinton's supposed murderous intentions four days in advance—before he was even sure that the man was an impostor? Why didn't he do anything to forestall them? Why aren't there more fingerprints on that glass? And who is Hector? When we've answered those four questions, we'll be well on our way to bringing your Richard back to your loving arms."

"Oh, if only you could!"

"He will, Kay," Rand had slowly taken a fancy to this brash young man. He inspired the Colonel with a certain reluctant respect.

"Thank you, sir. And now one more question before I sally forth and investigate. What do you know about your father's will? Aside from the museum that gets the card collection. I doubt if that would help us much on motive, unless you've seen any sinister curators slinking around here clutching rare and deadly weapons."

Kay almost laughed. "But I have!"

"Have what?"

"Seen a sinister curator. Only he wasn't sinister; he was just funny. He's named Warriner, and he was here for dinner last night. oh!" She stopped, slightly aghast.

"What's the matter?"

"Father liked him so much he asked him back here again tonight. I don't know how to get in touch with him. . . ."

"You needn't worry," Rand said helpfully. "He'll have seen the papers—he wouldn't want to intrude."

"I almost wish he would," Fergus meditated. "I could use an expert on playing cards who'd tell me about jacks of diamonds and such. But maybe I can get something out of Garnett's library. Now to get back to the will, Client—"

"I'm sorry. But I can't help you at all. Father never talked about his business affairs with me. He had ideas about the place of women—*you* know." The Colonel went "harrumph." "I'm afraid Uncle Teddy has, too. You'll have to ask Uncle Arthur about it—he might know. Or more probably Will."

"Right. Now keep your chin up, Client, and your eyes as bright as your hair. The O'Breen is about to solve his first murder case."

SEVEN

WILL HARDING TALKS OF PEACE

"If you don't mind, Colonel," Fergus said, "I'd like you to come along with me. I don't want to wear Kay out, and you sort of lend authority. Besides, I might want a witness later on to what people say."

Colonel Rand accompanied him gladly. He was beginning to decide that this confident young fellow had some talent, and he was curious to watch him at work.

They found Will Harding in the laboratory built on at the rear of the house and communicating with the rest of the building by a door at the end of the long central hall. Apparently the assistant felt it his duty to continue his dead employer's researches; or else the pure labor involved was a form of release from the nervous tension of the household.

"Mr. Harding," Rand began, "we are sorry to interrupt you at your work. But this is Mr. O'Breen, who is investigating Garnett's death at Kay's request. I'm sure you will help us, if only for her sake, to clear Mr. Vinton's name."

That was a polite way of putting it, the Colonel thought. He realized that the circumstances were such that the clearing of Vinton would almost inevitably involve the accusation of Harding, Willowe, or Miss Sallice; but he hoped that they might be too concerned to recognize the fact. All of them, of course, save the murderer.

Will Harding smiled wryly. "I'm sure I am only too willing to clear Vinton's good name, if that's what Kay wants. I'd ask you to sit down; but this laboratory wasn't constructed for social chats."

Rand looked around the large airy room. The mass of chemical apparatus meant nothing to him; an alchemist's paraphernalia could have conveyed no less. His attention came back to the young detective's questions.

They first covered the ground of the body's discovery. There was nothing new here; Harding's story fitted in neatly with Kay's. Then Fergus went on, "Look. These researches here—this laboratory—could you tell us just what it's all about?"

"Gladly. That is, as far as I can. Ever since I came here to live with Mr. Garnett, about three years ago, we have been working on an alexipharmical gas."

Fergus gestured a halt. "Hold on there a minute. Remember, we aren't scientists. You've been working on what kind of a gas?"

"Alexipharmical. Antidotal, to put it more simply. Mr. Garnett's idea was to double the protection of the civilian population against gas raids. Not only would everyone be equipped with gas masks; but at central strategic points there would be installed concentrated bombs of our gas. They might even be employed in private homes. When an attack took place, these bombs could be exploded, and our gas in the air would counteract the effects of the poison gas."

There was eagerness in Harding's face now. His words were precise, but his voice was rich in fervor. He took on a personality, a character that was ordinarily lacking in him. "It's a truly fine idea," he went on. "It is so rare to see a great scientific mind—and Mr. Garnett's was that—devoting itself to the cause of peace. But it was a difficult task. We still haven't solved it completely. There are so many possibilities in the attack; you have to take them all into account."

"If a practical military man may speak," Rand snorted, "it's a sheer waste of time."

Harding was aghast for a moment. "A waste of time to save the lives of defenseless citizens! To protect women and children against wanton marauders! Colonel Rand!"

"Harding's right," Fergus put in. "What do you mean, Colonel?"

"War against civilians," Rand explained calmly, "is absurd."

"Absurd?" The young assistant was scornful. "Is that the strongest word you can find for such atrocities?"

"No, no, no, young man. Leave your humanitarian angle out; there's still no practical value to this *Schrecklichkeit,* as the German high command called it during the war. They learned then what every decent military strategist has always known. Campaigns of terrorism are futile. No real advantage gained over the enemy, and serious disaffection springing up within your own ranks. It's no go."

"I know all that, sir," Will broke in with an eager ardor, partly tempered by regard for the older man's experience. "That's perfectly true on paper, and I dare say it may even work out that way. But still it is done, wicked though it may be."

"Look at the Basque provinces," Fergus added. "Look at Barcelona."

"Wickedness, my left foot!" Rand exploded. "It's sheer damned foolishness. Franco is nothing but a rotten bad tactician. This whole long-drawn-out Spanish war is proof that terrorism has no military value. You might call this entire affair a working laboratory experiment; if the terrorist theory were correct, the Rightists should have established a conclusive victory in six months. They didn't, and the theory is disproved once and for all."

Will Harding bit his lip. "I'm afraid, sir, I can't share your abstractly studious view of the matter. Human lives aren't pins on a chart to me. However, you called Franco a rotten bad tactician; I shan't say what else I think he is. But there'll always be rotten bad tacticians, despite all the military theory in the world; and we've got to be protected against them. That's where I come in," he added simply.

"Mr. Harding, I like any man who has strength in his convictions. Those convictions I may think to be misguided and misbegotten; but I respect the man. I respect you, sir; and I add to that respect a painful fear" (his voice sounded suddenly old) "that you may be right."

"Colonel!" Harding was taken aback by this sudden about-face.

"I and my generation of officers are outworn," Rand went on, speaking more to himself than to the young men. "It may be that we are the last of our race to know war for the glorious science which it was. The lower savages merely fight. The tribe with the most or the strongest men must win; there is no question of skill. But one of the first signs of rising civilization is the development of military strategy. Consider, for example, the Zulus of the past century, with their efficient impis and carefully planned campaigns. Numbers and strength become relatively unimportant to a civilized state. The enemy can not only be beaten down; he can also be outwitted. Remember Alexander's campaigns. Remember Belisarius at Daras, or Charles XII's invasion of the *flinterend*.

"And now? Now we are back with the Bushmen and the Igorots. Force and numbers are supreme—not the numbers of men now, but of planes, bombs, gases. And where one branch of civilization has withered, can the tree—" He broke off, almost ashamed of himself. This thought had been harrowing him for months, but he had never intended to speak it out. To cover his confusion, he produced an unusually fruity "harrumph."

This theoretical bypath had apparently led too far for Fergus. "How well along were you in your researches?" he asked.

Harding tore his thoughts away from Rand's reflections. "You never quite know about things like that. We might have gone on for years; we might have had a lucky break today which would have solved everything. Personally, I think we could have licked the problem in about another six months."

"And do you think now you can lick it by yourself?"

"I don't know," Harding admitted ruefully. "I hope so. It means a lot to me—oh, not just the fame and glory, but the whole idea. I'll try like the devil to lick it. And maybe I will. Though it's going to be hard without Mr. Garnett."

"You see what I mean, don't you? That if—I know this sounds Oppenheimish, but it has to be considered—if anybody—

picturesquely wicked Foreign Powers or whatnot—wanted to put a stop to your researches, they wouldn't have stopped at killing only Mr. Garnett. You can still carry on?"

"I hope so."

"Good. Now what did you mean by saying a while back that you'd tell us about the researches as far as you could? Was Mr. Garnett doing other work without you?"

"Yes. But I haven't any idea what it was. I know he used to work on in here after I'd leave him. Sometimes he'd even tell me to take the day off while he worked alone. But I can't tell you anything definite about it now. Later, if you want, I could go through his papers with you; I could tell, where you couldn't, if there were any notes that had nothing to do with this work of ours."

"Thanks. I'll have you do that. Now can you tell me anything about the terms of Mr. Garnett's will?"

"Not exactly. I do know that he made one three years ago, just after I came here, because I was one of the witnesses; but I never saw it. I do remember, however, that he used to keep a carbon copy of it in his desk. I came across it one day while I was looking for some notes. I saw what it was and managed to restrain my curiosity; but I think I remember where he kept it."

This will, Rand thought, should clarify the question of motive considerably; and the presence of this carbon should save time in the investigation. Chance was being considerate.

Harding led them down the hall into the study. While he began to rummage about in the desk, Rand surveyed with melancholy eyes this room so full of his dead friend's personality. Fergus paced the floor restlessly.

Abruptly the young detective paused before a shelf on which several decks of cards stood neatly stacked. They were apparently not a part of the collection, which was kept in the large steel case, but simply cards for use. They were well worn and looked modern in design.

He turned to Harding. "Just a minute before you find that. You remember that jack of diamonds—and why do serious students of cards always say *knave*?—that was beside Mr. Garnett?"

"Of course."

"Well, look. I suppose the police took it off with them, but do you know which pack it came out of?"

Harding looked at the decks. "I think it was that one." He pointed at one with a design of unusual crossed flags on the back.

"The Stars and Bars," Rand murmured with surprised interest.

Fergus examined the pack. It had not been shuffled, but was still arranged in suits. He laid aside the clubs, the hearts, and the spades, and took up the diamonds.

"Ace," he said. "My old man—the card-playing Irishman that he was—always used to call that card the *Earl o' Cork*. 'It's the worst ace and the poorest card in the pack,' he'd say, 'and the Earl o' Cork's the poorest nobleman in all Ireland.' Funny how some cards have names like that."

"I used to know a sailor," Rand put in, "who called the four of clubs the *Devil's Bedposts*. I never knew why."

Fergus laughed. "You sounded just like a character out of Chekhov then, Colonel. King of diamonds. . . . Queen of diamonds. . . . Ten of diamonds. . . . You're right, Mr. Harding. The jack is missing." He looked much more elated than you would have expected from such a simple discovery.

Once he had indicated the pack, Harding had returned to the desk. Now he came back to them with a sheet of paper. "Here you are."

"Just a minute first. These cards—do you remember if they were stacked like that when you found Mr. Garnett?"

"I think so. I couldn't say for certain."

"What I mean is—if a pack had been disarranged—scattered around—you'd have been bound to notice it, wouldn't you?"

"Why yes, I must have. I do remember noticing especially how orderly the whole room was." Harding seemed a bit puzzled by these questions.

Fergus's attention returned sharply to the will. "Nice simple little document. It starts off with several research institutions—bequests to carry on specific work. That doesn't help us much. Then the card collection—that's to go to the James T. Weatherby Memorial Museum, Providence, Rhode Island. I never heard of that."

"Mr. Garnett admired it greatly," Harding explained. "He said it possessed a finer collection even than that of the United States Playing Card Company; and he himself had a great many specimens that just filled in the gaps in the museum's exhibit."

"Thanks. But that isn't much help either. Now the personal bequests. Hmm— Ten thousand to Arthur Willowe. Not bad. And to you, Colonel, the library and the table and pieces for four-handed chess."

"Good," said Rand gruffly, and turned away for a moment.

"And Kay, of course is residuary legatee. Will that mean very much?"

"I should say," Harding replied, "it will mean a fortune." There was an odd note of regret in his voice. "Is that all?"

"That's the whole shooting match."

The laboratory assistant looked crestfallen. "I had hoped," he said, "that Mr. Garnett might have left me in a position to carry on his—our work."

"I don't blame you, Harding. Whatever the Colonel may say, as a practical military man, I'm all for you, as a common human being. It's a splendid idea, this gas, and I'd like to see you put it over."

"It doesn't really matter so much—the will, I mean. I think one of the foundations might help me."

"Good. That's an intention worth lighting a candle for." Fergus folded the carbon copy and slipped it into his pocket. "We'll have to check with Garnett's lawyer, of course, to see if the original has any codicils, or even if there's been a new will; but this is something to go on with. Thanks, Harding. And if you'll excuse us now—Come on, Colonel. I think our next step is Arthur Willowe."

Rand left the room slowly, with a backward glance at the many shelves of books. It was good that his friend had remembered him.

EIGHT

ARTHUR WILLOWE IS NOT HELPFUL

They found Arthur Willowe in his upstairs room. As they approached the door, Rand could have sworn he heard the clicking of typewriter keys; but when they entered the room, there was no trace of a machine. The Colonel was puzzled. At a time like this, the most trifling details seem significant. Was his normally acute hearing deceiving him at last, or was there some other sound which might be confused with that of a typewriter?

Willowe's was a pleasant little room, neat as a woman's and bright with sun. While Fergus made his explanations, Rand strolled over to the window and looked out at the fair Los Feliz hills, green even in winter. Magnificent country for walking; he must investigate it. There was a little balcony outside the window, with a cot on it. This, he supposed, was where Willowe took his naps.

"So you see," Fergus was saying, "anything you can say to help us would be a great boon to Kay. Now take for instance this business of all the doors being bolted. You know this house well—do you think anyone from outside could have got in?"

Arthur Willowe fumbled aimlessly with a deck of cards. "I realize that it would, as you say, be a great boon to Kay if you could prove that someone from outside came into this house last night; but I doubt if what I have to say could help you in the least. In the first place, Humphrey led a very retired life for the past year or so. Save for his trips to the east, he practically never saw anyone outside of the household. Except Vinton, of course. I cannot think of a soul from outside who might be a candidate even for suspicion."

"Nobody can know all of another person's life, Mr. Willowe," Fergus objected. "He could have had other contacts; you can't be so positive as all that."

"I am sorry, Mr. O'Breen, but I can. The doors were all bolted on the inside this morning, as you have been told. I am an orderly man, sir, if I am nothing else." He smiled bitterly. "I thought to check that as soon as Kay told me what had happened. So either Kay or Will Harding took pains to cover up for the murderer —which is ridiculous—or else the man never left this house—unless, of course, you are one of those fabulous detectives who perform miracles with locked doors."

"Miracles aren't my line, Mr. Willowe; but look. Supposing it was someone Mr. Garnett wanted to see privately. Garnett lets him in after the family has retired. They confer. Mr. X slips poison into the glass. Garnett lets him out, bolts the door after him, returns to the study, and drinks the poison. Wouldn't that be possible?"

Willowe gestured toward the window. "You see that balcony, Mr. O'Breen? You will notice that it overlooks the front door. I was sitting out there last night thinking over a—that is, simply meditating. I was there until midnight or a trifle past, and no one came or went. The medical evidence, I believe, shows that Humphrey must have been dead by then."

"How about the back door?"

"There is no bell there. In order to secure Humphrey's attention, your fabulous Mr. X would have had to make enough racket to rouse the whole household."

"But supposing it was someone scheduled to come at an appointed time? Then Mr. Garnett would simply go there and let him in."

Willowe automatically shuffled the cards in his thin white hands. "A possibility, I will admit. However, until you find any indication of the identity of your Mr. X, I think that you may disregard it." He began the layout for Canfield.

Fergus stopped pacing for a moment. "Then you think the murderer is one of the people in this house?"

"Is or was."

"What do you mean?" He resumed his pacing with fresh spirit.

"I mean that the man with the strongest motive is no longer here."

"The strongest motive . . . Then you know of others who have motives, even if not so strong?"

"Please stop that frightful pacing, Mr. O'Breen. No, I do not."

"Sorry, but I think better this way. None whatsoever?"

"Of course, I know nothing about Miss Sallice. She returned with Humphrey from one of his trips east while I was . . . ill. Beyond that none of us knows anything about her."

"Sallice . . . Sallice . . . Damn it, I've heard that name somewhere else recently." He paused a moment in silence, then turned sharply. "And how about you?"

"What about me, Mr. O'Breen?"

"What are you afraid of? Why were you hysterical this morning? In short, Mr. Willowe, just what's eating you?"

The cards slipped from Willowe's trembling fingers. "All right. I'll tell you what's 'eating me.' Your stupid slang phrase means something here. It is eating me—devouring me, if you will. Gnawing away like something fantastic and horrible and . . ." He checked himself, and concluded with terrible simplicity, "I am afraid of Humphrey."

Rand stared at the quivering little man. "Don't be an ass, man. Garnett's dead."

"That's just what I'm afraid of. His hate can be so much stronger now. And he did hate me. I think he kept me on here just so he could torture me—could keep referring to cars and hydrants and accidents and" (his weak voice all but broke) "Alicia."

"This is nonsense, Willowe. You weren't to blame for Alicia's death. An accident like that on a slippery road—it could happen to anyone."

"I don't know, Colonel. It was so—so like me. To do everything wrong. Maybe I am to blame, after all. But that wouldn't make any difference—whether I really was or not. Humphrey thought that I was, and he hated me. For a bit I thought it had changed. But now his hate is free of his body, free to return to me, and I'm afraid." He stooped over to pick up his cards, murmuring like a litany, ". . . afraid . . . afraid . . . afraid . . ."

Fergus turned away with a gesture which clearly said the hell with this. But as Rand and the investigator neared the door, Arthur Willowe straightened up. He seemed to have recovered himself, and spoke clearly.

"Very well, gentlemen. I shall tell you exactly why I am so afraid. I do not choose to be sniggered at as a mewling weakling. I have good cause; I had foreseen this murder."

Fergus whirled. "You knew it was going to happen?"

"To be more exact, sirs, I had foreseen the murder —but not its victim." And Willowe went on to tell all the cumulative little details of the day before, and how he had formed his theory that the life of Richard Vinton was in peril.

"I was wrong," he concluded. "Absurdly wrong. I can see that now. Vinton is alive, if in prison; and Humphrey Garnett is dead.

But when I think of the power that he has attained through death, I . . ."

Rand clapped a friendly hand on the old man's trembling shoulders. "You'll pull out of it, Willowe. Be strong. We'll be worthy of Alicia—both of us."

Arthur Willowe looked at him strangely. "That is what the dark girl said," he murmured.

NINE

CAMILLA SALLICE REMEMBERS A MOTIVE

"And what did you learn there?" Rand asked the detective as they came down the stairs.

Fergus shook his head. "I don't quite know. That strange hatred of Garnett's for Willowe gives us another motive—maybe. And that's a curious story about yesterday and Willowe's true-false premonition. But I don't know . . ."

They found Camilla Sallice on the sun porch. Her back was toward them, and it was hard to be sure; but Rand suspected her of wiping away tears at the sound of their approaching footsteps. He could not understand this girl; she seemed more affected than anyone else, almost more than Kay, by the death of Humphrey Garnett. It was as though this were the last of many sorrows and the hardest of all to bear. But why? he wondered. She had youth and beauty, and a curious exotic charm; why had she seemingly found her role in life a tragic one?

"Miss Sallice," he said, "this is Mr. O'Breen. No doubt Kay has told you about him."

She rose and faced them with a half-smile. "Of course. Please let me help you."

She seemed frankly ready to answer anything; and Rand expected the young detective to take up the offer promptly. Instead he stood still, staring at her intently until the silence grew uncomfortable.

"I beg your pardon, Mr. O'Breen," Camilla said gently, "but just what is this pantomime act? Love at first sight?"

Fergus waved the gag away. "No. At least, I won't be rash about the first part—"

"Mr. O'Breen! And in front of the Colonel."

"But the point is," he went on as though she hadn't interrupted, "it isn't at first sight."

She laid a hand dramatically between her agreeably full breasts and heaved such a sigh as only a contralto could deliver. "You know my past?" she murmured. "And you look such a nice young man, too."

"I don't get it," Fergus shook his head. "The past I mean is respectable enough—even a little too much so. But look. You sing, don't you?"

"Why, yes."

"I knew the name was familiar, but I wasn't sure till I heard you speak. That recital Maureen dragged me to—"

"Oh that. It was rather frightful, wasn't it? But they maintain clubwomen are very helpful to the Aspiring Young Artist."

Fergus grinned. "When Maureen told me it was a contralto, I expected something that looked like Schumann-Heink; and instead I got you. It was the one break I've had out of Maureen's club work; that black evening gown of yours saved me my weekly trip to the Follies Burlesque."

"I hope," Camilla added with a smile at the Colonel's modestly purple countenance, "that you noticed my voice a little."

"Oh yes. You were good—though the little people know I'd sooner have heard a good rousing come-all-ye than those dirges you sang."

"Thank you, Mr. O'Breen. Perhaps some time you might teach me some—what was it you called them?"

"Come-all-ye's. You know—"

For a moment Rand feared that Fergus was about to give a brief vocal demonstration, but Camilla cut him short. "I'll remember," she said hastily. "And isn't there something that you should be remembering, Mr. O'Breen?"

"What?"

"Why, that you're a detective and that I, presumably, am a suspect. Shouldn't we do something about it?"

She seated herself gracefully on the wicker chaise longue and waved the gentlemen to seats. Rand accepted; but Fergus indicated his preference to stand.

"Very well, if you wish," She busied herself with a cigarette and an overlong holder. "Now I'm afraid you'll have to ask me questions. I've been thinking as hard as I can, and I can't recall anything about Uncle Humphrey's death that might seem to help you. I went to bed as soon as we left him and fell asleep directly. But perhaps if you ask questions, I might know something I don't even know that I know—if you can follow that."

Fergus seemed to have recovered from his temporary interest in Camilla the Woman and his full attention had reverted to Sallice the Suspect. "All right," he said, pausing a moment from pacing. "I'll ask questions. Who are you?"

"I don't understand you."

"I said, in simple colloquial American, Who are you?"

"Why, I'm Camilla Sallice. Don't you remember? Colonel Rand just introduced us, and you went to a concert with Maureen. Which reminds me, if we must ask questions, Who is Maureen? Is she pretty?"

"Please, Miss Sallice." His voice held an unwonted note of authority. "Maureen is my sister, and let's not play games. Everyone I've talked with so far has admitted that he has no idea who you are, why you are here, or what your relation to Humphrey Garnett was. Now I want you to tell us."

Camilla laughed. There was a faint touch of bitterness to her laughter. "Is that all? I was his protégée."

"Which means just what?"

"A year ago I was singing in a night club in Washington. No, I'm afraid *night club* flatters it a little. A detective's accuracy might call it a dive. And singing didn't pay so well unless you made a percentage on drinks, too."

"A B-girl," Fergus commented.

"Exactly. Please don't look shocked, Colonel Rand. After all . . . Well, Uncle Humphrey was there one night, and he was much impressed by my voice. He thought it was far too good for such a place."

"He was right," Fergus admitted grudgingly. "But I'd like to hear you in a torch number."

"He thought I should have a chance at a real career, and he offered to help me. I was a little suspicious at first—any girl would be—but he finally convinced me of his sincerity. I came out here with him, and he's been paying for my lessons with Carduccini. I think I'm almost ready to make a real start now."

"And all this was just for the love of art and your beautiful voice?"

"Mr. O'Breen!"

"Please, Miss Sallice. Don't give me that. Any minute now I'll expect you to go into 'My mother was a lady.'"

Camilla smiled. "She was, you know."

"That's better. After all, a night club isn't a nunnery. You know the facts of life—birds and bees and stuff and things—and you know you're a damned attractive girl, in your cryptic way. And Humphrey Garnett wasn't a eunuch."

This time she laughed aloud. "I suppose, Mr. O'Breen, you're being complimentary in your own fantastic fashion. It's a bit hard to recognize, but I'll try to be grateful."

"Go on."

"All right. I quite see what you mean; I shan't play innocent. But I swear that there was nothing of the sort between Uncle Humphrey and me. I can't explain this to you or prove it; you'll have to believe me. But it would have been impossible. We—we felt so differently about each other."

"If you say so—" Fergus seemed only half convinced.

"I don't wonder that you're a little suspicious. I know Kay was, and even that poor dear old Mr. Willowe. But that's really all there was to it."

"You're fond of Arthur Willowe?"

"Yes. I suppose I am. He's so—so helpless. He feels he can never do anything well. He failed in business—he tried to write once—he couldn't even play chess with Uncle Humphrey. But he's been good to Kay, and he was good to his sister—at least, they tell me he was. And isn't that something in life—just being good to people?"

Fergus disregarded the philosophical point. "And does he return this fondness of yours?"

Camilla shrugged. "I can tell from your tone that you know he doesn't. It's just that he won't understand. He thinks that Uncle Humphrey and I—well, that I'd taken Alicia's place. If he only knew how dreadfully wrong he was—"

"Look. Let's take a different angle. Can you see anybody in this house wanting to murder Mr. Garnett?"

"Frankly, Mr. O'Breen, no. I know that this seems a strange thing to say when I was so fond of Uncle Humphrey; but I can't see him as the logical *victim* for a murder. There isn't any reason—unless of course it was Richard Vinton. He'd have been much more apt to be the murderer."

"You mean that Vinton is the murderer type—if indeed there is such a th'ng?"

"Not Vinton. No. Uncle Humphrey. I'm not being very clear, am I? But then I don't feel very clear. I mean that it would have suited his hard, intricate mind to figure out a perfect plot and put it into effect. And he could hate people—Mr. Willowe, for example."

"But you can think of no reason why anyone killed him?"

"No, I—" Camilla halted abruptly, and a dark shadow of fear passed over her weary face. "No reason at all," she said slowly, "unless . . ."

"Unless what?"

"It *is* possible. I hadn't thought of that. But I can see now. It's twisted and horrible and fantastic and yet it is possible. And it would be my fault . . . "

"What do you mean, Miss Sallice?"

"Camilla! You—you know something?" It was Kay standing in the open doorway, with Will Harding like a loyal and slightly bewildered dog at her side.

Camilla did not turn her head. She looked straightforth into the red west, and the setting sun transfigured her face in its glow. The hard lines were gone for the moment, and with them her mysterious bitterness; there remained only a strange look of exalted pity. "It's nothing, Kay," she said softly.

"But if you know anything, Camilla, you must tell us. You must!"

"Yes, Miss Sallice. If you can help us—"

Camilla turned to them at last. "I want to talk to you again," she said to Fergus. "But let me sleep on it first. I don't know . . . " And she walked slowly into the house.

"What a strange way to act," Kay observed hesitantly. "I've never been able to understand Camilla."

"I don't think you ever will," Fergus said. "You two don't tick quite the same."

"Whatever you mean by that . . . I came to tell you that dinner's almost ready, if you want to wash up or anything." She halted, then sent a brief glance of appeal to Harding.

"Excuse me," he said curtly, and followed after Camilla.

"Now, Detective. I wanted to talk to you alone. Tell me, please."

"Now, now. Don't expect miracles, Client. I can't just talk to three people—five, including you two—and up and say, in accents dire, 'Thou art the man!' I've got to think about it—work it out; I can't go off half-cocked."

She smiled a smile of urgent pleading. "But Fergus darling—oh, all right—Detective, then—can't you tell me anything?"

He paused in front of her. "I can tell you this: The fingerprints and the crumpled knave are both plants, and I can prove it. Trapping your Richard was as much the aim of this scheme as killing your father. And it's practically sure—steady now, Client—that the schemer came from inside this house."

He disregarded Kay's small gasp of horror, and plunged on. "This is going to be hard. It means that the truth may hit you quite as badly as Richard's arrest. So the point's this—do you still want me to go on? I mean, there's a good chance that mere proof of such a frame-up would get Richard off, without the need of proving who really did it. I've heard a lot about Lieutenant Jackson. He's intelligent and he's fair; we could probably persuade him of the plants.

"So I ask you, Client, straight out: *Do you want me to go on?*"

Kay looked at him earnestly. "You mean that it has to be—?"

Fergus nodded. "One of you? Yes."

"Should I—" She trembled a little under this burden of responsibility. "What do you think, Uncle Teddy?"

Colonel Rand put his arm around the girl's slim shoulders. After a slow "harrumph," he said, "It's up to you, my dear. All I can say is this: Mr. O'Breen seems shrewd, and the truth is the truth. It will prevail in time, perhaps, but judicious human aid has never harmed it. That's all," he added gruffly.

Kay tossed her head decisively. "All right, Detective. It's up to you. But there's one other thing that worries me."

"What's that, Client?"

Her voice was earnest. "You read a lot, in books and stories and things, about—" She hesitated. "Well, they say that . . . " She slowly gathered courage and blurted it out: ". . . that murderers don't stop."

Rand tightened the clasp of his arm. He hadn't thought of that. It was true, of course. To live here in a house where one of the inmates must be a murderer . . . He smiled and lied. "Absurd notion, Kay, my dear. A murderer's usually far too frightened to think of another crime in his life. It's purely a necessary fictional device to keep up the suspense a hundred pages after the first murder."

Fergus frowned. "I don't agree in theory, Colonel Rand—too many examples to quote against you—but I think in this case you're right. There are two possibilities in my mind—I haven't the necessary facts yet to make clear which is true. But neither way is Kay in the slightest danger. In fact, I'll stake my reputation as a fledgling murder expert on the fact that this is a case with one murder."

Rand couldn't decide whether the young man was being sincere or merely reassuring. But he could feel that Kay was shivering. It may have been simply because the sun had set.

TEN

COLONEL RAND EXAMINES A TAROT

This sudden sense of apprehension, Rand thought, might well be dissipated if he decided, in Kay's words, to wash up or anything.

He was right. It did help; but when he came downstairs again he did not go directly to the dining room. Instead, he turned into the study.

He could not help feeling that the key to the whole tragic problem lay there, in that room in which Humphrey Garnett had died and which still bore so strongly the imprint of his vigorous personality. Just what the Colonel was seeking, he could not have said. He wanted only to be there for a moment, hoping confusedly that he might, in some strange way, know what there was to know in that room.

All was familiar. No new knowledge was to be garnered from the books or the great chess set or the cabinet of playing cards. Moreover, this last and the chemical notes on the desk would require, he realized, far more technical understanding than he possessed to make clear whatever secrets they might hold.

Colonel Rand fingered his waxed mustache and called himself a particolored idiot for yielding to such a vague hunch. As though a mere empty room could tell him the depths of so dark a truth. He started to stride from the study, and then halted before a picture on the wall.

This was not familiar. It must be some recent acquisition of Garnett's which Rand had failed to notice when he was in the room before. It was a fine reproduction of an exquisite miniature painting, shaped somewhat like a playing card, but in no other wise similar to the cards which Rand knew.

In rich colors, tricked out with gold and silver, it represented what might have been an arbor of green boughs, but was clearly serving as a sort of improvised gallows. From the center of the top bough a man hung by a noose passed about his right foot. His hair fell downward in a great shock, and money bags dangled from his hands. His left leg was twisted in the air, giving the entire body something of the shape of a swastika. The whole had the effect of an abstruse geometrical joke played with an indifferent corpse. Beneath it ran the silver legend:

LE PENDU

"Ah," said a dry voice behind Rand. "I see that you appreciate the Hanged Man." The sentence was followed by the rustle of a discreet sneeze.

Rand turned about to see a complete stranger—an old man (seemingly a good fifteen years older than the Colonel himself), gaunt, stooped, and comfortably shabby, who smiled a dim scholarly smile of greeting and went right on talking.

"Of course you recognize the tarot series painted—in 1392, I believe—for Charles VI? Singularly fine designs. To some, the

Hanged Man is the most sinister of all the tarot cards, even more so than his immediate successor in the series, Death—of whom you may see a typical example here."

He extended his snuffbox, which bore an enameled design of a skeleton sweeping a scythe over a field scattered with broken heads and hands and feet. Above it stood the Roman numeral XIII. "For myself," he rambled on, "I fear I find the Maison Dieu the most ominous—possibly only because it seems so meaningless."

Rand stared at the intruder.

"There is something so economical about the skeletal sparseness of Death," the old man continued drily. "One inevitably thinks of Vendice's apostrophe—

*Does the silk worm expend her yellow labours
For thee? For thee does she undo herself?*"

This was too much for the Colonel. He emitted one of the great "harrumphs" of a distinguished career and followed it with a speech which demanded chiefly: Who the devil this fellow was, Who the devil he thought he was, What the devil he was doing here, Where the devil he'd come from, and Why the devil he didn't go back there. To be sure, there was a certain monotony in these satanic references; but the Colonel was far too perturbed to worry about fine nuances of style. That this outrageous individual should come and blather about the skeletal sparseness of death on the very spot where Rand's closest friend had died and that not twenty-four hours ago—this was too much.

Before his tirade was over, Kay and Fergus had come into the room. The stranger now turned to Kay in helpless appeal. "Miss Garnett, I beseech you. Protect me from this madman."

The Colonel grew purple. Taxicabs and police were nothing beside this outrage. "Madman indeed! My dear Kay, if you have no more respect for your father's memory than to let this blithering—"

"Allow me to explain, Miss Garnett. I called at your father's invitation to continue my study of his admirable collection. No one answered my knock; but noticing the door ajar, I took the liberty of entering. I observed this—ah, gentleman absorbed in the contemplation of the tarot reproduction there, and ventured a few remarks upon the subject. Whereupon he turned on me; and I veritably believe that had you not entered I should have suffered bodily harm."

Rand began to appreciate the situation. He looked at Kay. Despite the grave atmosphere of this house of death, she was struggling to repress a nervous giggle. Fergus had quite frankly averted his face. Rand could understand; the two of them must have seemed exquisitely ludicrous, senile gamecocks pecking at each other with furious words. He laughed and put his arm around Kay. "Sorry, my dear. We have enough to worry about without these silly interludes. Introduce me to the gentleman, and we'll forget the episode."

Kay smiled at him gratefully. "Mr. Warriner—Colonel Rand, Mr. O'Breen. Mr. Warriner," she explained. "is an authority on cards. Naturally, he was interested in Father's collection."

Warriner's anger had faded as rapidly as the Colonel's. " 'Authority', I fear, is too flattering a term for me. I am simply curator of the playing-card collection of the James T. Weatherby Memorial Museum in Providence."

As the two men shook hands, some curious lost fragment of memory worried Colonel Rand. There was something he should know about this man . . . ,"Had you known Garnett long?"

"Only by correspondence until last night. He knew our collection in the days before I took office. It was then that he resolved to leave his own to us on his death. It has always been a standing joke in our letters that I was the one man with a motive for murdering him." The curator emitted a single shrill high note, which probably represented laughter, and took out his snuffbox. "I hope I have not called inconveniently, Miss Garnett," he went on. "I thought that I was expected. Where is your father?"

Kay looked at him for a moment of unbelief. She tried to speak, but the words seemed to stick. "I came to tell you to come to dinner," she said, and hurried out of the room.

Fergus shut the door after her. "Sorry, sir," he said, "but I'm afraid you put your foot in it."

Confusedly, Warriner snapped his snuffbox shut without using it. "I do not understand."

"Humphrey Garnett was killed last night."

"So you can see, Warriner," the Colonel added, "why your standing joke fell a bit flat."

The curator tapped the reaping skeleton with an oddly lithe and young forefinger. "I am sorry," he murmured simply. "Death is always unwelcome to one's friends, however welcome it might be to oneself." He quoted in a soft monotone:

"We cease to grieve, cease to be fortune's slaves,
Nay, cease to die by dying . . ."

There was a brief silence; but anything unusual stirred the O'Breen curiosity. "Shakespeare?" he asked abruptly, "I can't place it."

"Shakespeare!" For once Warriner stood almost erect. "That, young man, is John Webster. Any fool can quote Shakespeare; only the refined palate can savor the delights of his so-called lesser contemporaries. Shall we in to dinner?"

Fergus followed him, looking for once a little abashed. Rand hesitated. He was not thinking clearly. Surely that bequest to the museum must be what he was trying to associate with the aged curator; he had never seen the man before nor, indeed, anything the least bit like him. But his teased memory was still unsatisfied. There was something else he should think of.

ELEVEN

PEOPLE TALK AT DINNER

Quite obviously everyone at the dinner table had memories of that dismal luncheon, and each of them had primed himself with a ready flow of conversation which would embellish the surface without touching the darker thoughts that lay deep within them all.

Fergus was chiefly responsible; he kept things going with a deftness which never made itself obtrusive. He chatted blithely on everything from amusing anecdotes of his detective experience to rowdy Irish tales from his father's repertory. It was a relief, Rand thought, to hear such stories told with an authentic brogue.

The others gradually relaxed. Kay chaffed Fergus with legends of his obstreperous childhood which she had heard from Maureen. Colonel Rand contributed fascinating details of great strokes of military strategy. Even the quiet Will Harding revealed himself in the surprising role of a connoisseur of limericks who experienced some difficulty in displaying the treasures of his collection in mixed company. Camilla, encouraged by this turn of the conversation, came forth with an amazing saga of her encounters as a percentage girl.

Maurice Warriner, too, sensed the desirability of General Conversation, and tucked into the table talk fascinating bits of card lore ornamented with obscure Elizabethan quotations. Only Arthur Willowe was silent. He was no longer hysterical; but fear still brooded sullenly over him.

Twice, however, this elaborately embellished surface wore thin. One occasion came when Warriner was describing the odd and ingenious playing cards which have been issued from time to time for educational purposes.

Will Harding was markedly interested. "Do you think they're really valuable, sir?"

"That would depend, young man. Some of the earlier

varieties—for instance, that amazing issue of Thomas Murner's in 1509—are quite rare; but most of the later ones—"

"No. I mean, pedagogically valuable. Could you really teach in that manner?"

"From the examples which I know, I would not trust them. I remember for example a soldier's piquet pack which was designed to teach easy English phrases to Frenchmen. The ace of diamonds, if my memory is correct, reads; *Le plus qu'il m'est possible—The more than it is possible to me.* That would hardly be of what you call pedagogical value." The old man paused, stared at his neglected food, and took out his death-bedizened snuffbox. "You're a very earnest young man, aren't you, Mr. Harding?" he asked sharply.

"What do you mean, sir?"

"You are intent upon serious values. You pursue a straight line." The curator poised a pinch of snuff neatly between thumb and forefinger. "It must almost be a relief to you now, to follow that straight line of research—alone."

If it is possible for a pale man to turn pale, Will Harding accomplished the feat at that moment. "Do you mean," he said slowly, "that I could—could rejoice in Mr. Garnett's death? Do you think I don't feel sick and empty because he isn't beside me in the lab? Do you think that any fine glory out of our research will mean anything to me when he isn't there to share it?" He was speaking with a soft intensity more terrible than any excitement could have been.

"I've got it!" Fergus cried abruptly.

Harding broke off. "Got what?"

"The limerick to top that last one you told. It starts:

*There was an old man from Bombay,
Who . . .* "

Fergus halted and looked around the table. "On second thought, Harding, I'll tell it to you later," But the limerick had already served its purpose. The spell was broken.

The other interruption of the carefully indifferent atmosphere came during the Sallice narrative. There was wine with the dinner, and Camilla had not neglected it. Her story carried with it a lusty relish—a broad heartiness which dispelled thoughts of death. Even the scholarly curator seemed delighted by it.

Only Arthur Willowe sat in glum discomfort. At last he spoke, just in time to kill the tag line of an episode involving a drunken but anonymous senator and the wife of a Lithuanian attaché. "My dear Miss Sallice, I have long thought that my mind would be relieved if I knew something of your past. I fear," he added primly, "that such is not the case."

Camilla refused to take the rebuke seriously. "Why, Mr. Willowe, I've only been telling you the most respectable aspects of my Long and Varied Career. Now if I told you about that place on the east side, you could really be shocked. Lawrence always used to call it the Swan, because it was such a wide-open dive."

Fergus pounced on the unexplained detail. "Lawrence?"

The dark girl seemed surprised by herself. "It's your own fault, Kay. You shouldn't have served wine. Whiskey, yes—even gin; but wine makes me talk. All right then, since I've said that much anyway: Lawrence Massey."

Rand sat up even straighter than usual. "Lawrence Massey! But my dear young girl, that is—"

"Yes, I know. Richard Vinton."

Dinner had stopped for the moment. All those at the table looked at the girl in amazement—all save Maurice Warriner, who was evidently quite unable to appreciate the danger of Camilla's conversational bomb.

"Don't start asking questions," Camilla went on. "There isn't anything to tell. His Dread Past used to be a secret, but it's in all the papers this afternoon."

"You knew then about old Vantage and the Cunarder—about the knave of diamonds?"

"Yes. That was always one of his favorite stories. It was strange too, Colonel Rand—hearing your name that way."

"My name?" Rand was puzzled. "But how could that—"

"I mean, when I heard Kay talk so much about you later. I kept wondering what would happen when you came out here and recognized him. Of course, you mightn't have at that; people don't always."

"How well did you know him?" from Fergus.

Camilla fingered her wineglass. "I used to see him around. He was on very good terms with my room-mate. She wasn't always home when he called. That's all."

"I know," Kay said quietly. "He—he told me all about it."

"Did he indeed?" Camilla smiled. "And that is very odd, you see, because he never recognized me."

Kay bit her lip. Colonel Rand gently touched her hand under the table. He understood. One has one's pride.

"But how could that be?" Fergus was asking. "I shouldn't think you'd be easy to forget."

"It was years ago, remember. For one thing, I was a blonde then. For another—well, I was young. That makes a difference."

Rand could see a gallantly Irish speech forming on Fergus's lips;

but professional interest took its place. "Was this what you wanted to tell us?"

Camilla, however, clearly felt that she had said too much already. "Was it what you wanted to know?" she countered lightly, and fell silent.

But with Arthur Willowe the account of her shocking past still rankled. "My dear Kay," he began to protest, "that your father should have exposed you to this—"

"Tush," Warriner interposed. He had been observing the scene closely with impersonal amusement. "Let us say that she had committed—whatever she may have committed. But that was in another country; and besides, the wench is dead."

"I'm not sure," Camilla murmured thoughtfully, "that I like that crack."

TWELVE

COLONEL RAND IS NOT A GENTLEMAN

Colonel Rand found the hours after dinner unsatisfactory. Kay, exhausted and nervous, apologized to the company and went off to rest. The Sallice girl vanished without even an apology. The five men, honoring the family tradition even on this night, retired to the study.

There Fergus began questioning Maurice Warriner on technical aspects of playing cards in general and particularly of the famous Garnett collection; and Rand, deciding that he could trust Fergus to separate the wheat from the chaff in all these learned details, engaged Will Harding in a game of chess. Arthur Willowe, of course, sat in a corner and played solitaire. He had visibly aged even since that morning, Rand thought; his pale hands trembled and were hardly able to lay out the cards.

Despite the painful scene at dinner. Harding was in top form. He displayed what seemed to Rand a truly exceptional chess mind for a young man. It was small wonder that Garnett had kept him on, even aside from his probable value as an assistant. Where in other matters, save for his fanatically enthusiastic pacifism, he was dry and retiring, as a chess opponent he inevitably commanded your attention and respect. It was only with great difficulty that

Rand, himself an excellent player, managed at last to force a stalemate.

He looked up from his absorption to see Fergus standing over the table.

"Didn't want to break up the game," the young detective said. "But Warriner's gone—said he had an appointment some place—and I've got to keep myself busy. So now, Harding, if you'd like to go over those notes with me and see what you can make of them—"

Harding was once more the dully efficient assistant. "Glad to, O'Breen."

"Want to listen in, Colonel?"

But again Rand decided that he would rather have a concise digest later. A cigar in the cool evening would do him more good now. The other two turned to the desk, only to find it already occupied. Unnoticed as always, Arthur Willowe had abandoned his solitaire and settled himself to write something on note paper.

He rose as the young men approached him. "The desk is yours, gentlemen. I have finished."

Rand, leaving the room, detected a harshly definite note in the old man's voice which disquieted him.

The hills proved as admirable for walking as he had hoped. You had all the beauty of the city's distant lights without the overpowering proximity of its noises. There was moonlight and a fresh breeze. A younger man might have become sentimental; to Rand it was simply a perfect night for exercise both of body and of mind.

A Watson, he reflected stolidly, is always supposed to have his own ideas on a case, if only so that the dazzling detective may refute them. So, as he strolled and smoked in the sweet of the night, he went over the possibilities carefully.

Opportunity, so far as was known, included the entire household. Motive was a more narrowing question. Vinton, of course—but for Kay's sake he must be eliminated. Kay herself—obviously absurd, despite the inheritance. Miss Sallice—he admitted that he was not wholly convinced of the innocence of her relations with Garnett. But what had she to gain by his death? Unless perhaps a codicil to the old will . . . And then too, what was this possibility which she had almost mentioned to O'Breen? Yes, assuredly the dark girl was, in some as yet unexplained fashion, a significant factor in the case.

To Will Harding, he resumed his chain of thought, Garnett's death meant only the loss of a good job. To Arthur Willowe—Rand paused. Ten thousand dollars would mean a great deal of independence—perhaps the first that he had ever known. And if he feared Garnett so much . . .

No, there were still too many questions to answer. You couldn't be sure yet; you couldn't lay your finger on one point out of so many and say, "There. That's vital." He frankly admitted to himself that he had no idea what Fergus' two definite possibilities were, nor why they should preclude another murder.

Reluctantly, the Colonel gave up his dutiful puzzling and turned back toward the house. The paths along which he passed had been deserted; long strolls in the hills are not popular in a city so overequipped with automobiles. But now he saw a figure ahead of him on the sidewalk—a tall, exasperatingly familiar figure. Rand quickened his already rapid stride.

The figure turned as the Colonel came abreast of it, and revealed the aged gentility of Maurice Warriner.

"Good evening, Colonel Rand," he smiled. "You too seek the beauties of the evening air?"

"It seems to be good for you, Warriner. I didn't recognize you from behind; you were holding yourself with such a firm carriage." But even as the Colonel spoke, Warriner's shoulders were sinking into their habitual hump. "Cigar?" Rand produced his case.

"Thank you, no. Even my vices are, I fear, archaic. Tobacco seems flat beside the sharp stimulation of snuff."

The two old men strolled for a moment in silence. "I thought you had an engagement this evening," Rand ventured.

"To be sure, sir. So I did. But my evening in the Garnett household has perturbed me strangely.

There's gunpowder i' the court—wildfire at midnight.

I wished to think a bit. I take it that that is why you too sought the consolation of evening?"

"Frankly, Warriner, yes."

"And what, Colonel, have you concluded?"

"I have concluded, sir, that there is damn-all to conclude. We have no facts, and far too many half facts. We must grope half-seeing; and despite the proverb, the one-eyed man has far less chance than the blind of arriving at the truth."

"Perhaps you underestimate yourself, Colonel. If I may permit myself to paraphrase:

Truth is a creature of so strange a mien
That oft revealed, she yet remains unseen."

"Well, sir, have your thoughts been more profitable?"

The curator slowed his pace. "I realize, Colonel, that I spoke out of turn at dinner. But I have known something of scientists and other research workers. As that earnest young man spoke so intently on such a trivial point, I suddenly understood a possible motive which the police, I fear, would not consider. I should not have spoken then; I see that now. But the more I think of this affair, the more that motivation seems plausible to me."

"Nonsense, sir. Harding's a fine young man. A bit dull, perhaps, but devoted to Garnett and his work."

"No devotion in mankind is stronger than devotion to glory. Self-preservation, it has been said, is the first law of nature; but one's self must be preserved immortally in the intoxicating alcohol of fame. Every man alive longs to be alone in splendor above the rest and ride in triumph through Persepolis."

The allusion escaped Rand. "Persepolis?"

"Surely you recall the great conqueror Tamburlaine speaking to his lieutenants in a moment of glory:

Is it not brave to be a king, Techelles?
Usumcasane and Theridamas,
Is it not passing brave to be a king,
And ride in triumph through Persepolis?

Tamburlaine helped Cosroe to attain fame and empery; then, inevitably, he brought about his master's death and supplanted him. Even so with Harding and Garnett."

Rand thought a bit. "It's no case for a jury," he said practically.

"No. That much I grant you. The frenzy of Marlovian verse would hardly make the case clearer to twelve good men and true. I beg your pardon, Colonel, for intruding my imagination on your practicality; and I give you a very good night. I shall try to keep my belated appointment."

But a thought had suddenly crossed Rand's mind. "Just a minute before you go, sir. I have never paid much attention to playing cards; but I have just thought of something that interests me as a military man. Perhaps you would help me?"

"Gladly, sir." Warriner stood impatiently.

"The playing cards which were manufactured for the Confederate States of America—that is, cards with the Confederate flag on them—are they of value?"

"Decidedly. There were not many of them manufactured, and most of those have been lost or destroyed. Emphatically, they are collector's items. But why—?"

"I believe that I have some among my various war trophies. My specialty, of course, is firearms; but I own a few other relics. All this talk about cards made me wonder."

"When you return to your home, sir, do me the favor of sending me a description. I shall be glad to tell you what I can about them. And now I must bid you good night. Remember Persepolis."

The tall, gaunt figure vanished in the evening. A brief sneeze sounded faintly as his steps died away.

Even as Warriner had observed, Colonel Rand was essentially a practical man; but he found even his practicality sorely bothered by the plausibility of the curator's reasoning. He remembered that one black moment in his military career when he had been passed over for promotion. Yes, a man might well commit murder to ride in triumph through that strange name.

Rand shrugged and went on toward the house.

As he drew near, he heard voices on the sun porch. Now eavesdropping should be the last act of a gentleman and an officer, retired or not; but he came closer because one of the voices was strange. He could not help thinking of their dire need for an outsider; and the voice of a stranger talking with Kay was too great a temptation.

". . . since before you ever met him," the voice was saying. "You've known that, I'm afraid, even though I've tried so hard to hide it."

"Yes," Kay answered softly. "I've known. And I haven't been very happy about it."

"When your happiness is all that I have ever wanted. Kay, my dear, I wouldn't have spoken even now. Perhaps it isn't fair. But we can't be sure about—about all this. For your sake, I hope he is innocent; but even if he is, that doesn't mean for certain that he'll go scot free. They may make out a case against him anyway. And I want you to know that—well, that I'm here. For anything you want."

"That's sweet of you." Her voice was clouded a little. "But why did you have to wait so long? If you'd said a little word even a year ago . . . But it's silly to think about that now. All—all this has only made me stronger. You see, my dear, I'm so much more to him now. And I love him very much."

The strange man's voice was humble and broken. "I shouldn't have said a word. But I couldn't—Oh, well." He seemed to regain his control. "We'll get him off somehow."

Colonel Rand swore silently. Stranger's voice, indeed! He recognized it now—Will Harding's. It was only that emotional stress had so far distorted it from its natural quiet precision. Rand mentally gave himself a severe and well-aimed kick. Eavesdropping on this poor young man, hopelessly confessing his love for Kay! And who wouldn't love her—Alicia's daughter?

The Colonel lit a fresh cigar, gave an especially loud "harrumph," and joined the couple on the sun porch.

Under the circumstances, conversation was forced and awkward. The group broke up with inevitable promptness. Harding retired to the study, to resume his work with Fergus; and Kay and Rand walked slowly upstairs to their respective bedrooms.

She was near tears as she kissed the old man good night. "Last night," she murmured, "I was saying good night to Father, and now . . . But at least you're here, Uncle Teddy; I can hold on to you. Don't leave me, please. Don't ever leave me."

Deeply touched, Rand retired to the room which had been assigned to him. But his involuntary eavesdropping, despite the hell it played with his gentlemanly conscience, was not over for the night. As he started down the hall to the bathroom, vested in the crimson tailored dressing gown which was the one flamboyant touch in his otherwise severe taste, he saw Camilla Sallice tapping on the door of one of the bedrooms.

He was still unfamiliar with the house. He could not be sure whose room that was, save that it was not the one he had just seen Kay enter. But as he reclined in a warm tub and lathered himself richly, he worried over the small problem. Then the answer hit him: That was the only one of the bedrooms, aside from his own, which he had entered that day. Besides, Fergus and Harding were presumably still in the study. Yes, by due process of elimination, the Sallice girl was paying a secret visit to Arthur Willowe. Though *secret*, he reminded himself, was a somewhat unfair word. There had been nothing surreptitious about her manner.

Nonetheless, he took a long time over his tub. It was a disconcerting little episode, in view of the marked hostility which Willowe had been displaying toward the girl. At last he left the bathroom, turning out the light, only to retire at once into the shelter of the dark doorway. Camilla Sallice was leaving the bedroom which she had entered.

The hall made a good sounding box. "Thank you, my dear," Rand could overhear—and there was no mistaking Arthur Willowe's thin voice. "You have made me very happy indeed—changed, perhaps, the course of my life. And now that I know your secret, it may be that I should tell you my own. Yes, Camilla, I will tell you." There was a curious mixture of pride and shame in the voice. "I am Hector Prynne."

"No!" Her rich voice was incredulous. "You? How fantastic!" She laughed deep in her throat—the happiest laugh which Rand had yet heard from her.

"There! Now we're even, aren't we?" And Arthur Willowe kissed the dark girl long and tenderly.

THIRTEEN

COLONEL RAND HEARS THINGS GO BUMP IN THE NIGHT

It was a very confused dream. There was something about a banshee in a yellow polo shirt and a knave of diamonds which stole a pieman (Rand was later ashamed to recollect that his subconscious mind could rhyme so outrageously) and a man who hung from a gallows by one foot and gestured *Heil Hitler!* with the other. Then the banshee and the pieman, who had by now found a yellow polo shirt of his own (with meringue on it), decided that the Colonel should be hanged too. So they took a long rope twisted out of strands of dry ice and tied it around his right foot. He didn't like it very much, but they kept pulling him on up. The blood rushed to his head in purple torrents, and his foot began to freeze off, chipping a little at the edges. The knave of diamonds held his Welsh hook in his right hand and began thumping things with it. As the Colonel's foot touched the iron top of the gallows, the knave's hook shattered a glass of Scotch and plain acid, no ice.

At this point the Colonel awoke. His right foot jutted chilly out of the covers and pressed against the metal frame of the bed. His head lolled over the edge, and blood tingled in it. He adjusted himself more comfortably and grinned. Nightmares were the just punishment of those who were too long to fit easily into an ordinary guest bed.

But his amused grin began to fade. Slowly he was growing aware that this had not all been part of a dream. That shock of broken glass still rang in his waking ears. And there came a faint distant bumping sound which could no longer be attributed to a malicious knave of diamonds wildly brandishing a Welsh hook.

Rand was sharply awake now. He could not locate the sound, but it continued, irregularly but persistently. He slipped out of bed and donned the crimson dressing gown. It had large pockets—quite large enough for the heavy (and somewhat outdated) Army revolver which he took from his suitcase.

The sound was downstairs, he realized, as he entered the upper hall. Everything was silent up here; down there the bumping sound persisted. His mind kept repeating, amusedly, that ancient Scottish prayer which Major Cameron used to quote with such relish:

From ghoulies and ghosties and long-legged beasties and things that go BUMP in the night—Good Lord, deliver us!

He glided down the stairs with an ease and deftness incongruous in one of his age and bearing. There was only one light burning downstairs, and that was in the study. He hesitated there for a moment. But the bumping noise did not come from that room; there was only the murmur of voices—Fergus and Harding still discussing Garnett's notes.

No, the noise came from farther down the hall. He tiptoed on, his hand tight on the revolver. This was like the old days of service again. His heart pumped a tense red flow of blood at a rate which, he felt sure, would have alarmed the devil out of his physician. He could hear Dr. Hagedorn expostulating, "But at your age, Colonel. . . ." He had no age now. He was a man of duty investigating a problem.

He paused before the closed door of the laboratory. This—he felt his trained nerves tingle as they had not tingled in years—this was the place. The sounds went on persistently, as though the intruder deliberately wished to proclaim his presence. Then, even as Rand waited, there came again that sound of shattered glass.

Rand's fingers ran lightly along the door jamb. He nodded to himself, satisfied. The door opened outward, and the lock was not quite caught. Noiselessly he pried it ever so slightly open. His foot slipped in between the door and the frame. Firmly he lifted the revolver from his pocket and held it ready.

Then his foot swung the door wide open at the same time that he whispered tautly, "Damn your eyes, sir, I have you covered!"

The beam of a flashlight shot square into the center of the open doorway. Rand saw the trick, but he had counted on it. That should have blinded him, which was why he had stood aside and let his foot do the work. He had not feared a shot; the fellow wouldn't dare rouse the household.

The flash went off again. The bumping had stopped now; there was nothing but a dark silence. Rand hesitated. He wasn't quite certain of the next move.

That move came from his adversary. In the half-darkness the Colonel saw a long thin body rush for the doorway. He threw himself forward and grappled with it. If he could pin the chap down—then call for Fergus— He had tossed the revolver aside; it was too dangerous at close quarters like this—it could be too easily turned against him.

As the two struggled tensely, Rand's hand felt about for the fellow's flashlight. It was too dark to distinguish a face. He could tell only that this was the body of a young and supple man—a dexterous fighter who was bothered (Rand realized with abrupt pain) by no artificial scruples against fouling.

His aged, if military loins ached with the shock; but he kept his hold. Condition, sir, he grunted to himself; that's what tells. His arms were rigid bars of muscle, and for a moment he held the intruder helplessly pinioned. But the condition of his adversary was not to be despised, and the young man had the added advantage of a faulty sense of honor.

It was this that won. For an instant of agony Rand released his hard-won hold. The other was gone in a second. Still gasping, Rand felt around for the revolver. He might chance it now. But even as his hand seized the weapon he felt one sharp heavy blow on his skull.

That was enough.

FOURTEEN

FERGUS APOLOGIZES

Colonel Rand awoke to find bright sunlight pouring into the room and Fergus O'Breen perched cheerfully on his bed. The polo shirt looked yellower than ever.

"Top o' the mornin'," said Fergus.

The Colonel was still not fully awake. "But I was *not* drunk last night," he objected feebly.

It took Fergus a moment to understand what that greeting signified. "Oh, you mean your head. It must feel like the torture of the damned. Sorry."

Rand lifted shaky fingers to his throbbing head. Not till he felt the bandage did he remember anything. Then slowly he recalled the thing that went BUMP in the night and the battle at the door of the laboratory. After that came some hazy recollection of people bending over him and a lot of badly organized hubbub.

"The damned scoundrel got away?" he demanded, with small hope of a negative answer.

"He got away," Fergus nodded. "But not before he went through the study too. I think that whole business in the laboratory was just to lure Harding and me out of the study. He had quite a time in there while we were busy with you."

"He was strong," the Colonel sighed in reluctant admiration, touching his forehead lightly.

Fergus swung one lean leg like an embarrassed schoolboy. "I hope you won't mind this, my faithful Watson. But that was me."

"You?"

"The O'Breen in person. Harding and I heard all that scuffle in the hall. The only weapon I could find was that brass ash stand, so I took it along. I saw somebody with what looked like a gun in his hand and I conked him. And it was you."

For a moment the Colonel wavered between fury and amusement. Amusement won out. "Serves me damned well right for coming out of retirement. It's a lesson to me, O'Breen, and I'm grateful."

Fergus grinned back at him. "I hoped you'd take it that way."

Rand looked grave again. "This man last night—you've no idea who he was?"

"None whatsoever. Everybody in the household seems accounted for. Except maybe the Sallice—she was alone. Kay had stopped by to say good night to Willowe, and Harding was with me."

"Mr. O'Breen, I may be old, but my memory, at least, is still keen enough so that I can distinguish a man's body from a woman's at such close quarters. I assure you that our invader was not the Sallice."

"Then it was somebody from outside. But who or why—"

"Did he get anything?"

"Harding checked. Nothing missing. The only things he might have wanted were in Harding's pocket—but I'll explain that later. It's time you had breakfast now."

"One more thing first—Kay . . . "

"She's all right. Nothing happened to her last night—except she fainted when she saw you there. Naturally it hit her—after all the other things she's had to go through."

Rand felt his aching head again. "She recovered well. I'm grateful for this bandage."

"That? That wasn't Kay—that was the Sallice. She went all-over tender and Lady-with-the-lamp-ish. You know," he added ruminatively, "that wench has got something."

"She hasn't told you her idea yet?"

"No. Haven't seen her this morning. But I don't know if we'll much need it now. You see," (the ancient Gaelic trumpets were sounding again) "I know what Garnett's secret researches were, I know who Hector is, and I know that there'll be no more murders."

Rand stared at him, wordless.

"Surprised? Just watch, Colonel. Nothing up this sleeve, nothing up this—and presto! This may be my first murder, but it'll be a honey. Now up with you, my shatterpated Watson, and hear all the fascinating facts."

A shower and a man-sized breakfast brought Rand to himself

again, despite the terrors and confusions of the night. As he lit the first cigar of the day, he settled back to hear Fergus's news.

The young man was pacing even more vigorously than usual. "As you know," he began, "Harding and I went over those notes of Garnett's last night. They were all in order, all dealing with the alexi-whatever-youcallit gas, excepting one bunch. Those weren't complete; they were just random notes that seemed to have got in with the others by mistake. The complete file must be hidden away some place—possibly in Garnett's safe-deposit box. Anyway, Harding had a go at finding out what they meant. He worked on it quite a bit, while I went over the card collection—with gloves. White ones, though—you know we're a superstitious race. And between that and my talk with old Warriner, do I know things about playing cards! Colonel, I could dazzle you with my erudition—and no Elizabethan quotations, either. Not even a pinch of snuff.

"But that's neither here nor there, except for Hector. Suddenly Harding jumped up from the desk and cried, 'Great scot! I can't believe it!' And a lot more shocked and sometimes shocking expressions.

"'Can't believe what?' I asked, and he explained.

"That is, he called it an explanation. It was a little too technical for me in spots, and I can't give you the McCoy on it; but it boils down to this: Humphrey Garnett's private researches were also on a gas—but it was a poison gas. When he worked alone, he was undoing all the work he'd done with Harding. And Harding says, from what he can make out of those fragments, that it would have been the most deadly and painful poison gas yet known. He was terribly cut up about it; he takes his pacific idealism pretty much to heart, and this was a bad blow. I can't understand it myself; how could a man work toward two such different ends?"

The Colonel poured himself more coffee. "I can understand it," he said, "because I knew Garnett. There was no inconsistency in that for him. Good and evil meant nothing to him as abstractions, even granting the ideas you and Harding hold that military preparedness is an evil. But we won't argue that now. Garnett was interested in the research problem itself, not in its outcome and use. And his devilishly ingenious mind must have delighted in finding a puzzle that could be worked both ways. It was like working out a chess problem. With one half of his mind, he'd try to concoct a 'good' gas which would counteract any poison known; with the other, he'd work toward an 'evil' gas which even his own 'good' gas couldn't lick. He was his own rival, and he couldn't have found a more worthy one."

"Hmm. I guess it does make sense, in its own screwy way. But I don't think you'd ever get Harding to look at it like that. Which makes me think that if he'd come across these notes earlier, as he happened on the carbon of the will, and figured out then what Garnett was doing on his own—well, you see what I mean? Only why should he hate Vinton so much that he'd try to frame him?"

Colonel Rand began to feel decidedly self-confident. Here was something else he could explain to the detective. "Because," he said (and his conscience hurt him a little), "he loves Kay."

"How do you know?" Fergus demanded; and Rand, somewhat shamefacedly, told of his ungentlemanly conduct in eavesdropping on the couple on the sun porch.

Fergus nodded. "That does fit in with what Willowe told us about Harding and his strange questions concerning Vinton. And I can't blame him, being with Kay all the time—though there's the Sallice, too. She's a bit more my style, but I won't criticize another man's taste. The only trouble is, it doesn't quite make good sense as a motive for incriminating Vinton. You'd think he'd see that a false accusation would be all that was needed to tie Kay to the actor forever. And that's the way it's working out." He paced a bit, frowning. Then his face cleared, and he went on. "Now as to Hector—"

"I also know who he is," Rand announced with a swelling of pride. "He is Arthur Willowe."

"The devil he is!"

But Rand told the brief episode of last night.

"Look. That may have nothing to do with it. And I may be wrong too. But here's what I found out. And now that I think of it, they may work in together. Remember when we were talking last night about how some cards have names—the Earl o' Cork and the Devil's Bedposts?"

"Yes."

"Well, in French decks all the court cards have special names—usually printed on the cards themselves. Nobody seems to know quite how they got those names, and they used to vary quite a lot; but now they're fixed to a given set, which any card collector, of course, would know by heart. They're very fancy names—queen of hearts, *Judith;* jack of clubs, *Lancelot;* king of diamonds, *Caesar;* and so on. And the jack of diamonds—well, you can guess that now."

"Is *Hector.*"

"Exactly. After Ector de Maris, half-brother to Sir Lancelot of the Lake—God knows why. But here's our problem, now that you've brought up your point—did your telegram say Hector, meaning the jack of diamonds, in order to indicate Vinton; or does that crumpled jack of diamonds mean Hector, indicating your Hector Prynne? You can have it either way. And another point that comes back to me out of all my crammed erudition—Eteilla, the first great authority on fortunetelling with cards, gives a special meaning to each card. The jack of diamonds means 'a selfish and deceitful relative.'"

"And Jackson pointed out that in less elaborate fortunetelling it means a blond young man. That, in our present group, could only be Will Harding."

"True for you. And still, as I told Kay, that card can't really mean anything. It has to be a plant; and if it's a plant, it must be aimed at Vinton."

"I'm not sure I follow you there, O'Breen."

"It's perfectly logical. Now look—"

But much was to happen before that explanation was concluded.

FIFTEEN

COLONEL RAND READS IN A MIRROR

Good morning, gentlemen." The interruption came in the deep warm voice of Camilla Sallice. She set an overnight case down in the doorway and came forward to the two men. She had changed, Rand thought; she seemed freer and more at ease. Not as though she had fully rid herself of her oppressive sense of tragedy, but rather as though she had found some means of making it bearable.

"Hello," Fergus greeted her. "Sleep well after life's feverous fits last night?"

"Well enough," she smiled. "It was all rather . . . disturbing."

Rand fumbled for a suitable phrase of gratitude. "I'd like to thank you, Miss Sallice, for this." He gestured at the bandage. "It was most kind of you."

"It wasn't anything, Colonel. I owe you some kindness."

"You owe me . . . ?" Rand frowned questioningly.

"We all do, I mean. You've brought a comforting sort of sanity into this household."

"Breakfast?" Fergus asked. "The cook's gone about her own pursuits, but we can furnish you with coffee, toast, marmalade, and a spot of whathaveyou."

"No thanks. I've had my breakfast."

"An illusion shattered. Here I thought you were the first woman

I've known who could look lovely before breakfast. You should see Maureen—it's an experience."

"Are you always so blithely complimentary, Mr. O'Breen?" She looked at him quizzically.

"Always. Only some times I mean it."

"As for instance?"

"As for instance, Miss Sallice—now."

"And do you always restrict your fine Irish style to words?"

There was a pause while the two young people regarded each other intently. Rand was not certain that he approved. To be sure, there was no denying the sleek dark attraction of Camilla Sallice; but a detective sould be impervious to such things. Deliberately the Colonel leaned across the table to find an ash tray.

The military bulk passing between them broke the brief spell. Fergus rose and hovered on the verge of an attack of pacing. "Decided what you've got to tell us?" he demanded efficiently.

"This, for the time being," she smiled with gracious melancholy. "I am leaving this house."

Rand went "harrumph" indignantly. "My dear young lady! At a time like this—"

"I'm sorry. I didn't expect you to understand, Colonel, although possibly Mr. O'Breen will." She looked at the young Irishman closely. "Yes, possibly. . . . You see, I simply cannot stay here."

Fegus stood still in front of her. Their eyes met fixedly. "I can't stop you, you know. I suppose I could tell the police—though I've no idea what they'd do about it."

"I haven't told anyone else that I'm going," she went on quietly. "It's simpler that way. But I remembered that you might need me. I don't want to hide away like a criminal. Here." She handed Fergus a slip of paper. "There is the address of my hotel. Please don't tell anyone unless it becomes necessary." She spoke simply and unemotionally, but her dark voice was rich in pleading.

Fergus hesitated. Rand had the sense of watching a struggle not expressed in their words. "I think you are being unwise, Miss Sallice."

"I think not, Mr. O'Breen. Good-by."

"Good-by." Fergus bit the word off sharply.

Camilla Sallice turned and gazed on Rand, as though her deep eyes could tell him what her tongue withheld. "You'll know some time," she said slowly, then added, like a tender echo of something heard long ago, "Dear Theo. . . ."

She was gone. Her heady perfume lingered to fight an invisible losing battle against Rand's cigar smoke. "'Dear Theo . . .'" he repeated in a soft whisper.

"'Theo'?" This was the sort of unexplained oddity which always caught Fergus' alert attention. "That's funny—even aside from her being so suddenly familiar. Kay always calls you 'Uncle Teddy.' That's what the Sallice would have heard."

Rand was lost in a brief reverie. "Only one person has ever called me Theo. . . ."

"And that was?"

"Please, Mr. O'Breen. It can have nothing to do with this. And yet it disturbs me."

Fergus stood for a moment undecided, then slipped the bit of paper into his pocket. "Well anyway, that's that. Now for a little chat with Hector Prynne."

The Colonel had roused himself afresh. "But first, sir, I have two questions to ask you, if I may."

"Yes?"

"First, why didn't you ask Miss Sallice what that motive is which she thought of yesterday?"

"Because, if I'm thinking straight, that's why she's leaving here. She's thought of something that we haven't, and she's afraid her reactions might give her away if she stays on here. She gave me her address expressly so that I could come and learn what her suspicion is. You see, she's read too many of these novels where the person who Knows Too Much is the second victim."

"That, sir, leads me directly to my second question. I seem to remember hearing you announce, through the haze of pain and confusion which I at first took for a hangover, that you knew there would be no more murders. How can you be so sure? I know that we were both very definite yesterday, for Kay's benefit, but this is between us."

"All right, Colonel. Look. This murderer had two objects. One was Garnett's death. The other, and just as important, was Vinton's execution for that death. Everything points that way—the telegram, the fingerprints, and the jack of diamonds—unless something comes of your Hector discovery. If he goes on to another murder in Vinton's absence, he'll draw official suspicion away from his victim. No, Colonel Rand, we're safe enough here until Vinton gets bailed out."

"And then?" There was a note of apprehension in Rand's voice. Involuntarily his hand touched his bandaged head. Last night's adventure had not been a good augury for peace and quiet in the household. Although he had escaped in safety, he knew instinctively that there was vicious danger in the man with whom he had fought.

"Then? Oh, I see what you mean. Yes, that would be perfect, wouldn't it? Our ingenious murderer waits patiently until Vinton is released and then boom!—another murder. Case against Vinton completely cinched. Nice and neat. Not a pleasant thought. But unless I'm terribly wrong, Colonel, that won't happen. I know it sounds plausible—terrifyingly plausible—but it won't happen." The young Irishman's voice was earnest and somehow convincing.

Rand rose, half-satisfied. "And now we interview Hector Prynne."

Fergus walked as far as the door without speaking. Then he turned. "Look. This isn't right. I'm a louse. I'm holding out on you, and you shouldn't ever treat a Watson like that. How would you like to see a confession of murder?"

Rand started. "A confession? What do you mean, sir?"

"Remember all of us sitting around in the study last night? You were playing chess with Harding, and I was talking about cards with Warriner. And of course Arthur Willowe was off in a corner playing solitaire. Then all of a sudden he gets an idea. He stops his patience and goes over to the desk and begins writing.

"Well, I was curious—the dominant O'Breen trait cropping out again. Remind me to tell you about the time my father was curious as to how a deck could hold five aces. So later I looked at the blotter. It wasn't too much help. I envy these detectives in books who find nice long pointed messages on blotters. Really all people ever blot is the last line on the page. This must have been a three-page note—there are three lines in Willowe's hand on the blotter, sort of crossing over each other in the midst of a lot of figures and stuff that must have been Garnett's. It's not too clear, but I think you can make it out. Here."

He took from his breast pocket a folded piece of blotting paper and handed it to the Colonel. "There's a mirror over there. I don't think there's much question as to what the lines say, though we might work up a little argument about what they mean. And now, my mustachioed generalissimo, let us off and learn the details of the second Hector."

But Colonel Rand stood still before the mirror, reading those three damning lines in Willowe's precise old hand.

The first read:

But now that the reality of death has come upon us, I

The second, sprawled in wider spacing:

    fore, since I know myself to be a murderer,

And the third was the signature:

        Forgive me!

                      Arthur Willowe

SIXTEEN

FERGUS GOES ROWING

The next five minutes were far too confused for Colonel Rand to do any straight thinking or even to be quite sure of just what was happening. It all started when they reached the foot of the staircase. Rand had often used the expression, "An idea struck him"; but he had never realized how literal it could be. Now he saw the young Irishman struck by an idea, and the result was astounding. First he stopped dead with his foot on the bottom stair, as though he were playing Living Statues. Then he groaned like something chained under a castle and muttered, "It couldn't. No, it couldn't. By Saint Columbkill, if it has . . . !" And with a hasty "Wait there!" he had dashed alone up the stairs.

Then, before Rand could even try to grasp the situation, Fergus was back, and the old soldier was being hurried out the front door and into the O'Breen roadster (which matched the polo shirt).

The classical ride in the taxicab had been a placid pleasure trip compared to this. For one thing, this was downhill. For another, no bored professional could equal an Irish amateur at reckless driving. Not until the traffic on Vermont had forced them to a quieter pace did Rand have any time for questions.

"What in the name of seven gods is this all about, young man?" he demanded, with bristles on every syllable.

"Gone," Fergus said briefly.

"Willowe?"

"Yes."

"But why are we—?"

"Taking it on the lam? I want to talk with the Sallice wench before she knows about it. I was wrong—holy Saint Malachi, how wrong I was! I never saw this possibility, and it was staring me square in the face, while I blithered on about— Oh, the poor foolish old man!"

"But surely that message on the blotter— If you knew that last night, you could have—"

"I'm so damned cocksure. It could have meant that too, couldn't it? And maybe it did at that. I still don't think so, but here's this fact for us. Oh, I'm off to a honey of a start, I am."

"Come, sir," Rand smiled. "Where's your blithe Irish self-confidence now?"

Fergus was silent as he executed a tricky left turn through traffic.

Then he spoke slowly. "Look," he said. "I'm going to let down my hair. I don't know why, but you seem a hell of a swell guy, Colonel, and it's easy to talk to you. You think I'm brash and conceited and cocky, don't you?"

"No," Rand said thoughtfully. "I think you're a rather sensitive young man who's been frightened by life into a spectacular performance."

"The worst of that is, sir, that I think you're right. There's a family tradition that there's bardic blood in the O'Breens. I don't know how true that is; but if there is, it came out in me. I used to want to be a poet; I still turn out some God-awful tripe for my own pleasure, but you're the first person who's ever known it. I took a hell of a ribbing for a while, and then I got the feeling of, 'Well, I'll show them.' I was too light for football, but I was, to speak with characteristic modesty, *the* basketball sensation that Loyola has ever known. People began to play up to me, and I took it in my stride. I put on this cocky act for the hell of it, and found it was the perfect bulletproof vest. But they're making better bullets now. . . ."

His voice sank. Rand was not quite sure what those better bullets might be, but he had a shrewd idea.

"You see, sir," Fergus went on, "I've got the fine Gaelic capacity for getting low as all hell; and I've got to keep myself high as heaven the rest of the time to make up for it. Maureen got roped into a psychology section at her club once and began Studying me with a capital S. She played around in her own quaint jargon and decided that I was quote an introspective extrovert with manic-depressive tendencies unquote. If that makes any sense, you're welcome to it. And that's that, Colonel. The hair-letting-down is over."

Rand's sense of duty had by now reasserted itself. "But Willowe?" he asked. "How about the police?"

"Don't worry. They'll be notified all right. That isn't my place. Remember: We don't know a thing about it."

As far as he himself was concerned, Rand thought, that was certainly true enough. He settled back in his seat and resolutely diverted his mind from Fergus' naïf self-analysis to the case before them. Willowe was gone. Then did that mean—? His enforced preoccupation with this problem blinded him even to the dangers of the peculiarly personal O'Breen style of driving.

The hotel was opposite Westlake Park. It was a vast, old place—quiet and a little dank. Rand didn't like the looks of the tenants in the lobby; they were mostly superannuated dowagers or arty young men. The hotel was in fact a haven of refuge, where the weary old and the ivory-towerish young alike sought refuge from the modern world.

"Have you got a Miss Sallice registered here?" Fergus asked the room clerk.

"How do you spell that? Let me see. . . . No, sir, I'm sorry. No one of that name here."

Fergus turned away puzzled. Rand snorted. "That's two of them gone! And you believed her little story? Yes, she'd be apt to run off and leave you her address! Why, at this very minute—"

At this very minute Camilla Sallice walked in the door of the hotel. A cabdriver followed with her suitcase. She stopped abruptly on seeing the two men, then hastened toward them.

"So you got here even before I could!" she exclaimed. "I am glad. I wanted to talk to you, and I couldn't—there. Just a moment till I register and then—"

"Register nothing." Fergus took her arm with polite authority. "We're going out in the park where it's a little more cheery and have a nice long talk. And then you'll be driving back to Garnett's with me. Here you are, Mac." He handed three bills to the driver and took up the suitcase. "That ought to cover it."

Camilla gently freed her arm. "I can at least pay my own bills, Mr. O'Breen."

"That goes on my expense account. I have to have some expenses, don't I? Come on."

The O'Breen vigor was even more noticeable in the open air. Swinging the suitcase lightly and whistling fantastic variations on his father's best-loved jig, he swept the other two unresisting into the park.

"Now, Miss Sallice," he began, pausing in front of a bench and waving her to sit down.

She looked about apprehensively and caught sight of a policeman strolling near by. "Please," she objected. "Not here. It's too—too public."

"As though a public place wasn't the surest secrecy for private conversations."

"No. I just can't. Let's go back to the hotel."

"That foul hole? Come on again."

He led her off once more. Rand followed, feeling somewhat like a highly astonished ocean liner carried along in the wake of a motorboat.

In two minutes the three of them were in the center of the pond which is called West Lake. Fergus had scorned the put-puts which were offered him and chosen a dilapidated rowboat. "You see," he explained, "rowing's the next best thing to pacing."

He rowed in good long smooth strokes. The lake was still and glistered in the bright winter sun. Blares of bad radio bands came from the miniature motorboats which scooted around them.

"Now," Fergus resumed, feathering the oars deftly. "Let's have it, Miss Sallice. We're alone enough here, the saints know. Now you can tell us why you've been hiding the fact that you're Kay's half-sister. Look out," he added; "these boats rock."

SEVENTEEN

CAMILLA SALLICE TELLS TWO SECRETS

Colonel Rand stared at the girl. The shot had gone home; there was no doubting that. "You mean," he spluttered impotently, "you're Garnett's daughter?"

She shook her dark head heavily. "No," she said. "Not Uncle Humphrey's—Alicia's."

The Colonel laid his hand gently on hers. It was hot and tense. "Alicia was married before—and I never knew it?"

Her deep voice was almost inaudible. "No, Colonel Rand. Not married."

He looked at her silently and tightened his clasp on her hand.

"I hate to tell you this . . . Theo," she faltered. (He understood now how she knew that name.) "But you do have a—sort of right to know. You remember—so many years ago—when you decided to—well, to be a gentleman and leave the field clear to Uncle Humphrey?"

Rand nodded. He knew words would choke him if he tried to speak.

"What you never knew," she went on, "was that he did the same thing. He left Mother then too. She didn't understand. It hurt her. Both of you. . . . She—she went a little wild for a while. She never told me who my father was. Whoever it was, he deserted her; she never saw him again after he knew I was going to be born. Her family took me away and put me in an orphanage. When Uncle Humphrey came back and proposed to her, of course they tried to keep me a secret. And while Mother was on her honeymoon, they had me moved to another place. They hated me; I was a blot on the family. And Mother never knew where I was."

The whole story was pouring out in soft low tones, scarcely to be heard above the blasts of the radios, but rapidly and forcefully as though it did her good to be rid of her secret at last. Rand patted her taut hand. "Go on."

"I ran away from the orphanage. I had a frightful life for a while. . . . But I'll spare you all that. Then, when I was over eighteen and I knew they couldn't make me go back any more, I went to the orphanage to find out who my people were. Then I went to Mother's home town. I slung hash there for a while—me, the granddaughter of the respectable Willowes—and I found out enough to know that my grandparents weren't the kind of people I could go to see. But I did learn Uncle Humphrey's address in Washington, and I wrote to Mother. They were just leaving for California. I saw her in one stolen visit and oh—she was dear."

Rand blew his nose viciously. "She was indeed, my child."

"But she didn't ever dare tell Uncle Humphrey about me; she loved him, but she was afraid of him too. She used to write to me all the time and talk to me about everything—that's how I knew about Theo and how much he meant to her. And she sent me money, but it wasn't always enough. And anyhow I'd started off wrong; it wasn't so easy to stop. Then I didn't get any more letters from her. And one day a man in the dive asked for me and said he was Humphrey Garnett.

"I was scared. I didn't know what he wanted. Then it seemed he'd found my letters to Mother after her death, and he'd traced me down. He'd learned from those letters what he'd never suspected—that sometimes he was too harsh with Mother. And he wanted to make it up to her through me. He did, and I loved him for it." Her story was finished, and the tears she had struggled so hard to keep back now overpowered her. Rand tried clumsily to console her; she was part of Alicia.

Fergus rested on his oars. "Thank you, Miss Sallice." His natural brashness sounded a bit dimmed. "I'm sorry as hell to have caused you this pain; but you can see that we have to know everything." He paused a moment. "But look here. Isn't anybody going to say, 'But how on earth did you know that?'"

Camilla smiled through her tears. "Dear Mr. O'Breen. You're so self-effacing, aren't you?" Fergus had the grace to look uncomfortable. "All right. I was surprised, and it all came over me so I couldn't even think. But how on earth *did* you know?"

"Thanks. It's no earthly use being a detective unless you can explain how good you are. I simply put together four things: The quarrel over your mother, Colonel Rand's reticence about the name 'Theo,' the sudden change in Arthur Willowe's attitude toward you, and the fact that once upon a time I took botany."

"Botany?" Rand echoed.

"The willow is of the genus *Salix*. When a mysterious girl with a phony-sounding name like Sallice is tangled up with a family named Willowe, it looks like more than a coincidence."

"You are clever, Mr. O'Breen. I changed my name because it sounded better in night clubs—they like things a little phony—and besides they always called me 'Willowe' at the orphanage until I was sick of the sound of it."

Fergus was rowing hard again. "I suppose all this is what you told Arthur Willowe last night?"

"Yes."

"When did you see him last?"

"Then."

"You didn't see him this morning?"

"No. I told him last night that I was leaving. I didn't get up this morning until just before you saw me. I knew he'd be taking his nap by then, so I didn't say good-by."

"Right. And now, what's all this Hector Prynne business?"

Camilla Sallice frowned. (It was an attractive frown, Rand thought. Everything about her seemed more attractive since he had learned the truth. It was partly the association with Alicia which transfigured her in his eyes; but it seemed too as though her somber, almost sinister quality had been purged by her confession.) "I—I don't think I ought to tell you that, Mr. O'Breen. I know I shouldn't like it if Mr. Willowe—if Uncle Arthur, I suppose I can say now, were to tell you my secret without my permission."

"But look, Miss Sallice. It's something we've got to know."

"Then why not ask him?"

Fergus feathered the oars again, which seemed to fascinate a swan drifting by. "Let me assure you, there are grave reasons why we cannot ask him."

Rand looked as perplexed as the swan. He regarded Camilla closely. The sun was bright and warm, but she shuddered. "Oh," she gasped. "Then he did do it!"

"He did kill Garnett, you mean?"

"No. Of course not. That's foolish. He couldn't have, not after the way he— Unless . . . " She grew less confident and hesitated a little. "He could have been just—just playing with me last night, couldn't he? The note and everything—it could have been all a story to fool me so I wouldn't tell it to the police."

"Tell what to the police?"

"What I thought last night—what I wouldn't tell you—what I thought you had come here to ask me until we began talking about—about me."

"You mean this notion you had of a possible motive?"

She nodded reluctantly. "Yes. It struck me all of a sudden last night. That's why I had to talk to Uncle Arthur and tell him all about me. I thought if that was true he'd show it when he learned the real truth and saw how terribly wrong he'd been. And now you—"

"How did he take your story?"

"He—he did seem confused by it. And then very sorry. But he was so nice. I thought then that I understood him, poor dear helpless old man that he is. But do you really think—"

"Just what are you driving at, Miss Sallice?"

"Why, that he must have thought that I was—that I'd taken Alicia's place with Uncle Humphrey. Bodily, I mean. He loved her so much; he would have been frightfully jealous. He and Uncle Humphrey hated each other anyway. That could have been enough to—" She halted. A direct accusation of murder was apparently more than she could bring herself to utter.

Fergus pursued his advantage. "Then you can see how very important it is for us to know everything we can about him. So tell us—why did he say, 'I am Hector Prynne'?"

Camilla laughed nervously. "But that's so silly. It can't have anything to do with—with anything."

"Tell us anyway," Rand urged, still somewhat puzzled by this whole Willowe situation. If the man had planned to incriminate Vinton for some strange reason, why should he flee now when his planted suspect was safely under arrest?

"I think it was just that he wanted to show his confidence in me—give secret for secret. You understand, don't you? So since he knew who I really was, he went on and told me who he was. But what difference can that possibly make?"

Fergus was rowing so eagerly that he just missed ramming a tiny island. "Go on."

"Well, you see, Uncle Humphrey wasn't very generous to Arthur about money. Not that there was any reason why he should be—Uncle Arthur didn't feel any resentment about that. But he used to want money to give to Mother occasionally—he didn't know that it was to send to me, but he trusted her in anything. He was too old to get a job, he'd failed in business, and he didn't know how to get money. So he tried writing."

"I've known guys who did that," Fergus observed. "Six months, and they were generally glad to get a job in a service station."

"He tried everything, writing away secretly in his room. He couldn't sell anything to what he called 'the slicks,' so he tried the pulp magazines. He wrote detective stories and horror stories and sport stories—and I don't think he'd ever seen a football game or a prize fight in his life—and they all came back promptly. Then he finally clicked in the off-color magazines—you know, things like *Naughty Nights* and *Risky Revels*. He went on and did some sexy novels for rental libraries. I remember I read one once; it was really shocking."

"He must have had great faith in his imagination," Rand grunted.

"He's sold quite a few things, and they've done well; but he's never dared tell anyone. He did want to tell Uncle Humphrey just to prove that he could do something; but he was afraid that that sort of thing might seem worse than not being able to do anything at all. So that was his secret."

"And he wrote under the name of Hector Prynne?"

"Yes. He sort of twisted that out of *The Scarlet Letter;* I think the idea amused him."

"Did Mr. Garnett ever learn about this?"

"No."

"How can you be so sure?"

"You know what Uncle Humphrey was like. If he ever had found out, he'd have been sure to taunt the poor old man about it. The chance would have been too good to waste."

"Did anyone else know?"

"Uncle Arthur said I was the first person he'd ever told; but Richard Vinton had guessed it. He found a page that had blown off the balcony; it had the Hector Prynne name on it, and he recognized it."

"When was this?"

"The day before yesterday, I think."

"Nobody else?"

"He used to get his Hector Prynne mail at a post-office box. There wasn't any way anyone could know."

"Then presumably nobody knew about it when that telegram was sent. . . . But to go back a bit—if you didn't mean Garnett's murder, what did you mean when you said, 'Then he did do it!'?"

Camilla paused. "I don't know now if this was really true or not. It might have been just a trick. . . . You see, he seemed so glad to know who I was. It was like having a part of Alicia that wasn't Uncle Humphrey's at all. He'd always felt he could never quite be close to Kay, because she was a Garnett; but I was different. It made him very happy, and he said he'd changed his mind."

Rand's head was throbbing again. The sun on the water was too bright; it was hard for him to follow this confused unfolding of secrets within secrets. "Changed his mind about what?"

"About—" She hesitated.

"About suicide, you mean?" Fergus prompted her.

"How on earth did you know?" This time she said it quite uncued.

"I read part of his note on the blotting paper, and besides I saw the ash tray. Old gag, the blotting paper. The Colonel here thought it was a confession of Garnett's murder; I thought it was his morbid remorse for having accidentally killed your mother. That ties in with his fear of Garnett. He was going to escape remorse and fear at once, and he had the note all ready. Right?"

"Yes. . . ."

"How was he going to do it?"

"He'd slipped some poison out of the laboratory—I don't know what, but he said it was quick and didn't hurt much. Then, when he felt—I can't make it clear, it was all so strange—when he felt that I almost *was* Alicia and forgave him in her name, he tore up the note and put it in an ash tray and shook out the poison on it—it was a powder—and set a match to the whole thing. It made a smoke almost like incense. . . ."

It was twisted, Rand thought, and yet somehow sacred. He could see the poor old man, shaken with his tragic devotion to his dead sister, receiving what was truly a sacrament of absolution from her child. In his blunt way, he could understand it. To the three men who had loved her, Alicia Willowe had meant something beyond life.

These thoughts were going too deep. Rand assumed as stiff a military posture as the rowboat would allow, delivered a too-casual "harrumph," and groped for a cigar.

"Fine," Fergus was saying. "It all works out." He had been maneuvering the boat to the dock. Now with a long pull he sent it straight at the waiting attendant.

"One more item for the expense account," he said as he paid off. "Now come on."

"Please," Camilla faltered, "could I have a drink?"

Fergus bestowed a broad grin upon her. "There, Colonel, is what I term a proper wench. She doesn't look at you wistfully, she doesn't make obscure hints, she just up and says, 'Please, could I have a drink?'" He tucked her arm under his. "Of course you could, my sweet, and indeed you shall. My father would do nip-ups in his grave if he thought I failed you. Come on."

Across from the park, wedged between a five-and-ten and a drugstore, stood a small café, whose windows proclaimed MIXED DRINKS and REAL MEXICAN FOOD. The cashier tossed a friendly nod at Fergus; he was evidently not unknown there.

"As a private investigator," Fergus announced as they settled into a booth, "I'm unorthodox as hell. Mr. Latimer wouldn't approve of me one little bit. I rarely drink on a case at all, and never before lunch. But this seems as good a time as any to start changing habits. What's yours, Miss Sallice?"

"Whiskey."

"Irish?" Fergus asked hopefully.

"Rye."

"Damn. I've been trying for years to find somebody who drinks

Irish whiskey. Honor of the race. But I don't even like the stuff myself. Colonel?"

"Scotch and soda."

"Why did I ask? Now if we can find—" He looked around the place hopelessly. Night life here, Rand decided, must be something spectacular; nothing else could give it such a dank, deserted look in the morning. Bars have hangovers too; and this one looked as though it might go out any minute and drink up the lake opposite.

Conversation lapsed until the two ryes and the Scotch highball appeared. Then Fergus lifted his glass and said, "Here's . . . ! You can add whatever you please to that."

"To your success," said the Sallice. She sipped the straight whiskey slowly. "I wish I knew," she said, "just what is happening."

"So do I," Fergus grunted.

"I mean . . . Uncle Humphrey was very close to me. They all are, in a way. And a think like this . . . Damn!" She set down the glass abruptly. "I thought that would help. It does generally. But it isn't any use." Tears were trembling in her dark eyes.

"I've a staunch, manly shoulder," Fergus suggested diffidently.

Rand looked at them for a moment and then rose. "Excuse me," he mumbled, and walked off. That was one advantage of bars. You could always excuse yourself and nobody thought anything of it. He had become curiously fond of the weary loveliness of Camilla Sallice in the past half-hour; but now, he felt, a young comforter would be more satisfying.

He stayed away as long as his excuse could plausibly justify, and at last returned to the booth. Comfort was comfort, but it was now high time that action be resumed.

Camilla was powdering her nose. Her face bore that strange expression of teary contentment known only to women who have just had a good cry. "My turn, Colonel," she said with a half-smile, and vanished.

Smiling, Rand stood and regarded Fergus for a moment. Then wordlessly he drew forth his pocket handkerchief and handed it over. Automatically the young man made a dab toward his lips, halted, then walked deliberately over to the bar mirror.

"Colonel," he pronounced on his return, "you are a cockeyed, insinuating, and malicious liar. There's not a trace of make-up on me."

"No. But you were quite ready to believe there might be. That's all I wanted to know."

Fergus shrugged impenitently. "I know. Now I get a sermon on Attention to Duty and Sublimation of the Impulses of the Flesh, with maybe five Our Fathers and five Hail Marys to round it off. But you're not a celibate confessor, Colonel. Think of your own youth. Remember," his voice grew warm with burlesque melodrama, "remember when that exotic and seductive International Spy, Valda Varazzi, approached you in her quest for the Papers. Picture her dropping her leopard-skin coat and slinking up to you in that décolleté evening gown. She draws near to you. She reclines on your shoulder. Her lips turn up to yours. And what do you do? I ask you, sir, as a gentleman of honor, what do you do?"

The Colonel finished his neglected highball. "Young man," he said judiciously, "even under the circumstances which you describe, I should never prove guilty of betraying my country's trust. No matter how décolleté the gown nor how exotic the spy. I should never yield up the Papers. But," he added, "I should certainly enjoy myself while the going was good."

Fergus grinned. "Thanks. You're a good guy, Colonel. But I wish I hadn't brought up the Valda Varazzi theme. I like this gal. I like her a hell of a lot. And I wish I'd met her some other way, so that I wouldn't have to be thinking every minute, 'This is all very well, but what does she want to get out of me?'"

"She may feel the same way," Rand suggested.

"That helps a lot. Well, it's all just one more reason to get this over with promptly. 'If it were done when 'tis done—'"

"But can it be done quickly?"

"Of course it can. It's practically done now, since that rowboat session cleared up the loose ends. Don't you see—"

"Ready, Fergus." Camilla looked freshened and almost gay. (It had been 'Mr. O'Breen' ten minutes ago, the Colonel reflected.)

"Ready, my sweeting."

"Where are we going now?" Rand asked.

"Back to the house. Jackson ought to be there by now."

Camilla grew suddenly pale again. "You mean the detective lieutenant? Why should he be there?"

"Sorry. Minor slip. Forget I said it." He paused to pay the check at the cashier's desk, then turned back to them again. "No—on second thought you'd better know. It might lessen the shock.

"You see, Colonel, when I told you that Willowe was 'gone,' I was just using a popular euphemism. Arthur Willowe has been murdered."

EIGHTEEN

MAURICE WARRINER RUNS

For once Fergus O'Breen's companions outdid him in curiosity. Both Rand and Camilla shot question after question at him; but he brushed aside their desire for information and gestured them into the car.

"You'll know all about it soon enough, children." (Rand bristled at the epithet.) "The less you know, the less apt the Lieutenant is to find out what I've been doing on my own."

He was silent all the way out Wilshire. Camilla was still dazed from the shock of Willowe's death. She trembled a little, and Rand took her hand. Her subtle scent was strong and her body warm, at once firm and yielding, in the confinement of the roadster. Rand was glad he was old; that enabled him to feel this simple paternal tenderness. But he couldn't help wondering how her tantalizing proximity affected the young Irishman.

Fergus spoke once as they turned on to Vermont. "There's one possible flaw." He seemed to be thinking aloud. "Warriner said something about the French pack having had other names for its court cards before this current official series. And I was so excited about Hector that I forgot to ask him more questions. If I'm wrong there and that card does mean something else . . . God knows what an intricate mind like that might conceive . . . I suppose I might get it out of one of Garnett's books; but still I wish Warriner would drop around again."

It was then that Rand recalled his talk with the curator during his stroll on the past evening. So much had happened since then that the interview had not recurred to his mind. "Warriner has his own theory about the murder," he said.

"So? He didn't say anything to me. When did you see him?"

Rand explained and told of their talk. "He's betting on Will Harding for your murderer," he concluded.

"Is he indeed?" And Fergus said nothing more for many blocks.

They were just turning off Los Feliz Boulevard when they saw him. Fergus drew the car swiftly to the curb. "Now's our chance. I'll check this one point, just to make dead sure, and then . . . " He leaped out of the car and started toward the retreating figure of the old curator.

Rand stared at the man's back. Something went *click!* in the recesses of his mind, and without even a premonitory "harrumph" he found himself shouting "Dalrymple!"

Fergus had almost caught up with Warriner when suddenly the old man halted abruptly. He turned and glared at the young detective as though he were the Angel with the Fiery Sword. Then he began to run.

Rand could hear Fergus' laugh—a mixture of amusement and wonder. Then he saw the young man set out after the old with long, easy strides. "Come on," the Colonel said sharply to the girl at his side. He opened the car door for her. She followed, puzzled.

Warriner was displaying an ability striking for his age. His shoulders were straight now, and he looked thinner than ever. He was running at a good pace, and Fergus seemed worried. It just wasn't right that a young man in his condition couldn't keep up with a doddering, snuff-taking antiquarian.

Without a word, the scene had suddenly become something earnest and deadly. It involved far more than the early names of the court cards in the French deck. Rand automatically felt for his service revolver, and deeply regretted its absence. To the occasional passer-by who turned a bemused head, there was only something grotesque about these two thin figures chasing each other down the street; but Rand felt that there was a sinister current running deep beneath this almost Keystone chase.

He and the Sallice girl were following as fast as they could; but in spite of Rand's well-preserved vigor, his running days were over, and even this fast-paced walk made his head throb anew. The two men turned a corner, and their followers lost them for a moment.

Camilla rounded the corner first. She turned back and stared at Rand. "They—they're gone."

Rand glanced about him quickly. Halfway up the block was an undeveloped lot, covered with close-growing trees. "There," he said. "Come on. He never goes armed. You needn't worry. There's no danger."

She looked at him uncomprehendingly, but followed without a question.

There was the sound of a furious scuffle among the trees—a thrashing of bodies and a dry crushing of leaves. Then the sounds ceased for a moment, and there came a sharp groan of pain. Camilla cried out.

"Come on," Rand said again gruffly. He wanted to think of words, but commands were more in his line. This time Camilla needed no urging. She dashed toward the clump of trees. Rand prayed that he was right about the man's habits. They never change.

Warriner lay on the ground at the foot of a tall eucalyptus. He wasn't moving. Fergus sat beside him, doing his best to look chipper while lines of anguish twisted his white face.

"The damned bastard fouled me," he muttered. "Sorry for the expression, Camilla—that must be what they mean by foul language. Sorry for the pun too—that's even worse. But I don't much like this sort of fighting."

Warriner stirred. At that the Colonel, with military efficiency, leaned over him and proceeded to shake him into some sort of consciousness. The old man's body was lithe and hard—not at all the dry mass of skin and bones you might have expected from his appearance; it was small wonder, from the feel of him, that he had downed even that ex-basketball star, Fergus O'Breen.

As the Colonel rose from his ministrations, his eyes caught the glitter of enamel on the ground. On an impulse he bent down again, slipped the small box into his pocket, and straightened up.

Fergus was glaring down at the curator. "What the hell did you get so excited about? Think I was going to arrest you for the murder? In the first place, I can't arrest anybody. In the second, you never even gave me a chance to speak. All I wanted from you was some dope on the old French pack."

Warriner's intelligence seemed to be coming back slowly. He sat up, rubbing his head in a manner which brought painful memories of the past night to Colonel Rand. "Gentlemen," he said, "I fear that you have discovered my shame."

"What do you mean?"

"I, sirs, am a victim. I cannot always be held responsible for my actions."

"You mean you're nuts?"

"No. I—I mean that I have required an artificial stimulus to pursue my work. You will recall perchance those delightful lines of the silver-tongued John Day—

Gold, music, wine, tobacco, and good cheer
Make poets soar aloft and sing out clear.

That may suffice for poets; they are an unaccountable tribe. But for myself I have found gold—what little I have ever possessed—music, wine, tobacco, and good cheer quite insufficient to keep myself singing clear. I needed more."

Fergus snorted. "So you took up snuff. So what?"

"Not snuff, sir; but my snuffbox."

Camilla Sallice, possibly because of her varied past life, was the first of them to understand him. "You mean, you've been taking—"

"I believe, madam, that the colloquial word is *dope*. It has been a help— No, those words are too mild; it has made life worth living. And the eccentric habits of an old gentleman make it seem plausible that I should bring out my enameled death in the most proper gatherings. But occasionally I find myself driven, almost without my own knowledge, to strange actions. I fear that you surprised me in one of my . . . ah, less rational moods. It took the staunch trunk of this eucalyptus to drive some sense back into my poor head."

Fergus frowned and viciously uprooted an innocent tuft of grass. "Which makes this," he announced, "beyond any doubt the Goddamnedest first murder case that any promising young detective ever tackled. It's got everything in it but a sinister Oriental, and I expect him to open the door when we get back to the house."

"We?"

"Come along, Mr. Warriner. I'll keep your secret dark; but I hope to the saints you'll never tear loose on me again, in your own quaint irresponsible way. God knows what will become of the future of the O'Breens if much more of this happens."

"I am not sure that I can accompany you, young man—"

"I think you'd better," Rand said with quiet authority.

It worked. He was by no means so out of practice at commanding as he had thought.

"About these cards," Fergus resumed as they started back to the car. "We'll just skip all that's happened since I thought of them. But you said that the jack of diamonds used to have several other names beside Hector. What were they?"

Warriner reflected. "Let me see . . . I can recall a very early French deck, around 1490, in which the knave of diamonds—accompanied there by a dog—is known as *Rolant*. I believe he was also called *Roger,* sometimes the *Valet de la Chasse*—he occasionally bore a hunting horn—and some curious—ah, yes, *Capitan Fily*. Then there is an eighteenth century English pack in which he is known as *Jack Sheppard*. As you may have noticed, that particular knave is a card often associated with crime and, if I may be pardoned the pun, knavery; the name of the great highwayman is not surprising, nor, indeed, is its connection with this shocking case."

Fergus had not heeded the last part of this learned discourse. He was murmuring to himself, "Rolant . . . Roger . . . Fily . . . Jack Sheppard . . . No, I *must* be right. . . ."

It was then that it happened. The curator's long thin leg moved with the rapid vigor of a whip. It seemed almost to curl as it snapped between Fergus' ankles. The young Irishman went down in a sideways plunge which brought Camilla toppling over him. Rand had no time to think of their unofficial prisoner. A car was speeding down the street headed straight for the two tumbled forms.

Fergus was on his feet almost at once, but the fall must have stunned the girl. Between them they half helped her, half dragged her to the curb. She clung to Fergus dazedly.

But the detective's mind was not on clinging brunettes. "The keys," he groaned. "I left them in the car. . . ."

The automobile which had threatened them had now drawn up sharply beside them with agonized brakes. The driver thrust out a red-veined face coming to a climax in a glowing cigar and growled, "What goes on here? Playing games?"

"Yeah," said Fergus, looking mournfully after the bright yellow roadster. "And we lost."

Fifteen minutes later they neared the Garnett house. Resolute trudging had left them tired and hot and not in the most peaceable of tempers.

"At least," Camilla observed after a long silence, "you can row a boat."

"I know. I know. Don't rub it in. I've slipped up badly, but how could I help it? God knows there's enough going on without an academical hophead to ball things up a little more."

"So you think that's what he is?" The girl sounded dubiously reflective.

"Why not?"

"I don't know. I've been around. I've run into funny customers in my time—"

"Customers is right." Rand noticed resentment in the tone of the young man who had so calmly accepted Camilla's story of her career only that morning.

"Don't start that," she snapped back. "My foul past is no secret from you, my fine broth. But I've known hopheads—"

"You can't just say broth."

"And why not?"

"You have to say broth of a something."

"All right. My fine broth of a Hawkshaw—how does that sound to you, my mad meddler?"

"I am but mad north-northwest," Fergus murmured. "When the wind is southerly I know a hand from a Hawkshaw."

Camilla stopped very deliberately, bent over a choice garden plot by the sidewalk, and scooped up a handful of nice soft soil. There was no doubt of her intentions; that polo shirt was so yellow.

Rand had been smoking quietly and wishing that he were not an elderly gentleman of military caste who wore a coat on all occasions. Now he summoned authority back to his voice and spoke.

"I know," he said, "that our tempers have been grievously ruffled by the heat and by the walk and by our singular misadventure; but need we be so childish?"

"After a pun like that . . ." Camilla began; but she thought better of it and dropped the soil.

"And I liked that car," Fergus added wistfully. "It's served me faithfully, man and boy...."

"That worry at least need no longer concern you, O'Breen," and Colonel Rand gestured ahead of them.

There, in front of the Garnett house, stood the empty O'Breen roadster.

NINETEEN

LIEUTENANT JACKSON ACCEPTS AN ALLY

It was Rand's old friend Number One who greeted them at the door. Camilla shivered and seemed to grow small as she looked at the uniform, and even Fergus was a bit subdued.

"Look," he said. "Has a man named Warriner come in here—a tall, thin, stooped old man?"

Number One looked down on him scornfully. "I don't see old men with beards when I'm on duty; but if your name's O'Breen, you're coming in here to see the Lieutenant, and right away too. No, not you!" He waved the others aside.

"That's all right, Colonel," said Fergus with calm assurance. "I'm certain the Lieutenant wants to see you too. Come right along. See you later, Camilla—and thank you." His voice was sincere.

Rand looked back as they went down the hall. Camilla Sallice's spurt of temper had deserted her; she now seemed terribly alone and forlorn in this house of death. With pity for her in his heart, he turned to see Number One glaring at him. "Well, at least you're sober this time," the policeman said.

Jackson was in the study again. He was alone and badly worried. He looked up as the men entered and snapped, "You're O'Breen?"

"Lieutenant, I am The O'Breen."

Jackson disregarded the correction. "All right. Now we'll get somewhere."

Fergus smiled. "Anything you say, Lieutenant."

"Where have you been?"

"The Sallice girl moved out this morning. I remembered some questions I had to ask her, so I went and asked them. I persuaded her to come back here with me."

"How did you know where she'd gone? Nobody in this house seemed to have the least idea."

"I found a piece of paper beside the telephone with a number jotted on it in what looked like her hand-writing. I thought she might have been calling a hotel about reservations, so I checked it."

"And pocketed the paper just to make things easier for us?"

"How was I to know you'd be coming out here? Which reminds me, Lieutenant, that I still don't know what bring you here—unless it's revisiting the scene of the crime."

Jackson looked at him shrewdly. "I've heard of you, O'Breen—heard quite a bit, in fact. That was good work you did in that arson case, and I've heard rumors about the way you put a stop to Rita La Marr's blackmailer. I wish to God I knew just where you stood in this business—with us or against us."

Fergus was pacing at a relatively temperate rate—apparently a partial concession to the presence of authority. "I'll be frank with you. I think you picked the wrong man when you arrested Vinton, and I'm trying to prove him innocent; maybe you'll call that working against you. But on the other hand, I'm trying to find the real murderer; and the saints know that ought to be working with you. You can call it either way. It might be simplest to flip a coin."

The Lieutenant leaned back. "All right. I'll be frank too. Supposing I tell you we're together on both counts."

Colonel Rand started. "On both?"

"Yes, Colonel. Vinton was released on bail this morning. He's here in the house now—got here just after we did. And I can tell you in confidence that there's very little danger of the charges being pressed unless we can learn something new and startling. That fingerprint business alone would give a good defense attorney—and Max Farrington is that—one honey of a chance to poke holes in our case. It's too risky."

Fergus paused in mid-stride. "All right. If we're working together, why not tell us just what's happened to bring you here?"

Jackson regarded him for a long minute. "I wish I knew," he said slowly, "whether I needed to tell you this. But here goes. Arthur Willowe has been murdered."

For Rand's taste, Fergus' reaction of surprise was just a trifle overplayed. The Colonel himself made no attempt at bluffing; Jackson's sharp eyes weren't on him.

"Yes, Mr. O'Breen, murdered."

"But how, Lieutenant? When?"

"As you probably know, Willowe took a nap every day at eleven o'clock on the cot on his balcony. That's where Miss Garnett found him. He used to sleep in the room itself; that cot was used only by him and only for these morning naps. It seems an odd arrangement, but nothing surprises me any more in this household. Anyway, the point is, everybody knew about this habit of his. While he was sleeping there this morning, somebody stuck a needle dipped in curare into the back of his neck."

"Just a minute, Lieutenant. Are you certain it was curare?"

"I admit that's hard to analyze. But it was one of the alkaloid poisons, and curare is the commonest. We'll have a definite report later."

"And was there curare—or any of the other alkaloids—in Garnett's laboratory?"

The Lieutenant groaned. "There was everything in that laboratory, O'Breen. I never saw such a hellish collection. And in a way this second death is my own fault. I should have sealed up that laboratory yesterday. But Harding insisted that he had some work to do, and I let him go ahead."

"You really think sealing it would have done any good?"

"Of course." Jackson looked suspicious. "What do you mean?"

"Nothing. Just that the murderer might have laid in his stock in advance. But as long as we're being frank, Lieutenant, do you know who killed Willowe?"

"I'm hanged if I even know why he was killed, let alone who did it. Unless, of course, he knew something damning about Garnett's death. He seems to have been the most inoffensively useless man I've ever encountered. And who was in the house? His niece, who seems devoted to him; the laboratory assistant, who had nothing at all to do with him; the cook, who's out of the question; and you two." He checked himself. "When did Miss Sallice leave?"

"A little after eleven."

"And Miss Sallice then, possibly. Though the Lord knows where she comes in. It looks as though this death must tie in in some way with Garnett's, but still—"

"And Vinton?" Rand asked.

"Vinton's accounted for. He left the jail with his lawyer, went straight on to Farrington's office, and got out here after we did. Even if Farrington's pulling a fake alibi for him, which isn't likely, the time element lets him out. He couldn't possibly have got here before Miss Garnett's call came through to us."

"One more frank question, Lieutenant." Fergus paused dramatically. "Were you ever center on the U.S.C. basketball team?"

Jackson jerked back in amazement, then let out a lusty shout. "Good God! Fergus O'Breen, the Fighting Forward—the man who made thirteen baskets in the U.S.C.-Loyola game!"

Fergus stretched out his hand. "Hiya, Andy!"

For a moment Rand was afraid the conference was going to turn into a contest of sporting memories. He was relieved to find that he was wrong. Both men were still deeply concerned with the business in hand.

"The personal touch helps," Jackson grinned. "I'd just about resolved to pool information with you anyway; and now that I remember the time you were practically a one-man team and licked the living be-jesus out of us, that decides me. Which wouldn't make any sense officially, but that's the way it works. Now get me straight, Fergus. I want you to play ball with me."

"OK by me, Andy."

"We've each got an advantage. I have the force of authority and the efficiency of routine behind me. You're on more or less of a personal footing with all these people and have a confidential in. Between us, we ought to get some place. Now if we could—"

Fergus caught his sideways glance. "Brush up on your mystery novels, Andy. What's a detective without a faithful Watson? Colonel Rand's been in on this with me from the start. He might as well stay on."

Jackson turned to Rand. "I must admit, Colonel, that I took the trouble of checking your arrival at the airport. Since that definitely eliminates you as a possible suspect, why then, if you're interested in sitting in on our conference—"

"I most assuredly am." Rand's head was worse, and he knew he presented an absurd figure with his bandage; but he was not going to miss a conference which might prove so vital to Kay—and to the memory of Alicia.

"Very well. Now perhaps the first point I ought to mention—you see I really am trusting you, Fergus, and going ahead with our own information first—is the will. Mr. Harding tells me that he showed you the carbon copy. If you've been reasoning from that, forget it. The thing's all wrong. The true terms of the final will—"

A knock on the door broke into the Lieutenant's speech. He turned and called "Come in."

This was a policeman Rand hadn't seen before. "We're having trouble, Lieutenant," he explained. "One of 'em's up and got plastered, and he's raising merry hell. Wants to talk to you right away, and says he'll tear the place down if he can't. What do we do with him?"

Before Jackson could answer, the problem solved itself. There was the noise of a hearty scuffle outside in the hall, and two men burst into the room. The first was Number One, red-faced and furious. The other, the vigorous belligerent drunk, was the mild Will Harding.

TWENTY

WILL HARDING IS SPECTACULAR

Even before the young assistant spoke, it was clear to Rand that he was very drunk indeed. This came as a surprise; he had seemed such an abnormally respectable young man—not even a smoker, much less an early afternoon drunkard. The drinks had given him strength; the way he dragged the husky Number One around with him showed that.

The two men spoke at once, Harding in drunken indignation and Number One in apology for disturbing his superior.

"Let him go, Hinkle," Jackson said sharply. "As long as he got in here, we might as well hear what he has to say for himself. Well, what's it all about, Harding?"

Released from the official grasp, Harding subsided abruptly. "It doesn't marrer," he mumbled thickly. "There isn't a Goddamn thing that marrers any more."

"Come on. Out with it. You forced your way in here to tell me something. What is it?"

Harding leered with bacchic cunning. "You wouldn't be underested."

"Underested?"

He shook his head slowly. "You wouldn't interstand."

Fergus laughed. "Go on, Andy. He wants to be coaxed."

"I'll coax him all right enough. Would you sooner have the boys take you outside and talk it over?" Jackson demanded abruptly. Number One looked as though the idea appealed to him.

Harding shook his finger waggishly. "Ah-ah, Lieutenant! That's naughty. That's the third degree, that's what that's what that is. The courts don't like that. No-o-o-o-o! But you're a nice fellow. I'll tell you. Only the trouble is, you like him."

"Like who?"

Drinking had brought out fresh aspects of Harding only dimly hinted at by his limericks of the day before. He now launched forth into a frank description of Richard Vinton couched in terms which would have made Jeeter Lester blush. It was not, perhaps, an edifying spectacle; but it somehow increased Rand's respect for the young man. He wasn't just milk and water after all; there was guts to him.

He paused finally, and Fergus broke into loud applause. The display, Rand admitted, deserved it.

But Jackson wanted something more specific. "Well, what about Vinton?"

"I'll tell you wharrabout Vinton. You turned him loose again, didn't you? You think he's a nice sweet airy-fairy Good Lillle Boy, don't you? Christ! Well, I'll tell you wharrabout Vinton! I'll—" He pulled a folded newspaper out of his pocket and stood for a long moment brandishing it in the air. He looked at once terribly dramatic and painfully ludicrous. Then in an instant all his force seemed to desert him. "Aw, the hell with it," he muttered, dropped the newspaper on the floor, and left the room, followed by the still badly perplexed Number One and his unidentified companion in uniform.

"Picturesque interlude," Fergus observed. "Now just what do you think that means?"

"Simple enough," Rand said. "He's jealous of Vinton. Seeing him and Kay together again got on his nerves. So he got stinking drunk and made a damned fool of himself. It needn't mean any more than that."

But Jackson had picked up the newspaper and was studying it. "It's this morning's paper," he said, "and folded to the theatrical section. What that could—Just a minute. Here's a paragraph marked." He read slowly.

> The creditors of what screen juvenile are rejoicing at his arrest on suspicion of murder, because the publicity will mean the formerly very doubtful renewal of his contract.

Fergus whistled. "I thought our little Richard was big time."

"You never can tell. Once you start slipping, you slip fast. This is a shrewd point; if he's cleared of all blame and scandal, the publicity should make him an invaluable property to his studio. A while ago this extra motive, if you can call it that, might have helped us; now it's just a nuisance. The fingerprints clear him on Garnett, and he couldn't possibly have killed Willowe."

"But it does show," Rand put in, "that Harding is exceedingly anxious to incriminate him."

"Yes . . . "

"But to get back to the facts of death," Fergus broke in. "Look, Andy. You were going to tell us about the will."

"Yes. As I was starting to say, there were two codicils. One was made two years ago—just after Alicia Garnett's death in the accident. It canceled the legacy to Arthur Willowe, and turned that ten thousand dollars over to Will Harding for purposes of research."

"And the other?"

"That was made about a year ago. It leaves twenty thousand

dollars in a trust fund to Camilla Sallice, on the condition that she goes on with her singing studies."

"Anything else to tell us?"

"Minor routine items. There isn't any doubt, for instance, that the poison was administered to Garnett in that highball. We analyzed the few drops left in the glass. And about that glass—there are smudges, probably glove marks, over Vinton's fingerprints, which was to be expected. And those fingerprints—which is another thing that made us suspicious of a frame—are exceptionally clear—much more so than you'd expect from a casual handling—even show a portion of the palm which we can identify by the pore markings."

"Anything more on Willowe's death?"

"We've identified the needle roughly. It's the same as several that are stuck in a pincushion on Miss Garnett's dressing table. I suppose anybody could have slipped into her room and taken it. One needle out of six or eight wouldn't be missed."

"Of course. All pretty inconclusive, isn't it?"

Jackson shrugged. "So far, I admit. But remember we're still working. I won't say the Los Angeles police always Get Their Man, but we don't do so badly. Now let's hear what you've found out."

Rand leaned back and watched the smoke of his cigar while Fergus told the results of their endeavors—Garnett's secret researches, Harding's violent pacifism, Willowe's false premonition, Warriner's theories and eccentricities, the secret of Camilla Sallice, and the possible double meaning of Hector.

Lieutenant Jackson listened with sharp interest. "So," he observed as Fergus paused. "You've done good work. Is that all?"

Fergus nodded. "That's all. Now have you any questions to ask—of me or anybody else—before I go on to explain who was the murderer?"

Jackson frowned. "Aren't you going a little fast, Fergus? Or is this one of the famous O'Breen ribs?"

"I know. You think I'm bluffing. Well, I'm not. I'm perfectly ready to explain the whole thing right here and now. But look. You know me, and you know I'm young and Irish. That means I'm theatrical. So how's about helping me out?"

"How so—helping you out?"

"Call this gang together and let me expound my solution—with all the trimmings and cranberry sauce. You know: Tent 'em to the quick; if they but blench, I'll know my cause. Not that I need that, but it does make things picturesque."

The Lieutenant looked at him for a puzzled moment. Then he grinned. "All right, Fergus. It's a tomfool idea, and I've got a terrible fear that you might make an idiot of yourself. But go ahead, so long as it's understood that this is strictly unofficial."

"Thanks, Andy. For a minute I was afraid that you were going to go all stern and hardboiled on me."

But the Lieutenant looked stern enough as it was. "Wait a minute; let me get this off my chest first. Don't go getting any ideas in your cracked Irish pot that I'm one of these obliging police detectives out of stories that are only too too happy to sit back and stooge for the brilliant young investigator. I want to crack this case. I know your record and I think maybe you can help me, even if you do pick a damned queer way of going about it. But any funny business out of you, and you're going to wind up in the can, basketball or no basketball. And you might find some trouble in getting your license renewed. Understand me?"

"I get it."

"That's OK then. Now who do you want for this grand finale?"

"The whole kit and kaboodle." Fergus ticked them off on his lean fingers. "The three of us, of course. Kay. The Sallice chick, Harding, if we can sober him up. Vinton. Might as well drag in Farrington if we can get hold of him."

"He's here now. Came out with Vinton. Anybody else?"

"Warriner. And I think that about washes up the list. Complete cast of characters."

Complete minus two, Rand reflected. He wished intensely that those two might also be present; he would give a great deal to see how Humphrey Garnett's brilliantly intricate mind would cope with the macabre problem of his own death.

"Warriner?" Jackson repeated questioningly.

"The curator," Fergus added.

"Oh yes. He was here earlier on the night of Garnett's death, I remember. But he can't have had anything—"

"Just the same, I want him."

"What am I supposed to do? Send out a dragnet for him?"

Fergus looked as though he had stepped through a curtain which suddenly turned into a brick wall. "You mean he's not here?"

"Why should he be? He's out of the question in this investigation. We haven't—"

"I know your Cerberus at the door didn't see him, but I thought after all— I mean, my car—" He stopped abruptly. That story, he seemed to be thinking, mightn't help much to bolster his reputation with the Lieutenant. "I guess it's not really necessary," he said slowly. "Can you round up the others for me?"

"That's simple enough. They're all right here in the house."

"Fine."

"And where were you planning on holding your séance?"

"The sun porch. Light and freedom. Clear thinking. 'Daylight and champaign discovers not more.' And when an O'Breen quotes Shakespeare, Andy, that means, in classical language, that all hell is about to bust loose." His natural exuberance was recovering from the shock of Warriner's absence; but the frown was not quite gone from his forehead.

Rand puffed his cigar in quiet confusion. Like the Lieutenant, he feared that Fergus was being overconfident—that his impetuous Irish brilliance was leading him to a rash promise which he might find it difficult to fulfill. Surely on this contradictorily insufficient and oversufficient evidence, and immediately on top of the still unsolved Warriner fiasco . . .

"There's just one thing," Fergus was saying, "that bothers me. It isn't vital, I'm certain. It can't be; everything else hangs together too neatly. But I don't like loose ends."

"Neither do I," Jackson commented drily. "Neither does a jury."

"It isn't anything as important as that. It's just my endless curiosity. What I want to know is—who was in Garnett's laboratory last night. You've heard about that?"

"I have. And that's one of the things I was waiting to hear you explain."

Fergus paced softly. "At first I had it figured this way: Everything else in the case points to somebody inside this household; and here's one bit of evidence that says: Aha, an intruder from without! What does that suggest to you?"

"One of the people here trying to throw suspicion onto an outsider."

"And that's what I thought too. But there were only two men in this house at that time, and both of them are perfectly alibied—Willowe by Kay Garnett and Harding by me. And the Colonel swears it must have been a man. If I could solve that little point . . . "

Colonel Rand roused himself. "If that is all that is holding you back, O'Breen, I think that I might help you. Our unknown intruder was a gentleman named Roger Dalrymple."

"It's against all the rules," Fergus groaned in desperation. "A new character at this hour!"

Jackson was less esthetic and more practical. "But according to what I was told, sir, you claimed after the scuffle that you were unable to identify him?"

The Colonel went "harrumph" and made rather a show of lighting his cigar; he didn't care to receive the spotlight of attention like this. "I have had occasion," he announced, "to meet up with Mr. Dalrymple once or twice before in my military career, and I recall especially his individual manner of fighting, which was learned anywhere save on the playing fields of Eton. But despite the foul blow which I received in last night's struggle, I was not certain until today. Then it came to me in an instantaneous flash."

"But why?"

With a complete lack of theatrical affectation, Rand paused to knock the overlong ash from his cigar. "You see," he said, "you gentlemen know this individual as Maurice Warriner."

TWENTY-ONE

A ROOM IS SEALED

Colonel Rand disliked strained metaphors, but this one suggested itself to him with irresistible force: Fergus snatched the bit out of the Colonel's very mouth and ran full tilt away with it.

"Of course!" he cried. "You and I, Andy, are damned downright idiots, and our staunch military friend here is a sturdy Gibraltar of perspicacity." He paused for a moment, as though to contemplate the audacity of his own idiom, then plunged ahead. "It was all so damned obvious. The man was overplaying every minute. He was just too wildly eccentric to be credible. The snuff and the erudition and the quotations from the lesser Elizabethans—it all had to be a gag, a performance played just a couple of inches beyond the hilt. You can see him saying to himself, 'Now how can I create a vivid and eccentric character?' And then, by God, he went ahead and did it, and we swallowed it whole."

Jackson made an authoritative bid for quiet. "Speak for yourself, Fergus. You're entitled to call yourself an idiot as much as you please; but remember I never saw this man. I didn't have any chance to draw these startling deductions you feel that 'we' should have made. And now if you please, Colonel, I'd like to know just who this Dalrymple is, and how you finally recognized him."

"Roger Dalrymple," Rand said quietly, "is what a reader of sensational fiction might call an international spy—a free-lance secret agent. I have no means of knowing which foreign power commands his invaluable services at the moment; his loyalty has always belonged to the highest bidder. But I am certain that it was the secret of Humphrey Garnett's two gases, and that of the poison gas in particular, which he was seeking."

"Then all that rumpus in the laboratory," Fergus interrupted, "must have been just a ruse to draw Harding and me out of the study so he could get at the desk. What a break for us that Harding had those notes in his pocket all the time!"

"But I still don't see how you can be certain," Jackson objected. "If you failed to recognize him at the time—"

"When I think of his hands," Fergus groaned, "I could tear up my license. They were lithe and strong—far and away too young for the rest of his body. And how he would forget his stoop sometimes, and the way he insisted on Harding's guilt—you can see how it would have suited his plans to get the assistant out of the way."

"All those things bothered me," the Colonel said. "And then this afternoon I saw him in a good light from the rear. He was walking erect; and no matter how effective the rest of your getup is, you can't disguise a back short of a hump. Involuntarily I called out, 'Dalrymple!'"

"So that's what started it all," Fergus muttered.

"All what?"

Briefly the Colonel told of the pursuit of Dalrymple-Warriner, while Fergus looked duly abashed.

"But it was ingenious," the young Irishman said as the Colonel concluded the story. "That alibi about dope, I mean. Admitting to one vice to hide another—"

Wordlessly Colonel Rand drew the enameled snuff-box from his pocket and laid it on the desk, where the reaping skeleton grinned up at the Lieutenant.

"This his?" Jackson asked.

"I picked it up after this morning's scuffle."

Jackson opened the box and looked at its powdered contents. Gingerly he sniffed, then with infinite caution touched a minute pinch of the dust to his tongue. "This," he pronounced carefully, "is, as far as I can make out, the purest Copenhagen snuff."

Fergus swore with quiet fervor. "And all of us being so nice to the dear old man and respectfully asking his advice on technical card problems. . . . Though come to think of it, we can rely on what he said about such things. He must have boned up on that subject and damned well, too; his act worked with Garnett, and God knows he would have tripped him up if anything had sounded phony."

"This alters the whole case," Jackson said decisively. "With a known professional criminal at large, we can't be too careful. He may not realize as yet that he's been spotted, despite his recent scare; we might still catch him as Warriner. And if not, can you give me, Colonel, a description of Roger Dalrymple that I can send out?"

"One moment, Lieutenant." Rand hesitated. "If you do find him, what charges can you hold him on?"

Jackson paused. "That's right. You know his past record, but we don't have any direct evidence of his present subversive activities. It isn't as though he's succeeded in nabbing the plans he was after. We might have him on breaking and entering, though I don't know how well your identification would hold up under good cross-examination. At least we can detain him as a material witness; that'll cut off his activities for a while, and in the meantime something may turn up that will pin the murders on him—though God knows why he should want to get rid of Willowe."

The Colonel shook his head. "I know his nature from the past, Lieutenant. Roger Dalrymple never kills. His is the fouler treason which butchers our country's men by the thousand—never the simpler, cleaner crime which destroys but one."

"That's as may be, sir; but even professional criminals change their habits occasionally. There's no telling what circumstances may force them to do. Now if you'll give me that description—"

Fergus and Rand exerted their best efforts, but the task seemed hopeless. If the man was so ingenious at impersonation, it seemed in the highest degree unlikely that he could be found under any description which they might give. What bothered Rand most was the presence of the yellow roadster in front of the Garnett house. Dalrymple, on escaping from them, had driven directly here. And after that—?

Had he, Rand pondered, intended one last desperate attempt to secure the plans, only to abandon it when he noticed that the police had once more taken over the house? If so, why had he left the car? Was it a nose-thumbing gesture toward Fergus or simply a logical desire to get rid of an encumbrance that might be too easily traced? And where had he gone from here? The forgotten song of the World War began to course through Rand's attempts at reasoning: *Oh boy, oh joy, where do we go . . .*

"One more thing." Jackson set down the telephone, through which he had been issuing his orders for the search for Warriner-Dalrymple. "With a man like that on the loose, I'm going to do what should have been done two days ago. I'm going to seal up that laboratory. I locked it this morning with Garnett's key, but locks don't mean very much to a professional. This is going to be a thorough job, and if there's any tampering going on, we'll know about it in time to head off the consequences."

Fergus muttered something about stable doors; it was fortunate, Rand reflected, that Jackson seemed not to hear it.

Number One was dispatched to seal the windows from the outside, while the Lieutenant and his two new allies went down the long hall to the dead man's laboratory, which grew like a parasite around the rear of the house. As from a parasite, too, there issued from this room an evil power which was slowly draining the life of this household. To Rand, there was something foully wrong about poison. You couldn't fight it; there was no sense of combat. It was worse than a bullet in the back. He would be profoundly glad to see this laboratory of death sealed away for ever.

"I'll be damned," Jackson exclaimed.

The laboratory door, which he had carefully locked so recently, now stood wide open. Inside they could see Will Harding, puttering aimlessly about among rows of glass objects.

"Of course," the Lieutenant went on. "He must have his own key; I should have allowed for that. And in the state he's in, he might do anything. Harding!"

The assistant turned, a beaker in his hand and a nebulous smile on his face. Cautiously he wobbled toward the door. "Sh!" he said. "They're playing games. Nice games. Mating games. Mustn't peek!"

"Is somebody else in there?"

Harding answered with a nod and a grin.

"And who," Fergus demanded wonderingly, "picks a laboratory for mating games?"

"Molecules," said Harding gravely. The word seemed to have much more than its proper endowment of l's.

"Nobody else?"

Harding peered vaguely around the corner of the L-shaped room. "Notasoul," he announced in something under one syllable flat.

"Come on, then."

"Wherewegoin?"

But Jackson was in no mood to humor drunks. "Watch him," he said curtly; and Fergus and the Colonel resolutely watched the assistant while Jackson locked the door again and affixed sternly official strips of tape around its edges.

"There," said the Lieutenant. "Hinkle's tending to the windows, and we've got this damned deathtrap sealed up for good and all—until, of course, the estate takes over."

Fergus surveyed the forbidding door. "Just tell me one thing, Andy. Are you locking out or in?"

Jackson frowned. "What do you mean? This is just a piece of routine I should have seen to at the start. Confidentially, I'm getting careless in my old age—this could make trouble for me if the Captain decided to fasten on it. And that's one more reason why I've got to crack this case damned soon."

"All I mean is, Andy, that it reminds me of the story my father used to tell about the room with the four-poster. But I wish you luck of it."

Jackson had started back down the hall, but he turned now. "And just what the hell does that mean? Is Mr. Vance cryptically enlightening the slow official brain?" He took no trouble to conceal his irritation.

"Easy there, my bucko. All I mean is this: Come Hallowe'en, Dad used to sit by the fire, when we had one, and tell us stories; and the one we liked best, even though Maureen used to wake up howling later, went like this—Once there was a man who slept in a haunted room, with a big curtained four-poster bed. Before he went to sleep, he looked in all the cupboards and rapped on all the paneling and then he locked the door and pushed the dresser in front of it. Then as he stood there, thinking 'Now nothing can happen to me,' he heard a voice. It was thin and cracked and high, and it came from inside the four-poster, and it was saying, with great glee, 'Now we're locked in for the night!'"

It was a simple story, and Fergus told it simply; but Rand was not ashamed to feel his back hairs stiffen. It was its very simplicity, there in broad daylight in that ordinary hallway, that made it horrible.

For a moment Jackson stared at the door. Then he wheeled and burst out, "And so—"

"—so what?" Fergus finished for him. "So when you lock a door you never know whether you're locking in or out."

"Nuts," said Jackson resolutely. "Come on."

Throughout all this, Harding had stood teetering back and forth, balancing the beaker precariously in a quavering hand. He grinned down at it foolishly; but as the moments passed that grin strengthened and hardened. It was a forceful and a bitter grin now. Suddenly he looked up at the others and seemed for a moment startlingly sober.

"Gentlemen," he said, "I give you the innocence of Richard Vinton!" At a gulp he drained the contents of the beaker.

TWENTY-TWO

LIEUTENANT JACKSON CONSIDERS THE CASE CLOSED

He'll pull through all right," the hastily recalled police doctor assured them. "Tricky stuff, that bichloride of mercury. A small dose can kill you, and a large one may make you just deathly sick. It acts as an emetic—cuts off its own toxic effect."

"Can we talk to him?" Jackson asked.

"I'd go easy. He needs rest. I'm leaving a nurse with him; he'll see that everything's as it should be. You can ask questions if you must, but don't let the man get overexcited."

"Well," said Jackson after the doctor had left, "it looks as though we're going to clear things up without your big scene, Fergus. We've narrowed it down to two men, and it isn't hard to say which is the one. Of course we'll keep up the search for your Dalrymple, Colonel; but just the same I think the case will be over as soon as Harding is well enough for a thorough grilling."

"I have always been amazed," Rand mused, "by the extreme consideration of the State for the health of those whose lives it intends to take."

"Come now," Fergus objected. "You can't seriously think that Harding—"

"It's all obvious enough," the Lieutenant replied. "In the first place, this was beyond any doubt a genuine attempt at suicide and not another murder. You were there yourselves; you saw it."

"Granted." Fergus smiled almost patronizingly. "Go on, Andy."

"There's nothing to go on about. Harding had all the motive you could ask for. Garnett's death gave him ten thousand dollars, left him alone to gain all the renown and glory of their researches, and what's more, according to his lights, freed the world of a monster who was creating war poisons."

"That, of course, is assuming that he knew about the second will and the secret notes."

"There's no way of proving that one way or another; but he could have known, you'll admit."

"All right, I'll admit. On with the reconstruction."

"Incriminating Vinton, if that had worked, would have left Miss Garnett free for him. But it didn't work, and that failure took all the glory out of his crime. When he learned we'd released Vinton, he went to pieces, drank himself practically out of his mind, made one last attempt at accusing Vinton to us, saw it didn't go down, and gave up. But he was so drunk that he poured himself too large a dose, and we'll have him on trial after all."

"The drunkenness, I suppose, had something to do with increasing the emetic effect?"

"Yes, Colonel. That sounds likely."

Fergus was pacing like a resolute robot. "Look, Andy. Can you honestly believe, in your official heart of hearts and mind of minds, that the guy who worked out this beautiful complex scheme is going to commit suicide and blow the gaff just because one part of it goes wrong? You can see the way this thing was plotted. There's a chess-problem mind behind it. There's intellectual pride involved. All that means every whit as much to the murderer as the material results of the crime."

Rand nodded. "That makes sense, Lieutenant."

"Maybe." Jackson was doubtful. "But to me this suicide attempt makes sense too; and I'm acting on it. I'll admit you can make out a pretty good case against Warriner, and I won't neglect that angle; but still—"

"Warriner!" Fergus almost laughed. "Who said anything about Warriner? His part in all this is easy enough; I can explain that when the time comes. But if you're going to close your eyes and ears—"

Rand fingered his cigar thoughtfully. "Mind you, Lieutenant, I am not advancing this as my own theory; but simply in order to shake you in yours. Any conclusion is the better for a little stiff jolting before it is reached. Can you be absolutely certain that Arthur Willowe did not commit suicide?"

"Absolutely. The medical evidence clearly shows that a man couldn't possibly have pricked himself in the back where that needle was found—unless, of course, he was a contortionist."

"That, Lieutenant, is the point of which I was thinking. I happen to know that Arthur Willowe, at least in the days of his youth, *was* something of a contortionist. Alicia—his sister, that is—has often told me of the acrobatic shows they used to put on as children; her brother, she used to say, was partially double-jointed, particularly in the shoulders."

Jackson frowned. "That is interesting, sir. I don't see it myself as a serious possibility; but it might be useful to a defense attorney."

Fergus halted for an instant. "No it mightn't, Andy. It's physically possible, yes; but not mentally—psychologically, as Maureen would say. We know that Willowe was contemplating suicide last night. At that time he wrote a three-page letter explaining his action—probably chiefly so it'd lessen the shock for Kay. Then, after he'd talked with the Sallice, he changed his mind and burned the letter. Now if—and God knows for what reason—he changed his mind yet again, he certainly would have left us another letter.

"No, Andy, Willowe was murdered; and that's my chief objection to your nice easy little solution. I can see why Will Harding might have killed Garnett—I'll admit he had at least three strong motives—and why he might have tried to frame Vinton for it; but I cannot see this second murder. Why did he kill Willowe?"

"Damn it, Fergus, I can't read the man's mind for you. I suppose it was because of something Willowe knew that would have given him away. The old man might have seen him leaving the study late that night, taking the acid from the laboratory, reading the secret notes—anything."

"Come on, Andy. That's out of a novel. *Why did he kill Willowe?*" The young investigator's Irish brightness was gone. He was tense and earnest now; and if Gaelic trumpets sounded, they rang forth in serious and mortal challenge.

"All right!" Jackson thumped a lean fist on the desk. "I'll tell you why he killed Willowe. He killed Willowe because the papers are on Captain Norris' neck and Norris was on mine all morning. He wanted an arrest. Well, by God, here's an arrest for him to put where it'll do the most good."

Rand was patently shocked. "You mean, Lieutenant, that you would send an innocent man—"

"Send him nothing! He'll be detained for questioning as a material witness. That's enough to quiet the papers—and Norris—and I can get on after Dalrymple. Once we've got him, this case will open up in our hands like a Japanese flower in water. But what we need now is immediate action, and this damned drunken young fool has given us the perfect lead. The D.A.'s office will go to work on him, but by the time they're ready to ask for an indictment, I'll have the whole mess sewed up just the way I want it."

Fergus' pacing had assumed a regular, constricted pattern, as though he found himself confined within an invisible cell. "This is none of my damned business, I know," he muttered. "Professionally, my job's over with now. Vinton is cleared and all is rosy. But he's cleared by the wrong answer, and I don't like it."

"We'll have the right answer within forty-eight hours—a week at the outside. We'll put the F.B.I. on his tail if necessary."

"But in the meantime," Fergus urged, "how about this poor dope? Do you think it's going to do him any good? Do you think it's going to help him land a job with a research institute if they know he was held on a murder rap—even if he is turned loose when you pull in Dalrymple?"

"He asked for it," Jackson said stubbornly.

"But supposing—supposing, Andy, you could sew the whole thing up right here and now. No bluffing, no fineigling—"

Slowly Jackson relaxed. "All right, Fergus. I'm only human, after all. As far as my part in this house is concerned, this case is closed. From now on it's up to Norris and the D.A. while I go after the lad with the snuff. But all the same I would like to hear just how you had it figured out."

"OK," said Fergus. "On the sun porch."

"So you're back to that cockeyed idea? I thought before it might give me a lead; but now I don't need it. You can spill your idea here and let it go at that."

"Look, Andy. Can't you be a good guy? Give me just this one break. I mean, if I make a damned fool of myself, there's nobody to blame but me, is there?"

"I wouldn't be so cocksure. False accusations can mean suits for malicious slander."

"And false arrests can mean suits too. I won't point out that they can mean putting an end to an innocent man's career or even to his life—that mightn't make such an appeal to the official mind.

I'd sooner gamble on the slander suit; better to have an action against the O'Breen Agency than no damned action in it.

"Come on. Let me go through with the scene the way we planned it. The nurse can come along too. Then if I lay an egg, you can take Harding off as soon as the doctor'll let you and go merrily along on your chase and just plain forget about my fiasco." His words were easy, but his voice was anxious and pleading.

"Let him have his chance, Lieutenant," Rand urged. "It's giving Harding a square deal, and you don't know—there may be something in O'Breen's plan that could help you. If you could establish a definite case now—"

Jackson was silent for a full minute. Rand could see him struggling between official rigidity and natural curiosity. "I guess," he said at last, "that in a town where they make movies anything goes. Next thing, maybe, I'll be drinking on a case, or smoking Régie cigarettes."

Fergus had stood stock-still awaiting the decision. "You mean it's OK?" His voice was quietly jubilant.

"Unofficially, yes. You can have your grand finale, Fergus. But I'm warning you—it had better be good."

Fergus said nothing. Somehow that was more impressive than the most confident assurances.

TWENTY-THREE

FERGUS GATHERS THE THREADS

Lieutenant Jackson looked around the sun porch at the assembled company. "I warn you," he began, "this is all strictly unofficial."

Rand followed his gaze. Unless Fergus' impetuous Irish brilliance had sorely misled him, here in this group was a murderer. It was not easy to believe. The Colonel noted, as he looked about him, how much these people had changed since the morning after the first crime. Kay looked pitifully older and much sadder. Camilla Sallice, despite her sorrow, seemed clearer and happier. Will Harding, tucked in on the chaise longue with the male nurse in dutiful attendance, still showed the shattering effects of his abortive suicide attempt.

Rand smiled curiously as he looked from the invalid to Kay and recalled how Harding's act had terrified her. In those first few minutes of uncertainty before the doctor's arrival, it had seemed as though all the other horrors of the case had been wiped out for her by this. Now—such is the disquieting reality of anticlimax—she kept her eyes averted from him and sat close to Richard Vinton. The actor, of them all, had come out best from the ordeal. Freed at last from the cloud of suspicion, he seemed another man. It was not only his bravado now; he looked strong and right. Rand could find it in his heart to forgive the chap for being an artist.

In this tense assemblage, only Max Farrington seemed out of place. The lawyer was as ever sleek and suave and confident—an abstractedly curious auditor at the session which was to mean life or death to one of the others present.

It was Farrington now who answered the Lieutenant, in his best If-it-please-the-court manner. "Since the police seem inclined to regret their unfortunate error in arresting my client, I see no reason why we should not co-operate with you."

Jackson smiled—almost, Rand thought, with a touch of malice. "It isn't so much a question of co-operating with *me,* Mr. Farrington, as with your boy detective here." Fergus winced visibly. "Bringing him in on this case was your own idea, remember—though I'm not saying it wasn't a good one. I don't know myself what hand grenade of deduction he's going to toss into your midst; I have my own ideas on the subject, but I'm giving him his innings before I take any action. And I request you—quite unofficially, I say again—to listen to whatever it is he has to say and to answer any questions he may ask you."

Fergus rose and resumed his walkathon. "With that formal introduction, I feel like an after-dinner speaker—which reminds me far too strongly that in all this fine hectic day we haven't had any lunch. And I ought to start off with, 'Unaccustomed as I am . . .' Which, as a matter of strict fact, is quite true. I'm not accustomed to murders, and I know I haven't got the right attitude. I don't mean to be flippant; but that's the way I am. It's worked before in other things; I've been flippant as all get-out explaining to a plush dowager that she really couldn't expect me to be much interested in chasing her paste emeralds when all the time the real ones were inside a roll of cotton in the medicine cabinet. But this is different; and so, to use another formula from after-dinner speaking, 'I ask your indulgence' if I sound a little too light and breezy every so often. I'm really," and his voice abruptly carried conviction, "sorry as hell that all this happened.

"Now that those formalities are off my chest, I want to ask a few questions. Mr. Vinton."

"Yes?"

"Did you at any time have in your hand the glass out of which Mr. Garnett . . . well, that glass," he concluded quietly after a glance at Kay's drawn face.

"Often, I suppose. But not on that night."

"Did you return to the study at all that night?"

"No." He spoke simply and convincingly. Kay looked at him with warmth and relief; having her lover back with her seemed the only bright spot in her present life.

"All right. I just wanted to make sure. You see, that could have provided another explanation. Now, Miss Sallice."

Camilla smiled at him; she appeared satisfied that matters were in good hands now. "Yes, Mr. O'Breen?"

"Look, before we go on with this, would you mind telling all these people just what you told us in the rowboat this morning? Not if you'd rather not; but I think it might—well, ease their minds a little."

Camilla told her story briefly and calmly. The scene that morning had eased her overcharged emotions; she could view it all dispassionately now, and tell it simply as an interesting narrative. Farrington looked bored by the recital, Vinton somewhat relieved, as though he had at last placed a memory which had been puzzling him, and Kay deeply sympathetic.

"You poor child," she said when the other girl had finished. "Why didn't you ever tell me?"

"Uncle Humphrey didn't want me to. He was possessive, you know; I think he wanted to feel that there was one part of his wife left that no one could share with him."

There was a little pause, quickly broken by Fergus saying. "Mr. Vinton."

Vinton shrugged. "I had thought that I was through with this sort of thing for a while. But go on, Mr. O'Breen. Glad to help you if I can."

"Mind you, I don't want to seem to be digging up your past; all of us here know that you've gone straight, and we don't want to hold your shipboard activities against you. But I've got to tell you something and to ask you something."

"Go ahead."

"What I have to tell you, you may know already from Kay: that Garnett hired me to check up on you—remember I didn't have any idea who you were, much less that you were Kay's fiancé—and that I managed to give him a pretty full report on your lurid past."

"This is an outrage!" Farrington spluttered. "Lieutenant, you are placing the conduct of this case in the hands of a man obviously prejudiced against my client!

"That's all right," Vinton said softly. "Let it go, Max. I can understand your position, O'Breen; it was a job, and you carried on with it. It's no more to your discredit than it is to mine when a producer casts me in something terrible. Now what did you have to ask me?"

"I gave Garnett this report by phone on the day he was murdered. But was there any possible chance that even before that Garnett knew what you had been?"

Vinton was puzzled. "That's hard to say. Acting a part isn't so easy in life as it is on the stage or screen. There you have the author's lines to go by, and as long as you're a good study with some talent it's smooth sailing. But in real life you have to compose your own lines as you go along, and it's easy to slip up now and then. I know that I did slip occasionally, and I think Mr. Garnett noticed it. I've seen him look at me very strangely from time to time. That's probably why he engaged you, and he may have done some thinking on his own in the meanwhile. In short, O'Breen, all I can say is that he might well have known who I was."

"That's enough, I think. Now Mr. Harding. I don't like to disturb you, but I guarantee that this will not be a particularly exciting question."

"Go ahead," Harding nodded listlessly.

"Last night you told me that Mr. Garnett had his own methods of guarding his secrets, or at least used to make cryptic references to such things. Now have you any idea what those methods were?"

"Was that only last night?" Harding tried to sit up and concentrate his attention on the question. "He did say such things, yes; but I'm not at all sure what he meant by them. No, I'm afraid I can't help you there."

"It doesn't matter; I've a pretty good idea myself, and we can check it later. Don't look so puzzled, Andy; it really does fit in. Now one more question, and then we go to work in earnest—fireworks 'n' everything. Client?"

Kay tried to smile. It wasn't much use. "Yes, Detective?"

"You said your father had serious heart trouble. How soon would that have been likely to prove fatal?"

"Dr. White said you couldn't know for sure about those things; but he warned Father that it might be within a few months."

"Who else knew about that?"

"I remember Father told us about it one evening when we were all sitting in the study. He seemed almost pleased, as though he had a strong new adversary now. I was really frightened. . . ."

"And who do you mean by 'all'?"

"The family—Uncle Arthur and Camilla and Will."

"And you, Mr. Vinton?"

"I don't remember whether Kay told me, or Mr. Garnett himself. At any rate, I knew."

"Fine. Now we can get going. Let's start out by looking for the motive that must have been behind this whole business. That means more than just a motive for killing Humphrey Garnett. It means a complex triple motive, and I don't think you'll find many people it could fit. In fact, I don't think you'll find more than one.

"The first essential of this crime was Garnett's death. Now who profits by that? I'm just being frank and logical, so for God's sake let's not have any indignant innocence. Kay, of course, as residuary legatee—which, I gather, means a great deal. Miss Sallice, for twenty thousand dollars. Did you know about that?"

"Yes. Uncle Humphrey told me when he changed the will. I remember we laughed about it and said by the time he died I'd be such a famous singer it wouldn't make any difference to me. . . ."

"Will Harding," Fergus went on, "for ten thousand. Now don't get excited—this is just some more frankness. Although you say you didn't know about the new will, you did admit, when we read that outdated carbon, that you'd expected some sizable bequest for your researches. Besides, still in the abstract, you could have learned earlier about the true meaning of Garnett's secret researches and staged that big surprise scene for my benefit. This would have added an idealistic hate to your motive and made it murder for profit and conviction at once."

"This is no way," said the male nurse, "to keep a guy quiet and restful."

"Sorry. I'll go easy. But we've got to get the facts clear. Mr. Vinton's possible motives have been subjected to more than enough scrutiny already. And I suppose, for the sake of the record, we ought to include the man you've all known as Maurice Warriner. Tell 'em, Colonel."

And Rand told them.

"The man is a menace!" Max Farrington exclaimed above the resultant excitement. "Why, Lieutenant, has he not been taken into custody? There's the answer to your whole problem!"

Jackson shrugged. "Take it easy, Mr. Farrington. We know our business, and if he's to be found we'll find him. But I'm not so sure the problem is as simple as all that. Go on, Fergus."

"Thanks, Andy. We'll take up that point later. But to resume this fascinating little analysis—there's one flaw about all these motives that depend on the will. None of these suspects was in dire and instant financial need; and all of them except Warriner knew about Garnett's heart. If the motive was nothing more than money, the murderer should have been willing to wait a few months and see if maybe the legacy would tumble into his lap as a gift from the gods of aneurysm.

"Now we come to the second essential of the crime—the framing of Richard Vinton. We can't doubt that such a frame was planned. The fingerprints, which seemed at first so all-convincing, are now Vinton's best proof of innocence. That glass was wiped off, or it would have shown at least Garnett's own prints and Miss Sallice's;

and no murderer is going to polish up a nice bright surface just to leave an unusually clear sample of his own prints. I thought that possibly Vinton might have been inveigled into handling the glass some time that evening after the other prints had been wiped off it—I mean, of course, before the murder, because it was handled later by someone with gloves."

Rand looked over at Vinton, and saw a sudden expression of fierce exasperation cross the young actor's face.

"Vinton's own evidence, however, disposes of that idea. The only conclusion left is that the fingerprints were forged with a stamp. Lieutenant Jackson has pointed out that they were far more clearly and regularly imprinted than you'd expect from ordinary handling. And despite all the popular ideas on the subject, the forging of fingerprints is perfectly possible. Check, Lieutenant?"

Jackson nodded. "It can be done."

"But there's even more convincing evidence of a plant, and that is the jack of diamonds which was supposed to be the dying man's accusation of his murderer. An accidental false trail from this card led us to Arthur Willowe; but disregarding that, we see that it must refer to the notorious episode on the Cunarder. And that ties in with the telegram, another part of the plant, and its reference to a mysterious 'Hector.' Hector is the name of the jack of diamonds in the French pack.

"Now the effect was supposed to be this: Garnett realizes he's been poisoned. He wants to leave a message which will proclaim his murderer's identity. He's already too far gone to write, so his lightning mind thinks of the jack of diamonds, which will mean Vinton-Massey to Colonel Rand, and he grabs that card. But the flaw here is that the pack from which the card was taken was not disarranged. That pack was sorted in suits and order, so that he couldn't have just grabbed the top card, seen that was the one he wanted, and let it go at that. He'd have had to burrow down to find it. But still that pack was stacked in perfect order, with the jack of diamonds missing from some place in the middle.

"So we can see that the crime was aimed at Richard Vinton just as much as at the ostensible victim, Humphrey Garnett. But now how about the third objective—the death of Arthur Willowe? The Lieutenant here can't think of anything better, so he says that Willowe was killed because, as they say in the classics, He Knew Too Much. Now I doubt that, but it's something you can't prove either way. If Willowe did learn something by accident, only he and his murderer know what it was. But let me point out this: In hearing of the Lieutenant's nominee, Miss Sallice announced that she had ideas of her own which she was afraid to tell me yet and that she'd sleep on them. And sleep she did, and nothing happened to her. I think the only reason why Andy holds on to this quasi motive for Willowe's death is that he knows damned well none of you had any other reason for wishing that poor old man out of the way.

"But," Fergus said theatrically, "I still claim that his death was an essential and integral part of the whole plot. By now, in this brief summary, we've learned a lot about the murderer. He wanted Humphrey Garnett dead, and for some reason other than or in addition to a legacy. He wanted Richard Vinton disgraced and put out of the way, preferably for good and all. He knew the poisonous contents of the laboratory well. He knew about Vinton's past. He wanted the death of Arthur Willowe. He had the intricate mind which could conceive and carry out an elaborate plot, and the orderly mind which would automatically straighten up the pack from which he'd taken a card.

"Does any one of you recognize that description?"

Rand looked around the circle. There was nervous apprehension on every face, but not that of guilt. It was the terror of wondering on whom the blow would fall. Even Max Farrington, despite his recent outburst, seemed completely captured by the power of Fergus' reasoning; and Jackson, though mental reservations showed in his frown, leaned forward absorbed in the narrative.

"There is one person in this household," Fergus resumed, "and only one, of whom all those things can be said."

Rand could bear it no longer. He brought forth his loudest "harrumph" to date and shouted, "Young man, will you come to the point?"

"Gladly, Colonel Rand." But Fergus could not resist one more brief pause. "That one person is—was—Humphrey Garnett."

TWENTY-FOUR

FERGUS TIES THE KNOT

"Hand grenade," Rand thought, was decidedly an understatement to describe this revelation. For a moment the entire group was paralyzed with shock. Then they all began talking at once.

From Kay: "Not Father! He never could have—"
From Camilla: "Uncle Humphrey! I can't believe—"
From Vinton: "By Jove, O'Breen, I think you've hit it!"
From Max Farrington: "Brilliant, O'Breen! Astounding!"

The restraining hand of the nurse kept Will Harding from joining in the excited chorus; but his gray eyes were strangely eager.

Lieutenant Jackson waited for a silence. Then, as the exclamations gave way to wordless wonder, he said, "Go on, Fergus. I'm reserving judgment; the idea's too damned dazzling right offhand. How's about a little reconstruction?"

"All right. Look. Here's how I size it up. Garnett puts together all Vinton's accidental slippings-out-of-character and adds them to Colonel Rand's familiar narrative of old Vantage and the card sharp. He engages me to check up on it; but even though he doesn't take his final step until he's had my report, he's pretty damned certain in his own mind. He resolves that no daughter of his shall ever marry such a man.

"But, he reasons, she seems to love the fellow very dearly. If he just ups and forbids the banns, she'll say, 'Father, I defy you!' and marry him anyway. Of course, he can cut them off from his fortune; but so far as he knows, Vinton is making good money in pictures and that wouldn't prevent the match. Besides, he wouldn't want to alter his will until he knew definitely that Kay would disobey him; and then, with his shaky heart, the very shock of her defiance might kill him, and Vinton would come into the money anyway.

"This point—I may be getting a little novelistic in my reconstruction here, but it still makes sense—reminds him that he has to die very soon at any rate; and he conceives this devilish idea of turning his death into a weapon against Vinton. He works out the whole elaborate scheme: the telegram, the playing card, the fingerprints. Then he realizes the danger that someone might see through it. How much more convincing the whole thing will be if there are two murders! Then no one will think the first one might be suicide.

"He's always had a complete contempt for Arthur Willowe. It doesn't matter a damn to him whether the ineffectual little man lives or dies. And if his death could be made to serve a purpose— So Willowe gets elected as the second victim. Some time on the afternoon before his own death, Garnett sticks that curare-tipped needle into the pillow on his brother-in-law's couch. He knows that Willowe won't lie down there until the scheduled time for his nap the next morning—long after Garnett himself will be dead. With decent luck, he counts on the needle doing just what it did do—sticking into the skin and being lifted out of the pillow when Arthur rolls over in death, so that it looks as though somebody had pricked him with it. What he doesn't count on is the fact that Willowe is bound to be caught up in the police investigation that morning and not get a chance to use his napping couch until the following day, when Richard Vinton is well out of the way as a suspect.

"This was one of his three serious slips. The other two happen when he makes his preparations that night. After he picks out the jack of diamonds from the pack, he automatically straightens up the cards again. And he's so eager to make the forged fingerprints stand out clear that he wipes all the others off the glass first. But he thinks he had the stage all set to represent himself being murdered by Vinton. If a poison container was to be found anywhere near the body, that might start people thinking 'suicide,' so he takes the glass back to the laboratory and pours the poison into it out there. At the same time he has another little task. There's the stamp with which he makes Vinton's fingerprints. If that's found, the whole damned scheme goes agley. What he probably does is melt it down in a crucible and get rid of it in a trash receptacle.

"Then he comes back to the study and drinks his death, in complete and perfect satisfaction. He realizes that Kay, being young and loving, might well have married a reformed rascal despite her father's command; but he knows that she will never marry a man who seems to be her father's murderer—especially, of course, if the State has effectively disposed of him. Garnett has solved his dilemma by merely shoving his death ahead a month or two; and incidentally he's worked out a problem which must have made his too intricate mind even happier than if he'd really succeeded in inventing that five-pack solitaire."

Fergus halted and looked at the Lieutenant. "Well, Andy?"

"It'll do for the time being. The press will love it, and it's enough to stave Norris off and give me a free hand. I can point out to him what a good defense attorney could do with that story if we tried to pull off an arrest now."

The grudging quality of this praise failed to alter the beam on Fergus' face. In his contentment at having solved the case, he had quite forgotten his dutifully conceived idea of appropriate sorrow. Vinton, Rand observed, looked frankly relieved that the ordeal was at an end. Kay, however, seemed painfully torn between joy at the end of all the suspense and horror at this frightful picture of her father.

"Of course," the Lieutenant went on, "we'll know a damned sight more once we lay our hands on Warriner. With a record like his, it'll take more than your theory to—"

"Damn!" Fergus snapped his fingers. "I left that out, didn't I? Sorry, Andy—you'd think I was trying to hold out on you. But I thought you'd have guessed by now."

"Guessed what?"

"Where Warriner is."

Jackson was on his feet. "You've known all this time?"

"Sure. He's right where he has been all along—right where you left him."

"Where *I* left him? Why, I've never seen the man in my—"

"I know. But just the same you went to a lot of trouble to seal him up in that laboratory."

Colonel Rand, when he recalled the case later, liked to forget the next quarter of an hour. Nothing else had brought home to him so sickeningly the dull fact of death. The loss of his friend Garnett had saddened him immeasurably; he had deeply regretted the passing of Alicia's brother, the sole remaining link to the days of his youth. Beside these sorrows, the death of such a petty villain as Maurice Warriner should have affected him not at all.

But he had not seen their bodies. Sight is more starkly convincing than hearing. It is one thing to hear that a man is dead and quite another to see stiff limbs, a strangled face, and popping eyeballs.

"Curare again!" Fergus had said instantly, and Jackson had nodded.

Rand had turned away, gagging, while Jackson had hastened to make the necessary calls to his headquarters and the coroner's office. What was it the poor rogue had said—"the skeletal sparseness of death . . . " He looked sparse enough now—his gaunt body sprawled on the floor of the closet, while his goggling eyes probed blindly for the secrets he would never find. . . .

Then they were back on the sun porch, and Jackson was explaining what they had found. Uncomprehendingly the others looked at him. It was the efficient Farrington who finally spoke.

"But I don't understand, Lieutenant. How did he get into the sealed room and who followed him there to kill him? And above all, why? Has this nightmarish case begun all over again?"

"Go on, Fergus," Jackson said wearily. "This is your party."

Again Fergus took the floor—and quite literally. "You've got it all wrong, Mr. Farrington. There's no John Dickson Carr touch to this—no locked-room problem at all. In a way I'm sorry. I've always wondered if those things happened in real life— But I'd better start at the beginning.

"It had to be, by elimination. Warriner had come to this house and left my car out in front. Now if, as was likely enough, he wanted to get rid of the car because it could be identified, he would at least have used it long enough to take him to safety; he wouldn't have dumped himself on foot right in the center of things. So it followed that he wanted something in this house. It also followed that he was still here.

"Now what did he want in this house? Answer: the plans. Where would he look for those plans? Answer: the laboratory. Remember he'd tried the study already with no luck. And then I thought of two things: We hadn't searched the laboratory; we'd just taken Harding's word that no one else was in there but some merrily mating molecules. And if you'll forgive me, Mr Harding, you were hardly a reliable witness at the time. The other item was the vague references which Humphrey Garnett used to make to the protection of his secrets.

"We know now what that protection was. The plans were hidden in a trick cubbyhole in a closet off the laboratory. The hiding place was constructed like a Japanese puzzle box, but with a difference: If you knew the right maneuvers, it opened readily; but if you just fumbled around, you released a little needle—a little needle dipped in curare—a poison, as you may know, which retains its strength admirably when dried and old.

"The rest is easy enough to reconstruct. Warriner slipped around to the back of the house and got into the lab, probably through the window. He'd undoubtedly been on similar errands before, and knew enough to spot a likely place for a cache. He'd have the closet door shut, in case anyone happened to glance in. Then the trap caught him, and he died alone there. A little later Harding came in and, of course, noticed nothing. Then we came along, and sealed up dead the very man we were frantically hunting for alive. Satisfied, Mr. Farrington? Andy?"

Jackson nodded. "'Death by misadventure,'" he quoted in anticipation of the coroner's verdict. "I guess that settles it." He sounded resentfully frustrated; it wasn't normal to solve a case and then have nobody to arrest. "Garnett's really the murderer again this time, but there's nothing I can do in my line about it."

Fergus surveyed his audience. "Any more questions?"

Rand tossed away his cigar. "Yes, Mr. O'Breen. One."

"Go ahead, Colonel."

"Why, with all your ingenuity, did you name the wrong man?"

TWENTY-FIVE

COLONEL RAND DOES HIS DUTY

Fergus stared at the Colonel. For once he was motionless and speechless. This wasn't in the script. No decent self-respecting Watson had ever asked a detective a question like that.

Jackson took over with sharp official interest. "Explain yourself, Colonel," he commanded. Involuntarily his eyes returned, with a glimmer of hope, to the invalid on the chaise longue.

Rand paused and went "harrumph." He was painfully embarrassed at taking the spotlight like this. It wasn't his proper role; but it must be done. He addressed himself first to Fergus. "You know, young man, you are basically a first-rate detective. You unearthed a great many valuable facts, and you drew some amazingly shrewd deductions. But you see, that was just what the murderer wanted you to do."

Fergus was touchily on the defensive. "OK," he said briefly. "Find me the flaws."

This sudden turn of events had brought confusion on the assembly. All eyes were tensely fixed on Rand. He fumbled for a fresh cigar and tried to make himself clear. "There are no flaws, Mr. O'Breen, up to a point. Your description of the murderer is exact—his motives, his desires, the very quirks of his mind. I was following your every step with rapt admiration. And I have rarely been so amazed as when you told us his name. Because, sir, as you will see, there is one other person to whom all that applies equally well."

"Who?" Fergus demanded.

"You credited Humphrey Garnett with three serious slips," Rand went on hesitantly. "That was where you went wrong. Those three items were not slips; they were essential parts of the plan. The wiping of that glass and the stacking of those cards were necessary, and the murderer had clearly foreseen that Arthur Willowe would have no chance to take his nap that morning. As a matter of fact, the only slips which he did make were connected with the glass and the deck; but you failed to notice them. It is a pity when you were right on so many counts."

"Damn it, you're as melodramatic as I am!" Fergus protested. "Come to the point!"

But the Colonel was prolonging his inevitable denunciation, not because it was more theatrical so, but because he could not make up his mind to go through with it. He loved Kay very dearly; it was hard to look at her and go on with this story. Duty, however, is a concept clearly defined in the military caste; with a puff and a "harrumph" he finally resumed his explanation.

"You see," he said, "I too had figured out this suicide-murder-frame-up idea. We were supposed to. But what convinced me that it was false was the card. That knave of diamonds was not—as you, young man, supposed—from an ordinary deck, although it did look modern in design. You must remember that the design of playing cards has altered almost not at all in the past hundred years, since the introduction of the double-headed court cards. And remember too, Mr. O'Breen, that when I looked at the deck I observed, 'The Stars and Bars.' For that was its design—the flag of the Confederate States of America. In other words, it was one of the decks manufactured, in England I believe, for that short-lived nation. They are not common, these Confederate decks; this was definitely a collector's item."

"One moment, sir," Farrington put in. "May I ask the source of your technical knowledge on such a specialized subject as playing cards?"

"My source, Mr. Farrington, is that lamented gentleman Maurice Warriner. As Mr. O'Breen has pointed out, even though Warriner was a fraud, his scholarly learning must be reliable if it enabled him to pass himself off as genuine with Humphrey Garnett. It is a pity that he is not here now to corroborate my statements; as it is, you must accept them until they can be authoritatively checked." Rand stopped. He was still seeing that pain-strangled corpse sprawled in the narrow closet. A bullet wound or even a bayonet thrust he was trained to understand and to accept; but poison— Though in war now, he reflected bitterly, even that . . .

With a marked effort, he controlled his thoughts and resumed his exposition. He was pleasantly surprised by his own volubility; he had been out of practice for so long. "Now even though my knowledge of playing cards is secondhand, I do know the collector's mind. I am something of a collector myself; firearms is my line. And I know that the items of your collection are sacred to you. Remember that Humphrey Garnett wore gloves whenever he touched his precious cards, and that he had willed his collection to a museum. No matter what villainous scheme he had evolved, it could not conceivably have entailed the mutilation of any part of his collection. If he had wanted to leave a false clue by crumpling a knave of diamonds, he must inevitably have chosen one from an ordinary deck, of which there were several in the room. To deface this particular knave of diamonds was rank vandalism and morally impossible to him, no matter what other crime he might have been contemplating. Someone else must have chosen that card."

"But how?" Fergus insisted.

"If I may indulge, Mr. O'Breen, in your method of novelistic reconstruction, what probably happened was this: Garnett was planning to look over his collection that evening; he was wearing the black gloves. He had taken out this Confederate deck, possibly to check some minute detail of design. The murderer entered. Garnett, unnoticed by his executioner, set the deck aside. Later, when the murderer, in accordance with his plan, was looking for a card for the false clue, he saw this well-worn deck, thought it an ordinary one, and used it. Both he and you, sir, should have realized that a worn common deck is not usually arranged in suits and order."

"But all this is psychological," Jackson objected. "I don't quite see what you're getting at, and you could never feed it to a jury."

"I know that, Lieutenant, though the point was enough to

convince me. But the murderer's other slip was far more serious. There is your tangible proof. Fingerprints, it is true, can be forged; but not the equally telltale pores of the skin."

Jackson swore comprehensively. "I'm a cockeyed idiot," he concluded. "I ought to hand in my badge for this. I'd got my mind so firmly fixed in another direction that I let that slip right past me. Then the murderer must be—"

"Exactly. Mr. O'Breen's detailed description of the criminal fitted Humphrey Garnett very neatly; but it tallies even more closely with Richard Vinton."

Kay was numb now; she seemed almost oblivious to what was happening. Camilla Sallice stared at Vinton in dark horror. Max Farrington shifted uneasily in his chair. Will Harding's pale face showed no malicious triumph—only a profound satisfaction that the truth had been reached.

Jackson rose and crossed to the actor. "And what have you got to say to that?"

"Nothing, Lieutenant. Why should I? It's absurd. Does the old boy mean I actually went out of my way to frame myself?"

"I mean just that, Vinton. You knew that if Garnett were murdered, as he had to be if you were to marry Kay and acquire his fortune before he could make sure of your identity, you would be the obvious suspect—particularly since I was certain to come out here for the funeral and expose your past record. So you took good care that you should be instantly suspected, and then released when it became obvious that the evidence was framed. You weren't sure if the police would detect that frame-up, so you had Kay engage a private investigator. If that too had failed you and you were brought to trial, you could have had a sudden brainstorm and convinced your attorney of the supposed plot against you. It would have made an excellent defense. That, in fact, would have been your best bet; for if you had once been acquitted, no evidence discovered later could have been brought against you.

"There were other advantages, too, to this arrest and exoneration. It meant excellent publicity and the renewal of your contract. Moreover, you were quite possibly a trifle worried about the unspoken rivalry of Will Harding; standing in peril of your life would, you knew, rivet Kay's affection and loyalty to you."

Rand's speech was interrupted by a strange sound. It was neither weeping nor laughter; it was more like some wail which The O'Breens of old might have heard in a banshee-haunted castle. He realized that it came from Kay, and he almost regretted his sense of duty.

Camilla rose. "You'll excuse us," she said gently. With her arm around Kay's throbbing shoulders, she helped the shattered girl into the house.

For a moment Rand thought that Will Harding would follow Kay; but the nurse restrained him with weary tolerance. Vinton, however, scarcely heeded his fiancée's collapse. He faced Jackson with that bravado so characteristic of him. "I suppose you realize, Lieutenant, that a second murder was committed while I was in jail?"

"That's no go, Vinton. O'Breen has explained to us how that was done, and the Colonel's made us see why. It strengthened your 'Garnett' plot, and it was timed to happen while you were safely in custody. But that won't help you now."

"And you'll remember that there was a mysterious intruder rummaging around in the laboratory last night. I suppose I did all that, too—possibly with ectoplasm?"

"That's been accounted for. It's no use trying to cloud the issue."

"But my dear Lieutenant, there's a great deal of use in pointing out the inconsistencies of this case. I may keep you from making a very serious blunder—to say nothing of preserving my well-trained lungs from the State's little reception chamber. How about that telegram? I suppose that Humphrey Garnett saw through my dire plans, dispatched that warning, and then, for all his colossal ingenuity, calmly sat back and let me murder him?"

"That's too easy, Vinton. You sent that telegram yourself. It was the first step in the whole frame. It went in by phone, and I know we can never prove definitely who sent it; but you won't get off on that."

"And I assume that Mr. Harding here attempted suicide for no other reason than to confuse you and add yet another element to the plot design? He could not, for instance, have had any serious crime resting on his precise conscience?"

Jackson looked questioningly at the invalid. Harding spoke softly, trying to check his emotion. "I think you know why I was such a fool, Vinton. I've thought all along you were the man, and I couldn't help thinking—though God knows it was a rotten thought—that with you out of the way . . . Then you came back. It looked as though you were cleared. I saw you and Kay together again. . . . I don't know—it was just too much for me. I started in drinking; and when you aren't used to it you get strange ideas. Things happen inside you, and you want to do things. . . ." His voice had grown deep and tense; it was now that voice which Rand had taken for a stranger's on the porch. Abruptly he broke off and turned to the nurse. "I think maybe you'd better take me inside," he said quietly.

Vinton smiled at his departure. "A touching scene. But I scarcely see that it affects our problem. I take it I may go too? You're surely not going to arrest me on this fantastic notion?"

But Jackson was resolute. "Fantastic or not, Vinton, I am. I'll admit I haven't been too bright on this case. The Warriner business, Fergus' brilliant theory, poor Harding's crackpot suicide attempt—and you're responsible for that too, if we come right down to cases—they got me all balled up. But this is the real McCoy, and I'm acting on it."

"Come now, Lieutenant—"

"Come now hell." Jackson was in no mood to be humored. "If you'd had the common horse sense to admit that you'd seen Garnett again later that night, so that he could have got you to handle the glass, you might have got away with it; but you tried to make us believe the prints were forged, and the pores blow that idea higher than seven kites. You're under arrest; you'd better make up your mind to that."

Vinton laughed. "Seven kites? My dear Lieutenant, seven kites is nothing to how high we'll blow your theory in court. What do you say, Max?"

The lawyer had risen and was holding his hat tentatively. "I don't know, Vinton. You see, this is a little out of my line. Hanly Warren's a very good man for this sort of thing. You'd better see him."

"Thanks," Vinton said harshly. "I will." For the first time that day his voice held a note of fear.

TWENTY-SIX

THE CASE IS CLOSED

And that," Fergus said, "is what did it." The two men sat alone on the sun porch. Vinton had been taken away. "Hanly Warren's never defended an innocent man in his life; that line just meant that Farrington knew his client was guiltier than all burning hell. And I doubt if even Warren can get him off this."

"Of course," Rand mused, "they'll try him only for Garnett's death. The evidence concerning Willowe is too weak. And I would not be surprised if he were guilty of a third murder, though the truth of that we shall never know."

"A third murder?"

"I am not too sure of Warriner and Garnett's trap. If he were coming to this house only for the plans, wouldn't he have waited until night, as he did before? I suspect that his motive was to see a person, and that that person was Richard Vinton."

"But why?"

"Warriner, with his technical knowledge, could very easily have figured out that point concerning the Confederate card. And with a man of his character, what would be more natural than to attempt a little blackmail? It is not improbable that Vinton knew of the puzzle cache—far more probable, in fact, than that Warriner happened on it so readily. It is the sort of ingenious device that Garnett might well have displayed proudly when the actor was still in his good graces. He liked an audience at times to applaud his ingenuity. Vinton could have explained to his blackmailer that he was short of cash, but that he could show him the hiding place of some valuable documents which would provide a worthy price for silence—knowing all the time how surely that curare needle would guarantee silence. . . . Yes, it is possible. . . ."

"And that reconstruction of Warriner's death was another of my bright ideas, wasn't it? So of course it's probably wrong." The cheerful self-confidence had died out of Fergus' voice. The Gaelic trumpets were silent. He wasn't even pacing now; he was slumped hopelessly in a chair.

"Lord, I made an unholy fool of myself," he groaned. "It was all so Goddamned clever and all just what I was intended to see. I'm an idiot. And I'm another idiot all over again to sit around being sorry for myself. This, I suppose, is what Maureen would diagnose as the depressive phase. But there's Kay to think about. This rotten mess has broken her up completely."

"I don't know. She can help to nurse Harding; that will take her mind off this burden for a while. And in time . . . " Rand smiled softly. "Of course, Vinton was far more glamorous. An actor and all that. But you will have noticed how, even in the midst of all this, she has always showed concern for Will Harding? And it would be so much simpler if he were to carry on his researches here—there's the laboratory and everything ready to hand. A perfect setting for a scientist and his wife."

Fergus perked up a little. "You know, that might work. He's kind of a nice guy underneath his dryness—if only he'd learn how to drink like a human being. I wonder if the Sallice would stay on here. Interesting wench, that."

"Gad, you Irish are mercurial—or is it only your youth? From dejection at professional failure you leap blithely to wondering about wenches."

"Why not? Maybe it's to make myself think that there's something left that I'm good at." Fergus' voice was almost bitter. "Not even a fee to console myself with; I wouldn't dare hand Kay a bill after this. Not that that worries me so much—I've spent only twenty-four hours on it—but think what cracking this case would have meant to my reputation!"

"Don't feel downhearted, man. You're not to blame. Why, in all my experience, I cannot recall a more difficult case. Small wonder, then, that a novice—"

Even in dejection, the O'Breen curiosity snatched at the unexplained statement. "In all your experience? I didn't know detective work was a regular part of army training."

"Well, you see . . . " Rand relit his still glowing cigar in modest confusion. "I was in the Intelligence Service. Acting Head of the Bureau in Washington for a while."

Fergus stared. "Why on earth didn't you tell me, sir? Why let me—"

"Because I thought you were on the right track. I was astounded when you went so completely wrong. I am retired from the service. Glory means nothing to me now. I feel no temptation to ride in triumph through Persepolis. No, another quotation of Warriner's is more apposite—'the wench is dead.' And my thirst for glory died with her. Cruelly odd that a rascal should utter such truths simply as a part of his deception. . . .

"So you see, Fergus, I was quite content to stay in the background and watch you get off to what I thought should prove a most promising professional start. In fact, young man, I still think so. You are all right. If ever I can recommend a possible client to you, I shall do so. Potentially, I think you are an excellent detective."

Fergus was almost himself again. "By the holy prophet Malachi," he smiled, "you make me think you may be right." He began to pace. "On my next case, sir, I solemnly promise you, you'll be confounded by what The O'Breen can do."

Colonel Rand smiled, wondered, hoped, uttered a brief silent prayer, and concluded by going "harrumph."

Fergus halted and extended his hand. "Look, sir. You've been swell. Thank you. And, as you ought to know, simplicity from an Irishman means more than all the blarney in Eire.

"And now, if you'll excuse me, I think I'll see what the Sallice is doing tonight. That's one thing I've got out of this case—I hope. That, and knowing you."

He dashed off, swinging his lean arms and whistling brightly his father's favorite jig.

Youth is indeed a strange and wonderful thing, Rand reflected, and fell to thinking of Alicia Willowe until the ash dropped from his neglected cigar.